Rendezvous

Dark
Passage

Rendezvous

Dark Passage

Richard S. Wheeler

A Tom Doherty Associates Book / New York

This is a work of fiction. All of the characters, organizations, and events portrayed in these novels are either products of the author's imagination or are used fictitiously.

RENDEZVOUS AND DARK PASSAGE

Rendezvous copyright © 1997 by Richard S. Wheeler

Dark Passage copyright © 1998 by Richard S. Wheeler

All rights reserved.

A Forge Book
Published by Tom Doherty Associates, LLC
175 Fifth Avenue
New York, NY 10010

www.tor-forge.com

Forge® is a registered trademark of Tom Doherty Associates, LLC.

ISBN 978-0-7653-8065-4

Forge books may be purchased for educational, business, or promotional use. For information on bulk purchases, please contact the Macmillan Corporate and Premium Sales Department at 1-800-221-7945, extension 5442, or write to specialmarkets@macmillan.com.

First Edition: February 2015

Printed in the United States of America

0 9 8 7 6 5 4 3 2 1

Contents

RENDEZVOUS 1

DARK PASSAGE 349

Praise for Rich[...]

Passionate, intelligently written, thoroughly entertaining historical fiction."

—*Kirkus Reviews* (starred review) on
The Richest Hill on Earth

Wheeler captures the roughneck atmosphere of the mining town and brings to life the social problems of the Gilded Age. . . . A multilayered world as versatile and enduring as the copper that inspired it."

—*High Country News* on
The Richest Hill on Earth

[Wheeler] is among the top living writers of Western historical novels—if not the best."   —*Tulsa World*

One of the best Western writers around today. He doesn't rely on epic battles or gunfights to tell his stories, relying instead on fascinating characters, vivid imagery, subtle action, and carefully drawn historical detail."

—*Publishers Weekly*

A haunting novel about hubris and its consequences."
—Larry McMurtry, Pulitzer Prize–winning author
of *Lonesome Dove,* on *Snowbound*

An exciting story of a young man coming of age and growing into a reality greater than his dreams."

—*Roundup Magazine* on *Rendezvous*

Wheeler is a genius of structure and form."
—*El Paso Herald-Post*

Wheeler continues to be one of the best of Western novelists/historians."   —*Salt Lake City Observer*

Rendezvous

For Frederic Bean,
treasured friend and fine novelist

Chapter 1

The moment had come. For this moment the jack-tar Barnaby Skye had waited seven brutal years. For this moment he would risk being hanged from the nearest yardarm or being hauled back to London in irons to a life in a cage.

All that had kept him alive was the dream of this moment. Night and day, on the high seas, or anchored near a shore, he had nurtured this dream until it roared in his head. The Royal Navy knew it and had set a watch over him whenever His Majesty's Ship *Jaguar* raised land. It was so this time. They had thwarted him in the past; this time they would not.

The Royal Navy had been his warden ever since a press-gang had "recruited" him at the age of fourteen, not far from the Thames and his father's redbrick warehouse. They had snatched a lad off the cobbles of London and stuffed him into a frigate of war. They had made him a powder monkey, his task to haul casks of gunpowder from the powder safe deep in the bowels of the warship to the gunners on the decks above. And they had turned him into a bloody slave of the Crown, howling curses at his powdered and periwigged captors.

He never saw his parents or his brother or sisters again. Neither did the Royal Navy admit to his existence, or grant him a seaman's rights, or give him a hearing. He became a whisper, a rumor, an amusing secret as the lordly captains rotated command, one after another. He also became a legend, a storied villain who schemed, who defied, who spent much of his short miserable life locked in irons, who scarcely ever set foot on land—the one exception being the Kaffir wars in Africa—and would never again set foot on land if the admiralty had its say.

Now the moment had come. He needed a moonless night or deep fog and had neither, but he would take his chances. The torrents of yearning, the need for freedom overwhelmed him but did not this time erode his caution. The *Jaguar* lay alongside Fort Vancouver on the Columbia River of the Oregon country, at the farthest reach of Empire. This was simply a courtesy call, a visit to the newest outpost of the Hudson's Bay Company, and another proof of British domination of Oregon. Even now, late in the evening, the commodore and most of his officers were feasting at the board of the hospitable Dr. John McLoughlin, the post's factor, no doubt toasting not one, but two empires, one of them mercantile, both of them predatory.

The watch had been doubled and Skye had been confined to the fo'c'sle as usual. Two sharp-eyed men roamed the deck of the frigate, waiting for such as Barnaby Skye to alter the light and shadow on the moon-washed teak. They patrolled the midships, rounded the taffrail, expecting a deserter to go over the side or off the stern. But that was not where Skye waited on this moon-clad night. He lay on the bowsprit, wrapped in canvas, looking like a fat sail. Just under him, suspended from the bowsprit, was his kit, his few possessions stuffed in a waterproofed bag.

The watch circled close—this time the bloody bosun McGivers—his gaze raking everything that was in or out of order. But it wasn't his fate to see anything unusual about the bowsprit, and he passed by with a weary clop of his clogs.

The gates of the distant fort opened, spilling yellow light. The commodore was returning. Skye judged this to be the moment, now or never—go now or lie in seagoing hulks another lifetime. The watch stood fore and aft, observing the oncoming shore party, McGivers not far away. Skye edged out from under canvas, dropped onto the rigging under the bowsprit, untied his kit, and stared at the inky water that gurgled past in the night, glinting moon back at him. He heard clipped English voices. The shore party was clambering into the jolly boat.

A beautiful spirit flooded through him, something akin to ecstasy. He eased into the furious cold of the river, his bare feet first, and felt the icy blast crawl up his legs and belly and thick chest. The shock stunned him. He let himself drift downstream, treading just enough to keep his head above the surface, feeling the cold suck the strength out of him. He knew he must not swim until he was lost in the night, a hundred yards at least from those watching eyes and keen ears. His young body could barely endure the murderous cold but his spirit soared like a soul rising to heaven. He could see the officers settle in the jolly boat, see oars probe the glinting water, and then he could neither see nor hear them. He dog-paddled urgently toward the bank until he could stand, and then staggered up a mucky grade, his body numb and his soul afire, water sluicing out of his heavy winter blouse and trousers. He shook violently, unable to stay the convulsions of his body. But that was God's good earth under his naked feet, clay and grass in his toes.

He intended to penetrate deep into the interior of

mysterious North America, into a wilderness scarcely known to white men, inhabited by wild savages, wild animals, and governed by wild weather. And after that, who could say? But now he walked north, because an eastbound vector would take him to the fort and under the surveillance of the watch. Shivering, he raced across croplands where the powerful Hudson's Bay Company grew its post provisions, stubbing his toes on stalks and weeds. He wanted a horse but saw none. Slowly he arced his way around the great fort, which now lay dark and silent in the night, a mausoleum of empire, and headed eastward well back from the river. After another mile or so, he paused to pull dry clothing from his kit, pleased that the oiled and waxed bag had turned the water. He wrung out his jack-tar woolens, donned his spares, and slid his wet feet into his boots. When he laced them up, he felt a surge of power: he was on land, he could walk, he was free. He pulled a sailcloth poncho over him, and trotted swiftly into the night, rejoicing, his heart tumultuous in his chest.

An odd feeling engulfed him. This was a sacred moment. Here in the deeps of a moonlit night, he tarried a moment to perform an act of emancipation. He tugged at some dead grasses, marveling at the feel of the brittle stems, and then he scooped up some of the soft soil and let it filter through his hands. This was the soil of a great continent: his soil, his grasses, his wilderness. He claimed the land, prayerfully and joyously. Henceforth he would be more than Skye, a last name spoken with contempt by the officers over him; he would be *Mister* Skye, a title the Yanks bestowed on any man here, even a commoner like himself, a mark of each person's innate dignity and worth. *Mister* Skye he would be ever more. This wilderness was his, he claimed it for the empire of his heart, and no force on earth would take it from him while he lived. The Royal Navy or Hudson's Bay might yet capture him but they would not take him alive.

They would come, of course. The Royal Navy would hunt him down, and soon. Hudson's Bay would come for him, too, and put word out among all its allied tribes. McLoughlin would hear of a wild man and felon, and not of a boy pressed off the banks of the Thames and treated as a slave. McLoughlin and all his traders would join the hunt and think of themselves as rendering a valuable service to the Crown. The prospect was daunting. So was the vast interior of this continent. So was the loneliness he faced.

Skye trotted eastward along a river road, hoping the dry clay would not record his passage. For now, distance was his sole objective. He wanted a dozen, nay a hundred, miles between himself and his pursuers. But he knew that ere long he would face new ordeals, feeding himself with nothing more than two hooks and a line, two ancient knives, and his hickory belaying pin. He had given much thought to his kit and now it would have to do: navy pea jacket and skullcap, raincoat-bedroll improvised from purloined sailcloth, a flint and striker pilfered from the galley, his razor and shaving mug, a large tin cup, some ship biscuits, tea, an awl, shoe leather, thong, fishing gear, and a small coil of manila. That was all. And even that had been hard to gather and hide in His Majesty's frigate.

He fled eastward, trotting, running, stumbling, barely pausing for breath. With the first gray of dawn he ascended massive bluffs until he was far back from the well-traveled river road, and continued onward, never stopping, his body responding to liberty even as his feet responded to the good earth. As the sun ascended on that April morning of 1826, he found himself in a vast land. An enormous snow-capped mountain vaulted upward from the south side of the river, and green slopes, mostly forested, rose from both sides of the river. He had scarcely remembered that land is rarely level. But again his limbs responded, as if they hadn't been punished by the hard night or the icy bath. Such was the rejoicing of his spirit that his stocky body knew no weariness. He danced on a ridge. He was free.

From time to time he eased back to some promontory where he could survey the shimmering river far below, and saw nothing on its banks. He was tempted to rest but refused to do so. He toiled eastward again, aware that his tortured passage along the bluffs would be much slower than passage along the river road below, and that his pursuers would gain on him this day. He wished he had stayed on the road, counting on speed to keep him hidden. But it was too late for that. He struggled through brush and forest, up and down giant shoulders, until at last he could go no further. He found a pine-clad promontory overlooking the Columbia and made a camp there where he could see for miles. He gnawed some ship biscuits and then he dozed.

They came in the afternoon, a well-armed party of seamen and officers along with some leather-clad men, no doubt Hudson's Bay guides and scouts. He couldn't make out which of the officers were commanding this little expedition or which of his shipmates were hunting him. But they marched by, pausing at every ravine to probe it. They were thorough and relentless, and no doubt cared little whether they brought Skye back alive or dead. Even from his aerie, he sensed their contempt for him, saw it in their thorough, studied manhunt. Then they passed upriver and vanished.

Something had altered. Now, once again, the Royal Navy stood between him and his liberty, and he didn't know which way to turn. His only weapons were his belaying pin and his wits.

Chapter 2

Skye waited restlessly until the jury of his peers vanished upriver. Thirst deviled him but he chose to ignore it. As a last resort he could descend some cleft to the river, drink and retreat. Instead he continued eastward along the ridge, so effervescent with joy that he scarcely noticed the protests of his body. Never in his life had he felt such ecstasy. The very earth was his father and mother and brother and sister and friend. His protector, too, hiding him in its rocky fastnesses.

He hiked warily, wondering whether he would run into some jack nastyface, perhaps a salt he knew, probing the ravines or studying the bluffs for signs of passage. He crawled out on promontories and saw nothing below but the glinting river hurrying its burden to the sea. He paused, letting the majesty of the place seep through him. This was better than seeing the horizon from a swaying crow's nest.

Thirst savaged him, and he knew he would have to descend and take his chances. He turned into a pine-shot ravine, sliding downward to a grove of new-leafed trees, yews he guessed, but he knew so little of those things.

And there he discovered a seep dribbling clear water down a rocky facade and into the grove. He cupped his hands and drank, learning something valuable from the moment: a burst of emerald foliage might be a sign of water. He would see the wilderness with wiser eyes henceforth. He had no doubt passed dozens of such springs.

He gnawed on hardtack, knowing it wouldn't last long or subdue the howl of his belly, and resumed his eastward journey. Eventually he reached a saddle divided by a tumbling creek that raced toward the Columbia far below. At the confluence of the creek and the Columbia stood a native village with some sort of fishing apparatus projecting into the river. From his vantage point he could make out brown natives wearing little more than loincloths—and the Royal Navy in blues among them, roasting what would no doubt be a salmon feast.

There they were, his shipmates, old hands, wolfishly hunting him down because they feared the lash. They were less than half a mile below, and all his leagues of walking had not freed him from the clutches of the King's avengers who wanted to make an example of him. He could not cross that arid saddle without being seen, and someone among them would raise the alarm. He pitied them. They wished him no harm but the Royal Navy knew how to bend humble men to its imperial will. Lads who had holystoned the teak deck beside him would be in that party below, balancing the harsh powers of royal officers against their rough sympathies. He studied them, discovering the unmistakable bulk of Smitty and the bent-over form of Hauk. Men he knew, set against him.

He peered about, looking for a way around. He discovered animals grazing above, and with them the possibility of village herders. To the north and east stretched treeless plains, offering little shelter.

He could not circle around by day. He could only wait or retreat. He edged back a hundred yards, making sure not to leave bootprints, and found an area of shelf rock veiled by brush where he could hide unless someone stumbled on the very spot. There he spent the rest of the afternoon, making occasional reconnoiters to a point where he could peer down upon the fishing village. The Royal Navy didn't budge. His shipmates had eaten, smoked, and were enjoying the sight of bare-breasted native women. Maybe that was all for the good, Skye thought. Their minds were on a different sort of chase.

He weighed his chances. He needed to eat and find a way past the tars. But what good could come from hastening upstream with the search party hot on his heels, guided by scouts who knew the country? He studied the fishery, a trap of poles that steered the salmon into seine nets. Beached on a gentle bank were several pirogues, dugout canoes, their paddles lying in them. With one, he could escape to the far shore—if he had the courage to walk through the village at night and take it. His instinct was to cross and then shove the dugout into the river so his passage would not be remarked.

He needed darkness. Moonlight would betray him. Give him the north star and he would navigate the inky river. He studied the village some more, noting a rack where salmon were being smoked. He waited impatiently for dusk—the itch to run, run, run mounting in him. But at twilight he was rewarded with information he needed: his erstwhile shipmates were settling down west of the fishery. The native huts clustered to the east. He spotted dogs, many of them gorging on the offal of the catch, and they shot fear through him. He didn't quite know when the moon would rise, only that in this phase it rose an hour or so later each night, and he would have to act early and fast after true darkness settled.

Restlessly, he bided time until he could no longer see the last band of blue in the west. The cookfires had dimmed. Midshipman Cornwall Carp—Skye recognized the choleric officer commanding this detail—would post a watch and the village mutts would form another sort of watch. Skye wondered what he would do if the mutts howled. Run for the pirogues, he supposed. But would he be strong enough to drag a heavy dugout into the river and escape?

He weighed, one last time, the alternative: hike around the village by night and continue up the Columbia on its right bank, a fox running ahead of the hounds. That made sense, too. And yet . . . the crossing appealed to him. The thought of some smoked salmon did, too. He wrestled back his terror and set out, retracing his way to the saddle and then cautiously working down it in taut darkness, his senses raw. The flutter of a night bird startled him. The scurry of an animal froze him. He reached the edge of the village, wary of the dogs, and studied the gloom for the Royal Navy's watch, but he saw nothing. His pulse lifted. The place was redolent of fish and smoke. He waited a long while, his gaze seeking the glow in the east that would signal the rising moon. He listened to the rhythms of the night, eyed the hulking native huts and fish trap, his senses filtering the shifting darkness that would tell him of the approach of a man.

Nothing.

It was time. He edged out onto the flat scarcely twenty

yards from the bivouac, discerned the fish processing area but could make out no fish. He finally found some on a wooden rack, lifted two, and eased toward the river. It reflected pinpoints of starlight off its ebony surface. He chose the nearest pirogue, carefully lowered his kit and the fish into it, felt about until he grasped a paddle and another and another. He lifted the stern of the vessel, found it heavy, and pushed hard. It slid a few inches, scraping loudly. His pulse catapulted. He tried again, and it slid some more. He peered about him, ducked behind the pirogue when he thought he saw a shadow emerge. But the shadow was only in his fevered imagination. He pushed and tugged some more, wild to break free, and at last eased the craft into the sucking water and hopped in just before losing it to the swift current, which caught it and drew it west. He settled himself, staying low, looking for signs of alarm and finding none. Then, safely away, he slid a paddle into the river and began his crossing, keeping the north star at his back.

He found the opposite bank too sheer to land, so he paddled upstream, fighting the muscle of the giant river, looking for a place to beach the canoe. A while later a beach hove into view, and he dragged the pirogue well up the gravel and out of harm's way. Once again, he felt ecstasy as he stood on dry land, his chances better now. And there to light his path was the lamp of the moon peeking over the mountaintops. He hiked eastward again, confident that he had given his pursuers the dodge, his kit slung over his back, and fifteen or twenty pounds of smoked salmon strung over his kit—enough to feed him for a while.

His body felt light and supple, his legs springy, his muscles fueled by his wild joy. Could any mortal experience

such exultation as this? He laughed, a big, booming eruption of delight that billowed out of his frame, and trotted
upstream on a well-defined trace. At dawn he found himself in much more open country, the arid bluffs farther
back and lower, the barren hills beyond them not much
higher than the river. He paused to study this new world,
look for signs of pursuit on land and water. But the gray
light revealed nothing amiss. He needed rest, so he turned
up a gully that descended out of the south and found a
grove of evergreens a half mile in. The generous pungence
of pines filtered through the quiet air. Here he would eat
and rest. Here he would take stock.

He found a small ell of rock and decided to build a
fire there. He had trouble with the flint and striker, having barely used the device before, but in time he set some
tinder smoldering, and with a few gentle breaths he
brought a tiny flame to life. He had chosen the site well.
The fire could not be seen from any angle. The smoke
would dissipate in the surrounding pines. He kept the
fire small and let it burn hot while he filleted a salmon
and ran the flesh onto a wooden spit that he held over the
hot coals.

The half-smoked fish didn't taste good, but he devoured
it as if it were a palace delicacy. Henceforth he would live
on salmon. He wouldn't have much else. He lacked the
weapons to kill game, and April wasn't the time to find
wild fruits and berries. But he had hooks and a line and
a river full of a legendary fish that fed whole tribes.

He lay back in the grass, satisfied for the moment. He
needed sleep. But he needed something else, intangible
but insistent in his mind: a future. Where would he go, and
what would he do, and what did he want to be? He scraped
dirt over the remaining coals, packed his kit in readiness

for a hasty retreat if he had to, and then let his mind wander like a homeless ghost in the cemetery of his life.

Long ago, he had been destined for Cambridge, where his father had been schooled in political economy before turning to the overseas trade. The boy, Barnaby Skye, had a lively interest in English literature and poetry and in his family's Anglican religion. He had entertained the thought of becoming a dominie if he didn't choose his father's profession. Then, in one dark moment on an overcast day in London, all his dreams were shattered and he no longer owned his own life.

Now he would fulfill his dream. He intended to cross this wild American continent, find his way to a comparable university on the Atlantic seaboard—Harvard came to mind—and achieve what had been his original goal. He knew little about the American college, except that it was respected and that it was located in Cambridge, Massachusetts, nearby Boston. The thought appealed to him. He had planned to go to Cambridge, England, but would settle for Cambridge, Massachusetts. He could pick up where he had left off seven years ago, work through college somehow, settle in Boston, and start a business. He had sustained himself with that dream, and now it was becoming reality.

But the thought left him restless. He was no longer that boy and wasn't so sure what he wanted now that he had, in a fashion, seen the world, if only from 'tween decks. The newly pressed seaman, Barnaby Skye, had fought bitterly in the bowels of the frigate just to survive, just to wolf his ration of gruel each day, just to win a little purchase on life. The boy had learnt well, fought the bullies, learned to give more than he took. But it had cost him a broken nose and numerous scars, the punishment meted out by harder, crueller, older men who built ruthless jack-tar empires 'tween decks, out of sight of bosuns and midshipmen.

He didn't know what he would do. Freedom bewildered him. For the first time in his life, he had no one over him, no one telling him how to spend his every hour. He ached with the burden of choice, ached to find someone he could share his dream with, anyone who might help him decide what to do with his life.

He dozed well into the morning, bolting awake with every shift of the breeze or catcall of a crow, and then settling back into the benevolent grass again while his heart steadied. No one came. He possessed the earth—and himself. That was it: for the first time in his young life, he owned himself.

He was troubled by a sadness that lay just below his wild delight in being free. He didn't know what he would do, or be, but he supposed the next months would teach him. He had never imagined that liberty could be such a burden.

Chapter 3

D r. John McLoughlin had had more than his fill of his demanding guest, Commodore Sir Josiah Priestley, but there wasn't much he could do except wait out the visit.

Priestley had all the hallmarks of his class: a fine wit, a scorn for commoners, a loyalty to the Crown that was more rhetorical than real, a smidgeon of learning in most of the branches of knowledge, and an assumption that all the world should treat him with the deference demanded by his station.

The commodore, in command of a small Pacific squadron consisting of three twenty-four-gun frigates, relics of the Napoleonic Wars, was paying a courtesy call to the new Hudson's Bay post, Fort Vancouver. There McLoughlin presided over a fur trading empire that stretched from Mexican possessions in California northward, and from the Pacific to the Continental Divide at the apex of the Rocky Mountains. Priestley had sailed up the treacherous Columbia with only his flagship, the *Jaguar,* leaving the two remaining frigates to display the war muscle of King George IV to the dissolute Mexicans farther south and then meet him in the bay of San Francisco.

The giant McLoughlin, born of Irish and French parents in Quebec, could be an accommodating host, and indeed had at first welcomed the visitors, sharing whatever luxuries and wines he had in his yet-unfinished fort on a flat north of the Columbia. He had more urgent things to do, chief among them putting the new Hudson's Bay Company division on a profitable footing. He presided over an area so vast it defied the imagination; an area largely unexplored, although his best brigade leader, Peter Skene Ogden, was swiftly mastering the country and locating the prime beaver-trapping areas.

On a less lofty level, McLoughlin was overseeing the planting of crops that would supply the post with its grain and vegetables, and was building the corner bastions of his fort along with comfortable residences for his chief men within it. He was also overseeing the post store and its profitable trade in peltries, all the while dealing as diplomatically as possible with his bullheaded and demanding superior, Sir George Simpson.

McLoughlin, a commoner and licensed physician who had spent years in the fur trade, mostly with the North West Company, had little use for titled nobles with all their conceits and blindnesses, but they governed his world and he had no help for it. And if he was a cynical adherent of the Crown, he nonetheless did his duty whenever called upon.

But now his sense of obligation grew thin. Priestley had intended to sail earlier. McLoughlin listened impatiently as Priestley explained in detail, with that nasal and shrill Hampshire voice of his, why his departure had been delayed.

"I should have hanged that wretch long ago. Pity I didn't. He's costing the Royal Navy a pretty penny, I say. Straight out of Billingsgate and with a coarseness to match. Troublemaker from the start, this Skye. Pressed in seven years ago, and refused to serve the Crown. Skulking brute with the mind of an ape and the habits of a pit bull. He's been the joke of squadron, you know. 'Oh,' they say, 'you get Skye this tour, Priestley. If he acts up, quarter him and feed him to the sharks.' Good advice, but out of the kindness of my heart I spared the devil his due. And now how am I repaid? He went over the rail! Over the rail! And I'm shorthanded. I'll give that watch a whipping when we're at sea. That Bosun McGivers! Right before the man's sleepy eyes Skye gave me the slip."

McLoughlin was hearing this the tenth or eleventh time. "I presume the navy'll fetch him back 'ere long," he replied, as he already had.

"Of course we will. That brute's scarcely set foot on land since we pressed him and doesn't know a thing. He won't get far."

"You were saying that some days ago. The party you sent downriver hasn't returned."

"McLoughlin, where can a man go? Up the river, that's where. Or out to sea, that's where."

McLoughlin disagreed. A deserter could go anywhere and lose himself in an unexplored wilderness. "He might strike overland—up the Willamette to the Mexican country, my lord. If I were in Skye's shoes, I'd make it my first business to escape the Crown's territories."

"Skye wouldn't be so smart. He hasn't the slightest knowledge of the local terrain. He's been below decks. How would he even know of the Willamette? Don't give him credit, McLoughlin. The man's an ape. And besides, he speaks only English, and barely that. Why would he go to Mexico? He couldn't even ask them for a cup of grog."

"Perhaps because you wouldn't expect him to go there, my lord."

"Ah, you mock me, McLoughlin. Insolence, insolence. But I'll let it pass. I wish to enlist you against this freebooter, this traitor to the crown. He's no ordinary deserter; he's arguably the worst man in the Royal Navy, incorrigible, reluctant to perform his duties, given to brawling, sullen and contemptuous of his betters. I want him back. On the small chance that my search parties don't haul him in, I'm charging Hudson's Bay with the responsibility of catching him, putting him in irons, and sending him to London for his hanging."

"We'll do our best, my lord."

"Of course you will. Anything less than your best will result in a report to the Admiralty and the Colonial Office. Catch him. I'm putting a ten-pound price on his head, dead or alive. It's to your advantage, of course. You don't want this murderous, ruthless brute loose in your country."

"He's murderous?"

"Why, I imagine he'd murder a thousand if he could. We prevent it by keeping him behind iron strap when he provocates."

"But he's killed no man?"

"What difference does it make? He has the penchant. He has that low brow, the mean cunning of the criminal class."

McLoughlin smiled. "Very well. I'll post the award. You'll give me a description, of course. If you don't catch Skye, he'll show up eventually at one of our posts. We have our ways, in HBC. I can enlist a dozen tribes, for starters. I can alert every factor at every trading post."

"That's not enough. I want more. I want an expedition to go after him if the navy fails."

McLoughlin poured some more darjeeling and arched a brow. "And who'll pay?"

"You will, of course. It's your duty to the Crown."

"I see," said McLoughlin. "You'll need to put this in writing, and I'll send it along to George Simpson for approval. I don't have the authority—"

"Tut tut, McLoughlin. Just do it."

"—to spend resources that are not included in company objectives. But we'll catch the devil if we can."

Commodore Sir Josiah Priestley's response was thwarted by the appearance of McLoughlin's clerk. "Excuse me, sirs, but Mr. Carp requests the commodore's attention."

"Ah, McLoughlin, news at last. I'll wager they have the bugger, or at least his head. Send him in directly."

A smooth-cheeked youth barely in his majority stepped

in, saluted smartly, and addressed the commodore. "With permission, sir—"

"Yes, yes, have you got the devil?"

"No, he gave us the slip. Not a trace. We penetrated several leagues upriver, as far as a native village. No luck. But one small clue, sir. The villagers lost a pirogue that night—maybe a mishap, maybe not."

"And you failed to follow up."

"Your pardon, sir, we looked up and down the river. It moves right along, you know."

"So you failed, Carp. I seem to have misplaced my trust. Or perhaps I overestimated your abilities."

The young man, holding the juniormost officer's rank in the Royal Navy, stood silently.

"It's all politics, McLoughlin. These useless sons of knights and barons get preferred over men of ability. Go, my boy. Tell Lieutenant Wickham we'll sail at dawn before we're fighting a headwind and rowing our way out."

"Very good, sir. I—I'm sorry. It's a huge country, sir—"

"Excuses."

The youth fled.

"So, my crew couldn't round up a common oaf. If the Admiralty'd give me a few good men, I'd have strung up the blackguard long since. Now, thanks to them, I'll look bad. Very well, McLoughlin. I'm expressly placing this matter in your hands. Hudson's Bay will pursue this Skye by all available means and report to the Admiralty."

"What does Skye look like, my lord?"

"Why, you can't possibly mistake him—the low cunning, the criminal brow, the wildness of eye—"

"Ah, my lord, is his hair brown or blond or black?"

"How should I know?"

"His age, then?"

"He's been in service forever. I inherited him. Three commanders before me inherited him. Who knows?"

"His eyes—are they blue or brown or gray?"

"I never examine commoners closely."

"His build, then."

"A brute, McLoughlin, an ape. And yes, there is something. Skye has a battered nose, broken a dozen times in his brawls. Look for a man who's all nose. That's all you need."

"Like me, I wager," McLoughlin said, aware that he had a royal nose, a nose that dominated his face like a hogback.

"No, McLoughlin, twice your nose; grotesque, I'd say. The monster of degenerate parents. Look for a physical degenerate and you'll have your man."

"What is he wearing?"

"Sailcloth. I've learnt that much."

"The charges, sir? Murder, theft, disobedience? Attacking an officer?"

"Worse than that. A habitual criminal, as devoid of civilization as the Arctic. A lone wolf. And desertion of course."

McLoughlin had a sneaking suspicion he might like Skye. Or at least admire him. But he set that aside. "I'll put out word. We'll have scores of men looking for the man or his bones."

"See to it," Priestley said, rising. "You have your company on the wharf at dawn to see us off. I'm going to press one of your trappers. When you give us Skye, you'll get your man back."

"My trappers? But—"

"No buts. HBC owes me a man."

"We owe you nothing of the sort."

"McLoughlin, I'm an officer of the Crown. I'd press you if I had to. Thanks to HBC's laxity, the ship's company is even shorter. We lost four men to scurvy."

McLoughlin knew better than to argue. He stood suddenly, stretching his six-foot, seven-inch frame, filling the primitive office with his presence.

"I will see you off in the morning," he said in a way that brooked no further discussion.

Then he escorted the commodore to the gate and had his men bar it. If they wanted to press an HBC man, they would have to resort to the ship's battery to do it, and then answer to the Admiralty and Home Office. Let that titled fool try.

Chapter 4

Rain, cold, starvation, and fear dogged Skye, sometimes all at once. A Pacific storm dropped snow on the mountains and a cruel drizzle on the Columbia, numbing him in spite of his woollen skullcap, pea jacket, and sailcloth cape. He lacked the skill to build a fire in wetness, and wished he had pocketed some dry tinder while he could. He regarded his ordeal as a lesson in wilderness survival, and would remember.

The thought of pursuit tormented him: time and again, he climbed an outcrop or low rise to study his backtrail. If not the navy, then surely some HBC man, a veteran of the wilds, would pursue and capture him. He saw nothing, but that didn't allay the imaginings of his fevered mind.

But worst of all was the hunger, which maddened him, reduced him to weakness. At times he even considered backtracking and turning himself in at Fort Vancouver. Anything for a belly full of hot food.

One desperate morning he whittled off a willow limb with his knife, grubbed about for worms, and rigged a fishing pole, using a navy hook he had pilfered from ship's stores. But the salmon ignored his bait. Then he tried one of the navy's ocean lures, thinking maybe salmon didn't eat worms or bugs. Over and over he drew the bobbing wooden lure through the water, but he caught nothing. That day he trudged eastward on an empty belly, dizzy from the want of food and fearful he would starve. What did he know about catching fish or killing game? What good were these big hooks and lures, intended for ocean fish?

He tried again that warm evening, hoping a fish would strike at dusk. He baited his iron hook with a caterpillar, tossed it as far out as he could, and let it bob on the river supported by a stick he used as a float. Moments later a silvery fish struck, almost yanking his crude willow pole from his grasp. He dragged in a salmon that weighed several pounds. Madly, he gutted and filleted it, tempted to wolf it down raw, but instead he spitted the fillets and set them to cooking. That evening he filled his complaining belly and cooked enough more to sustain him for a while. But he was unable to catch another fish although he tried until night overtook him.

He hiked eastward into dryer country, the river running through gloomy flats that oppressed his spirit. But here he enjoyed some spring sun. He knew the vagaries of fishing would leave him hungry more often than full, so he began a systematic hunt for other foods, scarcely knowing what was edible and what was foul. He could only sample roots and bulbs and wait to see if they sickened him. His best discovery was cattail roots, thick, foul-tasting, but starchy. He found them more edible if he mashed them between stones. In this fashion he managed to supplement his diet. But he longed for meat; any kind of fresh meat would have quelled his ravenous needs.

He scarcely saw game, only one or two distant does and a goatlike animal he thought might be an antelope. He found plenty of ducks and geese but lacked the means to kill them. He dug up plants, hunting for bulbs, but found nothing edible. Then one evening he stumbled upon a deer carcass, scaring off the predators feasting on it. Belly and haunches had been eaten out, but there was meat around the chest and forelegs. He built a fire from deadfall and set to work with his knife, slowly cutting strips and setting them over the fire on spits. This was a bonanza, a starving man's gold. He ate greedily and then cut more meat, intending to cook it and take with him what he could.

He was wildly lonely. The frigate had offered rough companionship. Here he knew only solitude, and it oppressed him more than he had expected. Even his days of confinement in the ship's brig had been marked by exchanges with his warders, the drift of conversation outside of his iron cage, the knowledge that he was never really alone, and he had friends 'tween decks.

At first he thought he could do nothing about his loneliness other than to dredge up memories. But as he walked eastward, he found himself enjoying the solitary life. To pass time as he hiked, he became an acute observer of his world and discovered that it was brimming with living things, and they spoke to him in their own way. The crows cawed his passage to each other. Ducks burst from cover when he approached and flapped into the skies. The birds became his scouts and sentries. If they burst from a tree, he paused to find out why. If they warned each other of his passage and followed along, hopping from bush to bush around him, he knew that probably nothing else was troubling them. The ears that no longer registered human voices began to register nature's subtle changes, and Skye knew such knowledge would help him survive.

One morning his newfound awareness of nature's rhythms kept him from discovery. He was walking through unusual silence, and felt it. He rounded a gentle hill and spotted Indians ahead cooking a meal, their three heavy log pirogues beached on a gravelly shore. There were at least twenty, all stocky bronze males, enjoying a breakfast drawn from the river. Their spears and bows and quivers lay about. He ducked out of sight, wondering whether he had been discovered. He retreated to a swale and hiked up it until he was well off the river road, and there he waited. He could afford to wait. He was a lone man going nowhere, on no schedule at all. But that didn't make it easier, and he knew he would need to learn patience if he hoped to survive.

He waited for what seemed an hour and tried again. They had left. He had not seen them going downriver, so he knew they were ahead of him and would continue to pose a menace. Maybe they might be friendly, but he suspected that Hudson's Bay would have a say in that. He scavenged their campsite, looking for anything useful, and found nothing except fishheads and tails. They tempted him. He had lost weight and his clothing bagged about his shrinking frame. He needed food and lots of it, much more than roots and bulbs and the occasional fish. He had exhausted the tea and hardtack and now had nothing at all to preserve him. He dreamed of bread and butter and beef and even burgoo, the oatmeal gruel that had been the jack-tar staple in the navy. His boots and clothing were showing signs of serious wear. Sooner or later he would have to stop dodging these people, walk into a village, and get help if he could.

But he didn't rue his escape. Indeed, with each passing day he rejoiced more. These days tested his mettle, tried his courage. He was a freeman, master of his destiny, even if his destiny was to starve to death. He wished he had counted the days since his escape, but he hadn't, and his mind stumbled when he tried to think back on his flight. But he knew a fortnight had passed, and he had made good his escape from the navy. His impulse to run, run, run had ebbed these last days, and now he intended to learn how to wrest food and perhaps clothing from this silent wilderness.

That warm spring day he set up his fishing rig and then whittled a thick sapling into a lance, pleased with its weight and heft. He sharpened its point, and practiced throwing it, not unhappy with the result, but aware of how much he had to learn about the weapon. He fire-hardened the wooden point and threw his lance at targets until his arms hurt. Then he checked his fishline and found nothing on it. He would go hungry again that evening, save for whatever roots he could choke down.

He collected his gear and hiked a few miles more across dreary plains until he came to a slough with fat geese swimming on it. Without a bow and arrow, or sling, or firearm, he would not be able to kill one. But perhaps if he sat bankside as quietly as he could for an hour, one might drift close enough to club. He settled on moist earth, close to thick cattails, and waited. The distant geese eyed him but never approached, and after an hour or so he knew patience and quietness wouldn't fill his belly. He was feeling miserable and at the end of his wits.

But he calmed himself. He had won the gift of liberty; he would subdue his body. Dusk settled without visitations from unwary geese, and he gave up. He had gnawed on cattail roots before, and would again. This time, though, he would do more. He pulled up quantities of the plant, cut off the gnarly roots, scoured the slimy surfaces, cut the roots into small pieces, and then patiently ground them into a fibrous pulp. He acquired two or three pounds of roots this time: real food if he could stomach it. He built a fire, boiled a few pulped roots in his large tin mess cup, and then set aside the mushy material to cool while he boiled more. He made a satisfying meal of the mash, and learned that patient preparation could yield edible food. This wasn't Eden, and nature's bounty could not be plucked off trees—but he had filled his stomach.

That evening he pulverized and cooked more of the starchy root, making enough mush of it to last a day or two if he should need it. A small reserve in his kit would lift his spirits and strengthen him. In the last light he doffed his boots and waded the slough, intending to camp on its far side and start off in the morning with dry clothing. He found a much-used campsite there, probably because of the geese and ducks in the slough, and rolled up in his sailcloth. Sleep came hard; he had never gotten used to sleeping on the earth.

A cold drizzle awakened him in the night. Miserably, he sat up, donned his skullcap and pea jacket, pulled the sailcloth cape over his head, and waited for better times. Sharp gusts of wind drove rain into his tiny shelter. In that brutal cold, his spirits slid to their lowest ebb. He was alone in a black and bitter night, wincing at every volley of icy rain, without a friend in the world, without anyone to love, without the ordinary comforts. He rummaged about in his mind, looking for succor against this bitter moment and finding none—except the long-remembered, half-blurred prayers recited from a church pew in his youth. He stumbled through these fragments, feeling hollow, and then enduring the numbing night.

Something came to him then, something important that he had ignored from the beginning. He didn't know how to survive alone. He could not live long on his own, without help. He could not count upon a stray carcass or the occasional catch of a fish whose habits he didn't know, or a diet of roots. He could survive only if he approached other people, trusted them, made friends, sought their help, learned their ways, and gave something in return. In short, he could not live a hermit's life. If he did not starve to death, he would go mad with loneliness. Only these tribesmen could show him how to garner food, or supply the companionship he craved, or shelter him from the elements. His God was telling him he wasn't alone in the world, and he should not be afraid.

Chapter 5

At first light Dr. John McLoughlin walked through the great gate of Fort Vancouver and instructed his men to bar it after him and defend the post if they must. He walked majestically down to the riverfront, where the

Jaguar lay anchored in navigable waters twenty yards off. The crew was unfurling sail to take advantage of a freshening southeasterly breeze. Sailing a three-masted, fully rigged frigate down the Columbia against prevailing westerly winds would be a tricky business.

He stood silently on the bank, waiting for Commodore Priestley to notice him, but for the moment the ship's master was overseeing his junior officers. Then at last Priestley observed the white-haired Hudson's Bay factor.

"Where are your men?" he shouted across the turbid water.

"Defending my post."

Unfurling sail high above caught the eddying breeze and flapped. The ship strained against its leash.

Priestly laughed. The commodore's threat to press an HBC man had dissolved in the night, as McLoughlin knew it would if he resisted.

"Not much of a hail and farewell," Priestley said. "The Royal Navy has a long memory."

The factor stood like a rock, silent and unbudging.

"Bring us Skye, McLoughlin."

"Permission to weigh anchor, sir," bawled a junior officer.

Priestley nodded. A crew turned the squeaking capstan, water dripped from the rising anchor cable, and suddenly the ship sprang free, heeling away from the wind and sliding down the half-mile-wide river, running like its namesake. In minutes it rounded a bend and disappeared.

McLoughlin returned to his gloomy office and lit a lamp. The *Jaguar* had reprovisioned at Fort Vancouver, taking on firewood, sugar, flour, tea, dried apples and vegetables, tobacco, whiskey, and sundries. Priestley had expressed outrage at the prices, never pausing to consider the pounds and pence of bringing such goods to a wilderness post. McLoughlin totted up the charges, drafted an invoice, and set it aside for the next express to his superiors. It would be a long time, if ever, before HBC collected from the Admiralty.

He turned to his post journal, and entered the departure of the Royal Navy, not failing to include the commodore's threat to press a man, the factor himself if necessary. Then he added a final sentence to his entry:

"Have decided to conduct intensive search for the deserter, Skye, apparently a man of criminal nature. Will direct that the tribes be notified, a reward posted, and my brigades and posts informed as fast as feasible."

He set down his quill pen. A favor to the Crown would not hurt HBC. And cleaning a criminal out of his district would be desirable. If the man survived, he would eventually show up. All this he would discuss further in a letter to George Simpson, governor of Hudson's Bay, up at York Factory headquarters.

He spent the next hour penning identical messages, instructing his factors to be on the lookout for a deserting seaman named Skye, stocky, big-nosed, powerfully built, probably in seaman's attire. If possible, they were to capture the man alive. The man would be tried, perhaps in London. They were also to post a five-pound reward and offer it to any tribe that brought Skye in alive—definitely alive and well. There would be no reward for a dead man. John McLoughlin did not intend to encourage the killing of a white man, or to give such a license to the various tribes that HBC traded with. He penned an additional letter to his gifted brigade leader in the Snake country, Peter Skene Ogden, saying much the same thing.

He summoned two of his senior French Canadian

engagés, Pierre Trintignon and Antoine Marie Le Duc, to his office and addressed them in his fluent French, the tongue of his mother. "I have decided to catch that deserter if possible," he said. "Which means sending expresses to the posts where the brute's likely to show up. Antoine, I suspect that Skye's heading up the Columbia—his other choice is Mexico—and you'll have the more urgent task. Take these expresses to Nez Perces House and Flathead House, and look for Ogden south of the Snake, delivering this express to him en route.

"Pierre, you take this express to Spokane House and continue onward to York Factory with an express for Simpson. You'll each take a mount and remount, and draw whatever provisions you need. The sooner the better."

"Ah, *oui!* And what does this Skye look like that the lord commodore wants so badly?" asked Le Duc.

"Priestley was rather vague. Odd how some men don't see what's before their eyes. Look for a man of powerful build, medium height, with a formidable nose—probably in seaman's clothing."

"Ah, *le nez formidable!* Such a man will identify himself without a word."

"This nose, I gather, rivals or exceeds my own nose," McLoughlin said, "and that makes it a nose unlike any other you have ever examined."

"It is so. I shall study *le nez.*"

"All right, then. If you run into Skye, bring him in. He probably isn't armed. He may be starving unless he's a canny woodsman. I want him alive. He'll have his trial, but I also want his story."

"This Skye, he makes the trouble, *oui?*"

"If Priestley is to be believed, yes."

"But you don't believe the commodore."

McLoughlin stared out the wavery glass window, one of the few glass windows in his post—or all the far west. "The commodore is a faithful officer of the Crown, but he sees commoners through the lens of his class. Skye is probably just as bad as Priestley makes him out. But I reserve judgment. I did learn that Skye was pressed into service as a youth and fought it. When you pull a man off the streets and make him the Crown's sailor, the man has a grievance." He smiled wryly. "Some men regard their lives as their own. It's a novel thought to feudal lords, even now."

"They pressed this Skye. *Mon Dieu!* Let the Crown press me, and there would be blood spilled."

McLoughlin thought the conversation had gone far enough in that direction. "Skye is no doubt exactly the blackguard he is made out to be. Pressed or not, he deserted."

"Maybe we should help him," Trintignon said.

McLoughlin didn't reply for a moment. "Bring him in and let Simpson and me decide that. Pierre, you take the north bank, which is your route anyway; Antoine, you ride the south bank. Have Gervais sail you across."

"I'll be gone before the sun reaches noon," Le Duc said. "This man Skye, he will walk into my snare. I will scatter bait and catch him like a goose."

"See to your safety. He's a brawler."

The burly Canadian laughed cynically.

His engagés took the expresses and vanished. Riding good mounts, they were likely to overtake Skye in days, or at least reach the posts well ahead of the deserter. HBC might preside over a vast wilderness, but it had its ways, and the veteran factor McLoughlin knew them all.

He debated sending a man up the Willamette to check for Skye's passage, and decided not to waste the precious manpower. If Skye was making his way into Mexican California, HBC would be well rid of him. But that was unlikely. The deserter would try to find refuge among the Yanks.

If any HBC man were to capture Skye, McLoughlin hoped it would be Ogden. Peter Skene Ogden would be a match for a dozen Skyes. The brigade leader had single-handedly rescued the faltering Columbia Department, and before that the faltering Nor'west Company, from certain ruin, using a combination of toughness and good humor while dealing with the company's free trappers, harsh discipline, an eye on the purse, and sheer strength of character. Ogden might even transform the deserter into a valuable HBC man. There were other valued employees with worse records behind them than deserting and brawling, and Ogden had nurtured industry and loyalty in them.

McLoughlin wondered how Ogden's brigade had done this season. The man's mission had been both hard and delicate: to trap out the Snake country so thoroughly that the slim pickings would discourage the Yanks, who were flooding into the jointly held Oregon country. The course of empire, both HBC's and Great Britain's, required that the Yanks be shut out until a boundary could be agreed upon. The Yanks were truculently insisting on the 49th parallel; Great Britain, with just as much determination, was holding out for the Columbia River as the boundary, which was why Fort Vancouver was built on its north bank.

If Skye ended up with an American fur brigade, it would be just one more problem for HBC. Ogden would know what to do: the man had a genius for cheering up sour engagés and winning the loyalty of bitter men. If

Skye was not utterly incorrigible, HBC might have a new man. That was a thought McLoughlin would not share with Simpson, whose blind loyalty to the Crown sometimes overrode good judgment.

But all that was speculation, McLoughlin thought. Ogden was due to return after the spring hunt south of the Snake, travelling right along Skye's probable escape route. And with any luck, he'd have Skye with him, the sailor glad to have some food in his belly. And if Skye slipped by Ogden, he'd run into the equally formidable McTavish at Fort Nez Perces, located at the confluence of the Snake and Columbia.

McLoughlin laughed softly. What was a poor hungry seaman to do against men like that?

Chapter 6

Antoine Le Duc rode up the left bank of the Columbia, finding nothing. The spring rains had washed the trail clean, but this seaman, Skye, would be easy to find. What would such a one know about wilderness? Le Duc rode easily, enjoying the fresh April weather, glad to escape the post, always happiest when he was prowling alone, unfettered by the will of others.

He led a rawboned pack horse and a spare riding mount. The three beasts of burden would give him speed and enable him to catch up with the sailor, if indeed the man had wandered up this bank. Perhaps the honor of capture would befall Pierre Trintignon, himself a wily French-Canadian like Antoine.

For two cheerful days Le Duc hastened eastward, and then, suddenly, he came upon a beached pirogue lying on a bank above a Klikikat fishery. It had been drawn up a gravel beach and its paddles rested in its belly. Ah! It all came clear to Antoine Le Duc. The sailor was either a fool or excessively scrupulous. The man should have pushed the dugout into the river after the crossing, and thus make his passage invisible. That made him a fool. Or else the fugitive had beached the boat so that it might be recovered by the Klikikats, and thus salve his conscience. That made him a fool also, but a fool with honor. Le Duc decided he liked his quarry. A pressed seaman who would desert the Royal Navy and plunge unarmed into the wilderness was a man after Le Duc's heart.

After that, Le Duc rode leisurely eastward through the deep canyon of the Cascades, where the Columbia breached a mighty mountain range. He saw no sign of his quarry on the rainwashed and sun-dried trail, but that didn't matter. Would such a man suddenly abandon his sustenance from the river and head over the mountains? Anyone experienced in the wilderness, like himself, knew that mortals, like any other animal, would go where passage would be easy and life could be sustained.

Soon, he found ample evidence of Skye's journey. The ashes of cookfires, a fishhead—so the man had hook and line—and a place where the sailor had hacked off a tree limb and whittled it into something. And bootprints, too. He was getting close. The man was eating cattail roots, leaving the fronds in heaps. *Alors,* a clever one. Le Duc knew that the Indians used the roots as an emergency food, and it was clear the sailor was answering the rumble of his belly in just such a way. It was worthy of respect.

Then one dusk Le Duc passed Skye. The man's boot-prints vanished up a coulee and did not return. So, the sailor was up there, well off the trail, imagining himself well concealed from pursuers. Le Duc smiled and continued onward. Let Skye discover him ahead, a lone voyageur roasting meat, the smoke of the burning fat drifting with the evening breezes. Skye's belly would lead him straight to the cookfire and then the fun would begin.

Le Duc wished to leave no hoofprints, so he led his horses well off the river road, an easy thing to do now that the river rolled through prairies, and headed upstream all that day. He found an antelope, shot it with one ball, and took the carcass with him. Antelope steaks would whet the appetite of a starving man.

He returned to the river road and made camp at an amiable place he knew, where a copse of trees supplied firewood, the prairie grasses would sustain his horses, and an arrangement of rock would keep the wind off the cookfire. An admirable place, where one could observe river traffic. He settled himself comfortably, hobbled the horses and put them on grass, hung the antelope, gutted it expertly, and hacked off some good flank steaks. Ah, the smell of meat. What the deserter would give for a bellyful.

He built a cheerful fire and let it burn low and hot before he spitted the meat and roasted it. The shadows were long and the sun was dropping, but Skye did not appear. Very well, then. The man would come at dusk, as cautious as a ferret. But Skye did not appear at dusk, either. Uneasily, Le Duc gathered the horses and tied them in camp where the desperado could not steal them. At full dark, Skye had not come in, but Le Duc sensed he was being observed, a sense well known to any voyageur. Ah, this Skye, an admirable rogue.

"Monsieur, I am a child of the wilderness, and I know you are out there, whoever you may be. One feels these things," he said conversationally. "I will take your silence for a hostile act, and prepare myself. If you mean no harm, come share the meat—I have more than enough—and smoke a pipe. I'm Antoine Le Duc, a Canadian trapper."

Le Duc listened intently. He heard movement but no one responded. No doubt Skye was taking a closer look. "Very well, you are as silent as an owl. That means you are no *ami, oui?* It is time for me to put out the fire and then you will not have the advantage."

"I'll smoke the pipe." The voice rose from the east. Skye had circled clear around the camp. Le Duc's respect increased.

"*Alors,* come have *le tabac,*" he said. "And an antelope hangs. Meat is plentiful."

The man emerging from the darkness was exactly as McLoughlin described him: medium height, stocky, powerful—and with a nose. Mon Dieu! *Le nez magnifique!* Never had Le Duc seen a nose so noble.

"*Bien, bien,* I am Le Duc. And you?"

The man hesitated. "I'm Skye. If you're looking for me, say so. If not, I'll share the camp."

"Why would I be looking for you, monsieur?"

"I thought you might be. I was a pressed seaman with the Royal Navy until I jumped ship a fortnight ago. If you intend to capture me, be about it. I've put everything on the table, and that's the way I deal with people. Well?"

"*Formidable!*" Le Duc said. "Let me start some meat. We'll need some more wood."

"No, you answer the question first. The meat can wait. Are you looking for me?"

"I am always looking for friends."

The seaman stared. "You've dodged my question. You're looking for me. I won't be taken alive. If you doubt it, try it." He turned away and walked back into the night.

"*Mon ami,* wait."

But Skye didn't. He vanished into blackness. Le Duc had to admire the hungry man's will. He could have feasted, but he treasured his liberty more. Surprised, Le Duc admitted he had lost the first round. This Skye was a *man.*

Le Duc sprang up and trotted into the darkness, in Skye's general direction. "Monsieur Skye. You are a discerning man. *Oui,* I am from Fort Vancouver. I was sent to find you. McLoughlin, the factor, sent me. Now come share the meat. You are starving. We will talk, *oui?*"

This met with such a silence that Le Duc wondered whether he had been heard. But at last Skye responded in that booming voice of his. "That's better. Now say the rest—that you intend to take me in."

"It is so."

"Now I'll repeat what I said. You won't succeed unless you kill me first. My freedom is worth my life. Go ahead and put it to the test."

He reappeared out of the gloom, squinted at Le Duc in the faint light of the distant fire, and walked to the camp. The man deliberately, carelessly turned his back and set a seabag or some sort of kit on the ground. The act tempted Le Duc to draw his dragoon pistol from his belt, but he didn't. Let him eat and talk, and then he would decide. Skye divested himself of his gear, including a hand-hewn lance, but he kept a single item at hand, a hardwood club with an odd flare in its middle.

"That's a belaying pin," Skye said. "Hardwood. Used to belay ship's lines. Anchor the lines. It's a weapon you'll be testing shortly, I suppose. But I'll eat first."

Le Duc sawed meat from the hanging antelope and set it cooking, and then, gauging his man, cut more. Skye looked ready for two or three servings. Le Duc added some wrinkled potatoes he had collected from the post's root cellar.

Skye didn't devour the food as Le Duc expected, but ate slowly, savoring it all. Le Duc studied his man all the while. Skye had strong, bony features, big hands, and an unexpected youthfulness. Le Duc had expected an older man, but this one was barely into his twenties, with a somber, silent nature that probably concealed a great deal of passion.

Le Duc pulled out his clay pipe and filled it, tamped it, lit it, drew and exhaled an aromatic smoke, and asked Skye if he wanted a pipeful. Skye shook his head.

"What are they saying about me?" Skye asked abruptly.

"I will tell you that after you tell me your story."

Skye hesitated. He seemed to hesitate in all his decisions, something that Le Duc filed away as valuable information. Then Skye described a life, in terms so stark and simple that it took only minutes. A fourteen-year-old boy destined to enter his father's mercantile business, pressed into the Royal Navy off the streets of London. A sullen powder monkey who never surrendered, fought his superiors, tried to regain his liberty, suffered years in iron cages, all while trapped in vessels of war that took him to Africa and the Kaffir wars, and the Bay of Bengal and the uprisings on the Irrawaddy. A rebel who was watched, who rarely put his feet on land, and whose hope of freedom withered—until now.

"Now tell me what they say about me," Skye said.

"Incorrigible, a criminal, a degenerate. Catch Skye and return him to London for court martial. There is a reward for you. Five pounds—alive, nothing dead."

"Then no one will claim it," Skye said.

"I could shoot you."

"Go ahead and try. I'm going to walk away. You'll have your chance."

"Ah, monsieur, it's simpler to wound, simpler to wrestle you into submission."

"If you can," Skye said. "I expect you'll try." He stood suddenly, the belaying pin in hand.

The challenge had to be met. Le Duc's pride was at stake. Not for nothing had Le Duc made himself king of the voyageurs, the right-hand man of the factor, the brawler who could bring anyone in HBC to his knees. Grinning, he sprang up and circled Skye.

"Monsieur, my soul awaits this moment of truth. Now we shall see. Now I'll pound you into dust and carry you back upon my spare horse."

Le Duc sprang joyously, intending to plant a boot in Skye's groin and end the matter in an instant. Instead, Skye's club hit his chest like a ramrod, staggering him and driving breath out of him. When the voyageur tried to yank the belaying pin from Skye's hands, the slippery hardwood offered no grip. He barged into Skye, but the club caught his knee, sending howling pain up his leg. Le Duc gasped. He had never experienced such agony. Next the club rapped his head until his ears rang and slammed into his right arm, rendering it useless. A beast!

It had taken only a moment. Skye stood unscathed, Le

Duc's body howled pain. Not a drop of blood had been spilled.

"Take me if you can," said Skye, who was scarcely even breathing hard. "I'm not going back alive."

"Mon Dieu," Le Duc muttered, massaging his useless arm, rubbing his hurting kneecap, and wondering whether his aching ribs had been broken. His breath returned in gusts. *"C'est magnifique. Sacrebleu!* A thing to remember. A story for the campfires. You are one of us. A man of the wilderness. A grizzly bear. Come to the fire and we shall pour some spirits I took the precaution of carrying with me for medicinal purposes, and I will tell you what fate awaits you."

Chapter 7

Skye lifted the flask, swallowed some awful concoction that burned his gullet, and spit it out, gasping for air.

"What is that?" he cried, his eyes leaking.

"Ah, Monsieur Skye, it is the elixir that lubricates the fur trade. Indian whiskey."

"It's the bloodiest vile stuff I've ever tasted. Have you some rum?"

"Ah, *non,* no one but John McLoughlin possesses any grog worthy of the name. But this is a noble drink, *oui? Formidable.* Pure grain spirits, with a dash of the Columbia River and a plug of tobacco for taste. Ah . . . one little drink and my right arm will work again, my headache will vanish, my ribs will repair themselves, and my knee will stop letting me know its displeasure. Two little drinks and I am the master of men."

Skye sipped again, wiped away the tears, and tackled another dose while a second meal of antelope haunch sizzled over the cheerful fire.

"All right, Le Duc, what's my fate?" he asked.

"Your commodore wishes for your safe return, and has persuaded our factor, the White Eagle, as the giant is called—the resemblance is pronounced—to reel you in like a fat salmon. Little did he know you can't be reeled, monsieur. In my saddlebags are letters to the factors at the posts—McTavish at Fort Nez Perces, Ross at Flathead House on the Clark fork of the Columbia, and another to Peter Ogden, who's leading a trapping brigade south of the Snake—which is on your route if you choose to escape His Royal Majesty's empire."

"I didn't know this was settled country."

"It is not. A few trading posts to get furs from the Indians, nothing more. A few brigades cleaning off beaver before the Yanks flood in. You'll reach Fort Nez Perces in a week or so. It's at the confluence of the Columbia and Snake. A formidable man, McTavish. He will shoot you if it pleases him. He is a cold, mean Scot, without the warmth and humanity of a Frenchman. Me, I would spare your life; a man deserves his liberty if he wants it more than life. But McTavish, he is a political animal, and will make meat of you if it pleases the company."

"I'll dodge the post."

"*Mais oui,* go around it. He will have the express I am delivering and will be looking for you. And so will all the Indians he trades with."

Skye sipped the fiery brew and contemplated that. "I knew Hudson's Bay would throw out a net."

He pulled the sizzling meat off the spit, let it cool, and then began gnawing on it while Le Duc drank and coughed and drank more.

"I'm getting my courage back, Skye. Whiskey courage. Soon I will try you again. *Voila!* I can move my right arm again. Next time, it won't be so easy for you. I shall be wary of the belaying pin. And you'll be sotted on this poison, an easy target."

"If you whip me, you still won't take me back alive," Skye said, gnawing meat.

"I will whip you. No man defeats Antoine Le Duc more than once or for long. I will show you what a man is."

Skye said nothing. He hadn't escaped a brutal life just to get into a contest of manhood with this voyageur. The more Le Duc drank, the more he was nerving himself to try Skye again—maybe with fatal results for either of them. Skye swallowed back the instinct to prove he was a match for any Hudson's Bay man—his pride was at stake—and considered.

He knew, somehow, that this was a defining moment in his life. He could guzzle more of that noxious brew, keeping pace with the voyageur, and then find out which of them ruled the roost. Or he could reach for better things. He had his liberty—if he could keep it.

He was still young, and probably much more serious than most his age. Years of oppression had left their mark on his moods. In all his years in the navy, he had fought when forced to fight, just to assert his right to a life, or to get food, or to stop the harassment of some petty lord of the 'tween decks. But not because he enjoyed hurting others, or lording over them, or playing cock of the walk. He would have preferred to read a book.

Quietly he arose, ignored Le Duc's taunts, and sawed

more meat from the hanging carcass. He didn't stop at one serving, but cut all he could—enough to last two or three days if possible. Le Duc drank, swore gallic oaths, and gathered his courage to provoke another brawl, but it didn't matter. Skye loaded the meat into his seabag, stowed his cape and other gear, gathered up his rude lance, and walked into the darkness.

"Skye, *merde!* Halt or I'll shoot."

Skye ignored the man and hastened into the blackness, veering to the right. He had told the voyageur his freedom meant more than life, and now he was being put to the test. Live free or die. He walked quietly, awaiting his fate.

"Va t'en au diable," the man cried.

The crack of the musket didn't startle Skye, nor did its ball strike him. The shot was bravado, fired into the air. He slid into the void of night and circled back, keeping an eye on the distant pinprick of fire until he was well west of the campsite, and then he rolled up in his sail-cloth. Let Le Duc sober up and ride ahead in the morning. There would probably be meat left over to cook and eat, and Skye was in no hurry.

It began to rain in the night, and Skye spent the last miserable hours before a gloomy dawn huddled under his sailcloth and feeling cold. He thought he was about half a mile inland from the river, but this was open prairie and if he rose and walked he would be visible. So he waited while the gray day brightened slightly. He could not see Le Duc or his horses, but still he waited. Let the man go ahead and warn the HBC. Skye would bide his time.

At last, he trudged down to the campsite and found no one there. The carcass was gone. Le Duc, with his wilderness instincts, knew exactly what Skye would do. The meat was probably feeding the fish in the river. Skye sighed. He liked the Canadian and knew the Canadian liked him, and knew Le Duc would redouble his efforts to bring the deserter to his knees.

Skye edged back from the river and hiked eastward once again, solitary but safe, his energies focused on preserving his freedom and renewing his life. The prints of horses preceded him. If they veered off the trace, he would be watchful. But he suspected that Le Duc would hurry to Fort Nez Perces and elsewhere, delivering his expresses, and never say a word about encountering the fugitive himself.

The evening with Le Duc had been rewarding. He now knew that HBC was looking for him, and he knew what lay ahead. He knew there was a reward for anyone who brought him in alive. That was all important, potentially lifesaving knowledge.

He hiked through a silent land and came late in the afternoon to a cold river rushing out of the south. He knew he would have to swim it. Unhappily, he doffed his clothing, stuffed it into his seabag along with his belaying pin, and wobbled into the water, feeling it stab his feet and ankles and then suddenly his thighs. The thunderous cold smacked him but there was no help for it. He swam furiously, feeling the icy water sap his energy and swirl him toward the Columbia, but at last, exhausted, he crawled up the far side, stubbing toes on rock, and dressed. He was chilled to the marrow and needed a fire.

He trotted eastward, trying to warm his numb body, and largely succeeded. But late that afternoon he rounded a bend and came upon an Indian fishery and village. Short, golden-fleshed people swarmed around him, looking him over, their countenances cheerful. Skye eyed them uneasily, wondering if they were measuring him for a reward from Hudson's Bay. But the men of the village didn't seem hostile. They crowded about, eyeing his warbag, his crude lance, and his clothing. The women smiled and studied him when they thought he wasn't aware. The naked children stared politely.

Wasn't this what he wanted? Wasn't this the succor that he knew he needed? Skye heartened at his reception, and tried some English on them. "Well, mates, do ye speak my tongue? Can we talk?"

They smiled blankly. One tried some hand signals that Skye took to be a means of communicating, but he could not make out the meaning. He thought he ought to give them something, anything, as a signal of his esteem. But he needed everything he possessed: he could not spare his awl or shoe leather or flint and striker or fishhook and line, or any of his ragged clothes. But yes, there was something he needed a little less than the rest: his coil of rope. This he extracted from his kit and offered to an older, wire-haired man whose bearing and dignity suggested he was the headman.

The muscular older man hefted the line, uncoiled it, found it a worthy gift, and grinned. This, in turn, evoked a flood of gifts in return, much to Skye's astonishment. The women hastened to their bark huts and returned bearing all sorts of things: a fine, tanned deerskin, a fringed leather shirt with dyed geometric designs on it, smoked salmon, and baked cakes made of some sort of meal. A bonanza. Skye bowed, expressed his thanks in English, and found himself being escorted to the center of the place where meals were cooking in big iron kettles that must have been gotten from Hudson's Bay traders.

That evening Skye feasted on all the fresh pink salmon he could eat, along with some sort of greens and meal-cakes. The women vied to please him, and he acknowledged each gift, each delicacy. A little boy edged close and finally ran a finger down Skye's giant nose, and Skye knew what it was about him that fascinated these people. They had never seen a formidable nose before. Perhaps they thought big noses signified power or importance. That dusk the headmen shared a pipe with him and he was ushered into a bark-walled lodge and to a pallet. Luxury, he thought, a respite from starvation and loneliness. He did not even know the name of this river tribe, or their personal names, but they had welcomed him generously. A dozen people, grandparents, parents, large and small children, called that hut home but Skye didn't feel crowded. Instead, he felt safe. He had not been in the bosom of a family since he was a boy, and now he lay in the close dark, aware of all those people, knowing he must never spin out his life alone.

Chapter 8

Skye pulled the elkskin shirt over his navy blouse and found that it fit well enough to use without alteration. It had a curious design, with leather fringes dangling from the arms. The skins had not been trimmed below the waist, and the fringes there hung unevenly, making an odd hemline around his thighs. It was well-used and soft, and permeated with tallow that would turn the rain. Bold zigzag designs in red and blue decorated the chest and back. He appreciated its warmth and knew a good leather shirt would be comfortable in the wilds, subduing the wind.

The headman's family stood around him, enjoying the spectacle. He prepared to leave but they insisted he breakfast with them, and once again he filled his belly, this time with some sort of fish cake that had berries in it.

Even that early in the morning, many of the village's young men were perched out on a rickety catwalk over the river, slender spears in hand, stabbing the occasional salmon that swam by. Skye watched, fascinated, believing he could fashion a spear out of his spare knife and a pole. If he found an abandoned fishery poking into the river, he would tarry there and try to spear salmon.

Several of the village men carried bows and quivers full of arrows, and Skye ached to possess the weapon. He had never shot an arrow in his life but he didn't doubt that necessity would teach him swiftly. He would learn well enough to kill game—or starve. Inspired to trade, he dug into his warbag and pulled out a treasured possession that he could nonetheless do without. He used his folding straight-edged razor now and then to keep his whiskers at bay. But now he needed a bow and arrows far more than a shaven face. He approached one of those who carried a bow, gestured toward it and the quiver, and then laid his shaving kit before him on the ground. He opened the razor and handed it to the man. The man gingerly ran a thumb over the blade and grinned. Skye's shaving gear included a battered white mug, some soap, and a shaving brush, and with all these and some river water he shaved himself while the villagers crowded about.

The man took the razor and handed Skye the quiver and bow. Skye rejoiced. With luck and some hunting skills, he might feed himself. He counted eleven arrows: enough to keep him fed.

He turned to his host, wondering what to give the man for his hospitality, and finally decided he could surrender his woolen skullcap. He handed it to the headman, who grinned and put it on. A swift command sent his wife hurrying into the bark hut, and she returned with a beaver-felt top hat, a trade item from Hudson's Bay. Much to Skye's delight, it fit, perhaps too snugly but it would stretch with use. The brim would shade his chapped face and keep the rain off his neck.

He ached to do more trading, especially for a horse, but he saw none. He doubted these fishing people had any. He knew what he would offer for one: his pea jacket. The new leather shirt would do for warmth, and summer was coming. After thanking his hosts with gestures he hoped would be understood, Skye departed eastward, enjoying his new wealth. He had a little antelope meat and some fresh fish—and a bow and arrows.

He examined the arrows, curious about their manufacture. They had been made from reeds and had sheet-iron points bound to the shaft with sinew. The points were trade items from Hudson's Bay. The bow had been fashioned of a blond wood that reminded him of yew, and was strung with animal gut. He would have to be careful with it because he lacked a spare string. As he walked, he nocked arrows and shot them ahead, getting the feel of the weapon. He collected the arrows as he passed by. He knew he had much to learn, and his efforts had been awkward. He didn't even know how to hold the bow and arrow. But by the nooning, he was getting better.

The country turned rugged again, and the river boiled between dark rock cliffs. The road veered sharply away from the Columbia and ascended a steep and much-used trail. Plainly these narrows blocked passage along the river and one had to detour around them. He could hear a faint roar as the Columbia bored through the gorge. When at last the trail took him back to water, he found himself in a land largely devoid of trees.

That evening he counted the day a good one. He baited his hook and line, and then practiced with his bow and arrows, gaining skill through the dusk. No longer was he helpless. But skill with a bow wasn't the same as being a hunter. He rarely even saw an animal. But as he penetrated these steppes day by day, he spotted distant herds of antelope, and once he saw wild horses. His first success with the bow was a humble one: he shot a raccoon. Greedily, he dressed the animal and then built a fire to cook it. The result was abominable, but the mouthfuls of soft meat helped sustain him. He counted it a milestone.

He had better luck with his fishhook and line, occasionally netting a salmon that kept him fed for two days. The weather warmed, and his passage would have seemed idyllic but for his constant hunger. He was plagued by loneliness, too, and ached to talk with someone, anyone. How far to Fort Nez Perces? How far to the edge of the Oregon country? How far to the American settlements? North America was a vast continent, but he had hiked eastward for weeks on end. Surely he would arrive at the Atlantic side soon. Or would he?

He was traversing a vast plain, broken by outcrops of dark volcanic rock and populated by horses that galloped madly away as he approached. He ached to capture one, but he knew little about them. He had never sat a horse.

His boots fell apart, and he repaired them with his awl and some thong. His trousers wore to pieces, and he sewed the rents and patched them with sailcloth. All this time he saw no one, and his loneliness ate at his spirits. Was this all there was? Would he die some lonely death in these empty wilds? What good was freedom if it came to nothing? He talked to himself, talked to the prickly pear cactus, talked to the crows that gossiped about his passage. Some evenings caught him in places without firewood, but he had learned to cook all of any salmon he caught and could make a meal of cold fish if he had to.

Then one day he lost a hook and line. It snagged on something and his line snapped. Skye found himself holding a pole with a foot of string dangling from it. With no more line, he might well starve.

He felt more and more oppressed as he considered the loss. He stood on the riverbank, drawn bow in hand, knowing the wealth of food that lay in those waters, maddened that he could capture none of it. He would have to turn himself into a hunter or starve. Immediately he hiked far away from the river, looking for game and finding none. When he returned at dusk, a terrible pessimism stole through him.

Standing there beside the mighty Columbia River with all its unreachable food, he asked himself why he had been set on earth. He had suffered in the navy, and now he suffered more. Did some people's lives simply take a wrong turn, never to be redeemed? Would he wander this wilderness until he died an early death? Would he be better off turning around, tracing his way back to Fort Vancouver, and turn himself over to John McLoughlin? It was tempting, if only because he would have companionship.

In the past he had occasionally fallen into bouts of despair, especially when he was locked in ships' brigs for weeks on end. He knew that there was only one cure for it: he had to drive the demon out of himself. He must never surrender to despair. He might now be in grave trouble, but he was not defeated. He reminded himself that he was alive and free. He had to help himself because no one else would. It was bootless to question the meaning of his existence, or why his had been a hard lot, or whether there was justice in the world. Such speculations never solved anything. He would keep on. He would suffer and starve if he must, but he would not quit and he would not surrender the liberty he had won at such terrible cost. With that resolve, and with a half-muttered prayer to the mysterious God who let him suffer so much, he started east once again.

The next day he shot an antelope. He could not explain it. The handsome animal stood on a slight rise, watching him approach, probably a sentinel for the nearby herd. It should have fled, but it didn't. Itchily, he nocked an arrow and eased closer, to perhaps thirty yards. A long shot for a novice with a bow. The antelope didn't present much target, facing him almost squarely. But he drew, aimed, and loosed his fingers. The arrow whipped true and buried itself in the animal's chest. The antelope took a few steps and collapsed.

Exultantly, Skye raced to it and found it was dying. He retrieved his arrow, pulling gently until it came free. He was a long way from the river a longer way to firewood. In fact, he didn't see a tree anywhere, but he knew a few grew near the water, often hidden from the prairies. The antelope was too heavy to carry and cumbersome to drag. Skye decided to lighten the load by gutting it, which took a while in hot sun. He didn't really know what he was doing, and doubted that his kitchen knife was the ideal tool. The carcass was still too heavy, so Skye slowly cut off its head, having trouble with bone and cartilage. Now at last he felt he could hoist the carcass to one shoulder, his warbag over the other, and stagger back to the river.

The half-mile trek exhausted him, but he reached the stony bank, washed the carcass and himself, and hunted for wood. He saw none. He stumbled a mile more along the river before he came to a crease in the land full of stumpy trees and brush, enough of it dead to give him what he needed. He exulted, and set to work at once, building a hot fire, butchering meat, and preparing for a feast.

He ate a bellyful of the tender meat, and toiled relentlessly at butchering the rest of the animal. He meant to cut it into thin strips and dry it if he could. The sheer toil amazed him. He lacked so much as a hatchet and had to break dry limbs off trees with brute strength to keep the fire going. He had to saw the meat patiently, being careful not to cut himself. And then he had to rig a grid of green sticks upon which to dry and smoke the meat.

Dusk arrived but he was scarcely aware of it because this bonanza of meat inspired unceasing labor. When he did look up at last, he discovered he wasn't alone. Half a dozen white men in buckskins stared down at him, and even as he reacted, he saw dozens more, including Indian women, join them. They multiplied, more and more of them crowding the hilltop along with pack horses and mules.

He had run into a fur brigade, but knew not whether it was British or Yank.

He paused, wiped the sweat from his brow, lifted his top hat, and waited.

Chapter 9

Peter Skene Ogden saw at once that this was the fugitive sailor, Skye, although the man was wearing a fringed buckskin shirt and a battered topper. McLoughlin's express, which Le Duc had delivered a few days before, warned that the Royal Navy considered this man a dangerous and incorrigible criminal.

Ogden had kept the information to himself. He had a cynical streak, and nothing aroused his amused skepticism more than the posturing of the servants of the Crown, especially the dread lords of the Admiralty. Ogden also had his own designs, and perhaps Skye would fit into them. Nonetheless, the man bore watching.

He hurried his trapping brigade down the long slope while Skye waited in the dusk, wary and silent. The man certainly fit McLoughlin's sketchy description. The nose—my God, what a nose—identified him.

"Ogden here. I don't believe we've met," he said.

Skye paused, his gaze searching, and then seemed to come to some conclusion. "I'm Barnaby Skye, sir. Call me Mister Skye."

"Mister Skye it is, then."

The brigade swarmed around Skye, eyeing him curiously. Ogden had taken these thirty trappers and camp tenders, plus their Indian wives, out last fall, and now was returning to Fort Vancouver with the winter's harvest of beaver pelts. They had trapped the Snake River country, garnering somewhat fewer than the three thousand pelts Hudson's Bay needed to turn a profit.

"I've some meat here," Skye said. "Just cooking it up. Help yourself."

"That's mighty kind. Fact is, we haven't seen a four-footed beast in two days. We're subsisting ourselves on salmon. All right, gents, divide it up."

An antelope wouldn't go far among thirty-seven men and women, but the whole brigade would get a serving. Ogden examined Skye's gear, finding only a bow and arrows. Offering that meat had meant sacrifice, which only heightened Ogden's curiosity about this notorious man.

"A man grows weary of salmon," Skye said.

"You heading somewhere, Skye? Any way I can help?"

"It's Mister Skye, sir. That title gives a common man dignity here in the New World. Any man can claim it, and I do. I've been known only by my last name since I was a lad of fourteen. I heard not even Barnaby, my Christian name, sir. Only Skye, as if a freeborn Englishman deserved nothing more."

"I share the sentiment. Call me Mr. Ogden," the brigade leader said, enjoying himself and Skye. "You're an Englishman. I'm a Canadian. We're bound by the Crown, then."

Skye said nothing, his face hiding some interior world from Ogden. It wouldn't do to push the man, Ogden thought. "We'll make camp here, if you don't mind. You've found the only firewood in miles, and there's plenty of grass for these half-starved mounts. I'm taking a lot of beaver back to Fort Vancouver. We've been in the Snake River country. You heading that way or heading west?"

"East, sir. Perhaps you can give me directions."

"Ah, directions to where?"

"Boston, Mr. Ogden."

"Boston?"

"It has a college I wish to attend, sir. Harvard. In a place called Cambridge. My schooling was interrupted long ago, and I wish to continue with it."

"But Boston's on the Atlantic coast."

"It's where I'm headed."

"Do you have any idea—no, obviously you don't. We have some tea I've been hoarding. I'll break it out. We'll have a cup and talk, eh?"

Skye smiled for the first time. "Tea. It's been a long time since I've sipped it."

Ogden could hardly believe his ears. In the space of a minute or two, Skye had demolished the reputation that preceded him. College. Boston. Sharing the antelope. Politeness and courtesy. Insistence on a dignified title. Either Skye wasn't the man the navy represented to McLoughlin, or else Skye was a master dissembler, capable of impressing people with the appearance of transparent honesty.

The man wandered the camp, looking itchy and uneasy while Ogden's brigade settled down for the night. He seemed a loner, unwilling to make friends with the voyageurs. But maybe that should be ascribed to his fugitive status.

Ogden let Skye wander while he set some tea to brewing in a fire-blackened pot. His Creole free trappers required constant attention. If he wasn't on hand to make sure the horses were hobbled and put out to graze, they might not be. If he wasn't around to set a guard, no guard would be posted. He had learned to command his trapping brigade with good humor, some jawboning, and an occasional show of strength. He wasn't a large man but he could mete out more than he took from any of them.

HBC had entrusted him with its most important trapping brigade precisely because he was good with the men.

The embarrassment of last season still aggrieved him. That was when the Americans had set up their rendezvous system and lured away twenty-three of Ogden's trappers by offering much higher prices—eight times the HBC price—for beaver pelts, while selling them supplies at moderate cost right in the mountains, so that the trappers didn't have to head back to a Hudson's Bay post for equipment. It had been an ugly season that had come close to bloodshed. Ogden despised his deserters, abominated the shifty Americans, coldly refused to leave the territory the Yanks were calling their own, and met threat with threat. At the same time, he had swiftly informed his superiors that many more of HBC's trappers would desert unless they were paid decent prices for their plews, as beaver pelts were called. The Creoles rightly protested that HBC had deliberately kept its trappers in bondage, working to pay off trading post debts that could never be repaid.

The company had reformed itself, more or less, and now Ogden led a brigade that had remained loyal and reasonably content—in a tentative sort of way. His mission had been to sweep the entire Snake country of its beaver, to keep the Americans out. He had done just that, ruthlessly cleaning beaver out of the country south of the Snake. But he was still shorthanded, and reliable men were a rare commodity in the wilderness. Maybe there'd be a place for Skye—if McLoughlin and HBC's governor, George Simpson, agreed. Which was a big if.

"Mister Skye, the tea's steeped," he said.

He handed the fugitive a cup. Skye settled on the ground, near Ogden's own small fire. They sipped contentedly, while Ogden wondered how to broach the various topics that came to mind. The trappers were all busy making camp, so they were more or less alone.

"I wonder if you know how far Boston is, sir. And what lies between."

"It doesn't matter, Mr. Ogden."

That answer, too, astonished the brigade's bourgeois, as the Creoles called him. Ogden tried another tack. "You're ill-equipped to cross the continent. It's nearly two thousand miles to the Mississippi River, and another thousand to Boston. Cold, heat, starvation, savages, disease, clothing falling off your body. Don't try it. If you'll hire on with HBC, you'll soon have enough to go east in safety and a chance of keeping yourself fed. I'll supply you right now, and you can work off the debt."

"That's a kind offer, Mr. Ogden. But I will go my way with what I have."

"It's suicide."

"Death, sir, can be the lesser of two evils."

"I see you're serious," Ogden said, impressed. It was mountain etiquette not to inquire too closely into a man's past. His brigades had been populated by wanted men, scoundrels, dodgers of all sorts. But by some sort of unspoken agreement, they all had a chance to redeem themselves here. What counted was what a man could do, the contribution he could make, and not what he had been. In any case, the harsh and dangerous life weeded out the malcontents and worthless men. Weak men didn't last long. They died or fled.

"This life can be so terrible that one is forced to put his hope on the next one. The lowest and darkest corner of paradise, Mr. Ogden, is the dream of a man whose every hope has been crushed." Skye stared at Ogden somberly.

"I am a free man. This wilderness is paradise itself. Every hour of my journey, my heart leaps and my soul rejoices and I sing my own hymns to our Creator."

Ogden, for once in his life, was speechless.

"I believe you already know much about me, and all this dissembling evades the issue," Skye continued.

"Why—"

"I am called a deserter by the Royal Navy and the company is offering five pounds to anyone who'll deliver me to Fort Vancouver alive. My capture will please the Admiralty."

Ogden laughed. "Somehow, you've met and impressed Le Duc, our express runner. The rogue never confessed to meeting you, but I know he did. He acted oddly. I met him ten days ago on the Snake River. He was on his way to Flathead Post, bearing the same express he gave me."

"No one will collect the five pounds, Mr. Ogden. Because I won't be taken alive. Try it and you'll find out soon enough."

Ogden shook his head, intrigued with this man. "I have no designs, Mister Skye. The fact is, I was hoping to make a trapper of you. I need every man I can get."

"That won't be possible, sir. I won't work for Hudson's Bay or any of the Crown's men, and I won't stay in British territory."

Skye's assertion certainly had a finality about it, Ogden thought.

"Well, sir, would you honor me with your story? If you want my opinion, the official version of events is usually concocted by men protecting their backsides. In your case, by a titled fool who commands His Majesty's ships more by politics and connections than merit. They all get along

all right—except in war, and then they serve the kingdom badly."

Skye ladled more tea from the pot and sipped it. "I'm
the son of a London merchant," he began, "intending to
join my family's import-export firm after a good schooling at Cambridge, Jesus College, my father's alma ma-
ter. It never happened . . ."

For the next half hour Ogden listened to a story of
desperation, obstinate courage, official malfeasance, despair, and sheer determination. This unfortunate might
have won his freedom in time had he smoothed things
over and done a lengthy stint as a seaman without further
blemish, but he had stubbornly resisted until he could escape. Maybe that had been poor judgment on Skye's part,
but he had been a fourteen-, fifteen-, seventeen-year-old
boy through the worst of it. Ogden wasn't sure but he
would have fought just as hard, had he been that boy.

Skye finished his story and stood up, gazing into a
cloudless night. "There's the north star and dipper, sir. For
the rest of my life, no man will ever keep these eyes from
seeing those stars. If I cannot leave my house or shelter
and see those stars at will, I will cast my life away as a
useless thing."

"You could have that life as a free trapper for us. I'll
arrange it. I can set things right with the company. If by
any chance it puts you in danger, I'll be the first to let you
know. You impress me. That's all I can say."

"Thank you, Mr. Ogden. I'm an Englishman and always will be. But I'm a man without a country now."

That sufficed for an answer, and Ogden knew his options had reduced to two: let him go, or watch him die
because the man would not be taken alive.

Chapter 10

Skye liked Peter Ogden but didn't trust him. He would know in the morning what Ogden's intentions were. At that time, the fur brigade would load its horses and head toward Fort Vancouver. And Skye, if he were left alone, would continue east.

Would they seize him at the last minute? He had no way of knowing. He had done what he could: told Ogden, with utmost seriousness, that they would never take him back alive. And he meant it. He would keep his liberty or perish.

He dozed restlessly that night, awakening with a start at the slightest shift of the rhythms of the night. He kept his larger kitchen knife at hand and would use it if he had to. But the night passed quietly, and even before dawn the camp tenders and the country wives, as the trappers called their Indian mates, were building cookfires.

It seemed a good time to go. Most of the trappers still lay in their bedrolls, although some were collecting horses in the gray dawn and throwing packframes over them. Skye rolled up his sailcloth and stuffed it in his warbag, gathered his bow and arrows, and returned his kitchen knife to a crude sheath at his belt. He would miss breakfast, but liberty was worth more than food.

"Mister Skye."

He whirled to find Ogden standing behind him, grinning.

"Stay and eat. You're a free man and you'll stay a free man. Shake on it."

Reluctantly, his mind swarming with suspicions, he shook Ogden's outstretched hand.

"I'm going to repay you for the meat. We've some jerky. I'll give you the rest of our tea. The Creoles don't care about it. They aren't Englishmen."

Skye nodded. "Obliged," he said. "I'm looking for some other things. I have one thing to trade—a heavy wool pea jacket—and don't know what it'll bring. I need a rifle or musket and powder and balls, a trap, fishing lures and line, hatchet or ax, a fishing net, blankets, horse . . ."

Ogden considered. "There's things the company can't do, such as take a contraband jacket in trade. And we're desperately short of arms. Five trappers lack firearms. Lost, broken, stolen. Then again, there's things the company can do. It can lose a trap. I've a Nez Perce fishnet I traded for some gunpowder. The company's short of horses, but most of the Creoles have their own. Maybe one or another will decide a warm coat's worth a plug horse."

The prospect gladdened Skye. He followed Ogden over to the cookfires, where two camp tenders were hustling up some grub. Ogden raided some panniers and supplied Skye with a canister of tea and several pounds of jerky. Then he headed toward another pile of gear and rummaged through panniers.

"Trade stuff. Most of it gone. Here." He handed Skye an iron hatchet blade, oddly made.

"War hatchet, the kind they like. You'll have to whittle a haft and wedge it in. That's about as much as I can get away with, Mister Skye. It's a trade for the meat."

Skye hefted the iron hatchet head as if it were gold, and then examined the trap.

"Here, let me explain a few things," Ogden said. "This is an American trap we picked up on the Malade. It's not even in my HBC inventory. It'll catch beaver, but you can use it for small animals as well. If you're going for beaver, you'll need castorum for bait, and you'll need to learn a few things."

Skye listened quietly while Ogden demonstrated how to set the trap, how to chain it in place, how to bait it, how to look for beaver grounds, how to check the trap. Ogden described how to cook and eat beaver tail, how to gut the beaver, flesh the hide, stretch it on a hoop and let it dry that way into a presentable plew. It all seemed too much to master, but Skye absorbed all he could, listening carefully. Ogden gave Skye a small, stoppered bone flask of castorum as a final gesture, and then led Skye to the cookfires. The fare that morning was salmon. The brigade, at the end of its trapping season, had little else.

The sun was rising by the time the cookfires were extinguished, and Skye knew he had only minutes to strike a trade. He pulled out his pea jacket and approached a Creole.

"Ah, you are Monsieur Skye," the man said. "I have the great honor. You gave us meat. I am your humble servant, Bordeau."

"I'm interested in a trade, Mr. Bordeau. How about this wool coat? Does it interest you?"

"Ah, such a warm coat always interests Bordeau."

"Try it on. It looks about right."

"Ah, but what is it that you wish to trade for? I am only a trapper, owing HBC all that I make."

"A horse and bridle and saddle."

"Ah, *non,* that is not possible. My two horses must carry me and my equipage, and I have none to spare. A pity. I would give two wives and a daughter for such a fine coat. Too much do I freeze my bones in these wilds."

Skye approached the other free trappers, one by one, with the same result. They all had their reasons, but it came clear to Skye that none of them considered the coat worth a horse and bridle, and so they had politely declined to trade. Skye caught Ogden grinning. Skye's efforts had become this morning's spectacle.

Skye considered trading for other things. A good warm coat should fetch him all sorts of items: moccasins, knives, things to trade to the Indians, gloves, leggings, spoons, forks, a frying pan. But time had run out. Ogden was putting his brigade on the road. The beaver packs were back on the gaunt, hard-wintered horses, the camp gear stowed, the trappers standing about, scratching under their buckskins for greybacks, or off in the bushes.

Ogden approached. "No luck, eh?"

"Mr. Ogden, I'm a lucky man. I'm free, and I'm outfitted, and I have you to thank."

Ogden smiled, mischief dancing in his eyes. "See that log? You sit on one side and I'll sit on the other. We'll arm wrestle. You lose, and I take you with me. I lose, and you get a horse."

Skye darkened swiftly. "Mr. Ogden, I'll arm wrestle, but not on those terms. No bet. Nothing, no one, takes me back—alive."

Ogden gestured Skye toward the log and sat himself on the far side of it. The trappers congregated. *Très bien,* what a morning! Skye settled himself on the other side, and dug his boots into the clay. The bourgeois looked to be slightly shorter but powerfully built.

Skye had done this before with many seamen, and he knew the tricks. So he was ready when Ogden clasped his hand and went for a victory with one violent lurch. Skye had intended to do the same, and the result was a brutal standoff. Skye felt his sweat rise and the muscles of his arm strain and hurt. He dug in and threw his weight into a victory plunge, only to lose ground. Much to his astonishment he found himself twisted the wrong way, his hand only six inches from defeat.

He felt the tremors as he twisted his arm upward an inch, then two. Now it was Ogden's turn to sweat. The dance in Ogden's eyes told Skye the bourgeois was enjoying himself. Two more sallies yielded nothing to either man. Then Ogden laughed, gathered his resolve, slammed Skye's hand onto the log, and kept it there long enough for the trappers to hoot. Then he let go.

Ogden danced to his feet, saying nothing, his face alive with delight. Men hoorahed and slapped his back. He shrugged them off and helped Skye to his feet.

"I let you go," he said.

"No," said Skye, "you let me live."

Ogden slapped Skye on the back, found a stick, and led Skye to some sandy soil, where he drew a map. "You'll follow the Columbia another forty or fifty miles pretty much east. Then the Columbia swings north, like this. Near there you'll reach the Walla Walla River and Fort Nez Perces at the confluence. Visit it or not, as you choose. You can follow the Walla Walla into the Blue Mountains and over to the drainage of the Snake, like this. But most of the country south of the Snake's unexplored. Or you can go up the Columbia until you reach the Snake, and follow it east, like this. It loops north and then dips south in a big arc. It's rough country and the trail will take you miles south of the river where it cuts through a long canyon. I don't recommend that route.

"You'll likely run into two tribes—Nez Perces and then the Snakes, or Shoshones. I can't say what they'll do to a lone man. They're friendly enough to a fur brigade with things to trade, but they're likely to steal anything they can get from you, so be on your guard. Watch out for Blackfeet—plains Indians, well dressed in gaudy clothes, good horses. They'll butcher any lone white man they can find."

"Is there a way to befriend the Snakes and Nez Perces?"

"A white man never knows. They live by their own rules. But they're likely to be friendly, especially if you give 'em a gift or two and smoke the pipe with the elders. If they ask you to smoke, do it. Just follow their routine exactly. It's a peace ceremony."

"Where'll the Snake River take me?"

"To the Americans. They're all scoundrels and black-guards, and I shouldn't send you to them, but they'll get you to Boston and maybe outfit you. They rendezvous in July down in Cache Valley—that's Snake country, and the Snakes'll take you there. They go to trade."

"Rendezvous?"

"A mountain fair. They—Ashley and his partners—send a pack-mule supply outfit from St. Louis and trade with the trappers for beaver pelts, which they take back. Long journey, over a thousand miles. It's your ticket to Boston. Your only ticket. You've got six weeks to get to Cache Valley."

"How do I tell the Snakes I want to go there? I can't speak their tongue."

"You won't have to. If you reach 'em before they leave, you'll be taken right along. They'll think that's where you're going anyway." He stood up. "Write me from Harvard, Mister Skye."

"I will, Mr. Ogden."

"And don't linger in British territory. HBC is an arm of the Crown. John McLoughlin's a bulldog. If he wants you, he'll get you sooner or later. Maybe next year, maybe in three or five years. Mark my words. Stay out of any place claimed by Great Britain. And if you stay in the mountains with the Yanks, watch out anyway. HBC has its ways, and if they want you they'll take you—dead or alive, right in front of a crowd."

"I won't forget."

Odgen clapped him on the back. "Good. Don't forget."

The brigade left immediately, and suddenly Skye found himself back in an aching wilderness, more silent and lonely than before. He watched the outfit climb the slope and vanish on the far side. He wanted to run after them.

He was alone again. Nothing stirred, not even so much as a crow. He felt desolated. Once again he realized how badly he needed company. Ogden had helped him. It was the first help he had ever received from anyone during his adult life. No one in the navy had helped him—or cared.

He wondered why Ogden had helped, and no good explanation came to mind. Skye had never thought much about getting along with people or what it took. Maybe that was because he was never free. But in Ogden he had found a friend.

Joyously he examined his new gear. The number four trap was heavy, and so was its chain. His hatchet head was heavy, and so was the small seine net, which had lead weights at the bottom and loops at the top for floats or a long supporting pole. The jerky, wrapped in an ancient piece of oilcloth, was heavy, too. He loaded all these things into his warbag, slipped his bow and quiver over his shoulder, and started east, toward Boston.

Chapter 11

Dourly, Skye examined Fort Nez Perces from across the Walla Walla River, wondering whether to go on in and risk trouble. It was walled by a stockade of upright logs planted in the sandy earth, and bastions loomed at opposite corners. A crimson flag bearing the cross of St. George in an upper corner flapped lazily on a staff. Skye supposed it was the Hudson's Bay ensign. It looked British.

The post stood on the Columbia's shore just above the confluence of the Walla Walla River. The country was so bleak it gave Skye a chill. For miles he had followed the river through arid, rough, treeless country unfit for habitation. Just why the post had been planted in such a locale he couldn't imagine—unless the Walla Walla was a thoroughfare into more bountiful lands. He thought he saw distant mountains in the eastern haze and wondered what they were.

He decided to go in. He needed instructions. He was dressed as a trapper now and his brown beard had sprouted luxuriantly since he had traded his razor. In addition to what he had started with, he was carrying a beaver trap and bow and arrows—hardly the equipment of a seaman. His heroic nose might give him away; it already had. But he would take that risk.

For days he had toiled upriver alone, carrying a heavy duffel now: the trap, seine net, and the rest. The bleakness of this empty land tormented him, awakened a hunger in him for companionship, the sound of voices. He forded the Walla Walla, which ran cold and hard with spring runoff, and climbed the sandy soil to the post, which slumbered in midday sun. He saw not a soul about the fort, although he could see someone hoeing in a distant garden plot that probably provided the post with its vegetables.

He plunged through the open gates and found himself in a yard, with what appeared to be the trading area immediately on his left. There he entered a low, dark, rough-made room with a counter and shelves lined with bolts of bright fabric, gray iron traps, casks and sacks of sugar and coffee and beans, and sundries. The scents of burlap and leather were pleasant in his nostrils.

"I've been watching ye through the glass for nigh twenty minutes," said an angular, red-haired, fierce-looking man with a voice that grated like sand under a horseshoe. "No living creature passes Fort Nez Perces unknown. Not even an ant."

"Then there must not be much else to do," Skye said.

"It's our protection, ye well know that or ye don't know the country."

"I don't know it."

"I'm Ross McTavish, factor here, and ye speak an Englishman's tongue."

Skye shrugged. "And you a Canadian's, I suppose."

"You're not giving me a name."

"Mr. Ogden told me Ronald Mackenzie would be here."

"He's not. Ye have it wrong. Mackenzie founded it, eighteen and eighteen, when he was still a Nor' Wester. Then it was run by Alexander Ross. And now I'm the man. This is mine, all mine."

"A Scots post, then."

"And what is the matter with that? Ye be a bloody roundhead Englishman and think ye rule the world?"

"No, I rule only my own life."

"Ye haven't given me a name, and I'll give ye no more time to think on it. If ye be not the deserter Skye, then prove it. It's the nose. McLoughlin said the sniffer would tell the hull story. And it does."

McTavish reached under the counter and whipped a dragoon pistol up at Skye. "Now then, set down the pack and walk ahead o' me."

"No."

"What do ye mean, no? Do ye think I won't shoot? Put down the pack!"

Skye stared into the huge bore of that weapon and wished he hadn't surrendered to the impulse to stop here. This fierce Scotsman was going to try him. He didn't answer. Instead, he deliberately turned to leave, and took two steps toward the door when a deafening blast erupted behind him and his topper sailed off his head.

"Stop or I'll be on ye, Skye. That was a warnin'."

He headed toward the door, heard McTavish leap the counter and plunge after him. Skye whirled, belaying pin in hand, and jabbed it hard as McTavish leapt at him. McTavish howled, pulled himself up, and rammed into Skye's torso. Skye rapped McTavish on the head and arms as he tumbled backward, not really wanting to hurt the HBC man, just to teach him a little respect. But the ferocious redhead wouldn't quit and used all four limbs, his skull, and his teeth, sometimes all at once. He tried to wrestle Skye's club out of his hand while not neglecting to knee Skye and bite Skye's arm.

Skye was losing his advantage, with McTavish staying well inside the swing of the club and twisting Skye's arms as they rolled over the earthen floor.

"You'll not have my name, not ever," Skye roared between gulps of air.

McTavish was giving him a fair beating. Skye had rarely been set upon by such a fighter as this one. His mountainous nose bled, and his right hand was numb. The belaying pin dropped out of it. McTavish was on him, twisting his arm back, back, back until it threatened to snap.

"All right," Skye muttered.

McTavish jammed all the harder. "Tell me you're Skye, ye bloody coward. Or lie to me if ye will."

"I'll say nothing to you." Skye peered up at the man through a haze of blood. His heart raced wildly.

"What does it matter? I've got ye. You're whipped and good. I'll ship ye to McLoughlin at Vancouver, that's what." McTavish eased off Skye and wiped blood from his face with his cuff. "Get up now."

Skye sat up shakily, uncertain which of his parts worked. His chest ached. His ears rang. The numb hand wouldn't hold a twig, much less his belaying pin.

"Ah, see here, this is a belaying pin. I've seen a thousand. Stolen from the Royal Navy. Deny that, will ye, Skye?"

McTavish picked up the pin and waved it menacingly. "What kind of lies did ye tell Ogden, eh? Try me and see if I believe a word." He picked up Skye's warbag. "Where'd you get this truck? Stole it, I imagine. Stole the bow and arrers, stole the trap. I've got ye red-handed, ye thief."

Skye's pulse settled and he recovered enough of his wind to talk a little. "I'm on my way to the rendezvous of the Americans. Ogden told me I could get directions here at the post."

"He hates the Yanks, and he'd tell ye no such thing. What do ye take me for?"

"Man who comes to conclusions before he get the facts."

"Well, are ye are aren't ye Skye?"

"Call me Mister Skye. I don't answer to Skye."

"I'll call ye deserter. Get going now. I'm locking ye up until I decide whether to hang ye or slit your throat."

It dawned on Skye that McTavish lacked the means to take him under guard back to Fort Vancouver. He doubted that the post had more than half a dozen men. He'd seen none within it, and only one out in the fields.

"A shot would be faster, McTavish."

"I dinna waste good powder and lead on a swine."

"I'm hungry."

"Then starve."

"Water, then."

"Help ye'self." He motioned toward an earthen pot with a metal cup next to it. Skye drank, left-handed.

While Skye poured water down his parched throat, McTavish pawed through Skye's possessions. "See here, a pea jacket. Now I have ye. And a fine buckskin hide—that'll help pay for your keep. And an awl—good for one beaver from the Indians. And a seine. Hatchet, two knives, cup. Good enough. It'll repay HBC for the cost of dealing with ye." McTavish carted every last item Skye possessed into a storeroom, closed the door, and turned the iron key.

Skye was tempted to bolt but knew he wouldn't get twenty yards in his condition, and wouldn't have so much as a knife to keep him alive even if he did outrun the factor.

"Write me a receipt, Mr. McTavish. A receipt for my possessions, if you will. Write that HBC confiscated these goods. Mr. McLoughlin would want that."

"Ah, ye live in a fantasy, Skye."

"Call me mister."

McTavish cackled nastily. "I'll call ye whatsoever I set my mind to. All right. Walk ahead of me now."

"Where?"

"That beaver press in the yard. I'll tie ye down good to the posts."

So they had no way to lock him up, no way to take him back under guard. That interested Skye. "I want my hat, Mr. McTavish."

For an answer he got a sharp crack of his own belaying pin across his arm. Pain shot through his shoulder and clear down his torso. Skye stumbled into one of the posts of the fur press and sagged there.

"Put your back to it and your hands behind," McTavish said. "I've cord here to bale the plews, and it'll bale deserters just as fine. I wonder what deserters fetch by the pound."

Skye hurt all over and was too tired to resist. But he had learned never to give up. He had spent weeks and months in ships' brigs, and now he would endure some more. "I'd like to sit down," he said.

"Stand up or I'll poke you up."

Skye felt rough hands wind cord tightly around his wrists behind him. Then McTavish tied Skye's ankles, too. Skye knew that in minutes his arms would hurt almost beyond endurance, and his tight-bound hands would prickle and go numb.

"Now, ye miserable deserter, I'll be taking your boots for insurance," McTavish said. He knelt before Skye and

unlaced a worn boot, yanking one and then the other off
Skye's feet.

"What are you going to do, Mr. McTavish?"

"I'll think of something unpleasant, Skye."

"Call me Mister Skye."

McTavish laughed, and left him there to bake in the
fierce sun.

Chapter 12

Skye didn't know how he could endure more pain.
His arms felt as if they had been ripped from their
sockets and his hands had gone numb. The day waned
and at least he no longer suffered its heat, but he doubted
he could stand much longer. If he slumped into his bonds,
he would hurt all the more.

Then, near dusk, a paunchy Creole appeared in the yard
and cut him loose. Skye fell to the clay, unable to make
his limbs function at first.

"Come, eat, *mangeur du lard*," the man said.

Skye struggled to his feet, staggered, and then followed
the man into a kitchen area with a hand-hewn trestle table and chairs fashioned from poles and leather. McTavish sat at the head of it, looking like a choleric country
squire just this side of apoplexy, while one other Creole
sat halfway down, well below the salt. The Creole who
brought in Skye sat down across from the other. Two
young and pretty Indian women were serving.

"There you are, you craven Royal Navy scum," Mc-
Tavish said. "Sit down there at the bottom of the table

where you belong. That's your gruel. Eat and don't complain. It's more than a deserter deserves."

Skye beheld a skimpy bowl of oatmeal and a wooden spoon. He set about eating as well as his numb hands and shaking arms would let him. McTavish and the Creoles devoured their plentiful roast beef, squash, bread, dried-apple pudding, and garden greens, all washed down with red wine.

Skye glanced furtively at the women, both of them dressed in patterned calico gowns rather than native clothing. Each wore a ribbon in her hair, and both were uncommonly beautiful, with strong cheekbones, glowing amber flesh, and shiny jet hair. He wondered whose mates they were, if anybody's.

McTavish seemed even more sour than he had that afternoon, and he ate furiously, sawing and torturing the beef as if to humiliate it, glaring at Skye, belching and muttering. It took the man scarcely two minutes to down an enormous helping, but the Creoles dawdled with their food, more intent on enjoying it.

Skye wondered whether the women would join the men at table, but they simply hovered about, serving seconds to all but Skye. He caught them glancing shyly at him, their gazes alive with curiosity.

"No wonder the Royal Navy suffers. If it's manned by the degenerate dregs of England like you, the King's foreign affairs are doomed. I could've whipped you with one arm tied behind my back, Skye. I ended up beating you with your stolen belaying pin. The King's navy's rotten to the core, a paper tiger, and you're the proof of it. Where'd they pick ye up? Out of some bloody penal colony?"

Skye saw where this was heading and kept his silence.

"Ah, I'm right, then! They took you out of some stinking gaol where they keep all incorrigibles. It was that or Botany Bay, no doubt."

Skye finished his oatmeal gruel, well satisfied with the plain dish.

"That's where they got you, then. Ye deserve to hang. Ye don't even speak back to me because ye know it's so, Skye."

"It's Mister Skye, sir."

"It's what I bloody well choose to call ye. Now, then, I'm putting you out."

"I don't understand."

"Of course you don't. Ye can't get ahold of the simplest idears because you're a degenerate with a brain the size of a pea. I'm putting ye outside the gates and I'll keep everything—your stolen goods and your boots. How's that for a verdict? Go, and don't come back."

Skye sat stock still.

"I can't take you down to Vancouver, blast it. If ye'd skulked in a week ago, I'd have sent ye down the river with the pelts. I sent Pambrun and Vincennes with the spring returns. And Pryor's taking trade goods up to Spokane House. There's but three men here—Gris, there, Souvanne, there, and me—and I can't spare a man and I won't be feeding you and guarding you and dirtying my post for a bloody month while I wait for relief. So get ye out, ye filthy deserter."

"That's murder."

"Of course it's murder. You won't last a week. Any good Creole or HBC man'd make it, but not some dross from a London lockup."

"Are you judge, jury, and executioner?"

"I am all of that, Skye. I'm also king. This is my bailiwick. My word is law and my fists enforce it."

"It's Hudson's Bay's bailiwick."

"I'll do what I please, and it pleases me to put you out. You're done? Go!"

Skye refused to move.

"I said go. Gris, open the gates and throw 'im out." The factor bolted up from his rude chair and loomed over Skye with cocked fists.

"If you're going to murder me, Mr. McTavish, you'll do it here, not outside your gates."

Skye's pulse leapt. He would fight here and die, then. But they would not throw him out in the cold, barefoot and without a kit. Without a flint and steel.

The Creoles stood reluctantly.

"Return my kit and I'll walk out. Otherwise, I'll fight to the death."

"*Sacrebleu,* McTavish!" Gris exclaimed. "I will get his kit and put him out. It is *assassinat.*"

But the factor didn't wait. Grinning, he closed on Skye, delight firing his burning blue eyes. "Teach you another wee lesson, eh, Skye? Show the Royal Navy's scum what a Hudson's Bay man is?" McTavish's voice rose high and crackled.

"It's Mister Skye, sir." Skye rose quietly from his chair. "And you'll have to kill me."

The Creoles were holding back, wanting no part of this. He ached from the afternoon's ordeal, from sunburn, and from his previous set-to with this vicious Scot. Anger percolated through him, softly at first, and then with resonance. Some obdurate courage rooted Skye to his spot in that dining hall. He knew that he would not leave that hall conscious—or alive. It came down to life or death, and so he waited.

McTavish paused, glaring at Skye, comfortable with his belly full of meat. The women watched silently. Skye could not say what sort of mood or menace or courage he conveyed in that taut moment, but McTavish paused.

"You mean it. I'd have to kill you."

"If I don't kill you first."

"Maybe I will."

"Try me. I've nothing to lose."

This was the moment, the hinge of fate. Skye waited. He would die here or not. But he would not die helpless and barefoot in the wilderness. He stood ready to kill McTavish with his bare hands.

McTavish glared unhappily, muttered something, his face reddening. "All right. I dinna want an inquiry. Mind ye, I'd as soon bash your skull in and throw you in the river, but I don't want to report it. Damn ye. Go to the Americans. You're not a worthy subject of the Crown."

"That's it exactly, sir. I'm not a subject."

"They're scum, like you."

"I take that as a recommendation."

"Deserter. Thief. Come along. I'll give you some of it back. I'm charging you for your stay. You'll not get a free feed on the company."

He walked to the store with an oil lamp in hand, Skye following. The redolence of fabric and good leather struck Skye, and he eyed those precious goods on the shelves with yearning while the factor opened the storeroom door with the iron key and pulled out Skye's kit.

"I'll keep that buckskin pelt. That's the price of the meal."

"How much is a good tanned deerskin worth, and how much is a meal worth?"

"What difference does it make? That's what ye'll pay because I say so. Don't tempt me."

"How much is the skin worth, and what's my meal worth?"

"By God, I'll not bargain with a deserter and degenerate."

"What do you pay the Indians for such a skin?"

"As little as I can, ye scoundrel."

"How much was a bowl of gruel worth?"

"To a starving man, plenty."

"What do you charge trappers for a bowl?"

"As many pence as I can milk out of 'em, Skye."

"It's Mister—"

"Get out before I shoot you. I've a loaded piece at hand."

Skye smiled. "Thanks for the hospitality. I'll remember Hudson's Bay. You have beautiful women."

McTavish snarled, but Skye took up his kit and checking it, threw the seine over his shoulder, hefted his belaying pin, and then remembered.

"Where are my boots, McTavish?"

"Where you can't get them, Skye."

"Then I'll take what's at hand to replace them."

"I'll kill you cold."

"Do that."

Skye set down his burdens and headed for the shelves, looking for something for his feet. He found no ready-made boots, and knew that he would not find any, half a world away from English cobblers. But there were hard-soled moccasins, perhaps made by French-Canadians. He reached for a likely pair.

"I'll kill you, thief." McTavish held his dragoon pistol in hand.

Skye paused, smiling. "Odd how I had just the same thought." He picked up the knee-high moccasins and found they were fur-lined.

The deafening shot grazed his hair and made his ears ring. Skye sprang forward, his belaying pin in hand, and knocked the empty pistol out of McTavish's grip. They circled each other.

"Try me," said Skye.

McTavish seemed to deflate. "I'll get your boots, and then get out."

He went after Skye's boots while Skye tried the moccasins, found them small, tried another pair that fit, and bound them tight. They had thick soles, maybe buffalo-hide.

McTavish returned with Skye's ancient boots.

"I think we'll trade, McTavish."

The Scot turned cunning. "Trade, will ye? Boots for moccasins?" He examined Skye's footwear and smiled suddenly. "You get the worst of it. Good navy boots. Ye be a fool."

"I came here to ask directions. How do I get to the rendezvous of the Americans?"

"It'll be good riddance putting you out of Crown lands, Skye. Go up the Walla Walla, cross the Blue Mountains at any pass you find, go down any drainage to the Snake, find the Shoshones before they go to the rendezvous, and let them take ye. And may the devil or some wild tribe destroy ye on the way."

"Thank you."

The factor walked Skye to the front gates and opened them. The night yawned ahead. "If I had my way, you'd be bound in irons and on the river to Fort Vancouver. Don't ever set foot in Crown lands or I'll come after ye. I'll tell you something: it isn't over. If you linger around the mountains, we'll catch you and ship ye back to London. HBC sits like a spider in the web, the sovereign over an empire. John McLoughlin's a great patriot, and he'd like na' better'n to put a deserter in irons. Some time, when you least expect it, we'll catch ye, Skye. So go to the Yanks to save your miserable life."

"I plan to, Mr. McTavish. I'm going to Boston and start college."

"You fooled Ogden, but you don't fool me," McTavish snapped.

Chapter 13

Skye found himself in a bountiful land as he hiked up the Walla Walla River, and his spirits matched the country. He had passed through fire and brimstone and had emerged from it alive and free. For the first time in memory, he lived each hour with sheer joy. This well-watered and mild country cried out to him.

The land! In his flight and hunger he had scarcely noticed the land. A childhood in London and a life in the prison of the sea had blinded him. But now, as he passed through a verdant and sweet country bursting with new life, the land bewitched him. Everything he beheld was a sweet mystery. He paused frequently, enchanted by the world about him. He marveled that he could name most of the plants and the creatures, and wondered where the knowledge came from. Poetry, perhaps. English poets had never ignored the land, and he had read them all.

Everything caught his eye and ear. The trill of a red-winged blackbird delighted him, and the whirring flight of a meadowlark. He paused to examine the fronds of weeping willows, and bent to inhale the acrid smell of a juniper. He lay for an hour on the grassy bank of the river, watching minnows dart, tadpoles swim, and a great humped turtle sun himself. He plucked the silvery sagebrush and rubbed its aromatic leaves upon his flesh. He watched squirrels, robins, raccoons, ants, red foxes, with eyes that had never beheld such wonders. He discovered that each creature had its own habits, and he could ferret them out. One dawn he discovered a doe with a newborn fawn at the river. The little creature wore white spots and stood on wobbly legs so thin he wondered how it could support itself. The doe picked up his scent and hurried her baby into red willow brush. Barnaby Skye smiled.

He absorbed this new world and loved it. Again and again he stopped to examine some new wonder, things as ordinary as a bee or a bright butterfly or a dragonfly. This was the good earth, and it awakened a new awareness in him. He wanted to walk this entire land, know it, possess it, nurture it even as it nurtured him. It dawned on him that he had been stunted and shriveled and warped by his sea-prison. The mortal soul needed the good earth and all upon it, just as much as any plant needed the good earth. He might have loved the ever-changing sea if he had not been a prisoner, and if it had not been a monstrous barrier against his liberty. But he could not put down roots into the sea. Here on this vast continent he could—and would.

Ever mindful that he needed to find the Americans in July, he continued eastward, but not in a rush, and always taking time to learn how to live upon the breast of the world. Bit by bit, he was becoming the master of his fate.

He experimented with various types of tinder for his fire steel, finding merit in the fibrous inner bark of dead cottonwoods. He learned to make his beds more comfortable by plucking away the smallest sticks and stones, and even to make a hollow for his hip bone. He practiced with his bow and arrows as he walked, knowing his skills were barely adequate. But one day he bagged a wild turkey, and several times he shot mallards, much to his astonishment. And he didn't neglect the sparkling Walla Walla River and its salmon.

If this was a paradise, it was also a land of unknown tribes, some of which might be dangerous. He found ample evidence of them: hoof and moccasin prints, and campsites. His Creole moccasins blended with these signs of passage and concealed his journey from knowing eyes. One day he found a discarded moccasin and put it in his kit as a pattern. He learned what he could of the ways the Indians fed themselves, noting what roots and bulbs they dug up, what trees and bushes showed signs of being disturbed, and what firewoods they used. Just by being observant, he learned the lore of the natives. The Indians had collected a tall herb with a cluster of half-inch-thick roots that he found edible. And they had dug up a low plant with bright white blossoms. This plant had a root that tasted bitter raw, but when he sliced and boiled the root in his tin cup, the white root tasted better. He discovered wild onions, and a small lily with purplish white blossoms that offered up a valuable root.

But the plant obviously prized by the local Indians grew

everywhere and had blue blossoms on foot-high stalks. Its bulbous root, the size of a small onion, proved to be without taste but filling and edible raw as well as cooked. Skye collected the bulbs and stuffed them in his kit. Nature was providing a bounty as the warm season progressed, and he stopped worrying about feeding himself. He didn't know the name of any of these foodstuffs, and vowed he would find out when he reached the Yanks. Names were important. He wanted to know the name of everything around him.

An occasional cold, rainy day taught him to study the land for shelter as he passed through, and to thatch brush huts from boughs cut with his hatchet. He learned to build a fire near a rock escarpment that caught the heat and radiated it back upon him. Windy days he had simply to endure, because there was little refuge in nature from the blasts of air that plucked at his flesh.

He experimented with his trap, chaining it down, baiting it with meat, and setting it two or three hundred yards from his campsites. He caught nothing, and wondered why. Perhaps it was his scent. He scrubbed the trap in the river, using a root that yielded a frothy substance like soap. The next morning a foul odor permeated the entire area, and he found a dead skunk in the jaws. He wondered if he could endure its flesh, decided he could not, washed the trap in the river, and fled the area.

He walked up the broad valley through golden days, seeing not a soul and glad of it. He wanted to be alone. His ordeal at Fort Nez Perces had scarred his soul, left a rancid memory of a fur company's arrogance, and deepened his hunger to reach the Americans. The river swung south through mounting slopes and east again, into foothill canyons. He was nearing the Blue Mountains.

He followed the diminished river ever upward through private canyons and hidden glens. The river turned into a tumbling torrent, icy with snowmelt, sometimes hidden from the surrounding slopes by its log-choked canyons. He came upon large swampy plateaus chocked with wildlife, moose and elk as well as deer. One day a huge brown bear with a cub scared him witless, and he backed away from the creek while she stood on her hind legs and snorted. After that, he habitually noted trees he could climb and lines of retreat. He had not won his liberty only to let himself be butchered by a wild animal.

He arrived at the headwaters of the Walla Walla, a mass of springs and soggy turf. From now on he would travel without a reliable source of water, and it worried him. He would need to keep his eye peeled for springs and seeps. He hiked the rest of that day through chill mountain air, finding no sign of a spring, and feared he might have to retreat to the headwaters. Some unknown distance ahead he would reach a summit and enter the Snake River drainage.

The pungence of pines intoxicated his senses; he had never smelled anything like it. But his quest for water preoccupied him, and he feared he would make a dry camp that night and hope his body would endure the drought. Then, as he wound his way around a steep north slope, he found the rotted remains of a snowbank, mottled with dirt and bark on its glistening surface. Meltwater leaked from its lowest point and he drank it, gasping at its cold. After that he hacked out several pounds of the dripping snow and packed it into his poncho.

He camped that night high in the Blue Mountains, warding off an icy breeze with a crackling fire of knotty pine, and satisfying his thirst with the decaying snow.

That night he slept cold even though it was the end of May, and finally built up his dying fire and sat in the pine-scented night, waiting for the sun.

The next dawn he swallowed some of his hoarded jerky and boiled some of his carefully husbanded bulbs in his little cup, using the last of his snow, and then set out again. He topped a saddle midmorning and descended a dry watercourse, wondering whether he had reached the Snake drainage. That day he hiked across a broad alpine meadow berserk with flowers. That evening he set up camp beside a foot-wide rill, and swiftly drove an arrow into a small deer, which ran, shuddered, stopped, and sagged to the ground a hundred yards away. He had never killed a creature that large, and felt a certain sadness he could not explain. It was odd, he thought, that a man who had fought the bloody Kaffirs would feel despondent about taking the life of a deer. It was as if the deer were innocent and undeserving of its fate, while the two-footed demons deserved what they got.

He dragged the limp yearling buck toward his camp, then thought better of it. He would leave it well away from his campsite. He attacked the carcass clumsily, eventually gutting it, up to his elbows in blood and gore. After two hours of sawing with his dull knives, he quit. He took ten or fifteen pounds of venison back to his camp, built a fire, spitted some of the meat on green twigs, and roasted it. It had taken an amazing amount of bloody work to make meat. Thinking back, he realized he had used too light a hand: next time, he would take his hatchet to a carcass and make quicker work of it. But that experience, like so many others these sweet days, had taught him much.

That night an unearthly howling awakened him, and he knew at once he was hearing wolves. He crawled uneasily to the fire and found a few live coals, which he soon fed into a hot yellow flame. Out in the blackness orange eyes stared back at him, one pair, two, then five pair in all, some holding steady, others bobbing, catching and losing the firelight. The sight raised the hair on the nape of his neck. He had no idea whether wolves would attack a man—no doubt the scent of meat had drawn them—but he took no chances. He put on his moccasins, grabbed his hatchet in one hand and his belaying pin in the other, and ran toward one of those pairs of orange eyes, roaring like a mad bull. The eyes vanished.

When he returned to camp he discovered that the wolves had pilfered the leftover meat he had cut. Unthinkingly, he had stored it near the fire—and not far from his head. Some bold wolf had come within ten feet of him. That ruined his sleep for the night, and he sat at the fire, feeding dry wood into it now and then, his mind filled with images of wolf packs hamstringing their prey, clamping their long jaws over vulnerable throats, and ripping open bellies.

He stirred with the first grays of dawn, much more aware that wilderness was no Eden. He hiked to the place where his deer carcass lay—and found no sign of it. When at last he found the remains fifty yards distant—nothing but well-gnawed bones now—he knew a large animal had been at work, most likely a bear.

Skye had gotten only one meal out of an entire deer. That was something to think about. He glared into the surrounding brush, and discovered he wasn't alone, even in the dawn light. A wolf stood watching, shaggy and feral, waiting to attack the well-gnawed carcass for whatever last bit of meat remained. It edged silently into shadow, sat on its haunches, and watched him. Skye had enough of wolves. He strung his bow, nocked an arrow, aimed, and let fly. The wolf exploded into the air, howled, and ran away with an arrow poking from its side. Skye followed the trail of blood but never saw the animal again. He had lost an arrow. He wanted a good warm wolf skin, and the next wolf to cross his path would donate it. He hated the wolves for reasons he couldn't explain. The wolves had done nothing but be themselves and yet they prompted a dread and rage in him. The bear had been bad enough, the wolves worse.

The next two days he descended the east flanks of the Blue Mountains, following a cheerful creek that rushed down awesome canyons that boxed him into their bottoms. He was plunging into arid country again, filled with broken volcanic rock. Then one morning he reached a grassy flat and discovered it was where the creek debouched into a larger river. And it was also the site of a large Indian village consisting of conical lodges of animal skins, such as he had never before seen. He didn't know who these people were or what his fate might be, but he had been discovered by bold half-naked children, and there would be no escape.

Chapter 14

Skye set down his heavy burden and waited. Children swarmed him, excited and curious, the boys slim and naked, the girls in leather skirts. Then men ran up, the women holding back. The men carried lances, bows, and arrows. He saw no firearms. These people were short, stocky, golden-fleshed, and had coarse black hair worn long. They stood erect and alert and conveyed a certain dignity. They studied Skye with obvious curiosity. He yearned to greet them but felt helpless. He could not speak to them, nor even let them know his intentions were peaceful. He held out a hand, but no one took it. They seemed to be waiting, and sure enough, emerging from the village was a gray-haired elder wearing ceremonial robes. A headman or chief of some sort.

The village lay alongside the Snake River on a grassy flat, in a mountain bowl. Out on the pasture oddly marked horses grazed, their rumps spotted, as if their maker had splattered white paint over them. But some lighter-tinted horses carried black or brown spots, and sometimes the spots covered the whole torso. Hundreds of these strange creatures dotted this basin, giving Skye the idea that this tribe knew horses well.

The headman wore a bonnet of eagle feathers that stood vertically, and also a white-man's shirt cinched at the waist. He surveyed Skye with eyes that revealed neither hostility nor friendship, but did convey a profound authority. Skye desperately wished he knew the protocols for this sort of thing. All he could do was talk.

"I happened upon your village," he said. "I don't know who you are. I'm heading east, toward the rendezvous of the Americans, and hope you can tell me how to get there."

No one understood. Skye stared at blank faces.

Maybe a gift. Skye swiftly considered the few items in his warbag, wondering which one he could do without, and finally settled on the canister of tea that Ogden had given him—something he treasured, but something not essential for his survival. He dug into his kit, found the enameled canister, and presented it to the headman, who accepted it without quite knowing what it was. He opened the canister, saw the tea, sniffed it, puzzled.

"I'll show you how to make tea," Skye said.

"Hudson Bayee," the headman said.

"No, just a man passing through."

Skye's shake of the head was understood, if not his words.

"Americeen?"

"Rendezvous."

"Ah." The headman had some inkling of something, and so did Skye.

The village men crowded around, examining the canister, admiring it more than what it contained. Women edged in now, peeking shyly at Skye, studying his gift to the headman. The ladies wore soft doeskin dresses, although a few were decked out in traders' calico, their dresses crudely cut but finely sewn.

The headman beckoned, and Skye picked up his kit and followed him into the village, which consisted of thirty or forty skin lodges, some brightly dyed with animal figures, all of them smoke-blackened at their apex. The village was redolent of salmon and meat and offal. The chief's lodge loomed larger than the others, and seemed to have more poles supporting it. Several handsome young women, apparently the headman's wives or daughters, stood about shyly. The headman spoke briefly to one, and she trotted away, vanishing among the lodges.

There they waited for what seemed a long time. Skye relaxed a little; no one had manhandled him or threatened his life. His gift had cemented his status as a guest— for the moment. The headman's woman reappeared, this time with an ancient white man in tow. The man seemed to be all or mostly blind, and stared out upon the world from milky eyes.

"Eh? *Bonjour,*" he muttered.

"Do you speak English?" Skye asked.

"Eh?"

Skye realized the old Creole was both blind and deaf. "English? Do you speak English?" he bellowed.

"Pierre Gallard, Nor' West," the man said, and slid into French again.

"Hudson's Bay?" Skye bawled into the man's ear.

"Eh? *Non, non, Nord Ouest Compagnie.*"

Skye understood: the North West Company, once a bitter and violent rival of Hudson's Bay and now absorbed by it. A lovely young woman appeared beside the old man, and Skye realized she was his mate. She, it turned out, could communicate better than he.

"Nez Perces," she said. "You Hudson's Bay."

"No, madam, I'm alone. I want to go to the rendezvous."

"Ah, *les Americains.*"

"Yes."

Swiftly she translated all this to the headman and villagers. It took effort, but in time she and he had exchanged information. He was in a Nez Perce village that had come here to fish. She was the wife of the honored white man, Gallard, from Montreal, and cared for him now that he was old and helpless. Gallard despised the English, and Hudson's Bay Company, but not Americans. Last year's rendezvous, the first, was the talk of all the tribes.

Skye asked for directions, and after much consultation, she told him not to follow the Snake because it ran through a terrible canyon, but to go around to the south of it for many days, and then pick up the Snake again where it came out of the canyon and ran through plains. The more she murmured, the better Skye understood her French. He dredged up words and phrases from his childhood, and from his occasional shipboard reading.

The headman thrust the tea canister at her. She examined its contents, smiled. *"Thé,"* she said, and explained what it was to him. He nodded and spoke to her at length.

"You guest," she said. *"Allez."* He followed her to the chief's portal and started to leave.

"Wait. What is his name? Will he trade for horses?"

She stared blankly.

He pointed to himself. "I'm Skye. Skye." Then he pointed at the chief.

"Ah! Skyeskye." She smiled and pointed. "Hemene Moxmox." Then she pointed at other leaders and village men: "Eapalekthiloom, Ealaot Wadass, Hematute Hikaith, Chelooyeen, Alikkees." Skye couldn't even pronounce the names, much less repeat them.

Skye remembered the word for horse, and yelled it into the old man's ear. *"Cheval?"*

Gallard nodded and said something to his wife. Skye dug into his warbag and produced his pea jacket, which he hoped to trade. She understood, and addressed her auditors at length. The headman took the blue woolen coat, examined it, tried it on—it was too long in the arms, but otherwise serviceable—and smiled. It would keep him warm next winter. And no one else in the village would have anything so magical. He talked at length with the Frenchman's woman, and then with his friends, and at last nodded. A nod, at least, seemed to be a universal sign that Skye took for a yes. He waited impatiently, hoping he had been understood, afraid that he had just given away his coat as another gift.

But the iron-haired headman spoke gently to two young

men, and these trotted off toward the fields where the herd grazed. Then he nodded Skye into his lodge. Skye discovered surprising comfort within. Its skin sides had been rolled upward a foot or so from the ground so that the spring zephyrs might percolate through and up the smoke vent at the top. Decorated parfleches held this family's possessions. Pallets lined the periphery. A stone-lined firepit occupied the center, but the fire was out this warm day.

Skye's dignified host walked around the firepit and placed himself opposite the lodge door. He beckoned Skye to follow and seat himself next to the host. Others in the village followed, seating themselves in a preordained order.

The headman withdrew an ornate pipe with a red stone bowl and a long stem from a leather bag, tamped what appeared to be tobacco in it, and waited. A young man appeared at the lodge door, bearing a hot coal wrapped in a leaf. It was passed to the headman, and in due course he lifted it with bare fingers, lit his pipe, and sucked until the tobacco was fairly ablaze. Then he lifted the pipe with both hands, chanting something as he did, in each direction of the compass and to heaven and earth. Skye knew this was some sort of important ceremony, perhaps a blessing of his presence in this village, and waited quietly. These people were in no hurry, unlike Skye, who itched to look at horses and select one.

The headman drew smoke, exhaled, and passed the pipe to Skye, who assumed he should do the same. Skye completed the ritual and passed the pipe along. The pipe went the full circle, no Nez Perce saying anything, then went another round, as a great peace descended on this group. Skye felt the peace, felt himself relax, and joined the quietness of spirit that seemed to occupy the lodge. He knew that this, too, was a lesson. Perhaps this smoking of the pipe meant something to all these American tribes. He would find out. Hundreds of questions had arisen in the last weeks, and he yearned to find the answers to them. For now, he had only his wits, his powers of observation, and perhaps whatever could be conveyed to him by an old deaf Creole and his younger Nez Perce woman.

These tribesmen had stopped time. Until this moment, Skye's focus had been escape, survival, and the future. Now, in this breezy lodge, among these elders, he experienced only the moment, without thought of his bitter past or uncertain future. The headman talked a while, sometimes addressing Skyeskye, who grasped not a word, and then suddenly dismissed his guests with a gesture. One by one, the men stood and ducked out into the blazing sun. Skye followed. There, tied to a picket stake, stood two handsome ponies, each with the peculiar markings these people cherished, one white with black markings, the other brown with white splotches across its rump.

This was a critical moment in many ways. Skye had never before ridden a horse. He had seen horses, the big British kind, chestnut or bay or black, often in harness.

The headman was eyeing him, waiting for something. Skye looked desperately for the old Creole or his woman, and could not spot either of them in the quiet throng. He studied the animals, looking for flaws, but he could scarcely tell a bad horse from a good one, and wouldn't know a horse that misbehaved from an obedient and eager one. Each wore a leather bridle of Indian manufacture. Skye realized they had no iron bits, and surprised himself by understanding that these devices were hackamores, and they could be used to start, stop, and turn a horse as well as an English bit and bridle.

He turned to his host. "These are fine animals. I don't know a thing about them. I don't even know whether you mean for me to pick one, or keep both. I lack a saddle, and will learn to ride them as you do."

The headman raised two fingers. "Skyeskye," he said.

Skye nodded, the universal gesture of affirmation. "Thank you, Hemene Moxmox," he said.

The chief nodded gravely. A small wave of his hand set one of the youths to demonstrate. The boy climbed easily over the back of the lighter pony, took the loop rein, and rode it in a loop. Skye watched intently. Then the youth rode the other in the same manner, and handed the reins of both to Skye. He took them as one would take the keys to a kingdom.

Chapter 15

Skye spent that night in the lodge of Hemene Moxmox. He didn't sleep well. Everything was so strange, not least of which was the intimate presence of the headman's wife and daughters, all of them crowded close. He heard movement in the night, breathing, snoring, people turning about. Someone left, and for a moment starlight appeared at the lodge door. Not even the crowded forecastle of the *Jaguar* was as packed and intimate as this.

But it was the presence of the women that troubled him. How did these people manage certain things? How could they all live through the nights without experiencing the stirrings that plagued Skye? A certain shyness tormented him as he lay there. He had suffered a living death in ships of war, and all the heat and need of youth had been ruthlessly suppressed. But now he lay within reach of several women, and his thoughts troubled and maddened him. He ached to leave the lodge.

Dawn crept in, but no one arose. He had already learned that these people weren't in a hurry and didn't count hours. They would arise whenever the spirit moved them. But Skye, restless and eager to be off, couldn't endure his buffalo robe pallet any longer, and slipped into the hushed morning. He wanted to be on his way; if he missed the rendezvous of the Americans, he didn't know how he might survive.

His horses had been returned to pasture by the headman's youngest son so they could graze and water through the night. A few horses stood beside the lodges of their masters, ever ready for trouble or use. Skye settled quietly in the brown grass beside the lodge, absorbing the village. He felt at peace there even though it was as strange a place as he'd ever visited.

He wasn't entirely alone. Here and there an old woman stirred, or someone headed to a brushy area. He supposed a village would have to move frequently to keep from fouling itself. But here there was land in such plenitude that moving from one locale to another offered infinite possibilities. A few dogs prowled, but these seemed to be the only night guard the village had. Most of the skin lodges had been erected in a large ring with a commons in the center. But here and there were other lodges situated without rhyme or reason.

He explored quietly, not wanting to disturb the dogs or the sleeping villagers. One lodge was empty, its door flap open. Smaller lodges, well back from the main circle, seemed to be occupied by single young men or the very old. Another, almost a hut, set well back from the village, puzzled him. Was it a place of banishment or taboo?

He studied everything around him, marveling at the uses of wood and bone and leather. Some of the ponies were hobbled, and he studied these devices, shaped like a figure eight, which caught the forelegs of the animals and prevented them from all but the smallest steps. He would need two, and if he couldn't trade for them he would have to manufacture them. Most of the horses were tied with braided leather cord—something he could weave himself. He had braided a lot of rope for the Royal Navy. Most of the horses were ridden bareback, but he saw numerous saddles, too, ranging from simple pads to elaborate seats with high cantles and pommels. Where could he get one for himself? And a packsaddle for his spare?

The curs sniffed him and growled, threatening to awaken the village, so he returned to the lodge of Hemene Moxmox and waited outside its door, absorbing the redolence of an Indian village. The sun was well up before anyone stirred, and then almost by unspoken command they all were up and bustling about. The headman's daughters appeared one by one and headed for the river and their morning ablutions.

Bit by bit, blue smoke layered the village as one woman after another stirred up coals and added firewood. They were taking their time about all this, too, and Skye realized it would be midmorning before he could leave. He decided to put the time to good use, and wandered freely, studying the manufacture of everything: saddles and tack, backrests, woven reed mats, buffalo robes, fish and meat drying racks, rawhide pouches used to carry goods, a

packsaddle that looked rather like a sawbuck. A partly
butchered deer hung high above the reach of dogs, but
the birds—especially a bold iridescent black-and-white
type—were feasting.

The headman's women fed him some sort of fish cakes,
no doubt salmon, on smooth slabs of bark, something to
eat with his fingers. The cakes had an odd, nutty flavor,
and he guessed the flour in them had been made from
some pulverized root or another. Hemene Moxmox stirred
about, occasionally eyeing Skye, but not trying to breach
the barrier of tongue that kept them from conveying their
thoughts to each other. It seemed best to Skye just to wait;
events would take their course, and meanwhile he was
studying everything in the village and learning swiftly.

When the time came, Hemene Moxmox's son brought
Skye's ponies to him, and now a moment of truth arrived.
He packed his warbag, gathered up his belaying pin and
seine and sailcloth, and stared helplessly at the animals.
A crowd had gathered, and while they were outwardly im-
passive, there were glints of amusement on those brown
faces.

Skye approached Hemene Moxmox. "Though you can't
understand me, I want to thank you for your hospitality.
I hope it's understood just by this talk."

The headman nodded solemnly.

Inspiration struck Skye. He had one more thing to give
the headman—his big, bulky seine net. He hadn't used
it for a while, and with a horse to help him go after game,
he could well part with it. He handed it to the headman,
after rolling it open a way. It had been made of traders'
cord, patiently tied together by one of the fishing tribes,
and had small lead weights along its bottom edge. "This
is for you, sir," he said.

The chief received the gift happily, his eyes alive with delight. He unrolled it, found it to be a majestic length and height, and spoke rapidly to several youths around him, who scattered into the crowd. The whole village, it seemed, had come to see Skye off.

Earlier, Skye had observed the youth swing gracefully over the bare back of the brown pony and ride him. The boy had done it in two stages, first up on the back in precarious balance, and then a leg over the croup. Skye set down his truck and gathered the rein. Then he leapt. The horse sidled away and Skye crashed into the earth. The crowd stared politely. Skye picked himself up and tried again. This time he catapulted clear over the pony's back, and tumbled to the earth again. No one laughed, and Skye fathomed that would be impolite—at least until the village guest was safely out of sight.

Ruefully, Skye eyed the crowd, knowing what they thought of his riding abilities. But then Moxmox clapped his hands. The youths appeared at once, each bearing things, which they laid before Skye. One was a small pad saddle with bentwood stirrups and a leather cinch. Another brought some sort of saddle blanket made of soft hide. Another brought hobbles and braided halters and lead ropes to Skye. And the last gift was a packsaddle and an ancient pelt for it. Swiftly the youths saddled the two ponies. Skye stuffed the hobbles and spare line in his warbag and tied it on the packsaddle.

Then they helped Skye up on the brown horse. It skittered sideways, almost toppling him, but he managed to stay aboard. Now at last the villagers grinned, some making odd clucking sounds while others simply cheered.

"Thank you, friends," he said, lifting his topper to them.

"Skyeskye," they replied.

The horse alarmed him with every step, but he resolutely steered it away from the village and onto a trail they pointed out to him, and in minutes he was riding alone, wondering how to manage horses, fearing a runaway, fearing they would stop dead or bolt back. But they didn't. They plodded steadily in a direction that took him away from the Snake. He realized he now had not only his own life and water and provender to worry about, but also those of his creatures. It would be entirely up to him to find grass and water, to rest them and keep them from injury, to examine their hooves and brush their backs. It was up to him to keep them from wandering or being stolen. To stay on board when they became excited or began to pitch him off. To track them down when they ran off. To catch them when they didn't wish to be caught. He vowed he would learn.

Every day was going to give him forced lessons in horsemanship, and he wondered if he would be up to the test. He rode quietly that sunny morning through a brown land of vast slopes and isolated green oases, always pausing at water. He soon ached in the saddle, and knew that these first days were going to be lived out in hellish pain.

But he was free. And he now had a mobility he never dreamed he might possess. He no longer struggled with his heavy kit, which rode easily on the animal behind him. Hesitantly, he kicked his pony into a trot. It danced along easily, jarring him with every step until he jerked the hackamore hard, and the horse settled into a lazy walk again. Next time, when he got his nerve up, he would try a canter. But for now he was more than content just to get to know his animals and master something about staying on a horse. He *had* to stay on; he doubted he would ever catch them again if he fell off. He studied his low rawhide saddle and found he could grip it if he had to, and vowed then and there to cling to it with an iron hand if he must.

He endured the pain until he could sit no more, and then slid off and walked, leading the animals and working the knots out of his legs and thighs. He marveled. Here he was, a British sailor who'd scarcely set foot on land since boyhood, leading two obedient horses as if he knew what he was doing.

He spent the rest of that day walking and riding, and in spite of his clumsiness he traveled many miles into dryer and harsher country. He had seen no one all day, but that didn't mean he was safe. A lone man with horses would be an invitation to trouble. But he would give trouble as well as get it if it came to that. He was learning, and the more he learned, the safer Barnaby Skye, formerly of the Royal Navy, would be.

Chapter 16

Skye pondered his fate as he made his solitary way eastward along a trail he hoped would take him back to the Snake River. He knew what he had been; he didn't know what he would become. He was still young, but unsure of himself. Why was Barnaby Skye set upon this earth? He could have answered that not long ago, but now he didn't know.

His solitude troubled him. For years he had been

stripped of his own will. The presence of other mortals around him had largely meant slavery, with only glimmerings of friendship from a few sympathetic shipmates. Now he was alone, free, sovereign, untroubled by the will of others—and desperately lonely. He needed friends, but had none.

The wilderness he saw about him, the vaulting slopes, the hot sun, a land scarred with angry black rock, made him pensive. Mostly it seemed benign but he knew that was an illusion, and every little while something happened to confirm it. Once his horse bolted, almost unseating him, when a rattlesnake coiled upward. On another occasion he ran into a bull moose with humped shoulders, and whirled his horses away when it lowered its great rack and pawed the earth.

He could not afford mistakes, and when they did happen, he knew he must learn from them and never need another lesson. Once, when he failed to hobble a horse properly, it dodged him until he walked it down. On another occasion the brown horse yanked a picket pin loose and drifted away. He learned from those episodes that the horses stuck together. He could ride one and the other would follow, helter-skelter. But he knew that if both horses got loose, he would be in trouble.

He learned watchfulness from his horses. When they stopped suddenly, their ears perked, their gaze focused on something, he knew he should be looking that way, too. Once they halted in brushy cover, and he was just about to urge them out of it when he spotted an Indian party in the distance. A dozen males, armed for war and painted in grotesque fashion, topped a distant rise and continued at an oblique angle. Skye's spotted horses had kept him from being discovered.

He had little difficulty feeding himself. He continued to harvest the bulbs of the blue flower and reduce them to starchy food. Each evening he staked and baited his trap a quarter of a mile from his camp, and often he caught something in it, a mink or weasel or chuck or raccoon. He butchered these into tasteless meat, and tried to preserve and flesh the better furs, especially the mink. He spent his evenings at that task, clumsily scraping with his dull knives, and then with a sharp piece of glassy volcanic rock.

He shot bobbing mallards or canvasbacks regularly, but they took a long time to clean and gut and cook. A pot of boiling water would have helped him pull the feathers, but he had only his large tin cup for a pot. Still, he occupied himself during the long spring twilights by preparing bits of food while he watched his horses graze.

The horses fascinated him. He needed to know all there was to know about them. They were shy, easily frightened animals, whose instinct was to flee rather than fight because they had few weapons other than teeth and hooves. One was sullen and did not like to carry him. That one became the packhorse, but he determined to ride it now and then because there would be times when he would have to. The other one, the brown mare, accepted him without sulking, but wasn't obedient or didn't understand what he wanted. He didn't know how to discipline her and decided just to be patient until he knew.

One day he struck a great river that had to be the Snake. It ran in a trench cut in volcanic rock, across a dreary plain with distant peaks in sight. A well-used trace ran along its south bank. He rode eastward through vast silences, acutely aware of his loneliness but not melancholic about it. He had too much to celebrate. He was free!

May passed into June. He was sure of that, though he had lost track of the days. He had a month or so to find the Americans, and not the faintest idea how to do it. If he did not find them, he would push ahead anyway. Somewhere, far to the east and across a continent, the Americans had forged a civilization out of the wilderness. He would find it.

He added an otter pelt to his growing collection of furs. If worse came to worse, he would have enough pelts to fashion into winter gear with the coming of the cold.

Twice he forded formidable streams flowing out of the south. There were well-beaten trails on both sides of each river. The Snake itself ran through an astonishing black canyon with walls so vertical that they denied him access to its water. From then on, he took every opportunity to work his way down to the river with his horses. Eventually the canyon played out and the river returned to the level of the plains. And still he saw no Shoshones—or anyone else.

The river swept to the northeast, and Skye sensed it would lead him away from the rendezvous. All he knew was that the trapper's fair would be well south of the Snake country. And then one day he did find a whole congregation of Indians on the move, perhaps even a village. He drew up his horses and waited while the vanguard approached. Then he lifted his hand in what he hoped was a friendly manner.

These were a less handsome people than the Nez Perce, plainly adorned, the women mostly stocky or fat, and the men lean and hawkish.

"Are you Snakes?" Skye asked.

A headman lifted a finger and described a wavy line

with it. Skye suspected it meant snake or people of the snake. Ogden had told him that was their sign.

"I'm looking for the rendezvous," he said, relieved.

"Ah, rendezvous," said the headman, his face lighting up. "Rendezvous." He consulted with other headmen, and then motioned for Skye to wait.

Had he found the right people? Skye and the village leaders gazed at one another some more, while the rest of the long procession crowded in. Skye thought there were two or three hundred here, innumerable horses drawing poles that carried the tribe's possessions. Many of the horses dragged the skin lodges he had first seen among the Nez Perce. These were not salmon-fishing Indians, such as he had seen on the Columbia, but a tribe that depended on the bison as well as the abundant fish. The men were well armed, some with muskets, the rest with bows, arrows, shields, lances tipped with iron points, and various war clubs.

"You Yank?" the headman asked, drawing his pony beside Skye's.

"British, mate. I am Skye." He waved a hand in a gesture he hoped would convey a sense of the heavens. "Skye," he said.

"Skye," the headman returned, duplicating his gesture. "Rendezvous." The headman summoned a gray man forward, an elderly Indian, but taller and gaunter than these stocky people.

"Perrault. I'm an Iroquois. I speak de Englees. What you want, huh?"

"What's Iroquois?"

The old man wheezed cheerfully. "Where you from?"

"London."

"You Hudson's Bay, eh?"

"No. I'm alone. I want to go to the Americans' rendez-vous."

"Ah, dat's where we go. You come. What's you name?"

"Barnaby Skye. And what's Iroquois?"

The old man cackled again. "Eastern tribe. Big civilized tribe. Me, I ain't civilized no how. I'm a trapper before I got sick and old. Canada and United States, that's where the Iroquois are from. New York, Quebec. I don't want nothing to do with Hudson's Bay. Them'd starve you to death. You HBC, I'd shoot you."

"These are Snakes?"

"You betcha. Mean bastards but I got a woman takes care of me. How come you here? You all alone."

Skye debated whether to tell Perrault, and finally decided to. "I was with the Royal Navy. I jumped ship at Fort Vancouver."

"Ah! You make a good free trapper then. Hate them damn British. You come with us and we make friends. Ah, Skye. I'll tell 'em you a big-water man. They don't know 'navy.' We holding up the parade now. Tonight, we talk. You got some whiskey?"

"I haven't anything."

"It don't matter. Soon comes rendezvous and then we drink whiskey until we get sick." He laughed.

Perrault talked at length with the Snake elders, who eyed Skye now and then. Skye had no idea what was being said or how much trouble he was getting into. But eventually they nodded at him to join them and the lengthy procession began again, retracing country Skye had passed through until they reached a river that flowed out of the south. The great caravan swung into that mountain-hemmed valley and made its stately way another five miles until dusk.

The village headmen left Skye to his own devices. He watched the women build cookfires while the youths took the horses to the thin grasses on the slopes. No one was erecting a lodge. He hunted for Perrault, and found him with three women, one older, the other two stamped in their mother's image.

"Ah, Skye, you got food, eh?"

"I have some otter—not very tasty but it's food."

"Good, we eat it."

"And these bulbs. I found they make a paste I can eat."

"Camas. Big food for Snakes. Taste like no damn good. I don't want none of that stuff. You get me meat and you make old Perrault and his women happy. Me, I got big belly. I got some French blood. French and Iroquois know how to eat meat and make love. Tonight, Skye, we eat big, then we all make love. I got some damn good women. You take your pick, eh?"

Chapter 17

Skye's blood ran hot but his memories ran bitter. He stared at Perrault's younger women and found them comely. They were stocky, golden-fleshed, cheerful, with bright black-cherry eyes and heavy cheekbones. One wore her straight blue-black hair loose; the other's jet hair had been done in braids that she tied with ribbons. He watched them, burning with sudden heat as they cooked a supper. Sometimes they gazed at him with broad smiles, almost coquettish.

Skye's life had suddenly plunged into a vortex of hunger, hope, need, and excitement. Women were a mystery to him. He could remember his sisters and his mother, but they were ghostly presences lost in the mists of time. He remembered the starchy girls he knew as a youth, in their pinafores and frocks, with all their politenesses and reserve. They had been fair-skinned, brown-haired or sandy-haired, their girlish figures buried in ruffles and layers of petticoats. About the time he was pressed into the navy, some of them were budding into women, giving him flirtatious glances, foolish and giddy girls suddenly shy around boys because they knew of things they hadn't known about as children. One of them, Molly, he had been drawn to, and she had filled the thirteen-year-old Skye with joy and terror and intense curiosity. What was this mystery? He had kissed her once and told her he would marry her someday. She had whickered and kissed him back, and they had held hands, happy and content.

Then ruffians had manhandled him into a cart, and he had scarcely seen a woman again. At sea he had the run of the ship, but when they approached port, the lord officers always managed to find some infraction and throw him into the bilge, where he spent days and weeks in irons, tormented beyond anything he could put into words, a young man with volcanic needs and rages and deepening bitterness. It wasn't misconduct that put him in the brig at every port; his masters knew his soul, his rage, his history—and what would happen if the boy got loose. It amused them to torment him.

So he rarely saw a woman in his seven years with the Royal Navy. Once in a while, though, Lady This or Dame That or Princess So and So came aboard, always on the arm of Admiral Lord Such and Such, and then

Skye would glimpse a female at last. They all looked indescribably beautiful to him, and their smiles set his heart to fluttering. Then they would go away, and another year or two would pass without his even seeing a woman in pastel silk or crinoline or linen, and all the while his young body howled.

His shipmates knew his torment and enjoyed torturing him. They came back after shore leave and told him lurid stories of easy women, seamen's conquests, bordellos and bagnios and easy times, women who cheerfully did this and that and ten times a night. Of Burmese beauties and Singapore sweethearts and Marseilles bawds, of bare-breasted South Sea islanders who wore only grass skirts, and gorgeous Chinese, and Greek harlots, and icy Spanish ladies who exploded like a canister of grapes, and uninhibited Filipinas and midnight black Kaffirs.

Skye heard it all, and these things hurt, as his boastful shipmates knew they would. Danny Boggs and Harry Peck loved to torment him. Even the bosuns and lieutenants loved to torture him.

"You missed it again, eh, Skye? Well, it's all your fault, laddie boy. Make yourself into a good seaman, and you'll taste the sweets," they would say.

But Barnaby Skye knew that no force on earth would reconcile him to his slavery. So he endured, hated, hurt, yearned, and tried to remember his sisters, his aunt Clarice, his mother, the sweet pigtailed girls he had met at tea parties and May fairs. These women were different from sailors' women. These women went to church, took communion, and got married and had families. Or were they so different? Maybe they enjoyed the mating, too. How could he know? Miserably, Skye pushed all his confused thoughts, his ignorance of females, his yearnings, aside when he could. But no young man in the prime of his life could put such things aside. The hungers returned again and again, brutal in their power.

Now he watched Perrault's women cook, watched their heavy breasts shift under their dresses, watched them talk and laugh among themselves. These were Shoshones, Snakes, savage women, wild and uninhibited.

He watched eagerly, alive with anticipation, wild to find out what this ultimate mystery was about. It had taken just one casual remark from the Iroquois breed to fan flames in him. Around him the Snake encampment settled for the night. He watched old men at prayer, hands lifted to the red sunset. A youth played a flute next to a beautiful girl, who pretended to ignore him. Skye discovered another odd thing: a lad and a maid stood facing each other, and then the lad drew a blanket over them both. There they stood, the boy's leggins and moccasins poking out under the blanket, along with the girl's skirts and moccasins. Were they kissing under there? He had no idea. No one bothered them. Perhaps this was the accustomed way for lovers to find a moment of privacy. He stared, fascinated. Then, at dusk, the youth drew the blanket off, the girl smiled and slipped away to her family.

Maybe that girl was like his sisters, who would be married now and have children. He could be an uncle. But he would never know his nieces and nephews, not even their names.

Men gathered in groups and smoked, rotating a single pipe among them, content to sit silently in the lavender twilight. The women retreated to the river—the Malade, the sick river, Perrault had told him—to perform ablutions shielded by thick purple night with only a band of blue lingering on the high black ridge to the northwest. Youths watched the horses. Perrault had taken Skye's two out to the pasture and put them in the care of the village herders. Skye wondered whether he'd ever see his horses again; he felt distrustful and didn't know why. These people had accepted him, and yet he wasn't accepting them.

The pungence of the new-leafed sagebrush eddied through the camp on the evening breezes. The first stars emerged, as if from a veil. Young men tied their ponies close at hand and set their bows and quivers beside their robes: this village had fangs, even in the midst of tranquility. A burst of embers fled a dying fire, momentarily illumining a group of women who were whispering to each other. Someone sang a monotone melody, or was it a prayer or a chant? The high nasal voice was an old man's and it sounded like the plainsong he had heard once in the cathedral. Skye wondered what these people believed and who their demons might be, and whether their morals were the same as white men's morals—or better.

"You want a pipe, Skye?" asked Perrault, and handed Skye a lit pipe without waiting for his response.

Skye took it silently, sucked the unfamiliar smoke—he hadn't acquired the habit, lacking the pence and the opportunity until now—and coughed.

The Iroquois laughed. "You don't know nothing, sailor," he said.

"I'm learning," Skye said. He had never said anything truer about himself. In the space of a few weeks he had mastered more things than he could name. And maybe this night he would master something more. Neither his gazes nor his attention drifted for long from the two young women, who had ceased their labors and were sitting quietly, still aglow with the day.

"Damn, we gonna have fun," the old Iroquois barked. "My old Molly, she likes to rut better'n me, almost, and comes after me if I don't make her happy."

Skye could hardly imagine it. He remembered shy pale girls with ringlets, starched manners and starched frocks, keeping a stiff distance from the boys.

"Too bad you don't got some whiskey, Skye. Maybe at rendezvous you give me some whiskey, eh?"

"How far away is that?"

"Two, three weeks mebbe. Got to go down to Cache Valley, near the big Salt Lake, Bear River. Then let the good times roll, ah, ieee!"

"Isn't it a fair?"

"A fair! Why, *garçon,* it be more. No words for it. It be games and cards and makin' friends and chasing the *petites filles.* It be getting a new fusil or traps or red cloth or ribbons. It be a good brawl, too, if one likes to wrestle a bear."

"Wrestle a bear?"

"Just talkin'. Them free trappers got the hair of the bear." Perrault sucked smoke, knocked the dottle out of his pipe, and laughed. "I guess it be time to go please old Molly afore she come after me with the scalpin' knife."

Skye found himself alone and taut as a strung bow. The younger women eyed him boldly, mischief in their faces, but didn't approach. They each unrolled a pair of blankets and made a show in the tumescent dark of wriggling into them. The two weren't more than ten feet apart, maybe fifty feet from Skye's bedroll. Was one closer to him by design?

A shyness tormented Skye. Was he supposed to crawl over there? Would one come to him? Who were they? Perrault's daughters? No, they looked to be pure Shoshone, probably stepdaughters, but who could say?

No such inhibition troubled Perrault and his woman. There, in the night blackness, the grunts and pleasures of mating filtered softly outward, and the night was not so dark that Skye couldn't see a little. The sight tormented him. This wasn't what he expected: nothing private, nothing tender.

He waited for quietness, but it didn't come. Perrault and Molly whispered and laughed and made noises. What did her daughters think of this? What would an Englishwoman think of this? Skye itched to throw off his cover, but sheer fear paralyzed him. He lay in the coolness, sweating, clenching and unclenching his fists. It was up to him. That's what it came to.

And then he went to her. He didn't care what he had been or who he was or what anyone thought. He didn't care whether she found out he had never done this before. It didn't matter that this dusky savage maid wasn't the pale blue-eyed lover of his dreams. His pulse lifted until he feared his heart would burst. He crept to the nearer of the daughters, expecting anger or a shriek, and sheer embarrassment. Instead, she whispered cheerfully, tugged him to the ground, and threw herself toward him. His hands found velvety flesh, wondrous to touch, and hers ripped at his clothing, while she cheerfully rebuked him with a noisy chatter that must have awakened all the neighbors.

And after that, he discovered a whole new world filled with shining joy and inexplicable tears.

Chapter 18

In the slate gray dawn, Skye stirred with the first light, as he always did, and noted a peaceful and utterly silent village, a mood that matched his own. The young Shoshone woman, whose name he didn't even know, lay beside him, naked under her blanket.

He had slept soundly after an hour of delirium and feverish exploration. Gently he arose and dressed. No one stirred, but he saw a Shoshone on horseback among the horses, ever watchful. Skye stretched his arms upward to touch the untinted sky, and then walked down to the Malade River. He had much to think about and things to relive and remember.

Now, he supposed, he had reached manhood after his long, bitter sojourn in the belly of the navy, like Jonah in the whale. He found himself beset by various strands of feeling: pleasure, relief, peace, guilt, fear, and loss. He wondered why he felt loss and what had been taken away from him. Perhaps it was his youthful vision of romantic love. What had happened here had nothing to do with love or tenderness or commitment. Certain youthful visions lay shattered; perhaps those English and Christian things he had soaked up in the Anglican church on Sundays, or in all the instruction and example of his parents.

He knew what lust was now. This mating was bereft of spiritual communion or any sort of friendship and tenderness with a woman. He supposed this Shoshone girl was wanton, but he had no comparison.

It didn't matter. He had enjoyed a fine, mad time, and the memory enflamed him. He had known ecstasy, trembling delights, and sudden peace. He had discovered the silky joy of a woman's flesh, and had responded with an explosion of pent-up need. He had learned his desires could build again and again, and that his bedmate's desires matched his own. He would never forget that night, or the sheer happiness of the moment, when nothing else mattered. Tonight there might be more. He would while away the slow daytime hours and hope for another turn, another embrace of smooth, golden flesh.

He wondered how to conduct himself now, and feared he would offend these people. Would she smile? Pretend that nothing had happened? Want him beside her as they wended their way southward to the rendezvous of the Yanks? What was politeness among these Snake people after moments like this? Or didn't it matter? There certainly were no secrets in a village without walls, and that was different from the way Englishmen lived. In England, a liaison would be discreet, and the lovers would say nothing or give nothing away, and everything would be closeted. But not among the Snakes. One could walk through a camp like this any dark evening and know most everything about everyone.

He washed himself in the icy river water, feeling the jolt of cold as he splashed himself. When he returned, the women were just stirring, though Perrault still snored on the hard earth. Far from being shy or demure, the three women grinned boldly, celebrating a good night, and chattered at him in a tongue he couldn't fathom.

They fed him something that had shredded meat, berries, and fat in it. He wondered what it was and how he could make some; obviously it preserved well in its gut casing. It would be a good emergency food on the trail.

His Shoshone lover and her sister enjoyed themselves,

glancing in his direction constantly, chattering among themselves about him, and laughing. He couldn't imagine what they were saying, and hoped it wasn't as graphic or coarse as the talk he had heard from his shipmates when they returned from shore leave. He fancied she was pretty: whatever she lacked in slenderness, she more than made up for with shining eyes. She was all aglow, as if all her feelings were sunny this fine June morning.

The sun leaped over the high eastern ridges, suddenly bathing the river bottoms in gold, but the village seemed to be in no hurry, and Skye fathomed that these people were rarely rushed. They would arrive at the rendezvous in their own good time and at their own speed. They were traversing a vast north-south valley hemmed by arid mountains with only a little scrub pine at their crests.

Last to arise, like some lord, was old Perrault. The breed stretched, made water, belched, and began joshing the women in his harsh tongue. Then at last he turned to Skye.

"She says you didn't know nothing but now you do." He wheezed cheerfully. "Haw."

"Uh, what's her name?"

"Her? It don't translate. Call her Annie." He addressed her in voluble Shoshone, and Skye caught only the name he was bestowing on her. "That other, she'll be Mariel, eh?" He laughed bawdily. "Ah, ha, good times for Skye."

"Mister Skye, sir."

Perrault wheezed and headed for the pasture where his horses were being herded. Skye elected to follow and catch his own. They weren't picketed, and he hoped he could slip hackamores over their heads and lead them back to camp.

He found the spotted horses easily enough, even amid

the hundreds in the Shoshone herd, but he couldn't even approach them. They threaded their way through the restless herd, nimbly staying well ahead of Skye, who grew hotter and angrier by the minute. After this he would tie one at his camp, or hobble them both, just as he always had.

There were several herders patrolling the horses now, and a handful of villagers catching horses. The Shoshones had no trouble with theirs. The women among them often walked right up to the packhorses, caught two at a time, and led them back to camp where they could be harnessed with those drags that Perrault called travois.

At last Perrault helped him, his eyes full of mirth and perhaps contempt. The old man had a way with animals. He walked straight up to Skye's brown horse and hackamored the animal in an instant. Then he caught the other and handed both leads to Skye.

"Haw!" yelled Perrault. "You got no experience at nothing. Wimmin, horse, it's all the same."

Sullenly, Skye packed his outfit, loaded it, and waited.

Some time in the middle of the morning, the vanguard finally started south, while the rest followed when they could.

They rode while the heat built, rested a while, drifted onward under a cruel sun. But Skye saw some sort of order when he looked sharply. The young men, the well-armed warriors, rode the flanks and rear; the headmen rode at the front. Hunters and vedettes were continually riding out and vanishing ahead or to the sides. Skye realized that the village was always on guard, and its relaxed progress was deceptive.

He steered his pony close to Perrault, who rode near

the rear, far behind his women, who were ahead in gossiping knots.

"You worked for Hudson's Bay, monsieur?" Skye asked.

"Ah! Dem no good bastards! Last year we quit. Yanks pay eight times more for beaver. I quit for good, bones don't like cold no more. Oh, Ogden, he mad plumb through, yellin' at us and makin' big threats like he near kill us. Say we owe HBC lots beaver. Damn! They cheat us, make us slaves so we go trade with the Yanks."

"You're not going back to Canada?"

"Non, non, *l'hiver,* too cold. My women, they take care of me. Molly, she be a widow, and dem girls, they need a good breed aroun'. I make a lodge for dem women, have me a good old age, eh?"

"I would think you'd want to go back to your own kind."

"You *Anglais,* damn, you don't know how it is. Dem Snakes, dey make you happy."

"Why do they call themselves Snakes?"

Perrault cackled. "Dem dumb Creoles, dey don't get it. The Shoshones use a wiggling finger—like dis—as their sign. It mean people dat live on curving river, like dis. But dem trappers, dey think it's snakes, and so dey call Shoshones Snakes. Call da river Snake. Eh? Whee! Pretty funny. Big joke. Snake people laugh."

"These people don't dress up. The Nez Perces wear finer clothing. Why is that?"

"Dere's another bad name. Dey don't pierce noses. Dey proud people, mean bastards, like to make war, steal Snake ponies. Mostly dey hate Snakes and Snakes hate dem. Shoshones, dey buffler people. Nez Perces, dey mostly fish-eaters but dey hunt buffalo each fall. When

it get cold, dey all go over the mountains and hunt buffler and fight dem Crows and Blackfeet."

Skye absorbed all that and took his lessons seriously.
Perrault was the key to understanding this country.

"What did we eat this morning?"

"Pemmican. Good trail food. Last damn near forever.
Ground up chokecherries or bufflerberries, dried buffler
meat, mix her up with fat and let it cool and put it in gut.
Damn, she keeps you going. Dem women make it good.
You like Annie, eh? Maybe you got her."

"Got her?"

"Yeah, you, me, we make a lodge. You young; you trap
a little, shoot buffler, and we got three wimmin for *l'hiver,*
eh? You get tired of one, you take Mariel, eh?"

The idea startled Skye. "Ah, I'm heading east, Mr. Perrault."

"Where da hell you come from? Some damn *Anglais,*
dat all I know."

Skye debated telling his story, and found no reason not
to. Swiftly, he described a young life under duress, his escape, and progress into a new life.

"Damn. HBC come after you. Dey rule the roost. Dey
catch you. You give dem the slip—dat pretty good. Dem
roosters peck de eyes out."

"They tried at Fort Nez Perces, but didn't know what
to do with me. McTavish was too Scotch to feed me."

"Don' go east. You crazy, *Anglais?* What you do dere?"

"I want to study. Get the education I've always wanted.
Go into business."

Perrault spat and said nothing. He kicked his ancient
pony and pulled ahead of Skye, an unmistakable gesture.

Skye rode alone the rest of that golden June day
wondering how he had earned Perrault's contempt. *Of*

course he would go east. And of course he would get into college—somehow. Work his way through. And of course he would win the life he had lost, and probably do better because of all his bitter experience. If he had learned one thing about this wilderness existence, it was the boredom that permeated everything. A life like this would stupefy him.

The cavalcade walked scarcely five miles that day, obviously in no hurry to go anywhere, and then settled into another camp very like the last. The hunters rode in, some of them with deer slung over packhorses. Somehow the meat found its way into most of the pots, along with roots and bulbs the women had casually gathered en route. The hunters were responsible for provisioning the whole band and not just their own lodges.

Skye tried to relax but couldn't. Why didn't they hurry to the Yanks' rendezvous? He needed to talk English, not with some ignorant old French-Iroquois breed, but people born to the tongue who could supply him with information. He knew almost nothing, and needed to know everything about going east.

His thoughts turned to Annie as dusk settled, and he waited for darkness with taut anticipation. Now that he knew what was in store, his craving was worse than ever. He didn't wait for darkness; he couldn't. In the gloomy afterlight and the hush of night, he crept to the nearer bedroll. But it was Mariel this time, and she burned with need equal to his, fierce and demanding, quite different from Annie and even more gifted in fanning his flames. She exhausted him. He had never known that sort of soft weariness.

Then he drifted to sleep, his thoughts probing this new wonder in his life. Sometime in the deeps, cries awakened him. Around him people sprang up. Men swiftly gathered their weapons and vanished into the gloom. Skye hadn't the faintest idea what all that was about and waited for Perrault to tell him. But the weathered old trapper took his time, and meandered about for a while, whispering to dark figures Skye could barely make out.

The old Iroquois finally squatted beside Skye in the starlight.

"Dem damn *Pieds Noirs*," he growled. "Dey got dem horse."

Chapter 19

Skye knew something of war, even if it was marine war. He would fight. He fumbled in the starlight for some clothing and his bow and quiver. He could see little, but finally managed to pull on his britches. No one had built up the fires for fear of an arrow or shot. He needed his moccasins, and discovered them near his bedroll.

When at last he readied himself and headed for the pasture where the horses had grazed, he knew he was too late. In that darkness he could not distinguish one horse from another. He would not know until dawn whether his own horses had been stolen.

He stood guard over the remaining horses, along with old men. His effort to help had been futile and late. No moon shone, and he could barely see the bulks of the nervous animals or the other village warriors about him. He could not imagine how the Blackfeet could even see enough to take some horses, much less escape along some line of retreat. He heard no wailing, no sounds of grief, and supposed no Shoshone had been hurt.

Eventually the quarter moon rose, and then it was easier to keep an eye on the herd and watch for intruders. An hour or so into the chill new morning the weary Shoshone pursuers returned, driving numerous sweat-stained animals before them. Many of the horses had been recovered. The warriors triumphantly drove the stock through the village so their prowess at war could be observed and honored by all. Then they dismounted and walked stiffly to their lodges, their faces grave.

"Ho!" muttered the old man next to him.

The rising light soon told the story. The pursuers had recovered twenty-one horses; only a few had been lost. Skye hunted for his own and found the brown but not the lighter one. He grieved the loss, and a knot of bitterness toward the Blackfeet formed in his breast. He would remember this. He looked over his brown and concluded that it had been left in the herd; it showed no signs of heat or sweat or hard use.

Around him the Shoshones talked in their own tongue, harsh and angry sounds that didn't need much translating. Skye hackamored and led his remaining horse to his campsite, and dourly began to load it. He would have to walk now, and carry his kit on the horse. Traveling to the rendezvous wasn't going to be much fun. Still, he had walked most of the way here, so he could walk some more. And the horse would pack his gear. It wasn't so bad.

And the nights . . . He eyed the two sisters, who grinned back at him, conspirators at taking turns. He needed to think about that. His shipmates would have boasted about it, but something in it troubled him. He didn't know these women. This most intimate act had been with strangers who couldn't speak his tongue. Something was missing.

He pulled his buckskin shirt over his head, found his topper and jammed it over his unruly hair, scratched at his luxurious beard, and thought he had failed his hosts this night. He knew nothing about the warfare of the savages and knew he had better learn fast. This was not the civilized world, with constables and sheriffs. He realized he had been lucky to come two or three hundred miles without being murdered or robbed. Whatever else this night and this loss of a valuable horse had accomplished, it taught him a hard lesson.

This morning the Shoshones were in a different mood. Those who brought the horses back were honored. They paraded through the village receiving their praise, which others were eager to offer. But even though Skye couldn't understand a word, he could sense the change. No longer was this a romp toward the rendezvous, but a solemn procession, with grim-faced young men, bristling with weapons—bows, quivers, lances, clubs, hatchets, knives—flanking the women and children and elders.

Skye walked along with Perrault's women, who were quiet this morning, but then old Perrault joined him, riding beside Skye as he walked ever southward.

"Ah, damn dem *Pieds Noirs.* Dey get eleven horse—dey get away. Dey get you horse, eh? You get another. Lots of horse. Go steal one. Dey get you horse, you go take another horse from dem. We gonna get even someday, soon as we trade for powder, fusil, lots balls. Den we steal fifty horse and kill a few of dem devils. Dey got lots of Nor' West fusils, guns dey get from the *Anglais.* But we get rifles at rendezvous, eh? You come along, we go take ten horse for every one dey get."

"Are they the worst tribe?"

"Oui, *du nord*. Dey strong, much bigger den Snakes. Dey pick on us, Crows, Flatheads, Assiniboine, Gros Ventres, all dem. You kill a *Pied Noir* and six more grow in his place."

"The men are all painted up. What does that mean?"

"It means lots of things. Dem that paints is ready for war. Dey all got their private medicine, lightning, stars, like dat. Good paint, make 'em strong."

"How do they make that bright red?"

"Dat's vermilion. Dey get that from traders. The rest dey get from plants and rocks an' mix wid grease."

"If they come again, I'll fight."

"Ah, you get yourself kill. You get a good rifle at rendezvous—mountain gun like a Hawken—and den fight."

Skye didn't reply. In the right circumstances, he could do more with a belaying pin than a firearm. He couldn't afford the mountain rifle, and anyway, he was bound for the east coast and the Yankees.

"How long to the rendezvous?"

Perrault shrugged. "Maybe a few days. Who know?" He eyed Skye. "How come you walking? Go put your stuff on my woman's travois."

"Travois? My stuff?"

"Won't hurt nothing."

Skye didn't need a second invitation. He waited for the women to pull up. Perrault barked a command, and even before Skye could loosen his load, the women were pulling off Skye's packsaddle and heaping his stuff on top of their folded lodgeskins. Skye watched long enough to see that his things were securely tied down, and then put his saddle on the brown, glad to ride again.

"Now mebbe you give old Perrault a few whiskey at the rendezvous, eh?"

"If I can," Skye replied.

The days passed uneventfully, but Skye used every moment to learn what he could, often consulting with Perrault. He studied the buffalohide lodges and admired their utility. They could easily be erected in minutes, were light and portable, were designed to handle a fire within and contain its heat, and could be made comfortable any season of the year.

He had never seen a buffalo, and itched to see the awesome black herds Perrault told him about. At first Skye scoffed; there could not be so many buffalo. But when he considered the number of hides in just one small eleven-pole lodge, he reconsidered. There were thousands of hides in this village.

He discovered that virtually every part of the buffalo could be put to use: its bones became tools, ladles, kitchen implements. Its hide could become a warm winter robe, and its meat could feed a lodge for many days. Its fat and meat mixed with berries could make pemmican, and the thick breast hide of the bulls could be turned into a war shield strong enough to deflect an arrow or spear or even a musket ball. He could make good moccasin soles from bullhide, and he could dry the sinew layered along the spinal cord into usable thread or a bowstring. He could stuff buffalo hair into a pillow or saddle pad, turn the scrotum into a rattle or a purse, or tan the soft hide of an unborn calf into a pouch.

He discovered that hunting these beasts was a great enterprise and sport, and that a fast and fearless pony, trained to draw close enough so its rider could drive an arrow into the heart-lung area just behind the front legs, was a prized possession and a source of wealth and food. He absorbed Perrault's vast buffalo lore, and realized that these tribes could scarcely exist without the animal, which was why the buffalo was greatly honored among them. Not even the salmon was prized so much as the buffalo.

At first he studied the practical, lifesaving, and useful things he found among these people: he studied war clubs, flint arrowheads, the traders' iron arrowheads, the way bows were made, and the wood used in them. He watched how the Shoshone made fires, what they used for tinder, and how they preserved a live coal long enough to start the next fire. He watched two women flesh a deer hide with scrapers made of bone and a bit of iron. He studied the roots and plants the women plucked and dug and used in their stews, the yamp and sego lily and camas, and the digging tools they used to wrench bulbs from stubborn soil.

He learned something about the medicinal herbs these people used, such as dogwood and yarrow for fevers, and the various stalks and leaves that would yield a dye, such as alder and bloodroot. He pestered Perrault endlessly, until the old Iroquois breed laughed or growled at him, but Skye knew that he had to learn, and fast, to survive, and that this tribe could teach him much of what he needed to know.

All these arts and crafts came naturally to a people who planted nothing but hunted and fished and gathered nature's own bounty. He knew if he could master even the half of what these people knew, he would improve his chance to survive his long journey across the continent.

He discovered that these people had religious and spiritual traditions that conformed to their way of life, but he could grasp little of them. He saw no sign of organized religion, but he discerned that each person had his own religion—Perrault called it medicine, an odd but fitting word—his own spiritual helpers, his own protectors and mentors. Some wore small totems, or little bags suspended from the neck; others wore amulets, often a small carved turtle of wood or bone. These things interested him less than the ones that he could employ to survive in the wilds, but he was curious about them. Perrault was little help on that score, and shrugged off Skye's endless questions, sometimes turning surly when Skye pushed too hard.

"You crazy," he snarled. "Damn! You owe me whiskey."

Perrault did tell him about one useful thing: the tribes could communicate with a hand language. Skye vowed to learn all he could; then, at least, he would have some way to communicate with these people. Maybe someone at the rendezvous could help him learn the sign language.

They emerged from the valley into a broad hazy land, with foothills rising to the east and arid drainages to the west.

"Pretty damn soon, now, Skye—ah, damn, *Mister* Skye. You be crazy."

Then one morning Skye sensed an excitement in camp. The Shoshones astonished him with their festival dress. The women decked themselves in quilled or beaded buckskins or flannel; the men wore all their war honors. A barbarous beauty pervaded the whole village, along with an expectation that Skye could feel as well as see in eager, joyous faces.

They paraded that grand July day, their horses mincing and dancing, their exodus orderly and spirited. Skye felt something mad and wild clear to his bones, and rode eagerly, scarcely able to believe the transformation around him. He didn't need to be told: today they would arrive at the rendezvous.

They turned east along a sluggish river, and followed it into a wide valley with grassy plains. It seemed a barren place to Skye, almost treeless except along the river. But a haze of blue smoke hung over this place, and the rolling grasslands were dotted with horses of all descriptions and colors. Lodges clustered near the river, intermixed with brush arbors that supplied shade. Skye could see two or three white men's tents of canvas, rectangular and angular compared to the conical skin lodges. As the Shoshones approached, they began to sing and dance. The warriors strung their bows and withdrew arrows from their quivers. Was this going to be a battle? Skye watched nervously, wondering what all this was about. And then, in one wild swoop, the Shoshones dashed madly into the rendezvous, a mock attack that was met by mock resistance from other Indians, and by white men who discharged their rifles into the skies and howled right along with the Shoshones. Then the Shoshones paraded through the whole vast encampment, whooping, displaying their gauds and war honors, strutting, whirling their horses.

Skye rode among them, astonished at all this, astonished at the odd-looking white men, most of them dressed in peculiar costumes, part European but largely adapted from the tribes around them. They sported beards as luxurious as Skye's. Some wore necklaces of bone, which won Skye's curiosity.

Perrault rode beside Skye. "Dem's Crows. Dey got here before us," he said. "Dat's de rendezvous, and now de fun start. Pretty soon dey all come sniffing around. Den dey give ribbons and looking glasses and calico and needles and knives an' stuff for my women and me. You get me jug of whiskey, and den you get one woman or the other any time." He slapped his bony knee and howled like a wolf.

Skye stared. Perrault was selling his women.

Chapter 20

Jedediah Smith dreamed of two things, adventure and wealth. A fortune would assuage the yearnings of his Calvinist soul and prove his worth before God and man. Adventure would test his mettle and make life sharp and exhilarating.

There in Cache Valley that July of 1826 he saw a way to have both. While the free trappers with Ashley and Smith's fur company began their rendezvous frolic, he was busy forming a new company to buy out General Ashley, who had at last made a fortune in beaver plews, and wanted to escape the fur trade before some new disaster laid him low.

The new partners and Ashley had been dickering all morning in their buffalo-skin lodge, but they weren't far from agreement. The lodge cover had been rolled up two or three feet, letting the playful breezes sweep in. That cooled the occupants and let them keep an eye on the glistening prairies just outside, where veteran trappers were sucking trade whiskey from Ashley's store after a year's parch, and swapping elaborate lies.

On hand also were Davey Jackson and Bill Sublette,

experienced mountaineers and participants in the great
Ashley-Henry venture that had probed up the Missouri
River in search of a fortune in beaver pelts. There had
been much to negotiate, but now an agreement was in
sight, forged by Ashley and the new company of Smith,
Jackson, and Sublette. The idea was simple, even if the
details were complex. The new booshways, as the free
trappers called them, were buying out Ashley, and would
pay him with beaver pelts the following year. If they sent
Ashley an express asking for more supplies, he would deliver them to this rendezvous site next July and return to
the States with the pelts.

Smith knew Ashley was getting the best of the deal:
the real profits in the fur trade went to its suppliers, who
charged several times St. Louis prices to bring the goods
a thousand dangerous miles to the Stony Mountains. But
Smith didn't expect the new partnership to suffer: in Jackson and Sublette he had two masters, canny veterans who
would lead trapping parties to the beaver in the fall, winter, and spring when the pelts were prime, and harvest
the wealth of the wilderness. They would do, along with
a handful of brilliant mountaineers, such as Bridger,
Harris, and Fitzpatrick.

The partners and Ashley broke for the nooning and meandered out of the lodge into the brilliant sun. Before them
lay a vast undulating prairie with enough grasses on it to
keep horses fat during the entire rendezvous. The Wasatch
Mountains rose to the east, their lower slopes dry and barren. Far to the southwest lay the Great Salt Lake, guarding a hostile desert beyond. Closer at hand, an emerald
band of trees and brush lined the river, supplying firewood, game, and shelter to the great trapper's fair.

The event had barely begun and would last five or six

weeks, until the wildmen of the mountains had squandered their last plew and the booshways were organizing and outfitting their brigades. Jed Smith—they called him Diah—was not one of those wildmen, and had blown nothing on trade whiskey—actually, pure grain alcohol seasoned with tobacco and spices and diluted with river water. He was one of them and yet he wasn't, a man apart, a man who daily read his King James Bible and sought the blessings of God upon his endeavors. And yet he was a man born to lead, born to adventure, and withal, tougher and more sagacious about wilderness than any of the others. The trappers trusted him more than any other brigade leader, knowing he would get them through. He understood the revelries and the animal hungers that fueled them so far from civilization, and never intervened or criticized, although he kept apart. The trappers, in turn, understood that about him and accepted his leadership without cavil, a bond built on mutual respect.

Buffalo stew bubbled in an iron pot, and he helped himself with a thick iron ladle. There had never been many of the shaggy beasts on this side of the mountains, and this rendezvous had doomed the last of them. But the Cache Valley abounded in deer and elk and antelope, and the mountaineers would wallow in fat meat.

So far, the rendezvous had been a quiet affair. When Ashley's pack train trotted in two days earlier, the trappers lined up at Ashley's tent store and bought jugs and cups of trade whiskey to allay a year-long thirst. The next days were devoted to serious drinking and gambling, usually euchre or monte, using greasy old cards that had survived for years in someone's kit. But they were really waiting for the Shoshones and Crows to arrive so they could begin the contests, the games, the wrestling, shooting, brawling, and other revels, such as the debauchery and whoring that took place largely at night. This was Snake country, and these were friendly Injuns who cheerfully lent or sold their comely daughters and wives to any trapper with a bit of foofaraw. That's when the midsummer's saturnalia would really begin.

Almost as if to answer his thoughts, Smith saw a stirring among the trappers. Someone came whooping in with news, and in minutes the word was bruited through the disorderly camp: the Snakes would be arriving in an hour or two. Bearded, buckskinned men, with visions of fair and dusky maidens dancing in their heads, laughed and howled and bayed at the sun. Tonight the party would begin.

But in his starchy way, Smith turned his thoughts elsewhere. The Shoshones would have furs to trade at Ashley's big store-tent, and Ashley would return to St. Louis with prime peltries—buffalo, elk, deer, otter, fox, as well as beaver—all handsomely tanned and valuable in the East. Next year, Ashley's store would be the Smith, Jackson, and Sublette store, and his own company would be dealing with tribesmen for those pelts, all for a fat profit. Smith reminded himself to invite the Crows and Bannacks and other tribes to come next summer and bring all the pelts they could produce. They all had furs to trade, and he intended to buy them. The Indian trade was especially profitable because they wanted so little for their furs—a little trade whiskey, a small hand mirror, a cup of sugar, a few lead balls, a few ounces of powder, some fishhooks, some calico, ribbons, and blankets.

By common consent the negotiations were adjourned that afternoon. The arrival of the Snakes was not a sight to be missed. They would be wearing their festival finery; their nubile honey-tinted maidens would be gauded out and painted; their bronze young men would be wearing their war honors, carrying their shields and lances, riding prized horses. Their ponies, many of them the spotted Appaloosa gotten from the Nez Perce, would be ribboned and painted.

Smith guessed there would be a few white men among them, probably Hudson's Bay booshways. The powerful HBC had fought the invasion of their turf by free trappers and now kept a baleful eye on the fiesty Yanks. Worse, the HBC had lost many of its trappers to the Ashley interests, and might be looking for ways to cause trouble. The Yanks paid a trapper good money for pelts instead of giving him a skimpy salary. An industrious trapper could earn several times more as a free entrepreneur than as an engagé, as the French-Canadians called them, and stay out of debt if he chose to.

"Well, Diah, now we'll see how the stick floats," said Bill Sublette.

"We'll make them welcome. Give their headmen some powder and galena. I want them to know that the partnership will be running the store next summer," Smith replied, his mind never far from business.

"I'll pass out some vermilion to cement relations," Sublette said. "I know most of their headmen."

"It'll pay off," said Davey Jackson. "I reckon we'll do better than Ashley and Henry, if only because we've got the experience under our belts. We've a notion what to do and not to do."

That was how they all reckoned it, Smith thought. He himself had gotten five thousand dollars out of his brief junior partnership with Ashley, and was plowing it all back into the new company. Where else in the United

States could a man make so much in a year? A few years like that and he could return to Ohio, marry, and live in comfort the rest of his life.

The thought made him itchy. Maybe he would not enjoy life in Ohio's Western Reserve, where the westering New England Smiths had finally settled after stops in upstate New York and Pennsylvania. Return? Not after he had heard the call of the wild. The wilderness was a temptation, not only to his flesh but also his soul and his pride. It was something to pray about, this demon in him. He knew he should return to civilization and settle down and become a deacon in his church.

He discerned a great stirring on the northern horizon. Trappers whooped and ran for their mountain rifles, anticipating what would come. Gabe Bridger grinned. Tom Fitzpatrick and the rascal Jim Beckwourth slid caps onto the nipples of their rifles while Black Harris and Louis Vasquez waited patiently, a faint smile on their weathered chestnut faces.

The Shoshones raced in, their warriors kicking lathered horses straight toward the camp, lances lowered, bows drawn, the whole lot howling like wolves. It was enough to terrify a pork-eater, as pilgrims were called. But Smith watched laconically, enjoying the fun as much as anyone else. On they came, screeching blood-freezing taunts, like an army from hell. Rifles popped, the balls puncturing the sky, as the Snakes swept into the encampment.

"It's a sight," Ashley said, standing beside Smith. "Makes a man want to reach for his piece and throw up a breastwork."

Smith nodded. The Snake warriors were curvetting their ponies, counting mock coup, and showing off like military cadets on a lark. Right behind them the main body of Shoshones walked in, chiefs and shamans, squaws overseeing the ponies that dragged the lodges, all gauded in bright trade cloth, blue and red and green, with horn bonnets and fringed leggins. What a sight!

But what caught Smith's eye was the lone white man, no doubt an HBC agent spying on the opposition. Ermatinger maybe, or the legendary Peter Skene Ogden, a man as shrewd and forceful as any Yank trapper, and then some. But this one didn't seem familiar. He was an odd duck, thick as a plow horse, wearing a beaver topper and a buckskin shirt, and riding a brown palouse. The young man examined Smith and the other trappers with a gaze that had palpable force behind it, a gaze that drilled meaning out of everything he saw.

What struck Smith the most was the man's somberness. Unlike the Shoshones, he was all business. The more Smith watched, the more curious he became about the stranger. Whoever the fellow was, he had made his mark simply with his raking examination of the whole rendezvous. Well, Smith thought, he would know the man's name soon enough, and probably his business as well.

The Shoshones chose a river site east of the rendezvous for their own, and the squaws set to work raising lodges and unloading the innumerable travois. Trappers crowded about them, eyeing the maidens with hungry gazes, eager for the great July debauch to begin. This night many a trapper would squander much of his year's income, the product of long, lonely hours wading icy streams and skinning beaver and sleeping on cold ground.

Smith hiked toward the new man, who was watching silently, his gaze piercing and cautious, as if he were fleeing a past or had perceived trouble here. The man was stocky and powerful, his face dominated by an enormous nose that had probably been broken more than once. The new man squinted at this strange world from blue eyes that revealed nothing of his mood or motive. He seemed ill-equipped, and had only a bow and quiver for weapons. But it wasn't his ragged exterior that intrigued Smith. This man radiated determination and will.

The man seemed to come to some decision, dismounted, and headed for Smith and Ashley in a strange, rolling gait, leading his brown horse. "Are you Yanks?" he asked in booming voice.

"Americans, yes, and you?"

"I'm a man without a country. I've been looking for you to get some information. How far is it to Boston?"

"Boston? Boston?" Smith stared.

"Boston, mate. I'm on my way to Boston."

"Why, she's just over them hills hyar," said Bridger. "Maybe a two-day hike. Just foller the turnpike."

"I was told it was a lot farther. I'll rest my horse for a few days and then head east. Hope you can tell me a little about it. It's Boston I'm heading for, and I need to make my way. If I can be of service for a bit of food, I'd welcome it."

Trappers crowded around the man. "What's your handle, friend?" asked Black Harris.

The man hesitated. Smith knew the signs. This man was a fugitive. "Handle? Ah, a name, yes. Skye, sir. Mister Skye. Call me that. Barnaby's the Christian name."

"You from England?"

The man nodded.

"This pilgrim's looking for Boston," said Bridger to the rest. "I told him straight, it'd be two, three days if the pikes ain't muddy."

"Yes, that'd do it," said Broken Hand Fitzpatrick.

The rest nodded solemnly.

"You have to be careful of buffler in Boston," Beckwourth said. "There's a city law against making meat on the streets. Other than that, Boston's just the place."

"Skye," said Smith, "why are you going to Boston?"

"It's Mister Skye, sir. That's how I want it."

"Well, then, Mister Skye, you might enlighten us."

"There's a university in Cambridge, near Boston, and I'm going there to finish my schooling, sir. I didn't catch your name, but I take it you're in charge here."

"No one's in charge, Mister Skye. These are free trappers, not employees. But yes, I'm a partner in the fur company."

"This fellow's going to Boston," yelled Black Harris.

"You don't say," said Louis Vasquez. "Boston, is it?"

Skye nodded. "Boston, sir. It seems to be less far than I thought."

"Just head east, and before you know it, you'll be matriculating," said Davey Jackson.

"I'm much obliged to you, sir," the Englishman said. "Is there a way a man could trade some labor for some food?"

"Nope, there plumb ain't," Sublette said.

Skye looked crestfallen. "Will labor buy me a rifle, or anything at all?"

"Go eat, man," Smith urged. "They're really telling you no man starves here, and no American trapper ever turns away a hungry man in the mountains."

"I have much to learn," said Skye. "Thank you."

"You just take your fill from that kettle, and then I want to talk with you, Mister Skye."

"Show 'im how to raise Boston," Bridger said.

Chapter 21

Smith watched while the Englishman downed a helping of buffalo stew, and another. The man was hungry, and that hunger ran deep. After that, Smith nodded Skye into the cool lodge and waited for the man to settle comfortably on the ground.

An Englishman asking his way to Harvard College certainly aroused Smith's curiosity. Especially one who probably was a fugitive.

"Mister Skye, those gents were funning you. It's their way. Boston is most of a continent away. I hardly know the distance, but it must be nearly three thousand miles. You'd hike over several ranges of mountains, cross the Continental Divide, head into dry plains that run six or eight hundred miles, reach the green basin of the Mississippi, climb eastern mountains, and arrive eventually on the Atlantic Coast."

Skye nodded. "That's what Mr. Ogden told me. I'm a seaman, and don't know the land, especially here. I started from Fort Vancouver and walked for three months. I thought I'd come a long way."

"The Hudson's Bay post," Smith said, carefully.

Skye stared out upon the sunny grasslands. "Are you connected with HBC, Mr. Smith?"

"No, we're all Americans here. They're our rivals. We've lured some free trappers away from them and they don't like it. Free trappers can earn a lot more from us than salaried trappers with HBC."

Skye didn't answer for a while. "You must be wondering about me, mate," he said at last.

"We gauge a man out here by what he is, and how he fits in, and not by any other standard."

"I'll tell you my story. It's no secret."

Smith nodded. He badly wanted to hear it.

Skye squinted uneasily, choosing his words. "Seven years ago I was pressed into the Royal Navy off the streets of London. I was fourteen, on my way to my father's warehouse—he's an import-export merchant—on the banks of the Thames. I never saw my family again . . ."

Smith listened for ten minutes and nodded. He thought it might be something like that. A deserter in the eyes of the Royal Navy and HBC. If the man was telling the truth, he deserved his liberty. But men had a way of justifying their bad behavior. Perhaps there was more. "And Harvard? What about Harvard?"

"I had set my cap on a university education before I was pressed, sir. Cambridge, like my father before me. He was a disciple of Adam Smith and the Manchester school, and wanted me to take up political economy. I leaned toward literature and teaching. Well, I'm free at last. I want to start school now. Pass my entrance exam. Work my way through, somehow, some way."

"Without means?"

"A man does what he has to. I'll find a way. For all those years I plotted and schemed and waited my chance. It was hard growing up. I fought for my gruel. I faced bullies. It was harder still learning guile, but guile is what freed me. It wasn't until I stopped making trouble that they gave me a bit of liberty on deck. And that's what I needed." He gazed out upon the roistering crowd. "Am I in danger of being caught here? Will they take me back?"

"Sometimes HBC men come to rendezvous."

"They won't take me. Not alive, anyway. The earth

feels good under my feet, sir. For seven years I never had earth under my feet for long."

"How'd you arrive here? What did you eat?"

"I had some fishhooks and line. Salmon, sir. I have a belaying pin and two knives, and awl, thong, and shoe leather. Also a flint and striker. I traded along the Columbia for other things. And also got help from the Nez Perces. The Royal Navy came after me, guided by some Hudson Bay men. I watched them from the cliffs. This is a big place, this America."

"You found the Shoshones."

"They found me, mate. I thought I was done for, but they were friendly."

"They're the one tribe in the whole area not beholden to HBC, Mister Skye. You were lucky. And your timing was lucky. They were on their way here for our rendezvous. This is the second."

"That's what Mr. Ogden said. He advised me to look for the Snakes."

"He told you that?"

Skye smiled for the first time. "He allowed that he doesn't care for you Yanks, sir. Now, what's a rendezvous?"

"Our free trappers trade their beaver pelts for supplies brought out from Missouri. That lets them stay here in the mountains."

"Missouri?"

"On the western edge of the United States, sir. The gateway to Indian Country. A thousand miles from here with nothing but empty plains, buffalo, and dangerous Indians in between."

Skye seemed awed. "No place a man can work for his keep along the way?"

Smith smiled. "By sheer luck, you came upon the only place." Smith wondered whether to tell Skye that he could easily sign on with Ashley and work his way to St. Louis. He could use another trapper, but he opted for honesty as was his wont. "Actually, General Ashley's returning to St. Louis in a few weeks with a hundred twenty-three packs of beaver. He could use any help he can get, and you'd be ensured of fairly safe travel. You'd never make it alone, especially a pork-eater like you."

"A what?"

"A pilgrim. A novice. An inexperienced man. It's a French-Canadian term, *mangeur du lard*. Actually, if you dodged the Royal Navy and some HBC guides, you're no pilgrim. You've got some mountain seasoning. Men are scarce here, and I'm willing to take you on. You've no trapping experience but I need camp tenders and would pay you well."

"I want only one thing: to start my life after I was robbed of it, sir. This General Ashley . . . would I be forced to enlist?"

Smith saw the drift. "He's an officer of the Missouri militia, not regular army, and this is his private business venture. No, you'd work for him by mutual agreement."

"He'll learn I'm a deserter soon enough."

"That's a risk. He'll be more inclined to wonder whether you'll be a loyal employee."

"Let me tell you something, Mr. Smith. All the while I was the King's prisoner, I never despised England or my people. I fought the King's wars against the Kaffirs in Africa—the only time I set foot on land in seven years—and on the Irrawaddy River in Burma, wars of Empire, sir, never doubting where my English loyalties lay, even if my private circumstance was unbearable. I'll want to see Ashley, and I'll tell him the whole story and let him decide."

"I'd advise waiting a while before talking to him. You may like the free life here—especially after all those years in a ship's bilge."

"All right. I'll wait. Now, while I wait, how can I earn my keep? How can I get an outfit?"

"An outfit would cost you far more than you could earn here, Mister Skye."

The young man looked crestfallen. Then he smiled. "Guess I'll be off, mate. Long road ahead."

"No, no, that'd be fatal. You stay and enjoy the frolic. Eat at my stewpot. Meet the crowd. Give as good as you get from 'em, and they'll respect you. If you need anything from company stores, see me. Your credit's good."

"I could buy blankets?"

"That and more."

"May I ask why?"

"I could tell you that I need every man I can get, and that would be true. But you impress me, Mister Skye. You've the makings of a mountaineer."

"A mountaineer, sir?"

"It takes a breed, Mister Skye. It takes men with uncommon courage and loyalty and common sense. The mountains kill the foolish. They freeze or starve or die of thirst or get snakebit or run into Injuns and don't know how to deal with 'em. The good men survive by sticking together through thick and thin. Life depends on it, working in pairs and groups. The loners die, far from help. You wander out now and meet these gents. They aren't ordinary. They're all graduates of what we call the Rocky Mountain College—it's a school where you graduate or die."

"Graduate or die!"

"That's exactly right. But, Mister Skye, even the best go under. Friends of mine have disappeared, or died alone, not through any fault of their own. Not all their mountain skills can save them from an enraged grizzly sow, or a party of Bug's Boys—the Blackfeet—looking for white men to scalp. Let me tell you something: not in all human history has there been a breed like this, surviving in a wilderness like this. They're resourceful. You could take away all their possessions and even their clothes in a cold night, and they'd survive. I've thought about it some: there's no general rule. Some survive by their wits, others by sheer willpower or determination. Others are uncommonly resourceful and inventive. You're one of those, I reckon. You got here; other men would be nothing but white bones by now. If you want, I'll ask General Ashley to take you to Saint Louis, but I won't do it for a few days. You have things to think about and things to see here."

The young man stood, uncommonly silent, his face full of emotions that Smith couldn't read.

"You go to Ashley's tent store now. Look over the merchandise. Get what you need and tell the clerk to put it on my account. Better yet, I'll tell him."

Skye seemed at a loss for words, and finally clamped Smith's hand in his own, blinked, and retreated into the July afternoon.

What was it about that man? What a terrible story, if it was true. Smith's intuition told him that Skye had the makings. A few items out of the company store would be worth the gamble to Smith, Jackson, and Sublette. But even if Skye elected not to stay in the mountains, Smith was ready to bet his last dollar that Skye would eventually repay the debt.

Chapter 22

Throngs of wild Indians and trappers mobbed the tent store. Skye decided to wait and observe, see what could be bought, what things cost, and whether he could buy the things he needed most: blankets, a good knife, a cooking pot, and an ax. The ax he would put to immediate use. Each remaining day of this wilderness fair, Mr. Jedediah Smith would find a pile of split firewood and kindling before his lodge, courtesy of Barnaby Skye.

The proprietors had arranged the store so that all the business was transacted over a rough counter on hogsheads at the front. Clerks examined peltries, set a price, and then traded for the goods lying in barrels and boxes and shelves and packs behind them. The Shoshones in their festival dress waited patiently, many of them laden with tanned pelts of all descriptions and buffalo robes. He liked these people who had invited him to journey with them. He had come along, and they had led him to this miraculous place that made his spirits soar.

Among the crowd were scruffy-looking trappers trading pelts for odd things—hand mirrors, gaudy ribbon, brass buttons, jingle bells, yards of bright cotton calico or flannel, strings of glass beads, knives, awls, hatchets, hide-fleshing tools, cups of sugar, molasses, beans, Chinese vermilion in waxed paper cubes, even needles and thread. Women's things, mostly. The trappers were going to have a time of it tonight.

Shoshone warriors traded for bricks of du Pont powder wrapped in waxed paper, small bars of galena, as lead was called here, or a pound of precast balls, bullet moulds, flints, flintlock rifles, strikers, knives, blankets, tomahawks, lance points, traps, and awesome quantities of murky amber fluid that looked like something left by a dog on a tree, no doubt spirits, sold by the tin cup. The revels had already begun, with man and woman alike swilling the stuff, gasping, and returning to the store for more.

At last Skye took his turn. A balding young man at the counter surveyed him.

"You must be the Englishman, Skye. I'm Osgood. Diah Smith told me to put your order on account."

"It's Mister Skye, sir. I'd like a pair of those blankets, a small cooking pot, and a good ax. Also a knife—one of those big ones over there."

"Arkansas toothpick. What else?"

"That's all, sir."

"Sheetmetal pot or cast iron?"

"Whatever's cheapest."

"Sheetmetal, half-gallon." Osgood shrugged and wheeled into the storage area, dodging other clerks. He dropped thick gray blankets and an ax on the plank counter, and then added a tin pot and knife. "That do?"

"Yes."

"They come to seventeen and four bits. I'll put it on your account."

Skye had no idea how much that was, but it seemed a lot. "I'll find a way to pay it, sir."

"A dollar a plew, seventeen beaver."

Skye wondered how he could trap and skin that many beaver in a whole winter. They were making a debtor of him. Angrily, he whirled away, determined to escape these designing Yanks while he could. But the thick, heavy blankets felt good in his hand. So did the steel ax, with its keen edge, and the cooking pot and sharp knife. Now he had a way to cook food, and several weapons: the bow and arrows, the hatchet, a throwing and fighting knife, the ax, and his belaying pin, which he could use in ways these landlubbers never dreamed of. He had fought Kaffirs and pirates with no more than a belaying pin, and had fended off knives and swords with it, his hand protected behind the flare of the hickory. Let them try him now: he'd show them what a man could do with an ax and a hickory stick. He eyed his treasures and calmed down. They hadn't singled him out and weren't trying to ensnare him.

He wanted to see everything, meet everyone, explore every corner of this summer saturnalia, but he put first things first. He headed for the thick cottonwood groves in the river bottoms, looking for dead limbs. He had found a friend and protector in Jedediah Smith, and he would repay the loan as swiftly as possible. He located a fallen cottonwood limb and swiftly chopped and split an armload of wood. This he carried to Smith's lodge, and then another load.

"That's kind of you, Mister Skye," Smith said.

"It's the beginning of a repayment," Skye replied.

"You'll make friends here."

"That's my intention. Is it safe to leave my kit with your trappers? It's not much, Mr. Smith, but it's everything I have. I'm with the Shoshones now, but I'd like to meet your people."

"Bring it over and camp here. They'll leave your kit alone, 'least the trappers will. The Injuns probably will, too, but lifting a few things is a sport for them, friendly or not. Especially horses. You set up your camp here, and

I'll keep an eye on it. See those brush arbors? Those frameworks covered with boughs? Build yourself one, get out of the sun, put your loot in it. It's a home, of sorts."

Skye nodded, and chose a smooth level spot. In his months of flight, he had become an expert, learning the hard way just what a small pebble or stick or a slight slope could do to a night's sleep.

He cut still another armload of wood and carried it to one of the cookfires where any hungry man could dip a bowl and fill his belly. Within an hour he had supplied wood to all four cookfires of the mountain men, a gesture that did not go unnoticed, though the men barely acknowledged it.

Satisfied at last, he wandered aimlessly through the rendezvous, noting that these wildmen didn't wait for nightfall to imbibe spirits. Most of them had a tin cup of spirits that they attacked now and then. A few were drunk and staggering about. Two had passed into oblivion, and lay like corpses in the midst of all the revelry. People simply stepped over them.

Skye had none, and could afford none, and had rarely tasted spirits in his life, having been a stripling when he was pressed, and a prisoner ever since. But he intended to guzzle some when he had the chance.

One thing he learned in his meandering: the white men and Indians alike used this summer fair to compete with each other. He watched, fascinated, as skilled marksmen, hefting octagon-barreled mountain rifles, put balls into tiny targets—as small as a knot on a tree—at awesome distances. Elsewhere he watched men throw their hatchets—called tomahawks by some—forty or fifty feet and hit their targets. Others threw knives with just as much dexterity and deadly effect, often betting beaver pelts or a cup of spirits on the outcomes. The Shoshones enthusiastically participated in what clearly were contests of martial skills, and he learned that a few Crows were also competing.

In the course of that afternoon, Skye discovered that behind these contests was the deadly serious business of survival. Each of these mountain men and their Indian rivals could call upon these skills and often did against two- and four-footed enemies. Skye knew he would master these amazing skills, and vowed he would make himself the equal of all these trappers.

Other trappers perched on logs or stumps gambled with grubby cards, playing games called monte and euchre, their wagering done with round beaver pelts, which he gathered were worth about a dollar. Others of this bearded and buckskinned gentry simply drank and bragged. The young fellow Bridger was one of these. He lounged against a stump, sipped whiskey steadily, and told the most outlandish stories Skye had ever heard.

"I mind the time I saw this hyar bull elk, and I thought to make meat, so I lifted old Thunderbolt and let fly. But durned if the ball didn't hit glass. It just tinkled down on the ground like a busted window. That elk, he was clear t'other side of a glass mountain and I couldn't drop him nohow," Bridger said. "What was worse, that thar mountain magnified him, so I was thinking that elk was a hundred yards away when actually he was fifteen miles. Now that war nothing compared to the river I came across once that ran uphill. It came barreling through a canyon and then run uphill a mile or two, so I made me a raft and it took me clear up a mountain."

It dawned on Skye that Bridger was piling one ridiculous tale on another just for Skye's benefit, though the

homely fellow never looked him in the eye or acknowledged his presence. They were testing him in ways he
could barely fathom. He laughed at Bridger's nonsense
and Bridger grinned in return. They asked Skye nothing about himself, and he volunteered nothing, uncertain about all this. How many of these fierce men would
be as fair-minded as Smith? One thing he knew: these
Yanks didn't hold to formality and status. No one was
looking down his nose at Skye.

He came across none of the Hudson's Bay observers
that Smith thought would be snooping around. Not a one
of these mountaineers spoke with the precise tongue of an
Englishman. But maybe Smith had meant Canadians,
both French and English stock. Of the French there were
many, most with black beards and thick accents. He heard
names that suggested Scotland, names that suggested
Quebec and Montreal. These were the HBC men Smith
had lured away from John McLoughlin at Fort Vancouver, men who had changed sides. Skye felt safe here, but
he wasn't entirely sure of it.

As dusk approached, Skye thought perhaps this assemblage would sit down to dinner, as Englishmen would
have. But nothing like that materialized. Men dipped their
bowls into the steaming pots. If a pot emptied, whoever
felt like it sawed at the fly-specked hanging meat and
started more stew. He discovered that these quartered
carcasses were buffalo, and that the choicest cuts were
humpmeat or rib. The mountaineers fed themselves whenever they felt like eating, roasting the best meat and stewing the worst.

But in the midst of this chaos, he discovered care and
precaution. That evening trappers collected the horses that
had grazed all day out on the prairies, brought them close,

and hobbled them in camp. This all might be midsummer's fun, but this camp had teeth, and it could defend itself in an instant. Skye saw the lesson in it and headed out to the fields to collect his brown mare. He caught it, brought it to his camp, and hobbled and picketed it close by.

He marveled. The Royal Navy had taught discipline; these children of the wilderness had that, and initiative as well. They prepared themselves for trouble without being asked. No man in command, not Jedediah Smith or Jackson or Sublette, or General Ashley, said so much as a word to any of them, and yet this festival camp would deal ruthlessly with any emergency.

The knowledge pleased Skye, almost as much as his keen observation of the underlying military genius in this ragtag army of trappers. He absorbed all he could of this odd gentry as he wended his solitary way through all their doings. With the advancing darkness, the trappers gathered into more intimate groups around low fires, mostly glowing coals that would silhouette no man and yet ward off the night chill. But there were gaps in the ranks. Men had vanished. He watched some of them take their leave, usually carrying their bedrolls and something else—a trinket or two, especially the round hand mirrors, or a hank of bright ribbon.

Skye felt the hot flood of his own needs, so recently awakened after the long drought in the Royal Navy. One by one the trappers slid into the night, heading for the Shoshone lodges. He chose not to try, and vaguely resented having to compete for Perrault's women, or any other women. This first night he would make friends and sample the spirits. He found a group of trappers sitting in a circle, most of them crosslegged or else simply squatting, a position they found comfortable, though it looked like torture to Skye. They were passing a jug around, and Skye knew he would have his chance for a swallow.

It was time to find out what these wild Yanks were like, and to sample some whiskey. He had rarely touched a drop of it in his cloistered life, but they wouldn't know that.

Chapter 23

Skye dreaded to open his eyes, but he knew he would have to sooner or later. His eyelids were all that protected him from the sunlight, which would lance into his throbbing head the instant he opened them and make matters worse.

Maybe if he lay quietly in his new blankets and refused to open his eyes for the entire day, the throbbing would depart from his head and the nausea from his tormented belly. He hazarded a small glimpse of the day and instantly shut his eyes again. It was as if he had been struck by lightning. He didn't want this day. He wanted to reel back time to the previous evening, before his first sip of that vile juice that swarmed down his gullet like a hundred hornets. He was feeling fine then. He doubted he would ever feel fine again. His new friends had ruined him.

He would have to get up and answer the call of nature. He couldn't escape that. Fiercely, he cast aside his new blankets and sat up, pushing down the gorge rising in his throat. Not far away, his fine friend Jim Beckwourth sat, grinning at him. Skye had made lots of friends last evening, but he couldn't remember the names of most of them. Fine old friends, the kind he had always wanted. They had passed him the jug and sat silently while he guzzled. He learned later it had been concocted just hours before from pure grain spirits, river water, a few plugs of tobacco, and some pepper for spice. Hooee!

He ignored Beckwourth and several other mountaineers who were gazing at him blankly, and crawled on all fours to some river brush, tottering like a cat with an arched back. He felt parched, and with every step he struggled to keep his belly from heaving. Last night he had taken sick, teetered from the dying campfire, and spewed out everything in his gut in one volcanic eruption. He was little better this morning. The sun crashed down on him, blinded him, and fried his brains.

He completed his ablutions, such as they were, and weaved back to his blankets, intending to collapse into them the rest of this July day. But his fine new pals would have none of that.

"Skye, if you don't get up, this child'll know you've gone beaver and we'll bury you," said Arthur Black.

"By God, Skye, if we bury you, we'll bury the biggest nose in Creation," said Beckwourth. "You have an Alps of a nose, a Stony Mountain nose. If all your appendages are the size of your nose, you're doomed to a life of pain and joy."

"It's Mister Skye, mate."

"Naw," said old Gabe Bridger, another of his fine new chums. "Man calls himself mister and the first thing ye know, ee's a booshway. What be 'ee front name?"

"Barnaby."

"No wonder 'ee got likkered up. This child never met a Barnaby thet didn't like to wet his dry with a snort or two. I known three Barnabys in my day, and you're jist like the rest."

"I thought it was Boston, Boston Skye," said Ferguson. "If it ain't, it should be."

"I knew a Boston once, but he gone under over on the Sweetwater," said Tom Virgin. "Hit's an unlucky name. It means manure in the Pawnee tongue."

They were at him again. They were at him all last night. There had been five or six passing the jug at various times, and it hadn't taken long to discover he had sat down with the wrong crowd, the elite veterans of the wilderness, and they were going to let him know it. At first they'd simply eyed him, but then they kept pushing that jug in his direction and urging him to take a good lick. He took lots of good licks.

"He's not going to make it. Let 'im be," said Virgin. "We'll put 'im in the river and float him down to the Salt Lake. That water's so briny it presarves carcasses. Skye, you get to be presarved forever in the mountains."

"No saltier than the sea, I guess," said Skye, and the men around him whickered.

"He'll be petrified salt. I seen an ol' coon turned into stone in six hour," said Bridger. "Over in the Yellerstone. He fell into one of them boiling pots, and when we got 'im out, he was solid rock from all that mineral. You think old booshway Skye'd look good as a statue?"

"Say, Boston Skye, 'ee know what day this is? The fourth day of July. You know what that means."

Skye shook his head. He hadn't the faintest idea.

"That means we catch a Brit, put 'im on a spit, and roast him to celebrate," said Beckwourth.

"Hey, that's some! We got us a live Englishman for supper," said Black. "This here's Independence Day."

Skye was getting the idea. "It's my Independence Day, too," he said quietly. "I'll join you, mates. I'm going to be an American like you. It's a country where a man can be a mister if he wants—and I want to. In England, the only misters are gentry and lords. A few months ago I made my own revolution."

"Ain't that some," said Virgin quietly. The mood changed swiftly.

Skye sat hunched and miserable, trying to ignore these fine friends and boon companions, but then Beckwourth brought him a mug of coffee, and he sipped the brew tentatively. He had rarely tasted it but he liked its aromatic, harsh flavor. They let him alone while he sipped. The coffee soon lifted his body out of its agony, and he opened his eyes again. His companions of the previous evening had mostly scattered but a few lolled about, repairing gear or whittling. Skye found an ancient pot over some coals and poured some more of the brew, feeling better as he stirred about.

Were these mountaineers like most Americans? Were Yanks mostly strange, hairy, slouchy creatures dressed in animal skins, with manners ruder than anything he'd seen among the limeys in the navy? Some, maybe, but not all. Smith wasn't like that. Tom Fitzpatrick had an Irish melody in his voice and good manners. Joe Lapointe talked a thickly accented English. Silas Gobel and Daniel Ferguson hadn't said much, unlike that blowhard Beckwourth, or that tale-teller Bridger.

Skye felt itchy and thin-skinned, and ready to show them a thing or two about a limey's bag of tricks. But they had drifted off, having wearied of their morning sport. They weren't a bad bunch but they had an edge, and they'd shown him he was a pork-eater. Skye pulled on his Creole moccasins and hunted around for a stewpot. Nothing much was cooking and he didn't feel like eating anyway so he abandoned the notion of breakfast.

The July heat boiled up and the sun was blistering the tawny earth on this July day. He needed to be alone. He jammed his topper down on his greasy locks and stalked to the riverbank, finding a trail along it that took him west onto lonely prairies where tall grasses danced in the bright winds. The more he walked, the more his legs behaved and the more energy he recovered. He slipped into a steady, long stride, the kind of stride that was the envy of any seaman confined to a teak deck. He stretched into a mile-eating gait, feeling the joyous and fertile earth under his soles. He felt a rush of dominion—he was a lord here, with no honorable sirs to stop him from walking any direction he chose to walk. Bit by bit, his body threw off the poisons of the previous night, and he felt himself again.

Then he beheld the girl. She sat on a boulder beside the river, watching him cautiously. He paused, studying this apparition. She didn't smile, nor did she reveal any emotion, neither fear nor friendship. She wore a plain buckskin dress over her slim figure. He thought she probably was no more than sixteen, if that, but how could one know? He smiled but she didn't. Perhaps he frightened her. He realized, as he stared, that she was uncommonly beautiful, with straight jet hair that shone in the white light, and delicate cheekbones and a fine, thin nose. She squinted at him, not quite suspiciously, but certainly with wariness. She wasn't Shoshone. He swiftly inventoried her dress and moccasins and face and knew she had been born to some other tribe, Crow perhaps.

Something about her stirred him. Maybe she was an Indian princess, a daughter of a chieftain, a haughty patrician among her people. She had the look, all-knowing, wise-eyed, strong-willed, swift to act and judge. He didn't know what to do, so he just stood there stupidly.

She looked so tender and young and virginal that he ached to get to know her. He wished he could just talk to this hauntingly lovely Indian girl.

He remembered a hand sign that Perrault had taught him. He would tell her that he was a friend. He lifted his right hand and held it, palm out, in front of his neck, his index and second finger pointing upward as high as his chin.

"Goddamn," she said in a dusky voice.

Skye gawked.

"You lost your tongue?"

"Ah, I was just passing by—"

"You are a Goddamn from Grandfather's Land," she said. "Across the waters. I have heard of you. You have the biggest nose ever seen. Now I have seen it. It is *big*."

"You what?"

"Sit down, old coon."

Gingerly, Skye lowered himself to the boulder and sat beside her. "You know my tongue," he said.

"The Goddamns stayed with us last winter."

"The who?"

"You hairy ones come, stay with Absaroka. We don't know your tribe until you tell us. Always, you call each other Goddamn, all the time, Goddamn, Goddamn, and then we know your tribe."

"Oh," said Skye, pondering that. "And they taught you English?"

"Taught me Goddamn. I know a little. American Goddamns, Canada Goddamns, same tongue."

"Ah, what is Absaroka?"

"Blackbird. Crow, in your words. Raven. I see you at trading store, and then some more times. I am looking for you to see the big nose."

"I don't know your name."

She squinted at him and said something he couldn't decipher. "What you call you?" she asked.

"Ah, Barnaby Skye. Mister Skye."

"Sonofabitch."

"Ah, can you translate your name? Into, ah, Goddamn?"

"Many Quill Woman."

The name seemed odd to Skye. How could he address this lissome girl as if she were a porcupine? "I think you're a princess," he said.

"What's that?"

"Daughter of a king or a prince."

"What's that?"

"Daughter of a chief."

"Ah! My mother's brother is Arapooish, chief of Kicked-in-the-Bellies."

" 'Kicked-in-the-Bellies'?"

"My people."

"But you said you were Absaroka."

"Sonofabitch!" she snapped. She looked offended.

"I will give you a name," he said.

"You give me name?" She smiled. "Hokay, damn, Mister Skye."

"In my country there's a little girl who's the daughter

of the chief, a princess. Her name is Victoria. I will call you Victoria."

She smiled wryly.

"How old are you, Victoria?"

She frowned, and then pointed to her fingers. "This many winters," she said, ticking off the count. It came to fifteen.

"Fifteen," he said. "I'll teach you the numbers."

"Hell, no. That's for winter. Now I sit here and make medicine. You like me?"

"Yes I do, Victoria."

"Good, Skye, pretty damn soon we have a lodge," she said. "I want a big-nose. You give ponies to my father, and we make more Kicked-in-the-Bellies, hokay?"

Chapter 24

Many Quill Woman liked the man sitting next to her beside the river, and knew exactly why. He had a certain gravity. Unlike the other pale-fleshed men, he didn't laugh much or slouch or talk too much. This one said little, but his eyes drank in everything around him. Some tragedy from his past clung to him; she knew he had endured something terrible and had emerged from it a man with strength and courage.

It frustrated her that she could say so little to him. When the American trappers had come to her village on the Elk River, which the white men called the Yellowstone, and spent the previous winter, she had learned their tongue—at least as much as she could. She didn't despise them the way the other village girls did, but tried to find out what she could. They were a strange and mysterious tribe, the Goddamns, and she doubted she would ever really fathom their ways. They came without women, and she wondered what the female Goddamns were like and why they were hidden away somewhere.

Some of them, like Ed Rose and Jim Beckwourth, were fine warriors and much esteemed by the Absaroka because they fought side by side with them in several skirmishes with the Siksika. But they told strange tales no one believed, and they wanted all the women in the village. The grandmothers enjoyed the pale men, and spent hours telling bawdy stories to them, and hearing bawdy stories from them, which made them all laugh and made the winter pass quickly. The trappers didn't conquer very many Absaroka women, though. Certainly not herself, though they tried.

The Absaroka had come to the rendezvous of the Goddamns to buy guns. Chief Arapooish had said they should, and had come himself with just a few lodges. They all bore many pelts to trade for the wondrous weapon that would help the outnumbered Absaroka keep their homeland. They lived in the most beautiful land there ever was or could be, a land of snow-tipped mountains, rushing rivers, sweet water, great plains filled with grandfather buffalo to feed and clothe and shelter them. But the Absaroka faced the cruel Siksika in the north, who were as plentiful as leaves on trees and who had gotten guns from the North West Company traders; and on the east the powerful Lakota, many times more than the Absaroka in number, threatened to overwhelm them and rob them of their rightful home in the center of the world.

So the wise Arapooish had led the People to ally themselves with the Shoshones and the pale men who had guns, and to welcome any of the trappers into their villages. And now, he and several Absaroka lodges had come over the mountains to this place where there would be traders with guns, and they had brought many pony-loads of beaver pelts, buffalo robes, deer and elk skins, ermine and otter. They had brought ponies to trade, too, because the Goddamns never seemed to have enough, and paid much for them—a pony for a gun. The Absaroka would go back to the Elk River with many guns and powder and balls, and iron arrow and lance points, and keen-edged hatchets, and flints and strikers, and awls and cloth and thread, and the Absaroka would be stronger and better fed and dressed because of these wonders.

She had seen this young man the day he arrived with the Shoshones, and something in him caught her attention. She had known from that moment that she and he would someday share a lodge; she had the inner vision that told her so. No white man had this inner vision, which is why they were inferior to the People. This man, Mister Skye, didn't see with knowing inner sight, but she would teach him how to look for the vision and see beyond what could be seen with the eyes.

She was glad he had found her there, far from the rendezvous.

"I teach you words, you teach me words," she said. If she was going to know this Goddamn better, she needed to be able to talk with him.

He nodded, but then he said, "Teach me the finger signs. I want to learn to talk with my hands."

That sounded like a good project to her, so she thought up signs to show him. She smiled, her face aglow.

She brought two fingers of her right hand to the right side of her mouth. Her fingers pointed left. Then she moved her hand leftward across her mouth. "Lies," she said.

"Lies?"

"Lies, two tongues."

He nodded and tried it. She laughed.

She clasped her hands in front of her with her left hand facing down and her right in the palm of her left. "Peace."

"That's good," he said. "Peace."

She held up all five fingers of one hand in front of her chest. "People," she said.

"Oh, that's easy," he replied. "People."

She eyed him mischievously, and crossed her wrists in front of her heart, her right hand nearer her body. She closed her hands, with their backs upward. Then she pressed her right forearm against herself and her left wrist against the right. "Love," she said solemnly, her eyes dancing.

He had trouble with that one, and she finally guided his hands until he could do it. "I'm not much good at love," he said.

She put the tips of her right fingers over her lips and inclined her head forward. "Be quiet," she said. "Now, Goddamn, this for you."

She closed her right hand and brought it to her forehead, thumb up, and then rotated her hand in a small horizontal circle, turning it up to the sun and then left. "Crazy," she said, her eyes alive with mirth again.

He imitated her. "I suppose I am," he said.

She pointed one finger of her right hand at him. "You," she said.

"That's easy." He pointed a finger at her. "You."

She touched the center of her chest with her extended thumb. "Me," she said.

"That's easy, too. Is there a sign for hunger?"

She held the little finger of her right hand alongside her stomach, and then moved the finger left and right. "Much hunger," she said solemnly.

"Show me yes and no."

She lifted her right hand in front of her to shoulder height, its fingers pointing up, her thumb on her second finger. Then she moved her hand down and left, closing her index finger over her thumb. "Yes," she said, and waited for him to do it, too. Then she extended her right hand in front of her, palm upward, and swung her hand to the right while turning it, putting her thumb up. "No," she said.

He wrestled with that a few times. "How do I say thank you, Victoria?"

She extended both of her hands outward, the backs up, and swept them outward and downward toward him. "Thank you," she said.

He did that. "I like you, Victoria. I hope you will give me many more lessons."

"Skye, you old coon, I show you how the stick floats."

He stared blankly and she laughed. Pretty soon he would have the signs, and pretty soon she would have Skye.

They strolled back to the encampment through a brassy afternoon, with the heat thick in her nostrils. She tried to teach him Absaroka words. There were so many, and she wanted him to master every one so they could talk and she could plumb his secrets.

She spotted an eagle soaring above and gave him the word, *mai shu'*. She named the wild rose, *mit ska'pa*.

She named the squirrels and the ravens and the hawks. She named their clothing, and then she named their body parts, eyes, ears, nose, chest, fingers, toes. She named the earth and sky and sun and stars.

All these he repeated, but she knew he was being dutiful rather than trying to learn them. He really wasn't interested in the Absaroka words, unlike the finger signs, which he made an effort to master. The signs he could use; her tongue he could not. She sighed. Maybe her inner vision had been flawed or she had not fathomed what she had seen. Maybe he would drift away with the rest of the Goddamns when this was over.

"You don't care about Absaroka words."

He didn't deny it, but gazed at her directly in a manner very impolite. "I need the sign language," he said. "You are a good teacher. The signs will help me when I go east."

"East?"

"Yes. I will not be here long."

She absorbed that, her confidence suddenly frayed. "Where are you going?"

He tried to frame a reply and couldn't, and finally shrugged. "I don't know how to tell you. But I have a long way to go."

She squinted. "And never come back to here?"

"No. I won't be back."

"You don't like it here? You don't like Absaroka? You don't like me?"

"I like you all. But this is not what I will do with my life."

"Sonofabitch, what you gonna do?"

He seemed helpless to explain. "Go to the big villages of the Americans."

"What there?"

"Go to college if I can. Someway, somehow."

"What's that?"

"I can't explain it." But then he tried. "Did your mother teach you how to sew a dress or tan a hide? Did she teach you how to cook? A college is where I will go to learn."

"You don't need college. I teach you everything. I teach you many words and signs."

"Yes, and thank you, Victoria."

He smiled. He hadn't smiled all the way back to the encampment and his mind was drifting elsewhere, to some shores of memory where she could never walk. She wondered about him, about the sadness written on his big, creased face, and radiating from his eyes. This Skye was a sad man.

"How come you ain't happy?" she asked, a little cross.

"I am happy. I have not been so happy since I was younger than you."

"What take your happiness away?"

"I was in a boat that sailed the water, and I could not escape."

"I would be unhappy, too," she said. "We live in a good land, the center of the world. There is no better place. Chief Arapooish has said it. To the north it is too cold, and to the south too hot and dry, and to the east too wet and flat and unpleasing to the eye. But here are mountains and forests and creeks to please the eye, and everything is just right for the Absaroka people. We love our land, which is just beyond the mountains on the Elk River, and we will never let others take it from us. We will die before we will surrender it."

"I understand. I would die rather than surrender my freedom. That is because it means more to me than life."

"Ah, Mister Skye, you are a man of much medicine," she said.

"Medicine?"

"Power. You could be a holy man. You maybe have the medicine of the hawks."

Skye laughed. She stared, amazed. He had been distant all the while they strolled back, but now his gaze met hers, and fires lit between them.

Chapter 25

Skye hunted for General Ashley. The time had come to make arrangements to go to St. Louis. He intended to work his way east in whatever capacity Ashley might use him. He'd heard that this rendezvous would wind up shortly, and Ashley was eager to get back. He had a fortune in beaver pelts that he would haul to St. Louis on the packhorses that had brought out the year's provisions.

He found the general at his tent, near his trading store, sitting on a stump and bent over a ledger. The man radiated a certain august presence that impressed Skye. The man's demeanor had helped him both as a politician and as an officer in the militia. He had a noble profile, and used it to advantage, often facing sideways from whoever he was addressing.

"A word if I may, sir," Skye said, his topper in hand.

"Yes, yes, let me add up this column," the general said, a bit testily.

Skye waited until the man finished and stared up at his visitor, his gaze assessive and neutral.

"I'm looking for a position—service to you on your trip east," Skye began.

"Who are you?"

"Barnaby Skye, sir."

"Oh, the deserter Diah Smith told me about."

"Pressed seaman, sir."

"It doesn't matter what your story is. The fact is, you deserted your post, failed your superior officers, your nation, and your shipmates."

"I served Great Britain for seven years, sir."

"Not voluntarily, so it's no sign of virtue in you."

"I fought for the Crown in the Kaffir wars and once in Burma, and was blooded in Africa."

"What you say doesn't matter. You deserted your post."

"General, how much does a man owe his government?"

"Whatever it asks."

"Seven years, sir?"

"More if required."

"If your government bound you to service for seven years, with no recourse, would you serve gladly—your life disrupted?"

"That's hypothetical. Your desertion is real."

"My question, sir—"

Ashley paused, softening slightly. "I would not serve gladly and I would seek avenues of redress. But desertion? Never."

"What if there's no redress?"

"There's always redress."

"Do you know that for a fact—about the Royal Navy?"

"Britain's a great nation—"

"That's not my question, general."

"No, I don't, but I can't imagine there's any truth in your cock-and-bull story."

Skye saw the way it was heading and abandoned that tack. "I'm looking for passage east. I'll work my way there in your service. I have a horse, and that would help you."

Ashley gazed sourly at Skye. "I can always use men. I have twenty-five, and three times that many packhorses, and there's always the threat of Indians or stampedes or trouble. I never have enough horses and men. But Skye, I expect honorable conduct from men in my service. If trouble comes, will you desert?"

"I fought the bloody Kaffirs side by side with the rest, sir."

Ashley stared coldly at him. "I'll think about it, Skye. I'll be leaving within the week."

"It's Mister Skye, sir."

"*Mister* Skye, is it?"

"In England, it's a courtesy not given ordinary men. This is a new world. As long as we're meeting as equals and freemen, you may call me mister, and I'll call you the same, or by your title."

Ashley smiled slightly. "And what would you do in St. Louis? Patronize the grog shops?"

"I'll work my way east, sir. I wish to go to Boston."

"Ah, and become a merchant seaman. New Orleans would be easier."

"No, sir, go to college."

"College? College?" Ashley was taken aback.

"You have a good one near Boston, and I'll find a way to get in and start my life again. Before the press-gang snatched me, I was headed for Cambridge, Jesus College, like my father before me, and his father before him. He's a London merchant, sir."

Ashley snickered nasally, apparently too astonished to

offer a rejoinder. Skye waited for an answer. If he should go with Ashley, it would be a long, brutal trip, not much different from his imprisonment in a royal man o' war. But it would take him east.

"Smith tells me you're a not a mountaineer," Ashley said.

"I made my way from Fort Vancouver, sir. I improved my lot the entire time, starting with little more than the clothes on my back, a flint and striker, and a few small items."

"Every bit of it Royal Navy property."

"Mostly mine. The rest back pay for seven years, sir."

"Theft."

"I never received a pence in the navy, sir."

"I don't believe you. You're a thief as well as a deserter."

"I was fined my entire pay and more, sir."

"For what?"

"Trying to secure my freedom."

"Diah says he's advanced you credit. I suppose you're going to run out on him."

"No, sir. Pay him out of service—to you, or to him, or however I can."

Ashley laughed, baring yellow teeth. "You're a rogue, Skye. You're planning to stick Smith with the debt."

"It's Mister Skye, sir. And unless you know a man's lying, you ought not to accuse. And unless you know a man's planning to steal from his benefactor, you shouldn't make that accusation either."

Ashley reddened. "I'm done with you, Skye. If I decide to take you—and I may be forced to because I'm shorthanded—believe me, you'll be watched day and night."

"It's Mister Skye, sir. I'll report to you daily until you decide."

Skye left Ashley's tent in a bilious mood. He hadn't expected that sort of treatment. He had heard the man was affable, a natural politician with an eye for a profit and plenty of daring when it came to taking a risk.

He stormed over to the headquarters lodge of Smith, Jackson, and Sublette, and barged in, finding Smith and Sublette.

"How much do I owe, and what can I do to pay it?" he barked.

"Well, it's Mister Skye."

Jedediah Smith retreated into silence a moment, and then showed those qualities that made him a leader of men. "Bill and I were just mapping out our brigades. We'll have three this year. How may I help you, Mister Skye?"

Skye felt the heat slide out of him and rotated his topper in his hands a moment while he collected himself. "I've come from an interview with General Ashley, sir. He's not inclined to employ me for—reasons of character. Very well. I have my own standards. You've fed me for several days and advanced me seventeen dollars of goods. What is the value of my horse, sir? Would that pay my debt?"

Smith eyed Skye contemplatively. "A good horse's worth a hundred to a hundred fifty in the mountains. They're so scarce it's a bargain. But I'm not inclined to put you on foot."

"I'm starting east in the morning and I'm going with a clear slate. I'll trade the horse for my debt and a good kit, including a rifle."

"You'll need your horse." He eyed Skye mildly. "I'll talk to Ashley. In the mountains these things have to be dealt with. Half his pack crew he recruited out of the grog shops of St. Louis. I don't know what's in his craw."

"Thank you, sir. I'd rather not travel with him."

Smith grinned. "Mister Skye, you've all the makings of a good free trapper, including the temperament."

"All I want, sir, is to resume my life. And I'll find the way, and do it honorably, no matter how long it takes. If that means paying you back when I get to where I'm going and find a means to survive, then I'll do it. But one way or another, sir, you'll be paid."

"You're not enjoying it here."

Skye shrugged. "There's nothing for me here. But yes, I'm enjoying it. I've never seen such sights. I have ambition, Mr. Smith, and this isn't the place for it. A university might be."

"I'll talk to Ashley. He's not being reasonable. He's leaving in a few days, mostly hanging around for any last pelts. Some trappers are still drifting in."

"He'll find me a faithful and hard-working man, sir."

"Mister Skye, you're a lot more than that, I'd wager. You think about staying in the mountains with my company. We need men. One can be a free trapper, or a camp tender, or a clerk. Camp tenders and clerks are salaried; free trappers sell us what they catch. They're independent businessmen. Davey Jackson's leading a brigade into the Snake country. Bill here's going over the Stony Mountains to the Crow and Blackfoot country, the Three Forks area—dangerous but untrapped. Virgin beaver country, but full of Bug's Boys.

"I'm fitting out a party to find a way to Mexican California. There's a river, the Buenaventura. No one's found it, but we know it's out there, other side of the Salt Lake. I mean to find it and take it west to the California mountains. The Sierra's full of beaver. I'm a man with big ideas, Mister Skye. If Ashley won't have you, we'd be more than glad to take you on."

It was opportunity—if Skye wanted to abandon a dream.

Chapter 26

The rendezvous was drawing to a close, but Skye hadn't an inkling about his fate. General Ashley put him off each day. If worse came to worse, he intended simply to start east on his own, hazarding whatever fate had in store for a solitary traveler walking across the continent. By all accounts, he could reach St. Louis, on the western edge of the United States, before cold weather set in. After that he could work his way east.

He found himself an outsider at the rendezvous. He didn't play euchre or Spanish monte because he had nothing to wager. His one encounter with the fiery trade whiskey made him chary of sipping any more of it. Sometimes he sat quietly among the trappers, listening to that awesome braggart Beckwourth spin his tales in a patois Skye could barely fathom, or Bridger tell comic yarns that usually ended up in raucous laughter.

But Skye didn't fit in. He had an innate reserve, bred into him from childhood, unlike these wild, exuberant, cocky Yanks. His was the lexicon of the sea, and theirs the lexicon of frontiersmen cut loose from all their moorings. He came to enjoy the hairy breed who combed the mountains, but he could never imitate them. He admired their vast confidence, their fierce loyalties—but he didn't admire their inflammatory ways, with emotions seething uncontrolled just below the surface. Twice during the rendevous he had seen knife fights, men threatening each other with death.

He made friends with them all, but knew he would be leaving soon for the states and would never see them again. As the rendezvous wore on, they welcomed him to their campfires, and he put names to a hundred faces, and found them a varied lot from all over the continent, bonded only by a ferocity and courage he had rarely seen in others.

He didn't participate in the endless contests because he couldn't begin to match the skills of these mountaineers. How could he compete against men who could throw a heavy knife squarely into a knot on a distant tree trunk, or fire their heavy rifles so accurately they could split the ball on the cutting edge of a distant ax set up as a target? How could he toss a tomahawk so well that it would bury itself in a stump fifty feet away? He marveled at these things, watched endlessly, learned a lot— and quietly practiced with his knife and bow and arrows.

But then one afternoon a pair of tomahawk throwers, Jeandrois Rariet and Tom Virgin, politely invited him to try. Skye decided to grasp the nettle, and they handed him a 'hawk. He'd been watching, and tossed the hawk in a fine true arc—but it landed wrong and didn't bite the tree trunk.

"You gents have great skills," he said.

"You have to, out here," Virgin said. "Try 'er again, Mister Skye."

Skye did, as haplessly as the first time.

After that, he found himself participating gamely in all

the sports. He was at his worst with the mountain rifles. The heavy weapons bucked in his grasp, ruining his aim, and he never hit a target. These men awed him, firing at the edge of playing cards, putting five shots into a fist-sized circle as far away as the eye could see, casually tossing knives or tomahawks with equal accuracy. He tried his hand, bumbled them all, took the joshing amiably, and ignored the taunts. They even bested him in the only area where he had acquired some skill—with his bow and arrows. Not a few mountaineers were splendid archers and could even compete with the Crows and Shoshones.

"I've never seen marksmen like you," Skye said to Tom Virgin.

"It's this way, old coon. Once that supply outfit pulls outa here, we got all the powder and lead we're gonna see until next year, savin' we go to some Hudson's Bay post and let 'em plunder us. So's there's none to spare. Some coons, they prefer flintlocks because there's always flint around, while other coons like caplocks because they fire when she rains. But them as has caplocks, they'd better have enough caps to last a year, or here's damp powder and no way to dry it. What it comes to is, we can't waste a shot. Naught a one."

"Why do you stay in the mountains and endure the hardship?"

Virgin spat. "'Cause it's fat times."

"You mean you make money?"

"Naw, I mean it don't get any better. You know what it's like to ride into some mountain park no white man's ever laid eyes on? What woodsmoke smells like early in a November mornin' when you're up and stretching and thinkin' breakfast? What it's like to cut into a juicy buffler hump and eat the best meat ever tasted by mortal man?

What she's like to be free of everyone, everything? What it's like to have to wrestle the world every day to stay alive? To have some old coons you can count on no matter what? Naw, you wouldn't know, but you oughter think on it. A mountaineer is a king in his own kingdom."

"I haven't even seen a buffalo, but I'd sure like to sample that humpmeat."

"Buffler's shot out around here. Never was much. But over yonder, other side of the Stonies, them buffler run in bunches so thick they turn the prairie black. You'll never see the like—herds so big you can't count. Hundred thousand maybe, maybe ten times that. No man can say. Meat on the hoof. Boudins—"

"Boudins?"

"Buffler gut stuffed like sausage and cooked up real good, or just eaten up. You run dry, some time, out on the prairies, you shoot a buffler and drink what's in the boudins, and it'll get ye out alive."

Skye nodded. Another survival item to file away, something to help him cross the prairies to civilization. "Thanks for the tip, Tom. Maybe it'll help when I go east."

Virgin scratched his enormous beard and squinted. "You plumb center sartin you're going east, eh?"

"Yes."

"You've the makin's of a mountaineer, but I guess we'll never know." He smiled. "Each to his own. Me, I'd croak if I had ta live back east again. I can't even stand being around St. Louis. Get to swilling grog and makin' trouble and pretty soon, the constable's got me. Out here, you don't have to make trouble because it's always makin' itself. I'm a free trapper, and that's the only life there is."

Skye smiled. There was indeed something seductive about the mountains, and at times they tempted him. But he could hardly imagine fashioning a life out of this sort of existence. What would he achieve? If he didn't die an awful death under a scalping knife, what would he have to show for a lifetime in the mountains? He had already lost seven years.

He headed, as he usually did, to General Ashley's tent but didn't find him there. He hunted for the man and found him out among the horses, looking dour. He and his packers were studying each of the general's horses, and not liking their condition.

"Not enough rest," said Ashley's top man.

"I hoped to buy some, but all I got was half a dozen miserable beasts from the Crows. They'll have to do," Ashley said.

Skye intervened. "Have you come to a decision, sir?"

The general turned to Skye, contemplatively. "We're leaving in two days. If you want to come along, I'll not say nay. We could use your horse. I'll trade the horse for your mess."

"I owe Smith, Jackson, and Sublette about seventeen dollars, sir. Perhaps you'd employ me for that and credit their account. I'll sell the horse for the going price."

"No, I won't do that. It's enough that I'm taking you safely east."

"Very well, sir. I'll probably strike out on my own soon."

"It's certain death."

"I've been talking to gentlemen here, sir. Tom Fitzpatrick has made the journey safely more than once. Once only a short time ago."

"Tom's a veteran of the mountains, Skye."

"It's Mister Skye, sir."

Ashley looked impatient. "How about selling me your horse? I'll pay fifty for it."

"The word is that a horse is worth a hundred and fifty here in the mountains, sir."

"We don't seem to come to any agreement, Skye. You won't ever again have the opportunity I'm offering."

"I've been talking to these men, sir. It seems that I can work my way south to Mexican Santa Fe and hire on with any of the traders on the trail between there and St. Louis, and still go east this year. If you want to hire me at the wage you pay your other men, I'll sign on. If you wish to buy my horse for the going price here, we can talk about terms." He turned to leave.

"I'll think about it," Ashley said, still dour.

Skye left Ashley, convinced the general of the Missouri militia wasn't going to give him a fair shake. He really didn't want to head south to Mexico, either. He might just as easily end up in a Mexican dungeon as in a trader's caravan, or so he had heard from these mountaineers. No, the best course would be to go east alone.

He found Broken Hand Fitzpatrick at his usual spot near the Ashley tent store, and approached the genial Irishman for some advice.

"Sorry to trouble you, mate, but I'd like to learn a bit about getting across the plains. You seem to manage it regularly, and keep your hair."

"Why, bless me, Mister Skye, ye have a way of complimenting that's music to me ears. I have a little luck and a little skill and a little caution, and it's gotten me through, but with a few scrapes. Like this hand, now . . ." He held up his crippled left hand. "The things you don't expect, that's what do ye in. A rifle burst, that's what did this. Expect the unexpected."

"Could you tell me what to expect—and all the rest?"

"Ye be wantin' to go back by your lonesome, eh?"

"General Ashley doesn't look kindly on me, Mr. Fitz-patrick."

Fitzpatrick laughed. "Any bloke that stiffs the Royal Navy is a friend of the Irish," he said. "Sure, I'll tell ye what I can. The Sioux are friendly, except when they catch a man alone. The Pawnee are tribulation and death."

"I wouldn't know one from another."

"In that case, ye'll need more than luck, Mister Skye. Ye'll need a cavalry company and a few cannon. Do ye have a weapon?"

"Nez Perce bow and seven arrows left."

"De ye know the sign language?"

"I've a few words a Crow lass taught me."

"Do ye have skill as a hunter?"

"No, but each night on the trail I set a trap and often catch small things. Not good to taste but it fills the belly."

"Agh, you've the makings of a mountaineer, Mister Skye. Do ye know the geography? Would ye know when ye reach Missoura? Do ye know how the rivers run, how the Platte runs into the Missoura near Council Bluffs? And how to find the trail that cuts that corner and gets ye to Westport, and from there to St. Louis? De ye know the tribes thataway, the Omaha, the Kansa . . ."

"You're telling me not to do it."

"Aye, I'm telling ye that, knowin' it won't do a bit o' good because ye'll do what ye have to. I never met a man so determined to get out of the mountains. You got anything against these mountains?"

"Yes, sir. They're barriers to a good life, and so are the vast plains I must cross."

"And, me English friend, what's a good life now?"

"A life of perfect freedom," said Skye without hesitation.

"And ye don't see it here?"

"No, these mountains are a prison, and the wilderness is a cage. No one here admits to the boredom, but I see it. These men have little to do. What do they achieve? Give me a great and proud city to grow in and educate myself and start a business, and the liberty to shape my life, and I'll be content."

"And all ye have to do is cross a continent," Fitzpatrick said.

Chapter 27

The rendezvous died two days later. At dawn, Ashley's men loaded one hundred twenty-three packs of beaver plus some bales of other pelts onto their horses, burdening each of them with two hundred fifty to three hundred pounds of dead weight. Everyone watched: the free trappers, the engagés of Smith, Jackson, and Sublette, the Creoles and Iroquois, the Shoshones and Crows, and Mister Skye.

A terrible silence pervaded the Cache Valley. Skye had expected the departure to be as exuberant as the arrivals, with whoops, gunfire, cheers, and catcalls. Instead, a certain gloom pervaded the great flat along the Weber River, abetted by an overcast sky that made the dawn somber. Another hard year would pass before they saw the next rendezvous, or guzzled trade whiskey, or bought the essentials and a few luxuries that would make wilderness life bearable again. By fall the coffee, tea, flour, sugar, molasses, salt, and beans would run out, and the mountain trappers would subsist once again on whatever nature provided. Friendships were being sundered, too; Ashley's contingent included a number of trappers leaving the mountains.

Skye was not among them. Ashley didn't want him. Skye had never been able to puzzle it out, but there was no point in worrying about it. Ashley had his own way of looking at things. Skye watched the general, mounted on a gaunt but well-bred charger, wave the long caravan into action, and the burdened horses walked down the Weber River, the teamsters beside them. At its confluence with the Bear, they would turn north, and then east, cross the Continental Divide at South Pass, descend the Sweetwater to the North Platte, and then east across a thousand miles of unsettled and dangerous prairie.

Skye could feel the loss and unease around him. As much as these mountaineers loved the wild life, they loved the replenishments from civilization, too, along with the news of the world. This was a moment when the men of the mountains weighed their options. They could catch up and go east if they chose. Or they could stay. It was up to each free trapper.

Skye didn't have that option. He found Smith in a pensive mood as they watched the long pack train, carrying a fortune in pelts, vanish around a river bend.

"If the general gets back safely, he'll be about seventy thousand dollars richer," Smith said. "If he doesn't, then we're in trouble, too. We'll have no resupply next summer. This business is all gamble."

"He has a strong force, well armed," said Skye.

"It's not just the Indians. Those horses might not last. They could be stolen. He doesn't have enough spares. Disease, cold weather, rain and mud—there's more things to go wrong than you can imagine, Skye."

"Ah, sir, I prefer to be addressed—"

"Yes, yes. I know."

"Sir, why was he so hostile?"

"The deserter business. He takes his generalship seriously, even if it's the militia."

"It didn't matter that I was pressed in?"

"Not with him."

"Mr. Smith, I'm told that half of Ashley's crew are thieves and murderers recruited out of the grog shops of St. Louis. He hired them willingly enough. Does he really think I'm worse than that lot?"

"It's in him to feel that way."

"Because he's a general of the militia?"

Smith shrugged. "Apparently so."

"I come from a nation where we're subjects of the Crown. Subjects—human fodder to be employed as the Crown chooses, with few rights and no heed paid to a man's dreams and hopes. I thought your Constitution and Declaration of Independence proposed a different—"

Smith laughed suddenly. "You don't need to make your case with me. I don't share Ashley's views." He surveyed Skye expectantly. "Well, Mister Skye, have you come to a decision?"

"Yes, sir. I'll be heading east on my own in a day or two. I'll get there somehow."

"Without a rifle, without knowing sign language, without hard experience. It's suicide."

"That's what Tom Fitzpatrick said. If I die, I die. I intend to get on with my life. If that means risks, then I'll take risks. I've taken risks from the moment I slid into the Columbia at Fort Vancouver. I'll take more."

"If I can't employ you, then I'd suggest you work your way south to the Mexican settlements. Taos, especially, and go with the next trading company. That's not safe, either: you'll run into Utes, Cheyenne, Comanches, and maybe some Lipan Apache. But it's probably better than going alone down the Platte."

"What'll happen here, now?"

"Most of us'll be moving out in a week or two. Shoshones and Crows'll drift off. Their trading's over."

"But you have trade goods, don't you?"

"Lots of them. We use them all year to barter for pelts or keep the peace or resupply ourselves. But by next summer, we'll be out of everything again."

"What are you going to do next, Mr. Smith?"

Jedediah Smith gazed westward, and Skye sensed the man was seeing virgin land, untracked wastes, surprise water holes, hidden trails. He smiled. "There's a river that runs across that desert somewhere, an arrow pointed at California. Ogden's been looking for it. I tried last year. It's not north of the Salt Lake, so it must be south. That's where I'm going."

"But what about trapping? Not many beaver in the desert."

"The Sierra Nevada, Mister Skye, the mightiest range of all, lies out there—somewhere."

Skye had the sense that Smith was more explorer than businessman, and wondered about it. A fur outfit needed pelts, not adventurers.

Smith returned from whatever uplands of the mind he had been visiting. "Davey Jackson's taking a brigade into the Snake country. He wants to push Hudson's Bay out. Bill Sublette's taking a brigade into the headwaters of the Missouri, Three Forks, Crow, and Blackfoot country.

Much the most dangerous of the brigades, but it's virgin country—never trapped. All he has to do is keep Bug's Boys at bay."

Skye knew the term. Blackfeet. "Tell me about them."

"The Blackfeet are proud, brilliant, numerous, and brutal. They'll torture you slowly—or rather, their squaws will—just to hear you scream. They've plenty of horses, skills at war, and rich country full of game. They're never hungry, never poor. They're well armed with trade fusils—smoothbore flintlocks they got from the old North West Company. But Mister Skye, a man can get rich there. Really rich. That's prime beaver country. That's a land that'll yield a young fortune to the trapper who gets there first. That's our ace. If Davey's outfit finds the British have gotten there ahead of him, and I run into trouble with the Mexicans, Sublette's our hole card. He's taking the toughest, bravest men he can find, men with mountain savvy, and they'll need their wits if they intend to keep their hair."

Smith was grinning at Skye, a question in his face.

"What could a man earn in good beaver country?"

"Enough to take him east and put him through a year, two years, of college. Maybe more. Of course, you'll need some items, especially a mountain rifle that fires plumb center, some caps, powder, lead, a horn, and several other things, including at least half a dozen traps. About a hundred dollars of goods, advanced against your harvest. It's a rich land for a man with the heart and soul to take what's there for him. Set a man up for years, maybe. A few free trappers are getting rich, depositing money in St. Louis."

Skye didn't take the bait. He smiled at Smith—the offer acknowledged with that smile—and drifted away. The morning was still young. He would have a few days to think about it. He wandered across the forlorn flat, over trampled grass and abandoned bowers, their leaves dry and brittle. The place had changed. A certain spirit, a breath of life and excitement, had flown away on the wings of Ashley's pack train.

The mountaineers didn't compete or gamble that morning, but sat about talking quietly, the boast gone from their voices, their thoughts on the fall hunt. There'd be little drinking tonight. Those who had a jug of precious whiskey would save it for some future time, maybe a winter bacchanal, guarding it jealously because it could not be replaced. But he knew most of the free trappers had squandered everything, saved back nothing, and were poorer than when they arrived two or three weeks earlier, even in debt to the company. It wasn't in them to hold back.

He found old Perrault and his women packing up.

"Ah! Skye, damn good rendezvous, *oui?* I got plenty drunk. Eleven times I get drunk, and don' spend a pence."

"It was good."

"You get drunk?"

"Once."

"Ah! You stay, you learn. You staying, eh?"

"No, I'm going east in a day or two."

Perrault made a motion that looked like a scalping knife rotating around his head, and leered. "*Au revoir,* Royal Navy," he said. "Dis ain't the sea, dis is de wilds, and you gonna find out how wild soon."

The women looked prosperous and grinned at him. They were festooned with bold ribbons, combs, bracelets, beads, necklaces, rings, and bright clothing swiftly crafted from tradecloth. They were packing new knives, tin cups, jugs of molasses, jingle bobs, arrow points, and a lot more things they had wrested from the trappers during their rowdy sojourn. The younger sister had smeared vermilion over her cheeks. Her eyes still shone, and Skye smiled back at her, remembering his nights with her, his exploration of all the mysteries of love that she and her sister had provided just for the pleasure of it.

"What'd you get?" Perrault asked. "Everybody get something at rendezvous. Shoshone all got stuff. Lots powder and ball, guns to fight Blackfeet."

"I have a cook pot, ax, knife, and a pair of blankets," Skye said. "And a debt to pay."

"Ah, forget it. Dey don' expect repay."

"I expect to repay. It's how I am."

"Well, we go now. Maybe not see you again. Damn, never see you again. You go get yo'sel' kill."

Skye nodded. "I don't expect to be back," he said.

Chapter 28

The gifts touched Skye. He had not received a gift since he had been pressed into the Royal Navy, and now he could barely cope with the flood of feeling racing through him.

He tried on the moccasins that Many Quill Woman had fashioned for him and found they fit him perfectly. Somehow, she had gotten the measure of his feet. These had been cut and stitched from elkskin as soft as velvet, and felt as if he had worn them for years.

She looked at him expectantly, her gaze sharp as a hawk's, to ascertain his pleasure.

"These are beautiful, Victoria," he said softly, rubbing

the supple leather with his hands. "I don't know how you knew my size."

She smiled. "I measure your feet. Do you like the beads?"

He admired the red-and-black geometric design she had patiently sewn into the leather, using trader's beads she had acquired at the rendezvous.

"Yes. These are beautiful."

"The design is a prayer to the four winds to take you where you will go."

She smiled, her brown eyes liquid with pleasure. He admired her lithe, taut figure, her sharp, angular features, and her hawkish gaze that seemed to penetrate into his soul and read his every thought. She had some way of fathoming everything around her with those remarkable eyes that saw through material things to the spirit that lay at the essence.

"I have more," she said proudly, and handed him another gift even more precious. Ten arrows.

"Victoria—" He couldn't speak. So she had seen his quiver, counted the seven remaining arrows, and knew he needed more. These were handsome arrows, long, with iron trade points bound by sinew over the haft, and three gray feathers anchored also by sinew to the rear. Each arrow was dyed with stripes of color around its shaft.

"The blue—it is for sky. The yellow is for sun. The four black lines—for you. I do not make these. The arrow maker make these. Big medicine. Now you have Absaroka medicine. Eiee!"

He slid fingers along the smooth surface, admiring the way a shoot of wood or reed had been scraped and planed into a straight shaft that would fly true.

"Absaroka make best arrows," she said proudly. "Now you eat, or go kill Siksika."

"Maybe these will save my life," he said.

She turned solemn. "Maybe so."

He felt bad because he had nothing to give her. He had subsisted as a pauper all through the rendezvous, living upon the charity of others. But the need raced through him and he knew what he would do. He plucked up one of his new blankets and handed it to her. It was gray, with black bands at the ends, thick and well carded, of English manufacture and phenomenally warm. These blankets came in pairs, and he would spare one for this lithe young Crow woman who had taken a fancy to him.

"I want you to have this. It is warm and well made," he said.

She took it, fondled it, her eyes alive with joy and delight. She wrapped it around herself, turning it into a robe or a capote even as she drew it tight under her crossed arms.

"See, Mister Skye? You make me happy."

She did look happy. He felt bathed in it. Something in her reached out to him, touching his core. She radiated a quality that seemed mysterious to him, as if she had magical powers.

"It will keep you warm when it is cold," he said.

"You make me warm," she replied, her face alive with delight. "Why do you go away? Is this not the best place, the center of the world?"

She knew his answer; they had rehearsed his reasons several times on their walks, or in their quiet moments beside the Weber River. She wasn't really asking; she was begging him to stay.

"I must go. It is my destiny." He felt uncomfortable. She had seen something in him and wanted him for a mate. She had made that plain. But he couldn't imagine himself tied to this dusky savage the rest of his life. He wanted a fair-skinned, blue-eyed English girl, or if not that, an American girl much like those across the Atlantic. She would be gracious and thoughtful and well schooled. She would be full of merriment and feeling and passion. She would become his wife gladly, and gladly she and he would raise a family. No . . . not this sharp-boned Crow woman, even if she seemed a cathedral in her own right.

He had tried to tell her about schooling, but without much success because the idea of formal education was outside of her ken. He had tried to tell her of his family, his father's business importing Chinese tea, silk, bamboo, rattan, copra, and ginseng while exporting British manufactured goods; of commissioning vessels to carry his cargoes halfway around the world; of a race of island geniuses who were dominating the sciences and arts.

His explanations had largely sailed past Many Quill Woman, and often her face darkened and softened when he spoke of it.

"We know nothing of these things," she had replied quietly once, and he sensed she was feeling defeat.

Now that surrender was in her face again.

"I will not be coming back," he said, not wanting it to sound so harsh, but not wanting her to have false hopes either. "But wherever I am, I will remember you, Victoria—do you like that name? Perhaps I shouldn't call you that."

"A name is a gift, Mister Skye. I like the gift. If I am

Victoria to you, then it pleases me." She paused, squinting at him sternly. "You have eyes for your own kind. I
see this. I have never seen a white woman. They must be
big and strong, not small like me. I know about this. I
have eyes for a good Absaroka man sometimes. A warrior with many honors. That would be good. Then I would
be proud. My man would give to the People. Many scalps,
many buffalo, many horses. He would feed the old and
hungry. I have eyes for a man like that. But I have eyes
for you, more than that."

"I would like to visit your village someday."

"Ah! The Kicked-in-the-Bellies. We have a strong village, and we have many Siksika scalps on our lances. You
see only a few of us here. Many did not come. Just the
ones with skins to trade for powder and guns and blankets and pots. We have many, and many children too. You
will meet them."

"I hope I do—someday."

"Soon, Mister Skye. I have the inner eye. My spirit
helper the magpie gives me the eye when I cry to see. I
saw you with my inner eye. You go away and come back.
The magpies are all around you, bringing you back. You
have bear medicine, and someday you will wear the claws
of the great bear—you call him grizzly—as your medicine. You will see. This I saw with my inner eye, so it
will be."

Skye didn't protest. Let the savage girl have her fancies. He had told her plainly what his future would be and
what he expected from his life. He only hoped she would
find some good Crow warrior and find happiness. But
he doubted it. He didn't know much about these American Indians but he sensed that Many Quill Woman was
not a typical young woman on the brink of marriage.

Something set her apart. Her destiny would take her in some strange direction.

"When are you leaving?" he asked.

"Arapooish say in the morning if the medicine seers tell him this is the right time to go back to Absaroka."

"I will see you off. And I will remember you because of the arrows and moccasins. How did you know my size?"

"You left a print in the dust. I make good moccasins. My father's wife makes good moccasins and I learn from her. You will take those moccasins into any Absaroka village and they will tell you what lodge they came from."

"And who made the arrows?"

"My father's brother Sees the Wind is an arrow maker. A holy man. He goes to the river to look for the right stalks. He catches the hawk for feathers. He goes to the distant cliffs for dyes. He blesses each arrow to make it strong and true. But I must tell you something. Do not shoot at the bear; the bear is your friend and helper. Send your arrows into elk and deer and antelope. Pray to each four-legged that gave up life so you could eat. Thank each one—this is what you must do when you kill. You will not have much chance to kill a buffalo, except maybe an old bull waiting for the wolves. But that is poor meat."

"I will remember."

She smiled suddenly, threw her new blanket over them both, and laughed. He started to pull it off, but she stayed him. "No, no, this is how Absaroka boy and girl whisper to each other."

Skye stood, astonished, half-embarrassed, under the small canopy of the blanket, while Victoria pressed close to him, their small world hidden from others, and yet all the more visible for being in plain sight of the whole encampment.

"There, Skye, this is how we do it."

She hugged him. He crushed her close, absorbing her sweetness and tartness all at once, something heady and private, as fragrant as roses in their privacy. She laughed and then ran a gentle hand through his matted beard. "Hairy man," she said. "We ain't got hair. You got more hair than a woman. Are all white men so hairy?"

Skye didn't quite know how to answer. The Crow warriors he had seen—for that matter, all the Indians he had seen—had little chest hair, and not much of a beard. "We're hairy people."

"Are your women hairy all over, too?"

Skye laughed uncertainly.

"You don't know. You are in that damn boat too long. Damn, Skye, you need a woman."

Under the blanket, the talk had taken a more intimate turn, and Skye was half enjoying it, half wondering how many dozen mountaineers were gathering silently around them, ready to hooraw him the moment the blanket came off.

"Good-bye, Mister Skye. You remember Victoria." She squeezed him hard and pulled the blanket away. Just as he suspected, a solemn conclave, including that rascal Beckwourth, Gabe Bridger, Tom Fitzpatrick, Bill Sublette, Davey Jackson, and even Jedediah Smith, stood in a circle and broke into applause.

Victoria squealed, glared at the impoliteness of these white barbarians, and ran toward her people.

"Them Snakes call me Blanket Jim," Bridger said. "Looks like I'll have to defend the title."

"Not for nothing did the Crows make me a chief among

them," said Beckwourth. "Last winter I multiplied their population by fifty."

"Very touching, Mister Skye," said Tom Virgin. "We allus knew you had the makin's of a mountaineer."

Chapter 29

The rendezvous broke up under a heavy overcast that matched the mood of the seventy-odd mountaineers. Something joyous had fled, and now the trappers and the engagés of Smith, Jackson, and Sublette repaired their gear, looked over their horses, and waited for the command of their bourgeois, or brigade leader.

Their life had emptied suddenly, and even though it was high summer they were thinking of icy streams, shivering through unbearable cold, starvin' times and rough encounters with Indians. Skye sensed the change of mood and was glad he wasn't a part of all this. They might be as free as meadowlarks, but their lives were hollow, too, and filled with long stretches of sheer boredom. They might master the subtleties of nature, or learn the tongues of the tribes, but this was hardly the place to find progressive ideas or commerce or the arts, all of which Skye fully intended to pursue. Tempting as the life was, he could never be a mountaineer.

It was time to be off. He had waited to the last to see what sort of opportunity might arise, but none had. He would go east alone and almost unarmed. He had come this far from Fort Vancouver; he could find his way down the Platte if he had to, thanks to Fitzpatrick's careful description of the route. He found Jedediah Smith packing his camp gear into parfleches and making ready to leave.

"Mr. Smith, I'll be heading for St. Louis now," Skye said tentatively. "When I get there I'll find employment and repay what's owed—over seventeen dollars, I believe. You have an account with General Ashley and I'll deposit it there."

Smith smiled mildly. "The mountains aren't for you, eh?"

"No, sir."

"You don't have the itch to see what lies in the next valley, or what a coon must do to get from here to there, or see some amazing sight never before witnessed by a white man?"

"Those are all absorbing things, sir. But I have other plans. It's a dream that sustained me for days and weeks and months in ships' brigs, a dream that kept me going when I holystoned the decks, or climbed the rigging, or gazed at a distant shore where I would not touch foot."

Smith nodded. "I have strong business instincts myself. Hope to leave the mountains in comfortable circumstances in a few years." He smiled. "But those aren't my only hopes. Here in America, Mister Skye, Yanks have a westering instinct. We settled the east and then pushed ever westward across an unknown land, always itchy to see what lay beyond the horizon. It's bred into us."

Skye sighed. "I lack the instinct. But I'll never forget this, and the fine men I've met here. You're friends."

"I won't try to dissuade you. But we're putting three brigades out and you could join one. We can outfit you and you could spend a year and come out ahead."

"I've thought on it, and I'll just take my chances. I'd be grateful for some directions."

"I'll draw a map."

Smith extracted a sheet of paper—a precious item in the mountains—and a lead ball intended for his rifle, and began to draw with it, much to Skye's surprise. The lead left a clear mark on the paper.

Swiftly Smith drew rivers and mountain ranges, his hand replicating some vast map in his mind. Skye marveled that this quiet young man knew such a large part of a continent.

"We're here in Cache Valley. You need to get to the Platte, which'll take you to the Missouri, which'll take you to St. Louis and the Mississippi. You have several options. You can go over to Bear Lake, and then cut east to the Seedskedee, and cross a wasteland to South Pass, then to the headwaters of the Sweetwater, and down to the North Platte, like this."

Smith sketched in a trail with dotted lines. Skye knew that sticking to it would be much harder.

"It'll be easy to find your way because you'll be following Ashley. You can't miss the passage of so many horses and men. It's also the fastest route east. But I'd suggest you go with Bill Sublette's brigade up to the Snake. He'll be cutting north at Henry's Fork, heading for the Three Forks of the Missouri, but he'll show you where to leave the Snake—at a place called the Hoback. You'll end up on the Seedskedee, and from there you'll go over South Pass—the Continental Divide, but you'll hardly know it. The Wind Rivers are just to the north, a majestic range, and you'll be passing around their feet. This'd take you out of your way—you'd lose maybe ten days—but you'd profit by traveling with experienced mountaineers and learning their ways, which I strongly advise. And of course, you'd be safer while you're with them."

"I'll do that, then."

Smith peered at Skye solemnly. "I'm sorry you're not staying, but I understand. Let's go talk to Bill."

Skye followed Smith out of the lodge and over to the partner's half-shelter. "Mister Skye's going east, Bill, and I suggested he go with you a piece to learn what he can. Head him for the Hoback."

Sublette grinned. "Maybe we'll make a trapper of ye afore we get shut of ye. I'm planning on winterin' with the Crow—with the Kicked-in-the-Bellies. You want to spend more time under that blanket, you just stick with old William."

Skye nodded. He shook hands with Smith, liking this man who had swiftly made himself a legend among those who knew him.

"Thank you. I'm in your debt. If you come east, look me up."

"Not likely, Mister Skye. East makes me itch and sweat."

Smith's brigade was the first to pull out, heading straight south toward unknown arid country. Smith intended to strike the old Spanish Trail between Santa Fe and California, but no one knew just where it was or how it ran.

Davey Jackson pulled out next, with a large group of free trappers and several women, a colorful outfit with lean, bearded men in gaudy buckskins, tough looking and sharp eyed. Every man had a mountain rifle and the skill to use it murderously. They were heading into the Snake country, looking for areas not trapped out by Hudson's Bay, intending to be a Yank presence in disputed land.

Then, midday, Bill Sublette's brigade abandoned the forlorn flat, with Skye riding along. His rested horse danced under him, and he had to relearn the horsemanship he had taught himself. He carried his warbag on his lap, but it didn't trouble him. He was on his way again, and that sent his spirits soaring.

Twenty-four veterans of the mountains rode beside him, including Bridger and Beckwourth. They rode without military discipline, each man in his own style, and yet these Yanks were fanged and strong, and could give better than they got from any passing band of Indians. They would have to be: they were penetrating Blackfoot country for the first time, and death rode with them. Some or all of these men would not return to the next rendezvous, and yet each had elected to head into the prime beaver country of the north, as yet untouched because the ferocious Piegans, or Siksika, or Bloods, barred the way.

Skye thought that the casualness of this caravan might not appeal to the lord generals or captains of the British army, who would have organized the company into formation and put vedettes out on the flanks. Perhaps Sublette would do that when they reached dangerous country, but Skye would be long gone. They would show him the path and send him on his way.

Thirty-one men; that was the strength of this brigade. There were enough, they said, to hold off a whole village of Blackfeet. Those mountain rifles, accurately fired, would keep even a massed enemy at bay. There were no women in this brigade; Sublette had forbidden it.

No one spoke. They had talked themselves hoarse in the rendezvous. That was the social time. This was the time to head leisurely north through shortening days and chill nights, mapping out beaver-rich creeks and rivers to trap later when the fur was prime. This was the time to enjoy summer warmth while it lasted in these northern climes, time to have fun, make buffalo meat and jerky, harvest strawberries and chokecherries and other wild fruit. Time to gird up for winter, fatten the horses, braid rawhide horse tack, tell tall stories. Skye had heard more than a few yarns, and realized that storytelling was one of the ways these men made time pass in a land without diversions or outside news. Adventure and utter boredom appeared equally in the lives of these mountaineers.

For several days they wandered north until they struck the Snake, and then turned upstream, traversing a flat country but never out of sight of towering distant ranges. Sublette often rode with Skye, gradually extracting from him the whole of his life in the Royal Navy and much about his childhood as well.

"I reckon an old coon like you'd think twice about returning to civilization, seeing as how you treasure your liberty," Sublette said.

"I treasure it. And I'm counting on your Yank government to protect it. But life is more than liberty. A man needs purpose and a dream, and my dream is to finish what I started and enter commerce."

Sublette didn't say anything, and Skye knew that his own preferences didn't sit well with these children of the wilds. The balmy days fled by one after another, hot midday, cool in the evenings, uneventful.

The river hooked around to the east again, and then one evening Sublette told Skye that they had come to the parting.

"Tomorrah we'll take Henry's Fork north and you'll stay on the Snake a while more, but not as far as Davey Jackson's Hole."

He stooped on bare earth and scraped a map with a stick. Skye had to find the route that had been traversed by the Astorians early in the century. If he found the right one, it would take him over a pass and down to the Seed-skedee. And then he'd face a long stretch of waterless wasteland until he hit a small creek at the western foot of South Pass . . .

Skye memorized the map in his head, knowing how hard it would be to translate to the real world what Sub-lette was scraping in the clay.

That evening, while feasting on a buck mule deer that Emanuel Lazarus brought in, the talk turned distinctly odd.

"Mr. Bridger," said Beckwourth, "do you think Mr. Sublette'd give us a week off?"

"No, Mr. Beckwourth, Mr. Ranne, and Mr. Fitzpatrick proposed it, while Mr. Reed, and Mr. Daw objected because they want to make the beaver come."

"A pity," said Beckwourth. "How about you, Mister Skye?"

"I'll be taking my leave tomorrow, mates."

"Mates? Mates? What sort of word is that? Call us mister."

Skye smiled.

"Time we elevated the manners around hyar," Bridger said. "Now, you ain't never to call me Gabe agin, though I'll accept Blanket Jim at rendezvous. From now on it's mister. High-toned, like Mister Skye hyar. Mr. Bridger, that's me."

With that, they all pronounced themselves misters and said the brigade was mightily elevated by the courtesy.

"Tell us again why y'ar Mister Skye," Isaac Galbraith asked.

"Because this is a new world," Skye said, simply.

"Yep, it's that all right," Beckwourth opined. "But mister ain't enough. Call me chief. Call me headman. Call me Lord Beckwourth, or baron or viscount or duke."

Skye smiled.

"Now, Mister Skye, old coon, onct ye get onto that Astorian patch, ye got to watch for the petryfied forest. Everything in her's turned to rock," said Mr. Bridger. "I saw me an elk turned solid rock there not long ago. And there's a marble grizzly rearin' up at the east end."

"And beyond the petryfied forest is the Amazons," said Mr. Beckwourth. "Two hundred seventy beauteous Injun women who won't let you pass until you pleasure 'em."

They managed all this until the fire died and the stars blanketed the sky, and Skye knew he had friends, and they were feeling loss at his departure. And he knew as well that he would feel a similar loss for these wild Yanks.

The next morning, one with a chill on it, they rode an hour to the confluence of Henry's Fork and the Snake, and there they parted. In the northeastern haze loomed a range topped by three spiky peaks.

"Them's the Tetons," Sublette said. "Snake runs right under 'em on the east side, but you won't go that far. All right, Mister Skye, keep your topknot on."

It was the mountaineers' blessing.

"Thank you, gentlemen. Keep your topknots on."

He rode away from them, a lone man in a wild, lonely land, with tears in his eyes.

Chapter 30

The Snake River divided itself around countless sandy islands and sparkled merrily through lush meadows or sudden patches of pine. It harbored along its banks more wildlife than Skye had ever seen, and in its transparent waters trout leapt and darted.

He found himself riding through an Eden that would have been the envy of Adam and Eve. He had little trouble filling his demanding belly now that July was fading into August and every bush brimmed with red, black, and silvery berries. He scared up deer and martins and elk, and once a yawning brown bear. He watched bald eagles circle above him and redtailed hawks dive for their dinner. Sunlight glinted off the cold complex waters, dazzling his eye. The screech of meadowlarks, kildeer, and red-winged blackbirds gladdened his spirit and told him that all was well.

The cheerful river ushered him across a golden plain and into somber mountains. Now the river pulsed through an intimate valley hemmed by vaulting pine-clad slopes, and Skye knew he must look for the vaguely described turnoff, Hoback River, that had been the route of John Jacob Astor's party heading for the Pacific coast in 1811.

He missed his companions, but the river had become his bosom friend, endlessly delightful to eye and soul. He was glad he had traveled a piece with Sublette's brigade, not only because it had cemented friendships but also because he had absorbed the ways of the mountaineers, an eager acolyte in the liturgy of survival. Skye had absorbed their innate, unspoken caution. Even though they might be talking to each other or seeming to pay no attention to the terrain, in fact they were constantly scanning horizons, studying dark blank woods, places of trouble and surprise. Without a word being spoken by Sublette or anyone else, they paused at defiles or river passages or at any place hemmed by brush or forest, and one or another would circle around for a hard-eyed look. These children of the wilds would not be surprised if they could help it.

He mastered their camp techniques, too. They grazed their animals until dusk and then hobbled and staked them close at hand. They built their small fires in hidden places, preferably under some branches that would dissipate the smoke. They scanned the heavens with knowing eyes, and prepared for a wet night if the omens told them to. They could thatch an effective shelter in a hurry, knew how to keep their spare clothing dry, and knew how to find dry tinder and build a fire where a drizzle wouldn't snuff it. Whenever they had spare meat, they hung it high and away from their camp, or jerked it if they had time. Occasionally they heard wolves, and constantly enjoyed the night-gossip of the coyotes, and sometimes counted their silences more important than the night-talk.

The wilderness and its omnipresent dangers had driven these men together; out in the wilds they were boon companions in a way that could not be replicated in the sullen cities. Skye had blotted up all of this during his brief sojourn with Sublette's men. He missed them so much it surprised him, and to counter his bouts of loneliness he focused on his future, examining his dream, over and over.

Boston was the great American seaport; there would be import and export businesses, very like his father's.

He would apply at once, knowing he could be useful. Those matters had been bred into his bones and he had heard his father's talk at many a meal. He would clerk, and save his pence, and apply at the college. He would study political economy as his father had done, and English literature, as he wanted to do. Then, someday, with a bachelor degree in hand—albeit at a late age—he would start his own business, win a wife, start the Skye family, and settle into an abundant life.

All these things he rehearsed and rehashed as he rode up the Snake, almost to prevent the bewitching river and the golden wilderness from seducing him. The Snake took him deeper into the mountains, and now he experienced sharply cooler weather, especially at dawn. Summer still reigned, but the higher he climbed the closer he peered into the future. He would have to hurry east. Sublette told him it would take three months to make St. Louis, and by then the nights would be cold.

He almost missed the Hoback River, taking it for an inconsequential creek, but he spotted a prominent blaze in a tree. The mountaineers had left their own road map. He turned his lively horse eastward and rode through an intimate canyon that made him uneasy because he felt hemmed in, almost like being in a ship's brig. He saw no sign of recent passage, though plenty of evidence that man and beast had come this way.

He topped a somber alpine pass one day, and began descending into what he understood would be the drainage of the Seedskedee—he wondered about the origins of that name. Once he struck that clear, cold river he was to descend it until he reached arid plains. With a little luck he would find a trail that would take him across a waterless flat to Big Sandy Creek.

He descended into an alpine valley where a river whirled through swampy flats. It wasn't a welcoming land, and he hurried through it, wanting a dryer and more comfortable climate. Nature was fickle, joyous one moment and sullen the next. This was a valley choked with brush, a place where he could easily be surprised, and that made him itchy. He urged his reluctant horse across numerous creeks, around mocking bogs, and along the edge of fearsome dark pine forests. Moose lived there, and he saw one after another standing in bogs, eating what grew close to water. This was country where winter came early and stayed long, a land locked by snow most of the year.

But the rushing Seedskedee gradually descended, often in a formidable canyon that made him feel imprisoned. One eve, just before the sun dropped below the western ridges, he located a good campsite on the river, a flat with tender grass, deadwood for fire, and some protection from the chafing winds. He slid off his brown horse and set his warbag and gear on the grass. He needed to stretch legs that had been imprisoned in the Nez Perce pad saddle too long. He wondered if he would ever get used to riding long distances.

They materialized out of the brush and woods, silent brown forms, a dozen, fifteen, all mounted, some wearing vermilion streaked across their cheekbones, others painted with subtler earth-hues garnered from nature. His heart sank. He lacked even his bow and quiver. Every one of them wielded a weapon, mostly drawn bows, but two brandished flintlocks. One had a war hatchet while another carried an iron-tipped lance.

Skye hunted his memory for the sign: *friend*.

Right hand. Palm outward. Index and second finger pointing up.

They stared. He tried *peace*.

Clasped hands. Back of left hand down . . .

Nothing. They eyed his horse, noted the gear on the ground, including Skye's bow and quiver. They talked to each other. Skye hadn't the faintest idea who they were or what might happen. A mountaineer might know, but not a British seaman. But then, suddenly, he had his answer: these warriors wore moccasins of smoked leather, almost black, something he had never seen before. *Pieds Noirs*, Blackfeet. His pulse raced. He sensed he was in mortal danger, maybe even moments from death. Six or eight nocked arrows pointed at him.

One of the warriors, apparently their leader, grunted something to the rest. That one bore a terrible scar across his left cheek and the edge of his mouth and two other jagged scars on his powerful torso. He had seen war. Skye knew the signs.

Two of them slid nimbly off their horses and walked straight toward Skye. But they didn't touch him. Instead, one grabbed Skye's horse. The other plucked up his warbag and quiver and bow.

"Stop!" bellowed Skye.

A fraction of a heartbeat later, he stared at an arrow driven into the soft earth between his legs. They were itching to kill him. He forced himself to calm down a little, but now his heart pounded crazily. Had he come all the way from the H.M.S. *Jaguar* to end up here, dying a lonely death in an empty land?

"I want my goods back. Leave that horse. I've done you no harm, but I'll fight if you want." Bluster. He had learned to defend himself in the Royal Navy with bluster. If he hadn't taken on the bullies, he would have starved to death or suffered abuse from his shipmates.

He thrust a finger at the headman. "I'll settle it with you," he said. "Get off that horse and we'll settle it." He had brawled enough in the navy; he'd brawl here if he must.

Something shifted in the brush behind him, a passing animal. The warriors stared into the thickets, seeing nothing. Skye ignored that, and walked furiously toward the headman, who sat his horse quietly, a deadly war ax in hand. One blow could cleave Skye's skull. Skye pointed at the man and at the ground, inviting the headman to get down and fight. The man stared back with expressionless black eyes, a faint triumphant glitter finally rising in them. He spoke low, the sibilants hissing from his lips.

Two of the warriors walked cautiously toward the red willow brush, and then one froze and barked something. In that moment, Skye was forgotten and a strange guttural grunt drifted from the brush. Skye stared, electrified by something he couldn't quite name. Then he saw it: a huge humped brown bear, erect on its hind paws, its nose silvery with age, eight, nine feet high, a monster, its small eyes focusing here and there, its wet nostrils flared. Skye had the sense that this monster could land on all fours and murder half these warriors—or himself—before they could run ten yards.

No one loosed an arrow, and Skye grasped why. An arrow might be little more than an irritant, something to turn this bear berserk. They all stood frozen, the warriors on foot and the rest on crazed horses that were becoming impossible to manage. Skye's horse fought the line, shaking her head violently.

In that frightful moment Skye did something he knew was terrible even to think about. He walked toward the bear, driving his limbs forward. The bear loomed higher and higher, awesome in height, its breath fouling the air, and Skye expected his life to end with a single swipe of a paw. Skye walked past the warriors on foot, closer and closer, his gaze and the grizzly's gaze locked. He came within twenty feet, then ten, his vector taking him past, rather than toward, the monster. He could not say why he was throwing his life away, only that he saw it as a small, frightful chance to escape. But these warriors were Blackfeet who preyed on isolated white men, and he had no other choice. They watched, mesmerized.

The bear snorted, the hairs at the nape of its neck erect. It snuffled and growled but stood as Skye walked past, its attention divided between Skye and the host of enemies before him. And then, suddenly, it shrieked. Skye had never heard a sound like it, and it drove shivers through him. The bear sprang, but not at Skye. It snarled toward the massed warriors, and Skye heard howling, the screech of horses, the thump of arrows finding their mark, and shouts of terror.

He ran until his wind vanished from his lungs, and ran some more, and stumbled along the trail he had recently negotiated, never looking back. And then, a half-mile distant—at least he thought it was that much—he did stare back, finding nothing. No bear, no Blackfeet. But that didn't mean anything. In terror, he raced further up the Seedskedee, splashing through tributary creeks, running until he dropped and the night cloaked him.

Chapter 31

Bear medicine.

The little Crow, Many Quill Woman, had discerned something Skye could barely fathom. The bear was his brother, his guide, his friend, his protector. She called it medicine. He tried to dismiss the savage superstition, but he couldn't. He had walked right by that enraged grizzly and survived.

The dawn chill numbed him. Gray mist blanketed the land, filtering the first light and rendering it pale and shadowless. He rose from moist ground, his body aching, yearning for a fire, warmth, food. But he had nothing.

He tried to fathom where he was. Pines loomed in the mist. He was somewhere on the upper Seedskedee. He had run until he dropped, and didn't know how far. A mile, maybe two. He stood, rubbed his aching legs and arms, and swung his arms to make heat in his body. He was ravenous. He had only the clothes on his back, his worn moccasins, and a sheathed knife at his waist. With that he must live—or die.

He started down the river again, needing to search the place of ambush for his gear. Perhaps it was still there. The bear may have driven off the Blackfeet. He needed flint and steel, bow and quiver, ax and hatchet, his blanket, and his sailcloth poncho. But anything, anything at all, would help.

The mist cleared as he hiked, but the relentless chill lingered. This was August and this was high country. Everything looked different in the morning light and he wondered if he would even recognize his campsite, which he had seen only in twilight. Wilderness was tricky and a man was hard put to say whether or not he had passed by.

At last the river entered an intimate defile and he knew he was drawing close. He had set up his camp in such a place, out of the wind and hidden from view. He passed through the red willow brush and came upon the campsite so swiftly that he had not been cautious. But the Blackfeet had departed. A horse lay on bloody soil, brutally clawed and half-eaten. These were bloody grounds. The stink of terror reached his nostrils.

His hair prickled, and he squinted hard into the shadowed brush, fearing the wounded bear or even the Blackfeet. He saw nothing and heard only the beat of his racing heart. He began a systematic search, in wider and wider arcs, hunting for something, anything, he might use. But the gory site yielded nothing. He tried to fathom what had happened. As far as he could tell, they had not killed the bear. There was no carcass or entrails. But had the bear killed any of them? He found no evidence of it, but wished he could read sign as easily as the mountaineers.

He widened his search and came up with a broken arrow with a bloody metal point. He kept it. The sheet-metal point would make a tool. He studied the arrow, noting its fletching and the dyes that marked it. This was a Blackfoot arrow and he wanted to identify it, sear its markings into his mind. He found what appeared to be the bear's trail through broken willow brush, and the sight made him prickle. The beast was leaking blood when it retreated. He hoped his bear brother would heal. How odd and savage it was to call the murderous grizzly his brother.

He widened his search until he knew for certain that the Blackfoot war party had left him nothing. Despair seeped through him. He could no longer build a fire, sleep warm, trap animals, fish, drive an arrow into game, escape the rain or sun, repair his moccasins, or ride to safety on his horse. He choked back desperation, knowing that despair wouldn't help him. What would someone like Bridger or Fitzpatrick do? He gently probed the ashes of the fire, hoping to find a live ember, but he found only cold black disappointment.

Flies swarmed the carcass of the horse. Skye realized suddenly that he had a mountain of meat before him—if he had the courage to eat it raw. He wondered if he could slice it thin and jerk it in the sun a day or two. Wolves or coyotes or something else had gnawed out its belly and demolished a haunch. Feeling queasy, he set to work with his knife, slowly ripping and cutting hide back from a forequarter until he could saw at the flesh. This would be a long, miserable task. His new knife had already dulled, making the work all the harder. He squinted about nervously, worrying that the Blackfeet might return, or the maddened bear, but he discerned only the quiet of an August morning.

All that afternoon he sawed at the carcass, eating tiny, digestible slivers of raw horse meat. He could barely chew bite-sized pieces, but he managed to down thin wafers of flesh, and gradually his hunger eased. Greenbellied flies swarmed, making his task miserable. Once he found himself staring at a pair of coyotes. He rose, roared, and they fled.

Then he discovered the Blackfeet had left something after all: his belaying pin. They probably could see no use for it. He hefted the smooth hickory shaft and knew he had an effective club. It gladdened him. He returned to his butchering, determined to make enough meat to sustain him until—what? Until he got help? Until he was ready to go east again? He dreaded the answer. Late in the afternoon, he realized he couldn't stay at this place of carnage all night, fighting off wolves and bears, skunks, raccoons, mountain lions, badgers, and whatever else would compete for the flesh of the horse.

He eyed his fly-specked pile of meat dourly, wondering how to carry it with him. Then he knew. Horsehair. He examined the long tail of the horse, discovering three-foot strands of durable hair. For once he was glad he had been a seaman. Swiftly he sawed off a mass of hair and knotted the strands into a web. He worked furiously, unhappy with the crudity of his efforts but glad to see something useful take shape. An hour later he completed a horsehair web that would carry the meat and might be useful in the future. He loaded his meat into it and stood.

He was ready to leave—but where?

He had come to the most paralyzing juncture of his life.

East across the plains with only a butcher knife and his wits? Or retreat back to the Snake and hunt down Sublette's brigade? Or try to find the Kicked-in-the-Bellies, his little Victoria, and some sort of succor?

He started east. Boston. That was his objective, after all. But fifty yards down river he halted. There would be no help—but constant menace—for a *thousand miles*. He stood miserably, unsure of his course. And then he knew why he could not go east: even if he managed to find food, his moccasins would wear out. He would be forced to hike barefoot across merciless ground bristling with cactus, rock, sticks, debris. He needed a horse, weapon, spare leather, an awl, and thong to survive.

He retreated to the campsite and watched two ravens

and a hawk flap away from the carcass. Had his dreams died here? No. He would go east when he could. For the moment, he needed the help of the mountaineers. He needed an outfit and that meant working for the brigade. Another year would slide by before he could pick up shattered dreams.

Reluctantly, hating every step, he headed upstream. Fate had decreed that he would not reach civilization this year. He had to find Sublette's brigade before he starved and before his sturdy Creole moccasins gave out. He hiked through dusk, retracing his route, splashing through icy rills and creeks because he could no longer ride a horse across them. In the last light he hunted for a place that might offer warmth, and found a spot. He settled at last against a south-facing rock that had absorbed the day's sunlight and now radiated it.

He cut tiny slivers of raw horse meat, chewed and swallowed them one by one, until he could no longer see. He unlaced his moccasins, hoping to dry them out, and settled down to wait for dawn. But a wind rose, whipping icy air through his buckskins, numbing his toes. And a light rain fell for a while, making him all the more miserable. If he didn't find shelter he'd die. He endured the stopped-clock night, working his arms and legs to drive away the numbness. Sleep eluded him. He was much too miserable. He heard the soft rustle of animals approaching and swiftly tied his net of horse meat high in a pine tree. Then he waited, his belaying pin in hand. But nothing happened.

Then, some time later, the cloud cover vanished and he beheld a sepulchral world lit by a pale moon. He would walk. Nothing else would do. He started up the gloomy river, stumbling through copses of pine and aspen, dropping into unexpected bogs, and sometimes pausing when a cloud bank obscured the pronged moon. A thousand desolating thoughts crowded his mind, but he furiously drove them back. He had not won his freedom only to surrender.

An odd purplish light tinted the land with the coming of dawn. Skye had no idea how far he had come. As the daylight intensified, rosing distant ridges and then painting them gold, he found himself in unfamiliar country. The Seedskedee meandered ever upward into bold mountains, golden in the low dawn sun. But he was lost. He studied the ground, looking for sign of his own passage. At some point yesterday he had descended a drainage, a lively creek, down to the Seedskedee, but he had crossed dozens of those and may have gone past his turnoff that would take him over the pass and down the Hoback to the Snake.

He studied the riverside trail carefully, finding no mark of passage, but he continued to ascend the river. The wilderness played tricks, making short distances seem endless. But now a deepening dread filled him. He did not know this country. The mountaineers understood it, but he had never set foot in it and didn't know the way out. He hiked up the river until he judged the sun was at its apex. He found some cattails, pulled them up, washed the starchy roots, mashed them with a rock, and gnawed on the tan pulp.

But he was lost. Everything seemed alike: pine forests, swamps, the burbling river, bogs, aspen groves, the scent of sagebrush in the air mixed sometimes with the heady scent of pines. Sudden drafts of cold air eddied past him, and occasionally he stepped into warm pockets, where he lingered to let his cold limbs warm, and his wet leathers dry.

But the stark truth was, he didn't know where he was, or where he was going, or what he should do. He was lost in all the ways a mortal can be lost.

Chapter 32

Skye knew he had come to one of those momentous crises that shape a mortal life. This journey had been filled with portentous events, things that would mould him for the rest of his days on earth. He was lost, tired, hungry, lonely, and without counsel. He had been robbed of sleep and his body felt leaden, dragging his spirits downward.

Despair was the enemy. Discouragement, defeat, surrender haunted him. He sensed he would never escape. He would die a terrible death here in a cruel wilderness. It had all come down to this, he thought bitterly. Was there no justice in the universe? Would those wigged and powdered lord admirals whose press-gangs had stolen life and liberty from him enjoy long and pampered lives while his bones moldered in a wild place?

He found a boulder heated by the early sun and sat against it, letting the wan warmth comfort his body. He closed his eyes, trying to summon courage. He had never felt so alone. And yet, as he sat there, he knew he was neither helpless nor alone. In all the years of his captivity he had never let his faith die: he had believed the God of Creation watched over him and would free him from his sea jail in His own good time. Now Skye was free—but where was God now?

He focused on that. He talked to God, told Him about the miracle of the grizzly that let him pass by, of food and succor that appeared when he needed it, of gratitude for being freed and alive and the master of his destiny. He didn't know if his babbling was prayer, exactly—certainly not the sort that was recited in the Anglican masses he had attended—but it was a conversation with his Lord, and he felt peace steal through him.

When he opened his eyes he beheld the wilderness, golden in the early sun, not enemy but friend. Some crows cawed mightily. He watched iridescent black and white magpies terrorize lesser birds. He remembered that Victoria had called the magpie her medicine-helper. He felt the first zephyrs of the morning eddy past him, redolent of sage and pine and the mysteries beyond the next ridge. The bright sun pummeled his leather shirt, warming it and him. Its rays caught his thick beard, fondling his face, and his hurts ebbed.

This was Creation, undisturbed by man, and the sight of it moved him. He hadn't expected that. This was not a dark and hostile Creation, but one that might serve him, nurture him, empower him, even as it empowered the many tribes who lived comfortably in the midst of it. Long before white traders showed up here, these tribes had drawn everything they needed, food and shelter, clothing, tools, meat, medicines, vegetables, seasonings, dyes, weapons, and more from this wilderness. The wilderness was his friend, his nourishment, his spiritual succor, his delight, his shelter, his fortress.

The day vibrated. Nothing felt quite as glorious as a late summer day in the high country. The heavens ached with joy. Skye stood, stretched, letting his new courage permeate his entire body. He knew he had come up the Seedskedee much too far and now he would retreat until he found the way to the Snake River. He sliced the last of his horse meat and chewed on it, finding the raw flesh foul. He spit it out. It had sustained him for a while but now he would need other foods.

He hiked downriver much of that morning and then found the turnoff. It showed signs of passage he had missed in the moonlight: his mare's hoofprints. He climbed the trail all that day, past grassy parks dancing in sunlight, past burbling rills and creeks, past aspen glades where every leaf quaked. He passed beaver dams and ponds, thickets of chokecherry laden with ripe berries. These he plucked and gnawed, sustaining himself even though the well-named fruit had a vicious taste that puckered his mouth.

He topped the divide and knew he was once again in the drainage of the Snake. As he traveled he came across campsites, and he paused to examine each one for discards, lost tools, anything helpful. And they did yield a small harvest. At one he found a bone awl. At another a pair of worn-out moccasins, too small for his feet but with some usable leather. At another place he found what he supposed was a flint hide flesher. He plucked it up. Flint was precious. A piece of steel might give him fire, cooked food, warmth. He thought of trying the back of his knife on the flint, but hesitated. If he broke his knife, he'd be in even worse trouble.

His left moccasin wore through and he cobbled a patch on it, knowing it wouldn't last long. And yet he kept on, sleeping under rock overhangs, dodging mountain rains, acquiring some cunning about wind and rain and cold.

He survived on what he could harvest, which was little
even in the season of fruits. But on the Snake River
drainage he found camas again and kept himself alive
by pulverizing its starchy bulbs. The camas were so
abundant that his desperate hunger eased and life brightened.

A few days later he found himself back at the confluence of Henry's Fork and the Snake. He arrived there on
a hot August afternoon and searched the river bank, seeking signs of passage. But rain had obscured any sign. Now
he faced decisions again. He could chase after Sublette's
brigade, plunging into new country, and quite possibly
never contacting the elusive trappers. Or he could retreat
to the Shoshone or Nez Perce settlements, places he knew
and could reach. He headed north to join the brigade and
win an outfit. Henry's Fork took him across a vast tree-
dotted plain with the three arrogant spikes of the Tetons
looming far to the east.

His trousers had worn to rags so he employed his bone
awl upon the rotting fabric, piecing them together. His
moccasins were failing, too, and even his leather shirt had
been pulling apart at the seams. The wilderness might
be his friend but it wasn't keeping him provisioned, and
he worried about the future in his mind, desperate for al-
ternatives. He had grown weary and listless, too, and ascribed the weakness to a lack of meat.

One early morning he spotted a group of riders so he
hid in a thicket of red willows. Some southbound warriors passed him by. Or maybe they were hunters. He
didn't know. They weren't painted. They had two horses
apiece, and from the little Skye knew about such things,
he supposed they were buffalo hunters, saving their fresh
horses for the chase. They didn't see him or suspect his

presence, and soon they were gone. The sun had been up
only a short time; maybe he could find their camp.

He followed the fresh trail northward for an hour or
so, and discovered the camping place beside the river.
Smoke coiled from a dying fire. A gutted yearling elk
hung from a heavy limb. They had eaten what they could
and abandoned the rest. Joyously, Skye added twigs to
the embers, blew gently, mumbled magic, and evoked a
fire. Then he scrounged for deadwood, having to search
wide and far because he lacked the means to hack it from
the surrounding cottonwoods, alders, and willows. He
butchered great, dripping slabs of red meat from a haunch
and skewered them with a green twig, his stomach rum-
bling with anticipation.

While the meat roasted, he cut more elk meat into thin
strips he intended to smoke into some sort of jerky, no
matter that he might spend two or three days at it. He had
not eaten like this for weeks and he intended to make the
most of his bonanza. Thus did he spend that sunny day—
eating, gathering firewood, cutting haunch and neck and
rib, smoking, and drying meat. He peeled the hide farther and farther back as he worked, and finally he spent
an hour at twilight cutting most of the hide free of the
hanging carcass. He found his fleshing tool and began to
scrape the inside of the hide, doing it awkwardly until he
staked the hide to the ground so he could get some purchase. It was slow, hard, unpleasant work, interrupted by
trips to feed the precious fire. By the time that darkness
engulfed him, he had cleaned much of the hide.

He foraged for firewood again, afraid that he would
lose the fire in the night, and eventually rounded up
enough to keep it going. He would sleep warm that night
for a change. He pushed ash over some live coals, built

up the fire, and settled down, feeling content at last. One war party had taken everything away from him, another had left him these gifts. Even here in these wilds, his fate had been decided more by other mortals than by nature. It was something to think about.

That night he slept on his new elkhide, welcoming whatever small relief it offered from the hard earth. He smoked meat all that night, rising instinctively when the fire needed tending. In the morning he roasted camas bulbs, pushing them as close to the flame as possible while he continued to smoke meat. He ate ravenously, his appetite whetted by the previous feast. Then he devoted the entire day to his tasks—preserving every scrap of meat that he could, scraping and softening the elk hide, collecting firewood, roasting camas bulbs until he had a formidable larder. He spent a second night at that fire, reluctant to surrender it but knowing he had to push ahead. Somewhere in this vast wilderness was a brigade of trappers who would welcome him into their ranks. And somewhere—he was hazy about the place—a slim girl living among the Kicked-in-the-Bellies of the Absaroka people would welcome him to her lodge, and perhaps to her arms.

He left at dawn, saddened to abandon the fire. His horsehair net was burdened now with smoked and dried elk meat, roasted camas bulbs, the discarded moccasins, the scraping tool, his belaying pin, and the stiff, rolled-up elkhide. The weight of all this was surprising, but it gladdened him: now he was a man of substance.

The overcast sky that morning reminded him that soon the season would change. Even now, in this high plateau, he felt the sharp night chill, which would soon deepen and last longer and longer as the sun fled south. He hurried north, sometimes intersecting tracks he thought might be Sublette's, but he didn't really know. Most of the trappers' horses were unshod, and most of the men wore moccasins, which made their passage little different from the passage of the tribes.

His Creole moccasins finally gave out, and he painfully fashioned new soles out of his elkskin, and anchored them to the worn soles with his bone awl and some thong. It took half a day, but he was not barefoot, and that was a miracle.

He ascended Henry's Fork, passing through a gorge into alpine parks laced with lodgepole, swamps, and broad grassy vistas. He saw abundant game but he had no means to shoot any, and was constantly reminded of how helpless he really was. He spotted buffalos one afternoon, a small group that included a bull and several calves, and he marveled at them. The monsters got wind of him and raced away at surprising speed. Skye knew he would not be feasting on humpmeat soon, not unless another miracle happened.

At the northern end of this plain he encountered austere pine-clad mountains, and after crossing a low divide he found himself staring at a gloomy lake. It took the better part of the afternoon to walk around to its outlet, and there he found the water flowing north. This water wasn't flowing toward the Snake; it probably was draining toward the mighty Missouri and Mississippi if he understood the geography. If he had passed into the Missouri drainage, then he had put the Snake country behind him, and he had entered the hunting lands of the Blackfeet Indians with only a belaying pin to defend himself.

Chapter 33

Hidden in a dense thicket of juniper well up a slope, Skye watched the Indian village parade by a half mile below. He had no notion what tribe this was—how could a British seaman know?—but he knew he was safest well hidden and far from the river.

For once he was grateful he didn't have a horse. The vedettes flanking the great migration would have spotted him instantly, or followed his fresh hoofprints. He supposed he was safe enough, although the sight of several hundred Indians, countless dogs, and endless numbers of horses, some dragging travois, shot fear through him.

By all accounts, these were not the same sort of Indian as those who inhabited the fishing villages along the Columbia, and even the friendlier tribes in this area—his mountaineer friends had listed the Crow, Flathead, Shoshone, and Sioux in that category, along with the Bannacks if their mood was right—could pose trouble for a lone traveler.

This village was migrating up the Madison River, away from the Three Forks country where Skye hoped to find the Sublette brigade. The last of the day's sun caught the clouds of dust raised by the passage of so many horses, and painted the very air gold as the village slowly wound past. But then the column slowly came to a halt at a riverside flat below Skye.

Swiftly, the herders moved the horses onto grass away from the glinting river, while nimble squaws unhooked travois and unloaded packhorses. The village would stay there for the night. Skye sucked air into his lungs and exhaled slowly. He was trapped, at least until dark, and maybe after that if there were sentries patrolling the herd, as surely there would be. Between the sentries and the dogs he would have a devilish time sneaking away. Suddenly the half mile between him and this crowd seemed like no distance at all. He studied the legs and feet of those antlike mortals so far away, hoping to discern whether these Indians wore the dark moccasins of the Blackfeet, but he could not say. Much too much space, and failing light, kept him from ascertaining that crucial fact.

He was thirsty but he couldn't simply walk down to the water's edge and sip that fine, clear snowmelt. Hunger bit at him, too. He had gone through his smoked elk and camas bulbs and had been finding precious little to eat along the Madison River.

There was nothing to do but lie patiently in the sunwarmed juniper, enjoy its resinous scent, and wait until darkness liberated him. Fires flared along the riverbank, one by one, miraculously blooming to life and radiating orange light into the purple twilight. Below, the herders were driving a multicolored mass of horses out on the flats. Wary brown warriors in breechclouts hobbled or picketed their horses close to the campsite. Lodges rose here and there, first a cone of poles and suddenly an entire Indian home. He eyed the skies anxiously, looking for signs of bad weather, and found some. Towering gray thunderclouds loomed behind him, and more blackbellied clouds were gathering muscle off to the south. So the lodges were going up this night.

From his haven, he began to enjoy this spectacle. Something powerful radiated from this village. These people looked after themselves, each to his own comforts and lodging, without direction. The warrior society that had been appointed to guard this village was posting its men around the area, all of them on this side of the wide river, making a safe cocoon for the women, children, and old people within. Once in a while, the eddying winds brought him the smell of meat cooking, which maddened him and tempted him to stand, walk downslope to the village, and surrender to his fate among friends—or foes.

Thus did he struggle with himself for a half hour or so, until something shocked him out of his reveries. He heard voices, so close that the low exchange lifted the hair on the nape of his neck. Not thirty yards away, in an adjacent juniper thicket, lurked four dusky savages, wearing only breechclouts and moccasins—smoked black.

Blackfeet.

He flattened himself to the earth, grateful for his worn leather shirt, his dark hair and beard, his begrimed trousers. If he could scratch his way deeper into the earth he would have. His pulse catapulted. He felt sweat blossom from every pore in his body, and in moments he had drenched himself with it. He lay motionless, waiting for the crackle of brush that would signal his doom. Here would he die. Here would the scalping knife circle his forehead. Here would be his last memory—perhaps of the violent pop as his hair yanked free of his skull.

But after the first rush of terror, he peered about him, slowly surveying his lot. Four Blackfeet. Maybe others were somewhere upslope, horseholders over the ridge. This would be a horse-stealing party. Sometime in the night they would pad down the sagebrush-choked slope, slip past or kill the night herders, and drive away as many animals as possible, probably fleeing toward the Blackfoot stronghold to the north.

So the village below was probably Shoshone or Crow. Maybe he could find a haven there, slipping into the village after dark. Maybe he could warn them—if he could make himself understood. But what sort of reception would he meet? Likely killed on the spot, an intruder rising out of the night. And how could he escape the alert Blackfeet hidden barely thirty yards away? No. He could not move, not yet.

Skye lay motionless, grateful for the ebbing light that gradually cloaked him in blessed darkness. Only once in his life had he been so close to death, and that time a wandering bear saved him. It took sheer willpower to lie motionless, calm his body, steady his pulse, stop his rank sweating, and prepare himself. He had only his belaying pin and his new knife. The belaying pin would help him; the knife would not.

He had some serious thinking to do. Somewhere above him there would be youths holding the ponies while the warriors worked down to the village herd on foot. He wanted a horse. The Blackfeet owed him a horse, and he'd like two or three more for good measure. A few horses would solve most of his troubles, and if worse came to worse, his transportation was edible.

He ached to grab those horses. He wanted a bow and quiver, too. He could either slip away in the darkness and hope not to get caught in the maneuvering when it all blew up—or he could hunt the hunters. He swallowed, trying to draw moisture to his parched throat, knowing what he was going to do, and marveling at his folly.

The night deepened, save for a blue band of last light riding the western ridges. The stars emerged as if the night sky were shedding veils. He listened closely, hoping to discern whether other Blackfeet occupied other thickets. But he heard nothing save for the occasional gut-turals of the warriors nearby. Slowly he rolled until he could stare upslope—snapping a twig as he did. But nothing happened. In the shadowy light he studied the black slope, wondering where the rest of the raiders lay waiting, and whether they could be taken unawares. His only advantage was that they wouldn't be expecting him; they would expect one of their own.

He strained his eyes and ears, trying to make sense of what lay around him, but couldn't. The darkness had deepened to pitch, and no moon illumined the night. Would these sharp-eyed savages strike in blackness so close they could not see their own hands? He would know, eventually.

His thirst became an agony, but he ruthlessly choked back the temptation to sneak away for a drink. This was his sole chance for a horse, for a weapon, for food and shelter, and he would take it. He had taken chances from the beginning, driven by his vision of liberty, a sunny up-lands of owning his own destiny. He had slid into the icy Columbia from the H.M.S. *Jaguar,* walked into Indian villages, wrestled the wilderness and its wild inhabit-ants, walked past a grizzly that could have butchered him with one swipe of a paw, all for his freedom. Now he would risk his life again.

Blackness lay thick upon the land. The stars vanished under the giant storm clouds he had seen at dusk. Dis-tant thunderheads flashed staccato white and purple, and sharp cold breezes nipped through his sanctuary, running icy fingers over his neck. He became aware, in the midst of all this, of a gradual increase in light. The gibbous moon had risen, shooting its glow in and around the storm clouds, rendering visible the murky flat far below.

Sure enough, the Blackfeet stirred. He heard them talk softly, and then creak out of their shelter, their movement veiled by wind and the distant rumble of thunder riding high peaks. There were six. Startled, he watched the enigmatic figures spread out and stalk downslope. Each carried a hackamore and reins of some sort.

He watched them descend, melding themselves into the tall sagebrush. He glanced sharply upslope, left and right, and then eased out of his thicket, his senses keen and sharp and clean. Off to the northeast, perhaps a quarter of a mile, was a saddle, probably a watercourse. The Blackfeet had come from there because it was the only place they could come from. He hurried upslope, angling north, taking advantage of the thick juniper as much as he could, wondering whether he was being observed from above. If so, he couldn't help it and would deal with it as best he could.

He paused occasionally to check on the progress of the horse thieves, but could no longer see them. The storms blotted up light again. He hurried upslope, his heart racing, pushing against sharp cold air. Then commotion rendered the night. Far below, a giant hand swept the herd into a gallop. Skye had no idea which way it was running, only that the thunder of many hooves ruptured the peace. He edged over the ridge and found dense aspen beyond.

And through the leaves, he discerned two Blackfeet and several horses.

Chapter 34

The tricky light gave Skye pause. Were there two or three? Did one hold a bow with a nocked arrow? Did the other hold the horses? He waited for the shifting clouds to reveal more, but time was running out. Down on the Madison River the rumble of hooves and the howls of Indians at war shattered the peace. Were the raiders coming here? Skye crouched deeper into the shade of the aspens, sorting it out.

A moment of moonlight gave him a glimpse of the valley before him. Both of the horse holders were mounted now, ready to flee along with the rest of the Blackfoot raiders. And the stolen herd was thundering closer, driven this way by the raiders. In a moment they would flood over the rim and through here. He waited witlessly, not knowing how to deal with this. If the raiders were coming this way, so would the village warriors in hot pursuit. Skye studied the terrain, looking for escape, but naked slopes hemmed this valley. He had best stick to the aspens. The raiders would drive their stolen herd up the valley and into the next drainage.

The first of the horses boiled over the saddle and he instantly flattened himself among the aspens, hoping the night would conceal him. A dozen horses, then another, twenty, thirty. He couldn't say. And herding them were the raiders, riding stolen animals they had bridled. The herd halted abruptly at the sight of the horse holders and their excited mounts, then milled and circled. The raiders shouted something, and the horse holders turned their mounts and led the herd down the long valley. Skye watched the Blackfeet race by and then waited for the village warriors to follow.

He almost missed the black horse, hovering in the darkness. Was it lame? Why didn't it run with the others? It whinnied sharply, and a moment later a wraith appeared at its flanks—a foal, born that spring. The mare nudged the foal furiously, wanting to catch up with the herd, but the foal didn't budge. Skye watched, mesmerized with possibility. The foal was limping. The mare wouldn't leave it. Maybe there was a chance.

Nervously, Skye eyed the skyline, expecting the village warriors to burst into view. The clouds obscured the moon again, plunging the whole tableau into murk. Maybe that was his chance. But what would he catch the mare with, and how would he hold it and ride it? He had only his belt. That would have to do. He eased toward the mare, which watched him alertly but didn't run because her foal couldn't. He talked softly, aware of the howls of war just over the saddle. He closed slowly, talking in a low voice, and then looped the belt over her neck, catching her even as the frightened foal limped away from him.

He was out in the open when the first of the defenders topped the saddle. He saw them, and then he didn't as the fickle light vanished again. He stood stock still; there was nothing else to do. The village warriors raced through one by one, their focus on the lost herd ahead and not upon Skye and a black mare off to one side, as inert as the trees and rocks.

Then no more came over the ridge and a quietness returned to the little mountain plateau. Slowly, Skye led the mare toward the aspen grove. The foal complained, but followed slowly, limping heavily. Skye drew the horses deep into the grove and quietly ran his hand over the mare, soothing the nervous animal. The mare pressed her nostrils into Skye and inhaled, gathering her own form of knowledge, and then nudged him.

Skye rejoiced, but he also puzzled over his dilemma. When would the foal be able to walk again? Was the mare broken to saddle or packsaddle? Without a hackamore or bridle or halter, how could he handle the mare or picket it at night? Would the pursuers return this way, or would they find another way back to their village?

He couldn't know.

He ransacked his memories of the Shoshone and Nez Perce he had seen. Some of them used the simplest imaginable means of steering or controlling their ponies. He recollected that many a child had looped a line over the nose of the horse, knotted it under the jaw, and used the two ends of the line for reins. That was all. He could do that. He could cut his remaining elkhide into strips and braid them into a crude bridle.

He ached to leave, but couldn't. He might have to suffer many more thirsty hours in this aspen grove before the village moved and before the injured foal was ready to travel, but the prize was worth it.

He had a horse—if he could keep it, and keep his hair.

One by one, he yanked the long fringes off the hem of his buckskin shirt and tied them into a short line that he anchored to the loop of belt around the mare's neck. And then he sat down to await events, holding her on a gossamer leather thread she could easy break. But she was content and let the foal suckle, and did not test his line. He sat through sharp cold, a few drops of rain, and deep silences. The riders did not return. The mare stood quietly.

With the first light, Skye studied the meadow and saw nothing at all but mist and grass and trees. He tied the mare to an aspen and slipped up to the saddle, where he beheld the village down on the Madison River. Guards circled the remaining horses. No one was packing: the village was awaiting the return of the pursuers. He returned to his own alpine meadow and discovered a nearby rill, where he drank greedily.

He thought of slaughtering the lame foal, and resisted the idea. He hunted the bottoms for something edible, finally settling on some miserable chokecherries. He plucked what he could, half afraid he would be spotted by returning riders, but no one came. He retreated to his aspens and gnawed at the bitter, mouthpuckering berries, barely able to endure them. They didn't alleviate his howling hunger. He bided his time by cutting elkhide thong and then braiding a three-strand line two yards long, and then tying it to the belt around the mare's neck. He had a stout lead rope, and a potential bridle.

At midmorning the mare seemed restless, so he cautiously led it out to graze. The foal barely limped now, and Skye hoped he could travel soon. He took the mare down to the rill, fearful of discovery. The mare drank, grazed, and stood quietly while the foal nudged her bag and drank his breakfast.

All that long day he lingered in the aspen grove, occasionally letting the mare foray to grass. Late in the afternoon he climbed to the saddle and discovered the village had left and was nowhere in sight. Joyously, he led his mare down to the campsite, looking for castoffs, lost items, food. He could almost feel the presence of the villagers there. Only a few hours earlier this place had been a nomadic home, filled with grandparents, children, men and women, chiefs, seers, revered oldsters, dogs, ponies. Now it was a naked flat.

He systematically scoured the whole area, finding one treasure after another, the losses of war. He found a hackamore and then another, a broken hobble, several broken rawhide lines, snapped apart when the stampeding began. He also found goods that had been deliberately abandoned, probably because there were no longer the horses to transport them. A good parfleche lay on the ground, and in it some pemmican. A rawhide packsaddle. Various moccasins and leggins. A red bandanna, which he immediately folded into a headband to corral his unruly mane. None of the moccasins fit him but he thought he could use the leather for patching. He found a hatchet in a pasture and rejoiced, running his thick thumb over its dull edge. He would sharpen it somehow. But the prize was a beaded fire-starter bag, handsomely fringed, lying in grass before a circle of rocks that had pinned down a lodge cover. Within he discovered a flint and steel and a nest of powdery tinder. Fire! That was like capturing the sun. Joyously he loaded all the loot he could manage onto the packsaddle and lowered it gently on the mare. She didn't mind. But the fire-starter bag he carried at his waist. Never again would he be without the means to kindle a flame.

He wolfed some of the pemmican and then started north, walking well back from the Madison River for fear of encountering more trouble. He was tempted to start for the East once again, but common sense overruled that. Given a rifle to kill buffalo or deer, a pair of blankets or a poncho against the weather, he might have endured the great plains. But autumn was tucked in the breeze and he had only the clothes on his back. He had learned enough about wilderness to know that his best bet was to join the brigade and let the future tend to itself.

He took the northbound journey in easy stages, letting the foal rest frequently. But the little rascal recovered much faster than Skye anticipated, and soon was dancing along beside his mother. It was a gray, skinny and proud and full of new life. A soft whicker from its mother brought it to her side whenever it pranced too far away. And as for the mare, it seemed docile and at peace as Skye led her northward. The mare was ugly, with a roman nose and crooked legs, but he loved her.

Skye felt rich. Never had he enjoyed life so much. The grasses had turned to tan, and the heavens were mostly clear and bold blue. Every thicket burst with berries, many of them unknown to him. He tried them all, cautiously at first, and then eagerly. He had lost track of the days, but knew this was September, a time when the whole of creation glowed and fruit burdened every limb.

He felt at one with the world around him, having at last arrived at his own accommodation with wilderness. This mountainous world seemed friendly, rife with possibility, alive with birds, small and large animals, fish, clear creeks, stately pines, grand ridges, towering clouds, whispering breezes that sometimes foretold him of the winter that would swiftly descend.

Almost every night the wolves howled from ridge to ridge, and sometimes just beyond his campfire. He feared them. They seemed bloodthirsty and vicious, and endangered his horse colt. One night when they lurked just beyond his camp, he sprang up with a roar and ran at them. A long while later they mourned from a distant ridge. His colt didn't make wolf-bait that night.

He worried more and more about finding Sublette's

brigade. He had seen no sign of it, although he studied the trails along the river for the prints of shod hooves or white men's boots. He was deep in Blackfoot country now, and walked cautiously, well away from the trails when he could, even though it meant climbing slopes and fighting through groves of pine and aspen. A man without a weapon was risking his life in this country.

The swift river drove through canyons, crossed broad flats, dominated huge valleys only to plunge into ravines that forced him to detour. And then he grew aware that he had reached a huge basin set in the midst of distant mountains. Grassy hills dominated the basin, but the white-peaked mountain ranges lay thirty, forty, fifty miles distant. It was mountain-girt, actually, with cottonwoods, aspen, and pine along the creeks. He spotted buffalo sign everywhere, and soon saw bunches of them, massed black against the golden fields of grass. He knew what this place was: Sublette had described it and drawn it into the clay as he made his map. This was the Three Forks country, the headwaters of a great river called the Missouri—and a favorite hunting area of the murderous Blackfeet.

The Sublette brigade would be here—if it was still alive. The whole area was overrun with beaver. Skye passed dam after dam along each creek. Whoever had the nerve to trap here could harvest thousands of pelts in short order. But perhaps it was still too early. Skye knew that these trappers didn't begin their fall hunt until the pelts were prime. Sublette wouldn't be here—not yet. He would be in some safe place, waiting for the cold.

But where was he? How could Skye find about thirty men in an endless wilderness? His life depended on it.

Chapter 35

Lakota! News of disaster raced through the village, and now the Kicked-in-the-Bellies gathered silently around the returning hunters. Some bore wounds, their bandages bloodred in the autumnal light. Some rode double because they could not sit their ponies without help. Another, Coyote Waits they said, lay in a travois near death. All that was terrible enough, but not so terrible as the four ponies that bore the dead, who hung over the saddles, the bare skulls of their scalped heads dangling toward Mother Earth.

Many Quill Woman watched bitterly, hating the Lakota dogs who had ambushed the Absaroka hunters. Never in her memory had the Kicked-in-the-Bellies suffered such a disaster, and she thirsted for revenge. Soon the howling Absaroka warriors would race out upon the plains to hunt down the Lakota and put an end to their victory dances.

Many Quill Woman knew every one of the dead. They were all of her Otter Clan. That made it all the worse, a terrible dishonor upon her clan, and also on the Lumpwood Society, whose young warriors these were. Their medicine had gone bad, and she ached with the shame of it. Someone among them had violated his sacred power, or betrayed his trust, or had touched what he must not touch and had not told the rest.

They were camped, this Moon of the Turning Leaves, near the confluence of the Yellowstone River, which her people knew as the Elk, and the Big Horn River, in the heart of the buffalo country. The buffalo brothers and sisters could almost always be found here, and indeed with each sun the hunters killed more and more, keeping the women very busy. This was the season to make pemmican and jerky against the winter, to scrape and clean hides that would become lodgeskins or winter moccasins or leggins, to feast on good humpmeat and tongue and bone marrow, and to store away plenty of salty backfat against the time when the Cold Maker ruled the earth. Later, when it grew cold, and the buffalo had grown their winter hair, there would be another hunt for humpmeat and bone marrow and backfat, livers and hearts, as well as warm buffalo robes to sleep in and for hides to trade to the white men for weapons and pots and knives.

But Many Quill Woman didn't want to think of that. Among the dead was Barking Coyote, who had eyes for her. She had spent many moments with Barking Coyote, sometimes in the bushes away from the village, liking him even if he was skinny and awkward. He was going to ask for her soon. Any day he would stake two ponies before her father's lodge, and leave a gift of tobacco and maybe a good pipe, and wait to see whether the gifts were accepted. But he wanted more honor first.

Now he hung lifeless from his pony, his eyes seeing nothing. An arrow driven into his chest had killed him. She stared at his naked skull and shuddered. He would wander the spirit world without a home, looking for his lost hair, the mark of selfhood, never content and never at peace. Barking Coyote's mother began to wail, and Many Quill Woman turned away. It was hard to bear death and loss without wailing. She had her own way of grieving, just by seething silently, angry because of loss and helplessness.

But many of the women wailed, and soon the widows would cut their hair on one side or chop off a finger at the first joint, making themselves ugly to show the world their true feelings. Two widows this time. The rest of the young men had not taken a woman.

These hunters brought back not a single trophy. No scalp dangled from their lances. They had counted no coup and had no proud stories of bravery to recite before the elders. The Lakota had won a total, brutal victory that would shame her village for years when the story was remembered around the council fires of the Absaroka. She felt mortified as she followed the mob toward the big lodge of Arapooish, Rotten Belly, the greatest of all the Absaroka. But even as they gathered before his lodge, he emerged with his face painted white in mourning. Nothing was said. The whole story lay upon those horses and the empty lances. This hunting band had gone out to kill buffalo, and ended up being surprised and killed by Lakota devils hiding nearby. That was a common enough event, but older warriors and hunters would have been better prepared for it.

The big-bellied, hook-nosed chief stared at the empty lances, devoid of any Lakota scalps, nodded and retreated to his lodge. That was all. They had given him the news. The families of the dead reclaimed the bodies and led away the ponies while all the village watched and the women wailed. Soon they would be building scaffolds and laying the dead upon them, wrapped in a robe, face to the sun, along with their bows and quivers for their spirit journey. The ponies would be slaughtered so that the departed would have a steed to ride on the trail to the stars.

Many Quill Woman watched until there was nothing

more to see, and then retreated to her father's lodge. She beheld her stepmother, Digs the Roots, fleshing a new buffalohide staked to the earth. This one would replace a well-smoked hide high in the lodge cover, which in turn would make fine, soft, brown moccasins capable of turning water because of all the grease embedded in the leather.

"Ah, daughter, the one who was playing the flute for you is gone," her stepmother said as she scraped. She had carefully avoided naming the dead, for it was improper to say the name or even think it.

Many Quill Woman nodded. "He was brave. His family will be proud," she replied. "He died a warrior and gave to the People."

"But he is gone to the ancestors. You will miss him, Many Quill Woman."

"It would have come to nothing," she said.

"Ah! I thought so. You have not been the same since the summer. You should not think about the Goddamns. They are a hairy, dirty race."

"One is different," she said. "I think about him."

She had been of two minds about the one who had died. The dead one was truly a good Absaroka from a prominent family with many honors in battle and two medicine-bundle keepers among them. He had seventeen winters and was just coming into his manhood. He had been a warrior for three years and had won honors. He had counted coup twice, and had won the right to wear a notched eagle feather in his jet hair. She had been honored by his attentions and the soft whisper of his willow love flute outside her lodge.

But ever since the summer rendezvous, she had been restless, and had moments when she wished the one who was dead would abandon her. She kept finding fault with the young man and knew she shouldn't. The one who interested her, Mister Skye, would be long gone now, off to his own strange world, but he seemed big in her mind, a relentless presence who filled her soul in the night. She didn't believe any of his story. Big ships with twenty sails on the Great Waters, villages so big it took hours to walk from one end to the other, guns so big they could shoot an iron ball too heavy for one man to lift, homes of fired clay so big many lodges would fit into one, streets paved of stone. She knew he had invented these things to entertain her. Nothing under the sun could be like that and she took it as his whimsy, not as anything real.

But he was different from the other pale men, more serious, more direct and truthful, more tender and honest. He didn't laugh much; she had barely seen his hairy face break into a smile. It was as if some terrible burden lay upon him that he could never set down. She didn't really know why she was drawn to him, only that he set her heart afire and she wanted to be his woman. She smiled. Maybe it was his nose. He had the chief of all noses, a nose to be proud of, a nose that made him a giant among all people.

She cut a snippet of black hair from the left side of her face to express her mourning for the one who had gone, but she did not cut half her hair the way a widow would. She walked to the pond where she could see her reflection, and saw how plain she looked. That was good. The cut hair would warn suitors off, and that was what she wanted.

Maybe Mister Skye wouldn't come. She had seen him walking over mountains after she had cried for a vision one moon earlier, and she placed great stock in that. But she didn't really know whether he would come back, and she knew all about false visions, the work of Coyote the Trickster. Even if Skye came with the trappers to winter with the Kicked-in-the-Bellies, and even if she met Mister Skye again, her parents would not approve. He would have nothing to give her father; he would also be a man without honors among the Goddamns, and her father would disapprove.

But enough of this! She put such things aside and hiked through the rustling grasslands to a distant hill where she went to be alone with the Spirits and to bring Magpie, her spirit counselor, to her. These days were bursting with glory, and she exulted in the golden warmth, the brown grasses humming in the fresh breezes, and the dome of the cloudless sky. Off to the southwest rose the snowy Big Horn Mountains, but other directions offered prairie and hills dotted with the sacred juniper and stunted jack pine. It was the most beautiful place on earth, a place to think about the First Maker, and his children Sun and Earth.

When she reached the crest she settled into the rustling grass, letting the breeze whip through her hair and eddy into her dress and over her slender body. She needed guidance, and felt something large but as yet undefined just beyond her knowing. She implored Magpie to show her what was there, just beyond. She begged her spirit counselor for the inner eye that would enable her to see past the visible world. Something large, something important and urgent was stirring her, and she desperately sought to know what it was.

She saw the familiar rakish bird fly by, a flash of white and black with iridescent blue tones. Magpie alighted some distance away, danced on one foot and the other, and broke into the sky, raucous and arrogant. Magpie was like Many Quill Woman, harsh and rowdy and not a bit sweet.

"Blessed is my counselor," she said. "You have come to share your wisdom with your daughter."

She felt her power, her destiny, too. She would not be like other Absaroka women, for she would teach herself the ways of war. She might be small and light and fragile, but she would be deadly. She thought at first that she would make war for the People like the great warrior woman Pine Leaf, because the People had lost so many young men to the Siksika and Lakota. Yes, she would learn the ways of war for her tribe and village, but she would learn war for other, mistier reasons as yet unclear.

She stayed an afternoon more, trying to sort out what could not be described in words, and then trotted back to her lodge and sought out her father.

"I wish to have a bow and arrows, and I wish to be taught," she said.

"You?"

"Yes, I have seen it. I must know how to fight."

"If you have seen it, and if you know it is a true vision, we will do it."

"I have seen it."

"You will war for the People, because we have lost so many."

She nodded.

"No woman may touch my bow or arrows or quiver or their war powers will wither. But I will get you a bow. The family of the one who was killed will give you one of his bows and will be pleased with your vision."

"I must tell you there was more to the vision. Yes, I must learn the warrior skills, but it won't always be for the People."

Her father eyed her sharply.

"For another Absaroka village?"

"No."

"For another People?"

"No, for myself and the one who becomes my man."

Her father stared a long while and nodded. "It is a good thing," he said uncertainly.

"Yes. This one will need me," she said.

Chapter 36

At first Skye saw nothing. He was examining the great mountain-girt basin from the top of a noble hill, looking for the Sublette brigade—and signs of danger. Puffball clouds plowed shadows across the giant land while zephyrs made the whole world vibrate and the late summer light shiver.

He knew he did not have keen eyes, or maybe he simply wasn't seeing what experienced trappers saw. During his brief sojourn with Sublette's men, he came to realize they read nature in ways he couldn't fathom. They saw meaning in the flight of birds or the way antelope fled. Silences meant a lot. The sudden cessation of birdsong could mean trouble. The scents on the wind told stories to them that Skye didn't grasp.

He lay in the shivering brown grass studying a panorama so vast he knew he could fathom only this small southwestern corner of it. But what he saw seemed a hunter's and trapper's paradise. Creeks and rivers laced this land. Broad meadows supported buffalo and elk and deer and antelope. Moose browsed the bogs. Willow brush and chokecherry thickets and copses of aspen or cottonwood gave shelter and food, and were the home of the beaver.

He waited patiently to make sense of all he saw as he squinted north and east. At last he spotted movement, small and dark and uncertain. But as he studied the faint motion, it came to him he was seeing a herd of running buffalo, maybe a hundred or so, and they seemed to be coming his way, although the distances made him uncertain. Yes, buffalo, black beasts over a mile distant, and more. Mounted riders among them, drawing alongside one. Sometimes a giant animal would stumble and fall, and the riders would leave it and race after another.

Indian hunters. Blackfeet.

The realization shot terror through him. The stampeding buffalo were heading in his direction, along with the hunters. He watched, mesmerized, not knowing what to do. He was in open country, grassy hills, without cover. Just behind him, his mare and foal stood in plain sight. He had been a fool to come here, throwing caution to the winds.

Sublette wouldn't be here in the heart of the Blackfoot hunting grounds—not yet. Not until the beaver were prime. They had explained it to him. Not until November, when the beaver had grown their winter pelts, were they worth taking. He was alone among hunters and warriors famous for casual butchery of any white man they encountered—sometimes with ritual torture to prolong the agony.

The herd grew closer and larger, and he was amazed by its speed. These big, clumsy beasts could run as fast as the fastest horse. He was trapped. All he could do was slip back below the ridge line along with his horses, and wait events. He retreated until he was out of sight of the herd, and clung tightly to the lead line of his excited mare.

He could hear the thunder of the herd just over the ridge, and once in a while he thought he heard the ululating howls of the hunters. They passed by. The herd had veered up the broad valley rather than boil over his ridge. He felt drained. Sweat soaked his leather tunic. He was not yet out of trouble and could not know whether a horseman would suddenly top the ridge and spot him.

Now Bug's Boys, as the trappers called them, were ahead and behind him, and his life wasn't worth a pence. He could think of nothing to do but wait for dark, which was a long time away. He didn't know which direction to go. He could run into the savages in any direction, at any time. He surveyed his situation, which wasn't bad, actually. He was simply high up the slope of a long grassy hill. Below, a creek ran somewhere. But he saw no cover other than a little scrub juniper. Well, that would have to do. He cautiously led his horses to a likely dark patch covering an acre and waited there. The mare grazed contently, no longer quivering with the sound of a stampede in her alert ears.

In the relative safety of the juniper, calm returned to him. For several months he had been transforming himself into a mountaineer. He had learned steadily, and now he would employ what he knew. He acknowledged he was afraid, and couldn't help the rush of fear every time he thought of the Blackfeet. And yet, the trappers dealt with that same fear day after day. They went about their daily toil with that fear never far from them. How did they do it? Skye marveled at their courage, and hoped to discover within himself the same fatalistic acceptance of danger along with their sharp, tough confidence that they could weather trouble.

He waited for several more hours and then, upon seeing no sign of danger, quietly walked eastward past giant foothills that guarded the towering peaks to the south. He knew from the crude maps drawn by Jedediah Smith and William Sublette that off to the east somewhere, over a high pass, lay the land of the Crow Indians and the Yellowstone River, the greatest tributary of the Missouri. There he might find safety, and maybe even Sublette. It would be the logical place for the brigade to wait for cold weather.

Two uneventful days later he reached what seemed to be the southeast corner of this giant basin, and beheld a sharp notch in the mountains, cut by a small creek. Signs of passage suggested the trail was heavily traveled, which worried him.

He turned into it, followed the creek beneath gloomy gray ramparts of limestone, and eventually topped the pass. At its crest he saw off to the southeast the most majestic mountains he had ever seen, jagged ramparts capped with new snow. He descended a long grassy valley and found himself a few days later on the bank of a large river he believed was the Yellowstone. It curved here, turning from its northward direction to an easterly one.

If he was right, this was Crow country, and while that didn't preclude the arrival of other tribes, including the Blackfeet, he began to feel less fearful. The river flowed at low ebb, and he found he could ride the mare through belly-deep water to a long semiwooded island that would offer him some concealment and protection.

He found a hollow near its eastern end where he could

build a small fire that could not be seen from either bank, and settled down for the night, plagued by mosquitos. He rejoiced to be in Crow country. His thoughts turned to the girl he had renamed Victoria. Suddenly she was present in his mind. He wasn't going to Boston, at least not until next summer, and her image danced before him, slim and fierce and tender. He wondered if he could find her, and if her family would welcome him when the cold set in.

His larder was reduced to cattail roots again, and he spent an hour collecting the miserable food. He kept smelling roasting meat on the wind, and ascribed it to his all-too-familiar hunger, which often excited fantasies of banquets.

"Well, dammit old coon, if you're goin' to come all this way and not jine us, then the devil with ye."

The voice behind Skye raised the hair on his neck. He whirled and peered into the dusk, discovering slope-shouldered Jim Bridger, old Gabe himself.

Skye roared. Bridger howled like a wolf. Trappers materialized out of the gloom and hugged Skye. The mare, picketed on grass nearby, reared back and broke her tether. Someone caught her. Skye fought back tears that welled unbidden.

"Why, old Mister Skye's a daddy, looks like," said one, observing the horse colt.

They escorted Skye to the other end of the island, taking his horses and gear with them. There Skye discovered Sublette and the whole brigade, much to his relief and joy.

And meat. Buffalo roasted over two fires. These mountaineers weren't concealing their presence, and the fires threw light on the far shores.

"He looks poor bull, don't he?" said Beckwourth. "I guess we got to put some tallow on him."

"He's been cavorting with Blackfeet women," said Black Harris. "That'll thin down a coon in a week."

Skye didn't argue. This outfit understood. Eat first and then talk. He ate. Succulent, dripping buffalo meat melted in his mouth. He wolfed down one cut, and another, eating with his fingers, juices running down his jaw and off his fingers. He had his fill and he kept on eating until he couldn't stuff another morsel into his mouth. Two additional quarters of a buffalo cow hung from thick limbs. He would soon tackle another pink, hot, dripping slab of the best meat he had ever tasted. But now he felt satiated, and that was an odd sensation.

They studied his plunder, what little there was of it, his mare and foal, his crudely patched moccasins, his mended tack.

"Hard doin's, eh, Mister Skye?" asked Sublette when Skye paused.

"I got here," Skye said, pride welling in him. "Pretty good for a limey sailor."

"Ye come over that pass?" Bridger asked.

Skye nodded.

"I don't suppose ye saw any Bug's Boys. Just limey luck."

Skye wiped his mouth with his buckskin sleeve. "I saw them but they didn't see me."

"Hull country's swarming with 'em. We come through at night, so damned many of 'em."

Skye nodded. Apparently he had done something even more daring than he realized. At ease for the first time in days, he settled back into a tree trunk and told them his story, beginning with his departure from the rendezvous, his loss of everything to the Blackfeet, the bear that saved him, his indecision and fear and despair when he was lost, his desperate quest for food, his wild moment on the Madison River when he was caught between a village he couldn't identify and raiders who came within a few yards of him.

"Poor doin's. Probably Shoshones, maybe Bannacks," someone volunteered. "Best not to tangle with Bannacks. Miracle you didn't get your ha'r raised."

They questioned him at length, and he asked them about their journey, which had been uneventful until they reached the Three Forks and found Blackfeet everywhere. After that they had slipped over to Crow country, the great bend of the Yellowstone, and had been here a fortnight waiting for the weather to cool, feasting on buffalo.

Sublette raised the question on all their minds. "What are your plans, Mister Skye?"

"To enter your service, sir."

"I thought so. We can use every man we can get. You'll need an outfit. We carry two or three spares; every year someone or other loses his plunder—traps, rifle, flint, and steel. We can outfit you."

"How will all that earn out, sir?"

"Camp tenders earn two hundred a year. Your outfit'll cost about a hundred. That means you'll have a mountain rifle, pound of powder and a horn, lead balls, thirty-two to a pound, half a dozen traps, a good skinning knife, blankets, and some odds and ends including a few yards of flannel."

"You'd make me a camp tender?"

"It's an apprenticeship, Mister Skye. Free trappers earn more, but you'll need to learn some things first. Beavers don't just come to you and offer themselves up. We try to have one camp tender for every two trappers but we're short. You'll skin and dress the pelts, dry 'em out, cook, keep the fires going, and herd the company horses and mules. It's hard work and these old coons'll give you all the grief they can. Next season, or maybe sooner if you're up and the beaver's coming, you can go out and trap and make a good living. You ever shot a rifle?"

"No, sir, except a few times at the rendezvous."

"Not even in the Royal Navy?"

"I wasn't a marine, sir. I was a powder monkey mostly and then a seaman."

"Well, you'll be getting some lessons in the mornin'. You'll learn the whole drill, from keeping your piece clean and dry to making meat. We'll burn a little du Pont. Old Fitzpatrick here, he's gonna turn you into a mountaineer. Let me tell you something, Mister Skye. Learn how to use that rifle. How to load fast and shoot slow and never waste a shot. A red man can pump six or seven arrows at you in the time it takes you to reload. So every shot counts. Believe me, before we're done with the Three Forks, you'll be put to the test."

Chapter 37

When the grass gave out, Sublette took the brigade off the island and into a broad valley of the Yellowstone that was hemmed by majestic mountains.

Skye marveled at its beauty. Never had he seen such a place.

"Up ahead a piece is Colter's Hell," Bridger told him. "With biling springs, hot water that shoots out of the ground, and the smell of sulphur. It's the doorway to

Hades. We all been there and peered in and saw the old horned rascal hi'self grinnin' up at us."

Skye smiled. He was onto old Gabe.

"You don't believe me, eh? Well, we'll go have us a sample." He turned to Beckwourth and Tom Fitzpatrick. "Old Barnaby hyar don't believe in Colter's Hell. I reckon we'd better go show him where a man can get a whiff of sulphur and brimstone."

"Skye, you don't believe in hell? We found it and we'll show it to you," Beckwourth said. "We'll show you where you can roast your pale white hide. This is where Old Bug himself lives."

"It's Mister Skye, mate."

"Well, you'd better tell that to old Satan," said Fitzpatrick. "The devil should address a man proper."

Skye smiled. This had been going on ever since he arrived. For days he had devoured good cow—the mountaineers made sure he knew good cow from poor bull—and sometimes elk or mule deer. For days he had slept warm under two thick blankets spun and carded in England. For days he had learned wilderness arts, fire tending, hide dressing, and how to shoot his heavy, octagonal-barreled rifle.

They had disabused him of various notions, such as that he should stand up to shoot. Instead, they told him to lie down or get behind a tree or log or rock, and make no target at all. He should steady the barrel on anything solid and squeeze the trigger sweet and true. They didn't have much powder or lead to spare, but a man who could shoot true could make the difference in a scrape, so they instructed him anyway. They taught him how to load fast, even how to load without measuring powder in an emergency; how to drive a patched ball home with the hickory rod clipped under the barrel, how to pour a little powder in the pan, how to scrape out damp powder after a rain because if he didn't he wouldn't be armed.

He progressed from clumsiness to some skill, occasionally hitting a distant target, and they pronounced themselves satisfied that he could make meat or send a few red devils to the spirit world. He wondered about that. He had fired cannon in war, and brawled in bloody mayhem, but coolly aiming at and killing a mortal bothered him.

Skye, Bridger, Fitzpatrick, and Beckwourth set off on horseback that golden October noon for the gates of hell, and told Sublette they'd be back the next day. Skye kept his counsel, expecting that all this was an elaborate prank on a pork-eater. But it would be fun, and he'd had little enough fun in his constricted life. They rode south along the Yellowstone, scaring up flocks of Canada geese and ducks and alarming a few snorty cow moose and calves.

Beckwourth was at his gaudiest—to impress the ladies certain to be dipping their toes in the boiling waters, he said—with elaborately quilled buckskins he had talked some Crow maidens—or matrons—into making for him. The fringes of both his tunic and leggins were extra long. He wore a great floppy felt hat that concealed his dusky face, and his untrammeled dark hair stretched far down his back, making him rakish. The man had style, Skye thought, and never more so than in his bawdy recollections of nearly the entire distaff side of the Crow Nation.

"Why," Beckwourth was saying, "I was so smitten by Bad Bear's buxom virgin daughter Raccoon, the Teton Queen I called her in honor of her assets, that I went to the chief and made him a proposition. 'Ol' Bear,' sez I, 'I want

Raccoon for my very own, and in return I'll be in your service, come war and come peace.' Well, Bear, he smiles, and sez he'd be honored, and he sent Raccoon over and I indoctrinated her in all the arts of amour for a fortnight, spending a pleasant January last winter. My reputation grew—deservedly of course—and next thing I knew, Bear's wife and three other daughters came into my lodge for their own initiation, and that's how I spent a pleasant February except that I was plumb exhausted and out of sorts by March."

Well, they were all marvelous liars: Beckwourth, that son of a white man and slave woman, most of all, and if that was what wilderness did, Skye supposed he would turn into a gaudy liar himself.

Bridger was steering them toward a conical peak to the southeast, and then into its foothills. Skye couldn't imagine a less likely place for brimstone and sulphur, and waited patiently to see how this great prank would end.

"We're getting close now, Skye. You can smell the sulphur. Wherever Bug is, there's the smell of burning sulphur," said Fitzpatrick. "This is just a sample, sort of an outlier. Hell's real front gate's another fifty miles south of here up on a steaming plateau where boiling water erupts and sulphur stinks up the air. I've seen old Bug hisself, and so has Bridger, but Beckwourth's so saintly Bug leaves him alone."

They were progressing up a bleak gulch with a small creek in it. The creek steamed in the crisp October air, which puzzled Skye. His husky colt poked a nose into the water and jerked back. They finally arrived at a place where water boiled out of a steep hillside and into pools, one below the next. Steam billowed into the chill air, and Skye realized the water actually was hot.

"Well, ha'r we are. I'll go pay Bug the admission," Bridger said, vanishing into brush. The rest were picketing their horses on the grassy slope and peeling off their duds. Skye watched, uncertain, wary of a prank. They'd get him down to the buff and then ride off. Yes, that was it. The whole elaborate business would teach him a lesson.

"Couldn't find the Divil," said Bridger. "Guess we go in for free this time." He began tugging on his moccasins. "I left him a message that ol' Skye was hyar, sampling the Divil's wares."

Next thing Skye knew, his comrades were poking toes into the pools, sampling them for heat, and then lowering themselves into the water with many a happy sigh. Where was the prank?

"Well, Skye?" Fitzpatrick, in waist-high water, addressed him. "Are you a shy fellow?"

"It's Mister Skye, mate."

"Well, this pool will boil off your cooties, and the next one up will boil you. Go down two pools and you can sit for an hour without getting lobstered."

Skye needed no more invitation. He dropped his grimy duds, stepped into the pool, and found himself immersed in just-bearable heat, which swiftly opened every pore and swept away every ache. He celebrated. Rarely in his brief life had he experienced a hot bath. He marveled at the water and wondered where it came from and what subterranean fires heated it. The water exuded a certain mineral odor, and Skye sensed that it had leached chemicals out of the bowels of the earth somewhere under this hot-bellied mountain. This was probably volcanic country.

That evening, they feasted on cow elk after Skye had collected wood and built a small fire for them.

"Actually, Skye," said Beckwourth, "we was elected to bring you hyar. The vote was unanimous."

Skye waited.

"You got the smelliest feet in Creation, and we was commanded to bring you here to clean your toes so you didn't foul up the whole camp."

Skye hardly knew what to say.

Bridger hiccuped and snickered.

Skye got the drift. "It's Mister Skye, gents. When you introduce me to the Devil, remember it."

"Bug wouldn't let 'im into hell, not with them feet," said Bridger.

They were making him one of them, but not without some initiation rites. Skye sensed how he stood with them. From their standpoint, he was an odd duck who talked with an accent and used sailor words and harbored a vision of going back to the civilized east. But he knew he had done something they admired, something that might have sunk even the most experienced of them. He had survived two encounters with the Blackfeet, picked up a horse and food and gear along the way, and somehow made it to the brigade through a wilderness he didn't know. They were going to put him through some more of this, but all the while they were teaching him everything they knew about staying alive in a land without roofs and constables and butchers and bakers. Skye glowed within. These were friends as well as mentors.

Leisurely they rode back to Sublette's encampment. The aspens had bloomed yellow and withered to nakedness, but the cottonwoods were just reaching a burnished gold radiance, somehow joyous and sad. The air had changed, and each breeze carried tiny knives in it. In camp, the pace quickened. Skye found himself jerking

meat, packing "Indian butter," which he learned was the
soft tallow that accumulated along the back of the buffalo—a delicacy that mountaineers as well as the tribes
cherished and ate raw. It preserved well, and Skye filled
leather sacks with it.

They trapped a few beaver just to have a look at the
pelts, and pronounced them not yet prime but getting there
fast. Skye learned to roast beaver tail and to flesh each
pelt and dry it on a willow hoop. Sublette kept him busy
but he still found moments he could call his own, and
these he used to master the arts of war as it was fought
here.

They showed him an Indian-made bullhide shield so
tough it could deflect arrows and even a rifle ball that hit
it askance. They taught him to throw a knife and a hatchet,
and he, in turn, showed them the sailor's weapon, the belaying pin with its flared cusp that protected the hand from
lance and knife. He surprised them in several mock fights,
deftly deflecting a wooden mock knife and a mock lance
fashioned from a stick, and thumping his adversaries in
the ribs, or neck, or knees, which set them to howling. He
knew little about shooting arrows or bullets, but when it
came to close quarters, he won their respect in a hurry.

"That Royal Navy's tougher'n I thought," said Fitzpatrick. "It can fight with a damned stick."

"It fights with cannon and mortar and sword mostly,
mate. But the seamen brawl with a marlinspike or
cutlass, and they're handy if we're about to be boarded.
Mostly the lads just pound on each other. Those sticks are
everywhere on deck; the rigging's wrapped around them.
All those lines off the masts end up wrapped over belaying pins."

They weren't grasping much of that, but they were

learning fast how to fight with a hardwood stick that protected the hand that held it.

Then one day the wind shifted and blew a cold gale that kept them from cooking because they couldn't keep a fire under anything. That night the temperatures dropped and it snowed sleety wet flakes. Skye hadn't thought much about winter camping, but now he did. He shivered under his blankets through a brutal night, wondering how he would survive that sort of ferocity. By morning he was numb and discouraged, soaked with snow, and colder than he had ever been.

The mountaineers joked about it, but he knew he'd die of the catarrh if he was subjected to much of it. Then he listened closer. They weren't really joking. They had a way of making their misery light by ridiculing it.

"Two months of hard cold work," said Beckwourth, "and after that, paradise."

"He's talking about them lustful and willing Crow women," Blanket Jim Bridger explained. "And them warm lodges with a hot little fire right in the middle, and thick buffler robes to lie in. Beats a dugout or tent or brush hut any time."

Sublette gathered them around the breakfast fire. "We'll head for the Three Forks," he said. "Beaver's prime now, and maybe Bug's Boys'll be in their lodges. But keep your powder dry. Pull those loads; I want fresh powder under every lock."

The lark was over.

Chapter 38

Cold was the enemy. It numbed and shocked Skye. He had been cold many times at sea, in unheated seamen's quarters, fighting North Atlantic gales, soaked with icy seawater. But on a ship there was usually refuge. In the wilderness refuges were few and took a long time to build.

November had barely started and yet it snowed daily, sharp blizzards that drove ice down a man's spine and numbed his fingers. He wondered how the trappers functioned at all, standing in icy creeks while they set their traps, going out each day to toil in bone-chilling cold, their hands too numb to set a trap or hold a rifle or pull a trigger.

Skye's leather shirt didn't serve him in this weather, and he yearned for the pea jacket and woolen skull cap he had traded long before. A few trappers had buffalo coats to warm them. The Creoles had blanket capotes, practical hooded affairs sewn from a trade blanket Skye knew he would need such gear fast or go under, so he ransomed his future to buy an old blanket capote from Broussard, a giant Canadian, and good gloves from Adams, one of the free trappers. Not even that was enough, because his feet froze. Many of the men had woolen or fur leggins, and so Skye bargained for a pair of these as well, and then rabbit-fur liners for his moccasins. By the time he was properly outfitted, he owed seventy dollars on top of his two debts to the company—one for the equipment he drew at the rendezvous, and the other for the outfit provided him by Sublette. Next summer, when debts and wages were squared, he would still be in the hole.

If this was November in the northern mountains, he wondered what January would be like. But by then the brigade would be holed up in Crow lodges, awaiting the return of spring and the second bout of trapping. His days were filled with hard work, which never ceased, although some brief interludes of warm weather made life easier. Sublette had led them over the pass into the Three Forks basin, and had set up camp close to the pass—an avenue of escape if they ran into Bug's Boys. This was Gallatin River country, and beaver flourished on every tributary, offering Sublette an incredible harvest.

Sublette made Skye the camp tender for Bridger and Fitzpatrick, and thereafter Skye was responsible for the horses of both men as well as his own, plus cooking, shelter, fire, and fleshing and drying the pelts. Skye felt lucky to work for two of the wiliest veterans in the mountains. He cut deadwood and kept fires going, fleshed and dried the thick pelts on willow hoops. He tended the horses, keeping an eye on them night and day, keeping them picketed and hobbled and on good grass. Once, when the snow rose higher than they could paw through, Bridger showed him something: he cut green cottonwood limbs and let the horses gnaw on the soft bark.

"They'll make a living on it," Bridger said. "We call it mountain hay. Had me two plugs that got so fat on it I had ta prop up their bellies on a cart."

Skye laughed. Old Gabe Bridger could never impart information without putting a twist on it.

Skye suspected his own mare was pregnant, which suited him fine. In his spare moments he haltered his rambunctious horse colt and began training it to lead and carry a small load. Occasionally he was given some free time, and then he hunted buffalo, which were plentiful in that vast basin. Bridger showed him how to creep in on them from downwind, and kill one with a single shot aimed just behind the forelegs. Thus did he contribute juicy humpmeat, tongue, and flank steaks to the brigade's cook pots. He also accumulated a few winter-thick hides, which he learned to stake to the ground and flesh and then soften and brain-tan into robes. He intended to sell them or trade them—anything to get out of debt and go east next summer.

It took days of miserable toil to flesh a buffalohide, and days more to rub brains into it and then soften it. But now he slept comfortably with good robes above and below him. He had a product the free trappers wanted and they bought his robes on tick. Skye discovered that a few buffalo robes draped over a framework of limbs could shelter storm-harassed trappers. And he turned one damaged robe into a wooly greatcoat, patiently lacing the parts together with thong.

Then, in December, the days turned warm again, even though the sun vanished in midafternoon. The weather amazed Skye. Just when he thought this country would be brutal it turned as mild as early autumn, and the whole brigade pulled off layers of clothing and stretched in the balmy air.

But William Sublette wasn't pleased. He called them together and issued a stern warning. "Bug's Boys'll roam for a week or two. I want the horses in camp every night. The camp tenders'll build a brush corral. I want the trappers to go out in parties of four, two armed and watching while the other two work. Maybe that'll bring less beaver, but it'll save lives. No man leaves camp alone, and no man goes unarmed."

Skye listened soberly. His buffalo-hunting forays were

at an end for the moment and his work redoubled with all the extra horse handling. That's how it went for a while until the day they found Polite Robiseau dead and scalped. He had left his colleagues a moment to use the bushes— and that was how they found him an hour later, his leggins down, his skullbone bare in the weak winter sun, an arrow protruding from his back.

His Creole trapping friends brought him to camp over the back of a horse, and they buried him under a cutbank because the ground remained frozen. No one said much of anything. The mountaineers' silence howled louder than words. His partners quietly divided his traps and gear, their faces inscrutable behind their thick beards, their eyes leaking grief.

But as soon as that was completed, Sublette and his veteran trappers wordlessly saddled their shaggy-haired horses, armed themselves, and rode out. Skye wasn't surprised. This platoon would strike back and hard if it could. He watched Bridger, Fitzpatrick, and the rest ride away, their heavy rifles in their laps, held in mittened hands. If it was war, they would take war to the Blackfeet.

In camp, Skye and the other tenders raised log and dirt and rock breastworks while they waited, and cleared away nearby brush that might conceal a warrior. No one spoke. The eight camp tenders had no leader, but every one of them was aware that menace lurked just beyond, perhaps in the pine forests, or high on the ridges. The Blackfeet were famous for their audacity. They were bold, daring, courageous, and skilled at surprise. Skye had heard plenty about them even in his short time with the brigade.

Skye eyed the camp tenders dourly. Four were Creole boys—Bouleau, Lapointe, Le Clerc, and Baptiste— perhaps fourteen or fifteen, new to the wilds. Then there was Scott, a sandy-haired ne'er-do-well, lazy and sullen, a runaway. He sat with his rifle in hand, doing little. Louis Pombert was an experienced Creole mountaineer who simply preferred camp duties, a good man who was building a log breastwork that would defend one flank. And also Manuel Estevan, a Mexican, good with horses, swiftly herding the animals into the camp and picketing them.

Skye did what he could, arranging the bales of beaver as a breastwork and adding saddles and gear—anything that would protect a man from an arrow. He'd been in battle, but he sensed the others hadn't. They toiled through the midmorning and then waited in a stretching silence for Sublette's force to return. The sight of the scalped Robiseau was heavy on his mind, the yellow skull bone and sliced flesh shocking to see.

The low December sun briefly topped the ridges and warmed the camp for a spell, making Skye sleepy. It seemed preternaturally quiet. A crow catapulted into the air and flapped away swiftly, electrifying Skye.

"They're on us, mates," he said. "Over there." He pointed across an innocuous expanse of snow-patched meadow.

"Who says?" asked Scott.

Skye didn't reply. He crept into the stronghold made of logs and beaver pelts and laid the heavy black barrel of his mountain rifle across it.

The Blackfeet came silently and in a rush, all on foot, about six or seven.

"Hey!" yelled Scott, diving for cover. Skye glanced at the fellow, who lay flat on the ground behind a log, his rifle useless unless he overcame his terror.

The rest of the men positioned themselves, rifles ready.

"Watch our backs," Skye yelled to Pombert. They were protected by a wide creek, but not much.

The first arrows struck from the rear, thudding close. Skye whirled. The ones out on the meadow were feinting; the main body of the Blackfeet lurked in the woods across the creek, well protected by trunk and limb and log. Still, any Blackfoot firing an arrow had to rise, aim, draw the bow, and shoot. There would be targets. Two arrows seared close, thudding into the pelts with sickening force that made Skye wince. He heard a rifle boom and saw a puff of smoke. Pombert, experienced mountaineer, was showing mettle.

Skye sighted down the barrel at a shadowy place he knew concealed a savage, and waited. A moment later he saw a flash of movement; the warrior rose and loosed an arrow. Skye caught him in his buckhorn sight and squeezed. Flint hit frizzen, the rifle whoomed, driving the butt into his shoulder. The Blackfoot cried and collapsed.

Skye ducked, poured powder, patched a ball, and jammed it home, and then poured powder into the pan and cocked his weapon, his heart wild in his chest. Around him he heard more booms, and more howls from the naked woods beyond the creek. The feinting warriors regrouped and howled from their side. Skye whirled. Someone had to keep them at bay or the camp would be overrun. They made a small target a hundred yards away, but Skye wanted to keep them far away. He settled his rifle on a bale of plews, picking a shadowy distant form, taking his time. An arrow thumped into the furs just beside him. He swallowed.

His shot sent another Blackfoot tumbling, and immediately the rest of the ones out on the meadow drew back. Skye found himself sweating, even in the December air.

Sourly he measured a charge and poured it down the muzzle, drove a ball after it, picked at the fire-hole which had been fouled, and looked for another target. He heard five shots explode like firecrackers, and knew that the ones in the woods were rushing the camp and that at least five of seven rifles were empty. He whirled again, finding a dozen of the devils at the creek and more pouring up to it. Pombert shot a Blackfoot, but that didn't slow their wading through the icy creek. Skye waited a moment more, until the first reached midstream, and then he shot. The warrior dropped into the river and stained it red. The Blackfeet around him howled but didn't stop. Scott burrowed deeper behind his log. Enraged, Skye dashed over there, grabbed the loaded rifle, and shot a warrior who was running into camp with hatchet raised.

"Fight!" roared Skye.

Scott whined.

A horse took an arrow, screeched and bucked. Blood gouted from a wound in its ribs.

A volley from the Creole boys slowed the charge through the creek, but it was too late.

Chapter 39

Blackfeet were everywhere. Most of them went for the horses, which were hobbled and picketed.

Three came at Skye. He dropped his empty rifle, picked up his belaying pin, and bulled straight at them. He knew what to do at close quarters. Murderously he whacked aside a lance, smacked the forearm of a man drawing a bow, jabbed at another lunging at him with a tomahawk. Skye whirled, braining a warrior behind him. Something seared his arm, shooting wild pain into his skull.

He spun and dodged, never a static target, inflicting mayhem with his hickory club. He saw Pombert fighting for his life, swinging his rifle against a big warrior armed with a lance. Skye ran to Pombert's help, with his own assailants hot on his heels. He jammed his belaying pin into the giant warrior, toppling him, and spun to face his assailants again. But others were swarming in from the meadow and the creek. It would be over soon.

He heard a volley. A warrior staggered. Others howled, clasped flesh wounds. Then Skye got caught up in the infighting again. A knife sliced his ribs. Another volley, and the Blackfeet suddenly retreated, gathering their dead and wounded. Sublette and his veteran mountaineers rushed into camp and out the other side, chasing the Blackfeet into the creek. The mountaineers urged their horses through the creek and kept after the retreating Blackfeet. Skye heard howls and shots from the woods, but the wall of timber concealed those events from him. He was bleeding from half a dozen places that stung wickedly.

Scott stood up and grinned, unscathed.

Pombert was all right. The Creole boys forted up behind packsaddles and supplies were alive but several leaked blood. Skye armed his rifle, then pulled off his bloody leather shirt and began stanching blood with a rag. He had no bandaging. Vicious hurts tortured him.

"Monsieur Skye, let me do dat," said Pombert. The veteran Creole swiftly cleaned and bandaged Skye's arm and then washed Skye's rib and shoulder wounds. "I will sew dis," he said. "You hold rag tight."

Pombert deftly threaded a needle from his kit and sewed Skye's rib wound together while Skye groaned at every prick. His side sheeted red, but the bleeding stopped when Pombert finished up. Skye's pulse slowly settled back to normal but he felt sick and feverish. He could barely breathe. One stocky young Blackfoot lay dead nearby, a hole in his bare brown chest, his sightless eyes malevolent. Skye had shot that one with Scott's rifle. The raiders had taken their wounded with them but Skye thought they had lost two dead and four or five injured, some of them gravely. That was a heavy loss for so small a party.

Scott loaded his rifle and grinned, as if to celebrate a victory. Skye stared blankly at the man and said nothing. Scott had been useless, and Skye made note of it without condemning. Some seamen in the Royal Navy ran rather than fought when it came to close-quarters fighting. Skye felt no moral outrage, only a sense that Scott would not be a man to partner with when it came to trapping.

Sublette's riders drifted back one by one. They splashed across the creek into camp and noted Skye lying shirtless in the cold with red-stained bandaging wrapped around his middle and his arm. Sublette dismounted and came to Skye.

"You all right old coon?"

"I will be."

"Anyone else hurt?"

"Go ask them. Pombert is all right."

"They steal any horses?"

"I don't know. Some of those devils went for the horses, but they were hobbled and picketed. Couldn't be stampeded."

"We'll count. I don't think we lost any, except the one

that took an arrow. I saw your mare and the colt. They're fine."

"Good. What happened in the woods?"

"We chased 'em hard. They headed for the pass and we chased 'em up a way until they set up a defense up there. We know you did some damage. They were carrying three, four wounded, dead—who knows?"

"You got here just in time. Two minutes more and we'd have gone under."

"I heard different, Skye. You were licking 'em."

"It's Mister Skye, sir."

"Yes, it's *Mister* Skye, old coon. And it'll never be anything else as long as free trappers are in the mountains."

Sublette patted Skye's shoulder and hastened to discover what else was amiss in camp. Skye heard him talking to Pombert, Estevan, and the Creole youths, and then drifted into oblivion. Sublette helped him to shelter and threw a thick buffalo robe over him, which he welcomed.

He woke at dawn to fever, his forehead burning even as his limbs froze. He felt weak as a newborn and wondered how he would manage his camp duties. But he didn't have to, At first light Sublette was hunched over him. "You rest, Mister Skye. We're moving tomorrow."

"I could use it, mate. Pretty sick."

Sublette nodded and Skye burrowed deeper into his robe. But then Bridger was squatting beside him. "You'll be fine, old coon. Meat doesn't spile in the mountains."

Skye hurt too much to laugh.

"I mind the time when I had an arrer in my arm, and I got Greenwood to pull her out. He had to dig out the point. It didn't infect because we were over six thousand feet. Below six thousand, everything mortifies."

"We're below that here."

Gabe Bridger whooped, stood, and vanished, only to be replaced by Fitzpatrick, who was running his hands over the belaying pin.

"Your club's ruined," Tom said. "Lookit this."

Skye squinted at the pin. Several deep gashes marred the hickory. A hatchet had chipped out a piece.

"That's probably how it was when I jumped ship."

"No, it was plumb virgin until now. I'd never seen one and I looked it over back at rendezvous. These scars were made today. When you're up, I want a lesson with it."

"Nothing to learn. They come at you, you hit and thrust and deflect. I didn't do it well or I'd not be sewed together now."

Fitzpatrick grunted, patted Skye on the shoulder, and wandered off.

Skye healed swiftly. Even the next day, when Sublette moved camp twelve miles to the Gallatin River, Skye managed to load his gear and ride. But no one would let him work. The camp tenders refused to let him build a fire, collect wood, cook, or butcher the buffalo that Bridger shot along the way.

Things changed subtly. They didn't forget to call him mister anymore. They were deferential, which bothered him. He had done nothing more than fight for his life in a tight corner, but now they were acting as if he'd won a war. And now they simply ignored the surly Scott, plunging the youth into deep isolation. Scott wasn't much, but a trapping outfit needed every man, and this outfit needed Scott to help keep camp. The young man exuded anger, envy, and a lot of other things Skye could only guess at, and spent a lot of time out of camp by himself. No one said a word about him, but every man in camp was monitoring Scott.

Beaver were plentiful, and for a few days the trappers brought back all they could carry. Then the weather changed. The wind rotated north, bringing gloomy overcast with it, and the temperature plummeted. Gray ice formed along the banks of the creeks. Skye dreaded and hated mountain winter. He could barely sleep at night, with every breath freezing in his beard and his body numb even under blankets and buffalo robes. As soon as he was able, he began building a real shelter, walling off an undercut rock cliff and laying up a rock fireplace that would resist the wind and throw heat into his refuge. Some of the veterans laughed at him and said they'd be moving about the time he finished—but they were the first to settle against the fire-warmed rock of the cliff when their daily toil was over.

At least it didn't snow much, though an inch or two fell now and then, and the horses had to paw down to grass more and more. No Blackfeet showed up but Sublette never let down his guard. This was their prized hunting ground; they would be back in force to revenge themselves for their wounds and deaths and dishonor. Bug's Boys never gave up. The free trappers went out in fours each day, armed and ready, but the deceptive quiet continued deep into the short days of December when the wan sun came late and fled in the middle of the afternoon, plunging the river canyon into a cold blue gloom.

Skye ate more beaver tail in those weeks than he wanted, and wished for some good buffalo hump. But the free trappers had turned industrious. This was the prime season, and from well before dawn to deep into the long nights they devoted themselves to trapping. They baited their traps with castoreum, the musk that drew beavers to the jaws of the traps, staked them in the icy water of half-frozen creeks, ran their trap lines, pulled beaver after beaver out of their ponds, and staggered back to camp with a heavy load of dead animals, too tired to say a word. Skye tried to keep up, to flesh each day's take and dry the pelts on willow hoops, but the hides froze and never did clean properly. He sensed that when the next warm spell and sunlight came, he would have to dress a lot of pelts over again.

All this was hard, dull, numbing work that lowered spirits and set men to dreaming of a hearth and comfort. Tom Fitzpatrick spent a week jabbering about bread. All he wanted was a taste of fresh, hot, yeasty bread. The Creoles dreamed of cognac or beer or women. Arthur Black wept for a lost love in St. Louis. Skye didn't dream of anything. He toiled through the wintry days, fought cold, suffered every time the wind blew or snow fell, and kept quiet. Somehow, next summer, he would go to the eastern seaboard. No sane man would stay in these empty, lonely, miserable mountains if he could escape.

One day Scott disappeared. Sublette and a strong party followed his tracks for several miles and found him near the pass, heading for the Crow villages, carrying a pack with some company sugar and the last of the coffee in it. Sublette brought him back and confiscated the sugar and coffee, which they were saving for Christmas. They would not have another sip of coffee until rendezvous—if then.

"I should have let him go," Sublette said to Skye. "He wasn't pulling his weight here, and we don't need him."

But Skye sensed that Sublette's anger cut much deeper, and that Josiah Scott's future in the brigade would not be pleasant.

In the middle of December, the gloomiest time in the mountains, Beckwourth began to talk about the famously available Crow women. He didn't boast. He simply raised the topic, mornings and evenings.

"Ah, Marse Sublette, think on it. Warm bufflerhide lodges, thick buffler robes, soft sleeping pads, hot little fires with hot little ladies, stewpots fulla buffler, full bellies, jokes you wouldn't hear no tight-lipped white woman tell. Ah, Marse William, it be time to make it over the pass before we're snowed in hyar. What a pity it'd be if the pass got snowed up and all your faithful old coons, excepting myself of course, took to blamin' you for their dire misfortunes."

Sublette smiled. "We're making the beaver come," he said.

And then it stormed.

Chapter 40

William Sublette knew he had tarried too long in the Three Forks country and would probably pay a price. The beaver pelts were piling up and he had stayed on, hoping to beat the weather. But now the weather was beating him.

Dan Ferguson and Peter Ranne hadn't returned. Their traplines were the farthest away, and the blizzard caught them. They were probably holed up safely enough, but Sublette didn't know, and when you don't know, you find out. But right now, the snow was deluging down, so furious and thick a man couldn't see much or walk a hundred yards without getting lost. He had no choice except to wait.

Sublette tried to remember what Ferguson and Ranne took with them, whether they had enough gear to hole up safely, build a shelter, climb into their buffalo robes, and wait it out. At least it wasn't brutally cold. That would come when the clouds cleared away. The trappers would have beaver tail for food—if they could build and keep a fire in such a swirl of snow. Both men were veterans of the mountains, and he shouldn't worry.

But he did. He was responsible for them, and every man in the brigade knew that he would employ the entire resources of the brigade to help any of them in trouble. From time to time they eyed him, waiting to see how far Smith, Jackson, and Sublette would go for its free trappers. He would show them, not to prove something but because every mountaineer owed that to every other mountaineer. That was the unwritten law of survival.

He stared irritably at the swirling snow. A foot and a half lay on the ground, enough to make travel hard work for man and horse. He was angry with himself. He knew he should have crossed the pass and holed up with the Crows long since. But the beaver harvest had been incredible, riches piling up each day, plew after plew out of streams that had never been trapped. He had thirty-two packs, and each pack was worth about three hundred when delivered to General Ashley at the rendezvous. Almost ten thousand dollars against the company's sixteen thousand debt.

He should have pulled out. They could be snug and happy in a Crow village by now, whiling away the days when the rivers and creeks were frozen over and the beavers were snug in their lodges. This storm would seal the pass over to the Yellowstone country, and it was unlikely they could get to the Crow villages until spring. The brigade faced a grim, cold stretch trying to survive in huts.

He heard the sound of an ax, and knew Skye was out cutting green cottonwood limbs for the horses to gnaw on. They could no longer paw through to grass, and the soft underbark was the alternative. Cottonwoods were the trappers' hay. But it took constant effort to feed fifty horses with cottonwood.

Skye worked at it constantly without being asked. He took care of his mare and horse colt, but he didn't stop cutting until the whole herd could gnaw at the lifesaving bark. Some sort of demon drove him. When the rest of the brigade was hunched around the fires, gabbing, playing euchre with ancient decks, that ol' coon Skye was out doing the work of three. He'd make a finer mountaineer—if he stayed in the mountains. Sublette squinted through the swirl at the distant man, doubting that the Englishman would. They would see the last of him at rendezvous.

He turned to Bouleau and Scott. "Go help Skye," he said.

"It won't do any good," said Scott. "We should wait until after the storm when we can work easier."

"You heard me."

Sullenly, Scott gathered an ax and followed the Creole out to the cottonwood groves. Sublette watched him go, his belly roiling. His brigade would never again include Scott. He had dealt with all sorts of men, including escaped criminals and loners and men ditching wives, and they had mostly turned themselves into mountaineers and trappers. But Scott was a shoddier sort of man, evading work, dodging responsibility—and a coward. He had heard all about Scott's conduct during the set-to with the Blackfeet. Skye hadn't said a word, but the rest of the camp tenders did.

Some of the Creoles materialized out of the white whirl, dragging firewood. He had put all the Creole camp tenders on that task, and warned them not to get out of sight. The whirling snow veiled the camp even at fifty yards, and filled footprints in minutes. There were plenty of things to worry about, such as running out of meat. Buffalo were plentiful around Three Forks, but getting to them in deep snows or blizzard conditions was another matter. It fell upon his shoulders to feed thirty men. Usually beaver tail sufficed. The trappers brought back the meaty, muscular tail of every beaver they trapped. But when they couldn't trap—such as now—starvin' times crept up fast.

"You worryin' again?" asked Beckwourth. "No good in it. After this blow is over, I'll just wade over and rescue them pork-eaters."

It was braggadocio. Jim Beckwourth knew perfectly well what it would take to reach the missing men.

"All right. I'll send you alone," Sublette retorted. "Your prowess is all you need. You have eyes that see through whiteouts, legs that never falter in drifts—"

"And a way with women that never fails," Beckwourth said.

"What's that got to do—"

But Beckwourth was laughing softly.

The cloud cover cleared off about dusk, revealing a fat moon that lit the snow-bleached land. The temperature was dropping fast and the horses' muzzles were rimed with frost. Sublette made his decision right then.

He found his veteran trappers crowded into one of the shelters.

"Let's go," he said.

They nodded. No one needed an explanation. They began bundling up, pulling on spare gloves, donning thick leggins they tied over their moccasins, pushing homemade beaver hats down over their long hair. Fitzpatrick cut kindling with his hatchet, until he had a bundle of it—enough for a brief fire, enough to start over if snow should douse a blaze.

His trappers and mountaineers would go with Sublette, twenty in all. And each would lead two horses. If that veteran outfit didn't find Ranne and Ferguson, the pair couldn't be found. The trappers loaded packs onto some hairy horses; other horses carried nothing for the time being and would be used to break trail through soft, treacherous, hock-high snow and even higher drifts. Skye dragged a fresh cottonwood limb to the herd and paused, watching the veterans load up.

"Mister Skye, I'm putting you in charge here. We're going after 'em. Don't know how long."

"Yes, sir. I hope you bring back good news."

The night glowed white. Overhead, stars pricked a jet sky, cold and distant. Sublette judged that they had five hours of moonlight and then would have to hole up until dawn, which would come late this time of year, days from the winter solstice.

He turned to Gabe. "You know what creeks?"

"Not exactly, but them coons were beyond us, and we were beyond the rest—up the Gallatin."

"All right. We'll rotate the lead. About a hundred yards for each man and horse, and then go to the rear."

They stumbled resolutely through the snow for hours, breaking trail, resting briefly, plunging through drifts, dropping into hollows unknown and unseen beneath the thick blanket. The moon quit them at a place without shelter, so they huddled in their robes, numb with cold and surrounded by blackness. Sublette knew his cheeks and ears and nose would be frostbitten, but there was no help for it. The night was thick and black and bitter, bad enough to make a man wonder why he had come to the mountains. But after a moment he knew why: not to get rich, but to test himself. He had seen something evolve in all his mountaineer friends—those who survived. It wasn't just confidence or resourcefulness, but something else. It was—how could he phrase it?—a fullness of manhood. The mountains spawned a race of giants.

The horses crowded close to each other for warmth, disconsolate under their loads, occasionally coughing. They were in good shape, largely because Skye had wanted them to be. Now and then a man stood, stretched, made his limbs work, cursed softly, groaned, and slouched into his robes again, pummeled by bone-chilling cold so bad that every slight eddy of air was a torment.

Long before dawn, they were off again, using the smallest hint of the coming day to navigate through the Gallatin River flats. When the sun did burst over the mountain ridges, the snow blinded them, and they squinted against the murderous brightness and pulled their hats low. In minutes his eyelids hurt, and every muscle around his eyes ached. The frost-covered horses walked wearily now, having gone long without food and water. Horses drank more water in the winter than in the summer, and wouldn't eat snow to allay their thirst. The Gallatin River had largely frozen over in the night.

The mountaineers let their horses drink at an open tributary creek and then dismounted and broke trail again.

"Are we close?" Sublette asked Bridger.

"This child don't think so. We got a piece to go."

"I've a mind to make camp, rest the horses for an hour, try to get something hot in us."

Bridger nodded and led them to a good spot, largely free of snow, where a fire could be built against a cliff that would throw the heat back at them. They cooked frozen beaver tail, fed the horses some cottonwood, warmed themselves, and then started out, knowing they could go only two more hours until darkness settled again. But the moon was already up, so they could continue deep into the night.

About dusk Bridger consulted with Fitzpatrick, and reported to Sublette. "This hyar's our creek. Ferguson and Ranne're over in the next drainage. But beyond hyar, I don't know."

"We're close, then. They'll be holed up around here."

They broke trail through unknown country that rose steadily. The horses had to be pulled and tugged now. Sublette's face ached, and he knew his fingers, cheeks, nose, and toes would be frostbitten a second time. Around him men cursed, slapped the offended flesh to drive life into it, and continued. They came to a large creek tending west, and decided that was the turnoff.

Sublette pulled his Hawken from its soft leather sheath, checked the priming, and fired into the quiet night. The roar shocked his ears. He reloaded, having trouble making his fingers work. They waited. No answering shot drifted to them. He tried again, and only silence replied.

"We'll go up this creek and fire every little while," Sublette said. The creek ran through woods, and the party stumbled over hidden logs and fought spidery branches the moonlight didn't reveal to them.

Then they heard the wolves, howling mournfully into

the night, back and forth, one bunch to the south, another
to the north. Sublette had the itch to murder the first one
he spotted. They were nature's killing machines. Half of
his men wore wolfhide hoods or hats because of the warm
fur, and that was the only use for a wolf as far as he was
concerned.

They fought their way up the drainage another two
miles before the moon quit them, and made camp in an
elk yard cleaned of snow. That night they built a bonfire
and warmed themselves half at a time, frontside and back-
side. But no one slept. No one had answered their periodic shots, and in that fire-breached darkness each was
wondering how Ferguson and Ranne went under.

Chapter 41

The rescue party did not return. Two bitter days rose
and fell without news. The sun barely crawled above
the nearby mountains and then plummeted into another endless December night.

Skye scanned the trails restlessly, his eyes watering and
hurting from the blinding light of the snow, but saw nothing. A vast silence permeated the mountains. He longed
for the call of a bird.

All the firewood and green cottonwood was exhausted,
and the camp itself was in peril. Meat was running low;
they needed a couple of buffalo and fast. Skye studied
the country farther down the tributary creek they were
on, tiring himself as he pushed through thick ridges of
snow. He came to a like place with plenty of cottonwood,

a little grass swept clean by wind, and open water. He would move there even if it was windier than the present camp.

When he came back he gathered the reluctant camp tenders, who hated being exposed to bitter cold, and told them they would move camp that day.

"Four or five hundred yards downriver. Not too hard, mates. Horses'll tramp a path for us. There's plenty of wood and feed, and we'll be that much closer to some buffalo."

"What gives you the right to boss us around?" asked Scott.

The man had been sour toward Skye ever since the battle with the Blackfeet, and now he sounded truculent. Every camp tender knew the answer; Sublette had put Skye in charge.

"Let's get moving," said Skye, not answering. "We've a lot to do."

"I said what gives you the right?"

"Mr. Scott, I'd like you to pick out six or seven horses, drive them ahead of us, make a trail. Follow my prints along the creek."

"I don't feel like it. That's too much work for this kind of cold. We should wait for Sublette."

Skye stared at Scott a moment, wondering whether to confront him, and then turned to Pombert and the Creoles. "We can be set up and warm before dark."

Pombert smiled and nodded. The Creoles drifted into their huts and emerged better dressed against the cold. They had all moved camp many times and hardly needed instruction.

"What do we do with the trappers' outfits?" asked Bouleau.

"Move them. We're each tending camp for certain trap-pers. Their outfits are your responsibility."

"I'm staying," said Scott.

Skye turned to the man. "Then stay," he said.

The rest started to dismantle the huts, pack gear, gather the miserable horses. Moving camp was a formidable business, especially on a day with a bitter wind to add to the misery. It would take hours to build new huts and throw the buffalo hides over them and start fires again.

Scott stared sullenly as the others began to work. But when Estevan and Lapointe began dismantling Scott's lodge, he howled. "Leave that there," he bawled. Scott loomed a foot over Estevan.

Skye's patience was running thin. Life in a wilderness camp in weather well below zero on Fahrenheit's scale was precarious. It was impossible to stay, but moving would be hard, cruel work. Scott stood six inches higher than Skye, and didn't lack brute strength, but if the matter had to be forced, Skye decided to force it.

"All right, Scott," Skye said, waiting.

"Think you can whip me, Skye?"

"It's Mister Skye, mate."

"Think you know what to do? You've been in the moun-tains a long time and know what to do?"

Skye didn't reply. He stepped closer. He would hurt Scott, but he didn't want to. He had learned a few things in the Royal Navy.

"Well, aren't you the tough one, throwing weight around," Scott said.

That was good. Scott was using words rather than fists. Skye stepped closer. "Get to work, or try me if you want."

"I never take orders from a stinking Englishman."

Skye stepped closer until he was almost chest to chest.

"Show me," said Skye softly. His breath plumed the air. He stood ready, waiting for Scott's move.

"I quit," said Scott, whirling away. "Tell Sublette."

Skye watched the man retreat. Scott had nowhere to go and would be back in an hour. Skye nodded at the rest and they began the miserable exodus. They toiled through the brief day, dragging gear, driving horses, cleaning snow away from the sites of the new huts, trying to start fires when the sparks off their flints died before they nested in tinder. Skye finally sent Pombert back for some live coals because none of them could start a fire with flint and steel.

Scott packed his horse, pulled his thick robe around him, and smiled.

"I'm going to the Shoshones," he said. "Tell Sublette he owes me and I'll collect at rendezvous."

"If you make it."

Scott glowered. "You think I can't."

"It's a long way."

They all watched his back until he vanished. Skye didn't like it. Sublette would blame him for provoking the trouble and losing a man. But the camp had to be moved, and Skye thought he had waited a day too long at that.

They still weren't settled when the early dusk overtook them. Skye grimly chopped firewood first—that was the critical need and the key to surviving the next fierce night. They picketed the horses on the cleared grass, worked at building buffalo-robe huts with numb fingers and frozen ears, and finally crawled into their new huts, frozen, exhausted, and hungry.

Scott didn't return. Skye wished he would, not because

the man would help out but because the man would kill
himself through his own misjudgment.

The next day dawned clear and breathtakingly cold.
None of them dared venture beyond their three-sided
huts, built to trap the heat of the fires before them. Skye
had never seen a winter's day like this; blinding bright,
cruel, and murderous. Sublette didn't show up all day. In
an odd way that comforted Skye. The booshway wouldn't
quit until he had given Ferguson and Ranne every
chance.

Then, at dusk, the trappers quietly rode in, frost-rimed
men on silver-patched horses, hunched deep in saddles,
buffalo robes over their laps and legs. Skye watched
anxiously as they drifted in one by one. Sublette studied
the new camp, nodded, and tried to dismount, falling into
the snow because his limbs didn't work.

The other trappers tumbled off, unable to stand or function. Skye helped them down and to the fires. Pombert and
the Creoles rushed into the cold to help. Sublette warmed
himself at the nearest blaze without saying anything. The
result of the search was obvious to all.

Skye dreaded the questioning he would receive once
the trappers were settled. But what happened couldn't
be helped.

"This is a good place," Sublette said. "Where's Scott?"

"He quit. Headed for the Shoshones."

"Why?"

Skye sighed, wondering what to say. "Wouldn't move."

"Did he test you?"

"Yes."

Sublette nodded. Skye waited for more, but there wasn't
any. He supposed it was a rebuke. A better man could

have talked sense to Scott. Now the company had lost a man.

Chastened, Skye returned to his camp tending. The trappers looked half-frozen, too tired to eat, and miserable. They had brought a frozen elk haunch with them, so the camp tenders set to work roasting it. Later, when they all had feasted and warmed before the roaring fires, Sublette told his story.

"We checked three drainages and never saw sign of those ol' coons," he said. "We plumb froze to death, fought drifts, weathered hard nights, but we kept looking. Covered a lot of land. None of us was keen on giving up. They're dead or alive—we don't know. Probably gone under. We're feeling lower'n a snake's belly. They were good men. I'd trade a thousand Scotts for each of 'em," Sublette said. "They made the beaver come."

"Your men look bad," Skye said.

"Frostbite mostly. I got some flesh going black. I hope it doesn't mortify. Every one of us has some frostbit flesh."

"It don't spile in the mountains," said Bridger. "If our flesh falls offen us, we'll freeze it and keep it for poor doin's and eat it when we need it."

No one laughed.

Skye found himself wanting some encouragement. He had moved the camp and now man and animal were better off. He didn't hear it from Sublette or the trappers. But neither did they complain. Maybe they expected him to do it. Maybe that was why Sublette put him in charge. Skye pondered that in the orange firelight, wondering why the esteem of these men meant so much to him. He would abandon them next summer, but here he was, nursing every sign of approval. Maybe it was just that no one had ever approved of him. Maybe it was because these mountaineers were taciturn, especially in weather like this that put a man on edge. Or maybe their minds were simply occupied with Ranne and Ferguson, each of them wondering what had become of their veteran friends. If death could overwhelm two of the wiliest men in the brigade, it could overwhelm any of them.

The next days were among the worst in Skye's young life. If anything, the cold was worse. It didn't matter how many fires a man surrounded himself with; he was always on the brink of freezing solid. Nothing in a fo'c'sle, or high in the rigging on a bitter day at sea matched this cold and misery. Ranne and Ferguson didn't come in, but no one expected them to. Man or horse couldn't travel without frostbiting their lungs. They couldn't hunt, either, and Sublette put them on short rations. If they couldn't make meat soon, they would be eating one of the horses. Beyond the physical misery, gloom overtook them. The sun scarcely appeared. Men were too cold to talk, and sunk into their icy robes.

Skye kept himself occupied just by dreaming of his return to civilization. Wilderness had nothing to offer him, except a few seductive weeks in early summer when the sheer joy of the warm season lifted him. But all he really had gotten out of this was boredom, toil, fear, and anger.

Christmas came and went, but no one celebrated it, and half of those in camp weren't aware of it. Then one day, in the space of an hour, it warmed. Skye marveled. One minute he had lain in his robes, waiting for life to begin, a while later he threw off his robes, felt delicious warm air eddy through his buckskins, felt a wild liberty build in him, the freedom of a man emerging from prison, and stepped into a mild afternoon.

"Chinook," said Bridger. "I mind the time we were plumb froze to death, and down to stewing shoe leather for soup, when the Divil comes up outa them geysers on the Yellerstone and heats up the country almost to biling. So hot in January we was drenched in sweat. I had me a bath and went courtin' Injun wimmen."

"How long do these chinooks last?" Skye asked.

"Maybe long enough to get us to a Crow village," said Sublette. "Let's go."

"You mind if I leave some shelter and fixings behind for Ferguson and Ranne?" Skye asked.

Sublette shook his head. "They've gone under, Mister Skye."

"I'd like to leave a shelter up, and hang some pemmican from a limb. I'd like to leave some kindling, and I'll leave my flint and steel."

"Don't ever be without flint and steel. If they're alive and have their rifles, they won't need flint and steel. Any man with a rifle has both."

Skye considered it a revelation. He had never thought of a flintlock and some gunpowder as a means of starting a fire. He still had much to learn.

"Sure, ol' coon, you leave a camp for them," Sublette said. "Half shelter, dry firewood, some beaver meat hung high up. If they're alive, they'll know where to find us— with the Crows. And if they aren't alive, we'll donate the camp to the Blackfeet."

"I just have a feeling," said Skye, wondering why he thought they were alive and holed up in a place he could almost envision.

"You're a mountaineer, Mister Skye," Sublette said. It was the compliment that Skye had craved for days.

Chapter 42

The brigade fought its way over the pass to the Yellowstone country, and it was like arriving in the promised land. The chinook winds were even warmer on the east slope and had eaten away most of the snow.

But man and beast needed a rest after wrestling with soggy six-foot drifts, so they camped on the great bend of the Yellowstone again. They were in dire need of meat, so Sublette sent every hunter out while the rest made camp. One by one they drifted back around twilight, all of them emptyhanded. The game had vanished. Deer and antelope would be herded up for the winter—somewhere. Buffalo would also herd into groups—somewhere. Anything else that might make meat was hibernating or had fled south.

They ate the last of their emergency pemmican, scarcely two mouthfuls apiece for the twenty-seven men left in the brigade, and settled down for the night with empty bellies and a sense of foreboding. The horses fared better on brown bunchgrass that grew abundantly north of the river.

Skye knew from bitter experience what life was going to be like without food, and set out in the twilight to remedy the situation. He hiked along the riverbank until he found what he wanted, an inlet covered with dead, brown cattails, their stalks decaying on the ground. He cut through the frosty soil and examined the roots. Yes, they were edible—smaller and harder than when they pumped life to the fronds above, but they would make a food of sorts. He dug several pounds of the roots, washed them in the bitter-cold river, and got back to camp just before dark.

He lacked the means to turn roots into flour, the way the Indians did, but he found some smooth river rocks and a flat rock surface, and began mashing the roots into pulp. Then he boiled them in the company cookpot, drained off the water, and ended up with a tan mush that tasted bad but was thick and starchy. Some of the others watched him disconsolately, scarcely aware that he was producing food. They were meat eaters.

When the mush had cooled he ate some of it, enough to satisfy his hungers, and set some aside for breakfast and lunch. The only man among them to pay attention was Tom Fitzpatrick, who watched, tasted, and smiled.

"I'm always looking for ways to get along," he said. "This is one I didn't know about, ol' coon."

"They kept me alive when I had nothing. I mashed them when I couldn't boil them. I had no fire for weeks."

"All the better to learn about," Fitzpatrick said. "We could feed this camp if we had to."

"Don't know that most of 'em'll touch it," Skye replied. "Not my favorite taste."

Fitzpatrick smiled. "We call it the Rocky Mountain College. Some learn their lessons—and the rest go under."

Fitzpatrick helped himself to another finger-load, and settled down beside Skye for some serious eating.

"What do you think happened to Scott?" Skye asked.

"He would've headed for the Shoshones. Probably made it because of the chinook."

"What do you think happened to Ranne and Ferguson?"

"I'd guess they're denned up with a b'ar."

"Alive?"

"I think so. B'ar would be warm. They couldn't hear our shots from in there."

"What if the bear woke up?"

"They do all winter. But they're not full of fight. Couple ol' coons could go in there for a snooze, long as they were quiet about it."

"Are you whistling in the dark, mate, or do you put stock in it?"

Fitzpatrick grinned and shrugged. "The wild world isn't what we think. I've gone alone from the mountains to Saint Louis. A man who's resourceful can make it."

"Why're you here, mate?"

"It's a calling. Maybe I'd have been a priest. This is religion."

"Religion?"

"This is holy, Skye. Don't you feel it?"

"No. It's mostly boredom, fear, pain, discomfort—and starvation. What's wrong with a roof over your head? Pretty women?"

"Rules, Skye, rules."

"It's Mister Skye, mate."

Fitzpatrick laughed and helped himself to more mush. "That's a rule I could do without. But as long as it's rooted in a sentiment that would please any son of Ireland, I'll accept it."

"I'm going east next summer. What advice have you?"

"Don't count Indians friends when they're friendly, and don't count them enemies when they threaten you. Avoid them unless you can't help a meeting. Every encounter means trouble. The friendly ones want every item in your kit, the rifle especially, but they'll settle for your horses or a kettle or all your knives. Take some twists of tobacca with you. Tobacca's a peace offering, and it binds them if they accept it. But don't count on it. Don't count on anything. This evening I was counting on an empty belly and now I'm full. I'm indebted."

That night the wolves howled. Skye had never heard such wild yelps, eerie screams, yapping sounds. Maybe he could shoot one in the morning. He didn't relish eating dog but he relished an empty belly less.

Sublette and the hunters saddled up before dawn, intending to ride straight toward the northeast where the wolf chorus had erupted and kept on all night.

Skye wished he could go. His duties locked him to the camp.

"Start the cookfires, Mister Skye," said Sublette. "That yapping last night was buffalo talk."

"How would you know that?"

"You'll learn it if you stay in the mountains."

Skye watched every free trapper and hunter in the outfit throw saddles over shaggy horses, which looked fat inside their hairy coats. Skye knew better. His mare was ribby under that matted hair, and his colt was worse. The horses wouldn't have much energy in them this time of year.

That afternoon they rode in—without meat, looking dour. Seventeen had left, but ten returned. The others were still out prowling, and might stay out overnight.

Skye waited patiently for Sublette to unsaddle and picket his horse.

"The wolves downed an old bull so poor there wasn't much to begin with. Naught but a skeleton and half-eaten hide now. Loner bulls like that, they leave the herd to die. Or the young bulls drive 'em out. Fitzpatrick says you made some paste out of roots. Got some?"

Skye dug into his pot and handed Sublette some of the mush.

"Gawdawfulest stuff I ever put between lips," the booshway said. "You damn Brits don't know what food's supposed to taste like. Line up the camp tenders and go harvest a pile of it."

Skye laughed.

He dragooned the camp tenders and set them to work along the banks of the Yellowstone, digging up roots out of half-frozen bog areas. They didn't get much, and grumbled the whole time, but ere long they had reason to be grateful. The hunters returned with nothing, mad and cussing and ready to chew out anyone who complained.

That night the whole brigade dined on a few mouthfuls of cattail root, duly pulverized and boiled and seasoned with a little salt. They didn't say much, and the ridicule that Skye was expecting never erupted.

"Poor doin's." That was all anyone said. But Skye sensed respect. He had conjured up a meal of sorts, and the English pork-eater had shown the mountaineers a thing or two.

The next day the wind shifted north and they knew they had better hurry to the Crow villages before the next blast of arctic air. They packed without breakfast. They were plumb out of everything now, and full of self-pity, gnawing hunger, and rage. The hunters set off; they would rejoin the brigade down the Yellowstone a day's journey.

They rode with the wind, the slivers of icy air on their backs, numbing their necks, bullying the weary horses. At the nooning Skye boiled water and served it. The brigade groused but drank the hot water.

"I always knowed that when it comes to cooking, Skye,

you're some," said Bridger. "This hyar's the best concoction ye ever did serve us."

An hour later the mountain veterans taught Skye a thing or two. A ravine choked with buffaloberry had survived the predations of birds, and the company set to work collecting the remaining silvery fruit. But it came to mouthful apiece. Skye was growing faint.

They halted at a place where the river plunged through a narrows hemmed by grassy slopes. The hunters and trappers found them there, and had nothing to offer.

"The trouble with winter is that the game herds up, and you got to know where they yard," Beckwourth said.

That observation didn't feed anyone. Skye had one more idea. He borrowed a fishhook and line from Tom Fitzpatrick and wondered how to manufacture a fly. The Yellowstone was running low and transparent, and he thought it would yield some trout. He found a bit of frayed leather, odd threads dangling off it, and worked his hook through it. It didn't look like an insect. It didn't look like anything.

Behind him the camp tenders built fires close to the limestone cliff and put up half-shelters because it looked like the weather would turn in the night. Mare's tails had corrugated the heavens all day. The brigade was in a surly mood, and demanding that Sublette send an express rider to the Crows. Food for some foofaraws, powder, and lead.

Skye hardly knew one freshwater fish from another and no one had ever described their habits to him. But he thought a mouthful of trout would help, so he rigged a pole, dropped his bizarre thing into the Yellowstone, wiggled it gently while there was daylight enough to attract the denizens of the deeps.

And felt a hard yank.

A minute later he beached a fat trout.

"You damn Brits don't know what good food is," said Sublette, eyeing the three-pound silvery fish. Skye grunted, freed his hook, thrust the flopping fish at Sublette, who held it as if it were a hot potato, and dropped his line into the river again.

In the space of an hour he caught four more, and then the light faded. That came to only a few mouthfuls per man, but they all were fed after a fashion. And the Yanks weren't making fun of him this time, although they cussed the fishbones and opined that there were good reasons most tribes hated fish.

"Thank you, Mister Skye," said William Sublette. "This is the miracle of the loaves and fishes, Royal Navy style. I am coming to admire the British pallet. But you forgot the sauce."

"Get out the traps," said Skye, "and put the fishheads in them, well away from camp. It was something I learned to do on the Columbia."

Sublette stared, nodded, and gave the command. Skye thought they might catch breakfast.

Chapter 43

The fish-baited traps yielded an otter, raccoon, and fox. William Sublette watched the camp tenders swiftly gut and clean the animals and salvage the meat. There wasn't enough to feed twenty-seven starving men much, but each man would have a few mouthfuls of gray meat—if he could overcome his queasiness about eating it.

The cold had returned, but it wasn't as severe as the spell they had endured in the Three Forks country. A nippy northwind probed at Sublette's clothing, finding ways to chill his neck and ears and ankles. He ached for summertime, when the mountains glowed and a man had few worries. The hot fires in each of the four messes warmed frontsides but not backsides, and the men were in a foul mood.

The camp tenders set the meat to roasting over the fierce fires after carefully setting aside the offal, which would be used tonight to bait traps again—if the hunters failed once more. Sublette sometimes thought this brigade was cursed with grief. It had lost too many men, endured too much hardship. And it would have been much worse off without Skye. The Englishman had found ways to feed them more than once. Miserable food, things the free trappers despised—but things that kept them alive. Skye was showing every sign of being a natural mountaineer and a leader.

Beckwourth was having his usual good time. "I don't think I'll eat otter," he said to Skye. "I prefer roasted camp tender."

The men had been bantering with Skye these past weeks, a sure sign that the Englishman had become one of them. Sublette watched Skye work, admiring the man's industry and resourcefulness.

Every man got a few bites of meat that morning. Some whined about it but no one refused it. The mean wind sliced into them all—this upper Yellowstone country was famous for its winter winds—and Sublette was eager to get going, put the wind to their backs, and hasten to the Crow villages.

Once again the brigade packed and loaded their horses.

The hunters fanned out, more determined than ever to make meat and lots of it. Their senses and instincts, always keen, had been sharpened this morning by deep hunger that verged on starvation. Sublette thought they would succeed this hard day.

He waited for Skye to load his gear on his mare and start east once again under a weak winter sun that promised more heat than it gave. He fell in beside Skye, choosing to walk rather than ride, so he could talk with the Englishman.

"Mister Skye, what are your plans?"

"The same as always."

"You know, you'd have a future with the company if you would stay in the mountains."

"I'm sorry to disappoint you, Mr. Sublette."

"You're a natural. You found food when a brigade full of veteran mountaineers couldn't find any. You wisely moved camp when you had to, in spite of the serious grousing of a misfit."

"I did what I had to. We were out of firewood and feed."

"They tell me you dealt with Scott very well—patiently at first, giving him a chance to cool down, and then firmly. Faced with a fight, he caved in."

"I lost a man."

"No, good riddance. You did what you had to. A good leader does just that. Scott resented you ever since he proved himself a coward in the fight. They all saw it, and they all saw you. After that he was just looking for ways to cause you grief. I was expecting something like that when I put you in charge."

"It seems a man's every act is watched and reported to you."

"A brigade is a close-knit outfit, Mister Skye. Reported

isn't quite the word. I have never asked or expected men to report about the conduct of other men in the company. But because this is wilderness, and we're never far from trouble—starvation, sickness, Indians, thirst, thunderstorms, hail, freezing to death, drowning—these things are chewed over, and rehashed, and chewed over again. It can't be helped."

"It's the navy all over, mate. When you fight beside men, they look you over and you look them over."

Sublette nodded. They hiked along the north bank of the Yellowstone after detouring around a canyon, and now passed through a forest of bare cottonwoods. Rugged white-tipped mountains rose in the north, separate from the great spine of the Stony Mountains that lay south of the river. This was the raw, noble, harsh country the Crows called home, glorious in the summer, vicious in the winter.

"You may have surmised that I'm leading up to something, Mister Skye. You've proven yourself even in the brief time you've been with us. Next summer, at rendezvous, I'm going to propose to my partners that you become a brigade leader. There would be a base wage of eight hundred dollars and bonuses based on the number of pelts your brigade brings in. With your skills, you would probably be rich in three or four years."

Skye squinted at the distant mountains, which were dazzling in the morning light. His blue eyes, nested in hollows of reddened and weather-chafed flesh, seemed to seek visions in the thin winter air, and concealed from Sublette the thoughts that were crawling through Skye's mind. "I'll think about it, sir," he said at last.

Sublette wouldn't be deterred. "Mister Skye, I well know your lifelong vision of educating yourself and going into business. It nursed you through years of grief. And nothing I'm proposing now would keep you from it if you eventually want to pursue it. But you've a chance here to establish yourself for the rest of your life. Will you at least think it over?"

"Yes, of course."

Gunshot drifted on the wind, faint but unmistakable. The sound gladdened Sublette. It didn't signify war or trouble; it signified game. "Hear that?" he asked Skye. "That's meat."

Skye smiled.

An hour later they came to a noble stand of cottonwoods beside the river, and found the hunters waiting there, fires already going. It was only midmorning, but the brigade was about to feast.

"Fat cow," said Bridger, who had been out with the hunters. "In fact, three fat cows and one calf, and as many as we want. Two, three miles yonder." He pointed north.

Fat cow! Word whipped through the brigade. Fat cow!

Sublette swiftly dispatched half a dozen camp tenders to help butcher and haul the meat. They would take it all and the hides, too, good gifts for the Crows. Butchering and transporting four buffalo was a major undertaking. They had come only a few miles this day, but so what? Starving men would have fat cow, and the horses could use a rest.

"Mister Skye, you stay. Unload and picket the horses on whatever grass you can find. We'll stay the night. This hyar campsite even has a name. Big Timber, named after those noble cottonwoods yonder by Lewis and Clark— actually Clark, coming down the Yellowstone with Sacajewea and a few men, heading east to meet Lewis at the confluence of the Missouri."

Skye knew nothing of that, but he nodded and set to work, unloading the horses and picketing them one by one on brown grass where they could make a living. A vicious wind wailed through the naked branches of the cottonwoods, shooting ice into Sublette's flesh, but he didn't mind.

Fat cow!

Sublette stepped off his horse, unloaded and picketed it, and then cut deadwood from some nearby cottonwoods. It would burn hot and fast. Cottonwood smoke was foul compared to the resinous smoke from pine wood, but it made a good fire. He kept his Hawken rifle at his side, as always. Just when you thought you might be safe from the red devils, that's when they surprised you. But he had little fear of them now, in the dead of winter, when they would be telling stories in their lodges.

He noticed that Skye wasn't armed, and thought to tell the man. There were things Skye needed to learn.

"Mister Skye, where's your rifle?"

"With my gear, sir."

"Have it with you. Someday that practice will save your life. And no matter what you're doing, eye the horizons constantly."

Skye nodded, collected his rifle, checked the charge of powder in the pan, and set it close to him while he picketed horses.

By the time the first of the meat arrived—several huge chunks of haunch laced to the saddle—Skye and Sublette had a camp set up.

"Shall I start roasting it, sir?" Skye asked.

Sublette shook his head. "It ain't hump. Set it aside."

Skye looked disappointed but said nothing.

Together, they pulled the red meat off the packhorse

and set it aside. Sublette felt his belly rumble. He and Skye could be cooking this meat right now; he and Skye could be feasting, filling their empty bellies at last while the rest were butchering. But the thought of humpmeat, fatty and tender and laced with flavor, stayed him. Even starving men should wait a while for humpmeat. Or tongue. That was another feast. There was a lesson Skye would learn soon enough.

Another burdened horse arrived, bearing a green hide with a huge chunk of meat and bone within, along with a tongue. Sublette opened the parcel and eyed the meat happily.

"Mister Skye, that's hump. Run a cooking rod through it and start it roasting over a low fire. You'll see that it's worth the wait. And then start the tongue cooking."

"My stomach doesn't agree, sir."

Sublette laughed. "Damned English don't know fat cow from poor bull," he said. "You see how that meat arrived special—all wrapped in a hide? There's a mountain message in it."

Sublette helped Skye rig up the fire and block the wind that was whipping the flame. "I've camped here at Big Timber half a dozen times and every time the wind pretty near drove me out," he grumbled.

No meat arrived for a long time, and then the whole brigade arrived at once, packhorses loaded, crude travois dragging huge hulks of buffalo.

"We been samplin'," said Bridger, whose cheeks were bloodstained. "Best lights I ever bit into."

Skye looked appalled.

"Raw buffler liver, Mister Skye—it's a mountain man's sweet. This child'll show ye next time. And maybe we'll roast some boudins, too, as long as you're a pork-eater."

"You actually eat raw meat?" Skye asked.

"Mister Skye, we got vices ye never heard of. We'll teach ye the whole lot of 'em, one by one," Bridger said. "Now whar's that hump we expressed down hyar? I'm plumb sick of yore vittles—raccoon and swamp roots. This child don't eat coons and roots, you hear me?"

But Skye was grinning. He pulled the dripping hump-meat off the fire and began sawing down to the bone, sending aromas into the wind that drove Sublette half mad. The meat, blackened on the outside, remained pink at the center and dripped juices. Solemnly, the brigade gathered around the cookfire to observe all this.

"Ye don't get any, Mister Skye," said Bridger. "Ye got to cook the next hump, yonder, and then ye can have our leavings. That's what ye desarve for feeding us dead fox and marsh roots."

"That's right," said Tom Fitzpatrick solemnly. "We've all decided that you don't get any. You can stick with your dainty British cookery."

Sublette watched Skye redden and then relax, and then bellow. "Mr. Bridger, Mr. Fitzpatrick," he roared, "cook your own bloody meat."

Old Gabe Bridger—who was scarcely older than Skye, actually—cocked an eyebrow, grimaced, looked exceedingly pained, and then hoorawed.

No pork-eater was Skye, Sublette thought. He was a mountaineer now.

Chapter 44

"The pale men are coming!"

Many Quill Woman heard the village crier, Buffalo Hoof, chant his message among the lodges of the Kicked-in-the-Bellies. Swiftly she drew a thick buffalo robe about her and slipped through the low lodge door into a wintry day.

She saw no trappers, but that was as it should be. Even in winter, the village wolf soldiers had detected the pale men far away, and reported the news to the chief, Arapooish, and the elders and seers. By the time the pale men entered, the village elders would be gathered before the chief's lodge to receive them.

Tonight there would be feasts and merriment. The People of the Raven had little to do in winter but tell stories and have good times around the lodge fires.

She waited impatiently, giving place to the warriors and elders as a young single woman should. Had he come? She would know soon. But she already knew, having seen with inner vision. Even though Skye had talked of going far to the east and the big waters there, he would come. She smiled. Magpie had known more of his future than he himself had. Magpie was a true counselor who saw all things and led Many Quill Woman to her understandings. Magpie didn't go south in the winter the way other birds did, but stayed right there, making a living even in the cold season.

Swiftly the lodges emptied themselves as the people dressed against the icy wind and gathered in the harsh sunlight to witness this event. Maybe the liar Beckwourth would be with them again. Beckwourth called himself an Absaroka chief, which amused her people. But he was a brave warrior and had fought beside her brothers in wars against the Siksika, so they would honor Beckwourth and supply him with women. Beckwourth never had enough of them. Many Quill Woman hoped that her father entertained no such notions about her. Let Beckwourth winter with Pine Leaf again. They were made for each other. The thought made her smile. Pine Leaf, the revered warrior woman of her people, didn't really like Beckwourth either but Beckwourth didn't know that.

How handsome was her village this year. They were fat because they had made a fine fall hunt, and had many robes and parfleches full of pemmican and frozen buffalo quarters hanging high above the snapping jaws of dogs. They had traded many beaver pelts at the rendezvous and now the warriors were decked out in crimson or blue, and women were wrapped in thick blankets with black stripes at either end, and had tied their straight hair with ribbons gotten from the traders. Oh, how she loved her village, with smoke curling from its many lodges, and fat horses gathered nearby, safe from the Siksika dogs. Here were great men and seers, the proudest of the Absaroka people, choosing to live in the village of the great Arapooish, vanquisher of the Siksika, terror of the Lakota, and the only chief in many years who blessed his people with good times.

She saw the pale men enter the village, and as always they excited curiosity. Where were their women? Why did these men come to the mountains without their wives and children? This thing had baffled her people and none of the elders or seers could explain it. Somewhere, these trappers had hidden their women. Most of the Absaroka had never seen a pale woman. Many Quill Woman had never seen one, and she suspected they must be ugly and mean, so the pale men were ashamed of them. It was said that the pale women were kept in a hot land far to the east because they could not take cold weather, and there the pale men repaired now and then to add to their families. What a strange custom.

The Goddamns made a great show, riding in procession into the village, escorted by the Kit Fox Society, the young warriors doing the policing of the village this winter. The Goddamns did not sit proudly on their ponies, with backs straight, like any Absaroka man or woman. These pale men slouched, and spat—a terrible insult—and even looked directly at the Absaroka instead of averting their gazes as politeness required. Still, they made a great spectacle, and Many Quill Woman thrilled at the sight of these barbarous men, so empty of manners and so lax in their conduct that they scandalized her people.

Their terrible beards plumed their faces until one could scarcely see the face hidden by them, as if the beards were masks to conceal these men from the eyes of the seers, who plumbed the depths of all mortals. They wore magnificent hats and headdresses, all of their own design, obviously their secret medicine. Some were made of fox or beaver or otter, some made of buffalo or the material they called felt. They carried their heavy rifles in saddle sheaths, usually fringed and decorated. But not one of them dressed like another, and each was so different that she could hardly say that they were all of one tribe.

She watched eagerly, awaiting the sight of the one she ached to see, and wondering if she would recognize him behind his beard. She would. She would know his blue eyes and his big nose. She spotted Beckwourth—ah, how he was smiling, his brown eyes dancing with delight. And she spotted others she knew from previous visits, all bristling with beards. Many passed, strange men, and then she saw him near the rear, just as he saw her.

Her heart soared. "Mister Skye!"

"Victoria!"

He had come. Her inner vision had told her he would, but she had doubted and now was ashamed. His gaze bored into her, searching her, noting everything about her, and she flushed with warmth, even in the biting cold. But he had stopped the procession and he knew suddenly that he must move on. There were welcomings to be completed before she could greet him.

She raced toward the great lodge of Arapooish, twenty-two poles, big enough for six wives. There would these pale men be welcomed. She felt aglow. She could not say why she felt so happy. Skye was not a great man among them, and he was near the rear, giving place to the leaders of the brigade. Why did she care? Maybe a witch had cast a spell, or even an evil spirit from under the waters, swimming among the fish in the places of the dead.

The leaders of the pale men dismounted before Arapooish and the elders, leaving their horses to the lesser ones like Skye who stood back, a man without status among them.

Beckwourth did the honors. He could speak the tongue of the People.

"My esteemed chief, Arapooish, Rotten Belly, we have come to offer you gifts," he said, enjoying himself. But Beckwourth always enjoyed himself, even when he shouldn't. "Here, behold the tobacco," he said, handing her chief a twist. That was ceremony. The gift of tobacco signified many things, but most of all peace and friendship. Her chief nodded, and his son, Arrow, accepted.

"And here, behold the blankets," he said. The one called Sublette, leader of the brigade and a trader, handed the chief two beautiful green blankets with black stripes at their ends. Rotten Belly handed these treasures to his son.

"And these are for the beautiful wives and daughters of Arapooish," Beckwourth said. The trader chief handed hanks of bright ribbon—bold blue, yellow, red, green, orange—to Arrow.

"And behold this, great chief of the Absaroka."

This time Sublette brought forth a heavy rifle from his pack, along with a horn of powder and a bar of the soft metal.

"Ah!" The Absaroka warriors crowded close. This was a noble offering from the pale men. "Aieee!"

This gift the chief accepted with his own strong hands. He hefted the shooting stick, cocked it, examined its beauty, and smiled.

"My friend Beckwourth, we welcome you to our happy village. We are as brothers to you, and you have sealed our friendship with your splendid offerings. Together in battle we are a match for Siksika or Lakota even though they are many more than we are. May you enjoy your time with us, and may our lodges shelter you from the fury of the Cold Maker. The women will erect our council lodge for you, and it will hold many Goddamns. The rest of the pale men will stay with their old friends and share our lodges. But tell me, Beckwourth. When will the pale men bring their wives so we may see them and try them?"

Beckwourth smiled. "Maybe soon, Rotten Belly. We are far from them, and must bring them a long way."

"Well, we await them. We are eager to see them, and often we wonder about them. I want one or two, and will give many robes for one. Come now, escort your headmen into my lodge, and we will smoke the pipe and counsel for a while." He eyed the crowd. "You women who are hospitable and of good heart toward the pale men, put up the council lodge, that these friends of the Absaroka may find warmth. The Cold Maker roars."

She watched the chief's lodge swallow the Goddamn headmen. Fitzpatrick, Sublette, Bridger, Beckwourth. She knew every one of them from other times. Arapooish's wives sought shelter in other lodges while the great ceremony of the pipe proceeded. Many women rushed to put up the poles of the council lodge, pull the massive buffalohide cover up the cone of poles, and pin its sides together with willow pins.

Now she was free. The sacred ceremony of the pipe might continue within the chief's lodge but all who were witnesses to the arrival were released. She sought Skye and found him beside a mare. He had cared for her, and she was fat, and so was the spirited little gray stallion at her side.

"Goddamn Skye sonofabitch," she said joyously.

He gaped at her as if he were buffalo-witted.

"Don't you know me?"

"Victoria. Of course."

"You come. I tell you so."

Skye smiled wryly. "You knew better than I did."

"You get many beaver?"

"No, I am a camp tender—I don't trap. Not yet. But how are you? Are you a warrior's woman now?"

The Goddamns were so ignorant. Anyone could tell from the way she wore her hair loose that she wasn't. The women who had men braided their hair. Couldn't he see that? "No damn good," she said. "We talk. I like my name, Victoria. I will take it. Come."

She beckoned him to her lodge and he followed, leading his horses. "Come, come, come," she said, irritably.

Then she presented him to her stern father, Walks Alone, and stepmother, Digs the Roots, who waited before the lodge huddled in their robes. They had met him at the rendezvous and had steered her away from him—and all pale men.

"This is the Goddamn for whom I waited," she told them in her tongue. "Magpie gave me the inner eye to see the man within the face-hair. He is from another tribe of Goddamns, across the Big Water. Skye is his name, like the heaven above us. What a great name, for the whole home of stars and sun and moon. He will be great among them in a winter or two."

They nodded, reserved and curious. Then her father urged caution. "He is not great among them. He came near the end of the procession, one of the last and least. This is not good. We will ask Red Turkey Comb to see what must be seen, and I will make him a gift of a pony for it."

Victoria pushed back her annoyance and responded dutifully, as befit her station. "Yes, that would be good. We will learn about Mister Skye. Nothing escapes Red Turkey Comb."

Her father nodded, ushered Skye into the lodge, and performed the ceremony of the pipe with the man, while she and her stepmother, or little mother as one was called, and sister and brother observed silently.

Her father was welcoming Skye, but she knew that it was a formality. He had higher hopes for his oldest daughter.

Chapter 45

Skye marveled at the beauty of the Crow village. It nestled under sandstone bluffs, within an arc of a laughing creek, protected from the bitter winds that whistled across the rolling prairie above it. Each lodge was shielded by willow and chokecherry brush that further subdued the winds. The blackened peaks of the golden lodges leaked lazy smoke into a stark white, gray, and tan world.

Wherever Skye turned, he found the genius of these people making life bearable and comfortable. They had chosen a perfect site to winter. Cottonwood and willow forests offered plentiful firewood to feed the hearths of the lodges, while tawny bottomlands supported the village horse herd, and the sandstone escarpments on both sides of the creek corralled the horses.

They had put him and the other camp tenders and clerks in a sixteen-pole lodge made of twenty-seven buffalo hides sewn tightly together. It had taken a dozen women to raise the heavy lodge cover after they had erected the tripod and laid the other lodgepoles into its apex. After that they had spread buffalo robes on the ground within, layers of them until the icy earth no longer bit those who lay upon it.

Skye swiftly learned how to manipulate the leather ears of the lodge to harness the breezes and draw out the smoke of the small lodgefire. The women had hung an additional shoulder-high dew cloth from the lodgepoles within, which made the lodge so warm that a man could sleep without burying himself in robes. He had never seen a European tent half as comfortable.

Those first days he explored the village, examining lodge after lodge, admiring the artistry that brightened the lodges with figures of animals or geometric designs, or what he supposed were medicine symbols, household gods blessing those within. The veteran trappers had wintered with these Kicked-in-the-Bellies for several years, and had found berths in many lodges. Some had even been adopted by families or into the tribe.

He counted forty-one lodges, and using the mountaineer formula of eight to a lodge, calculated that something like three hundred and twenty or thirty persons inhabited this village. He felt its power and comfort and protection, felt its ancient knowledge of all the ways to find meat, or preserve food for emergencies. He felt the power in the bows and quivers of its warriors, and in the warrior societies that vied with each other for honor. He walked freely among these people, exchanging smiles because he couldn't talk with them.

He did not escape work here. As a camp tender he was responsible for cutting copious amounts of deadwood from the cottonwood groves, for the fires never ceased consuming fuel. He was also responsible for several horses as well as his own, and looked after them each morning.

Within a day or two after he arrived he felt a euphoria such as he had not experienced since boyhood. He could not explain this exultation, only that it coursed through every fiber of his being. Instead of cowering before a brutal northern winter and suffering its numbing cold, he found himself enjoying each bright day. The long nights bloomed into yarning and storytelling parties around hot lodgefires of the hospitable Crow. Most days, the sun warmed the intimate valley for a while, brightening the world of these cheerful people before vanishing mid-afternoon behind the western bluffs. But the winter didn't seem hard.

How could a man be melancholic in paradise? Yes, it was that, in its own magical fashion. He slept warm on three buffalo robes, and not even the presence of a dozen others disturbed his slumbers. He could not remember a happier time.

Each misty dawn, when the sun was rosing the bluffs, the village hunters, along with the trappers and mountaineers, saddled their winter-shaggy horses and rode out to make meat. It took constant effort to feed so many mouths.

In some ways, hunting was easier in the winter, except when the weather turned foul or bitter. The animals herded up, the mule deer and antelope forming into bands for mutual warmth and protection. The buffalo gathered into small herds in valleys where they could escape some of the wind. In heavy snow the buffalo could be driven into snowbanks, mired and surrounded, but these days, without much snow on the prairie, the hunting was harder and required more cunning.

The guns of the mountaineers contributed mightily to the village's larder that January of 1827, and that made them all the more welcome among the Absaroka. Massive quarters of buffalo hung from stout limbs, along with the carcasses of deer and antelope. Only elk were scarce this winter.

Skye heard about it all but was not free to hunt. Not yet. As the juniormost member of the brigade, he had the most work, and William Sublette did not neglect to keep him busy chopping wood for the brigade's hosts as well as the big lodge that housed the camp tenders. Even so, Skye had more free time than he had ever known. Time to explore, learn the ways of these brown people, master their arts and crafts and weaponry, and try to make friends even without the employment of words.

One twilight he pulled a buffalo robe around him and slipped outside for a breath of fresh air. Stars winked in the slate sky. He realized he was happy. He had never known what it was like to enjoy life.

He heard the wolves patrol the ridges. He often did. They boldly probed the camp most nights, the smell of meat drawing them in, but the frozen carcasses hung well above their snapping jaws.

"Goddamn Skye, I have waited for you to come, but you do not," said a low sweet voice beside him. He whirled. She was there, wrapped in the black-banded gray blanket she had been wearing about the village, the one he had given her.

He had been avoiding her, and she knew it.

"Victoria—"

"You have given me a good name. I have told the seers that this is my name now."

Somehow he felt snared by an invisible web that was spinning about him, and it troubled him. He had other plans, dreams spun in a ship's brig to keep him alive when he had no reason to live. He could not let this slim savage demolish them.

She studied him—one could take it as a glare, so intense was her gaze—from brown eyes that radiated irritability and love in strange harness. Jet hair framed her sharp features. The hair vanished under her blanket, along with the rest of her lithe figure. He had never thought of beauty in these terms—only in pale, blue-eyed English terms—and found her all the more intoxicating because she awakened something unforeseen in him.

It wasn't just Victoria that was intoxicating him. This wild sweet liberty, this coming to manhood in the mountains, this strange sovereignty over his own life and destiny, far from organized society—all these things had stirred something so profound that he was having doubts about everything he believed in.

She waited patiently for him to speak, but he could muster no answer. How could he tell her that he didn't want her attentions?

"Sonofabitch, Skye, I go now." She turned to leave.

"No—Victoria—"

"I am cold. I came to invite you to the lodge of Red Turkey Comb. He is a seer and a man with great power and will help you find vision. Then you will know what you must do and what powers have been given you. He will see you if you offer him a gift. Have you something to give?"

Skye didn't. He could scarcely be poorer. "No . . ."

"Yes you do. He is old, and his fires need wood."

"Wood?" Skye veered toward the council lodge and plucked up an armload of cottonwood limbs he had cut that day. He wasn't at all sure why she was taking him to a shaman, and it would probably offend his own beliefs, but he was curious. What could a savage mystic do?

She smiled and led him toward a humble lodge set apart from the rest of the village. There she scratched gently on the door flap, and they heard a muffled voice from within, which she answered in her own tongue. Then she gestured him in. He pulled aside the flap and penetrated into a dark lodge with only embers in its firepit. The shaman sat beyond the coals, silent and barely visible.

Skye set the wood down while she said something to the old man. He nodded, beckoned Skye to sit on his right. She settled herself across from the old man in the place of least honor according to custom, and loosened her blanket. She wore a white doeskin dress, brightly quilled in geometric patterns. She fed some of Skye's wood into the embers. In a moment they blazed and swiftly warmed the lodge, the flickering light playing off her brown face and glinting in her hair.

"Red Turkey Comb is pleased with the wood. He had none this night, and now he will be warm."

Skye realized how much a simple gift could mean, and knew that he would leave an armload for the old man each day. As the light bloomed, he took the measure of the shaman. This one was not at all ascetic in appearance, but a heavy man with sagging flesh and a measuring gaze.

The shaman listened quietly to Victoria for a while.

"I tell him about you. I tell him you confused and don't know what to be. He think he help you be."

That confounded Skye but he kept quiet. She would have to do the talking. He could understand some Absaroka words, but he couldn't describe his life or his hopes to this old man.

Time passed and the evening deepened, but the shaman didn't hurry. The old man touched Skye's hand and closed his eyes. Then he tamped tobacco in a short clay pipe, plucked up an ember with a leaf, lit the tobacco, and smoked.

Then Red Turkey Comb closed his eyes and chanted something that sounded like a supplication.

"He is asking the grandfathers and The One Who Made All Things to give you vision," she said. "You must prepare yourself with your own pleading. Talk to the grandfathers."

Skye nodded. He didn't know where his life was taking him, and perhaps this wattled old shaman might give him answers.

Now and then the old man eyed Skye contemplatively, his gaze searching and direct. Skye felt he had no secrets left, for the old man had fathomed all there was to know of him.

Then, for a long while, Red Turkey Comb closed his eyes and sat so still that Skye wondered whether he had fallen asleep, as old people do. But then he returned from wherever he had been, and began talking softly to Victoria.

"He is honored to have such a man as Mister Skye visit him and seek to know the medicine that flows out of him," she translated. "He sometimes has little to offer, but this time it all came to him clearly, as bright as summer sunlight . . . Mister Skye is a friend of the People, and with his mighty arm will help the People against the Siksika and Lakota. He will be honored by all the Absaroka, and welcome in any village of the People."

She smiled. This was good news to her, even if it excited wild doubts in him.

"Mister Skye will become a name known to all the People of the grasslands. He will be a name known to his own tribe. He will fight many times, sometimes to save himself, but more often to help his own tribe, or the Absaroka, or—his women."

"Women?"

She nodded. "That was what was spoken."

"A wife and daughters."

She smiled and said nothing.

"But I'm planning to go east."

She translated that to Red Turkey Comb, and then translated his voluble reply.

"The past is a broken bowl and cannot hold broth again. The dream that sustained you was a good dream because it gave you life and hope each day on the big waters. But it is gone, and a new destiny is yours. You will be honored. Even the Siksika and Lakota will speak your name with fear. Even the grizzly bear, your brother, will honor you."

Skye stirred restlessly, not liking that.

"Goddamn Skye, you got big medicine!"

Skye nodded skeptically, unsure of what to do next. But the old man stayed him with a wave of the hand, and dug through a parfleche behind him. Then he handed Skye a necklace made of giant grizzly claws, each arched and lethal-looking, and five or six inches long. They were strung on a thong and separated by blue-enameled wooden trade beads. Victoria gasped and then translated.

"Wear this. It will tell the People of your powers," she said.

He handed it to her, and she knotted it behind his neck.

"There is no greater sign," she said.

Red Turkey Comb stood, a signal that this interview was over, and Skye and Victoria bundled themselves and pierced into bitter cold. Skye knew, in the dark, that something had changed.

Chapter 46

Something portentous had happened to Skye in the lodge of the shaman, Red Turkey Comb, but he couldn't fathom what it was. He knew little of Indian belief, and distrusted even that. He tried to make light of the prophetic vision about him, but couldn't. Somewhere, floating just back of his thoughts, was the understanding that his life had changed so his future would, too.

He wore his bearclaw necklace uneasily, feeling odd emanations from it, powers he ascribed to savage superstition that he would soon put behind him. Living in a Crow village could do that to a man. Sometimes he pulled the necklace over his head to examine it and run his fingers over the dark, lethal grizzly claws. Whoever had fashioned this necklace knew the power of those claws. The root of each had been encased in blue tradecloth, and a small hole had been bored in each to take the thong of the necklace. The lustrous blue beads separating the claws added to the beauty of this insignia of power.

But more than beauty stirred him as he ran his blunt fingers over the necklace. He felt stirrings of things he couldn't put a name to. He remembered walking past the towering grizzly on the trail, past claws just like these that could have shredded his vulnerable flesh, and yet the bear had let him pass, a friend and brother. Now these claws were a bond. He and all the bears of the world were brothers. He had somehow taken into himself the powers of the bear, its strength and resourcefulness, its lordship over all the other creatures that walked.

Was he now a bear? No, he was Barnaby Skye, but a

man infused with something new and transforming. He saw it at once in his daily contact with the Absaroka people. Word of his visit to Red Turkey Comb, and the old shaman's seeing, swiftly spread through the Kicked-in-the-Bellies, the news on the lips of the village crier and the source of gossip everywhere. Skye sensed it. The young men, once indifferent or hostile because Skye had spent so much time with one of the most desirable maidens of the village, now stopped and exchanged greetings, and paused to admire his necklace.

Somehow the bearclaw necklace invested Skye with power and prestige and made him an important man among these people. Even Victoria's family was treating him differently, the father less solemn and distant, her brother less imperious. Skye had done nothing to merit this attention, and supposed it was merely pagan superstition at work. In any case, he would be leaving the mountains in a few months. The necklace would be an entertaining curio to show his classmates someday.

He supposed his trapping friends would swiftly put the new camp tender in his place, but it didn't happen. Beckwourth, for instance—the one veteran he thought would make light of the necklace with his usual barbed wit—examined the necklace solemnly and told Skye to live up to what was given him. Sublette studied the necklace, smiled, and added his own mysterious prophecy: "Guess you won't be going east after all, ol' coon. That's good. We need you."

Skye started to protest but fell silent. He wasn't so sure he wanted to go east. He had been thinking about what the shaman had told him. The bowl had been broken and it would no longer hold his old life in it. Who was he now? He worried that in his mind as he went about his tasks, cutting firewood each day, cooking, checking the horses. Who was he? Or rather, what did he want now?

Once, exasperated with himself, he borrowed a small round mirror, a favorite trade item, and studied himself in it, trying to find himself in his own image. He examined his giant nose, long and thick like a hogback ridge, and he found his blue eyes and angular features. But he no longer saw the London boy, and even the sailor was barely a memory. He could no longer conjure up his seaman's life, his tiny bunk, his sullen obedience—most of the time—to imperious officers, his wild, birdlike joy when he had climbed high in the rigging and could see a world that extended beyond the wooden hull of his ship.

Gone now.

In his looking glass he beheld a hardened man with a knowing face, a man ripped from civilization and unlikely to return. An ugly, bearded man in fringed buckskins, who wore his hair loose, or anchored with a red bandanna. A man whose chest bore an ensign that made him a king or a prince in these Absaroka lands. He recognized a new man, and he knew he had been transformed.

Another arctic blast drove them all into their lodges, but now he found himself a frequent guest at the lodge-fires of these people, sometimes with Victoria, often not. The Crows came to him as he cut wood, invited him with gestures or a few words of fractured English or a few Crow words, and then he would spend an evening with one or another clan, often accompanied by veteran trappers. There, in the intimacy of the lodges, he would devour buffalo rib roast with a dozen others and then listen to stories. How these people loved to spin stories! He swiftly gathered there was more to it than entertainment. These tales conveyed tribal history, taught lessons, explained spiritual mysteries, reaffirmed the power of First Maker and all their other Above Ones, and told of the beginning of the world and the creation of the People.

Then, sometime late in the evening, it befell the grandmothers to tell their own stories, and Skye at first could barely believe what he was hearing, and thought his limited knowledge of the Crow tongue was deceiving him. The old women, some toothless but always grinning, eagerly began wildly bawdy stories, swiftly convulsing their audiences with their humor. How could this be? Skye listened uneasily, glancing at the assorted wives and daughters who were enjoying these unabashed tales about mating, the size of genitals, getting caught with someone, sexual prowess, boastfulness about things that Skye had never heard discussed in mixed company.

And there was Victoria at some of these parties, laughing wickedly at these tales spun by grandmothers. She wasn't like a British girl, either innocent of such things or feigning ignorance. She had always stirred him, and ever since he had first gazed upon her at the rendezvous he had wanted her. But in those summer days, when he knew he would be leaving the mountains, he had set aside those feelings because she was different from the Shoshone girls he had dallied with. He couldn't explain it. Now, in the confines of the lodges, and with a new future being born in him, those feelings flooded back. But of course it was not love, he told himself. How could he love a savage?

But he could. The more he and Victoria learned how to talk to each other, often in a patois of Crow and English words enriched with gestures, the more entranced he was with her sharp-etched humor, her swift tenderness, her many ways of nurturing him, and the promise of delights unimaginable that brimmed from her eyes. He had been a lone man too long. He thought of sharing a lodge with her in the winter's cold and in the high days of summer. He thought of her smooth brown body beside him, her yearnings and his joining in the night, a life together, a family—

How startling it was to think of children. His and Victoria's children! All his days, he had thought of himself as a son, not a father. The realization that he was a grown man, free, no longer just a son, no longer tied to England, astounded him. In all the years in the Royal Navy he had perceived of himself as a youth, but now that frozen image was melting away in the rush of events. At age twenty-one, he was capable of siring his own family, sons and daughters, slim and dark like their mother, blue-eyed like himself. He was a man.

The cold spell dissolved one February day in a rush of warm west winds, and he ventured out again, along with the rest of the Absaroka people. The sun was returning, bit by bit, and the high plains glowed in the afternoons, the brown grasses absorbing the warmth. The air remained chill but was sweet and dry. Soon now William Sublette would tell his brigade that the spring hunt would begin; the ice was melting in the creeks and the beaver would be swimming out of their log homes. The realization made Skye restless. He didn't want to leave this paradise where winter had been tamed and the Absaroka told and retold their stories and he had made many friends.

He did not want to leave Victoria. With the milder weather, they spent more time away from the village, and the sight of her in her gray blanket always melted his heart. They had touched a little—some innate delicacy had made this bonding different from the ones he had experienced with the Shoshone women—but now he ached for her and he was flooded with visions of her with him in the thick, warm buffalo robes. He wanted to hug her and never let go, and he knew she felt the same hungers.

But of course the Absarokas were never alone. Each lodge housed grandparents, a man and his women, children, brothers, sisters. The act of love was done in company, and that was how those things were well known to all. A lodge was black at night, without windows, but the soft noises of love told their own tales to all. How could he endure that? Would he find it intimidating to love her only a few feet from her parents—even if they were married Absaroka fashion? He could not say, but he desperately wanted a lodge of his own, and a sweet privacy with her.

One day William Sublette told his brigade they would leave for the Three Forks country early in March, and trap until the beaver were no longer prime. That was only days away, and the news tore through Skye's soul, wrenching him.

Skye thought about Victoria, and how they had come to each other from such different worlds, but also how they had weathered into each other, spending golden moments, experimenting with words, sometimes saying nothing at all in contented silence. He had to act now or he would lose her. Victoria's parents could give her to any Absaroka warrior at any time. There were many who would gladly leave ponies before the lodge and had eyed Skye as a rival. It was now or never. He wasn't sure it would be a good match—the differences were real. But he loved her. He had never loved anyone before, but he knew he wanted her, would always want her, and would be desolated if he lost her.

He walked out to the herd, which was up the creek a mile or so, and found his mare and yearling colt among them, shaggy, thin, but not in bad shape, all things considered. She shied away from him, but he persisted in walking her down, and eventually he caught and haltered her. The colt came along.

He looked the yearling colt over, finding it big, well-developed, dark and cocky. It had scarcely been handled. But after a while it let Skye touch him, rub its ears, run a hand along its neck under the mane, scratch its jaw. Then Skye slipped a loop over its neck and held tight when it yanked back. The colt stopped resisting sooner than Skye had thought, and let itself be haltered, as it had been the previous summer. He led the colt, tugging firmly when it resisted the pull of the lead rope, breaking it to halter.

He lacked a comb to curry the colt, but perhaps it didn't matter. He had a fine, strong yearling with a friendly eye and a good way of moving. He hoped it would be enough. He led the colt away from its whickering mother, led it back toward the village, led it through the village lanes, now teeming with people who were scraping hides, smoking, fletching arrows or enjoying the mild weather—to the lodge of Victoria's family. And there he tied the pony to a picket, his heart riding on the work of his fingers.

Chapter 47

One memorable afternoon Daniel Ferguson and Peter Ranne walked into the village leading their burdened packhorses. Word raced through the lodges, drawing trappers and the Crows.

Skye heard the news and ran toward the newcomers, not believing it. But there they were, in good flesh, showing no sign of unusual hardship. Even their horses looked pretty decent, though their thick hair could be deceptive.

The trappers whooped and hollered and carried on in a way that Skye, with his British reserve, would never quite get used to. A crowd of Crows gathered, just as curious as the brigade. They had heard the story of Ferguson and Ranne's disappearance and probable death during the bitterest days of December.

"Knew we'd find ye hyar," Daniel Ferguson said. "Only the pass kept us from coming over. Fifty-foot drifts or ye can call me a liar."

"Maybe ten-foot drifts, ol' coon," said Sublette quietly, cheer radiating from him.

"No, fifty footers. No child could get through, so me and Peter, we made snowshoes."

"How'd ye get the horses over?"

"I made snowshoes for mine. Peter made skis for his hosses, and they were some, except his nags couldn't stop on a downslope."

Beckwourth guffawed. Bridger grinned. Skye could see that Bridger was thinking up something equally outlandish, but for the moment Ferguson had him buffaloed.

"What happened, Daniel?" Sublette asked, an edge sharpening his voice. "We went looking. It went hard. We near froze before we gave up."

Daniel Ferguson peered innocently about him, enjoying the crowd. He lifted his beaver cap and took his time, knowing he was the cynosure of their attention.

"You got some tobacco? I could use a smoke," he said.

"Not until rendezvous."

Ferguson looked disappointed. "That was all this child lacked, was a good smoke. We plum had everything else any ol' coon would ever want. We was having fat times, excepting that we lacked a pipeful. That sure was a sore point."

Skye listened skeptically, amused and impatient. This old trapper was going to drag out his story for an hour.

"I had every trapper out looking for you," Sublette said, pointedly. The booshway wasn't going to stand for this much longer.

Ferguson leaned upon his mountain rifle, surveyed his audience again, and apparently judged that it wasn't going to get any larger. "Well, sir, it be like this. Me and Peter, we seen that old storm a-brewing and black-bellied clouds a-comin', so Peter, he says to me, 'Let's git.' So we lit out because that was a mean storm and we were a piece from camp. We didn't git far before it was snowing and blowing, but we pushed along, slipping and sliding, leading our nags and hauling beaver. We got down out of the drainage all right, and got out to the flat country all right, but the snow was coming and I was feeling testy. So I said to Peter, I says, 'I know a place to go. I saw her once when I come through hyar a few winters ago by my lonesome, dodging Bug's Boys.'"

He paused, letting it be understood that he knew the Three Forks country better than the rest of them.

"Instead of comin' back to camp, we just hightailed on down the Gallatin until I see what I'm lookin' for, a big billow of steam right in the middle of all that falling snow, snow coming down in buckets so we can hardly see a trail.

"So I says to Peter, 'Ol' coon, we've arrived in the middle of summer.' He looks at me like I've gone beaver, but he leads his nags, following me, and pretty soon the steam gets so thick a man can't hardly see, and I says, 'Peter, we're at the gates of July.'"

All this took translating. Skye had never quite fathomed the argot of the trappers, but as near as he could tell, Daniel Ferguson was saying the pair had not only abandoned the area they were trapping, but had hiked far down the Gallatin River instead of heading for camp.

"Hot springs!" bellowed Ranne. "He taken me to hot springs, biling up outa the ground, letting off steam so thick a man couldn't see his own hand. This child stood on the banks of a pool with green grass growing around it, and the horses soon took to it. Snow falling all over, steam rising, snow vanishing into the steam, and heat coming at me.

"Well, old Daniel and me, we unloaded them hoss, unloaded our gear, unloaded our plews, stripped buck naked, and tippytoed into that thar pool until we was plumb up to our noses in hot water. That water, she felt so good it was better'n rendezvous. Pretty soon I'm so warm I've gotta go down to the cooler end of this hyar pool. It's snowing, and a few flakes land on my hair, but no matter. It's like walking through the pearly gates. I had me a soak, and old Daniel had him a soak, and pretty soon we got to thinkin' we should head back to camp—but we can't. We can't get out. It's too cold out. The snow, she quits, and a breeze comes up so sharp and cold that I'da freezed up solid if I stepped out.

"I look around, and it's plain this place is known to somebody; there's a few shelters around, an old lodge standing, some buffler hides over frames—things like that. A Blackfeet resort, that's what I'm thinking, and I'm glad it's January and all them Bug's Boys are hiding in their lodges. So I says to old Daniel, 'Old boy, it's getting too late and too dark and too cold. I guess we'd just better suffer all this misery and go back to camp in the morning. Them horses is fine—they got all the green grass they can swaller, growing along the banks where it stays warm.'"

Ferguson nodded. "I reckoned we'd fetch pneumonia if we climbed out and tried to go through all that snow back to camp. So we stayed the night. Next morning, it was clear and so cold a man'd freeze just trying to put his duds on, so we just hunkered in that hot water. I was getting a little wrinkled, like a raisin, but it didn't matter. I was getting so hongry my belly was a-howling, but we couldn't get out. I thought, old boy, this hyar's how ye'll go under, starvin' to death in a hot pool ye can't get outa."

Ranne broke in. "Them elk is what kept us a-going. They come for the heat. They see us and don't care. They come just to stand in that pool up to their bellies, and stay warm on the coldest day of the year. Steam's billowing up, but we see elk all over, keeping their toes warm. So, Daniel, he swims over to the bank to get old Jezebel, his rifle, and he kills us a cow elk. We got eats—if only we can get out and gut it and carve on it and build us a fire— but we're plumb stuck in the water. It's so cold we can't even think about cooking elk over a fire, and we're thinking maybe we could bile some elk in our pool, but it's not that hot. So we just stay up to our noses, and feel our skin wrinkle and cook, and starve."

The booshway interrupted. "We were looking for you. It frostbit every man," he said, tautly. "We searched every drainage, fired shots and got no answer, looked for a message—and finally left, every man among us thinking you'd gone under."

"I know, I know. But we couldn't get out of that pool," Ferguson said.

"And besides," said Ranne, "we got us some company."

Skye could see the few Crows who knew some English try to explain all this to the crowd of Kicked-in-the-Bellies solemnly taking in the palaver.

"Company?" asked Beckwourth. "Probably Bug's Boys."

"Bug's Girls," said Peter Ranne.

That sure got attention.

"Twelve of 'em," said Daniel Ferguson.

"Beeeuties," said Ranne. "All about seventeen, eighteen, and fairer specimens of the Wilderness Tribes no coon ever set sight upon."

Some of the Crows growled.

"Ahhh, got to the meat of the story," said Beckwourth.

"They didn't see us old boys at first on account of the steam, so they set up their two lodges, all the time jabbering and carrying on, and pretty soon they doff their blankets and capotes. And then they doff all the rest, and stand there plumb beauteous in the mist, the fairest damsels we ever did see . . ."

"And then this old coon sneezed," Ferguson said.

"And they seen us," Ranne said. "They squeal, and then look us over, and then they decide we ain't takin' scalps and come on in. Well . . . it be some party. I don't reckon

I ever been to a nicer party. Men and wimmin get along better in hot spas."

"We got to know 'em all. They's Piegans, they say, off for a lark. They was sociable, and they invited us to share our elk in their lodges after the plunge, and so Daniel, he gets one lodge and six beauties, and me, I get the other lodge and six beauties, and that's how come we never did get back to camp."

Skye listened, rapt, and couldn't quite imagine why the trappers were laughing and hooting and making light of the story. Unless it wasn't true . . . was this a mountaineer joke? The part about the hot springs seemed true enough—but what about the Blackfeet women? Had they arrived in a blizzard? Had they invited the trappers into their lodges after a plunge?

Skye watched Beckwourth and Bridger slap the missing trappers on the back and make sly jokes. Those Yank mountaineers had their odd ways. Skye could not say why bawdiness made him uneasy. Maybe it was simply that he had spent so much of his young life in a ship's brig that he never learned much about women. All he knew was that for him, these things were serious and sacred, and he hoped Victoria would feel the same way. Maybe he alone in the world thought that a man and a woman should form a union of hearts before they formed a union of bodies. Maybe the world would laugh at him. He knew the Crow people would. Maybe Victoria would, too. Wasn't she born to them?

The Crow, still translating, all broke into broad smiles, for this was a story tailored to delight these bawdy people. Skye realized that it didn't matter whether the tale was true; there was so much fun in the telling and the imagining.

Only William Sublette didn't laugh, and then he finally surrendered, too, the torment of the search forgotten in the joy of seeing two boon companions alive and well after several brutal months of winter.

It turned out that the wayward trappers spent those months at the hot springs, minus their fantasy women, feasting on the animals that came there to escape the bitter cold, trapping beaver in nearby flowages, and generally having a grand time until they could make it over the winter-bound pass to the Crow country.

Skye searched the crowd for Victoria, wanting to know what she thought of all this. But he didn't see her. He wandered back through the village to the lodge of her parents, his thoughts far from the two returned trappers and their alleged bacchanal. The yearling was gone; it had been accepted by her father and mother.

Chapter 48

In one dazzling moment Skye knew his life had forever changed. He peered at the lodge, somnolent in the winter sun, and at the place where his colt had been tied, and wondered. No one came to greet him. Perhaps no one was within.

He thought of Victoria, his promised one. He ached to sweep her into his arms and crush her to him. He ached to talk with her, feel her sharp voice in his ears, rejoice in her wild humor. Now he wanted to hear her whispers in the night.

"Victoria!" he cried, but the lodge did not reply.

"I love you!" he cried, but the busy Crow village ignored him.

What did it all mean? What would happen? He looked about, seeing the ordinary life of a winter-bound village. Smoke drifting from lodges. Curs meandering from lodge to lodge, sniffing cookfires, looking for bits to eat. He saw old men wrapped in blankets shuffling from one place to another. Was this the life he had committed himself to? Had he made a desperate mistake?

A worm of regret crawled through his belly. What had he done? Had he tossed aside a life of achievement just because some hot desire boiled in his loins?

He sighed. The bowl had been broken and no longer held his life within it. Whatever he had been—English youth, seaman, prisoner, merchant's son—all that was gone. There was only the present and the future. Only Victoria. Only the mountains. Only the trapping, the rendezvous, the life of a wilderness vagabond.

A grandmother shuffled by, paused, grinned toothlessly, and touched his bearclaw necklace. Then she patted him on the arm. The necklace meant something to them all. Or rather, Red Turkey Comb's perception of his power and destiny meant something to these people. Surely it had meant something to Victoria's father, who had accepted his single colt. A beautiful maid like Victoria might have won a bride price of many horses and a stack of other gifts from an eager suitor.

He had bear medicine, but what was that? Did it mean only that he was strong? He couldn't answer that, but maybe in time he would know. The grizzly was king of beasts. Skye knew he was no king of beasts, and no match even for the warriors of this village, or the hard mountaineers in his brigade.

He drifted through the village, looking for Beckwourth, who would know what all this meant. No one among them knew the Crows better. Beckwourth would probably be in the small lodge inhabited by Pine Leaf, the warrior woman of the Absaroka, who had been Beckwourth's lover for years. According to the legend, Pine Leaf had vowed never to marry and to become a warrior for the Crow nation until she had revenged the tribe for past losses. She wasn't large but she was nimble, a fine archer and horsewoman and lancer, and had fought brilliantly beside the male warriors, often rallying them when all seemed lost, and becoming a famous woman among all the plains tribes. A maiden she might be, but no virgin, and she had welcomed the rogue Beckwourth into her arms, something that Beckwourth bragged about amidst all his other bragging. Skye wondered if a tenth of what Beckwourth said about himself was true.

Skye found the lodge next to a grove of giant cottonwoods, and scratched gently on the door flap, as was the custom. Beckwourth himself pulled the flap aside.

"Mister Skye," he said. "Come in."

Skye entered and waited while his eyes adjusted to the darkness. He beheld Pine Leaf sitting crosslegged, wearing a simple doeskin shift. She motioned Skye to sit at her right, the traditional place of honor. Beckwourth, lean, mottled brown, and mocking, settled down on the other side of her.

"Do you know the beauteous Pine Leaf?" Beckwourth asked.

"We have met."

"Ah, behold a woman known across the Plains. She has counted coup more times than most warriors in the village. She has turned routs into victories. She has bestowed her favors on Beckwourth and no other. Beckwourth treads where no Crow chief or warrior treads." Beckwourth laughed softly.

"I am honored to be in the presence of such a great one," Skye replied slyly.

Pine Leaf obviously understood all this, and smiled. Scars laced her lean, hawkish face and bare arms, giving credence to her reputation as a warrior.

They bantered a while more, and then Skye turned to the issue that had brought him. "My colt has been accepted by Victoria's father. What happens next?" he asked.

"Accepted, eh? Why, you do what comes naturally." Beckwourth grinned, his even white teeth gleaming in his dusky face.

"I need serious advice, sir."

"If you don't know how to do it, you shouldn't get married."

Skye stared at the lodge door. Beckwourth wasn't going to help him. The rogue would make a joke of it, turn something sacred into carnal humor.

But Pine Leaf intervened, and began talking quietly in the Absaroka tongue to Beckwourth. Skye could understand just enough to catch the drift.

"She says it's time to teach you about the customs of the Absaroka, so I'm delegated. She says Many Quill Woman's a mighty big catch because she's so pretty and has good medicine; half the young men in the village'd give every pony in their herds for her, but the other half think she's got a sharp tongue and don't want nothing to do with her. She's plumb mean to 'em. That mouth of hers is some."

Skye laughed. Victoria's sharp tongue was one of the things he loved about her. She could gut a braggart faster than she could gut a deer, and one of her targets had been Gentleman Jim Beckwourth himself.

"Now, here's the way the stick floats. Many Quill Woman's gonna disappear until the big day. You won't lay eyes on her until then. Her daddy'll send word to you to fetch her at an appointed time—likely, sundown, day after tomorrah. And there she'll be, all dolled up in finery."

"What do I do then?"

"Skye, is your brain solid wood?"

"It's Mister Skye, sir."

Beckwourth grinned malevolently. "You haul her off to your lodge and honeymoon."

"But what of the marriage ceremony?"

Beckwourth chortled. "It isn't like that. You get Many Quill Woman, you take up with her."

"No ceremony?"

Beckwourth shook his head. "Oh, her pap'll have the town crier announce it and they'll have them a parade. And when you wander over to the lodge, he'll give you a few things—the family's gifts to the new couple."

"Such as?"

"Well, it's traditional to give a small lodge, and some ponies to haul it, and the furnishings, along with the bride."

"A lodge? Ponies? I just gave them my colt."

"A bride's family don't stint to set her up, Skye."

"Will there be a feast? Any formalities?"

"Mebbe so. They'll show her off to the whole village. Mebbe ride her through the village, her brothers leading her horse. Let all the village see her in her finery. And they'll show the whole village what they're gonna give you—the lodge, the ponies, and stuff. Mebbe stop at Arapooish's lodge for a little showing off."

"I haven't anything but the clothing on my back. I'd hate to come to my own wedding looking like this."

"Mebbe you should talk to Sublette. You should be looking your best."

"Do I bring her parents a gift?"

"You already have. That little stud colt told 'em you want their daughter. Now, Skye, there's a custom you should know about. From now on, never speak to your mother-in-law, Digs the Roots, and she'll never speak to you. If you see her, look away. If you need to talk to her, send the message through someone else. Mothers-in-law got nothing to do with sons-in-law. Not ever. Except me, of course. I talk to Pine Leaf's maw all the time. These Absaroka let me do whatever I want because I'm a chief. Me and Pine Leaf, we run the wars around heah."

"But you're not married."

Beckwourth laughed gently. "You're bright sometimes, Mister Skye. When it comes to mothers-in-law, these Absaroka are a lot smarter than you white plantation owners."

Skye shrugged. He knew nothing of that. In England he had been too young to consider such things, but he remembered his grandparents, and all the love they had bestowed upon his parents and himself and his sisters until his grandmother had died in her early fifties.

Skye visited a while more with the rogue, and then retreated into the cold twilight, enjoying its peace and the quiet of another winter's night. The earliest stars had punctured the veil of the heavens and glittered above. This aching, mysterious wilderness had become his world, and he was more familiar with the barking of a wolf than he was with the rumble of a passing hansom cab. The starkness of the land appealed to something wolfish in him, something lonely and uncivilized, something that could not be broken to harness. He hadn't known, when he slid into the Columbia long before, that he was saying good-bye not just to the Royal Navy, but to civilization. He grew aware of the necklace on his breast, a device imbued with mysterious power that made him a man among the Crow people. He touched the claws, feeling their sharp length, the violence in them, the sheer animal force they conveyed to him.

He thought of Victoria, as fierce as the land and as wild, the ferocity of her love and loyalty so bright and bold that it had blistered his pallid British ideals. She was a savage woman to match the savageness of his heart. Now she would be his mate. Once he would have chosen some oatmealy English girl, now he would be bored by any woman who hadn't lived close to death and starvation and war and the wild beasts of the fields and forests.

Skye looked into the darkening skies and saw Victoria. He peered into the shadowed cottonwoods and found her there. He studied the ridges where the wolves and coyotes and painters prowled, and saw her spirit striding beside them. He saw her in the icy haze, in the glowing lodges emitting sour cottonwood smoke from their nestled poles. He saw her in the sweetness of the village, in the umber faces around the lodgefires at night, in the exquisite quill-work on a bodice, in the rabbit-fur calf-high moccasins these people wore through their winters. He saw her in the ancients shuffling through their night errands, and in the children scurrying to their homes at the end of a day.

He did not know what would happen next, or when he might be permitted to carry her away with him, off to some private place, where he could hold her in ways sweet and sacred. But he would know soon.

Chapter 49

Skye found himself in a whirl of activity he little understood. Victoria simply vanished, and he wondered which of the many lodges hid her and why he could not see her. February petered out and March rushed in on cold winds and bold blue skies.

The old women of the village smiled at him now, and the children gawked as he passed by. Beckwourth told him that Victoria's family was prominent; her father was an important subchief who had counted many coups and was a leader of the Lumpwood Warrior Society.

Skye learned that Victoria's own mother, Kills the Deer, had died two winters earlier, that Victoria had a brother and two sisters, that Victoria belonged to the Otter Clan, and that her family was the caretaker of one of the village's most sacred medicine bundles, which was opened each spring at the first thunder.

He wondered why the family had accepted his single pony and not the lavish offerings of so many of the village's young men eager to win a beautiful maiden from an important family. He couldn't entirely ascribe it to the word of the shaman, Red Turkey Comb. There had to be more to it than that. Skye did not know and supposed he never would know. There would always be a gulf between the Absarokas and himself.

One afternoon he found William Sublette and sought the brigade leader's counsel.

"She'll be the only woman with the brigade, sir. Does that bother you?"

"Bother me? She'll make the work lighter, Mister Skye. And keep you in the mountains where you belong. She'll do what I couldn't do: give you a reason to be a mountaineer. Davey Jackson's brigade has a dozen Metis women in it. We put the Creole trappers with wives in his brigade because it would face less trouble over there among the Shoshone and Nez Perce. We're in dangerous country here, Skye. You and your bride know that."

Skye grinned. "What we're getting is another warrior, sir. She's a good hand with a bow, and I aim to teach her how to shoot—after I learn."

Sublette smiled. "I'm counting on it. Now, Skye, there's something all the old boys want to give you. Come along."

Dutifully, Skye followed the brigade leaders to the council lodge that housed so many of the engagés. There they had all assembled, grinning mischievously as they lounged around the lodgefire, and Skye feared he'd get a hazing of the sort reserved for bridegrooms.

But they sat about awkwardly, even shyly, tongue-tied for once. Even the veterans, like Tom Fitzpatrick, suddenly looked awkward.

Finally Peter Ranne cleared his throat, looking like he was being led to the gallows.

"The coons reckoned a man should have himself some fancy duds for his wedding," he began. "So, the outfit, we got you some skins sewn up by the women hyar. Weddin' skins, that's how we call 'em."

They unfolded a fringed elkskin shirt, tanned to a soft gold, with quillwork across the chest. The shirt was wondrously crafted, and decorated with bear paw insignia.

"Put her on," yelled someone.

Skye did, marveling at the fit and the gentleness of the

leather. They gave him fringed leggins, too, matching the golden shirt, and then a pair of high moccasins with bull-hide soles.

Suddenly Barnaby Skye was overwhelmed. These were friends. They had dug deep to offer him a treasure like this. These were the best friends he had ever known.

"I—thank you," he said, hoarsely. He could not say more.

"You're a straight shooter, plumb center," said Bridger. "You got a maiden a man'd die for. Hyar now, wear these skins—at least until ye get to your little honeymoon bower and take 'em off."

Men laughed, and Skye sensed a yearning among them. Certain Crow women they could have for a bit of foofaraw. Love, marriage, ties to the tribe were something else, something large and tender and misty in their hearts. These mountaineers had opened their purses and wrought a miracle. He marveled that the village women could have sewn and quilled the shirt and leggins so swiftly.

"I've talked to Arapooish," Sublette said. "Tomorrah, Mister Skye, you'll be married. The next day, we're off. Sorry to cut short your honeymoon, but the streams are thawing and there's beaver to trap."

"It won't stop our honeymoon," Skye said.

"Ye'll be plumb tuckered out," volunteered Black Harris. "Tending Victoria and tending camp."

Men laughed. One by one they stood, stretched, slapped Skye on the back or shook his hand. He had expected a rough and raucous hazing from these ruffians of the mountains, but they had celebrated his happiness tenderly and shyly, with a wistfulness in their manner.

"Well, old child, ye come a long way," said Bridger.

Skye nodded. Could the man about to take a bride be the same man who had slipped into the icy waters of the Columbia, determined to escape slavery or die?

He wandered the village itchily that afternoon, trying to fathom its mysterious ways, sometimes lonely, sometimes angry that he couldn't find Victoria, sometimes feeling left out because no one told him anything, or what he should do, or where he should be, and when. Couldn't these Absarokas even tell him what to expect?

But then, in his restless wanderings, he discovered a small new lodge apart from the village, erected in a park surrounded by cottonwoods. The lodgepoles had been newly hewn and debarked. The lodge, of fine buffalo-hide, bore the track of the bear, brown prints around its lower perimeter. Skye knew, suddenly, that this was a gift, his new home. Tears welled up unbidden, and he was glad no one saw them.

He slept in fits that night, doubts crawling through him like worms. It wasn't too late to stop this. He could back out. He could finish up his time with the brigade and go east. He could hew to his ancient dream. What business had he with a savage woman and savage people? The dangerous wilderness would only murder him in time—or bore him, or leave him an outcast, forever cut off from his own kind.

But then in the deeps of the night, he knew he would not stop this wedding. The seaman, the deserter, the old Barnaby Skye, never had a life, and he was abandoning nothing important. The new Barnaby Skye would have everything a man could ever want.

That bracing morning, marred only by overcast, he washed in the bitter-cold creek, shuddering while he cleansed himself, and dressed in his new buckskins.

He marveled at their golden beauty and warmth. Carefully, he lowered his bearclaw medicine necklace over his head and straightened it on his chest. The cruel claws fanned outward, emblematic of something that Red Turkey Comb, and all these Crows, had discerned in him. That something was what had won Victoria. The necklace seemed a heavy burden to him in a way, binding him to these people even as it required that he live up to the message embedded in those claws.

The men around him watched silently, somehow pleased by the sight of their new comrade Skye decked out in mountain finery and ready for his bride.

The morning ticked by and nothing much happened, although Skye discerned swift furtive activity in the village. He paced through the herd, checking up on his mare, walked the creek, and then returned to his lodge. A wan sun drove off the overcast, and by noon a bright warmth had settled on the village of the Kicked-in-the-Bellies. Then, midafternoon, the village crier, an old man with great bellows, rode among the lodges, bawling his message for all to hear. Skye stood before the council lodge, still uncertain. But even as he waited along with his mountaineering friends, who had all gauded themselves with red bandannas and ribbons for this occasion, Skye beheld a parade. At least it seemed like one. Victoria's father, Walks Alone, and brother in all their ceremonial regalia slowly rode by. Their groomed horses shone in the winter sun and danced proudly.

Skye's new father-in-law radiated power from his stocky frame. He wore a buffalo-horn headdress and carried a lance wrapped in red tradecloth. A small medicine bundle hung from his neck. His son, Victoria's brother, wore two eagle feathers downward, ensigns of war prowess, and passed by proudly. He was older than Victoria but her sisters were younger.

Behind them rode Victoria, looking so beautiful that Skye's heart lurched. She was regal. Her small, spare frame radiated pride and joy this nuptial day. Her black hair glinted in the coy sunlight, two braids falling over her breast, each braid tied with a bright blue ribbon. A streak of vermilion divided her forehead. For this occasion she wore a loose dress of whited doeskin, so full in the skirt that she could ride astride her glistening dappled horse. Intricate green quillwork decorated the bodice, and the pattern was repeated along the fringed hem that fell over high bead-decorated moccasins. She was fragile, proud, joyous, and commanding all at once, and something tender radiated from her.

Skye saw her and loved her. She pretended not to see him at first, but then she gazed at him. That glance, so direct and searching, shot a flood of love and eagerness between them. He ached to reach out and help her off her lively mount. A boy followed, leading three horses, each of them laden with buffalo robes. Others of her clan followed, each in dazzling ceremonial dress.

The villagers crowded close, exclaiming at the lavish parade, studying Victoria, eyeing Skye, whispering and smiling. Others walked by, men and women dressed in dazzling finery, one after another. The Crows were a handsome people, he thought. And in their own fashion they were clad in their form of military dress uniforms and ballgowns, artfully fashioned from tradecloth, beads, quills, leather, feathers, and dyes. He loved them; his heart sang out to each of these relatives as the parade wound by.

It did not stop before his lodge but continued toward the great lodge of Arapooish, who waited there along with his many wives and children. The parade didn't stop there either, but continued to the small lodge of Red Turkey Comb, where the old shaman greeted them with a simple nod, and then around the village, four times in all, for that was the sacred number. Then, at last, Victoria's father drew up his horse before Skye.

A great crowd had collected. All the village, it seemed. Skye didn't know what he should do and hoped they would prompt him. But it turned out that he didn't need to do anything.

They helped Victoria dismount and brought her to him. He had never seen a woman so beautiful or radiant. Her golden flesh glowed. Her bright dark eyes saw only Skye and held him in her vision. He saw love. He beheld her slim figure in the soft, delicate white doeskin, and then he reached out to her, clasping her small hands in his big ones. She smiled. Her hands felt right and good in his. He gazed upon her until the world fell away and he saw only her, and saw her joy, and knew that what he was experiencing was sacred.

Then the youths who had followed her in the procession presented Victoria and Skye with three fat horses, two of them dragging travois laden with wedding gifts: robes and horse tack, a willow flute and drum, moccasins, parfleches, gourd rattles, a reed backrest, the tawny pelt of a mountain lion, half a dozen snowy ermine, elkskin gloves, and several pairs of moccasins. Villagers exclaimed. Victoria smiled. She said nothing, as if for once she was required to hold her sharp tongue in abeyance.

Skye didn't know what to do or say, but he had been around the tribes enough to know that he could add his own ceremony to theirs, and they would honor him for it, and enjoy his contribution. He raised a hand.

"My friends, my brothers, my sisters, my parents, my children: with this union I have become one of the People and you are in my heart even as Many Quill Woman has entered my heart. To her I pledge my love, my life, and all that I am and will be. She is my love, now and forever. And you are my clan and my family."

"Sonofabitch!" said Victoria.

The trappers laughed. The crowd smiled.

A few Absarokas began to drift away, and Skye sensed that they were unhappy the pale man from across the sea had taken the belle of the village from them. But others lingered on, especially the old women, wreathed in smiles and filled with blessings. Skye couldn't understand their words, but he certainly grasped their messages.

His mountaineer friends awkwardly shook hands or clapped him on the back or permitted themselves a bawdy comment that set Victoria grinning. And then they, too, drifted away in the late afternoon quiet. The wedding festival was over. It had been a parade, a way of making the event public. Stops at the lodges of the chiefs and criers and shamans. A display of a family and a clan's glory. Some gifts for the couple.

He and Victoria gazed at each other in the gathering silence, and she smiled.

"Well, Mister Skye?"

He could not speak. He drew her to him, and she responded.

"Let's go to the lodge," he said.

"We got horses."

"They can wait."

She laughed bawdily, but she plucked up the halter lines and tugged the horses along the way to the little lodge in a quiet corner of the woods. "Somebody gotta have sense," she said to Skye. "We picket the horses, and then you show me what a goddamn grizzly bear you are. Eiieee!"

She laughed until she doubled over, and Skye couldn't understand why it was all so funny, but he roared.

Chapter 50

Many Quill Woman slid out from the warm robes, wrapped a fine red blanket around her nakedness, and stepped into the cold dawn to welcome the day. She loved the first light, the sacred moment when the Sun Father caressed the breast of the Earth Mother.

She loved the quiet, the mists of night, the grayness that slowly yellowed and rosed into color. She peered sharply at the slumbering camp, her senses seeking anything amiss. She saw and heard nothing. The horses dozed. The trappers slept, all but one. But this was always the most dangerous moment, the time when the Siksika dogs howled down upon the unwitting to murder and steal. William Sublette knew it, too, and habitually arose before first light to watch and wait. He was a good chief.

He stood before his hut, absorbing the rhythms of the new day there at the Three Forks, the beaver-rich wetlands where the streams joined to form the Big River, which the pale men called the Missouri. He nodded. She hurried to the leafless brush, braced for the cold water that would drive the langorous night from her lithe body, and performed her ablutions.

Numbed, she hurried back to her small lodge, dropped her blanket, and dove into the thick robes, nestling against her hairy man. White man had so much more hair all over than her people, and it amused her. She had married a hairy bear. He stirred and drew her to him until her small breasts pressed against him. They would not mate now; they would draw strength and love from each other to nurture them through the day.

His big paws traced the lumps of her spine, his rough hands pleasuring her smooth flesh. She caressed his cheeks, toyed with his growing beard, and played with his shoulders.

"Victoria," he said, and she was gladdened. She loved her new name. He had said it was the name of an English princess who would someday be queen of his people across the Big Water. She marveled at that. The Absaroka had never had a woman chief.

"No goddamn Siksika this day," she said.

"Someday they'll come. It's still too cold."

"I'll kill some."

He hugged her tight. "You're good with your bow. We'll do some more shooting, and soon you'll be better than I am with a rifle."

That pleased her. He was teaching her to shoot and she was very good as long as she could rest the heavy barrel on something solid. Someday she would be a warrior woman, like Pine Leaf, and help her man in times of trouble.

She nestled her head into the hollow of his shoulder, content. These two moons had not been easy, and she hadn't anticipated the strange, bewildering world she had entered when she and Skye had become mates. The very morning following their marriage the big chief Sublette had marched his trappers westward into Siksika lands, and she had barely found time to say good-bye to her people. It had torn her heart to leave her Kicked-in-the-Bellies behind and head away with these pale Goddamns into a fate and life she couldn't even fathom.

That tormented dawn after their wedding, following a sweet and merry night in which she made Skye groan and laugh and cry, they had heard the call of the chief, Sublette, outside the lodge. Muttering darkly, her bearman had dressed, and she had thrown on an old calico dress, grabbed a blanket, and then had swiftly dismantled the new lodge, storing the seven lodgepoles travois-fashion on one pony, and the lodge cover and their few possessions on another travois. Around her, bearded trappers, breathing frosty plumes in the icy air, wrestled packs onto mules, saddled, damned the First Maker—that was the thing that always amazed her—and departed when the sun was well up and the sleepy Absaroka village could observe their passage.

Ah, those first days were hard! Even now, she hated to remember them. There had been so much she hadn't thought about. She was the sole woman in a brigade of the pale men. And she found herself responsible for the sole lodge and household among them. The rest of these hardy wild men slept under blankets in the frosty night, or built half-shelters of canvas, or erected crude huts. They were crazy. She and her man would enjoy the comfort of a tiny lodge with a fire in its belly to warm them.

She had no one to talk to except Skye. Maybe a word sometimes with Beckwourth, who mangled her language and privately laughed at her people. But no other woman. She ached to chatter with Absaroka women. That was how the chores vanished and the work was made light. But there was only Skye, and often he was so busy cutting wood, or skinning and stretching beaver pelts, or cooking, that she couldn't even talk to him. She had wan-

dered disconsolately through the camp each day, waiting
for the nights, desolated with her loneliness, an alien
among these wild men.

They had treated her well enough but they didn't understand her and she didn't understand them. And Sublette eyed her, or the lodge, as if waiting for the chance to
condemn, or to tell Skye he was delaying the brigade, or
that Skye and his woman were burdening the whole outfit. She knew that, and it chilled her, so she wrestled
ferociously with her chores, the horses, the erecting and
dismantling of their little lodge. She would not bring
shame upon her man.

Nor was that the end of the trouble. They had eyed her
hungrily, and studied Skye enviously, their thoughts filling their bearded faces. They all wanted a warm lodge
and a woman, but there was Skye, the least among them,
with both and it made them bitter. She saw it, even though
they spoke another tongue. Some of them made Skye suffer. He was camp tender, and they made him work all
the harder and found fault with all he did. She knew
enough of the Goddamn tongue to know they were shooting word-arrows into him. But he smiled and said little.
Only when they crossed a certain line, saying things
about her, or how Skye and Victoria spent their nights,
did her bearman rear up and make them back away.

She liked that. Skye had been slow to anger and endured all sorts of demeaning things—if they were made
in jest. But he was brother of the grizzly, and sometimes
he became a bear, and the trappers learned that Skye had
his limits and could roar if they pressed him too hard.

They brought in many beaver—this untrapped country
was thick with them—and Skye worked until he dropped,
fleshing and stretching, cooking beaver tail, cutting wood,

cleaning camp. She assuaged her loneliness by helping him, taking over much of the cooking, making moccasins for the trappers, chopping cottonwood limbs, and sometimes hunting in her free moments, using her bow and arrows expertly to bring down an occasional doe or buck.

After a while she had been rewarded with a different sort of look from the chief, Sublette, and then smiles, and then affectionate greetings. The men changed, too. Now Bridger or Fitzpatrick would pause at her fire and exchange insults with her. She discovered they loved insults, and she had hoarded up an armory of bad words to cuss them with. The Absaroka didn't have any bad words, but the Goddamns did, and it tickled her to loose them like thunderbolts whenever they came around her.

As the old moon passed, and the new one came, she knew she had won them. She was still lonely. Her heart cried for her people. She ached to hear her own tongue instead of this awful English she despised. But things were better, and the trappers were happy because they were making beaver and hoarding up some money to squander at rendezvous on spirits and women and shirts and blankets and shining new traps and rifles. She ached for the rendezvous herself—because then she could be with her own people. All she wanted was friends.

She drew tight against Skye, and he responded.

"You know, Victoria, marrying you was the best thing I ever did," he said. "You've given me a new life—and it's better than the one that filled my dreams so long."

And then she wasn't lonely, at least for the moment. And because he was happy, she was, too.

"Mister Skye," she said. "There's you and me, you and me. You got bear medicine. I got the magpie. Sonofabitch!"

Author's Notes

This novel inaugurates a new Skye's West series in which Barnaby Skye is a young mountain man in the Rockies. The new series will cover the period from 1826, when he arrived in North America, to the time he became a guide in the late 1840s. The first eight Skye's West novels were set in the 1850s and 1860s, when Skye was a guide and a western legend.

Jedediah Smith, who appears in this story, was not only a giant of the fur trade, but one of the preeminent explorers of the unknown American West. After the 1826 rendezvous he embarked on a long, perilous journey in which he sought a route to Mexican California. He found one, but at great cost. By the time he returned to the 1828 rendezvous, he had lost nearly all his men, first to Indians in the Mohave desert, and then to Indians in what is now Oregon. While his men were more or less under arrest in California, he made a perilous trip to the 1827 rendezvous to report to his partners, nearly losing his life and those of his two companions en route. He himself died a few years later on the Santa Fe Trail, the probable victim of Comanches.

I have depicted legendary mountain men such as Tom Fitzpatrick and Jim Bridger fictionally here, but have attempted to portray their well-known traits accurately.

—Richard S. Wheeler
August, 1996

Dark
Passage

For Tim and Tammy Gable

Chapter 1

It had never occurred to Barnaby Skye that domestic discord could ruin a rendezvous or even threaten his future as a mountaineer. Even less had he imagined that it would transform his life. But his young Crow wife, Victoria, was unhappy and on the brink of leaving him, and that was how the trouble began.

He was summering on the Popo Agie near its confluence with the Wind River that summer of 1830, enjoying the great annual gathering of his trapping friends, the thing they all had ached for during the long bitter year. This was the long-awaited shining time. During all those wintry months he had dreamed of these sweet and carefree days when there was nothing to do but soak up sun, eat good buffler hump, play euchre or monte for wild stakes, tell impossible yarns to greenhorns, buy beads, bells, ribbons, and mirrors for the glowing Indian maids, get the sad news about all the coons who went under or quit the mountains, load up with shining new traps, good center-shooting rifles, thick blankets, calico shirts, keen knives—and a few good jugs of whiskey to lubricate it all.

Paradise, at least at first. Never in Skye's memory had there been such a summer. The playful zephyrs cooled him, while occasional thundershowers kept the grassy river bottoms green. The arid benchlands to the north had browned under the hot sun, and now they shimmered in the rising heat. But beyond, tantalizing like an eager lover, rose the mountains, blue and cool and sweet, where a man could suck air into his lungs and rejoice just to be alive and free, without civilization or law or politics or masters to rein him in.

But Victoria was unhappy.

During each of the previous rendezvous, she had borne his little communions with the whiskey jug without complaint. But not this time. Like most of his trapping brethren, he had stocked up on trade whiskey at the canvas emporium of Smith, Jackson, and Sublette and gone on a bender for several days—three, to be precise. Vile stuff, that trade whiskey—grain alcohol, river water, some pepper and tobacco for taste. Worse than monkey spit. When he finally recovered his wits, he felt nauseous and the sunlight intimidated him.

That's when Victoria squinted at him, pursed her lips, and plunged into a hostile silence. He ignored her. If she wanted him to quit the jug, she might as well forget it. He was himself, and couldn't change.

"I want to go visit my mother and father. I haven't been with the People for four winters," she said, looking up from her cook pot one July morning.

"We could do that. Stay a few days right after this breaks up."

"No, I want to be with the People again. Many moons. Maybe always. I am one of the Kicked-in-the-Bellies. Arapooish is my chief. So I will go back—until the next rendezvous, anyway."

He surveyed her, worry coiling through him. He didn't want her to leave. He was hitched to the fur company for a living, and wherever they sent him, that's where he would go. He'd been a camp tender, and had done so well that they had finally made him second in command, the camp clerk and assistant to the partisan, or bourgeois, as the Creoles called the brigade leaders. That was something, rising like that. His pay had gone from two hundred to three hundred a year, too.

Skye sulked. Women! How could any man get along with one?

He eyed her furtively, admiring her lithe, compact figure and her dusky flesh and her taut, clean-boned face and the jet hair she wore in long braids. She was his miracle, and every trapper in camp envied him. From the moment he had fallen for her, while yet a bumbling British seaman who had just fled the Royal Navy, she had worked magic in him. She had given more than love: fierce loyalty, an education in the ways of the Plains tribes, tenderness, his first experience of a shared life, and more. She had lightened his chores as camp tender, brain-tanned every buffalo and elk and deer and moose hide the meat hunters had brought in, which eventually added a hundred dollars to their annual income when they traded the peltries at rendezvous, and had sewn handsome, comfortable skin clothes and fur-lined moccasins for him, year by year.

But now she was threatening to leave him. Well, not that exactly. She wanted him to live in her village for a time. He couldn't imagine what to do about it or how he'd make a living there. She said they didn't need to make a living if they lived with her people. The Absaroka had more than enough of everything. But he said he needed to buy powder and lead, flannels, good four-point blankets, knives, skillets, tin cups, coffee, beans, sugar, flour, and salt. And besides, he owed the company a hundred and fifty dollars and that sum was expanding by the jugful.

She glared at him as if he were crazy.

He should have been happy. That's what rendezvous were for. Six or seven weeks of pure, unbridled fun with the wildmen of the mountains, along with assorted Indians from all the surrounding areas. All except Blackfeet, the ever-present menace to them all. But here, on the Popo Agie, were Nez Perce, Shoshones, and plenty of Crows, though not most of Victoria's village, which was hunting buffalo after a hard and hungry winter.

He glowered at the world, oblivious of the breezes toying with his long hair, his stocky body alive to the delicious warmth of the early summer, even if he was hungover. The sprawling camp lay quiet in the morning light, smoke drifting lazily from a few cookfires, most of the mountaineers still on their buffalo robes after another night's debauch that usually ended around dawn. Skye saw no guards. Did all these veterans of the mountains trust the world that much? Would no Indian venture to steal a horse or a hundred horses? Did all catastrophe cease when these knights gathered?

Skye eyed a knot of men under a nearby brush arbor, and knew they were deciding his fate and the fate of most of the mountaineers gathered at the rendezvous. There sat the owners of the fur company—William Sublette, Davey Jackson, and that legend, Jedediah Smith, back from his three-year adventure to California and the Oregon country, still alive although almost no one else on that expedition had made it. Skye shuddered. He had desperately wanted to go with Smith, but if he had done so he would be lying in a grave.

With the partisans sat some younger men: Tom Fitz-

patrick, Jim Bridger, Milt Sublette, Henry Fraeb, and Jean
Baptiste Gervais. Skye had an inkling what that was all
about. The partners were selling out, just as Ashley, before them, had sold out, and the younger bunch was buying the company. He'd already heard enough to know that
the outfit would be called the Rocky Mountain Fur Company. Just what that boded for him, Skye couldn't imagine, but he knew his future was all tied up with their
palaver.

"Well, dammit, Skye, you going to eat or do I throw
this to the dogs?" Victoria asked.

Skye ate. She glared at him, registering every bite. He
didn't thank her for heating up the buffalo stew. He ate
lightly, his stomach roiling from the previous night's
excesses.

"Can't eat? You were pretty goddamn drunk," she said
maliciously. "Maybe you starve to death."

"What's in your craw?"

"Whiskey"

"I'll drink if I want. This is the only time all year I can."

"Except when you take jugs with you."

Skye ignored her, sipped some scalding coffee—itself
a once-a-year luxury—and fled. If she was going to go
back to her people, he wished she'd be off. He was tired
of the nagging.

He didn't like this rendezvous anymore. The others had
been the best moments of his life. He'd come to the mountains a refugee from the long arm of the Royal Navy, a
man who'd grown up in a watery prison, but here in the
mountains he'd become a new man, learning the craft of
survival better than anyone else—because he had to. He
had no place to run. This last year had been the best.
Smith, back from his terrible trip to the coast, had met

Jackson and Sublette in Pierre's Hole in August—they had been looking for him—and then set out on a hunt northward toward the Blackfoot country, up into the lush Judith Basin, south of the Missouri River. And Skye, along with Victoria, had been along, blotting up the art and genius of the one man who seemed immune to all the perils of the wilderness.

Skye knew that for as long as he lived, he would consider Jed Smith the finest mountaineer and explorer of the times. A season in Smith's brigade had taught Skye all the things he needed to know: how to make camp in a defensible place, how to listen to nature, how to find forage where there seemed to be none, how to conjure food from the naked earth, water from a desert, shelter in a barren plain. How to discern the presence of animals, birds, and Indians. All those things were what made the Bible-reading Smith a man apart. And the things that spelled the difference between life and death, comfort and misery, nourishment and starvation for man and beast. And there was Smith yonder, fixing to desert him, quit the mountains. That was the gossip, anyway.

It riled up Skye some. He itched to have a sweat. Victoria had introduced him to the sweat lodge, especially when Skye needed to boil the booze out of his pores and clean his body. Now he wanted one that would clean his spirit, too, of all its dreads and angers. He didn't know how to do that, especially with all those partisans throwing the dice of fate. His fate. Who would he work for and what would the wage be? And who would be his brigade companions? That mattered most of all.

Nothing much happened during the mornings at rendezvous, and this one was no exception. Victoria vanished with the packhorse on her diurnal woodcutting mission, which took her farther from camp each day. From the slope of the hill where Skye stood, he could see several hundred lodges, scores of brush arbors—structures resting on poles and covered with boughs to provide shade—and vast herds of horses dotting the browning grasslands. Every week or so the rendezvous moved a mile or two to provide the ponies with fresh pasture, so it was slowly crawling up the purling Popo Agie and toward the blue crests of the Wind River Mountains, which were not visible from where he stood, blocked from view by layer upon layer of brooding brown foothills that censored beauty as if it were sin. Not even the company store—or American Fur's rival outfit—was doing any trade, and its clerks lazed in the mellow sun of a July day. Skye watched a red-tailed hawk as it hunted along the brow of a hill, and emptied his mind of everything.

But at noon things changed. The partisans emerged from their shaded arena and headed for the stew pots. Sky intuited that the bargaining was over. It surprised him that Milt Sublette and Tom Fitzpatrick headed straight for him. They looked to be all business.

"Mister Skye," said Fitzpatrick, "you're speaking to the new owners of the company. We're calling it the Rocky Mountain Fur Company. It's no longer Smith, Jackson, and Sublette. Bill Sublette, anyway. Milt's joined us."

"Well, that's some doings." Skye lifted his top hat and screwed it down again. Ownership didn't much matter to him, as long as he had a living.

"Milt and Bridger and I are headed north with a strong party. Fraeb and Gervais are taking a brigade south. How'd you like to take out a smaller third brigade? We're making you a partisan, and we're offering five hundred for it."

"Five hundred? A partisan?"

"Mr. Skye, you've proven yourself for four years. You're a veteran. Smith recommended it, says there's no one better qualified or more likely to make a successful hunt. You're a team, you and your Victoria. Jed said he had the best outfit he'd ever had, never lacking for anything, including safety."

"She's sure some," said Milt Sublette. "A she-tiger."

"I, ah, I need to think it over, gents," Skye said. "Victoria—"

"Nothing much to think over, old coon. We'll put you on the roster as brigade leader."

Skye didn't answer. He didn't have an answer.

Chapter 2

Skye broke the news to Victoria when she returned with her packhorse laden with firewood.

"That's a lot of money, Victoria," he said. "A brigade leader. They like us. They say you're as valuable as I am."

He stood there, top hat in hand, hoping it would be all right. But she glared at him and silently unloaded the wood, dropping it near her cookfire in front of their small, tattered lodge. He had the feeling she was torn asunder.

"We can afford lots of good things," he said. "You want more four-point blankets? One for a capote? You want more cook pots? You want a rifle? We could even buy a horse, maybe."

She kept her silence, glancing at him now and then as she started a fire with a coal borrowed from a neighboring blaze, and then led the runty dun packhorse—a wounded war pony she had nursed into serviceability—back to the herd. Skye stood alone, the wind raking his face, the sun punching needles into him, a man with no refuge except the one walking a horse to pasture.

He didn't know what to do. In her silence lay a message, and he suspected that she would leave him if he stayed with the company. He loved her, but he wanted that job as partisan. He'd come a long way, the youthful fugitive from the Royal Navy who had survived by sheer luck until he stumbled onto the Americans and succor. If he quit the outfit and went with her to her people, he would feel incomplete. If he stuck with the outfit and he lost her, life would darken. She had made their small lodge a paradise. Within its buffalo-hide walls were food, warmth, thick buffalo robes and blankets, shelter from blizzard and rain and cold—and companionship. Once they had learned each other's tongue, they talked and shared, laughed at fools, admired brave men, dreamed, hugged, and coupled. He was not alone.

No child had issued from their union, at least not yet. He feared he was barren, that those long dark maddened years aboard a royal frigate, the bad food and foul air and sickness, had undermined his youth and health. If Victoria only had a child or two, she wouldn't feel this way; instead, she had little more than drudgery and a life as an alien among strange white men, with only Skye for a friend. She lacked even one woman friend. He understood her agony and knew why she was poised like a doe to flee.

He waited for her to return from the pasture. There were many Crows at this rendezvous, some of them related to her, and she would be with them. She had spent every spare moment with them ever since they set up their lodge on the green flats along the Popo Agie. He had seen her laughing with them—no doubt telling wicked stories about the strange white men—and each day she spent more time among them. Hour by hour, as the rendez-vous spent itself, he was losing her.

His own summer celebration went sour. This time, the rude jokes weren't funny. Bridger's wild tales were all familiar. The contests didn't appeal to him. He wasn't much of a shot compared to some of the masters of the long rifle, and although he could throw a 'hawk or a knife with some skill, the veterans of the Rocky Mountain college could whip him easily.

Each year he'd heard the same complaints about pirati-cal prices at the company store, and each year the free trappers had bought new outfits anyway, grumbling all the while they fondled their new Hawkens and blankets and powder horns and flannel shirts. This year they had a choice between the American Fur Company's outfit, run by Henry Vanderburgh and Andrew Drips, or the usual one, but the competition didn't make life any better for the mountaineers. Both outfits charged all they could get.

He yearned for a book or two and a quiet time under a tree, reading. He had heard more than enough tales about grizzlies, Blackfeet, and starving times. No one talked about liberty, or the affairs of nations, or fiction. They didn't even know who their president was, and didn't care. No books came out with the outfit this time, and only one St. Louis newspaper, which most of the moun-taineers couldn't read anyway. Skye wandered restlessly among his friends and rivals—some of them antagonistic toward him because he had climbed the company ladder a few rungs—discontented, crabbed, and half annoyed be-cause he wasn't having a good time.

July slid into August. The nights turned cool, and the days were dry. The oppressive night heat lifted, and a man could sleep in fresher air, with fewer mosquitoes and flies to torment him. Fitzpatrick and Milt Sublette began forming up the pack outfit that would haul the plews and skins back to St. Louis. Trappers traded the last of their pelts or went into hock another year to put an outfit together. Skye bought another jug of trade whiskey, running his debt to three hundred something.

One day the Crows left to hunt buffalo around the Yellowstone, and the next day the Shoshones and some Nez Perce pulled out for the Snake country, while a few Sioux and even a few Cheyennes headed south or east. These enemies and rivals of the Crows and Shoshones respected the neutrality of the trade fair—up to a point. They would gladly butcher each other a mile from the Popo Agie. Victoria watched them leave, her face pinched and her thoughts unfathomable. She and Skye had all but ceased talking, and he had long since been feeding himself because she was no longer around to cook for him.

He watched her angrily. She would take off after the Crows, and good riddance. He didn't need her anyway. Bloody woman. He'd get another. Lots of pretty Indian girls just itching to make a lodge with a white trapper. One was as good as another.

But he didn't really believe that. Victoria's glares and silences—and furtive tears—tore Skye to bits. He knew she was staying on until he made a decision one way or another. But the moment he chose to lead a brigade, she'd be off to her people and that would be the last he'd ever see of her.

One evening he climbed a foothill to think. The air was thick with smoke from forest and grass fires somewhere else—the summer had turned into a scorcher—and he stared into a blood-red setting sun that looked angry and ominous. He already knew what he would do, and it desolated him. He hated being put into this dilemma. Hated his easy surrender. But he was sour on the whole mountain fraternity with all its adolescent braggadocio. Maybe they were all brave and daring men, but they were mostly ignorant, narrow, and mean, too, most of them meaner than the limey jack-tars he'd rubbed shoulders with, and they were a mean lot.

He came off the hill bathed in red, the blood of the sun dripping off him, and headed for Tom Fitzpatrick, who was smoking a pipe, his back befriending a shaggy cottonwood.

"Ah, mate, you mind if I sit and talk?"

Broken Hand, as the world knew him, nodded Skye to join him. "It's a fair night," Fitzpatrick said. "One of the last, I imagine. Smith, Jackson, and Sublette are taking one hundred ninety packs of beaver to St. Louis next week. Milt, Bridger, and I'll head north with a strong brigade. Fraeb and Gervais'll head south." He turned. "You've been acting like a bee stung your butt."

"I'm giving up the company."

That did surprise Fitzpatrick. "A man's reasons are his own, I suppose."

"I'll lose Victoria if I lead a brigade."

Fitzpatrick nodded, sucked his briar pipe, and studied the dying sun. "Where'll you go?" he asked at last.

"Her people."

"Well, now, this is luck. We're thinking to send you up the Yellowstone with a brigade. We thought with your connections ye'd do a deal of trading with the Crows. Maybe you'd better think this over."

"I did, sir. I'd bloody well lose her."

"I'll confide something to you. Beaver pelts can earn a fortune, and we're facing tough competition from rich men—Pratte, Berthold, Chouteau—who bought the western division of the American Fur Company from John Jacob Astor. They have a brigade in the field this summer, up north. Led by two experienced men, Henry Vanderburgh and Andrew Drips. They're building a post—Fort Floyd—at the confluence of the Yellowstone and the Missouri—a perfect spot to control the mountain trade. And they're planning another on the Yellowstone and the Big Horn. That'll be for the Crow trade. Just put a canoe into water here and you'd end up there. And that's not all, Skye. Our friend Jim Beckwourth—he's a headman with the Crows now, for American Fur. They're paying him a reg'lar salary to steer the Crow trade to that outfit. We'd hoped your brigade could stem that."

"I've made up my mind."

Fitzpatrick grumbled impatiently. "How much do you owe the company?"

"Over three hundred, sir. But I'm outfitted. I thought I'd pay it off next summer with peltries. Victoria tans a fine robe. I don't much like trapping, but I'd get it paid off."

"Suppose we were to employ you to steer business our way. Keep it away from Beckwourth. Bring the Crows to us next summer—Powder River it'll be, and that's Crow country. Take a small trading outfit with you."

"It won't be easy to match Beckwourth, sir. He's been in the mountains since the Ashley expeditions."

"It's worth a try. AFC's paying Beckwourth—we know that. Probably three hundred to steer the tribe their way. They've also given him a trading outfit. He's picking up pelts. You and your lady'd be worth the same to us."

"You'd trust me?"

"The mountains bring out a man's nature."

"Beckwourth's a chief, I hear."

Fitzpatrick nodded. "That's right. But you're married to a Crow from a prominent family. I'll have to talk this over with the partners. I think it'd be a good move to put you there.

"It wouldn't be easy. American Fur's building posts, and Beckwourth can get trade goods whenever he needs them. We can supply you only once a year. We'd give you a small outfit—mostly shot and powder, arrow points, knives, awls—things you could carry on a single pack-horse. But mostly we would want you to become an important man among them, win their loyalties, and bring them to us next summer, laden with beaver and robes for trading. In other words, beat Beckwourth at his own game. Do whatever it takes, compete on any terms."

"Well, there might be something in it. I'll talk to Victoria. Maybe she'll like the idea."

"A word of caution, Skye. American Fur's a rough outfit. They'll do anything to whip you. Maybe even resort to violence. Blame you for whatever goes wrong. Beckwourth's certainly capable of ruining you. You'll be facing a gifted man, a fine warrior, cunning and smart—and a man without scruples."

That troubled Skye. "I have scruples, sir."

"Best forget 'em."

"No, I can't do that. I live by my ideals. I'll not do anything dishonorable."

"No one's askin' you to."

"That's got to be understood. Let me say it plain. My word is my bond. I'll not lie, cheat, slander, steal, or kill. I'm a peaceable man and I hate war. Especially for the sake of commerce. If Beckwourth whips me by resorting to those things, then I'll be whipped. There are deeds I won't do, not for anything. But I think I can whip American Fur. And I think the Crows would like a man who lives by his own standards. If that's not enough—then I'm not your man."

Fitzpatrick stared a long while and then shrugged. "The mountains are a hard place," he said. "Your rules don't apply."

"My rules apply to me."

Fitzpatrick grinned suddenly. "I like that, Mister Skye. I like that indeed. I'll talk to the partners."

Thus, willy-nilly, a deal was forged. Victoria didn't object at all. Now she'd have Skye in her village, among her people, and she'd still be able to get blankets and beads and knives and hatchets.

"Dammit, Skye, this is good," she said, looking cheerful for the first time in months. He knew, and rejoiced privately, that she couldn't bear to leave him, either, just as he couldn't bear to leave her, and this new position was a miracle and a cause for rejoicing.

Then one austere August day, Skye watched the old partners, the masterful Diah Smith, Bill Sublette, and Davey Jackson, start a large pack train eastward. The next day he watched Fraeb and Gervais head toward South Park and the high Rockies. And then Bridger, Fitzpatrick, and Milt Sublette leave for the Blackfoot country with a powerful brigade two hundred strong.

He and Victoria loaded their lodge onto a travois, burdened two packhorses, saddled two riding horses, and headed home, and all the while Victoria laughed and babbled like a merry brook.

Chapter 3

Victoria, Many Quill Woman, rejoiced. The pony beneath her was taking her home.

Home to her father, Walks Alone.

Home to her little mother, Digs the Roots.

Home to her brother Arrow, and to her sisters, Makes the Robe and Rosebud.

Home to her people, to the land of plenty, where buffalo and elk and deer abounded, where clear cold water dashed from the mountains.

Home to the center of the world, which the Absaroka would possess forever.

Home to her father's brother Arapooish, Rotten Belly, great chief of the People.

Home to her own tongue, which tripped lightly through her soul as she rode.

She could not contain her gaiety, and laughed and mumbled as she and Skye traveled through a cloudless August day. She felt weightless, afloat upon a gauzy cloud, no burden at all upon the ugly little pony. She felt lithe and young, her body perfect, her spirit hovering above her, like her counselor, Magpie, who flew along beside her, an ever-present guide.

Her man seemed more somber. He took them down the Wind River, but well to the west of the river bottoms to avoid dangers along that great artery. Soon they would reach the Owl Mountains, where the river vanished into an impassible red-rock canyon, and there they would detour over the crest of the mountains. When they reached the river again it would have a new name, the Big Horn, and it would be nestled in red and yellow rock.

She glanced boldly at Skye. He rode peaceably, almost carelessly, but she knew it was an illusion. His eyes never ceased their study of distant horizons, the heavens, rocks and barriers and gulches that might conceal danger. He took in all of that, weighing and assessing. In their four years of marriage, he had transformed himself from a man who rode boats upon the big waters to a seasoned and careful warrior. His new Hawken rifle rested in its quilled sheath, always at hand. But that was nothing compared to the terrible bear claw necklace he wore upon his chest, the ensign of his medicine and power.

She examined Skye, finding satisfaction in the sight of him. She especially admired his nose. Was there ever such a heroic nose? He wore his long hair gathered into a ponytail, the way of the warrior, and upon his head was the medicine hat that had become his Sacred Way—a top hat, the pale men called it, black felt, scuffed and battered, with a small brim below it.

He paused on a slope, stopping just under the ridge so he could peer ahead without being seen. This heartened her, this innate caution. He would deliver them safely to the Yellowstone country and the village of her people. This time he lifted a hand, and she stopped her pony at once. Behind her, the packhorses stopped too. He had seen something. She slid off and walked to where he sat his horse, just below ridge level. She peered east and saw what he had seen, the dust of many horses on the river, heading north, their own direction. A large and fast-moving party, without lodges. Warriors or hunters. And they would have vedettes to either side, probably one very close.

Not Crows. She knew where her people were. The Absarokas at the rendezvous had told her. She and Skye could stay put, probably unseen in this dry drainage, but if the vedettes cut their trail, they would not be safe. She looked at Skye anxiously. He watched and waited, squinting into the noonday glare, and eventually he pointed. To the west, a small group of horsemen—mere black dots— rode through the dry sagebrush-shot country. She and her man were between the main body and the sentinels.

"Nothing to do but go powwow with 'em," Skye said. "I'll fetch some tobacco."

She watched Skye ride back to the gray packhorse, dismount, and dig through the panniers. Tobacco came in various forms, the most common being the plug, or twist. He pulled out several.

Moments later they topped the ridge and were instantly spotted. Skye led her directly toward the smaller group of riders, while dread stole through her. These were not pale men, but one or another of the Peoples. If Siksika, or Blackfeet, she and Skye were doomed to a slow death by torture. But they were far from the land of the Siksika, and more likely these were Sioux or Cheyenne, who might or might not torment them.

They met on a windy hilltop. Four warriors, none young; small, wiry, lithe, broad faced, wearing only breechclouts—and war honors, eagle feathers in their jet hair. But they weren't painted for war, not displaying their personal medicine. None had a rifle. The bows of three remained unstrung, but the fourth—the headman, apparently—carried a strung bow with a nocked arrow. He could kill her husband before Skye had his Hawken half out of its sheath.

She didn't know who these people were. Not Sioux or

Cheyenne. Maybe Arapaho or Ute, far north of their usual haunts. Maybe going to make war on her Absaroka. She glared at them disdainfully, letting them know what she thought.

But her man made the peace sign and offered a twist of tobacco—sealing the peace, if accepted—to the leader. The burly warrior studied Skye, glanced briefly at her, and then focused on Skye's magnificent bear claw necklace, given him four winters earlier by Red Turkey Comb. The medicine necklace told the world his was the power of the grizzly bear.

The elder took the proffered twist of tobacco. Skye, who had learned something of the finger language, asked them who they were. Victoria watched closely, as puzzled as Skye.

Pawnee. Ancient enemies of the Sioux. Friends of white men. Friends of the Absaroka, sometimes.

"Aiee! Pawnee, Skye," she exclaimed. "Goddamn!"

He didn't know much about them, so she explained that these people lived to the southeast, along the Platte River, and hunted buffalo. Maybe friends—if they didn't steal everything in sight.

"I never met one," Skye replied. He turned to the elder and signed for a smoke. But the elder, his eye upon the distant column, motioned Skye to come. They would join the main body.

Reluctantly, they headed for the distant ribbon of water. They were alive, anyway, and no one had stolen anything—yet.

"I never was much good with the sign language. Maybe they've got someone we can talk to," he said to her. "Tell me about these Pawnees."

She didn't know much, but she did remember one thing:

they worshiped the Morning Star, and every year they captured a maiden from another tribe and ritually sacrificed her to Morning Star. She glared at these burly Plains people, suddenly cold within. She'd kill a few before they laid hands on her. She didn't know of any Absaroka girls who had been sacrificed, but that didn't mean there weren't any.

Before Sun had gone much farther through the sky, they reached the main body—perhaps fifty warriors, traveling with many packhorses and travois laden with good robes and peltries.

Their arrival halted the procession, and all the Pawnees crowded around. They were good horsemen and rode spirited animals. None seemed menacing to her; she felt more at home in any Indian camp than among the pale men.

Skye was taken to their chief, a lean, corded giant whose experience of war was etched in the scars on his body—an ugly welt across a forearm, another across his ribs. Then a mixed-blood warrior pushed through. He had brown hair and gray eyes, and a freckled, mottled flesh.

"Le Duc," he said, and began talking in the tongue of the Creoles. Skye shook his head. But Le Duc knew a few of Skye's words, and so they communicated.

"Cut Nose," Le Duc said, pointing to the headman. "Pawnee war chief. Me, Antoine Le Duc, Le Duc fils, engagé."

"Barnaby Skye, Victoria—Many Quill Woman, Absaroka," Skye replied. All the while, Cut Nose listened and waited for translations. In time they got the story. These Pawnees had come to trade robes for rifles, blankets, pots, and knives at the pale men's fair but arrived too late, and now were looking for the pale men. And they had decided to visit the Absaroka as long as they were so far from their villages. And maybe steal some Sioux ponies.

"We are going to the Absaroka. The Kicked-in-the-Bellies. Come with us," Skye signaled.

Cut Nose wanted to know where the traders had gone.

"Back east, with many pelts. Some north to the Missouri—Big River—to trap. Some south, to the Wall of Mountains, to trap."

Le Duc explained all that.

"We will visit Arapooish, Rotten Belly," Cut Nose said. "You are our friends, our brothers. You are welcome in our camp. We will smoke the pipe of friendship tonight. We are friends of the pale men, 'Mericans, traders. Yes, you, us, we are like two stars side by side."

Skye didn't like it. Victoria could tell that. Her man was a lone bear. But there was nothing to do but join these Pawnees on their adventure into distant lands.

She would be the lone woman in camp. She eyed the Pawnees mistrustfully. Who knew what such strange men would do? Skye would protect her, if he didn't start sipping from his jug.

Pawnees along with the Skyes started north again, finding the trail that would take them over the Owl Mountains. The trail led far west of the place where the river vanished into a sinister gorge, up through arid land dotted with juniper that seemed to grow in rawboned rock. They descended all afternoon through red-rock country, her own Absaroka land, the Big Horn basin, and would camp that evening at a famous hot spring where her people had come for healing and prayers. But she didn't like it. She would have liked to soak in the hot water with Skye, but now with all these Pawnees around they'd just set up a lodge. There wasn't much game around the spring, and she hoped the damned Pawnees had some meat.

They made camp at dusk in a green valley girt with red rock and junipers. She didn't like the look of the thunderclouds building over the mountains, so she set up the lodge while Skye took the horses to the nearest pasture and hobbled them. Grass was thin there. Something crabbed at her; unruly suspicions, dark doubts. She dropped the trading packs just inside the lodge door.

The Pawnees cooked a deer and shared the meat. Some of them slid into the healing hot waters as dark descended. She didn't like any of this, but Skye seemed happy.

Later, long after she and Skye had gone to their robes, she awakened with a start. She'd been hearing something and then nothing. She poked her head out of the lodge. The clouds had dissipated and a quarter moon cast pale light—on nothing. The Pawnees were gone. She stalked the camp, finding not a trace of them, and knew, suddenly, that the Skye horses would be gone, too. Along with their packs—everything, including the trade items entrusted to them by Broken Hand Fitzpatrick.

Angrily she walked through the moonlight, confirming her darkest suspicions. The treacherous Pawnees, well known as the great thieves of the prairies, had stolen all the Skyes possessed—and five hundred dollars of trade goods.

"Goddamn," she said, hating to tell her man they had nothing.

She stormed back to the lodge, finding Skye up, sitting in the deep dark.

"Thieves!" she bawled.

"Everything?"

"Everything. Our horses."

"The trading packs?"

"Gone."

Skye sighed, registering that. "Now I owe them five hundred more. Where'd they go? Could you make it out?"

"Not enough light to see. But not long ago. I can still smell the dust."

Skye stalked the abandoned camp angrily, seeing for himself.

"What are we going to do without ponies?" she asked.

"We'll walk," he said.

Chapter 4

"**W**e'll carry what we can on our backs," Skye said. "It isn't so far. Ten sleeps to my people."

"That's not where I'm going."

Victoria registered that and looked unhappy. "You will not catch them. They have many horses."

"I'll try."

"You are alone; they are many."

"When I was a boy in the boat on the Big Water, I was alone. They would not even let me have my gruel—my food. So I fought them for it. They beat me, but then they let me eat. Maybe I will lose, but I must try. It's a law of my life that I must try."

She nodded. "Maybe you will get everything back. Maybe you will die."

Skye surveyed the abandoned camp in the light of earliest dawn, before the sun rose. No trail led north. So the

Pawnees had slipped away in the night, back from where they had come. South to the plains. Away from the Crows. All the talk about visiting the Crows was smoke.

"Victoria," he said, "I have to go after them, away from your people. You may as well go north. This is your country. You'd be safe enough. We can rig up a pack for you. Maybe I can make some meat for you to take with you. There's berries, chokecherries . . ."

It angered her. "Wherever you go, Skye, that's where I go, dammit."

"You could visit your people. I'll come later when I finish this."

"Maybe I wouldn't see you. You and me, Skye. We will find the Pawnee thieves."

"It could be dangerous."

"You got bear medicine. Big, big medicine. Me, I got some medicine, too." She grinned at him. The idea of a daring raid on their tormentors appealed to her.

"I thought you wanted to get home to your people."

"I do. But goddamn, Skye, we're gonna walk into the village with some war honors, Pawnee scalps. You, you'll be a big man among us."

He shrugged. Being a big man had never appealed to him, nor had he ever sought status. Swiftly they inventoried their few possessions. They had the lodge, which they would have to cache and hope to recover later; two summer robes; the clothing on their backs; his rifle and powder horn and fixings; his sheathed knife; her bow and quiver of arrows; her flint and striker. They had what they needed.

They found no place to hide the lodge, so they left it. But before doing so, Victoria hung a small medicine bundle from the lodgepoles, her amulets, some sage, some sweetgrass. The Peoples would leave it alone. They left the robes within; they were too heavy to carry. Then they headed south, back to the Owl Mountains. She carried only her quiver and bow; he cradled his Hawken in its fringed, quilled leather sheath, her gift to him.

Hunger bit him. His stomach growled and complained, and he kept a sharp eye for anything they might eat. She walked wordlessly beside him, every step taking her away from her village and her dream of reunion.

The day turned hot and they staggered through boiling air, crossed the Owls, and reached their base and the Wind River by nightfall. The trail of many horses led ever south, but they had not seen their quarry all day. The Pawnees could be twenty miles ahead for all Skye knew.

They slaked their thirst, and Victoria managed to find some roots and berries. They had no pot but she roasted the roots—prairie turnips, he thought—over coals. That meager fare would have to suffice.

That night, snugged close for warmth, she ran her small hands over his back. "You some hell of a sonofabitch man," she said. He laughed. One thing a Crow woman loved was a good warrior.

She laughed, too, oddly happy. He had come to understand something: she liked having him to herself and not sharing him with all the trappers and mountaineers. Now at last she had Skye without all the rest of it.

He awoke in the night, responding to the rustling of some creature, but saw nothing. She lay beside him, awake. He judged that it might be two or three in the morning.

"Let's go," he said.

"Damned spirits," she muttered. "Bad place. Someone died here."

Hunger tortured him now; his belly howled. But he pushed that aside. They could gain hours on the Pawnee. If they were like other Plains people, they would be in no hurry to start in the morning. He and Victoria could be seven or eight hours closer by the time the Pawnees saddled up. But they would not be able to see the trail, and would have to trust that the Pawnees were heading toward their own country, having done all the mischief they could.

He splashed icy water on his face, gasped, felt the water trickle through his beard, while she silently prepared herself for the day. Then he hoisted the heavy Hawken—the big mountain rifle had been built to withstand abuse, which is why the trappers loved them—and they started south again, with only the Wind River to guide them.

Fool's errand, that's what it would come to, he thought. But it was something he had to do. Some things were iron rules inside of him, and this was one. Maybe he would fail, but they would not forget Mister Skye.

The trail took them over the foothills of the Wind River Mountains, which lay in their path like giant tree roots. The slopes winded them, but at least they could make a living out of buffalo berries and the bitter chokecherries, though all the berries in the world wouldn't do much for the gnawing in his gut.

He pressed forward relentlessly, sometimes worrying whether his mate could maintain the pace. But she walked grimly beside him, her face a mask, enduring hardship in the way of her people. All that brutal day he pushed along the trail, knowing that they were gaining ground. The Pawnees were in no hurry, and their travel was leisurely. The horse manure was fresher, the evidence of passage—bent grass, sharp prints in sandy soil—more immediate.

At dusk Skye and Victoria climbed an endless slope, topping it in the last light, a streak of blue behind the mountains signaling the death of a day. And below, a mile off, a fire. They stared at it, suddenly aware that decisions had to be made.

"I guess we'll walk in," he said.

"And die."

"Maybe not. I'll keep my sheath on the rifle. You keep your bow on your back."

"Maybe they just kill us."

"Maybe," he said. "But if we go in armed, we'll face thirty or forty nocked arrows."

She muttered something to herself, and they started down the long slope, stumbling in darkness, not trying to conceal their presence. A few hundred yards from the fire, some of the Pawnee materialized, alert and ready to kill.

"Well, we're back, mates," Skye said, forcing himself to sound cheerful. "Thought we'd join our good friends the Pawnees."

They didn't understand a word, but that wouldn't matter. Swiftly the warriors enveloped them, eyed their weapons, peered into the darkness looking for others, for ambush, for trouble. Over the fire, a deer haunch roasted, spitting fat into the flame. That was all Skye thought about. He headed straight for the haunch and sliced slivers of hot, roasting meat from it, wolfing some, handing some to Victoria.

"How come you here?" asked Le Duc, the breed.

Skye ate. Filling his belly was the only business he wished to conduct. So he smiled, sliced more meat, fed

Victoria, and continued to satisfy the howl of his stomach. Finally he wiped his mouth, sheathed his knife, and examined the Pawnees. Every horse had vanished. Whatever remained of the stolen packs and pack saddles had vanished.

"Come to fetch our horses and packs," he said to Le Duc. "I guess if you Pawnees are friends, you'll return them, eh?"

"What horses? I see nothing."

Skye lifted his topper and settled it again. "Well, this is some," he said. "Let's go ask the headman there. Go on, ask him."

Reluctantly, Le Duc spoke to the headman, and the headman replied.

"He says we don't have nothing."

Skye grinned. "Tell him he does not speak truly, and if he's a friend of white men, he'd better try again."

Le Duc spoke again, and the headman's response was stony silence. Pawnee warriors glared, and Skye noticed that some had bows in hand.

"Tell him he's no match for bear medicine," Skye said, touching the magnificent bear claw necklace on his chest. "Tell him he can have this necklace if he's telling the truth."

Victoria cussed at him.

Le Duc tried again. "He says he's telling the truth and give him de bear claws."

"Tell him that if he's lying, the bear claws will kill him within one moon because he will not be worthy of such medicine."

"Sonofabitch," Victoria said.

The headman stood, undecided and unhappy, and then walked into the darkness without a word.

Skye guessed he had just won, but wasn't sure. "Le Duc, we're fetching our horses and gear now. If you don't give us our own back, we'll take others. If we don't get our gear back, we'll take more horses."

Sullenly, the breed translated to the warriors, who stood stock-still. No one moved. Skye examined them alertly, knowing the moment of truth had arrived, and if he guessed wrong, he and his beloved might not walk away.

"Take us to the herd," he said.

No one moved.

"All right, we'll find the horses ourselves. But first we'll collect our gear."

He deliberately walked the periphery of the camp, where the firelight faded into night, and saw nothing at all. No one stopped him. He guessed that they were astonished that a lone man and woman would challenge thirty or forty able warriors. Wherever the gear was, he couldn't find it.

"What're we gonna do, Skye?" Victoria asked.

"I don't know from one moment to the next." He hiked back to the fire, which cast wavering orange light upon these powerful soldiers of the Pawnee tribe.

He stood in the midst of them, his voice scornful and withering. "I thought we were friends. You told me you were coming to visit my wife's people. Instead, you're liars and thieves." He spat on the ground. "That's what, two-tongued, miserable, thieving curs. I'll tell the Absarokas about the lying Pawnee. I'll tell the Shoshones and Bannacks and Cheyenne. Let 'em know all about you."

They would translate his tone of voice, at least. But none moved.

"Skye," whispered Victoria. "Watch out."

Skye whirled as an arrow thudded at his feet.

"Get out," said Le Duc. "They say go."

So he had lost after all. He was jeopardizing Victoria as well as himself. Wordlessly, he stalked away, this time with a large escort of Pawnees, determined to see him far from their camp. They halted after ten minutes or so, muttering something at him that he took for a lethal threat.

"Thanks for the meal, mates," Skye said.

He and Victoria hastened through the blackness, veering sharply left to dodge any treacherous arrow. But no one followed. He had failed. They would put up a massive guard this night and in the days to come.

"They gonna talk about this a long time, Skye," she said.

"But we didn't get anything back."

"Big medicine," she said.

But big medicine wouldn't replace their losses.

Chapter 5

The ignominy Skye knew he would face when he reached Victoria's village didn't make the hard walk any easier. He had dreamed of returning with all the ensigns of success: horses, packs, Victoria handsomely accoutered with every imaginable luxury—four-point blankets, pots, knives, awls, conchos for her belt, looking glasses, beads, and all the marvels that bespoke success and comfort. That and a trading outfit that would make him a treasured guest.

Instead, he would walk into the village as a pauper. He would greet her parents as a pauper. He would try to compete against Beckwourth and the American Fur Company as a mendicant, with nothing to show for his four years in the mountains.

But that was the future. Now, on the trail, survival occupied every moment. Victoria's moccasins were wearing out. His shirt was rotting. They were never far from starvation. They were helpless against enemies, rain, cold, brutal heat. They trudged wearily back to the Popo Agie, the plains desolate now, the grass grazed to the roots from the time a thousand horses sojourned there during rendezvous. They trudged north along the Wind River, retracing their steps, the land dry and game scarce. They survived on a hare one day, a badger another, vile meat that gagged him.

Victoria never complained. She not only radiated cheer—he ascribed that to the imminent visit with her family—but oddly, she seemed to love and admire him all the more, even in his defeat. He couldn't understand it.

They toiled over the arid, scowling Owl Mountains once again, and down to the hot spring nestled in the rough red-rock country. Their lodge had not been touched. The sacred bundle still hung from within. Victoria retrieved it, rejoiced in its medicine, and they settled into their home—for the night. She cut moccasin leather from one of the robes they had left there and sewed a new pair, awkwardly using his knife as an awl, cussing all the while. She cut a chunk of the summer robe to take with her, knowing that she would need to repair footgear again before they had walked ten sleeps to the Yellowstone— the Elk River, as her people called it.

They stuck to the bottoms of the Big Horn River, working north through a harsh, naked land, and were rewarded with some game. Skye first surveyed the sage flats, saw nothing menacing, and risked a shot with the Hawken. The boom emptied into silence, and a yearling mule deer crumpled. That midafternoon they filled themselves with the dark, soft meat, which they roasted on green willow sticks, and ate again at dusk, and again in the sharply chill morning. Summer was waning. They would sleep cold before they reached her people.

They traversed a depressing and monotonous basin, eating the venison, and then struck greener country east of the Beartooth Mountains. When they reached Clark's Fork of the Yellowstone, Skye knew they weren't far from Victoria's band. He had been there before with one of the brigades, and knew the country. The closer they walked toward the Yellowstone, the more exuberant Victoria became, sometimes laughing or talking softly to herself in her own tongue—the words sweet and melodious, utterly different from her harsh English. She bloomed, laughed, found prairie turnips and other edible roots Skye couldn't name, all the while helping him hunt and keep an eye out for trouble.

But as her spirits soared, his sank. His leggings were in tatters, begrimed and falling apart, rotting day by day, his fringed coat foul with grease. He would arrive in her village half-naked, filthy, unkempt, and starved to a shadow. He looked at his grimed buckskins, his hands caked with dirt for want of soap other than the thick root of the yucca she dug and pulverized for him, his greasy boots, his worn calico shirt, and he beheld a vagabond who had never escaped his misfortune. He had dreamed of triumph, of walking proudly through the camp behind the town crier, showing them all that their Many Quill Woman had a *man*.

Each day, the snowcapped blue peaks of the Beartooths loomed closer, while the Pryors vaulted smoothly upward in the east, and each night the cold crept deeper into their camp, forcing them to keep a fire going all night because they had nothing else with which to protect themselves. But the storms held off. There were always blessings, and one of them was a dry August and September.

The very hour they struck the stately Yellowstone, its icy waters braided by gravelly islands and its banks thick with cottonwoods, they discovered a distant party and hid on an island, unable to tell friend from foe. But they were not discovered. There would be traffic on that great artery, most of it unfriendly, and they would have to be much more careful.

Here game abounded, and they shot what they needed, while Skye worried about his declining supply of powder and ball. His pig of lead, bullet mold, and spare powder had all fallen into the hands of the Pawnees. He might have to buy powder from Beckwourth and watch the man laugh at him.

Still, it did no good to worry about the future. They were traversing grand country, the valley of the Yellowstone running here between tan sandstone cliffs, the bottoms green, the foothill slopes dotted with jackpine, the distant blue peaks noble and exhilarating. Already snow had crowned them, yet it was still summer in the river bottom.

This was Absaroka, land of the Crows, and this would be his home, his refuge, for at least this winter, and maybe much longer. He realized that now Victoria was usually in front, ten or twenty paces ahead, whirling forward with a girlish joy at returning to her people. He rejoiced in her happiness, and yet it seemed to be saying that he wasn't enough; life with him didn't fulfill her. She needed her people even more. A worm of bitterness slid through him, but he dismissed it. He would not let some petty jealousy erode the bond that had transformed his life.

The Crows, this season, were at the great bend of the Yellowstone, the very spot where, in early 1827, he had found Sublette and the trapping brigade that saved his life. The place was a favorite resort of the Crows, abounding in game and good grass, as well as a safe and defensible site. Then, one glowing September day, they forded the Shields River flowing in from the north, hiked west a few more miles, and spotted the drifting smoke of cookfires.

Victoria was home. She laughed and cried, and urged Skye to hurry, hurry, that last mile along the river flats, across grassland and around mottes of cottonwood, past a multicolored herd of Crow ponies, until at last a village guard, a young member of one of the warrior societies, halted them, his gaze first on Skye and then on her.

"I am Many Quill Woman," she cried. "And you were just a boy when I went away."

Skye was able to follow that with his rude knowledge of her tongue.

"Yes, Grandmother, I am the younger son of Beaver Tail, and my mother is Iron Awl. And this is the man you went away with." His gaze, which raked Skye's bedraggled attire, said all too much.

"We have been insulted and robbed by the lying Pawnee," she retorted acidly. "Come, and I will tell the story to the elders and our great chief, Rotten Belly."

The youth nodded, turned his spotted pony, and accompanied the two visitors through the village, past smoke-stained lodges, tripods bearing medicine bundles, strips of buffalo and other meat drying upon racks, women fleshing buffalo hides staked to the earth, old men sunning, groups of younger men watching the hawks and passing a lit clay pipe from one to another, and women grinding up berries to put into pemmican, the trail food and winter emergency ration.

And with every step a crowd gathered behind them, some examining Skye's tattered buckskins with ill-concealed malice or horror. Was this the fate of the proud daughter of Walks Alone? The one who married the *mah-ish-ta-schee-da,* the yellow eyes, as these people called white men? Skye could do nothing to change their impression of him, so he ignored them all, anger brimming in him at his fate, and proceeded toward his ritual welcome into the village. His feelings were not far, just then, from the hard, isolated, savage feelings that had filled him during his endless captivity in the Royal Navy. He wouldn't let them bother him. He would live and fight and pay no attention to the contempt swirling around him.

Victoria's family engulfed her. Walks Alone, Digs the Roots, Arrow, Makes the Robe. She jabbered with them, their words tumbling so fast Skye couldn't make them out. But except for an occasional glance in his direction, they ignored him.

"Ah, Mister Skye, you fixing to pay your respects to Arapooish?"

Skye turned and found himself facing Jim Beckwourth, who smiled easily at him from coal oil eyes. The veteran mountaineer, known to these people as Antelope, certainly looked as though he owned the place, the ease and grace and status apparent in his finely wrought buckskins, which he wore with a certain flair, and his elaborate manners. Beckwourth had become a war leader, perhaps even a chief.

"I do know the tongue," Beckwourth said. "And even a smattering of your limey one. I'm delighted to see you here in this corner of paradise."

Skye followed Beckwourth toward the great lodge of the chief, located closer to the riverbank and surrounded by a half-moon of lodges that formed a park, or public square, around Arapooish's majestic twenty-one-pole lodge. Antelope walked with an easy grace, wearing his soft-tanned buckskins and Indian ornaments, including war honors, as if he had been born to these people.

Skye was tempted to explain his desperate circumstances to the mulatto—if that's what he was, which Skye doubted because the man showed no sign of mixed blood other than a somewhat swarthy complexion—but decided to narrate the story to the chief, if the chief wanted it. One thing Skye didn't want was sympathy, and neither did he want to make excuses. He had been outwitted by the Pawnees, was paying for his stupidity, and that was all there was to it.

"Well, Mister Skye, you've come a piece, I gather," Beckwourth said, probing.

"A piece."

"One's fortune reverses in the mountains. One moment, one is an emperor of the wilds, the next, one is a pauper. I have a certain small influence here, and perhaps I can be at your service."

"Perhaps you can, mate. We had a bit of misfortune."

Skye liked the Missourian, whose grace and choice of words bespoke education and breeding. Among the mountaineers, Beckwourth had won a reputation for courage, loyalty, and mountain skills. They said around the campfires that he was the son of a Virginia aristocrat, although he had grown up in frontier Missouri, where his father had brought the family.

"Pawnee lifted everything I possessed, except for my rifle, which was at hand."

"I thought it was something like that. Well, that's not unusual here. You have friends among the Crows, and I can no doubt supply you with some necessaries, including some DuPont and galena. I trade it, you know. I have some connections."

They found the Crow chief standing before his lodge wrapped in a red blanket. Once again Skye marveled at the headman, who was huge, lean, rawboned, formidable, and whose gaze took in everything, not missing Skye's tatters. Around the chief the elders gathered, gray-haired men, patient, curious, and in no hurry.

The chief raised a palm in welcome, while Beckwourth translated. Skye wondered if the wily Missourian could be trusted not to embroider the story. Or invent one altogether. Beckwourth was a famous embroiderer, but no more so than half the men in the mountains. In the end, Skye decided he did trust the man. Antelope Jim actually was well known for fair dealing and honesty, and his wild yarns were well understood to be a form of entertainment not intended to be taken seriously.

"It is the husband of my brother's daughter, returning to us. You are welcome here. Come, you will tell us your story," Arapooish said. "But first, we will smoke."

It took the better part of an hour. They listened to Skye recount his story, his decision to come live with Victoria's people, the encounter with the Pawnees. In simple terms, he described his and Victoria's determined pursuit of the Pawnees, entering their camp, his effort to

shame them into surrendering their booty—and his failure. Skye noticed that Victoria and her family had come
and were among the auditors. That was good, he thought;
it would keep Beckwourth's translation from meandering.

He glanced at the passive Crow faces around him,
unable to fathom whether he was in disgrace or merely
contemptible in their eyes. Every face was a mask, not
least the chief's.

Then, the story done, Skye sought to retire from this
august company. But the chief stayed him with a wave of
the hand. Quietness settled over the throng. Children,
grandmothers, sharp-eyed youths, old men, and impas-
sive warriors stared at him.

"Now hear me," Arapooish said. "Mister Skye, you
have done a brave thing. The People will gladly help you.
I will give you a new name. You will be known by it
among us. You are now Man Not Afraid of the Pawnees."

Skye saw Victoria clap a hand to her mouth, and it
dawned on him that the name was an honor. He might
be dressed in tatters, but his name was gold.

Chapter 6

James Beckwourth—also known as Medicine Calf,
Antelope, Bull's Robe, Enemy of Horses, Red Fish,
and Bobtail Horse—contemplated the fate of his old
friend Skye and decided to help. The presence of Mister
Skye in Rotten Belly's village would be a joy; a pair of
white men whiling away the winter, lavishly entertained
by adoring Crows.

Whatever the world said about Beckwourth's blood, he knew himself as a white. His father, Jennings Beckwith, came from Virginia aristocracy, while his mother was a quadroon, one-quarter black, and the intimate companion of his father for many years. It had been a marriage, though not one ever recorded or solemnized. Beckwith had raised his son as a white, teaching him his letters and making the youth a full member of the large family living on the harsh and dangerous Missouri frontier. Technically, even that bit of black blood made the boy a slave, but his father had, on three occasions, filed manumissions, making sure that Jim would be a free man.

Jim had come up the Missouri River and into the Rocky Mountains with the second of General William Ashley's fur-trapping expeditions, in the fall of 1824, served with Ashley and his successors, was a courageous and imposing trapper, fighter, and enterpreneur, well admired by all his mountain friends. He had come to the Rockies two years ahead of Skye but had made more of his sojourn, becoming by degrees one of the elite of the mountains, with all the prowess of Bridger, Fitzpatrick, Black Harris, or any of the other veterans of the wild whose very names struck awe in the greenhorns who occasionally drifted west.

Beckwourth had been familiar with the Crows from the beginning of his mountain life, and in 1828 he joined them. They thought of him as one of their own, having heard a wild tale from the veteran Caleb Greenwood that Beckwourth was a lost Crow child, found and raised by whites. His swart appearance did nothing to discredit the whimsical story that had started as a joke, and when Beckwourth did arrive in Arapooish's village he was greeted by his supposed father, Big Bowl, as a long-lost son and showered with robes, buckskins, furs—and women.

Since then, life had been a lark. Black Lodge, one of the most honored warriors in the village, gave his daughter Stillwater to Beckwourth for wife, but the Crows being Crows, Beckwourth soon acquired six or seven other women including his remarkable friend Pine Leaf, a lithe woman warrior. How could any mortal be so fortunate?

He, in turn, swiftly gathered that the way to progress from nonentity to honored member of the tribe was through war honors. So he organized raids against Crow enemies, especially the Blackfeet, stole horses, killed an occasional enemy warrior, counted coup, and performed deeds of derring-do that would be told and retold around tribal campfires and during councils. That was how he acquired all those names—honors, really, bestowed by a grateful chief upon an unusually gifted warrior who had come to live with the People. Beckwourth's leadership had enhanced the security and prowess of the Absarokas and made them a terror to their enemies.

From this pinnacle of success, Beckwourth eyed the newcomer, seeing a friend—and potential ally. Beckwourth had drifted far from his old friends who had come west with General Ashley to gather beaver pelts. He had joined the rival outfit, finding lucrative work with the Upper Missouri Outfit, that portion of the American Fur Company that had been purchased from John Jacob Astor by powerful entrepreneurs including the St. Louis Chouteaus and their French relations. They were mounting a ruthless assault on the Rocky Mountain Fur Company by building trading posts along the Missouri River and using them to penetrate the mountains and monopolize the lucrative beaver trade, which could yield a fortune to anyone with the nerve to take the terrible risk.

And they were paying Beckwourth handsome wages to steer Crows to American Fur's trading posts. His four hundred a year bought him every imaginable luxury among the supplies brought upriver by keelboat, including quantities of various fine liquors, all illegal in the Indian territories but a staple of American Fur Company's provisioning.

Beckwourth knew his man; Skye's affection for a jug of corn whiskey had become a byword of the rendezvous. And now a little of that elixir would, he figured, purchase a valuable ally. Thus did Skye appear one evening shortly after arriving in the village at Beckwourth's lodge, where Stillwater greeted him with a shy smile and then vanished.

"Ah, Mister Skye, I see your fortunes have improved. Here you are in fresh buckskins, with some meat on your ribs, and the world looking rather more amiable," Beckwourth said.

"It's that, mate," Skye agreed. "And thanks to some powder and lead from you, I've been able to help provision Victoria's family."

"But you're far from where you were."

"I'm a poor man, Jim. But I've been a poor man before."

"You lack a horse."

"I lack everything. I'm dependent on Victoria's people."

"That might be remedied."

"I intend to remedy it. I'll not be a beggar. I'm in debt to the new outfit, and I'll pay them."

"A worthy sentiment. We'll drink to it." Beckwourth rummaged among his possessions and extracted a jug. Smiling, he uncorked it and handed it to Skye. "Elixir,

Mister Skye. A rare thing in the mountains except at rendezvous. I've been saving it for a special occasion, which is now."

Skye eyed the jug eagerly, and then guzzled and coughed.

"Bloody stuff," he muttered, wheezing. "It seems, ah, rather young."

"Very young. In fact, concocted this afternoon of grain spirits, a plug of tobacco, and assorted flavors."

"Trade whiskey."

"It brings in the beaver."

Skye wheezed. His eyes leaked. Beckwourth sipped lightly and returned the jug to Skye's eager grasp. Skye sucked hard, gasped, roared, wept, and coughed. "It'll be smooth sailing soon," he said. "But it takes a bit to put wind in the sails."

Beckwourth got down to business. "Mister Skye, what brought you to our fair metropolis?"

"Victoria. She was plumb lonesome for her people."

"Your loyalty's admirable. You gave up life with your friends, your boon companions, from the moment you walked into that rendezvous of eighteen and twenty-six. That's a moment I won't forget, you and the Shoshones. You excited some curiosity, my friend."

Skye took a swizzle, coughed, blinked, and smiled. "That juice is panther piss. Grizzly sow juice. It's a limey's paradise."

"Actually, it's castorum."

Skye coughed and laughed. Castorum was what mountaineers used to bait the beaver traps. "Mr. Beckwourth, what are we negotiating here?"

The man was not a lummox, Beckwourth thought.

"Perhaps a partnership."

"I'm partnered with Rocky Mountain Fur."

"I thought so. Are we rivals?"

"It looks that way."

"You were outfitted by Fitzpatrick, and in return you'll steer Crow trade toward RMFC. How much do you owe them?"

"Three hundred. Plus the trade goods I lost."

"And you've nothing for it, thanks to the Pawnees. A bit of a mess. Maybe something can be arranged."

"I'm already into you for powder and lead, Jim. There's a robe or two right there. No, nothing can be arranged."

"Why not? American Fur'll pay off your debt and outfit you; it'll be entirely honorable. You will meet your every obligation. And we'll simply steer peltries and trade to Fort Floyd. Kenneth McKenzie's going to be well stocked when he's done outfitting the post."

"Every obligation but one, mate. My word. Bridger, Fitzpatrick, Milt Sublette, Gervais, and Fraeb have my word."

Beckwourth smiled lightly. Skye was not a man who would tamper with his word. It was an asset in the man, and had been noticed in the mountains. "Then we'll be rivals. But I doubt that you'll deliver one pelt to your colleagues."

Skye shrugged, remained silent, and swallowed one last gulp. Then Beckwourth corked the jug and slipped it into a parfleche.

"Mr. Beckwourth, you set a fine table."

They laughed.

"My friend Barnaby, how are you going to deliver? You've an obligation you can't possibly meet. You've not a trap or a horse. You have no influence. You've no reputation among these warriors. You walked off with one of the prettiest girls in the village and made enemies. But now you're going to persuade the whole Crow nation to trade with your fur company, which doesn't even have a trading post."

"I fled the Royal Navy with much less than I have now."

"I'll give you some advice. The way a young man advances among the Absaroka is by war honors, counting coup, proving himself an effective warrior and defender of the People. Now, rivals we may be, but I'm always looking for good fighting men to go with me on raids. Maybe you'll make some progress. I'm a war leader. I'll invite you next time I go out. You want horses? The Blackfeet and Sioux have a-plenty. Yours for the stealing—if you don't get killed. You want influence? Count coup, take a few scalps, beat an enemy. You want power? Shoot buffalo and give the meat away. You want plenty of women—the women here'll throw themselves at you, the fairest maidens, all yours—"

"I have Victoria, mate."

"But surely—Skye, there's not a virtuous woman in the Crow nation. They don't believe in it. They expect you to dally with them. Pretty soon Victoria'll find her pleasures, and you'll find yours."

Skye stood suddenly, his face dark with something, and he plunged into the twilight.

Beckwourth smiled. There were white men like that. A few months in Absaroka, and they were all transformed. The Crows played an amusing mating game, serial adventures, one after another. What else was there to do all winter? By his own reckoning, Beckwourth had shared his robes with seven such beauteous and available ladies—and could have enjoyed a dozen more were it not for his fascination with that lithe cat of a woman, Pine

Leaf. She was the storied woman warrior of the Crows, the slim terror at his side in battle who had twice saved his life. And the only Absaroka woman who held herself aloof from his formidable charms. At least, so far.

Well, Skye would soon learn how life was lived among the Crows. And then he would forget about steering beaver to the opposition. War and women; Beckwourth had plenty of both and intended to have even more.

Chapter 7

Skye felt the rough bark of the cottonwood against his back and the sharp September air eddy around his beard as he watched twilight thicken over the Crow village just below. This brow of a hill had become a favorite resort of his, a place to think and plan and hope. Sometimes Victoria joined him there, but not often. He saw little of her; it was as if she had returned to her life as a Crow maiden, almost as if he didn't exist.

Perhaps he didn't. He wondered whether their union had been a mistake. Things had been difficult ever since he and she arrived in Rotten Belly's village with little more than the clothes on their backs. Her parents had provided them with a home, but even that was awkward. According to custom, he could not address his mother-in-law, and his marriage was suffering. He could not bring himself to make love to Victoria while her parents and a sister slept a few feet away, not even though that was perfectly acceptable and expected among them.

He had learned the Crow tongue to some degree, but

that didn't make him a friend of other young men his age, who preferred to socialize with their own kind. He talked with Beckwourth now and then, which helped mitigate the loneliness he felt. He knew now how Victoria had felt during their years with the trapping brigades. She had been desolately alone among white men. Now it was his turn.

The oncoming cold worried him. Even now, in the twilight, he felt its bite. The peaks had already been dusted with white. He had only an old summer robe for warmth, which he wrapped about him as he contemplated his fate. Below, the cookfires glowed and blue smoke eddied over the camp. The village of the Kicked-in-the-Bellies was a happy place, strong, secure, and comfortable there on the big bend of the Yellowstone. The beauty of it struck him; there, in a corner of the mountains, layer upon layer of blue and black vaulted upward, while at his feet lay an orderly collection of tawny lodges, their tops blackened by smoke. The Yellowstone glinted in the last light, while the reflections of the first stars danced on its swift dark water.

He had spent his days hunting on foot because he lacked a horse, and he had occasionally made meat for Victoria's family. In those cases he usually borrowed a packhorse, one that would tolerate the smell of blood and death, and if he was lucky—mostly he wasn't—he brought back his quarry, usually a mule deer. These additions to the larder were welcomed, and the hides, which Victoria tanned, kept him in powder and lead and moccasins. Beckwourth bought any dressed skin that Skye could provide.

But it wasn't much of a life, and with winter racing toward him, he ached for a lodge, some horses, a pile of blankets, some thick buffalo robes—and privacy. He hardly knew where to turn.

He watched a lean figure toil up the slope toward him, and recognized Beckwourth. The man who had adopted these people as his own dressed like them. His long hair had been coiled into a knot at the nape of his neck, and from it poked two eagle feathers, his war honors. He had wrapped himself in a red Hudson's Bay blanket with black stripes.

"Knew you'd be here, Mister Skye," he said.

Skye nodded and motioned Beckwourth to sit.

"I'm taking a little party out in the morning, and thought to invite you. I'll lend you a horse and saddle, and I expect before we're through you'll have several more. We're heading north, toward the Musselshell or the Judith country, and our plan is to reduce the horse herds of the Blackfeet, count some coup, and make all the mischief we can. It's a grand opportunity for a man to win some prestige and maybe walk off with all the booty he can handle. You might even get a lodge out of it. Should be a lark, Barnaby. I'm taking twenty men, the best in the village, including Rotten Belly's sons. You be ready at dawn. Should be out four or five days. I'll bring a good robe for you. You'll have a chance to use that mighty Hawken if all goes well."

"And if it doesn't?"

Beckwourth smiled. "You'll have even more chance to use the Hawken."

"I don't look for chances to use my Hawken on two-legged game."

"Well, it isn't likely"

"Let me think on it. I'll let you know directly."

Beckwourth nodded and retreated down the slope.

A bold band of blue behind the western ridges was all that remained of this day. Skye knew that before that sliver of light disappeared, he would have to make a fateful decision.

He watched Beckwourth stroll down the slope and felt that he was being pushed into a corner. He had known this decision would come sooner or later, but he was still unprepared for the moment.

He sat in the gathering chill, his eyes on the winking cookfires but his mind elsewhere. He remembered the Kaffir wars, fought in the name of empire, planned and executed by the lords of the Horse Guards. The sailors and marines had traveled upriver, pursuing the bloody natives until the Kaffirs turned the tables on them and nearly enveloped the whole force. A hail of spears had decimated the marines; the fierce natives had then attacked with machetelike weapons that could slice off an arm or cut a head in two. Many a jack-tar and redcoat had died in those weeks, all for empire.

He had fought Burmese river pirates from 'tween decks, watching shot pour through the gun ports, rake his shipmates, blind Will Fellowes, pulp the face of Higgins, blow off Billy Burns's right hand. All for the Crown. He had watched maimed men, the detritus of war, receive their discharges and begin a life as mendicants, wearing their medals on their shabby coats. No hope. He had seen tears, heard howls of pain, listened to the onslaught of death as it captured a man. He had held a dying seaman named Harry Combs in his lap while the man sobbed out the Lord's Prayer and bled out his life.

No, he didn't like war. But that didn't mean he wouldn't fight. It only meant that there had to be grave reasons, larger than commerce or personal honors. That was a distinction the Crows didn't understand. For them, waging war, stealing horses, trapping enemy hunters, all had a preemptive quality: do that to the Siksika or Lakota, and the Absarokas would be all the safer.

But which side had started it? And was a horse raid offense or defense? A new provocation or a retaliation for old troubles? The tribes didn't lack scores to settle. He had always believed he would fight ferociously in defense of those he loved, but he would never start a war. But that didn't make sense out here, when strife among the tribes was ongoing, unending, deadly, and involved the very survival of each tribe. His old, European notions of just war didn't work very well here in a wild land where a tribe warred or died away.

There might be good in it, as Beckwourth predicted. He might return in a few days with horses, a captured lodge, scalps, prestige, power, wealth, medicine, and a say in village councils. He might yet be able to serve Rocky Mountain Fur, repay the lost trade goods, win the respect and allegiance of the war chiefs, Rotten Belly, the headmen and shamans, and bring them all to rendezvous next year with loads of pelts to trade. That would be a grand thing, leading the Crow nation to the rendezvous and the trading tent. If he could do that, the Rocky Mountain Fur Company would forgive him what he had lost.

The night had lowered. He stood, stretched the stiffness from him, wrapped his summer robe about him, and descended into the village, enjoying the savory tang of the woodsmoke in the still air. He paused at Beckwourth's lodge to tell him that he would be ready at dawn, and went to his people. He found Victoria in her parents' lodge and decided to bare the issue at once.

"Beckwourth invited me to go on a horse raid at dawn—and I will go."

She stared at him, the firelight glinting in her black eyes.

"I'm not one for picking fights. But this will help your nation. There are a lot more Lakota and Siksika than there are Absaroka. Maybe I can help even things up." He smiled tentatively.

She beamed, delight swimming in her face.

"I'll need to borrow some things. A horse, for one. A robe."

"I will ask."

"I might not come back."

"You have bear medicine, Skye."

He needed more than bear medicine. The Blackfeet fielded some of the best mounted warriors in the world, and the seaman Skye knew he was no match with lance, club, arrow, or sheer horsemanship. He wished he had her easy confidence, but he didn't.

Victoria's mother ignored him, as she was required to do, but Victoria's father eyed him amiably from his place of honor at the rear of the lodge. With a glance at Victoria, Skye explained his intent to her father and asked for those things he might need in war: a fast horse, a war club, a robe to cover him at night.

"And what does your medicine say, Man Not Afraid of the Pawnee?"

"Grandfather, I have not examined my medicine."

"Your ways are strange to us. When you know, come to me."

Skye understood. He would seek help. He pulled aside the lodge flap and walked into a chill night. He needed to find a small gift, anything, and remembered what had been warmly appreciated before. He hiked into the murky cottonwoods, waited for his eyes to adjust, and then hacked at dead limbs with his hatchet until he had an armload.

These he carried to the small, isolated lodge that was the sole worldly possession of the seer, Red Turkey Comb. He scratched gently on the lodge, the polite way of announcing himself, and eventually heard the old man's voice inviting him in.

He ducked inside and found the frail old man sitting in a cold lodge, entirely without light.

"It is the husband of Many Quill Woman, Grandfather," he said. "I have brought you some wood."

"Build a fire so I can see you. Then we will smoke."

Skye did, patiently striking sparks into tinder, until finally a tiny pinch of it glowed, driving the darkness back. He blew on it until it burst into a tiny flame, and swiftly added twigs. It took a long time to build a lodge fire for the old man, and even then the icy lodge didn't warm much.

In time, the fire burned merrily in its pit, but the old man didn't seem to notice. Skye realized Red Turkey Comb was not far from blindness.

They smoked, and then the shaman waited.

"I will go with Antelope on a horse raid, Grandfather," he began. "They ask me what my medicine tells me."

"Grizzly bear medicine."

"I don't follow you, Grandfather."

"Yours is the way of the bear."

Skye touched his bear claw necklace, symbol of honor and power among these people. "Sometimes I am a bear, Grandfather, and sometimes I am not."

"No, Man Not Afraid of the Pawnees, you have the

bear spirit. That is your path. I will tell the war leaders that you follow the way of the bear."

That puzzled Skye. "What is the way of the bear?"

The old man coughed. "The bear fattens in the fall, before he goes to sleep."

Skye waited, quietly.

"It is right for you to go with Antelope. You saw truly that this is so. Follow your path, Man Not Afraid of the Pawnees. You will become a blessing for the People. Go now, and tell Walks Alone I wish to talk with him. I will tell Walks Alone that his daughter's man follows the way of the bear, and it is a good way, and he will be proud of his daughter's man."

Chapter 8

Skye marveled at Beckwourth. The war leader had an unerring instinct about where to find their quarry. For three days, Beckwourth had taken them north, arriving one noon in a mountain-girt basin he called the Judith country. The whole grassy plain was dotted with buffalo as far as the eye could see.

"Where there's meat, there's Blackfeet," he told Skye. He led them west, staying low and out of sight, every warrior alert. By dusk they had reached a rough water-chiseled land under a brooding butte, a place somehow melancholic and foreboding. That was when Bad Heart, one of the Absaroka warriors, paused, sniffed, and announced that smoke was on the breeze, which was eddying in from the northwest.

"We are close," Beckwourth said. "And now, Barnaby, you will see a horse raid. Somewhere nearby, probably in a river valley we'll reach shortly, we'll find a hunting party hunkered down for the night out of sight of the buffalo so as not to alarm the herd. They'll have their best runners with them. A good buffalo runner knows how to gallop close to a running buffalo so the rider can sink an arrow into the sweet spot. They're fast, and they're valuable—and they'll be ours!"

Skye nodded. Night settled while Beckwourth held his warriors in a small hollow, well hidden. Then, in full dark, he led them north again, through a chill night when the stars glimmered in moving air. He left the group and went ahead on foot, returning a half hour later.

"Just as I figured," he said to Skye. Then in the Absaroka tongue, which Skye could at least follow, he explained. The Blackfeet were camped in a creek bottom hemmed between steep bluffs, out of sight of the buffalo. Their horses were being kept in a natural canyon with night herders penning them in. Two prized horses were in the camp itself, saddled and ready for emergencies. There looked to be about fifteen Blackfoot hunters at the fire, plus two herders keeping an eye on the horses, which weren't picketed because they were in a natural pen. But he found a rough passage to the top of the bluffs; the horses could be stampeded up and out. He and several Crows would descend on foot, surprise the herders, and drive the horses over the top. Others, on top, would steer the stolen horses south.

"And you, Barnaby, will settle on the edge of the bluff where you can see the camp and keep 'em pinned down with that big Hawken of yours. Shoot anyone who tries to follow."

Skye nodded.

After that, the long wait began. Beckwourth didn't want to start the affray until the Siksika were asleep and the night was well along. Skye sat quietly, his back to a tree, wondering whether he could shoot a buffalo-hunting Blackfoot who was simply gathering meat for his people. He had shot at Indians many times, and yet this was different. Always, in the past, he had shot to defend himself and whoever he was with. But not this time.

His bones ached from the cold, and time dragged. But finally Beckwourth nodded. His party left their horses with young horse-holders and crept into place. Skye settled on the bluff, trying to locate the camp in the deep mysterious dark, wondering whether the Blackfeet had more sentries out and whether he would find out too late—when a knife or arrow pierced him. Some embers glowed; a sliver of moon gave just enough light to see the vague shape of things.

He waited tensely, hearing soft disturbances in the dark, then the movement of many horses, and suddenly, the victorious howls of the Crows. Everything happened at once. The Blackfoot herd stampeded up the bluff, Crow horsemen on top steered it south, the sleeping camp erupted, and Skye saw faint, blurred movement below. A Blackfoot untied his pony and swung onto it to give pursuit. Skye shot, dropping the horse and throwing the rider. The boom of the Hawken changed the complexion of the night. Swiftly he moved to a new locale, knowing his muzzle flash had revealed his position, reloaded, and fired at another mounted rider giving chase. He missed. He reloaded again, and shot a third time, right into the embers, which shot sparks and light into the dusky camp. Other Blackfeet were running, gathering quivers and bows and lances, hunting for horses, swarming toward their herders, who lay in the grass, either dead or dying.

He'd seen enough. The Crows and Beckwourth were already half a mile away, and Skye knew he would have to get out fast. He reloaded, trotted back from the rim, mounted his borrowed horse, and rode south, steering his horse toward the howling of the Crows and the thunder of the stolen herd. A while later he caught up and rode down the long dark night to the music of the hooves.

Thus they traveled until exhaustion overtook them and Beckwourth decided they were out of danger. They rested until dawn and then examined their booty. Forty-one horses, some of them magnificent. One scalp, too. And several coups. No losses, no wounds. A great victory! Beckwourth had proven his medicine prowess once again.

"That big mountain rifle of yours kept 'em at bay, Barnaby," Beckwourth said. "You did just fine. You've won some war honors now."

"I think we were lucky," Skye said.

Beckwourth laughed. "Look at those ponies," he said. "There's some buffalo runners in there. That's more horses than we've gotten out of a raid in a long time."

The multicolored horses did look magnificent. Some of them bore the medicine markings of their owners; a white handprint on the chest, or yellow stripes painted on the side, or amulets plaited into their tails. One magnificent black caught Skye's eye. He would give anything to own that one.

The solemn Crow warriors kept a sharp lookout for pursuit, but no one came, and late one October afternoon they returned to the Kicked-in-the-Belly village. Beckwourth was ebullient. As far as Skye could fathom, the rest took war too seriously to exult, but he did catch the flash of joy and pride in their eyes. The Siksika had lost a lot of horses and one herder. The other herder, it turned out, had warded off his assailant and fled into the darkness. A victory, yes. But there would be revenge, somehow, someplace, and the tables would be turned.

They paused just outside their village. Skye watched the warriors paint up, using the small kits of paint they had taken with them. They would enter the village in triumph this time, wearing their medicine insignia, wearing their war honors. They didn't neglect their horses either. They groomed the ponies and painted them. This would be a great day for these people. Skye watched, sensing how important this ritual was to these fellow warriors, sensing the pride, status, power, and honor attached to this ritual. But Beckwourth outdid them all, garbing himself like an oriental potentate.

When at last they were ready, Skye marveled. These warriors reminded him of a hundred bagpipers in their plaid kilts, their pipes howling defiance and death. What was grander than a victorious army dressed for a parade?

Villagers swarmed to meet the victorious warriors, crowding the lane leading to Chief Rotten Belly's lodge, where they would each, under the seal of absolute truth, tell their tales to the elders, the chiefs, the shamans, and the delirious crowd who had come to celebrate. At first the village women looked sharply for signs of tragedy, the empty saddle, the horse carrying a burden, a wounded man, death painted upon the faces and chests of these greathearted men. But they found none. This party had gone out into the dangerous world and returned in glory, driving forty-one horses before it. Nineteen men, forty-one warhorses that had once belonged to the despised and dangerous Siksika. Forty-one duns, browns, chestnuts, appaloosas, paints, and the proud black, as dark as coal, that walked with an easy gait and a calm that wasn't evident in some of the other nervous animals. That one fired Skye's imagination, and he felt a pang. There was a horse.

Leading this marvelous assemblage was Beckwourth himself, grinning, wearing the softest white buckskins, a bone necklace over his chest, his hair tucked into a knot that bore two downturned eagle feathers, white and black. A scarlet sash completed his ensemble. He was thoroughly enjoying himself and absorbing the waves of acclaim that washed over him as he passed women and children, old men, yearning boys, and even the blind, who had been led to the parade so they, too, might experience this splendid event.

Skye rode through the village, marveling at the uproar. Horses neighed and whickered, boys yelled, women howled, the town crier, leading this assemblage, bellowed his news and repeated it. Across the way, Skye spotted Victoria, her face flushed with joy, eyes shining, her gaze rapt as she absorbed this great moment of triumph. Her eyes were on the gaudy Beckwourth, but then she spotted Skye and smiled. He nodded to her, enjoying her delight. She was with several other young matrons, a flock of them, crooning their joy.

Beckwourth smiled at many women, and Skye knew that every smile was an invitation and that the Crows sometimes could not count the presence of one virtuous woman in a village. It galled him suddenly. Where was faithfulness and loyalty among these wanton people? He eyed her darkly, hoping that four good years had forged a bond.

At the lodge of Arapooish the crowd collected to hear the whole story. The chief wore a single braid this day, which fell loosely over his brown chest. He wore only his breechclout and leggings, though the air nipped at him. One thing about old Rotten Belly, Skye thought: the man had a certain presence. He looked like a chief, acted like a chief, inspired confidence and awe, as a great chief should.

In a leisurely way, playing to the eager crowd, Beckwourth described the foray. Three suns to the north, in the rough country near Square Butte, they had spied a herd of buffalo one evening, and also a hunting party camped on a creek. They were Piegans planning a good hunt at dawn when they would have light enough to make meat. Some Piegan boys guarded the herd, which had been nicely pinned into a creek bottom by bluffs that were almost impossible to scale. . . .

This was a great victory, better than any so far this season, and Arapooish commended each of them and gave Beckwourth a new name, Night Man.

Beckwourth, still astride his prancing brown, raised a hand. "To each of my brave warriors, I give two ponies. To my friend Mister Skye, husband of Many Quill Woman, I give two horses. The black horse to ride, and another to pack. Two horses do I give the young man who has come to live among the Absaroka."

The people relished that. Any grand act appealed to them. They exclaimed. Victoria sighed, her eyes more on Beckwourth than upon Skye.

"Take the black and pick a horse, Mister Skye," Beckwourth said in the Crow tongue.

Skye did, easing into the herd, finding a braided halter on the calm black. The horse led easily. He chose an ordinary dun for the second horse, not wanting to deprive any of these worthy fighters of a coveted animal.

"Mr. Beckwourth," he said. "I thank you. You do yourself honor. With these I will hunt the buffalo and bring meat to this village. You have made me a wealthy man."

"It is well said," Arapooish added. "We will dance this night."

The crowd returned to the cook pots and lodges while Skye gently worked his hands over the powerful black, admiring the strength of the stallion, its graceful stance.

"Sonofabitch," said Victoria. "Some damn horse."

"Tomorrow I'll put it and the packhorse to good use."

"Antelope looked so proud. Was ever there such a warrior? I saw the sun pouring from his eyes."

She was paying too much attention to Beckwourth. Or was he paying too much attention to her? The prettiest, most desired maiden in the village not long before? She was even more the beauty after a few years with Skye. Something dark stabbed at him, and he pushed it aside as unworthy jealousy.

She smiled, winked, patted him on the arm, and drifted off. She had been like that lately, not unhappy with him but distant, absorbed in the thousand strands of life that occupied her village.

That evening he borrowed a pad saddle and braided hackamore and tried out his new horse. It glided easily, turned obediently, stopped with the slightest tug of the rein. He urged it into a trot, then a fine, powerful gallop, and knew he had a fleet horse, probably a buffalo runner, and that he could trust it. He wasn't much of a horseman, having spent most of his years imprisoned on a sailing ship, but ever since joining the trapping brigades he had made a point of learning what he could, mastering horses, grasping their nature, riding, packing, picketing, grooming, caring for their feet. He was a passable horseman, but less a hand with a horse than any of these warriors, who had made horses an extension of themselves, so that warrior and pony became a single entity.

He examined the packhorse, too, satisfied that it would carry whatever burdens he placed upon it. Then he took the horses out to pasture in the hills north of the river, intending to leave them with the horse herd guards, doubled this night because of the possibility of retaliation. On second thought, he decided to tie them at the lodge. Early, before the village stirred, he would be off on a hunt. With each buffalo or elk or deer, he added to the security of these people.

In the darkness he summed up his perceptions. He had done well this trip, won war honors, obtained two fine horses, and gained some status in the village. But Beckwourth had gained much more by leading a spectacular raid without any loss, by bringing back many horses, and by giving Skye the black, the best horse of all. The Crows loved a magnanimous giver.

Skye wondered if he could ever overtake his rival.

Chapter 9

The next dawn Skye saddled the sleek black, haltered the dun, and rode into the sunrise. Victoria's family still slumbered in their lodge. Not a soul stirred. Smoke drifted from the blackened tips of a few lodges. When he reached the periphery of the silent village a subtle change came over him. He was abandoning its safety and plunging into an uncertain and dangerous wilderness. Frost rimed the brown grasses. It would be a fine day to hunt.

This day he would try to find game and contribute to the well-being of the Kicked-in-the-Bellies. That would not be easy. The band had been at the great bend of the Yellowstone for some while, and the country had been hunted out. Soon they would make their winter camp in the Big Horn basin, but for the moment they would remain in their favorite grounds.

He enjoyed the powerful walk of his black horse. The animal seemed as eager for adventure as he. This was as much a journey to improve his condition as it was an effort to make meat. The Crows honored a good hunter, though perhaps not as much as a successful warrior. Skye had no great hunting skills because he had spent so much of his life as a sailor, but he had determination and that would suffice. The nippy air exhilarated him, and the bountiful and everlasting land, layered in blues and purples and browns, evoked within him a feeling so rare that he reined the horse briefly just to treasure the moment. Here he was, a free man, living entirely by his wits, rejoicing to be alive.

He began to study the ground, looking for the signs of passage: the delicate hoofprint of a mule deer in the frost; the nobler prints of an elk; the surprisingly delicate prints of a massive buffalo. He found nothing, but didn't really expect to. Part of the joy of the hunt was the search, he against nature under the bowl of a bright autumn sky. What more could a man ask?

Still, as he worked eastward along the Yellowstone, he found no sign of game. He paused at a spot where the river glittered over some shallows, and decided to ford it and work his way up into the foothills, far from the great artery of the river.

The well-trained black took to the ford without balking, but Skye had to tug the lead rope of the dun. They crossed without getting into deep water because the river was at its seasonal low, and he rode up a creek valley. He had learned much in his four years on the wild continent; everything meant something. The sudden bolt of a bird, silence, the circling of hawks, the skimming of hills by a hunting eagle, all signaled things that could scarcely be translated to words. By noon he still had found no game. He paused under a barren cottonwood to let the horse graze and to let the faint warmth of the mild sun permeate his soft buckskins.

He rode through an afternoon without luck. Once he saw some tan-and-white antelope on a distant slope, but they edged away as he drew close. Then he saw a pair of gray mule deer at the edge of an aspen grove. But they vanished.

He walked his horse across drainage, topping ridges, looking for some shaggier, as the mountaineers called buffalo, but this was not his day. When the sun began to drop to the western mountains, he hastened back to the village, his Hawken unfired. It had, actually, been a splendid day, one he cherished. But he would enter the village once again with nothing to show for his effort.

He placed his gear in the lodge of his in-laws, hung his sheathed Hawken from the lodgepoles, and slipped on his camp moccasins while carefully avoiding his mother-in-law. They saw he had nothing to show for the day's hunt, but said nothing. Walks Alone gestured toward the iron kettle that contained a supper, but Skye

declined. Victoria wasn't present. He retreated into the
sharp air, took his horses to pasture—a mile from the
village now because every patch of grass had been grazed
into the dirt—and entrusted them to the herders, doubled
now because these people feared Blackfoot retaliation.

Skye walked back to the village in gathering darkness,
straight to the small lodge of Beckwourth, certain she
would be there. He scratched on the lodge flap politely,
listening to the muffled chatter within. One thing about
Beckwourth: he was a spellbinder in several tongues.

"Come in, Skye," he said, and Skye wondered how
Beckwourth knew who was there. A tiny fire, no larger
than a teacup, illuminated the lodge. And there was Beckwourth, Stillwater, Pine Leaf, Walks Into Wind—and
Victoria.

"Home is the hunter. Loaded down with meat," Beckwourth said, swiftly surveying Skye.

"Not this time." Skye turned to Victoria. "Your family
has meat in the pot."

She shook her head. "I have eaten, Mister Skye. Antelope has given us buffalo tongue."

Skye bit back the anger in him. He nodded curtly.

"Have some, *amigo*," Beckwourth said.

Skye teetered on the brink of stalking out, but finally
surrendered to his complaining belly and fished some
slabs of fine, juicy tongue out of the blackened iron
kettle.

"Antelope has told us of the great whiskered fish in the
land where he was a boy," Victoria said, making peace.
"It is all lies. There are no such fish."

Beckwourth smiled, his coal eyes glowing. "I'll
take you there and show you, my beautiful friend."

Skye bridled. The man was flirting with his wife

right in front of his face. Was this how it would be in this village? He chewed on the meat, anger percolating through him. Beckwourth would drive him to a showdown some time soon. All this was deliberate. Beckwourth was making a show of his position and power and gallantry.

Nothing in Skye's life had prepared him for this sort of threat. His years as a pressed seaman had plunged him into an all-male world. Women were mysteries. Victoria was the only one he had ever been close to, and she was a Crow, whose ways he barely understood. During his years with the trapping brigades, none of the trappers had ever crossed a certain line; he and Victoria had been serene in their marriage and companionship, and the mountaineers honored their union. But here was Antelope Jim, enjoying Victoria, winning her smiles, and probably enjoying Skye's discomfort.

Skye choked back his anger and anxiety, and tried to make himself at home around that tiny fire, which Beckwourth occasionally replenished from a small pile of kindling.

"Victoria is the most beautiful thing that ever happened to me," Skye said quietly. "I met her at that first rendezvous and loved her from the moment I saw her." He gazed quietly at his wife. "And I think she felt the same way about me. We couldn't even talk with each other, and yet we communicated. These have been the best years of my life."

Victoria rewarded him with a smile, and for a moment he thought everything was fine.

"I envy you," Beckwourth said. "So fair a woman, the dream of every fine young man in the village. Truly, Victoria, you had your choice of anyone here. And you chose my most estimable British friend. Let me get out the jug, and we will toast Victoria."

"No," said Skye. "We will not toast Victoria now."

Victoria glanced back and forth, not quite sure of what was happening here, spoken in the English she little understood.

"She chose me, mate," Skye said, an edge in his voice.

"Ah, Skye," she said. "I remember."

"Let's go, Victoria."

"But, Skye, we haven't even started telling stories yet."

Skye knew that storytelling was one of the great entertainments of these people—and that no one told a better, funnier, wilder story than his rival across the little fire.

"I thought we'd take a walk. And then go to the robes. I'll be hunting again in the morning."

"Ah, the robes!" she said, and everyone laughed. "You go sleep, Skye. I will listen to stories."

"Victoria. We'll go now."

She smiled at him across the tiny fire and didn't stir.

"Have a good hunt, old friend," Beckwourth said, something calculating in his face.

Skye was suddenly aware that he wasn't really wanted there—and that the moment he departed they would be talking in the Absaroka tongue again, and that later in the night the stories would become bawdier, which was how the Crows amused themselves. He had heard these stories, some of them wildly inventive, some thinly disguised gossip, all of them told in mixed company, which embarrassed him acutely. And where did they lead? In the end, to liaisons, the participants eyeing each other contemplatively through the storytelling, their bodies howling to them.

And there he was. He had just dealt himself out. The dreaded possibility that Victoria would succumb, or abandon him, or return to her people's ways, ate at him like acid as he nodded curtly and retreated into the night. He had rarely felt so stupid or jealous.

The night sky was clean and black, with hard white stars stabbing light from the dome of heaven. He stumbled through a hushed blackness with nothing to light the way. Most lodge fires were out, and no moon guided him. The night was as desolate as his soul.

Still, he had acquitted himself well. He had told Beckwourth, with all the dignity he could muster and all the earnestness in his soul, that he loved Victoria and prized her above everything else in his life. Surely his friend—if Beckwourth could be called that—would respect that. Surely Victoria would, too. . . .

He stumbled across the rim of a lodge and veered into the night, hoping his eyes would adjust. So black was this cold night that he feared he would wander into the wrong lodge. They looked alike in the darkness, vague cones with a forest of poles on top. He paused, trying to orient himself. He was lost in his own village. More by instinct than by sorting things out, he veered leftward, somehow made out Walks Alone's lodge, and crawled through the flap into the utter darkness, enjoying the sudden warmth that persisted even though the fire had long since died. No one stirred. He crawled to his robes—borrowed robes, actually, provided by his wife's parents—and dug into them. But he could not sleep. He tried hard to banish the terrible fantasies crawling across his mind: Victoria and Beckwourth, Victoria and Beckwourth, his friend and his wife . . .

She did not come home, and he did not sleep.

Chapter 10

Skye awakened with the first hint of light up in the smoke hole. Victoria lay beside him. He wondered when she had come home and why he hadn't noticed. The evening's dreads eddied through him. Had that damned Beckwourth seduced her? Did she still love him?

He swung out of his robes, pulled on his worn moccasins, and crawled outside into a predawn half-light. The camp stank in the still air. Why hadn't Rotten Belly moved it? Skye walked down to the river and relieved himself, feeling his joints ache from the chill. He would hunt again this day.

He stood there in that terrible quiet, wanting succor. Where was God? In that faint band of blue light to the southeast? Skye prayed briefly, hardly knowing what to say to a deity who could give him anything he asked for— but didn't. "Send me a buffalo, so that I may win the esteem of my hosts. I don't know these people; guide me through the eye of the needle."

He sensed the presence of someone beside him and discovered Victoria's father, Walks Alone. "I will hunt with you today," he said.

"I would like that."

"I will show you things. We will talk."

Skye sensed that all this was good. Maybe the shaman, Red Turkey Comb, had said something. Maybe Walks Alone had simply taken things into his own hands. They would talk. Skye could grasp the Absaroka tongue after four years with Victoria, but his father-in-law knew no

English. They would get along, and there were the hand signs to fall back on.

They walked together out to the herd and nodded to the sole night herder. Skye found and caught his black easily, but couldn't locate the dun in the half-light. Walks Alone caught his best horse, a buffalo runner, and a pack-horse as well. In a while, when the sun rested coyly beneath the horizon, they rode north up the Shields River valley, staying close to the western foothills.

Walks Alone carried a full quiver on his back and his bow in hand. Skye carried his Hawken in his fringed and quilled sheath, hung from the saddle and tucked under his leg. They didn't speak, content with the companionable silence, their senses alert for game. But there would be nothing so close. A hundred hunters a day had streamed out of the village for months, many in this direction.

When the sun finally broke over the eastern mountains, tinting the sky blue and the vast countryside brown and black, the mood changed. A day had begun.

"Among the People," Walks Alone said, "a man with a disobedient wife is without face. The village makes jokes about such a one, and the jokes are cruel. Many Quill Woman does not obey you."

Skye felt a certain helplessness. "And how do I make her obey?"

"You must punish her."

"Is that how the People do it?"

"Yes, it is the custom to beat a woman who does not obey."

"We are talking about my wife?"

"You must beat her. Then she will respect you."

"Then she might run away to someone else."

"That would be good; you would no longer suffer such shame."

Skye digested all that, his instincts rebelling against it. "Among yellow eyes, it is rarely done, Grandfather." He used the term of utmost respect, "grandfather," which designated his father-in-law as a teacher, a wisdom giver.

"How do your women respect you, then? And why do we never see a pale woman? Yellow eyes hide them from us, and we think maybe you have none and want our women."

"There are many pale women. The man is the head of the marriage but the woman is not a slave, and she may do what she will. A husband and wife become companions and make decisions together."

"Among the People it is done differently. A man must protect his family, and they must be obedient for their own safety."

"Grandfather, is it not the right of each of the People to follow his own path? I follow my path—that which has been given to me by my own people."

Walks Alone nodded. "That is your right. But it won't protect you from gossip or malice among the Absaroka. There is much gossip about you and Many Quill Woman. It brings unhappiness to my lodge."

Skye scarcely knew how to respond to that. It had not been easy to live with these Absarokas. A lodge offered no privacy. People lived in unusual intimacy. Skye had not enjoyed Victoria's embrace since they had moved into her parents' eighteen-pole lodge. Two sisters, a grandfather, her parents, and assorted visitors conspired to ruin his lovemaking. Once, when he and Victoria had ridden through the narrows where the Yellowstone burst out of the mountains, they had come to a sunny meadow, got off their ponies, and joined together with all the old fire and joy.

But the family had not shared Skye's compunctions. Often, at night, he could hear Walks Alone and Digs the Roots coupling just a few feet from him, sometimes screened by a hide barrier strung up in the evening, sometimes not. The women went about their toilet nonchalantly, as if Skye weren't there. The daily cycle of life within the lodge hinged on the master's whim. When Walks Alone felt like sleeping, he put no more wood in the fire and drew his robes around him. The rest did, too. When Walks Alone felt like staying up, the rest stayed up. When any had to get up in the night, the fact was known to all. Walks Alone's elderly father, Standing Weasel, wandered in and out all night. All that had been hard enough, but the custom prohibiting Skye from addressing his mother-in-law, or even gazing directly at her, complicated matters all the more.

He was mad with need for privacy, wild to possess a lodge of his own, a sanctuary for Victoria and himself. He had been catapulted from years on board a royal warship with no family to life with too much family, and it took a strange toll on him.

And now Walks Alone was telling him plainly that they were not pleased with him. Well, he thought bitterly, he was not pleased with them; he was coming to regret this whole lash-up. He wasn't an Indian; he didn't really want to live in this sort of intimacy, without space or privacy, where everything about him was known and he knew more than he wanted about the rest. How could he be himself in such a circumstance?

Nor was that all. The lack of privacy assailed him from unexpected quarters. Sometimes one or another of Victoria's sisters vanished for a time, sometimes overnight, sometimes to the menstrual hut. And sometimes unexplained people stayed in the lodge; a boy, probably some kin, occasionally made himself at home. Yet no one told him who the child was or why he was there. Probably he was an adopted son; the children of the village were constantly being adopted by other families, and children were constantly acquiring new parents. Yet no one explained any of that to Skye.

In the midst of all this enforced society, Skye felt a deepening loneliness. He had only the dubious friendship of Beckwourth. All this was a lesson. He knew now how Victoria must have felt all the years in the white men's fur brigades. And how courageously she had adapted herself to a way of life so strange. No wonder she rejoiced just to talk with someone who spoke her language. It had been years since he escaped the Royal Navy, but now his thoughts turned to civilization. Maybe it was time to head for St. Louis and whatever the future might bring. There he would pay off his debts and make something of his life. And he would forget Victoria.

But to think it was to know that he would not forget her. She had come miraculously into his life during a time of change. The thought of her wry good humor restored his determination to make something of himself among these strange people. His mind teemed again with questions. He would ask his father-in-law how a young man made his way among the Absarokas. There would have to be some way.

But before he could form a question, Walks Alone reined his pony and signaled to Skye to stop. They had been traversing undulating barrens not far from the foothills of the western mountains. Walks Alone had seen something. He signaled Skye to wait and then steered his pony up a long grassy draw with a halfhearted rill running along its bottom. Skye saw nothing.

The Crow dropped off his pony, tied it to a juniper bush, and glided up the side of the draw. Then at last Skye saw the quarry, a cow elk standing on the ridge with only her head showing. She was watching Walks Alone, but didn't move. Walks Alone didn't approach directly, but angled in a way that gave the impression he was ignoring her, all the while drawing closer, until he was within bow range.

Skye marveled. He had not seen the elk, but now was receiving a valuable lesson. Walks Alone continued to veer toward the ridge, apparently paying no attention to the elk, which was growing restless. Then, swiftly, he drew his bow and loosed an arrow. It struck the elk's midsection. She staggered but did not fall, and headed upslope toward the foothills, gouting blood. Skye rode up while Walks Alone returned to his pony and mounted. Then, silently, they followed the trail of blood, which crimsoned the grass ahead of them with bright red drops. The elk had vanished ahead but left a clear trail. It would not be a clean kill, and she would suffer.

For a mile, two miles, more, they rode their ponies into the foothills, past the first pines and past some slender aspens that had lost their leaves. Sometimes they found no blood and could only guess where the elk went; other times the elk's flight was clear. Walks Alone ignored Skye, focusing entirely on the chase until at last they found her, still standing, her head lowered, her belly red. Walks Alone drew his bow and loosed another arrow, this one piercing the elk, which shuddered and folded to the earth.

Skye and Walks Alone rode the rest of the way and

studied the lifeless elk, a fine cow, heavy with fall fat. Walks Alone slid off his horse and circled the elk. Then he lifted his arms and sang something. Skye knew the Crow was apologizing to the spirit of the elk for taking its life. He thought maybe that was how it should be, and a better way of viewing hunting than the ways of the whites.

Walks alone neither gutted nor butchered the elk. He retrieved one arrow, which slid out easily amidst a bloody flux, but couldn't free the other. He headed for a nearby aspen grove and cut two saplings with his hatchet, and then trimmed them. He was making a drag, a travois, and would take this elk whole back to the village. It probably weighed six hundred pounds, far too much to carry on the packhorse. Artfully, the Crow lashed crossbars to the poles, using thong, and then anchored the drag to the packsaddle. He positioned the drag downslope from the elk, to make things easier, and then he and Skye dragged the elk, bit by bit, onto the travois. It was exhausting work, and they could move the elk only a few inches at a time. But at last they loaded the elk. The saplings bowed under the weight.

"We will go back now," Walks Alone said. "The People will rejoice. We will have a feast."

"I would like to keep on hunting," Skye said. "You go on."

"But we have hunted this elk together. The People will honor you."

"It was your victory, Grandfather. The honor is yours, not mine."

Walks Alone studied Skye, something kind in his eye. "You are a man of truth," he said. "This elk gave her life to me. That is what she told me. Be patient and ignore the bad words in the village. I have received wisdom from the seer, Red Turkey Comb, and understand your ways. He says you are the kin of the great grizzly, the most terrible of all creatures, and someday you will show the People how a grizzly bear defends its nest. Your time will come and then the People will honor you."

Skye wondered whether it would. He stood quietly while Walks Alone started back. The packhorse slowly dragged the burdened travois, which threatened to snap under the weight. Skye watched his father-in-law go, feeling an unfamiliar affection for him. Soon there was nothing but two deep furrows in the soft earth, and Skye was alone.

Chapter 11

Victoria's father, with the help of three others, hoisted the fat elk on a stout cottonwood limb. He sawed off the forelegs and fed them to the dogs. With a practiced hand, he gutted the animal and set the offal aside. Then he peeled the fine, thick hide in swift jerks, cutting gently where it adhered to the carcass, all the while enjoying the company of some of the village headmen, who had come to admire the elk.

Victoria watched somberly. This had been her father's kill, not Skye's. Her man was still out hunting. He wasn't good at it and didn't have the cunning that any good hunter possessed. She felt embarrassed that he was not present, sharing the moment. But she had been embarrassed a great deal by him recently.

When the hide finally pulled loose, her father folded it and gave it to her. It was so heavy she could barely hold it.

"Make a good elkhide coat for your man," he said. "The Cold Maker is coming and he has nothing to wear."

She nodded, knowing it would be good to do that. She could stake and flesh the hide that afternoon, and let it dry. Then she could hair it and brain-tan it and soften it. This was a prize elkhide, unblemished, soft, fine-grained. It would make a fine coat and some winter moccasins and maybe more than that.

But it should not be a gift from her father. Skye should be wearing the hide of an elk he killed. She watched her father a while more. He was cutting haunch meat and giving pieces to the friends who had helped him. Her brother, Arrow, was helping him. Walks Alone would give most of this elk away. He was a great man in the village of the Kicked-in-the-Bellies, and the more meat he gave away, the greater was the respect he would win. He cut pieces and sent them to his brother the chief, and to the seer, Red Turkey Comb, and to the small lodge of Makes Sun, who was old and feeble but took care of three old women, his wife and her sisters. Boys hung about, eager to perform this service for the headman who had killed the elk, and he would give a little to them, too. But when he was done with the giving, there still would be meat in the lodge kettle for several days.

How adept her father and brother were with the knife, and how fast they butchered the elk. Soon it would be bones for soup and gristle for the dogs. Knives were miraculous tools, and so were axes that cut wood, and awls that punched leather, and iron kettles that cooked meat and didn't break apart over a fire. Her people could no longer get along without such marvels provided by the yellow eyes. She wondered what it had been like for her grandmothers, who cut meat with knives of flint or bone, poked leather with bone awls, and cooked meat by boiling it in leather containers over heated rocks or burying it in hot ashes lined with grass.

She toted the heavy hide to her father's lodge and reluctantly staked it to the ground and began fleshing it. She preferred flint fleshers to the metal ones made by white men. Slowly she scraped the bits of meat and white fat from the hide. She didn't really want to do that, not because it was hard work but because she didn't want to give the elkskin coat to Skye. She had another one in mind. Skye didn't deserve such a fine, flawless skin. Antelope would know better how to wear it. He had a way with clothing. He would see at once that the leather was perfect, soft, golden, and clean, and would wear the coat in a way that told the whole village it was the best coat of all. And all would know who made it for him.

But she worked on the coat for Skye anyway because her father had commanded it and because she cared about Skye. She toiled through the cold afternoon—the weather was changing—and ignored her friends. Across the way, young men smoked and lounged and sometimes turned her way with amused glances. She knew what they were thinking: she chose Skye when she could have picked a better one. Her brother, Arrow, had joined them, his smirk even larger and more obvious than those of the others. He had no use for Skye or any white man.

"Where did this fine hide come from, Many Quill Woman?" asked Turtle, one of her old beaux.

"It came from my father."

"Ah, and not your man. He has no medicine."

"He has been named Man Not Afraid of the Pawnees."

Turtle laughed. "No one is afraid of Pawnees. I am not afraid of Pawnees. I am not afraid of Siksika or Lakota, either. I will fight them anytime."

It was strange. Among his own kind, Skye was an honored man and a leader. He had done brave things, fought well, won the esteem of many. Beckwourth admired him. The headmen—Bridger, Fitzpatrick, Sublette—rewarded him. She had been proud of him then. But now, in her own village, she saw that he was without power. His name should be No Medicine, because that was what had happened. He had none; somehow, he had violated the grizzly medicine given to him, and now he was as powerless as a child. It saddened her. She could not say what had happened, only that he didn't belong in the village. Maybe she would set his belongings outside the lodge door. Then he would go away and she would be free to pick someone else. She needed to think about that.

Skye rode in empty-handed, just ahead of a swirl of snow. Wearily he dismounted, eyed her and the half-fleshed hide, and entered the lodge without a word. He put his Hawken within, along with his powder horn and the rest of his kit. Then he emerged into the sharp cold, rubbed the black horse with dried grass, and checked its hooves.

"I never saw an animal. Hunted north, in the foothills."

"You have bad medicine. The grizzly has turned his back on you."

He paused beside her, forming words, and then turned away. She had heard them all. He led the horse out to the herd. She watched him go. He walked wearily, and wore clothes that had been given to him, and led a horse that

had been given to him by a war leader with much medicine.

She was cold, and tired of fleshing, so she rolled up
the half-fleshed hide and took it into the lodge, where it
would stay warm and she could unroll it again. Her heart
was not good. Everything annoyed her this cold, blustery
eve, and most of all Skye.

Tonight she would go listen to stories again in the lodge
of Antelope. Maybe Stillwater would be there, maybe
some of the other women. Antelope surrounded himself
with women. He had invited her to arrive just after dark,
which came early this Moon of Heavy Frosts. The lodge
of her father was wearisome this evening. Skye and her
mother avoided each other. Her father sat and smoked,
tired out by all the butchering. She ate the boiled elk hastily, saying nothing at all to her man, and then wrapped
her fine Hudson's Bay blanket about her and ducked into
the night.

If Skye had power, he would give her a big lodge, with
many robes, and have many fat Absaroka wives, much
meat, and eagle feathers in his hair—war honors. And
he would not have to deal with his mother-in-law. Jim
Beckwourth had medicine. She liked that.

She scratched Antelope's lodge door politely and was
invited in. He sat before a small bright flame, bare-
chested, muscular, his tawny flesh much the color of an
Absaroka's flesh. A necklace with a blue stone in it hung
over his chest. He had loosened his wavy jet hair and it
hung loose. He wore leggings and fine, beaded moccasins made for him by one of his many admirers.

"Ah, my fair Victoria—which do you prefer, Victoria
or Many Quill Woman?"

"I am Victoria; so I was named."

"A beautiful name, the name of a princess. Your presence graces the lodge of Antelope this fine evening."

"Where is Stillwater?"

"I sent her away."

"That is strange, Antelope. What of the rest?"

"Pine Leaf will not come this evening. And Walks Beside the River is not going to be with us a few days. And the others—" He shrugged.

"You sent them away!"

He smiled. "I told them that this night I would take Victoria to my robes."

"Oh!" She didn't dislike that. He had made his intentions known long ago, and much had passed subtly between them for days. But she thought she would tease him some.

"What makes you think I would go to the robes with you?"

"You want a man, and I am a man."

"You are saying Skye isn't a man."

Beckwourth shrugged. "Skye is a great man and an old friend. But we are rivals now. He wants to take my business from me, and I want to take his wife from him."

"Is that the way of friendship?"

He grinned. "Of course it is. I will give Victoria what she lacks."

"I don't lack anything."

"You lack my attentions. I am a gallant man and famously successful with women. Every man in the village admires me. I have had more wives than anyone else, and they tell other wives to try me because they have such a good time."

"How you boast!"

"Now or later?"

All this amused her. How fine it was to receive the attentions of such a one. Who among the People hadn't tried this now and then? Even before she was old enough to bleed, she had learned all about these things from the grandmothers. They told funny stories that made everyone laugh, and they knew exactly what they were talking about because they had done these things themselves. That was what separated the Absaroka from other tribes. The Absaroka knew how to amuse themselves. She decided she wasn't in a hurry, and she would make him work for his reward.

"I have come to hear stories," she said. "This evening you promised more stories. You said you would tell about the fire-boats that come up the river. I have never seen one."

"You don't want stories."

"Of course I do! And I would like some of your whiskey, too. If you are going to take me to your robes, I want stories and whiskey."

"No, whiskey will make you stupid. It is much better when you have all your senses. Then you will have such a good time you will tell the village that Antelope is a great man."

"How you boast! All you want is conquest. For you it is like war honors. Like counting coup. Like wearing another eagle feather in your hair."

"Ah, Victoria, it is so. But my hair is down and there is no feather in it."

He fed some small sticks to the blaze and pulled her to him. She pulled free and drew her red blanket around her.

"Maybe sometime," she said.

"So, Skye wins this night. But not for long. You will come to Antelope soon."

Chapter 12

In the morning, just when Skye was debating whether to try hunting in a hunted-out land, the town crier, old Pretty Louse, made his decision for him.

"Now listen, Kicked-in-the-Belly people. With the next sun we will move to winter camp. The camp chief has decided. The council of old men has decided. The weather prophet has told us this is the time. We will winter on the Rotten Sundance River! Pay attention now, all of you. Buffalo have been seen there."

Pretty Louse wandered off to cry his news elsewhere. Skye knew that river by another name, Clark's Fork of the Yellowstone. He and Victoria had briefly followed it and crossed it en route to this camp. In some places, where the bluffs defanged the wind and the cottonwoods and willows grew thick along its banks, the river would make a fine wintering ground, especially if some buffalo were around.

The move was fine with Skye. He had grown weary of the big bend of the Yellowstone, weary of feckless hunts. That day he combed and groomed his horses and checked their hooves. Then he tried to help the women, but they shooed him away. What was women's work should not be done by men. He didn't know quite what the line between men's and women's occupations was, and counted it as another blunder they would hold against him. There had been many of those lately. The whole village lived by a web of traditions and laws he barely fathomed. He wandered over to the small lodge of Red Turkey Comb, but the

shaman politely declined Skye's assistance and said
he owned nothing anyway.

Early the following morning the village formed into a
caravan, somehow creating order out of bedlam. Skye
brought his dun packhorse to Victoria, who squinted silently at him and then loaded it with their few possessions.
Even its packsaddle was borrowed. He hoped he might
travel with her this day, and perhaps the companionship
would bridge the deepening gulf between them. But she
busied herself, avoided him, helped drop the lodgecover
and load it onto a travois, loaded the family parfleches
upon packhorses, gathered lodgepoles into bundles and
hung some from each side of two ponies—and ignored
his efforts at conversation.

Walks Alone and Arrow had ridden forward, where a
vanguard was forming. Skye saw at once that the great
men of the village—the seers, Rotten Belly, war chiefs,
subchiefs, war leaders like Beckwourth, were gathering.
The procession would be led by Father of All Buffalo, the
camp chief, with Rotten Belly close behind. Skye thought
to ride picket duty out on a flank but was sharply turned
away by a leader of the Kit Fox warrior society, whose
duty and honor it was to protect the flanks as the caravan
proceeded. That left the rear, so he rode back to where the
horse herd milled—there weren't many because most animals were employed as transportation—and there he discovered youths, barely men, guarding the animals. They
eyed him coldly. Behind them, forming a rear guard, were
more of the Kit Fox warriors, who had the honor of guarding the village this day—or maybe this trip.

Within the forming column Skye saw all the rest: wives
and daughters, children, old men and women, infants in
cradle boards, little ones in baskets tied to travois, older

ones sitting behind their mothers. There was no place for him, a man without status among these people. He scarcely knew where to turn. To ride beside Victoria, and her mother, and her feeble grandfather, and her sisters, would shame her and him. To ride among those who didn't want him among them because he possessed few war honors would be to suffer rebuke.

Mysteriously, without any command, the village began its long journey amidst cries, the lashing of whips, the bellowing of horses, and the barking of a hundred curs. The great procession wound its way eastward along the Yellowstone River. Horsemen sat their ponies on almost every ridge and promontory within sight, guarding the People. Skye had seen villages in transit, but still he marveled. This was a festive occasion, and these people had gauded themselves in fine style, with bright tradecloth sashes, red headbands, jingle bells, beribboned manes, eagle feather bonnets. But all this didn't lift his spirits; he felt utterly out of place, not even welcome among his own lodgemates. He scarcely knew where to ride. He had a valuable weapon, a Hawken that could reach farther toward an enemy—or game—than anything else in the village, and yet the closed ranks of the Absarokas nullified its power.

So he rode his fine black horse in a sort of no-man's-land, well to the left of the column—the river flowed on the right—but far from the mounted vedettes who protected the vulnerable side of the column. And no one paid him the slightest attention, least of all the woman he called his wife.

They camped that night on a cottonwood flat beside the Yellowstone. In the morning they would begin a long detour around a gorge that boxed the river for several miles. The women broke out trail food—pemmican—because the vedettes, who doubled as hunters out on the flank, had made no meat that long dusty day. Everyone was in a festive spirit—they loved to travel, and every bend of the river brought its own excitement, even though they had seen all that country many times. Many of the women built wickiups of brush and covered them with robes for a shelter, electing not to raise a lodge.

Not until the early dusk was he certain he could even stay among Victoria's people. Some robes had been laid out for him, and he rolled himself up in one upon hard, cold ground. At least Victoria was beside him. Maybe there were other things to be thankful for, too. She had not whiled away time with Beckwourth all day.

"Victoria—"

"I am tired."

"You have a fine village. I have never seen such a great people."

She stared at him quietly, her eyes not cold this one moment, smiled, and then pulled her robes tight about her.

It was a long, chill night, but the weather prophet had been correct: no storm passed over them to make life on the trail miserable.

Skye awakened at the first hint of dawn, relieved himself in the river, splashed icy water over his face and beard, and stood quietly, watching the light thicken beyond the steep hills in the east. These dawn moments, when the whole world lay hushed, were holy to him, the time he saw into himself the best, and the time he understood and loved others the most.

He sensed the presence of another even before he turned to discover the seer, his friend, Red Turkey Comb, beside him. The man reached to Skye's chest and touched the bear claw necklace.

"You have bear medicine," he said.

Skye nodded, unable to think of a thing to say.

"Today you will ride with me."

"I would enjoy your company, Grandfather."

The seer nodded. "Ride with me and they see."

Skye wasn't certain what the shaman meant. But it didn't matter. This day he would ride with the one in the village who accepted him wholly.

"I am the least of the prophets," the older man said. "So I ride where there is least honor."

"You are the greatest of the seers, Grandfather."

"I will not say it about myself. This sun we will ride behind the rest, and just ahead of the horse herd. That is the place I choose."

"Then I will join you there, Grandfather."

The seer nodded. "I will tell you the ways of the Absaroka, the people of the fork-tailed bird. It is good for you to learn the ways and beliefs of the People."

An hour later, after a breakfast of jerky, Skye found Red Turkey Comb riding one horse while leading two packhorses that dragged his entire possessions, including his small lodge, perhaps fifty yards ahead of the boys herding the horses. They rode companionably through the morning, speaking little. Once in a while one of the Kit Fox Society warriors rode close, staring at the shaman and at Skye, and then returned to picket duty.

"They see you with me," Red Turkey Comb said. "It is good. You are a blessing and a gift to the Absaroka people, Man Not Afraid of the Pawnees."

"I feel as if I'm not helping your people much."

"You follow your path, and the People do not understand it."

"Not just the People. My wife doesn't understand it."

"She is young, and her head is turned by others."

"I am losing her."

The seer remained silent a moment, and then spoke. "You will lose her if you let her go. You will not lose her if you don't let her go."

"Would you explain that, Grandfather?"

"If you want to keep Many Quill Woman, you will do what you have to do, and what your medicine tells you to do."

All that was a mystery to Skye. But the old man closed the subject by turning to another. "I will tell you the ways of the People, so that you may become one of us. You should know that many things are sacred to the People, gifts of the First Maker, the mystery of all Creation. This land is sacred to us. It is the center of the world. To the north it is too cold; to the south too hot and dry. But here, on the edge of the mountains there is water and wood and the sacred buffalo, our meat and warmth and lodges. Let me tell you, husband of Many Quill Woman, that he who walks with reverence upon the breast of the earth shall be rewarded. He who respects all that is, the four-foots, the winged creatures, the spirits of the rivers and hills, the grasses given us to feed our ponies and feed the buffalo—such a person will be welcomed on this earth by all the spirits and will have friends everywhere. The Absaroka people have friends in the sky and on the earth, in the forests and on the waters."

Skye listened for hours to the poetry of the old man, absorbing the wisdom of a people who did not feel that the world was a hostile wilderness but a warm, providing, friendly place where they were welcome. Skye marveled. For him, the wilds had been a place of struggle, desperation, bare survival, and vulnerability to the elements, animals, enemies . . .

Thus they rode, toiling over steep slopes until they came to a hot spring where the villagers paused to refresh and wash. The purling hot water, rising out of the base of a cliff, astonished Skye. Women crowded the banks, but long before everyone had washed or refreshed, the camp chief was urging the village on again, and the police society was prodding the procession forward.

That night they camped at a place where majestic cottonwoods lined the river and a tributary stream rushed out of the south and emptied itself into the Yellowstone. The Crows called it the Diving Water River, an appropriate name. Skye helped the shaman off his horse, and together they raised the lodgepoles and wrapped the lodgecover around them. Skye chopped an armload of firewood for the seer before heading to the lodge of Victoria's people. A cold wind followed by gray overcast had chilled the village. There would be no wikiups sheltering the village this harsh night.

"Thank you for your company, Grandfather," Skye said. "You have taught me much about the ways of the People."

He picketed his horses on good grass close to Walks Alone's lodge. There seemed no point in running the horses out to the common herd with so much grass underfoot.

"Tell the man who is Victoria's husband that we have a stew and he should eat," said Digs the Roots. That was as close as a mother-in-law could come to addressing her son-in-law, but even that represented a major change.

Victoria quietly repeated her mother's request, though there was no need for it.

After their meal, Walks Alone shared a pipe of red willow kinnikinnick and tobacco with Skye and Arrow.

Skye sensed that something had changed. A revered seer had taken the Englishman for a friend, and now his in-laws, as well as others, were treating him with courtesy.

He wondered how long it would last. A shaman's example had restored Skye to the Kicked-in-the-Bellies, but it had not won the Englishman any more honors or made him a man of parts in the village. Compared to the illustrious Beckwourth, he possessed nothing—except a treasured wife.

Chapter 13

The column halted. Beckwourth did not at first know why, but he pushed forward among the headmen and saw the rider. Far ahead, accompanied by two of the Kit Fox Society warriors in the vanguard, rode a stranger, a white man.

The camp chief, Father of All Buffalo, awaited him, along with the war chiefs, headmen, and Rotten Belly himself. They had made good time for several days, driven east by a sharp west wind that harried the horses and drove spikes of icy air down their backs. Beckwourth wished the seers and weather prophets had moved them to winter grounds much earlier.

The stranger wore a thick blanket coat and a hat made of glossy beaver fur, and protected his hands in crude gauntlets. Beckwourth couldn't quite place him. But as the man drew closer, Beckwourth guessed he was Creole, one of the Canadian or St. Louis French in the fur trade. The man reined up at last before Rotten Belly and presented the chief with a plug of tobacco.

"Beckwourth," the man said.

Rotten Belly turned, summoned Beckwourth to his side.

"Ah, there you are, *mon ami*. I am Bissette, American Fur. We haven't met. Would you translate for me?"

Beckwourth turned to the chief of the Kicked-in-the-Bellies. "This man is Bissette, from American Fur Company, and he wants me to translate. I will tell you what he wants and tell him what you say."

Bissette plunged in. "We have start a post at the wedding of the Yellowstone and Big Horn, Monsieur Beckwourth. Kenneth McKenzie makes the trade with River Crows and he desire to serve the Mountain Crows, including your people. So he occupy old post of Manuel Lisa. Maybe he build good post someday. He say, plenty of blankets, powder, lead, rifles, knives, awls, good things. Buffalo are thick on the Big Horn, plenty of wood and grass a little to the south. Your people can winter there, one day's ride from ze post, make buffalo robes, trade for good things, have fat hiver, winter, ze Absaroka get rich, many guns, much meat, and happy times, *oui?*"

That suited Beckwourth just fine. He translated all of that, making sure that the camp chief, Father of All Buffalo, whose decision it would be, heard every word. Many of the village people were crowding in now, wondering about the halt and the visitor. He made sure that all of them heard the good news, too. He was employed by American Fur to steer these people to them and now he would do it—leaving poor old Skye helpless, to boot.

The camp chief listened sourly, his medicine and wisdom challenged by this proposition. "We will go where the spirits have told me to go," he said.

"Grandfather, your word binds us all," Beckwourth said. "But it would be good to send a few of our warriors back with this man Bissette, to see for themselves if the buffalo are thick on the Big Horn River." Bissette looked puzzled, so Beckwourth translated the exchange.

"Ah, monsieur, tell them zat McKenzie's trader, he make a gift to the headmen, one pair four-point blanket to each headman, more to Rotten Belly and Father of All Buffalo, much tobacco, *oui*? If they no like place, if no buffalo there, zen they go to Clark's Fork like you say."

Beckwourth explained all that. "Think on it," he added. All this would result in deliberation. These people would not make a momentous decision without pondering it. "Many buffalo, a warm camp, plenty of wood and grass."

And so the column halted while the headmen debated. In either case, the camp on the Big Horn or the camp on Clark's Fork, they had a long way to go. They were passing through rough country now, where the claws of the mountains stretched down to the Yellowstone, forming steep pine-dotted canyons. They were close to the Buffalo-Jumps-Over-the-Bank River—or the Stillwater, as white trappers called it.

Beckwourth knew better than to intervene while the seers and headmen, whose office it was to decide such matters, discussed the issue, so he dismounted, stretched his legs, and turned his back to the vicious wind out of the west. Bissette's proposal was a good one. The village would winter fifteen or twenty miles from the new outpost, an easy ride, and bring in good peltries—beaver, robes, ermine, wolf, all winter.

Beckwourth spotted Skye out on the fringe of the crowd of spectators and strolled over to him.

"What's this about, mate?" Skye asked.

Beckwourth flashed his wry smile. "About trading. American Fur's set up shop on the Big Horn in an old cabin put up by Manuel Lisa, got it manned and provisioned. Bissette says there's plenty of buffalo and good wintering grounds south of there on the Big Horn, so he's inviting the village to winter there, get fat, arm themselves, and bring in pelts to American Fur Company. . . . Don't feel bad. Rocky Mountain Fur paid you to do your best. You did your best."

"It's not over."

That struck Beckwourth as pure blindness, but he simply smiled. Poor Skye would not persuade a single villager to hang on to his pelts and trade them at rendezvous next summer.

The villagers stood stoically as the headmen sat in a circle on the frozen ground, quietly debating. Beckwourth could only wait. He knew better than to push the issue.

Younger men looked over their horses or grazed them. Women settled on the ground, wrapped in robes and blankets, and hugged their children. Beckwourth found a boulder that deflected the wind, and settled against it. He spotted Victoria, and she smiled at him. In a way, he hated to take her from Skye, but in another way he loved every moment of it. Victoria was the prize. Not only was she the prettiest of the Absaroka girls, she was the wisest, the most traveled and schooled. And she spoke English, more or less, after the years in the fur brigades with Skye.

The headmen and seers seemed to be taking forever. He wandered back to their circle and listened to the deliberations. Father of All Buffalo was resisting; the rest wanted to go to the place where buffalo were thick and they could turn every robe and pelt into something valuable.

Finally Rotten Belly intervened. "We are divided. I will say this. I will send four wise men to the Rotten Sundance River and they will look for buffalo and wood and grass. And I will send four wise men to the Big Horn, and they will look for buffalo, grass, and timber. We will decide at the place where the Rotten Sundance River flows into the Elk River."

Beckwourth translated for Bissette. "They'll send a party back with you to look over the Big Horn, and another party will work ahead and look over the Clark's Fork, and they'll decide at the junction of the Yellowstone and Clark's Fork in a week or so."

"Ah, it is less than we hope."

"No, we'll see them on the Big Horn—if the buffalo are there."

That was how it played out. Father of All Buffalo didn't look happy, but the council had not rejected his winter ground. Beckwourth watched four veteran war and police and camp leaders of the People ride east with Bissette, and watched four others, all appointed by Plenty Coups, ride ahead to the Clark's Fork area.

The village didn't get much farther that day. A worsening of the weather caught them. Temperatures dropped sharply until not even a hooded blanket capote turned the cold. They had made no meat this trip, and the stocks of trail food were declining. All the more reason to head for the buffalo, Beckwourth thought. Father of All Buffalo had waited much too long to move camp.

He and Stillwater set up their small lodge under a sandstone escarpment to escape the vicious wind that night, and then he rubbed down his fine brown horse. A temporary village of sorts had sprung up along the Yellowstone, the People huddling against the bitter weather. It would be a great night to have company, but he knew Victoria wouldn't enter his lodge until they were well settled in their winter camp. Travel was exhausting, especially for women, who bore the brunt of the work, raising and lowering lodges, packing up and unpacking, wrestling with sullen horses, caring for children, dealing with dogs, butchering any meat their men brought in, and trying to put food in the mouths of their families.

The next several days they struggled east in relentlessly cold weather. The only good about it was that it didn't snow or rain or mire man and beast. Beckwourth was ebullient. The more desperate their circumstances so late in the year, the more likely they would be to winter on the Big Horn, close to American Fur's outpost. The traders would ship many packs of beaver and robes downriver in the spring—and Beckwourth figured it would net him a raise.

On a gray day with flakes of ice in the air, they reached the confluence of the Yellowstone and Clark's Fork. There, the party sent up Clark's Fork awaited them, and their news delighted Beckwourth. No buffalo that direction, but plenty of deer. There was no reason to tarry there; the Big Horn awaited them, but Rotten Belly decreed that they would stay and hear the news from the other party when it returned. The village chafed at the delay, wanting to settle in for the winter. But grass was plenty, and the weary horses and mules could fatten on it while the village waited.

Then, one evening two days later, the Big Horn party rode in—and drew a crowd. One, Man With Many Horses, had been seriously injured in the thigh, which was covered with bloodstained leather bandaging. His woman,

Sweet Root, cried out and helped her man off his pony. They all soon had the story. The Crows had ridden to the Big Horn, found that Bissette had spoken truly: there were buffalo everywhere, wintering in small herds that occupied adjacent valleys. The old trading house was located on the flat just west of the confluence, and each man had received a twist of tobacco as a gift from the American Fur Company.

But the rest of the story was darker. Returning to the village, they had been set upon by Piegans, a dozen roaming horse thieves out of the north, and had barely escaped. Only because one of them, Big Moon, had a musket that reached beyond the Piegan arrows had the outnumbered Absaroka escaped. An arrow had lodged in the thigh of Man With Many Horses, and he had bled almost white.

What now? Beckwourth saw the chance and stepped forward, addressing Rotten Belly as well as Father of All Buffalo and other headmen. "Let us camp where there is ample meat, and we can trade robes for guns. Then I will personally lead a party against the Piegans to avenge this terrible thing. I will take many scalps."

No one disagreed. In the next gray dawn, they would start for the Big Horn.

Chapter 14

And so the Kicked-in-the-Belly people wintered on the Big Horn twenty miles south of the American Fur Company outpost, in a sheltered bend of the river where thick cottonwood forest supplied firewood, brown grasses stretched in every direction, and high bluffs baffled the wind. Buffalo were plentiful, even as the trader at the outpost, Samuel Tullock, had said.

But no sooner had the village erected its lodges than a storm howled in, dumping a foot of snow on the village. Father of All Buffalo, never reconciled to the change, nodded knowingly Women fought drifts to cut firewood with their hatchets. Others cut brush and packed it around the lodges to subdue the relentless wind and protect man and animal. The herders checked the horses now and then and hastened to their lodgefires, knowing no thieving enemy would be out in such weather. Horses, huddled rump to wind, pawed through snow for brown grass or stood quietly and endured the caked snow or their backs and whatever else life brought them. The days grew short, and Father Sun hovered low in the south and vanished midafternoon.

Only at night, when the temperatures plummeted and the stars looked like chipped ice and the snow squeaked underfoot, did the weary, bone-cold People relax their constant labor to settle in. In those times, they gathered together to gamble with sticks, or tell stories, or smoke their special mixture of red willow bark and tobacco, or make clothing to subdue the icy breath of the Cold Maker. The new winter would be long and hard, but most of all boring, confining an outdoor people to tiny leather cones.

But as harsh as winter was in these days of endless darkness and twilight, the Absaroka people didn't much mind. The village seemed almost magical, especially in the evenings, when lavender light crept over the snow and vanished in the tree-blackened bluffs, and orange light from the lodgefires glowed luminescently through the tawny lodgecovers, turning every smoke-stained lodge into a street lamp. This was a land of plenty. Beside or within each lodge was a pile of dry firewood, dead cottonwood limbs. From the few trees within the village, frosty quarters of buffalo and mule deer hung, fresh and ready for the black cast-iron cookpots gotten from the traders.

A few hardy hunters supplied the village with ample buffalo meat. The lumbering animals didn't run well in snow and were easy to pick off in box canyons or narrow draws. Skye was among the hunters. From the moment the Kicked-in-the-Bellies arrived on the Big Horn River, he had saddled the weary black horse and ridden out for meat. He shot several buffalo, employing his Hawken at a distance to save his horse a risky chase over snow-covered, treacherous ground. He shot carefully, aiming for that vulnerable heart-lung spot just back of the forelegs, preserving his precious caps and powder as he had learned to do with the fur brigades. After each shot, Walks Alone and Arrow lifted their numb hands to the gloomy sky and prayed to the departing spirit, apologizing for taking its life to feed themselves. Their profound spirituality affected Skye. He liked a people who so respected all life that they would apologize to the killed animal. Then he and Walks Alone and Arrow butchered the bison and dragged bloody quarters back to camp on a groaning travois, one at a time.

Skinning a carcass was itself an ordeal that took time and numbed the hands. Once they had skinned one side, they had the brutal task of turning the buffalo over to skin the other, no mean feat because the hump prevented it. Sometimes not even the three of them could turn over a carcass, and then they had to use a horse to help them.

Once, just as they approached a cow lying in a pool of reddened snow, the buffalo struggled to her feet, snorted, sprayed blood from her mouth, lowered her massive head until her horns were swords, and thundered toward Walks Alone. Skye was just then ramming a new charge home. Swiftly he extracted the hickory rod, fumbled a cap over the nipple, and shot into the chest of the pain-crazed animal. It dropped just before careening into Walks Alone, whose retreat was slowed by the snow. They stared, shaken. Skye reloaded with shaking hands, not bothering to clean out the fouled nipple, and then they set about gutting the lifeless animal, each of them working in wary silence. During those hard winter days, when they toiled from the late dawn to the early dusk, Skye sensed that he was being accepted, though no word was ever spoken. The hunting had bonded the men of the lodge.

The women soon had five prime winter-haired buffalo hides to flesh and tan, but the grim weather prevented them from making robes. The hides were stacked outside Walks Alone's lodge, stiff boards of hair and skin. Frozen meat hung from cottonwood limbs, enough to feed the lodge for two moons with juicy hump meat, delicious tongue, and spicy backfat that seasoned every pot. The big white guts were carefully washed and packed with shredded meat and fat for future use. And one by one, the buffalo's very bones were cracked open and the delicate marrow scraped from them for a sort of pudding that set their mouths watering. These were good times, despite the numbing cold. Walks Alone and Digs the Roots were happy. The hides were future wealth. Skye's position among his in-laws improved a little. His Hawken had ensured a fat and happy winter.

Around the wavering fire, the women toiled endlessly.

Victoria completed the elkhide tunic for Skye, embellishing it with blue quillwork across the breast, the blue for sky. She presented him at last with a golden coat, while her father smoked and watched.

"Here, dammit," she said, holding up the shirt. "I make this for you."

It fit him well, and warmed a body too lightly clad.

"It is beautiful, Victoria," he said. "Now I am warm. You have chased away winter. You are good to me."

Then she surprised him by extracting a pair of elkhide moccasins, cut high to turn the snow and lined with the soft pelt of a rabbit.

"My mother make these for you," she said.

The moccasins were much needed, and wrapped his cold feet in instant warmth. "Tell the one who is your mother," he said, politely avoiding her name, "that I am pleased and honored and wish her the blessing of a happy lodge and plenty to eat and many grandchildren."

The last evoked a sharp look from Victoria as well as her parents. Their marriage had been barren, but in Arrow's lodge, three children had been added to the People. It had been something to hold against Skye.

In some ways, the camp on the Big Horn was the best of times. Other lodges were enjoying the same bounty. Wolves circled the camp, shy by day but bold at night, driven half mad by the smell of meat hanging well above their snapping jaws. Skye often listened to the wolves at night, aware of how thin the buffalohide wall of the lodge was against the full ferocity of nature.

The deep cold and darkness enforced intimacy, and at last he spent hours with Victoria. At first he tried to engage her in English, but her responses were always in Crow, and he realized it was impolite to address her in a private language in the midst of her family. Everything spoken between them would be for all to hear. That was still a nagging problem with him, and made him yearn all the more for his own lodge.

Each day he took generous cuts of buffalo to his friend Red Turkey Comb, and brought armloads of dry wood scavenged from the surrounding hills. And each day he paused to visit with the old man, often wondering why the seer stayed so much alone in his small cold lodge during the most social time of the year. The shaman had been steadfast in his friendship, and Skye wished he could do more for the man whose vision embraced things unseen by others.

"Your time will come, and then the People will know who you are," the shaman said one afternoon. "The bear sleeps in his den all winter, but when he awakes the world trembles," he said on another occasion.

All these things Skye filed away in his mind, wondering what they might mean. He had come to the Crow village because Victoria needed the company of her people, but this old sage was telling him that he would have a larger destiny among the Crows.

Whatever the future might bring, Skye was fairly certain it would not include future employment with Rocky Mountain Fur Company, except perhaps as a trapper or camp tender. Beckwourth had been quick to exploit his new advantage now that he was close to a source of trade goods and could easily deliver peltries to the trading house on the Yellowstone. His lodge had bloomed into a small store where a Crow could trade buffalo robes, beaver pelts, fox, otter, wolf pelts, weasel, ermine, and even deer hides for almost anything—lead and powder, rifles, awls, knives, bells, blankets, calico, flannel, salt, sugar—and whiskey. Alcohol was illegal in Indian territory, but that had never stopped American Fur Company from supplying it. Beckwourth was suddenly doing a lively trade in jugged Indian spirits—actually grain alcohol, river water, tobacco, and a close of cayenne pepper for flavor. Whatever the elders thought of it, they averted their eyes. Beckwourth was a headman, an authentic hero among the people, and a gracious friend of most of the senior warriors in the village.

What was winter for, if not to gather in lodges through the long dark afternoons and evenings, laugh, tell tales, gossip, gamble—and now drink the water-that-makes-one-crazy. Skye registered the subtle change in the village and knew that some of those parties, most of all Beckwourth's own, had grown wild. And even as those parties drew crowds, so did his supply of robes and pelts grow. His periodic trips to the Yellowstone, laden with furs, told the tale.

Skye had lost the Crow trade and could never get it back. Worse, now that the camp had settled into its long winter's night, Victoria had started once again to frequent Beckwourth's lodge.

Chapter 15

These were good times for Jim Beckwourth, yet he was not content. What more could a man ask for?

First there was the beauteous Stillwater, boon companion in his robes and devoted to making him happy and comfortable. She was a bright-eyed, honey-fleshed woman with blue-black hair she wore in a single braid, often with a yellow ribbon tied into it. She was also fun, and had a belly-shaking laugh that erupted through his lodge now and then.

Secondly, he had Pine Leaf—after a fashion. She was the slim young woman who had become famous as the woman warrior of the Crows, having vowed revenge upon the Blackfeet who had killed her brother. She was fast, lithe, adept with lance and bow and arrow, and had come to Beckwourth's aid several times in pitched battles, once saving his life. Pine Leaf had vowed never to marry, but that didn't prevent her from enjoying lovers, of whom Beckwourth was the most prominent. He had often asked her to marry him, and she had always replied, "When the pine leaves turn yellow."

Which they never would.

Of all the women he knew, he loved Pine Leaf the most. Stillwater was all for having more wife-sisters around to share the work and provide companionship all day. If Beckwourth did manage to acquire more wives, she would be the senior and most important one, the sits-beside-him wife, seated at the place of honor beside him in the lodge. And she could boss around the younger and lesser women to her heart's content, which she intended to do.

It came down to Victoria Skye. He wanted her as much as the others, and her refusals only spurred him to find the way to win her. He wondered why, in the midst of success, he could not be content. He pondered it, looking for answers. Was he trying to prove something? He couldn't say. He knew only that some worm kept eating at him, making each of his triumphs bitter because it didn't fulfill him. If he couldn't take Victoria from Skye, then nothing else mattered very much.

No woman among all the Absarokas had been more perfectly formed or walked the earth with more grace and poise. No other woman was more splendidly dressed or did finer quillwork. And only Pine Leaf outdid Victoria when it came to armed struggle, because Skye had taught Victoria all he knew of lance and knife and muzzle-loading rifle. Beckwourth envisioned a lodge filled with beauteous women, a veritable army of women, and maybe even a few children, too. Even now Stillwater bloomed with child.

It wasn't that he wanted to wound his friend Skye; he liked Skye, and liked talking English with Skye now and then. And he respected Skye's prowess as a mountaineer, for the Englishman had proved himself over and over to be resourceful during starving times, danger, war, and brutal weather.

He was halfway rich, thanks to all the trading he was doing. Some of the villagers chose to trade directly with Tullock up on the Yellowstone, which was fine; Beckwourth got the credit for steering the Mountain Crows to the little outpost that American Fur had set up there. But more often, the villagers bargained directly with Beckwourth, and he scrupled to deal fairly with them and charge slightly less than the company did, or at least offer more for a pelt or hide or robe. Whenever the hard winter permitted, he rode north, with packhorses bearing his furs, and exchanged them for more trade goods, always making a little in the process.

He profited especially from the illegal nectar of the fur trade, smuggled countless leagues up the Missouri, well hidden from the watchful eye of the army at Fort Leavenworth. American Fur contrived to have a few barrels of pure grain spirits on hand, carefully concealed in a bunker yards from the Yellowstone post in case some wandering official—or rival—should show up. At this priceless fountain, Beckwourth regularly replenished his jugs—and then added the water and plug tobacco and spices that turned spirits into Indian whiskey. And this he sold at his little soirees, usually after supplying a free sample just to prime the pump. It was amazing how the pelts accumulated in his lodge from just one little party.

But that wasn't what was on his mind one January afternoon when he decided to have another party. Victoria was. He mixed more of his trade whiskey and announced to Stillwater that he would have another party that evening and he would invite all the grandmothers to tell their bawdiest stories.

"Oh, I would like that," Stillwater said.

"I will invite Victoria Skye—Many Quill Woman. Maybe a little whiskey will warm her cold heart."

"You're not going to get her into the robes."

"I'm going to try."

"I'll tell her that Antelope is the greatest lover in the village. No man makes a woman happier."

"That should entice her."

"I would enjoy a time in the robes, too, but I am getting big."

"So I noticed."

"I will turn my back and listen. I will see whether you are the same with her as you are with me."

"Are there any better among all the Absarokas?"

"I wouldn't know," she said, and laughed happily. "Maybe I will find out sometime. The women say that Standing Otter is a great one."

"Ha! His otter wouldn't stand long."

"Maybe I'll find out. Then I will be able to tell you."

"Then you'll know why you married Antelope."

That evening he welcomed twelve guests, who entered his lodge, respectfully nodded toward the hearth and its sacred hearth spirits, proceeded by custom to seat themselves in a circle around the small, hot fire, and await the libations of Antelope.

Among them was Kills the Dog, the old woman, wife of Sees at Night, who was renowned for telling the bawdiest stories known to the People. No woman was her match, although some said that Pretty Eyes was close. But Kills the Dog was much older and more experienced, and knew just what sort of story to tell on a cold January night. What else was there to do in the deep darkness of winter but tell stories?

Thus Kills the Dog was escorted to the place of honor, next to Beckwourth himself. She had grown fat with age, and that made her wobble as she stooped around the circle of the lodge and settled herself. Beckwourth surveyed the rest cheerfully. Bad Medicine, a fine warrior and hunter with plenty of pelts to trade; Lame Dog, another one of Antelope's war companions, a famous drinker and womanizer; Two Horns, a gorgeous young virgin, half sister of Stillwater; Pine Leaf, of course, a seductive tigress; and Many Quill Woman, whose good humor contrasted so sharply with the dour Skye. There were many others, of course—those who loved a good cup of whiskey, various female candidates for Beckwourth's attention, and a couple of good storytellers, both old women.

"Ah, friends, let us bless the Cold Maker for making us come together on a bitter night. Now we will have a party. I will pass the jug around; take a good drink to warm your spirits. After that, we will tell stories. Kills the Dog promises to tell you the worst stories that ever assaulted your ears."

Kills the Dog smiled toothlessly.

Beckwourth uncorked his jug and passed it first to Kills the Dog, who took a mighty swill, coughed and sputtered, and passed it to the next. No one refused such a generous largess, a gift worth a pelt if one took a long guzzle. Beckwourth eyed Victoria with interest as she swallowed slowly.

"Sonofabitch!" she said in English.

The jug made the rounds and returned to Beckwourth, who corked it and set it next to a tin cup. When anyone wanted more, a pelt would come around the circle, and Beckwourth would fill the tin cup with his concoction and send it to the buyer. By the time it reached the buyer, it was usually much diminished by samplers along the way. Which was fine with everyone.

"Now, Grandmother," he said to Kills the Dog, "tell us a story."

Kills the Dog licked her lips, shook her head, and said that the cup needed to go around a few more times. Only then would her stories melt the wax in their ears.

So Beckwourth invited another grandmother, Elktooth, to begin.

"I will tell the story of two young people whose families did not want them to marry," she began. "But they lived long ago, and were among the first to come to this country where the Absaroka belong forever. One was Pretty Fox, a beautiful virgin, the younger daughter of Makes the Birds Fly. Pretty Fox had eyes only for her beloved Buffalo Hoof, but her parents told her she could not marry until her older sister was married, because her older sister had a bad temper and no man wanted her. So Pretty pined and waited, and Buffalo Hoof decided that the best way to have Pretty Fox was to marry both sisters at once."

This was a good story, and Beckwourth settled back to enjoy a fine evening. Soon the grandmother came to the crux of the story: both sisters were married to Buffalo Hoof but no sooner had they moved to the lodge given them by the village than they quarreled about who should be the first to enjoy Buffalo Hoof in the robes. The older sister said it was her right; the younger said she was the one Buffalo Hoof loved. So Buffalo Hoof, who was a magician, put them both asleep, and when they awoke neither knew who had been first, and he wouldn't tell them when they asked.

"Ah, I would not put any woman asleep," said Beckwourth. "That is a bad story."

"You would put me to sleep, Antelope," the old woman retorted.

That was how the evening went. Once in a while the Cold Maker shot icy air down the smoke vent, pushing smoke into the lodge, and then Stillwater had to go out and adjust the smoke ears, because the wind was coming from all directions. But that was all that marred a splendid evening. The cup went around many times, and by the time it was time for grandmother Kills the Dog to tell her terrible stories, she could hardly speak.

Beckwourth watched Victoria enjoy herself. Skye's wife was laughing with all the rest, and her eyes glowed. She sipped every time a cup passed by, and then swore mighty oaths she had picked up from the trappers.

That was all fine with Beckwourth, and when at last his guests had their fill of wild stories and departed one by one through the oval door covered with a flap of buffalohide, he detained her.

"Tonight you enjoy the robes with me," he said in English. "Stillwater says she is too big now, and she says you should enjoy my attentions."

"You got too many attentions. Goddamn, maybe sometime, Antelope, but not now," she replied, not soberly. "I got to keep Skye warm."

And then she drew her blanket tight around her and plunged into the night.

Chapter 16

A harsh wind rattled the lodge of Walks Alone, and Skye knew the day would be mean. Victoria slept late into the morning, exuding the stale odor of spirits. Skye had studied her somberly as she lay curled in her buffalo robe. She was not the girl he had married. Not much was left of the bond they had forged during his years with the fur brigades. Spirits were his own demon, and they were becoming Victoria's as well.

She awakened as he gazed at her, stared crossly at him, and rolled over. Then at last she got up, straightened her doeskin skirt, tied her beaded buckskin leggings around her calves, pulled up her moccasins, and drew her red blanket about her. She vanished into the cold and returned minutes later, still silent and avoiding contact with him.

Her mother and sisters had gone somewhere, probably to collect wood, a relentless and demanding task through the winter. Her father had settled into his backrest and stared at the small fire, idled by winter.

Skye wanted to talk to her. He had things to say, things building up in him for a long time.

"Victoria, we'll go get some firewood," he said.

"It is cold."

"Then we will brave the cold."

"It is women's work."

"Then we will do women's work together."

"Dammit, leave me alone."

"We will walk along the river."

Irritably, she pulled a blanket about her, pulled a thick shawl over her head, and drew gloves over her hands. "It is too cold," she said. "I do not feel like a walk."

He drew a buffalo robe about him, and put on a thick beaver cap, and they exited the lodge, smacked hard by a brutal wind that pierced their clothing.

"You see? We go back now."

He took her elbow and steered her down toward the river, over glazed snow and treacherous drifts, until they hit a regular path near the bank—in fact, the trail north to the trading cabin.

She walked in stony silence, radiating rank hostility toward Skye. He couldn't help that. His marriage was in grave trouble and he was going to talk about it. The vicious wind would punctuate his every sentence, and maybe that would have more effect than long counsels around a cheery lodgefire. Also, he wanted to talk English, which was not possible when they were among her family.

"You are going to tell me not to go to Antelope's lodge."

"No, I'm going to ask you. I won't tell you."

"You should tell me. All men tell their women what to do."

"I prefer to ask you. Then, if you agree, I have your consent."

"Goddamn, I don't understand you, Skye."

"I said I'm going to ask you and I mean it. It has nothing to do with obedience. If you obey without wanting to, you will not think of me as a friend and husband."

"No, I think maybe you care about me if you tell me no. Maybe I keep wanting you to say, 'Goddamn it, Victoria, do not do this or you can find someone else.'"

"You are not my slave, Victoria."

She glanced at him sharply. A gust of wind lifted her blanket from her, and she cursed. "Let's go back," she said.

He shook his head. "I'm going to tell you what I believe. We've never talked about it. I know what you and your people believe, and what you think is right. But now I want to tell you about what I profess and honor, and what I was taught by my elders. Then maybe we can understand each other better and make a better marriage."

She didn't reply.

The pain of coldness was good. The whole bleak scene before them, the black river running between sheets of ice along the banks, the spidery web of naked gray limbs, the overcast sky, the occasional outcrop of tan rock, the dark junipers and pines, matched the spiritual winter of his soul.

"For years when I was trapped in the Royal Navy, the ones above me told me what to do, and I did it because I would be punished if I didn't. I especially hated that life because it wasn't my own. That is one way of life. A marriage can be like that. Some white men's marriages are like that. A man tells a woman what to do, and she does it. Your Absaroka marriages are mostly like that. Some women enjoy it. They want to be told what to do. If their man says, Don't go to Antelope's lodge, they obey. That may be the way of your people, but it is not my way."

"Maybe you don't know women. If you don't tell a woman what to do, she don't respect you."

"You will respect me more if I ask you. And it is a mark of my respect for you. You will always have the right to choose. Some white men give that respect to their women. Some don't."

"Where the hell are white women? The *mah-ish-ta-schee-da* have no women."

"The yellow eyes will bring their women someday. They live mostly in villages and cities."

That gave her pause.

Skye felt the cold begin to numb his cheeks and nose, and wondered whether to turn back. He was more vulnerable to this sort of penetrating cold than she. He decided he would endure. On this morning he would endure anything, bear anything, suffer anything to save his marriage. He hastened the pace to stir his blood.

"Where are we going?" she demanded.

"I hope to a new place of the heart."

"You going to make me?"

He laughed, and she glowered at him.

"I am cold," she said.

"Yes, you are cold. The words are well chosen."

"Maybe I'll go back now."

"I want to talk more about our marriage."

"You not gonna make me walk?"

"Not if you don't want to. I want us to walk side by side through life because you want to walk with me."

She stared and drew her blanket tight about her. But she did not turn around. That was good.

"Your people and mine have different ideas about marriage. For us marriage is very sacred. We marry forever, all of our lives. Yes, we can escape a bad marriage, just

as you can. We can get a divorce, but it is difficult, especially in England, where I come from. But we try to follow the laws of God, and he wants us to stay married.
When white men and women marry they make sacred
vows to love and honor each other all their days, through
good times and bad; to be faithful and caring; to follow
the Christian faith together. All this is done in a church,
the House of God, so that those who make the vows do
so in the presence of God—the First Maker, as you call
God—so everyone knows that this is holy."

"Goddamn! No wonder all you come out here and
escape the women. For us it is different. Sometimes it is
no damn good and then we put everything outside of the
lodge door to tell the other it's no damn good."

"Yes, that is it. Your ways and my ways are different.
I am married for better or worse. I hope you will be, too,
because that is how love works. If you love me when times
are bad, and I do not provide for you, and I am not a great
man in your village, then you truly love me. And if I keep
on loving you when you drift away and will not be my
friend and lover, then I truly love you."

She had no response to that at first, but he could see
she was registering it, thinking about it.

"If marriage is sacred among the *mah-ish-ta-schee-da*,
then why does Antelope collect women? Why do all the
mountaineers buy Indian girls at the rendezvous?"

Skye didn't have a very good answer to that. But he
tried. "What is sacred to the yellow eyes is not accepted
by all of them," he said, choosing his words carefully.
"Nothing requires them to believe anything. It is up to
them. The very ones who come out here to the wilderness—"

"What do you mean, wilderness? This is my home."

"Well, if I could show you how people live in cities, you'd know what I mean. This all seems like a country where no one lives."

"But it is full of people."

Skye didn't argue that point. These people lived in portable towns and left little mark of passage. "Anyway, the ones who come here are usually the ones who reject all those things. They come here to escape. Most do, anyway. Jed Smith—you met him—he's a believer."

"That is a bad religion, then. It is too hard. It drives people away."

"Some would say so. I think the rules are mostly good. The rules about marriage are good. They are good for the children, good for the women and men."

"Do you think our ways are not sacred to us? Or bad?" She was angry. "You think you are better than us?"

"Your ways are sacred, Victoria."

"I am cold," she said.

He stopped. His face was stinging from the bite of the wind. Going back, with the wind, would be more comfortable. "All right. It is cold." They turned back. "Now you know that I will never tell you to do something. I am not your chief. I am asking you now not to go to Beckwourth's parties. I don't know what he has in mind, but I don't trust him."

"You are goddamn strange, Mister Skye. An Absaroka would not let his wife disobey him."

This walk had all been for nothing. But he had, at least, told her for the first time who he was and what he felt. "I want you and love you. But I also know I may not be wanted. I don't fit into your village very well. The future is up to you, not me."

He left the rest unsaid. If she didn't want him, she

would put his gear outside the lodge someday, and he would suddenly find himself a single man again.

They walked in silence, the wind harrying them back, so that the return was shorter than the outbound walk. It had been a good walk. He didn't know whether she would accept what he said, or him. The more he dwelled upon the customs of the Absaroka people, and the customs of white Europeans, the more he believed that there was an unbridgeable chasm between the two people. He could not become an Indian. Maybe he wasn't much of a church-going Christian, but those were nonetheless his sacred beliefs, and if he let go of them he would be a man without a center. There were many customs of the Crows he could easily accept and enjoy, things that would trouble most white people. But he could not turn himself into an Absaroka, or any Indian.

They reached the lodge, and she turned to him, searching his face. He saw perplexity in hers, but not anger. She took his hand in hers and lifted it to her face.

"Goddamn, Skye," she said, and then ducked through the lodge door. He followed, not knowing how it ended.

Chapter 17

A chinook swept away the snow in hours, and the Kicked-in-the-Belly people emerged from their lodges, shed their blankets and robes and gloves, and stretched in the wan, welcome sun. The Cold Maker would soon return, more furious than ever, but for a few days the People would enjoy the blessings of mild weather.

The strange warmth seemed heady to Skye; the winter had been long and bitter. He rejoiced as the snow melted into the thawed ground and he took long hikes along the Big Horn soaking up the sun.

No sooner had warmth come than warriors dreamed of horse raids and glory. Now, for a while, they could carry their lances, bows and arrows, tomahawks, and clubs out on the plains, extending the dominion of the Absaroka people over a fiercely contested land. Jim Beckwourth quickly seized upon the warmth to assemble his long-delayed foray against the Siksika. He progressed from lodge to lodge inviting the finest fighting men in the village to go with him; there would be ample powder and lead for anyone with a musket or rifle, thanks to the American Fur Company.

He found Skye sunning himself beside the river.

"Ah, friend Barnaby, the time's come to even the score. We'll catch the Blackfeet in their lodges and make them pay. I'm leading a large party on a raid, and I'd be most honored if you supplied us with your keen sharpshooting."

"Weather might not hold long enough."

"War honors mean a lot to these people, my friend. You've the makings of a headman."

"And if we lose? Men die?"

"It's unlikely. Are you coming? We need that Hawken."

"I think I might."

Various of the Crows were standing about, but they could only surmise the nature of the English-language exchange.

"Good. We're leaving at once while we have the weather. A couple of eagle feathers in your bonnet wouldn't hurt, you know. And a few coups. It's all a game, Skye."

"War's no game, mate. I've seen more killing and wounding than most men. And I rarely saw a need for it, except against pirates."

"We'll catch them in their lodges. They don't fight in winter."

Skye had a reply to that but kept his counsel. A raid would improve his lot in this village, especially if he returned with a few ponies and more coups.

Skye felt at odds with himself. He owed it to Bridger and Fitzpatrick and Sublette to go out and make war on the Blackfeet. Of all the tribes of the northern plains, the Blackfeet posed the greatest danger to the Rocky Mountain Fur Company. They had been armed and motivated by the British to attack Yank brigades, and now the American Fur Company had started trading with them, along with Hudson's Bay, supplying even more rifles and knifes and lance points. The Blackfeet were a proud and powerful league, brilliant in war, a terror to all the surrounding tribes. Anything Skye could do to subdue them would earn him praise and thanks at the rendezvous.

"When are you leaving?"

Beckwourth flashed one of those smiles that had made him a reputation. "Get your gear," he said, and headed over to the lodge of Pretty Weasel to invite the man to the party.

That very hour, the invited warriors, thirty-eight in all, including Pine Leaf, gathered their war ponies, put together their fighting gear, their leather bags of war paint, a little jerky or pemmican, flint and steel, hooded capotes, leggings, spare moccasins, war shields, braided lariats to deal with stolen horses, and a winter robe or a pair of blankets to sleep in. Then they assembled beside the river while the People watched silently. Skye joined them, mounted on his winter-gaunted black horse, with the dun for a spare.

Skye sensed something was amiss when he told his father-in-law what he would be doing. Walks Alone stared stonily at him. Beckwourth had not sought the blessing of the war leaders, or the consent of Rotten Belly, or a reading of the auguries by the shamans. It was rare not to dance, to supplicate the Above People, to make medicine, to consult the spirits, to read what lay beyond the sky and wind and earth.

But the interlude of the warm winds would be short; they must act at once or not at all. It wasn't that the warriors ignored their medicine. Many paused, arms upraised, to sing a war song, to open medicine bundles and examine what was within, to go off alone to talk with the Ones Above. Indeed, one of the invited men, Barking Wolf, turned away, saying his medicine had warned him of death and cold. He was no less a man among the People for following his medicine.

But the moment arrived that very noon when Beckwourth, Skye, and the proud warriors rode out of the village on their shaggy war ponies, first to supply themselves at the trading house on the Yellowstone, and then to strike north and west, across two hundred miles of rough prairie and intermountain basin, to the heartland of the Piegans.

The old men of the village, the women, the chiefs who stayed behind, the youths who weren't invited—and who would defend the village in the event of attack—studied the departing band. Beckwourth was leading nearly a fifth into battle on winter-weakened horses, going such a distance that they would surely risk death by freezing, storm, or starvation, when the chinook died. For what? Because a Crow had been injured in the thigh last November?

But there was honor in all this: the old men might disapprove—and yet, in some ambivalent way, the whole village exuded pride at these daring men, and would richly honor their success when they returned. If they did return. Skye wondered.

As the war party rode out, Skye discovered Walks Alone watching, and beside him Victoria, wrapped in her blue blanket, staring at him, her solemn expression ineffable. They had reached some sort of accommodation. She had neither gone to another of Beckwourth's drinking parties nor given Skye her boundless love, as she had when they were among the fur brigades. He hadn't lost her, here in this Absaroka village of hers—nor had he recovered her affections. Some fresh war honors might help, and he admitted to himself that that was the real reason he was going.

They rode north under a fitful and low sun that somehow belied the eerie warmth of the chinook and reminded him that this was January. Still, by day, at least, the weather remained pleasant, though cold crept back as soon as the sun plummeted in mid-afternoon. This group of Absaroka warriors was uncommonly silent, as if they were all wondering about the wisdom of a sortie fought without the blessing of the People. Maybe death would ride beside them this time.

Beckwourth followed the same route he had taken the last time, taking his Crows through the bleak gateway that divided the Belt Mountains on the west and the Snowies on the east, and into the snow-swept Judith country. The weather held, though some days a high overcast reminded them that Father Sun was powerless against the ferocity of the Cold Maker.

Beckwourth headed straight for the square-shaped

butte that served as a landmark. A somber creek there would take them to the Missouri, which would have to be forded, no small matter in the middle of winter. They had no trouble finding game, which was herded up and easy to kill because the deer or antelope were weakened, slow, and faced decaying snowdrifts in every direction. Each dusk they roasted deer or antelope, picketed their horses on thin brown grass, and then lay in the icy dark, not wanting to give their presence away with a night fire.

By the end of the third day, Skye sensed that the chinook was about to end. He could not say why. Everything looked and felt the same. But the air had a different scent, the arctic smell he knew so well. They were traversing a desolate land of great bluffs and valleys, barren, brown, gray, and patched with dirty snow.

At midafternoon, with the light failing, Beckwourth began looking for a place to camp. They weren't far from the Missouri, and not far from the heartland of their enemies. Skye surmised that their leader would settle for a spot a mile or so ahead, where some cottonwood mottoes offered firewood and a respite from the raw wind. They lay on a creek between steep bluffs.

The Siksika struck without warning. One moment the Crows were riding quietly north lulled by the soft clopping of hooves; the next, swarms of bright-clad Blackfoot warriors were racing their little ponies down the tan bluffs, howling the Devil's music. Ambush. And a bad place. Beckwourth reacted instantly, motioning his band forward to the woods, where they could find shelter and erect a defense. But no sooner had they whipped their gaunt horses toward the woods than another swarm of Blackfeet burst from that cover, with wild howling punctuated by the dull bark of smoothbore musketry and the rumble of hooves.

Trapped. Attacked on three sides. The Crows started to mill, uncertain of direction. One swift glance told Skye they were facing eighty or ninety Blackfeet, who held the high ground and largely surrounded the Crows. Beckwourth saw the situation, too, and turned his pony east, where the creek flowed between cutbanks that would pose a barrier on one side.

So much for Beckwourth's optimism, Skye thought. Some Kicked-in-the-Bellies would die this day. Skye spotted a buffalo wallow and raced toward it, while around him swirled the melee of battle. It was time to put his Hawken to use. It reached farther than the Nor'wester rifles the Blackfeet had traded from Hudson's Bay. But it wasn't much of a weapon to use from the back of a galloping horse. He reached the wallow, dropped off the black, and sprawled on the half-thawed mud, feeling ice water soak his leggings. He paused a moment to slow his pulse and aim, then fired. A distant warrior was smashed off the back of his spotted pony. Swiftly, Skye loaded, a guessed-at charge of powder, a patch and ball, rammed down the muzzle. A cap over the nipple. He lowered his rifle, his elbows solidly supported by the frozen mud, saw a Blackfoot looming over his Crow friend Running Duck, squeezed a shot—and saw blood blossom in the warrior's shoulder. Running Duck dodged the war club and escaped.

The nipple was fouled. Skye stabbed at it, scraped away the stinking powder residue, reloaded, and shot again. But time was running out. He would be overrun in a few moments. He loaded, sprang for the black horse, which was trotting rapidly toward the retreating Crows, and saw it might be too late. A Blackfoot was cutting him off from his horse. Skye whirled, aimed the Hawken point-blank, fired, and hit the horse rather than the rider. The pony collapsed instantly, throwing the warrior. Skye barreled in, clubbed the man, and then raced for his horse. He had run out of time. Half a dozen Blackfeet were closing in. He reached the black, clambered slowly, much too slowly, aboard the frightened horse, and urged it south toward the retreating Crows. An arrow pierced Skye's buckskin tunic, tearing at him but otherwise doing no harm. The howling behind him served better than spurs or whips to drive the black forward, and then suddenly Skye found himself temporarily alone.

He tugged the black's rein, slowing him down, husbanding what little energy remained in the bony animal. Ahead of him, the Crows were retreating pell-mell toward home, a defense abandoned. He glanced behind him, discovering knots of Blackfeet on the ground, scalping two Absarokas. In spite of their great advantage, they were not pursuing. Maybe the Hawken, a weapon they knew and dreaded, was staying them.

His rifle was empty. He tried desperately to reload while on the run, but his hands were numb, he was shaking, and he could barely sit his horse. Except for his belt knife, he was unarmed. But it didn't seem to matter just then. For whatever reason, the Blackfeet weren't giving chase. He peered about, not quite grasping what was happening, and then saw what he had missed in the fading winter light: a bank of ominous black clouds had massed across the western sky, blotting out the residue of sunlight. Within an hour, the warriors would be fighting an enemy far worse than the Siksika.

The retreating Crows were a sorry sight. They had lost

horses, and some rode double. One badly wounded warrior, apparently unconscious, was held in the saddle by another less injured one. In the thickening darkness it was hard to see. Beckwourth was all right, and leading the pell-mell flight out of that valley of doom.

They found no shelter in the Judith country when the wind quickened, the air turned sharply cold, and then stinging crystals of snow drove into their necks, numbed their ears and hands and feet, and collected on their robes. There was nothing to do but keep on going, running down the wind, away from the Blackfeet and the howling storm, which began blowing murderous gusts of lacerating snow into them. The ground whitened; they lost all sense of direction, but walked grimly onward, the horses exhausted and sullen, the injured warriors near death.

Beckwourth finally hit a patch of woods on the Judith River and they found some small shelter in it. Building a fire was out of the question in the blizzard and darkness, but at least they could rest the horses, feed them cottonwood bark, and try to gather their strength while rolled in robes that did little to turn the bone-numbing cold. Skye's whole body ached. He needed fire, fast, instead of a howling wind, penetrating snow, and shocking cold. In utter darkness he wallowed about, trying to make camp with hands that wouldn't respond to his bidding. His colleagues were doing much the same, but he couldn't see them. He finally pulled his Hawken from its sheath, released the black to make whatever living it could, and crawled deep into a thicket of junipers, which brushed his face and stabbed at him. There, in a sheltered hollow, he pulled his thin robe over his head and tried to rest, lying on gnarled roots that tormented him, hoping he would survive until dawn.

It was the coldest and longest night in his memory. He wondered if his fingers and ears and toes and nose would survive the frostbite. He and the whole party were at death's door—and for what?

Chapter 18

Out of the howling snow late one gloomy day came Skye and the army of the fallen, each man and horse snow-caked, the living hunched in their saddles, the dead frozen over their mounts. They came softly, their passage muffled by the veils of snow, the sight of them curtained by layers of white gauze. No one perceived their arrival; no one was out in the midst of the Cold Maker's revenge for the stolen days of comfort.

But for a subtle shifting of the silences, no one within the Absaroka lodges knew of their arrival, so their entry went unremarked until the few with keenest senses wondered, poked their heads through the oval lodge doors, and beheld disaster. The news passed among the lodges, but slowly on a day that paralyzed life and held it hostage. A woman sawing buffalo meat from a hanging carcass saw them, wailed, but her soul song died among the sheets of snow. She stared, spellbound, as if she were seeing spirits, not mortals. She began to wail, her mewling sharp in the brittle air.

Bitter cottonwood smoke hung over the village, driven to the ground by the avalanche from the sky. She watched them make their way to the great lodge of Arapooish, for they must report in exact detail all that happened, even in the midst of misery. She beheld Antelope, Beckwourth, in the lead, followed by two snow-caked ponies bearing dead men, and then the rest, some of them humped against the jolting of their horses in a manner that told her they were wounded.

"Eee!" she cried, and this time other heads poked through lodge doors, and a somber, blanketed handful of people followed the fallen army to the lodge of their chief. Now at last the wailing of the women crescendoed beyond the censorship of snow, and the village came alive, erupting from the lodges as swiftly as they all could gather robes and capotes and blankets about them to stave off the Cold Maker's deadly attack. By the time Antelope's war party had gathered at the great lodge, half the village had gathered around.

But Arapooish took his time. He already knew, and the waiting was his statement of anger and sorrow. Even as the fallen army waited, the tallykeeping women somehow discovered the names of the dead, and the widows wailed.

Skye hunched deep in his saddle, wanting only to reach the warmth of a lodge. His hands were useless, his ears blackened with frost, and his toes little more than a memory. Beckwourth sat his fancy pony, the hood of his blanket capote off, his head bare to the snow, waiting for the stragglers. Some, maybe most, were suffering frostbite or fevers. None among them bore scalps on a lance, or wore the ensigns of victory, or had painted up. None drove captured ponies before him. Some rode double.

At last Arapooish emerged, gaunt and rawboned, wrapped in a thick black robe, his obsidian eyes alive with some emotion Skye couldn't fathom. His wives and children, swaddled in bright blankets, arrayed themselves around him. It was up to Beckwourth to talk, not an easy task for a defeated war leader. But Beckwourth, formidable in all ways, was up to it.

"My chief and friends, we found the Siksika as we had intended, on a fine day, near Square Butte near the Big River, on our way to the ford where we might cross to the land of the Piegans. There, actually, the Piegans found us, traveling through the valley where we had ambushed them not long ago. The good weather had enticed them from their lodges, just as it had drawn us out of ours, with dreams of victory."

"They came down upon us from both bluffs, howling their curses, catching us without cover. When we ran forward we met with yet another bunch blocking our passage. But we fought bravely, for these are the best men among us, and retreated, taking a toll of the enemy. But there were many of them, a hundred to our thirty-eight, all well armed by Hudson's Bay, and deadly. The husband of Head-and-Tails Robe and the husband of Little Horns received their mortal wounds at that time, and the two sons of Sings at Dawn died later and are here."

Now the women wailed, sorrow for the widows of the fallen, grief for the warriors, gouting from them.

"Plenty Wood, Light Robe, and Old Skull were wounded, but they are here with us, alive in spite of the efforts of the Cold Maker. Behold them. We lost five horses. Mister Skye, Man Not Afraid of the Pawnees, killed one Piegan, or so we believe, and fought bravely, slowing the attack. And so he has a coup."

"We retreated while a storm gathered and the enemy headed for shelter. We were caught in the storm, without any place to hide from it, and most of us have been frostbitten."

No one spoke. Snow whirled down.

Arapooish nodded. "So it is," he said, and returned to the warmth of his lodge. The abbreviated report was done. Skye observed the wives and parents of the fallen, all grief-stricken, some weeping. Most of the fallen had large families, brothers, sisters, children.

Skye wished he had resisted the temptation to enhance his status in the village. It was foolhardy. He had counted coup—the sole warrior to do so—but at what price? He wondered whether his frozen body would ever recover. He looked for Victoria but didn't see her. It was hard to know who was who, so wrapped in robes and blankets were the spectators.

Somberly, the village boys led the ponies away from the encampment. There, in the cottonwood groves, the youths would chop green limbs and let the ponies gnaw on them. The softer bark was good fodder. The families of the dead lifted their men off the ponies, finding that they had frozen into an elbow and could not be properly laid on a death scaffold without thawing. The cottonwood groves would soon hold upon their limbs the bodies of two warriors.

Beckwourth walked proudly back to his lodge, ignoring his frostbitten feet and the stares of the shamans, ignoring especially the calm assessing gaze of Red Turkey Comb. Pine Leaf and Stillwater helped him.

The snowflakes drove needles of pain into Skye's face, and he retreated swiftly to Walks Alone's lodge, where he discovered gloom. Digs the Roots, Victoria, Rosebud, and Makes the Robe wept. Walks Alone had sunk into his backrest and stared numbly into the cold, wavering fire. Walks Alone's old father had burrowed into his buffalo robe and was staring at nothing, probably dreaming of warmth and sun.

Victoria silently pulled Skye's thick moccasins from his feet and began massaging the numb toes, which shot prickles of pain through him. He wondered what she thought of all this.

The storm abated in the night, and at dawn Skye beheld a frigid world, the sun glaring off white snow, the temperature so low it bit his face and numbed him even in the small time it took to relieve himself in the willow brush. But at least the village had come alive; it would endure whatever it was forced to endure. The cold was harder on women; it was up to them to gather wood, and they half froze for the sake of warmth. Paths began to appear from lodge to lodge, several to the river, which remained open in places; many to the brush where Skye had gone.

Within the lodge, his father-in-law greeted him pleasantly. "Your medicine was good. You counted coup. You are a good warrior."

Skye nodded.

Victoria said, "I am sorry you went with Antelope."

That surprised him.

"All this was seen," said Walks Alone. "The seers knew. Yet the young men did not open their eyes or ears. It was bad medicine. It was bad to leave in haste and return in sorrow. It was wrong."

Skye gradually realized that he had risen a few notches in their esteem, while Beckwourth had fallen. By insensible degrees, Beckwourth's leadership would wither. Warriors would decline to go out with him. The gossips would find fault. The women would shake their heads and warn their daughters that he was a man of bad medicine. It would take mighty deeds, many coups, many horses, for Antelope Jim to regain what he had lost among his people this winter.

Skye saw the change most visibly in Victoria, who tentatively began conversing with him, always in Absaroka, usually cheerfully He had not experienced her cheerful chatter for a long time.

And, Skye thought, all this might just open the door for the Rocky Mountain Fur Company.

The next bitter-cold afternoon, the village bundled itself and followed the grieving families out to the burial scaffolds, which stood ready in the limbs of two majestic cottonwoods. The dead had been thawed and straightened out and bound with their possessions within a good buffalo robe. Their faces had been painted according to the ritual for the dead, the symbols representing their clan, their warrior society, their coups and honors.

Skye followed. He didn't really know the dead, except as names. Yet he felt constrained to pay honor to the fallen, and braved the brutal weather, Victoria beside him. Against all temptation to hasten this business, the families took their time, enduring what had to be endured. Most of the village attended, but he saw notable absences. Except for Skye, none of the frostbitten had come, including Beckwourth, who had frozen two toes. But Stillwater represented that lodge.

The elders sang, the notes brittle in the icy air. The bundles were lifted to the scaffolds, faces to the heavens, and left there to be reunited with the nature from which they had sprung. No one spoke the names of the dead, for that would provoke the spirits of the departed. At last they trailed back to the village, Skye hobbling on aching feet.

He had fought and suffered for Victoria's people. And now he wondered what it meant.

Chapter 19

Beckwourth endured his frostbitten toes, which had turned dark and painful, and pondered his fate. He was one to learn from his mistakes, and he knew now that his rash exodus with a war party, without consent of the high chiefs and seers of the village, had damaged him and his enterprise. But not seriously. The Absarokas had a native affection for any of their number who would take war to their enemies. When the dust settled, more would remember him for his daring winter raid on the Siksika than for the losses to the village. The winter keeper might even call this one Winter of Antelope's War and record it on his buffalo robe.

He was not without resources. He had the might of the American Fur Company behind him. He had already led the Kicked-in-the-Bellies to a lively trade for pelts, leaving Skye and his employers in the dust. But fences needed mending. Throats needed lubricating. The winter had been long and hard. He would give some extravagant gifts to the chiefs and headmen, and he would entertain as never before. He liked being an important headman of the Crows. He even looked like one of them, no doubt because he was one-eighth black, the child of a white man and a quadroon woman, his delightful mother who lived quietly with his father outside St. Louis.

That bit of black blood served him ill back in that world but served him well here. If he had stayed in Missouri, he would have run into strange walls, sharp, questioning moments, swift rejections. Here it was quite the opposite. That slight tawny tint of flesh made him one of the Absaroka. Where else in the world could a man have several wives? Where else could a man lounge, hunt, make love and war, and be taken care of by adoring women? Ah, life was good in the mountains.

"Stillwater, we are going to have storytelling parties," he said to his ever-accommodating mate. "Prepare the lodge."

"I like parties. Will you serve spirits?"

"More than ever before, and without a tally."

"You will have many young men, then. Only the Old Bulls"—she named a society of traditionalist elders—"will be unhappy"

"I will give them tobacco. It is the peace offering."

"You will invite the women."

"I always invite the women. Soon you will be my sits-beside-him wife, and you will have less work. I am going to fetch Many Quill Woman to my side."

Stillwater smiled. "She is a good choice, but she has a sharp tongue."

She would be a fine choice, and he could talk English with her, which was more than he could do with Stillwater or Pine Leaf or the others. He would take her from Skye. What the Briton really needed was the company of white men again. He was buffalo-witted among these people, didn't know how to become one of them in spite of his war honors. Take his Victoria from him and he would drift away, and so would any threat from the Rocky Mountain Fur Company.

Beckwourth began his rehabilitation by hobbling to the lodges of the headmen and giving plugs of tobacco to them. These were accepted, and the ceremonial pipes that followed sealed his acceptance. The Crows were not going to abandon a valuable and well-armed war leader like

Antelope. He visited Arapooish, offered tobacco as well as a good knife, and received much the same acceptance, plus a good buffalo tongue meal proffered by the chief's several wives and daughters.

He limped to the small, isolated lodge of Red Turkey Comb, and there altered his routine. He was admitted into a chill dark lodge, the fire little more than embers. But that was how the seer, ever the ascetic, preferred to live.

"Grandfather, I bring thee tobacco, and more. I bring the sorrow in my heart that I did not seek your medicine, your vision, before I led the brave young men of this village to a winter war—and defeat. I seek your counsel now."

The old man closed his eyes a moment, accepted the plug, whittled some into the bowl of a long-stemmed red-bowled medicine pipe, found an ember, plucked it up barehanded, lit the tobacco, and puffed slowly, never saying a word. Antelope knew that things had not been settled.

But at last the shaman handed the pipe to his visitor, and Beckwourth drew the fragrant smoke. They had made peace.

"Tell me what is in your heart," the shaman said.

"I wish to restore myself to the graces of the elders, Grandfather."

"What else?"

"I am a trader. I wish to prosper in my trade and supply the Absaroka people with good things."

"And?"

"I was a notable war leader among the people, and I wish to be again. I am ambitious for honors."

"And?"

"That is all that is on my mind, Grandfather."

"I think there may be other things."

"I can think of none."

"Very well. It is as you say." He drew smoke and exhaled it and watched it drift out the smoke hole above. "Hurt no Absaroka, and be kind to guests of the People. Do no harm to rivals. Give the people nothing that would destroy their senses and honor our ways. Keep the peace of the village and put the People ahead of your own ambitions. This is all I have to say to you."

Beckwourth found himself dismissed, and retreated from the smoky lodge to the clean bright air of a February day. The old man had all but forbidden him to continue his parties.

That very evening he invited a dozen people to his lodge and greeted them joyously as they filed in. Victoria Skye was among them, and he rejoiced. She still was the most beauteous of the Crow women, the only one who could speak his tongue, and the one with the most vital inner life, thanks to her exposure to another world.

"This is a good night," he said when his guests had settled. "This night I will pass the cup around many times, and we will tell the best stories."

And that was how it went. He charged nothing for the spirits, and the stories evoked laughter and sometimes controversy. That evening flew by, and he knew he would soon have the people back in the palm of his hand.

As winter decayed and the timid sun cut holes in the snow around rocks and trees, Beckwourth's parties lubricated the life of the whole village. The Kicked-in-the-Bellies were having a grand time. Beckwourth's trade increased, and he frequently rode up to the outpost on the Yellowstone with packs of robes and pelts and returned with more of the goods and spirits he needed to foster trade. But these were running short. He could no longer get sugar, coffee, tobacco, or blankets at the post. And Tullock told him they were out of spirits.

Even so, Beckwourth had the Crow trade locked up. He eyed Skye almost with pity those days. Skye never came to the parties, and Beckwourth discerned that the man was embarrassed by the bawdiness of the Crows. But the Briton was hunting daily, often shooting buffalo at great distances from the village, but somehow managing, along with his in-laws, to bring meat and good winter-haired hides back to the village. These hides, tanned by his wife or mother-in-law, were starting to accumulate, and he soon would have enough for a lodge of his own. Each of those thick winter robes was worth two lodge skins, and as soon as his women had finished with their preparation, Skye would have his own lodge—and probably the renewed loyalty of the exquisite Victoria.

It was time to act. Beckwourth invited her one evening when spring lay tantalizingly close and all the teeth had been pulled from the Cold Maker's jaw. For this great oc-casion, Beckwourth accoutered himself in his gaudiest glory. His wife washed and oiled and braided his long black hair until it hung in two glowing cords, cleaned his best golden elkskin outfit, and quilled his new moccasins. He took a sweat to steam the winter out of his pores, and enjoyed the ferocity of the steam as well as the sacred rituals, the sagebrush and sweetgrass, the holy chants, that accompanied the ritual, for the Crows purged soul as well as body when they sweat. Then he dressed, added a red sash, tucked his two notched eagle feathers, won in mortal combat, within his blue headband, rubbed the astringent sage over his body as a perfume, and awaited her.

She arrived at sundown, as invited, and found only Stillwater and Beckwourth present.

"Ah, my dear lady, lovely woman, whose beauty rivals even Stillwater's—welcome. Would you care for spirits?"

Victoria surveyed the almost-empty lodge—usually it was packed for Antelope's parties—and smiled.

"And how is Skye?" he asked solicitously.

"He is much in favor. He brings the People much meat and shares it. We have many hides. The headmen invite him to smoke with them."

"Yes, he makes progress. Good for him. But all those hides must wear you out. Tanning a robe is hard."

"The women do it together."

"Are you happy?"

She smiled. "I do not hear Magpie, my spirit-helper, scolding me."

Stillwater ladled good buffalo tongue from a pot and handed the horn bowl to Victoria, and then another bowl to Beckwourth. His wife smiled again; Beckwourth always enjoyed Stillwater's smile, which spoke of merriment within her soul and a generous spirit. He had found a good wife in her.

They ate quietly and then settled back into the multiple robes that formed cushions across the floor of the lodge and held the cold at bay.

"Many Quill Woman, we have a proposal. My beloved Stillwater and I want you to join us as my second wife."

Victoria didn't startle. She had been expecting something like this. She simply nodded.

"Stillwater wants company; she would love to share the cooking and cleaning and sewing with one she cherishes. I would honor you as my woman, love you both equally, and keep you well clad and comfortable. I am a rich man. I am honored in the village. I am still learning the ways of your people, but with each day I am closer to being the Absaroka you would want as your man."

Victoria kept her counsel, and Beckwourth scarcely knew where he stood.

"Now, Skye is a good man. He toils each day. But he does not seem at home among your people. I am at home. Be my wife. Put Skye's things outside the lodge. He will go away, for he has no one else."

"I will think about it."

"Well, it is good to think, but I want an answer now. Tonight we will share the robes, and I will show you that Antelope is a man who makes a wife happy." He turned to Stillwater. "Isn't that so?"

"Ah, you are too much for me, almost. I need to share you with her so I can have some peace."

They laughed.

"Tonight," Beckwourth said. "Tonight in the robes. With the next sun, you can put Skye's things outside of your lodge."

Victoria sighed. He was sure he had never seen a fairer beauty, perfect at the age of twenty. She set him to burning with as little as a smile. Tonight they both would burn.

She examined him and Stillwater, who was beaming with joy. He could almost see her mind racing back and forth like a rabbit between coyotes. A cauldron of anticipation boiled within him.

"I will be your wife, Antelope," Victoria said.

Chapter 20

She was not in the robes beside Skye that morning. He realized she hadn't come home. He stared sharply about the lodge. His mother-in-law looked away. His sisters-in-law were not about. His father-in-law was eating.

All this was normal enough. The Crows drifted endlessly from lodge to lodge. Their children were almost interchangeable, staying at one lodge and then another, foster and real parents almost indistinguishable. But Skye didn't like it. He arose dourly, pulled on his moccasins, drew a robe about him, and stepped into a wintry morning. An inch of fresh snow covered the older and dirtier layers. The gray sky spread gloom over a hushed landscape.

He didn't know what to do. Doubts crawled like maggots through his soul. She had gone too far with her parties. Probably had gotten drunk on Beckwourth's spirits. He walked to Beckwourth's lodge, on the other side of the encampment, making tracks in snow. Smoke curled lazily from the vent. Someone was up. Stillwater was probably fixing something to eat.

He scratched politely on the hide next to the doorflap, the Indian way of knocking. No one answered for a moment, and then Beckwourth replied, his voice muffled by the lodgecover and liner. His response, in the Crow tongue, asked who was present.

"Skye."

"Come back some other time."

"Is Victoria there?"

A long pause.

"Yes."

"I want to talk to her."

"No."

The response triggered a rage in Skye. He eyed the doorflap. It might be buffalohide but it was as sacrosanct as a locked door. It was unthinkable to violate it.

He yanked the flap aside, flooding the lodge with snowy light. Victoria was sitting in the robes, bare, her dress, leggings, and moccasins cast aside. Beckwourth wore nothing. Stillwater was at the fire, cooking.

Skye stared, pierced to his bones. "I'll kill you," he said to Beckwourth.

"Get out."

But Skye didn't. Victoria cried and dove under the robes, pulling them over her head. Stillwater screamed and backed away from the fire. Skye had invaded their lodge without invitation.

"Get up and I'll kill you," Skye said, his fists balled. He started for Beckwourth, who whirled away. Skye followed him around the fire. He was going to catch Beckwourth and fry his hide in that fire, hold him over it until the man hurt as much as Skye hurt. Victoria screamed. Stillwater fled into the snow.

Beckwourth reached his wife's cooking items and clamped his hand over a knife.

"We'll do this outside," he said.

Victoria cowered under the robes, weeping.

Skye glanced at her, grief running so deep and wide through him it was like a spring flood, sweeping all before it. "Get out," he said to her. She drew a robe around her honey-fleshed young body and fled barefoot into the cold, wailing.

Skye had no knife. He had not expected to use one this winter dawn when he had first stepped outside.

"Get out of my lodge, Skye. We'll settle this outside."

The blade sliced air between them.

"I'll kill you," Skye said.

Beckwourth stepped toward the center, where he could stand. "For what? She's divorcing you. She's going to be my second wife."

Those words stung like whiskey in a wound. "You took her. You destroyed my marriage. Step out and we'll see who's marrying and who's dead."

Beckwourth grinned. He ambled back to the robes, pulled on his breechclout, tied on his leggings, drew a soft flannel shirt over his lean frame, pulled on his moccasins, and motioned Skye out.

Skye stepped out first and didn't give Beckwourth a chance to right himself as he crawled out the oval lodge door. He bulled into the man, throwing him into the snow. Beckwourth rolled to his feet unscathed, knife in hand. Skye found a long piece of kindling to deal with the knife—he had fought knives with a belaying pin in the Royal Navy, and now he and Beckwourth circled round and round, thrusting and parrying. The dead limb wasn't much of a weapon, and Skye had to hold it with both hands. But he was mad, and backed Beckwourth into a crowd of silent Absarokas. Victoria wasn't in sight.

Beckwourth lunged; Skye cracked the wood over the man's arm. The shock sent the knife flying, and Skye thrashed into him, knocking him back. Beckwourth fought hard and easily. He was taller than Skye, longer-armed, but lighter. Skye knocked him into the snow again and landed on him, his rage flowing like a river, his thick fists hammering, even as Beckwourth hammered back, threw Skye off, and gouged at his eyes. Skye was scarcely aware of the bite of the snow, the gathering crowd, the moaning of the women, and sobbing of Stillwater. He saw only his tormentor, and he hammered at the man, at the same time taking whatever Beckwourth delivered, oblivious to his own pain or punishment. He didn't care how he hurt; he cared only to hurt. They rolled, one or another on top, one or another bucking the other into the slush.

The imperial voice of Arapooish cut through the mayhem. Skye ignored it. The voice repeated itself sharply. Skye didn't give a damn. He was giving more than he got from Beckwourth. His fists ached from hitting Beckwourth so hard, and Beckwourth was hurting.

Hard hands yanked him away. He fought maniacally to free himself, but more hard hands stayed him, and he found himself caught and being hog-tied by the Kit Fox warriors, the village police this season. Beckwourth had ceased resisting and stood, panting. Snow slathered off his soaked clothing.

Stillwater wept, great tears flooding her golden cheeks.

There had been no satisfaction in it. Victoria was gone; this man had slept with her and stolen her. He could pound Beckwourth to pulp and not put his life back together again. Skye sagged, suddenly hollow, his rage dripping away like the melted snow trickling down his bare back.

The chief said something. Skye was too upset to understand the tongue and stood, dazed, while rawhide thongs imprisoned him. He saw Red Turkey Comb, wrapped in a gray blanket, watching him sharply. He saw the village chiefs, the headmen, the elders, the shamans, the powerful scarred face of Night Owl, chief of the Kit Fox police. They didn't need explanation. It was all clear.

They were waiting for Skye to clear his head, for Skye's

wildness to ebb. Then at last the chief spoke, slowly so Skye could understand.

"You have violated the peace of the village. You have entered a lodge without being invited. You have stamped upon our customs and laws. You have fought with a war leader. You have shed blood—it is there upon the snow. Therefore, hear me now. You will leave our village. You may not return to the Kicked-in-the-Belly people. You will get your things—all that is yours. You will get your horses. You will prepare for your passage from us. The Kit Fox Society will see to it."

Skye felt bone cold. His elkskin clothing was soaked. He felt as cold within his breast and heart and mind as he did within his body. He walked wearily through the emerging dawn to the lodge of Walks Alone, followed by the police and by his erstwhile father-in-law. He saw his friend Red Turkey Comb turn away. Vaguely, among the women, he spotted his in-laws. He reached the lodge, put together his kit, pulled on his belt with scabbarded knife, hung his powder horn, and carefully lowered his bear claw necklace over his cold, soaked shirt. Then he filled his bag with his possibles, the spare moccasins and mittens Victoria had made for him, a beaver hat, his battered top hat, and his flint and striker.

Then he rolled up two robes—a fair-enough exchange for all the buffalohides just outside the door—and stepped back into the cold world. Victoria had vanished. Just as well. He couldn't bear the sight of her now. Not after seeing her sitting naked in Beckwourth's robes, her golden bare shoulders, her bare breasts and legs and feet, her long black hair loose and tangled, beautiful, shocked by the intrusion. He would see those things in the nights ahead. He would see them as he rode down trails. He would see them writ upon the sky. He would see them on his death-bed and on his way to hell.

They had gotten his horses for him, and they had put one of Walks Alone's saddles on the good black, and on the dun a packframe, which held a large slab of frozen hump meat, enough to keep him fed for a week. Walks Alone was giving him that much, anyway. Walks Alone's face was inscrutable, but Skye felt sorrow lay behind the blankness. Walks Alone and Arrow had become his friends and workmates.

They would not look at him. He could not say good-bye. He mounted the black, studied the faces of these people he loved, and rode away, towing the packhorse behind. The Kit Fox warriors followed, two by two, saying nothing, leading him far beyond the village, north up the river a mile or two. Then they halted and wordlessly let him continue. They stayed there. He was soon out of sight.

He would ride a while and then build a fire and try to dry out his sopping leather tunic. He didn't much care if he lived or died. Everything inside of him had died in those moments of dark revelation that dawn. He didn't know what to do, or where to go, or why to live, or how. And it didn't matter. If he didn't survive this winter odyssey it wouldn't matter.

It would be a mild day once the sun got up on its haunches, but that didn't matter. He rode cold and alone the long silent miles to the Yellowstone. When he came to the fur company cabin, he paused, not wanting the company of anyone. He had lost Victoria, and no company could replace her. Maybe someday he would remember the good times, the days under the clean blue skies when she rode beside him, the times they gazed at each other, saying more with a glance than any string of words. He would remember the silky beauty of her flesh, the crush of her lips, the laughing banter she made with the other trappers, the swift clean butcheries that turned game into food.

Maybe someday he would heal, and remember his Indian wife of four years, a girl in her late teens, barely twenty at the last. Maybe that would be the best way to remember her, a girl not yet twenty, the image frozen within him as he grew old.

But maybe it would be best not to remember her at all, because it hurt too much to even speak her name, as he was doing as he led his horse along the river.

"Victoria," he said, and nothing answered.

Chapter 21

In his short life, Skye had suffered all sorts of wounds. His nose had once been broken, swelling his face into an aching pulpy mass. He had been flogged thrice in the Royal Navy, ten lashes less one, and his back still bore the scars where his lacerated flesh had knitted itself into ridges. Each lash of the whip had shot raw red pain through him, spasming his young body, forcing howls from him. He had once suffered dysentery during the Kaffir wars, and lay dehydrated and feverish, wishing he could perish rather than endure the raging sickness and weakness of his flesh. On board the frigate he had fought brutal seamen, larger, meaner, crueler than he ever imagined, and they had pounded on him until his flesh ached and his bones hurt and his head rang. Here in the mountains he had frozen and boiled, starved until he was mad, been knocked senseless in a scrape with Cheyenne dog soldiers, and awakened sick and nauseous and seeing double images.

All these he had borne, and none of them had affected his will to live. In fact, many of these insults to his body had kindled the rage to live and triumph and be a free man. He had not surrendered.

But now he wrestled with a new kind of wound, one far more piercing than anything he had ever experienced in his young life. He could scarcely find words for this wound—betrayal, loss, anger, despair, desolation, rejection, breach of trust. Words didn't describe the plunge of his feelings, as if he had been thrown into the abyss. Physical pain was an old and known enemy that he dreaded but understood. But this pain of the soul he didn't understand. He was born under a curse, and whatever small handhold he had purchased on the cliffside of joy had crumbled, and he was falling, ever downward.

He paused at the small log structure at the confluence of the Big Horn and Yellowstone, resurrected for the season by American Fur. The present tenants had repaired the roof and covered it with a foot of sod. He saw small portals on the two sides visible to him, but these held no glass. Hides scraped thin enough to pass light filled each small frame. He had been in rude huts like this one, immersed in perpetual twilight even on a bright day.

He stared, not knowing what else to do. The cabin stared back solemnly. He had never been here. He tried to think but couldn't. His mind had numbed and narrowed down to blankness and instinct. He knew he should try to reach one of the Rocky Mountain Fur Company brigades, but that was really not an option. The largest brigade, led by Bridger and Fitzpatrick, was wintering in the Three Forks country, the headwaters of the Missouri, on the other side of a vast and snowy range of mountains that locked him out until spring. He might, if he could find snowshoes, negotiate the icebound pass that would now be choked with twenty or thirty feet of snow. He might with a backpack manage to ascend and descend, endure the icy blasts and treacherous fog on the ridge, and reach the Gallatin valley without his horses or kit. But he had no snowshoes or cash to buy some. The other RMF brigades were even farther. One was wintering down in South Park, actually in Mexican territory, and the other, in the Snake country, was equally out of reach until the spring melt.

None of that made any difference. He sat his black horse, staring at the blind-eyed cabin, watching blue smoke eddy from a fieldstone-and-mud chimney. The cabin gave him no answers.

"Well, come on in or be gone," came a voice from the dead cabin. "We don't take kindly to varmints aiming to do us harm." Skye saw the muzzle of a rifle in a slit.

Skye nudged his black forward and stopped at a hitch rail in front of the place. The massive hand-sawn plank door swung open and he beheld a potbellied red-maned giant with a pair of dragoon pistols in hand.

Skye stared inertly, neither dismounting nor talking.

"You ill?"

Skye didn't respond.

"Well, get down, dammit."

Skye shook his head. He had no business here, no business anywhere. He turned his horse and tugged his dun packhorse around. Nothing mattered.

But the red-haired giant sprang out the door, cursing,

and yanked the black's head around. "Now get down and abide a wee."

Skye heard Scotland in the voice. And saw Scotland in the face: freckles, fierce blue eyes, crags and ridges running across brow and cheek.

Skye sat the black, paralyzed. "I'll go," he muttered.

The Scot glared into Skye's face. "You're a man staring into a grave," he said. "You're sick."

A second man, this one dark and cross-eyed, with a luxuriant black beard, appeared.

"Help me get this mountain of dead meat off his plug," the Scot said to the other.

They pulled the black's head around and took the reins from Skye, and waited for Skye to dismount. But Skye sat.

"We'll lift ye off," the Scot said.

Skye let himself be lifted off. He was confused. Why were they doing this?

"Take the plugs out to the pen and bring his kit in. We'll get some tea into the mon," said the Scot.

Skye had yet to say an intelligible word. They steered him into the place. It wasn't much; a small room with rough-hewn shelves on the far side, earthen floors, gummed by spit and sweat and grease, and scabrous gray logs. A few trade goods on the hand-hewn shelves: pots; knives; awls; powder and ball; jingle bells; blue, red, and green beads; bolts of chambray; iron lance points; steel arrowheads; hatchets. A rude counter of splintery cottonwood. A low opening to a rear room where a fire burned. A perpetual gloom about the whole outfit.

The Scot herded Skye into the rear room, half of it stacked with robes and hides and exotic pelts, the rest reserved for bunks and a cooking area around the rock fireplace. On each side was a plugged gun port. The hides and pelts and robes exuded dead animal smells, rancid and thick and choking.

"I'm Tullock, American Fur," said the Scot. "My partner's Pierre Bonfils. And who are you?"

Skye stood, dazed. He couldn't bring his name to his lips. He didn't want anyone to know his name.

"You sick? Get some heat into you thar," he said, gesturing. "Your leathers are soaking. You must be colder than a grave. Give us that shirt and we'll dry it."

The golden elkskin shirt with fringed sleeves, Victoria's fine quillwork on it in blue and red patterns. Skye stared.

"Your shirt, man. You're cold."

Skye shook his head and sat down before the fire.

"You have a name? You Skye, down with the Kicked-in-the-Bellies? You fit the description."

Skye nodded.

"Well, that's progress. You hungry? We got us more frozen buffler here than we can eat in a month."

Skye shook his head.

"You in some kind of trouble? Sick?"

Skye stared. A faint heat penetrated the clammy cold of his elkskin shirt.

"You know Beckwourth? Our man down there?"

Skye stared, rose, wrapped his robe about him, and headed for the door.

"Hey! You come back here. You're not fit to go out."

The burly dark man caught Skye at the door and forcibly steered him back.

"Let go of me," Skye said.

"Well, at least ye can talk," the Scot said. "Something's happened to ye."

"I have to go."

"Na, laddie, don't ye be going now. We'll pour us a bit of whiskey I've been hiding from Pierre. Something's happened and ye need a dose."

The Scot pulled a grass-filled tick from his plank bunk, revealing a jug wedged against the cottonwood log.

"Sacre bleu!"

"Real whiskey, not the other. Ye need a few droughts of medicine, that's what I'm thinking. Ye act like ye've seen the Devil, old Bug himself."

Tullock uncorked the jug, poured a generous slug into a tin cup, and handed it to his guest. Skye sipped, coughed, swallowed, and sipped again. The spirits, taken neat, scorched his innards. Silently he handed the cup back to his host, who sipped and passed the cup to his partner.

"It's getting dark and you had better stay here tonight, Skye."

Skye nodded. "It's Mister Skye," he said.

"Eh?"

Skye felt the spirits permeate his body, even as heat from the fire dried his buckskins. "Forget it," he said.

"Now, what's the trouble, mon? Are ye ill?"

"Thank you for the spirits," Skye said, and rose. "Time for me to go."

"No ye don't, laddie."

"I am a free man."

"You're a sick man. Ye'll stay, and we'll see what the morning brings."

It didn't matter. Right now, in the warm dark of Beck-wourth's lodge, Victoria was probably coupling with her new mate. The images filtered through his mind. She would enjoy herself with Antelope. Maybe more than she had enjoyed herself with her husband of four years.

She had abandoned him, just like that. He was like most people, struggling to make some small sweet life out of nothing, but surrendering what little they possessed piece by piece by piece.

He began to doze, the spirits working in him. He was conscious of someone pulling a robe over him, of his hosts boiling some buffalo tongue in a pot suspended over the fire. The heady smells of cookery filled his nostrils.

But it didn't matter. Nothing did, or ever would.

Chapter 22

Skye did not know where he was. Dim light filtered into a log room. A banked fire exuded a residual heat from under the ash. Then he remembered and wished he hadn't awakened. Someone stirred out in the trading room. He threw off the robes and stood. His hosts were not in sight.

Stiffly—he felt ill—he drew a robe about himself and walked into the better-lit room, where Tullock was standing at a counter entering something in a ledger with a quill pen.

"Ye lived, did ye?" the trader asked, surveying Skye's face.

Skye nodded, and headed into an icy dawn. He found the Frenchman out there chopping wood. There would be a fire and breakfast soon.

Later, he poked at a slab of buffalo for breakfast. He wasn't hungry. The traders eyed him curiously but didn't probe.

"I'll be going now, mates. Thank you for quartering me."

"Nay, mon, ye'll be staying a while. A fever eats ye, and it's not a fit day."

"I'm going."

"And where, may I ask?"

Skye shrugged. He would go until he froze to death, and that was all he envisioned or wanted. He rolled up the robes, collected his kit, and headed for the rude door.

"If a mon's bound and determined to die, not much can save his mortal soul," Tullock said. "But if a lad's a wee bit uncertain, he ought to stay put. Buffalo meat we have aplenty."

They were curious about him, but it didn't matter. Skye continued his preparations.

"Where are my horses?" he asked.

"Enjoying some cottonwood bark for breakfast. If I let ye at them, I'd be an accessory to murder, seeing as how you're bent on destroying yourself."

Skye set down his kit.

"That's better. Now have some meat and get close to the fire. I have a wee bit of good tea, and we'll brew it up and get it down ye."

Skye sipped tea—it tasted just fine—and slipped back into his buffalo robes. They left him alone that day. No one came to trade, and the traders whiled away their time chopping wood, playing monte, and observing the unchanging dull weather. Skye's body mended a little, but the pain of having to live deepened and cut like a knife wound. In a way, the pain was good. It prodded Skye, harried him, forced him to contemplate Victoria and come to grips with events. But it didn't change anything.

That afternoon he rose, washed his face, brushed his leathers, and ran a bone comb through his unruly hair, while his hosts watched silently.

"I'm better now, mates," he announced.

"Well, Skye, tell us your plans."

Up to that moment, Skye had none, but suddenly he did. "I'm heading east," he said.

"East? The States? Not without grass for your horses and a wee bit of sun on your back."

"Tell me the way."

"The way is to recover your mortal soul, recapture your mind, become master of whatever lies within ye. That is the way."

"I'll be all right once I'm on my horse. I go down the Yellowstone to Fort Union, eh?"

"Fort Union's not so easy as that. It's on the left bank of the Missouri. A lot of water between you and it. A mon goes east in a keelboat or maybe a pirogue or even a raft or bullboat—if he's willing to brave the Rees—the Arikara—who pump arrows into passing white men. If I were going east, I'd wait at Fort Union for the spring and go down with the crew on the keelboat that supplies the place each year. Hire on to take the peltries back to St. Louis. Ye could find employment and succor there. Kenneth McKenzie needs all the hands he can get."

"I'm obliged not to, mate. I'm bound by debt and contract to the Rocky Mountain Fur Company."

"A good outfit, with sterling men. I count Bridger and Fitzpatrick and Sublette among the best in the mountains. But these things can be dealt with, Skye."

"Mister Skye, sir."

"Yes, so I remember. Mister Skye. Fortunes change. These things are understood. We could buy out your debt and outfit you and you'd work for us. Your name precedes you."

"I don't want to stay in the mountains."

"What happened there with Arapooish, may I ask?"

"A private matter."

Skye said it with such finality that Tullock didn't probe further.

The next morning Skye thanked his hosts and left. They had described a ford just below the post that would take him to the north bank of the Yellowstone, and they described another ford on the Missouri that would take him to Fort Union—if he was lucky enough to locate the ford. This time of year, even the mighty Missouri offered crossings. If he couldn't find the ford, he was to proceed to the bank opposite the post and fire his rifle. They would come for him with a barge.

He plunged into a bright day under a brittle blue sky, the hint of spring enough to make travel bearable. He was glad to be alone again. He didn't want the company of anyone. The silence engulfed him. He was passing over an empty land. The river hurled its way to the Missouri, and ultimately the Gulf of Mexico, usually running in a broad valley between sandstone bluffs. The country was anonymous and dull, without notable landmarks, without soul-lifting beauty, colorless, oppressive. It suited his mood. Usually he followed the river road, but on one occasion he had to detour widely around a vast ice jam that had dammed the river and sent it over its banks.

For food he sawed at the frozen buffalo meat, wrapped in duck cloth, he carried on his packhorse. He saw only ravens to remind him that life existed, and was glad. He didn't want to see life. This country was as empty as the seven seas, which would be his destiny. This river would take him to New Orleans, and New Orleans would take him to sea, either in a merchant vessel or in the United States Navy. That is how it would all play out: a lone man, walking the hard decks in an empty world until he died. For a living he would do what he knew how to do, live under sailcloth, be driven by the wind, and surrender his stunted will and ignore his fractured dreams.

Somehow he would pay back Rocky Mountain Fur. For a while, they would receive small deposits from him out of his seaman's wage, and when that had been settled, he would be a lone man, without obligation or tie or family or friend. And that is how he would remain until they put him ashore, or wrapped him in sailcloth, added some ballast lifted from the bilge, and slid him into the lapping waves. He knew the sea. All his life he would be at sea.

He rode quietly through March and then found himself one day at the confluence, a small sea of currents where two great rivers married. Tullock had told him to ride west, past Union, a stockaded fort with opposing bastions erected close to the river, to a place a mile upstream where the river widened and rilled over submerged rock, visible only this time of year. But he could not find the spot, and when he bullied his reluctant black horse into the river at likely points, he plummeted deep into a channel and could barely get himself out. The river and its banks had a relentless sameness that defied a newcomer to locate the place of passage.

So he retreated to the post, which brooded darkly across a ripple of sun-dotted water. He was pulling his Hawken from its leather sheath to alert them when he heard a faint shout on the wind. Someone on the far bank had noticed. Skye waved his rifle and waited. Presently Creole boatmen poled a scow across and boarded his horses and himself. No one said much; they eyed him curiously as they worked their poles. One's gaze halted at the bear claw necklace.

He debarked on a well-trampled levee and pierced Union through tall gates, finding a yard and buildings under construction within. The Creoles were not far behind. The place rivaled Fort Vancouver, and Skye had an uneasy stirring of fear. Would he be clapped in irons here and shipped away?

But no such thing happened. Two clerks, each in a black broadcloth suit, materialized. The attire astonished Skye. He had not seen a gentleman in a suit since his days in the navy. Not only that, but their boiled shirts were snowy, their hair and bodies were groomed, and even their boots bore fresh blacking. What sort of place was this?

They, in turn, surveyed a young man in worn buckskins, unkempt and haggard and grim. "Sir? Welcome to Fort Union. Do we know you?" asked one.

"No. Mister Skye," he said.

"Ah. We do know you. I'm Largent, chief clerk, and this is Bonhommais, second clerk. Please, sir, let me fetch Mr. McKenzie."

Skye permitted himself to be led back in. Engagés instantly led his weary horses to a hayrick and unburdened them, while Skye watched uneasily. The imperial designs of Americans were as plain here as the imperial designs of Britons out at Vancouver. And betwixt the millstones fell unlucky mortals like himself.

Still, he was not without weapons; his sheathed Hawken in hand, a hatchet and Green River knife at his waist, and the will to be free—or dead. They led him to some apartments, humble enough at first, but then into a dining hall with accouterments that stunned him. A long table, cov-

ered with a snowy linen cloth and thick linen napkins, had
been set with Limoges china, crystal goblets, silverware,
pewter platters, and bottles of French wine. And standing at the head of this astonishing wilderness apparition
was a powerfully built man Skye thought might well be
a duke but knew at once was the Scots-born lord of this
wilderness empire, Kenneth McKenzie.

Chapter 23

Skye had not seen such a man as Kenneth McKenzie
since his youth in London, when he occasionally
glimpsed the peers of England. But here, improbably,
stood a man radiating power, with a pugilist's face, a
body beefy and imperial, and a gaze that owned the
entire universe within the man's vision. He wore a fawn-
colored waistcoat under a green cutaway, and pinstriped
trousers over gleaming boots. His hands were the size of
sledgehammers, and Skye didn't doubt that the lord of
this corner of the universe could employ them with martial intent. But all that was prelude to something larger, a
palpable force of will that brooked no resistance. He was
a dread and absolute sovereign of this wilderness empire.

"You arrived during our dinner hour, which was
impudent," he said. "What is your name?"

"Mister Skye, sir."

"Oh, yes, the opposition. Well, Skye, be off now. We'll
put you up if that's your intent."

"It's Mister Skye, sir."

"Oh, yes, I've heard about you. We'll humor you. But

a gentleman's title is reserved for gentlemen, namely my senior men here." He waved at a raft of human penguins in black worsted even now gathering at their ornate chairs in military rank.

Skye had already had enough of this place. He would make his way down the river to New Orleans without the help of these popinjays. He turned to leave.

"Just a minute, Skye, I haven't dismissed you."

Skye ignored him and headed toward the double doors.

"Skye! Where are you going?"

Skye didn't stop. Two beefy clerks detained him, clasping hands upon his arms. Skye didn't wrestle free.

"When you address a man civilly, with ordinary courtesy, you will receive your answer."

McKenzie laughed. "*Mister* Skye, where are you going? Why did you come here? Why are you not plotting and scheming to steal our Crow trade from us?"

"Mr. McKenzie, if you will kindly let me go now, I'll be off. If you are a gentleman, then conduct yourself as one."

The rebuke astonished McKenzie. "Mister Skye," he said, "I'm going to eat now. I'll instruct my staff to feed you in the mess, and put you up. You may leave if you choose, but I would like an interview with you after dinner. I'll summon you in a while."

The tone had changed. Skye nodded. He was hungry. He departed as the clerks gathered about their dining chairs, waiting for the signal to be seated.

A servant took Skye across the yard and into a mess hall next to the kitchen. The fur company's employees— engagés, they were called—had long since eaten, not observing gentlemen's hours. But, upon direction from the old servant, the cook dished up leftovers, including a substantial buffalo stew—and bread. Skye had not had bread in his hands for many years, and the yeasty loaf was indescribably delicious.

He ate quietly, reflecting on recent events. McKenzie was a legend, and Skye had heard much about the man around the campfires of the brigades. He was a well-born Scot who had come to the New World as a youth and entered the fur trade, first with the old North West Company, and then in partnership with some Americans, and finally as the most important man in the Upper Missouri Outfit, mistakenly known as the American Fur Company. He was related to Alexander McKenzie, the first white man to cross the North American continent.

Kenneth McKenzie was ruthless, brutal to the opposition as well as his own men, and got things done without scrupling much about how he did them. He operated his satrapy with absolute authority, down to fining, imprisoning, flogging, or banishing anyone he chose without the slightest pretense of a trial. He had justified this on the ground that he operated in a dangerous and lawless wilderness far from the reach of courts and sheriffs and prisons. His stated goal was to rub out the opposition and reign supreme on the upper Missouri.

Skye wondered whether the man would even let him out of Fort Union. Skye had been a prisoner before, incarcerated by men who had designs on his labor, or who simply loathed him, or who enjoyed the power to toy with the liberty of another mortal. He suspected that all three motivations threaded through the skull of his host, especially because Skye alone had questioned McKenzie's manners, if not his civility. Skye sighed.

After his bountiful dinner, the ubiquitous servants took Skye to a small guest room—not the barracks, as Skye had expected. That pleased him. He was in no mood to be sociable. He found himself in a room with a bunk, washstand, and wooden chair brought a thousand miles up the river. Even this crude quarter offered more civilization than he had seen in North America.

Deep in the evening McKenzie summoned him, and he followed a servant who threaded across a corner of the yard and deposited Skye in an apartment under the stockaded wall of Fort Union. Another lackey steered Skye into a large private room heated by a cheerful fire. Here, too, luxury abounded. A blue Brussels carpet decorated the plank floor; oil portraits graced whitewashed walls. A desk, stuffed chairs, footstools, sconces for oil lamps, a shelf with gilt-stamped leather books upon it, all contributed to a certain patrician aura. The man in the center of this wildly incongruent life stood quietly, awaiting his guest. He offered a hand and Skye shook it.

"Mister Skye, have a seat there. I am about to have a snifter of brandy, as is my wont. May I pour you the same libation?"

"Yes, sir."

McKenzie handed a snifter to Skye, who sipped and marveled.

"Now, then, why are you here?"

"I am leaving the mountains. I intend to go to sea, which is my trade. I came to ask whether I could go down the river with your keelboat this summer, working my way for passage. Until then I propose to work here for nothing but room and board. That's why I wanted to see you."

"Abandoning your post, are you?"

"No, sir. Chief Arapooish forbade me the village."

"He did, did he? Did you do murder?"

"It's a private matter, sir."

McKenzie stared. "Well, I'll get the story from Beck-wourth. But you've let down your masters."

"I've disappointed them, yes."

"And you'll not repay them."

Skye rose, irritated. "I'll leave in the morning."

"Sit down, blast you. What sort of crime did you do? I could put you in prison, you know. We've a gaol here, or I could send you down under indictment."

"You could imprison my body, sir—for a short while."

"That's a strange reply. If you go down the river by yourself this time of year, you'll die."

"That may be the better of my options, sir."

"Death? You're a desperate man."

Skye turned. "I'll be out of here as soon as you swing open the gates."

"Oh no you don't. You don't escape the clutches of Kenneth McKenzie so easily, Skye."

"I have nothing more to say."

"Stubborn cuss. Very well. You failed Sublette and Fitzpatrick. You were sent to the Crows to worm business away from us. Why should I employ such a man?"

"I'm withdrawing my offer of service. I'll go alone."

McKenzie guzzled a long, fiery bolt of brandy, and wheezed. He set down the snifter and glared. "I don't know what to do with you."

"Then don't do anything. I shouldn't have come here."

"You intrigue me. What's all the story I don't know and you're not telling, eh? All right. I know who you are. I know the name of every man in the mountains, or nearly all. You were offered the chance to be a brigade leader last summer. Ah, don't look so startled. Kenneth McKenzie has ears everywhere. Do you suppose Beckwourth has never talked of you? You chose to come to the village of your wife. Where's she?"

"She's not my wife, sir."

"Well, squaw. Harlot."

"She is neither of those."

"Marital discord. That's it. Woman trouble."

Skye stood, poised to leave, mute. A few minutes with McKenzie had persuaded him that he would be better off taking his chances with the Indians and winter on his own.

"How much do you owe your masters?"

"I was indebted nearly three hundred, employed at two hundred for the winter with the Crows. I intended to pay the rest with robes tanned by my wife. Also, five hundred in trade goods were stolen by the Pawnee. I am liable for it."

"That's a lot." He surveyed his guest thoughtfully. "Men are scarce here, and you made a name for yourself out in the field. I could put you in Vanderburgh's brigade."

"Thank you, but that would not be honorable. I am obligated by debt and contract and my own word."

McKenzie laughed.

Skye began to boil. If this didn't stop, he would land on McKenzie and give better than he took, even if he ultimately went down the river in irons. He stepped forward, bristling. "I'm as good as my word. And I'll back my word with these." He lifted his fists and edged toward the man. They were of a height, both blocky, both hardened by mountain life. McKenzie was a little older, but showing a paunch that suggested too many brandies and too much time at table.

Stunned, McKenzie set down his snifter but didn't lift

his fists to defend himself. Instead, he lifted a silver bell and rang it.

An engagé, a big Frenchman, ambled in.

"Escort this man to his quarters."

Skye wheeled away, leaving both men behind him, stepped into a sharp night, found his way to his quarters, rebuilt the dying fire with a cottonwood stick, and settled in his robes, wondering how a man in the mountains could become a seaman.

Chapter 24

In the morning they took him to the mess, where he encountered about twenty men, mostly Creoles, and served him a steaming bowl of gruel and tea. The oats tasted just fine, and the tea was a treasure. The others sitting on the bench seemed to know all about him and greeted him amiably. Word obviously flew around a fur post. These men bore the wounds of a hard life. One lacked two fingers. Another had been scalped and wore a skullcap. Yet another had a peg leg strapped to the stump of his right leg, while another wore a black eye patch. They were served by an Assiniboine woman—wife of one or another of the men—who lacked an ear and an eye and bore a slash across her brown face. Despite all that, she was pretty, and she smiled at him, her face bright with curiosity.

Some of these laborers would tend horses and cattle, others would hunt buffalo, still others would continue to build the post—two buildings were being constructed in the yard. One or two others would salt or season the pelts and press them into packs for transport down the river, while one or two others would cut firewood and distribute it to the various stoves or fireplaces within.

Skye thought he could do some of those things—if he stayed. He would prefer to risk his life traveling to St. Louis in late winter than to face the hauteur and contempt of McKenzie. After the hearty but simple breakfast, they took him to McKenzie's lair. This time the man wore a black cutaway instead of the festive green one, but otherwise looked much the same, beefy, florid, and Scots to the bone.

"I can use a man," McKenzie said without preamble. "I'll hire you."

"Maybe, maybe not, sir."

"I set the terms; you don't."

"My terms are these: twenty dollars a month until I go down the river with the keelboat. After that, crewing on the keelboat in exchange for passage. The accrued wage will be sent to General Ashley, agent for my employers, as payment on my debt. I will not compete with my employers. That is, I will not deal with the Crows or trap in Vanderburgh's brigade."

McKenzie stared so long at him he thought the man hadn't heard.

"Berger needs a man," the factor said. "Would you trade with the Blackfeet?"

"Yes, sir. Fitzpatrick and Sublette have no dealings with the Blackfeet." But he had misgivings. He would be befriending Victoria's enemies. But what difference did it make?

"We have an outpost on the Marias. Berger and a man or two are trading with Bug's Boys. If they succeed, I'll send Kipp to build a post next fall. They've built a cabin—that's all it is—and it's vulnerable. But the Blackfeet want to trade, and Berger's fluent in the tongue, so I think you'll be safe enough. We opened up trade just this fall. Berger brought forty of them here, and we did a good business. I'll send you there. He needs help. You're too valuable to put to work here laying up cottonwood logs or cutting firewood. Three months on the Marias, then bring the returns here by pirogue, and then join the keelboat crew in July. Twenty a month, the funds to be credited to Rocky Mountain Fur through Ashley. Subsistence for you and your horses, and an outfit as needed. What you lose you pay for. You will use your horses on company business. I am sending some resupply to Berger on your packhorse. Tell him we don't have much left here, but there's powder, lead, knives, blankets, awls, beads, molasses, and a bolt of flannel. I am entrusting you with supplies. Live up to my confidence in you."

That faint praise came as a surprise to Skye. "All right, sir."

"Maybe by July I can persuade you to stay."

"No offer would do that."

"I'm going to find out what happened, Skye—ah, Mister Skye."

"Mr. Beckwourth will tell you."

McKenzie looked irritable. "Go to the trading room and get what you need. Sign for it. You can read and cipher, I take it?"

"I was preparing to enter Cambridge—Magdalene—when the Royal Navy press gang took me."

"Likely story."

McKenzie dismissed him with a wave. "Be off now. It'll take you a week by land. You'll be driven far from

the Missouri. You'll ford the Milk and several lesser trib-
utaries. Berger's post is on a flat close to the confluence
of the Marias. Take this letter with you. It will tell him
about you."

Skye took the letter and headed for the cheerful trading
room, staffed by cynical black-clad clerks who looked
to be more prosperous than their fur company salaries
would permit. He selected a pair of four-point blankets, a
small brass kettle, half a dozen beaver traps, a ball mold
and bar of galena, and some DuPont powder.

The post seemed to anticipate his every move, such
was McKenzie's genius. In the yard his saddled horses
waited, the packhorse laden with his robes and the resupply. He added the gear he had drawn from stores and
rode into the morning light, once again a man alone. No
one saw him off, but he didn't doubt that many eyes
watched.

What had he done? He couldn't say for sure. He was
only trying to survive, far apart and two or three snowy
barriers from his former employers. Someday, the ledgers
kept in St. Louis would record payment in full by the
Briton who left the mountains.

Bug's Boys. He had met them only in battle, and all
too often at that. Now he would trade—take in their beaver and pass through the trading window muskets and
powder and arrow points and knives and lance points—
with which to slaughter his friends and wage merciless
war upon Victoria's people. Oh, what had he done? Had
he just sold his soul to the Devil?

He had learned a little about the Blackfoot Federation—
the Piegans, or Pikuni, as they called themselves, the
Bloods or Kainah, and the Siksika, or Blackfeet proper,
all speaking the same tongue, all proud, warlike, power-

ful, and brilliant. Every neighboring tribe feared them. But most of all the Yank trappers feared them; any encounter would become a fight to the death, war waged with the most relentless, cunning, gifted soldiers in the mountains.

He traversed an empty land, a solitary figure riding across snow-patched plains. Far distant, the Missouri oxbowed eastward in a broad, low valley, almost featureless. Skye scarcely knew where he was going, but he couldn't miss if he stayed with the great river. He saw no signs of passage, no hoofprints in the frozen mud, no tracks of deer or antelope, no startled ravens breaking for the skies. He felt dwarfed by the surrounding emptiness, as small as he had felt at sea. Wind bit at him, found every pinhole in his clothing, but he ignored it. He had come to live in nature by enduring it. When you knew you couldn't stop the wind or warm the air or abolish the rain, you endured. By the end of that March day he wondered whether he had made any progress at all. Nothing had changed. He steered his weary black and packhorse down a long, shallow coulee toward the river bottoms, where he would probably find wood and a place to escape the wind. But he was not lucky that night. The flats were as barren as the country above, and he knew he would roll into his blankets and robes with little more in his belly than some gnawed jerky.

All the more reason to leave the mountains. His thoughts turned to Victoria and then shied away from that topic. He wanted to draw a curtain across all of that, but couldn't. An ancient love persisted. In the weeks since he had found her with Beckwourth, he had slowly recovered a will to live. He still told himself he didn't care whether he lived or died—without her life wouldn't be worth living. But it was in him to keep on, no matter how bad things were, just as he had kept on as a seaman.

He did better the next night, warming himself in the reflected heat of a sandstone cliff, boiling Darjeeling tea in his new brass kettle, drinking it while it still scalded. He had plentiful cottonwood beside him, and the horses were staked close at hand on abundant brown grass. But such was the land that he swore he had made no progress at all from sunup to sundown. Nothing had changed. The mute river ran distantly, often out of sight, mysterious in its trench in the plains. No one was abroad.

He forded the Milk, a shallow opaque river dividing stands of naked trees. He kept his gaze sharp and expectant; predators gathered at such places, but he saw none, and knew that he probably would not survive an encounter with a roving band of warriors, no matter that the American Fur Company had opened trade with the Blackfeet. He eyed his back trail nervously. Behind him was a telltale wake of hoofprints pressed in the midday mud and frozen to stone each evening. Anyone could find him, and no doubt would.

The country turned rougher, and he often camped beside a half-iced creek instead of finding his way down to the river. The hills crowded in, the empty flats vanished, and he could no longer see his fate hours before it engulfed him. Now, amid slopes and wooded groves and rock, he faced ambush and surprise.

Then one day he struck a large stream flowing southeast and followed it toward the great river. It was either the Marias or a good imitation of it, according to what he had been told. He found the cabin just north of the Missouri, and beside it a whole village of Blackfeet, their smoke-stained lodges emitting lazy coils of sour cottonwood smoke. Bug's Boys! He rode uneasily through them, even as they stared silently at him. They were a gorgeous people, proud, tall, honey-fleshed, slender, and attired in blankets and bonnets that featured shades of blue. These people plainly loved blue, or else it had some sort of religious significance to them. He had seen many an Indian in his mountain years, but these were far and away the most handsome he had ever encountered.

An old mountain man lounged in the doorway, watching him. This one had been baked the color of an ancient saddle by the sun and wind, and his face was framed by a mop of snowy hair that hung loose to his shoulders. But he was more or less clean shaven; the man probably scraped himself once a month.

"Mr. Berger?"

"I don't know the first word, but the second's me."

"I'm Barnaby Skye, sir. Mr. McKenzie sent me to help out."

"Well, ain't you the politest devil in the hills. You talk like an Englishman. A greenhorn for sure. Don't know that I need help. Got these Piegans hyar, peaceable and trading plews. But they'd as soon slit my throat, the way they think about us. You bring any trade goods? I'm scraping bottom."

"Mr. McKenzie sent some, all he could spare. He told me to help you this spring and then help bring the returns down the river."

"You know the tongue?"

"No, but I'll learn it."

Berger spat. "I need a whole pack train of goods and they send me a greenhorn with one packload of trinkets. Well, git down. That horse'll come in handy until it's stolen. What do you do?"

"I have trapped and hunted mostly. Been a camp tender."

Berger spat again. "You bring any spirits?"

"No, sir."

The next wad of spit landed closer.

"I guess you can cut firewood."

"I can do that and make myself useful, if that's what you want. I cooked plenty as camp tender."

"Camp tender for who?"

"Jackson, Sublette, Fitzpatrick."

"You desert them?"

"No, sir. I can't reach them until the snow melts."

"Likely story. I'll hear the rest of it later. I guess I'm stuck with you. You just keep your mouth shut, don't rub them Piegans wrong, and mind your manners with their women. They ain't loose like the Crows."

Chapter 25

Victoria boldly moved into the lodge of Jim Beckwourth, determined to have a happy time. She relished her new life as Antelope's woman. Stillwater was big with child, so Antelope devoted all his amorous attentions to Skye's former wife, giving her little gifts almost daily. A yellow ribbon one day, a string of beads the next, a jingle bell another day; needles and thread, a new awl, a sharp knife. Stillwater delighted in having a younger wife with her to share the work, especially now that she was so heavy and everything was harder to do.

And Stillwater cherished being Antelope's sits-beside-him wife, with seniority over the new one.

Of course, Antelope did not abandon his long-standing romance with Pine Leaf, the woman warrior, and sometimes he left both of his women in the lodge and went visiting for a night. Those were the only times Victoria was unhappy. Lithe, beautiful Pine Leaf, the sister warrior who fought beside Beckwourth and had saved his life, was a rival that Victoria couldn't hope to equal in his heart.

He continued to call her Victoria—Skye's name for her—and she knew why. Every time he pronounced that name, it was with a sense of victory. He had not only vanquished his rival in the trading business but had taken Skye's wife from him as well. The thought made Antelope very happy and it amused Victoria, too. Sometimes he joked about it and they both laughed. Odd how it had all worked out. Skye had stolen her heart long ago, but when she brought him here to her people, he proved to be nothing, and wouldn't even go out and steal horses or make war. She put him out of mind. Antelope filled her thoughts.

She was very rich. Antelope had more of everything than anyone else in the village. She had everything an Absaroka woman could ever dream of: her new man was a war leader with many coups to his credit, and he could wear the notched feathers of an eagle. He sat in the old men's councils and his voice was heard. He had many women, which proved his greatness. He was the best host and party-giver among the Kicked-in-the-Bellies, and people rejoiced when word came to them to come to his lodge for a merry evening. He always had spirits, and quietly took in robes and pelts as he filled the cups.

Mostly the village nodded and winked and laughed at

what happened to Skye. Everyone but the Old Bulls, the society of grandfathers who devoted themselves to the religion and traditions of the People and disapproved of change. But there weren't many of those because they were always making life so painful for everyone else. The Old Bulls would stare at her when she passed, but that was nothing. She loved being young and Antelope's lover and full of life and the woman of a great leader.

She had eyes for Antelope, but she had eyes for others—Young Horse, for instance. They had been eyeing each other at the parties, and maybe someday she would see what he had to offer. She had lost her virtue, but what Absaroka woman hadn't? That was the big joke. And what had the loss cost her? Nothing but Skye, who was gone now. Antelope was a true Absaroka even if he had been raised as a yellow eyes, but Skye never was anything but a yellow eyes. She should have known better than to marry him, but she was just a girl back at that rendezvous, and full of romantic ideas. Now she was a knowing woman; she knew all there was to know about a man, and yet she was only twenty winters.

There was one other who stared at her, and he wasn't an Old Bull. The shaman, Red Turkey Comb, kept his counsel, but she knew he disapproved—and that the old man influenced her father. But she did not need her father or the shaman anymore now that she had Antelope. She remembered the long months with Skye in her parents' lodge and how frustrating it had been. He did not fit. She wondered what she had ever seen in him. She was glad she was in Antelope's lodge now. She avoided her father and brothers and sisters and grandparents, and especially avoided the old shaman, often walking in a different direction when she saw him. It made her angry, all this silent disapproval. She would live her time on earth as she chose.

At least she hadn't lost her mother. Often, Digs the Roots and Many Quill Woman slipped away together to chop firewood, and then they talked.

"You are better off. The one you were married to," she said, properly avoiding Skye's name, "had no understanding. Now you have a good one, this one who has another wife. The one who is your present man, he will give you all you could ever want. He is good with a woman, which is why he has many. Half the girls in the village would like to be that one's woman."

Victoria giggled. "Skye's feet smelled like skunks."

"The yellow eyes are dirty," her mother said as she hacked at a dry limb a long way from the village. Firewood was growing scarce in this last decaying gasp of coldness.

With the budding of leaves came the budding of war dreams among the men of the village. There were scores to settle, especially with the Siksika. Antelope sensed the time had come, even though many days were still chill and horses mired themselves in the muck.

"I'm going to go looking for Piegans," he announced to her one day in the Moon of Budding Leaves. "I'm taking Pine Leaf with me, and a few others I trust."

"Why Pine Leaf? You should fight with men."

"Because Pine Leaf is a great warrior woman, and because we are happy together on the warpath."

A stab of jealousy cut her. "Then take me. Skye taught me how to make war."

"You're ninety pounds soaking wet."

"What does that mean?"

"You're too small."

"I can hold the horses. Skye taught me to shoot."

"War isn't for women. What chance would you have against a big, tough Siksika twice your size and weight?"

She fell into silence. She hated it when Pine Leaf intruded on her new life. She had taken a dislike to Pine Leaf, even though Stillwater liked the warrior woman.

"I'll bring you back a scalp," he said. "Count coup just for you."

"Ha! The only coup you count is on Pine Leaf."

Antelope laughed. "That's a good way to put it," he said.

"I'm going, even if I have to follow along behind the rest of you."

He turned serious. "No, I will make sure you don't."

But when the dawn came she threw her blankets over a pinto that Beckwourth had given her, gathered her bow and quiver, strapped her knife to her belt beside her flint and steel, found some jerked buffalo, and defiantly joined the rest, some thirty hard, watchful warriors who eyed her coldly. But she didn't care. Antelope sighed, relented, and let her come. She would give a good account of herself, and as long as she was along, Beckwourth would be forced to divide his time between her and Pine Leaf.

The warrior woman immediately joined her as they rode north in a brisk wind. "What does Magpie tell you?" she asked.

"Magpie does not tell me anything."

"You have come to war without knowing?"

"Yes!" She had not sought medicine wisdom, nor had her spirit-helper come to her. She had cast aside the powers that had been given to her. "Don't criticize me," she snapped.

"You may die. Or they may capture you and use you and then torture you to death slowly."

"I will show you who's the better warrior woman," Victoria said.

"I go to war against the Siksika because of a sacred vow. I will avenge the death of my brother, and many Siksika will die at my hand. It is not for myself. It is for the People. A sacred calling. I will never marry. My life is not given to any one man. It does not matter to me who I am, only that the People be safe and strong. I do not live for me. This came to me in a medicine vision when I was not yet a woman. What is yours?"

"I will not tell you."

"Let me be a sister to you, then. You can help. Sometimes women come along not to fight but to tend the wounded, find food, hold horses. I will show you how it is on the warpath. You are young and need a grandmother—a teacher."

"I am going to fight. I will show Antelope who is the best between us."

Pine Leaf gazed at the rebellious girl and rode away silently. There would be no friendship on the warpath between these two. Victoria was delighted. She didn't want to live in Pine Leaf's shadow.

That evening, deep in the Yellowstone country north and west of the winter village, they camped in a ravine where they could strike a spark into tinder without suffering the wind to extinguish the tiny glow before they could breathe it into flame. Brown grass, flattened by snow, matted the slopes, enough fodder for the ponies. Victoria had neglected to bring a picket line and knew she was in trouble.

"I need a picket line," she said to Antelope.

"Lots in the village," he said.

She didn't dare ask the other warriors and certainly not

Pine Leaf. She ended up turning her pinto loose. It wouldn't drift away from the rest but would be hard to catch at dawn. That evening she would begin to braid a line out of something—maybe the antelope skin she used as a saddle pad, or the edge of one of her robes. But she had gotten off to a bad start, and raged silently. She didn't like this, but the worse things got, the more stubborn she became.

She sensed the warriors were expecting her to feed them, but she scorned them. She chewed on the tough jerky and made do with that. She would be a warrior, not a camp follower.

The men had changed. These were the same men who lounged in the village, smoking, gambling, hunting, laughing, enjoying their children, eyeing all the wives and single girls, giving gifts. But now they were all strangers. She had never been on the warpath before, and the change in them excited her. They were moody and silent. Above all, they communed with their spirit-helpers, with the One Above, with those things around them that would influence their fate. Some fasted. Some observed strange rituals, walking in a circle, or lifting a hand to the sliver of new moon, or chanting to the setting sun, or removing their medicine bundles, opening them, minutely examining the totemic items within before retying the bundles and hanging them at their breast. Most of them sang their own medicine songs, devised to inform the spirits, or plead, or boast, or recite honors, or repeat a vow.

She watched, amazed at the transformation in these men. One thing she now knew: war was serious and these warriors took it seriously. Somehow all the war fever of the village had little to do with this, out upon the breast of the earth, where a warrior might fight and die.

Chapter 26

Jim Beckwourth had ambitions, but not the ordinary kind. He didn't mind money or comfort or power, but these were not what his soul yearned for. He could take or leave wealth, didn't need to be a chief, and was as much at home out on the trail as in a comfortable warm lodge. Assorted wives and sweethearts were always welcome in his life, but he could manage without them if he had to.

What James Pierson Beckwourth lusted for was legend. Somewhere along the way, he had discovered that a reputation was exactly what satisfied his yearnings. So he began creating one. He did not wish merely to have a great reputation as a mountain man or a Crow warrior. No, he wanted his reputation to transcend all those lesser things. It would not do merely to be known among the Crows as a fine warrior. He needed to impress his mountaineer friends that he was the best of the best at everything. The best hunter, best warrior, best womanizer, best child-begetter, best shot, best knife fighter, best scalper, best scholar, best tracker, best leader, best guide, best horseman, best dresser, best looker, and best storyteller and friend the West had ever seen. He modestly supposed he was not quite all of these things, but if he nurtured the legend a little, people would think he might be.

Fame was, after all, a heady delight for a young man who had technically been born a slave, even though his father had raised him as a free man. Back east, such a person, even though he was only an eighth a man of color and looked entirely white, had little hope of winning any sort of reputation at all, except perhaps as some sort of rascal. But here in the free and wild wilderness, reputation was the narcotic that filled his veins with joy.

A reputation took nurturing, pruning, and planning. It was not, after all, some weed that might grow and bloom all by itself. And so he had begun, way back in his fur brigade days, to let his colleagues know of his prowess at virtually everything, from reading and writing to shooting his Hawken. It required only a little embroidery, and he was always careful to stick closely to what everyone knew was true. He was not alone at this, either. Most of his campfire colleagues were past masters at the art of inflating their derring-do, especially when whiskey lubricated their tongues.

James Beckwourth knew well enough that fame had to be accompanied by deeds, that while he could embroider, he could not defraud or he would lose the whole game. And so, among the Crows, he was always ready to lead horse-stealing parties, acts of war that won acclaim with minimal risk. It wasn't hard to slip into a sleeping camp and make off with horses, or fire a few shots at awakening enemies, or even count coup. And that was what he was about on this adventure.

It did not hurt to have not one but two women along vying for his attentions, the famous fighting woman Pine Leaf and beautiful Victoria, Many Quill Woman, who had learned plenty about war from Skye. Some of his Crow colleagues no doubt disapproved, but so what? The women only added to his luster.

His objective this time was not to steal horses from the Piegans but to continue north to the Sweet Grass Hills and beyond to steal horses from the Bloods, the most formidable of all the enemies of the Absarokas. The Crows scarcely even respected the Piegans, especially the Little Robe band, which usually lived in a sort of unwritten truce with the Crows. But the Bloods, the Kainah, were a different matter. They were powerful, ruthless, daring, proud, colorful, and masters of mayhem. Counting coup against the Bloods was a dream that burned and smouldered in the soul of every Crow warrior. Let a Crow defeat a Blood and he would be great among his people, storied and feted, adored by the women, admired by every youth yearning to go to war.

The Bloods, then. They roamed country a little north of the Piegans, but forayed south now and then to torment the Crows. Beckwourth intended to catch them at their spring hunting grounds around the Sweet Grass Hills, and if not there, then across the medicine line into British territory, which was home to them. This would be a long trip, with the possibility of a long retreat and a long pursuit if the angry Bloods came after them. But that only made the prospects more enticing and ensured the glory of all the Crows. They were strong enough to thwart the Bloods, especially with Beckwourth's big Hawken that could deal death at a thousand yards, many flights of arrows distant.

Day by day they rode north through an early May chill, ever watchful for the enemy. They cut the trail of war and hunting parties on two occasions, the hoofprints embedded in the moist soil of springtime. Later in the year, when the sun had hardened the earth, it would be far more difficult to read as much from the passage of horses. But with cunning and care they made their way north unmolested except by a two-day cold rain that caught them on grasslands far from firewood and shelter and numbed them into misery. They were traveling for war and had not brought their heavy robes. Little Tail, one of the finest men among them, soon took sick, fevered by disease, and discovered that his medicine had failed him. They left Little Tail in a hidden swale, where he would endure until the sickness passed. It was a bad omen, and many of the Crows ascribed it to the presence of women.

Their passage took them across a vast and lonely prairie broken by occasional buttes and oddly formed hills. They reached the Missouri and tried two well-known fords before they found one that permitted passage. Even then they had to swim their horses through twenty yards of swift cold current, early spring runoff, and lost a horse in the process. Another bad omen. The shivering party gathered on the north bank, stripped off sopping leather clothing, built a miserable fire that threw no heat because of the wind, and tried to dry itself out. Some of Beckwourth's warriors eyed the women sullenly but said nothing. If either of the women belonged in the hut of the time of the moon, then the whole party was in danger from evil medicine. Pine Leaf never fought during those times, so the warriors eyed Victoria with dark suspicion and avoided her.

Beckwourth laughed. He believed in nothing, or almost nothing other than the explosive force of powder and the lethal effect of a lead ball. Victoria was an asset. She would hold the horses when the warriors crept on foot toward a Blood herd, and she could fight if she had to, using her own lighter bow and arrows. She had soldiered without complaint, making the brief camps comfortable.

One day, from an observation point halfway up the side of a butte, they spotted a whole Blackfoot village on the move, the motion almost invisible against the shadows of puffball clouds plowing across the land. Closer inspection revealed vedettes far out from the main body, two of them passing under the butte. Beckwourth, as war leader, opted for concealment, though some among them would have liked to swarm down on the vedettes and take scalps. No one among them could say whether these were Piegans or Bloods, or less probably Gros Ventres, Crees, or Assiniboines.

They pierced deeper into hostile country, their senses alert and nerves ajangle with the sudden flight of any bird or the slightest shift of the silences. Far to the west the white spine of the Rocky Mountains formed a rampart. For all the members of the Blackfoot Federation, those mountains meant home.

The next day they discovered a large herd of buffalo grazing in a shallow basin, and were just contemplating a feast of tongue and hump meat when the herd stirred. Something at its farther periphery agitated the black creatures, and the stirring spread into a sinuous movement, and then a slow trot, and finally a rush, as the huge animals began stampeding, their speed astonishing and improbable for such lumbering creatures. The source of all this soon became apparent. Blackfoot hunters were running the herd southward, darting among the great beasts on their swift buffalo ponies, drawing close enough to punch a lethal arrow into the heart-lung spot just behind the forelegs. Only the excitement of their hunt, and the mile distance, choked with buffalo, kept them from seeing the Crows.

Beckwourth watched, delighted even though they would not make meat just then, knowing they had escaped detection. He drew his men into a shallow gulch just out of sight, prepared to fend off the warriors who would want to catch and kill the buffalo hunters, steal their ponies, count coup, and go home triumphant. It would be an easy victory—but not against the Bloods, if Beckwourth's instincts were true. These hunters were Piegans, and they were probably tied to the passing village.

"These dogs, these Piegans, are too easy," he said, preempting the discussion. "They aren't worth chasing. We will go for the Bloods, and we will return with more honors. What is a coup against a Piegan? Nothing. We will show the People how to make real coups."

"I will count coups against these," said Sitting Man.

"No, that would betray us to them."

"I will count coup. It is the way given me. I will take some scalps and their buffalo runners. I want a fast horse. This is my way."

Beckwourth didn't like it. As war leader, he could forbid it—and face the consequences. Or permit it—and face the consequences. To prevent a warrior from acting upon his medicine was a grave matter, one that could sour the rest of the foray. But to give in might lead to discovery and defeat by overwhelming hordes of Blackfeet.

"Go, then, Sitting Man," Beckwourth said unhappily. "But they will follow your trail back to us."

Sitting Man didn't wait. He climbed onto his pinto pony, made medicine a moment, singing his war songs, and rode south, a lone knight.

Beckwourth had no choice other than to put distance between the war party and Sitting Man. The buffalo were long gone, and nothing but a swath of trampled, muddy grass told of their passage. He eyed the distant cloud-shadowed hills uneasily, saw nothing, and rode north as hard as the horses would move across soft and treacherous earth. He headed into the middle of the trampled area, hoping to conceal his party's passage, and rode north, ever north, to the land of the Bloods.

Far ahead, across a featureless plain, lay the Sweet Grass Hills, three great buttes rising over three thousand feet above the plains, the center butte much smaller than the massive ones east and west. Somewhere northwest of the hills, in the shadow of the Rockies, they would probably find Bloods—or Bloods would find them. But to get there they would cross a land without stories. Nothing ever happened there, nothing that could be told and retold. Nothing on that hollow plain spoke of time, or habitation, or events. So they would ride through a place without time.

An eerie isolation surrounded the hills, which perhaps was why the Blackfeet thought they were the habitation of spirits. One could gaze upon the dark buttes and see the spirits congregated there, unhappy, fearsome, isolated, and maybe vengeful, too. Beckwourth didn't like the looks of the hills, and neither did his warriors. The quest for glory had turned dark.

Chapter 27

Death wove a red thread through Skye's every hour. Berger's little post was subject to every whim of the Blackfeet. The Piegans suffered it simply because it was a convenient source of white men's goods, much closer than the Hudson's Bay posts far to the north.

Not that the Piegans liked or trusted the Americans, with whom they had been at war ever since they had skirmished with Lewis and Clark. Many a warrior entered the cabin not so much to trade as to measure the heads of those within for the scalping knife. If the traders survived, it would be only because of Berger's formidable presence. He refused to be intimidated. But as the scanty supply of trade goods dwindled, and the pile of robes, prime beaver pelts, and other skins mounted, the Blackfeet took more and more liberties, wandering behind the crude counter, daring Berger to cause trouble, pilfering whatever they could.

Skye knew that he and Berger and the Creole, Arquette, wouldn't last ten minutes in a fight. Not with scores of warriors lounging about ready to burn the rough cottonwood log cabin and fry its occupants. But peace held, perhaps because Berger assured the Blackfeet that the American Fur Company would build a larger post there and sell more goods for better prices than Hudson's Bay. That slender thread was all that kept their topknots on their skulls. That and Berger's fearless diplomacy.

The little outpost did not deal in whiskey even though spirits were the most lucrative—if illegal—business of all. Berger knew full well what a jug of Indian whiskey— raw alcohol, river water, and a plug of tobacco or pepper for taste—would do to these tribesmen who weren't accustomed to spirits. They were explosive enough sober; with drink in them they would pay no heed to tomorrow and butcher the hated Yanks just for the joy of it.

At Fort Union an Indian could show up at a small window after dark, any night, and trade a pelt for a cup. But Fort Union could defend itself even from a mob of whiskey-crazed warriors on a drunk. Its stockade was all but impenetrable. So the only risk in the illegal liquor trade was discovery by the United States Indian commissioners.

Skye yearned for a jug, but Berger kept not even a drop

for his own use. Skye woke up each morning wondering if he would survive the day. His task was to cut firewood, which took him far from the post and subjected him to the whim of any Blackfoot who decided to kill him. Another of his tasks was to feed the horses any way he could, putting them out on the tender spring grasses and watching over them while they grazed, or cutting grass and bringing it to his animals, which were penned behind the cabin. He expected them to disappear at any moment, with the itch of any Blackfoot, but the theft didn't happen. Still another was to hunt, because the post's provisions had long since been exhausted. Berger traded goods for meat now and then, but the food supply had become precarious and monotonous.

Blackfeet came and went. Some days a whole village would erect its lodges around the cabin; other days there wasn't an Indian in sight and Skye could do his chores without the underlying terror that usually accompanied them. Skye was assigned the meanest and most dangerous tasks because he was junior, while Arquette sorted and pressed beaver and other furs into packs, and cooked as well. Berger lounged, traded, meandered among the Blackfeet making friends as much as possible. He did not neglect to hand out small gifts—a plug of tobacco here, a few beads there, a knife to a chief or headman.

Skye tried to learn the tongue, but confused it with the Crow, and had trouble. Still, he figured every word he mastered was a word that might help him in a pinch. "Arrow" was *aps'se*. "Water" was *oh kiu'*. "Wind" was *su po'*. "Fire" was *is'tsi*. The Marias River, close at hand, was called *Kaiyi Isisakta,* which really meant "Bear River." He mastered fifty, then a hundred words, but Berger never let him trade. That business was too delicate and the Blackfeet too unpredictable.

So Skye headed out each morning with his packhorse, walking past the handsome lodges of these people while enduring their curious silences, chopped cottonwood limbs, bundled them on his pack saddle, and returned, amazed to be alive. He took his Hawken, but Berger instructed him not to use it except as a last resort. He was to stand firm, prevent theft of his horse if he could, show no sign of dread or fear if he could, and hasten back to the post.

Then, for a while, the Blackfeet vanished. They were off on raids, hunting, visiting relatives in other bands, marrying, making ready for the Sun Dance, which they held at the time of the summer solstice, going on vision quests, opening sacred medicine bundles—the beaver bundle was opened about this time each spring, Berger explained. That was fine with Skye. His sojourn at this vulnerable little outpost was coming to a close and he was still alive, to his astonishment.

He debated whether to pull out, head across the opened passes, find Bridger and Fitzpatrick, report for work, confess his failure with the Crows. It was tempting, but the thought of Victoria stopped him cold. He was done with the mountains. Any hope of healing the hole in his heart lay in some Yank place like St. Louis or the mysterious cities to the east. No, he wouldn't do that, nor would he betray McKenzie. He would not add that black mark to all the rest.

More Piegans arrived, thirty lodges led by a burly old chief with five or six wives. Skye had never seen such tall, handsome Indians. They exuded pride, beauty, power, arrogance, assurance, and lordship over all this country.

They drifted south during the brief summers, making trouble for their neighbors. Their lodges had been gaily decorated with moons and fallen stars painted around their bases, bright insignias suggesting clan and medicine painted on the sides. These people favored blues of all shades in their dress, beadwork, and even on the parfleches.

Swiftly they traded prime beaver plews for Berger's powder and lead, lance points, kettles, arrowheads, knives, and awls. By the middle of May they had reduced Berger's stock of trade goods to a few items, mostly awls, flints, fire steels, knives, and beads, which made Berger uneasy. Empty shelves only tempted the Indians with visions of blood and fire. It was time to get out of there, build some bullboats and float the pelts down the Missouri to Fort Union on the crest of the spring runoff. Skye, with his horses, would take a load overland, a dangerous business for a sole white man during the high summer days when every warrior of the northern plains was out roving, looking for adventure and plunder and coups.

Berger talked at length to Little Crow, the chief of this band. He seemed more amiable than many of his younger warriors, who apparently considered the traders disposable now that the post had been largely emptied of the miraculous goods white men traded. Little Crow genially announced that his people would summer west of the Sweet Grass Hills where the buffalo were thick, and maybe raid the cowardly Crows on Elk River—their name for the Yellowstone—for horses, or join the Bloods on a joint venture southward for plunder. The medicine was good; the seers were brimming with fierce optimism; the weather was fine, the land full of grass to fatten ponies; and all the young men were itching for honors. Who could resist? The fierce Blackfeet were the best of the best on the plains and would take many scalps, capture many children and women, and torture hundreds of Crows to death, the sound of their howling proof of their cowardly natures.

They left after three days, and Berger decided it was time to head down the river. He elected to build two large bullboats to carry his packs of fur to the fort, one man in each boat. Some additional furs would go back upon Skye's packhorse with Skye. Berger set Skye to cutting willow saplings for the bullboats, while he and Arquette prepared a stack of raw buffalohides by trimming the edges. All this required brutal toil. Skye buried the ends of the saplings in the earth, forming an elongated circle, and then bent them over and lashed them together into a framework that looked like an inverted bowl. The hides, properly dressed with fat, sewn tight, and sealed with pitch and tallow, would form the skin of the bullboats and would last long enough in the water to get the furs and traders to Fort Union. Maybe. The light boats were treacherous, hard to maneuver, and likely to capsize in white water.

Rain stopped the work. It came in cold gusts, sheets of icy water that drenched a man and set him to shivering. They swiftly ran out of firewood, and Skye was elected to cut some, which he did between spring showers, often getting soaked in the process. Arquette nursed catarrh, while Berger coughed and cursed, and Skye wrestled with bilious fever between his cold bouts of woodcutting. But he persisted. His three months as an engagé for American Fur Company were drawing to a close, and soon sixty dollars would be applied to his debt to Rocky Mountain Fur.

The only good thing about living among the dangerous Blackfeet was that time flew. Danger honed a keen
edge on every minute, and he scarcely thought about Victoria, or loss, or the emptiness of his future. It was enough
to survive among tribesmen who were itching to take his
scalp and leave him soaking in his blood until wild creatures ate his meat and plucked out his eyes. But when he
did think about her, he knew that his pain had not lessened, love had not dwindled, and his anger at her and at
Beckwourth had not abated. Time had healed nothing.

By early June they were able to work on the bullboats
again. Time was growing short. They needed to reach
Fort Union with the season's returns by July 1, when the
keelboat was due from St. Louis and scheduled to load
and turn around as fast as possible. They finished the
sturdy, flexible frame of one boat and began lashing
the hides together with thong and fitting them over the
frame. This too was hard work. The seams, including
every hole made by an awl, needed to be caulked with
pitch drawn from a pine, and the hides soaked in tallow to
waterproof them. They finished one boat, and it looked so
fragile and makeshift that Skye, the seaman, wondered
whether it would survive a mile of water. They began the
second, only to discover they lacked hides and would
have to find and skin some buffalo. That or build a log
raft, which was itself a risky way to carry the hides. Rafts
tipped over in rough water, soaked the hides, and resulted
in even more disaster than bullboats.

So Arquette and Skye hunted buffalo while Berger
guarded the post through the high sweet days of June. The
hunt was fruitless. Buffalo had long since gathered
into great migratory herds and drifted off to prime
grasslands to calve, fatten, rub off ticks and fleas on any

useful tree, wallow in mud puddles to clean their hides of varmints, and fight off the wolves that silently shadowed the herds, looking for the injured, the old, the isolated calf.

Berger cursed his subordinates for their barren efforts and decided on another expedient: he would trade for packhorses and send the furs back overland, two men with horses, while he navigated with the sole bullboat. There wasn't much left to trade, but he figured he could get some horses out of what was left. One rifle—his own—would get him half a dozen horses with packsaddles thrown in. All he had to do was find some Blackfeet.

Chapter 28

Many Quill Woman—the name Victoria was fading fast—looked for a sign as the Absarokas rode past the Sweet Grass Hills. She sensed that those gloomy forested slopes were the habitation of the dead, the place where the spirits of the Siksika came to live as shades in the other world. The peoples of the plains knew each others' stories. In her village were two captive Blackfeet women who had become wives, and several captured children who would be raised as Absarokas. In the villages of the Siksika, the Lakota, the Cheyenne, and other tribes there were Crow women, sometimes wives, more often slaves. And so the stories were shared, and each tribe well knew the sacred rites of the others.

She looked for the spirits but saw none. Maybe she was wrong. The Siksika believed the spirits of their dead went to the Sand Hills to wander forever—but maybe these weren't the Sand Hills. These hills rose in utter isolation, surrounded by emptiness, and spread night out upon the sunny plains. A place like that deserved respect. She spoke gently to the grandfathers and grandmothers whose shades surely resided there. So many of them; others walking the spirit trail, arriving each day. She felt the coldness of death pass through her, and hurried her pony westward, eager to put the hills behind her. This was not a good land, like that of the Absarokas.

The others in her war party eyed the hills somberly. If these hills weren't the abode of the Siksika dead, they certainly should be. Maybe some of the spirits who resided there had been sent to this place by Absaroka arrows and lances and war clubs. This was not a good place for an Absaroka to be, with the eyes of the spirits upon them, ever watchful.

She was having misgivings about coming with Beckwourth. She wasn't afraid of death, like the yellow eyes. Life was short. One could die for the People and be remembered. But she wasn't a warrior and knew little of the ways of death—except for what the one who had been her man had taught her. In this kind of land, where there was no place to hide, even a horse holder was as vulnerable as a warrior who crept into a Siksika camp.

This was not a good land—it lay open and barren and without history, and the white wall of the mountains in the hazy west rose like the end of the world. Her Absaroka world had no end, but this Siksika world stopped in the west. This was a cold land, too, and there was no place to hide from the cold. Even now, well into spring, cold gusts whirled down off the distant mountains and sliced heat out of her lithe body.

The others rode quietly, saying nothing, their thoughts upon war, their silences profound. Pine Leaf rode apart, isolated, small, odd, like a doll. Many Quill Woman had never seen the woman warrior like this, and now she understood the sacredness of Pine Leaf's vows to kill Siksika. Something flat and hard emanated from the woman warrior here in the land of her enemies.

Many Quill Woman summoned her courage. She had seen no magpies this entire trip. Usually they flocked about, raucously following the passage of horses and men. She knew her spirit-helper had turned her face away. Bad medicine. But Many Quill Woman knew she would continue. She would ride with Beckwourth even with bad medicine. That was how much she enjoyed her new man.

That's what she told herself, anyway. But in softer moments, doubt flooded her, fear and a cold dread. Even now, they might be observed. Or Sitting Man might have given away their passage. She thought Beckwourth should have commanded Sitting Man to come along and not chase after the hunters. But now it was too late. She doubted that any of them would see Sitting Man again.

Black-bottomed clouds spun off the distant mountains and rolled over the prairie like dark stones, bringing with them the little death of the sun. She did not like the clouds or this land, and wondered whether the Absaroka warriors did. Even Beckwourth had grown quiet, the loquacious storyteller and party-giver oddly solemn. How could they steal horses when there was no place to hide? Well, it worked both ways. If there was no place for Absaroka to hide, then there was no place for the Siksika to hide either.

But nothing disturbed their passage. They rode through a quietness that began to grate on her. Would not even the west wind make a noise? Was this the land of the dead? Twilight settled over them, veiling their passage, shrouding them in the funeral clothing of night. They would halt at some creek, water and graze the ponies, and sleep without a fire, huddle under their horses if it rained, and then arise to hunt their prey before dawn.

Beckwourth led them into a shallow draw running a trickle of water. The draw put them well under the surface of the plain and protected them from the all-seeing eyes of the Siksika. Maybe with the next sun they would find the Bloods, the Kainah, and then they would wait quietly for the cloak of another night to hide them when they filtered into the herds and stole fine fat ponies. They were well concealed; there would be no need for guards this night, hidden in a crease of the prairie.

They picketed their ponies on stakes. Victoria employed the line she had braided out of much of her robe. Her brothers the warriors seemed uncommonly quiet this night. She lay in the chill of the draw, wishing she could escape the flow of cold air down it, staring at the many stars in the heavens, each star the spirit of one who was gone forever. Like Skye. She tried to abolish his name from mind, but his name was there. He was like the dead now; she should put him out of mind, if she could.

Few of them slept. One could hear sleep, hear the sigh and fall of breath, but not now. The ponies were nervous, wheeling on their pickets, snorting softly, their nostrils catching the scent of something—wolf or man or bear. Who could know? It would be a long night.

She tossed the whole night. The hard cold earth bit her. She could not find a level place in the draw. She swore owls drifted past her. Owls were sacred, and their presence portended death. Shapes in the night changed, loomed over her, retreated. Surely these were the Siksika spirits from those brooding hills. Her bones ached. Why had she come on a warrior's mission? What a foolish young woman she had been. Why had not Red Turkey Comb said anything? Where was Magpie?

The wolf cry in the predawn light wasn't a wolf, and all the Absaroka knew it. She bolted upright in the murk. An arrow struck her buffalo robe. They had hunted for the Bloods but the Bloods had found them first. She saw, or thought she saw, Blackfoot warriors on either side, loosing arrows into the Absarokas below. One brother grunted, cried something, and then groaned. The groaning stopped. She froze, unable to decide what to do. Around her the Absarokas were struggling out of their robes, reaching for their bows and quivers, stringing bows. She heard another thump of arrow on flesh, and someone toppled with a terrible cough and a sigh.

Fear paralyzed her. Near her, Pine Leaf was yanking her pony's picket pin from the ground and easing over the back of her fear-crazed pony. Pine Leaf steered the pony straight upslope at the warriors who were loosing arrows from above, recklessly steering toward the enemy. Other Absarokas followed her, and Many Quill Woman heard the sounds of desperate struggle from that quarter. She stared, astonished. Most of the Absarokas were fleeing down the draw on foot or horseback. She saw a horse stagger, whinny, grunt, and roll over slowly. That was her salvation. She raced to it, fell behind the still-heaving body, strung her bow, pulled an arrow from her quiver and nocked it, and tried to discern the enemy, who were gliding downslope on foot, barely visible in the curtains of darkness. She rose, loosed an arrow at a crouching warrior on the slope. It missed. She ducked behind the carcass and nocked another.

Goddammit, where was Skye?

She heard Antelope howling like a wolf, his voice unmistakable. He was rallying his men against this unseen enemy. A dozen Absarokas raced in his direction. But the arrows came thick and fast, finding their marks. Many Quill Woman saw another Absaroka stagger and fall and writhe on the bloody grasses. She knew that one, Diving Hawk, husband of her friend Little Weasel, and a new father.

Someone fired a rifle, the crack shocking in the silent cusp of day. She saw forms darting downslope, crouching, looking for targets, loosing arrows. They spoke the tongue of the enemy. One stopped, threw up his arms, and tumbled. So one Siksika dog died, anyway. She would kill another. She would kill before they killed her. Where had her people gone? She could see none, but she heard the low thud of hooves across the throat of the earth. Where were her warriors? Where had Antelope gone?

She heard the sounds of struggle up above, on the plains, grunts and cries, howls of rage, horses coughing and collapsing. For the moment the war departed from her. Those who had crept down the slopes had run back up again. The light thickened into a soft gray, enough to make things out. A half dozen Absarokas lay dead or groaning. They would lose their scalps soon enough—and so would she. But she saw several Bloods—if that's what they were—on the slope, some looking dead; another was sitting with his leg cocked sideways, useless. She suddenly realized she had to find her people, find Beckwourth, get a good horse and flee. Wherever the fighting was, it wasn't in the draw. Black lumps sprawled on the slopes told her of death. Weeping, choking, gasping, groaning, singing, told her of dying. Suddenly war took on a new perspective for her. This was real; the victory parades through the village had never been real. How would she feel with an arrow in her chest, unable to breathe, her world turning over?

Beckwourth had raced up the draw, the one direction that offered salvation. She would follow. She abandoned the carcass, felt an arrow pierce her skirt, tumbled to earth, and tried to find the arrow's source. The injured Blood on the slope was still fighting his battle, and his arrows were lethal. Another smacked the grass inches from her nose. She bolted forward while he armed himself. She turned, loosed an arrow at him, and it struck his bow, spoiling his aim. His arrow vanished somewhere. She raced up the draw, heart pounding. Where were they?

She splashed through the rivulet at the head of the draw and felt the icy water soak her moccasins. She climbed a short steep embankment that took her to the undulating plains, and freedom, and beheld bloody light across the eastern horizon. She saw no one for a moment; the running battle had taken both sides far away. Her heart slowed. She wished she had run when Antelope called, jumped on any pony instead of lying behind a dying horse.

A warrior loomed out of nowhere. He was leading a lame horse. She saw in a flash this one was a Blood, and he would kill her with the knife in his hand. She drew her bow, but he lunged, knocking her flat with his shoulder; a club just missed her face. She tumbled to earth and scrambled aside to avoid the blade.

But the thrust didn't come.

Chapter 29

They stared at each other. Her heart raced. The Blood was mature and powerful, and he bore the marks of war. A scar cut across his cheek, from the corner of an eye to his mouth. But for it he would be handsome. He stood over her, enjoying his triumph.

She would die. The knife in his hand was poised to cut her throat. She ached to kill him, but his moccasin rested heavily on her chest, crushing her into the earth.

She didn't want to die. Not after only twenty winters. But helplessness stole through her, the helplessness of a baby bird caught in the hand. She did not rebuke herself for coming on this ill-fated venture. There wasn't time. She needed to summon her wits and begin to sing a death song, but words deserted her.

Something shifted in his eyes, and he lowered his hand to his side. It wasn't mercy she saw, but something else. And then she knew. He would enjoy torturing her later. The Siksika were good at it. She would die slowly, her flesh roasted and peeled from her living body, her screams involuntary no matter how hard she sought stoic death. She ached for the blade and its swift sure mercy.

He took his foot off her and said something she didn't understand. The pain where his foot had crushed her chest throbbed. He smiled darkly, picked up her bow and snapped it in two, pulled the knife from her waist sheath and left her there. She knew if she moved, or fled, he would be back in an instant. He studied the distant prairies, listening for the sound of strife. His lamed horse had ended the battle for him. He studied his horse, lifted a foreleg; the horse screamed its agony, and he let go. In one blurred motion he slit the throat of the horse. Red gouted from its neck. It shivered, sagged, and dropped heavily to the ground, its limbs flailing, its body convulsing.

The Blood warrior walked downslope toward the wounded or dead Absarokas. She watched him, filled with knowing. The man was powerfully built, with flesh the color of honey, jet hair worn in a single braid, and wearing leggings and moccasins and breechclout, but nothing save a medicine bundle above the waist. A second scar puckered his left arm. He was older than she, and he had seen many battles and won many honors.

He approached Little Otter from behind. The Absaroka lived, but soon wouldn't. An arrow pierced clear through his chest. The Blood grasped Little Otter's two braids, lifted them high, and ran his scalping knife clear around Little Otter's head, across his brow, over the ears, around the back, and to the brow again. Little Otter groaned. The Blood yanked mightily on the braids, and the scalp popped free with a sucking sound. The Blood watched the Absaroka sag into the ground and left him to die slowly, his spirit homeless evermore. The Blood lifted his fresh scalp and offered it to the heavens, seeking the blessings of the rising sun upon his victory.

One by one, the Blood scalped the rest of the dead and injured. Six scalps in all, a great victory for the Blood; probably his greatest ever. He would tell the story of many coups to his people soon. Many Quill Woman watched her friends die. Without scalps their spirits would wander through eternity and never walk the trail to the stars. Now this empty plain, without history, had a new story.

The sun crimsoned the new grass and then lifted off

the breast of the earth. All this had happened between first light and sunrise. Off to the east, the Sweet Grass Hills brooded and mocked. The hills had seen the Absarokas all along and had told the Siksika where to find enemies.

So this was how her young life would end. In unspeakable pain and torment. They would soon return, probably bearing more scalps, and then she would know the fate of her people. She would count the scalps and know. Then they would turn to her, the survivor. Her fate would be decided entirely by the one who captured her. He held the power of life and death over her now, and none of the others would intervene. They might all use her, one by one, and then cut her throat. They might beat her until she couldn't endure the pain, and they would beat her the more. They might take her with them for a while, and torture her this evening, sport around a campfire, her shrieks blotted up by this empty silent land until she died. And the death would be a mercy.

She knew their tortures. A favorite was to jab splinters of pine into the victim's flesh and then ignite them and watch living flesh roast. They might cut off her fingers, joint by joint, slowly, so she didn't die quickly. They might suspend her by her feet from a limb, the blood rushing to her head, and then cook her head over a fire. Or they might simply beat her to death, each of them counting coup, kicking, hitting, cutting, until she passed out of this world and into the spirit land. If only she had her knife she could plunge it into her breast. But she didn't. She lay aching, dreading, aware of a fate that she had brought upon herself.

Magpie. The bird settled near her, pecked at something in the grass, and flew away in a burst of black and white and iridescent feather. Why had Magpie come now, when all was over? To watch her die. Many Quill Woman had ignored her own medicine-helper, and would pay. And Magpie would remind her as she died in pain what it was to ignore what had been given to her.

She discerned a knot of horsemen in the distance, returning slowly, and she knew the rest of the Bloods were gathering at this scene of triumph. There were about twenty. So her Absaroka party had been the stronger, but the courageous Bloods had attacked and won on this day, taking advantage of the land they knew so well, and the night, and maybe Beckwourth's recklessness. She had heard only one shot during the entire affray; it had been Beckwourth's. These Bloods lacked firearms and fought with arrow and club, war ax and lance. A rifle cost many robes, many beaver pelts, and few could own one. Only a few chiefs, with many wives tanning robes, had rifles.

Sorrow swept her. Foolishness! She had been swept along by giddy girlish dreams, Beckwourth's seductions, bad company. She might yet live, but she was doomed. She lay quietly on the grass while the Bloods rode in, stared at her, talked with her captor, and gazed at the six scalps. They lifted a lance that bore three more. She feared she would find Beckwourth's beribboned braids, or Pine Leaf's lighter colored braid, but did not see them. Nine dead, no doubt more wounded. This was the worst tragedy her village had known for many winters. Horses, too. The victors drove a dozen Absaroka ponies before them, including hers. She knew them. Some still bore medicine paintings on them. The Bloods had triumphed in many ways this day: horses, scalps, and a captive to torture.

They wrapped their dead one in a robe and lifted the body onto a horse, which sidestepped nervously, smelling blood and death. Her captor kicked her hard in the ribs, shooting pain through her, and motioned her to stand. Now they all stared at her. She was lithe and pretty, and she knew that they were seeing a woman to use, a woman of the hated Absarokas to use and torment and kill. They brought her a horse and she mounted, her body aching. Some came and punched her, counting coup. She was cold, but they gave her no robes. It would be a long time before the sun was high enough to warm her, and she would still be cold. She would never be warm again, and when her time came, she would die cold, even if they killed her with fire.

They rode west, she knew not where, her captor leading her horse with a braided lead rope. They stopped only to water the horses at a creek and drink some themselves, and then were off again. They gave her none, and her body cried with thirst. All that morning they rode toward the western mountains, each step taking her farther from her people.

They began talking to each other at last, their talk almost cheerful in spite of the dead man among them. It had been a good fight this day, and the Bloods were the lords of the plains. Many coups had they counted. They shared pemmican but fed her nothing. She grew faint and didn't know what was worst: utter hopelessness, dread of the torture to come, or thirst. The day warmed, and blossoms bobbed in the zephyrs. The sun stroked her doeskin skirts but did not warm her.

They stopped early on a sizable river she did not know, one lined with cottonwoods and willows—firewood for what was to come. She watched Magpie flit from limb to limb, dodging behind leaves, swooping just in front of her horse. Magpie had come to watch her die. Her captor motioned her to step down, and she did, collapsing in the dirt beside the river. He said something, kicked her, and she rose. He pushed her toward a stately willow and lashed her to its trunk. This would be the place of her torment.

They ignored her, built a fire, staked the ponies on tender spring grasses, washed themselves, went into the bushes, devoted themselves to their prayers, their medicine, each in his own way. They trod this land with a lordly step, knowing themselves to be invincible. These people were much taller than hers, with hawkish faces, not the moon faces of her people. They had thinner noses and some of their eyes were gray instead of black or brown. She loathed them all the more for their proud manner, their handsomeness, their arrogance.

She grew dizzy, bound to the rough bark by tight thongs, and wished she would slip away into the spirit world. It grew dark, and she sensed anticipation among them. They eyed her now and then. They looked to their horses, examined the ones they had won at battle, made their medicine. Night came, and this night would be the night of all nights.

She watched their war leader, their headman, who issued quiet commands that were instantly obeyed. This night the horses would be well guarded. He sent three of his warriors into the deepening darkness. They would wander among the ponies this night, and none would fall to the Absarokas. They were warriors first, and whatever entertainments they had planned for her came second.

Her captor came at last, freed her, and led her away from the tree. So they would not torture her there. The warriors gathered about her now, and she understood what would happen this night. It was written upon their faces.

Chapter 30

Her captor took her broken body to his village, but she was elsewhere. He had granted the Absaroka woman a reprieve—for the moment. Her fate would be whatever his whim might be. He could, even after she spent months of faithful service as a slave, choose to kill her and no one would interfere. She had become property.

She sat upon a pony, oblivious of the world. Her mind drifted away from its moorings and her thoughts turned to sacred things. She hurt, but not even that mattered. Her dress had rents in it that let in air and male gazes, but that didn't matter either. What would they see that they hadn't seen?

She rode through a fine spring day but it didn't lift her out of her long drift into a spirit land. She had had nothing to eat for two suns, and it dizzied her. If she fell off her pony and they brained her with a war club, that would be a mercy. She was parched as well; they had not given her water. Her heart raced because of her thirst.

Then, at noon, they reached a creek that ran between barren banks, not a tree or bush in sight. Her captor untied her hands and pulled her to the ground, commanding something. She crawled to water and they let her drink. She sipped a little, and it tasted good. She cupped her hands and drank more, and more. Water was the ultimate blessing. A person could endure hunger, but thirst raked a body. The effect was immediate. With water came the will to live if she could. Around her warriors drank and left her alone. She took care of her needs, always in plain sight, and then went back to the creek to drink some more, soak her lithe body in water. Then she washed, not caring what they thought: her face and hands, her neck and limbs, her violated torso. Then she drank again.

The water even assuaged her hunger a little. They did not feed her because they were almost out of trail food and had shot no game. A warrior expected to go without if he had to, and she shared the warrior's fate. The water restored her body to her, with its pain and shame. Now, at last, in the brightness of a summery day, she studied them. They were very like her own people, most of them dressed only in breechclouts, some with leggings and moccasins. They had started to paint themselves, each daubing color according to his medicine, drawn from small kits they carried with them. The colors had been found in nature, mostly from vegetation and blooms, but sometimes from the clays and rock of the earth. They were painting for victory this occasion. They could not be far from the Kainah village.

These were seasoned veterans of the warpath. Her captor was one of the youngest, she thought, but still a veteran warrior. These were tall people, muscular, their color ranging from amber to copper, their skills at war evident in their every gesture, in their elaborate war shields made of the thick neck hide of a buffalo bull and capable of deflecting arrows and even a musket ball that quartered into them. Their medicine was powerful: otters, lightning, falling stars, bears, geometric designs, crimson, blue, white, tan.

Her captor motioned for her to mount, and after she did he tied her hands with thong so tightly it slowed the blood to her fingers. This time he tied a braided rope around her neck, and mounted his own horse holding the other end. The device would symbolize her captivity when they rode through the village.

How often she had stood in her own village while the warriors rode in, their paint, their war emblems, and the burdens on the horses telling their tales without words. How often she had watched the arrival of a captive being brought to the Kicked-in-the-Bellies, and had spat at the victim, heaped insults upon whoever it was, woman or man, and enjoyed the thought of the beatings the enemy would justifiably receive. The Absaroka didn't torture, not the way some people did, but the captive would suffer abuse—kicks, pummeling, starvation, exhausting work, cold, lack of clothing, discomfort. It was all the just reward of making war against the Absaroka.

Now all this would be her lot. She should be angry but she was beyond that. Anger required energy, and she had none left. But she might still be proud. Let a noose dangle from her neck; she would show the Siksika dogs that no noose and no abuse had broken a Kicked-in-the-Belly woman. She would sit so imperiously that they would know what she was, know that nothing they could do to her would break her pride or shame her. They would see her pride and wonder whether torture would shatter it. They would see her pride and envy her. The women in particular would torment her, cut her hair, jab at her, prick her flesh with knives, disfigure her, whip her, leave her naked to the cold. But they would not break her pride.

The war party paused at the edge of the village, which lay in a half-moon along a river they would ford to reach it. There they were greeted by the village wolves, the sentries always on guard against surprise. The villagers began to gather across the sparkling river, women, children, old men, and boys itching to be warriors. The boys would do her harm as she rode by, pelting her, jeering, running close with a stick to count coup, maybe even driving blunted arrows from their small bows into her. She had seen boys in her own village put out the eye of one captive and open the wounds of another until she bled over her skirts. She braced for that.

Then the war party descended the gravelly banks of the river and they forded the low, glittering stream, which rose only to the pasterns of the horses. Her captor jerked his line, yanking her by the neck until she nearly fell, but she clung to the mane of her pony. To fall was to die, because he would not stop dragging her. What better entertainment than for the village to witness the death of an enemy? She clung, absorbed each yank of the cord, kicked her pony forward to gain some slack in the braided cord. Now they were walking through an aisle between crowds of people. This was a large village; the Bloods were many.

The women began to keen; she knew that sound. Their eyes weren't upon those fresh Absaroka scalps dangling from lances but upon the burdened pony at the rear of the procession, upon the paint that told all who had eyes that this great victory was not without a price. The Bloods eyed her coldly, and she eyed them back, gaze for gaze, glare for glare, the stares locking. She did not surrender to their gaze. A rage to live rose in her; she was among the enemy and that became reason enough to survive. She would show these hated people what it meant to be Absaroka.

The boys she dreaded soon began walking beside her, shouting at her from both sides. She gripped the mane and held on. A rock stung her ribs, knocking breath from her. Then a youth darted close, a war club in hand, and swung it. The club landed on her shoulder, knocking her clear off her pony. She tumbled to the grass, felt the yank of line on her neck, flailed dizzily as the club found her skull, and then felt her head snapping under the tug of that cord. She crawled forward, not fast enough. Boys kicked at her, screaming their taunts. She grabbed hold of the line, let herself be dragged by it until she could put her bare feet under her. The line never stopped; her captor never slowed. She bounded up and forward, found her footing, and careened ahead. Her captor had speeded up, enjoying her desperation. The boy's war club found her back, knocking her to the ground, where she writhed. This time the line slackened. She heard a sharp male command, and the boy retreated. She was too spent to continue; hurting, tired, starved, so faint she couldn't even get to her knees. The Bloods swarmed about her, some taunting, others silent. She had to get up or die. She pulled herself to her hands and knees, staggered to her feet, felt blood welling from her head, pushed back tears and rage, and found herself glaring at the tormenting boy, a lean laughing youth on the brink of becoming a warrior. She slapped him. He was so astonished he didn't respond.

Then the village women swarmed in, pummeling her, knocking her to the ground. She felt pain welling up in her until it burst in her skull, and she fought and clawed at the swinging feet and hands. Then something hit her on the head, and she saw whiteness. She did not lose her senses, but she lost time and place in a wash of bewilderment. Everything hurt. She heard a sharp command, and the pounding slowed and then stopped. She lay bleeding on the grass. Someone carried her somewhere, darkness, a lodge, silence. No one tended her. She lay in gloom, wanting oblivion, her last strength gone. She had not known a mortal body could yield such pain to its possessor.

No one was about. She lay there, the ache not diminishing, the Bloods celebrating. Some were drumming and singing or dancing. She heard the steady heartbeat of the drummers. This night they would be celebrating a great victory, each of them telling of his role, boasting of his prowess, calling down his medicine. Those rich in captured ponies would give them away, one for a youth, another for a widow, one for a woman with many children, and the best buffalo runners and war ponies for their friends, their colleagues at arms. She heard the beat; the throb of the drums matched her pulse, and when the drums quickened, so did her pulse. She was grateful for the darkness, and wanted night, blackness to enfold her.

She did not know how long she lay there, only that it had been long. Then she grew aware of some stirring. Her eyelids were so swollen she could barely open them to see. Her captor sat in the place of honor, opposite the doorflap, leaning into a reed backrest. A woman handed him a bowl and a bone ladle. He quietly ate stew. They noticed Victoria staring but offered nothing.

She drifted into darkness again. She was allowed to lie in the place of least honor, next to the lodge door. No one gave her a robe. Ants crawled over her. She grew aware that this lodge sheltered others, mostly women, and two or three children, who whispered, pointed, poked her, and laughed. If she lay very still, almost not breathing, the pain lifted a little. To breathe was to hurt. She thought a rib might be broken; her shoulder was numb, and she could not move her left arm. Her head throbbed. A lump had formed on the side of her head, another just above the back of the neck. She could barely swallow, and she could not turn her head.

She lay adrift, the night passing through her brain like

dark clouds, the stars glittering and then vanishing, the moon racing. She thought of Skye, long lost, and loved him as she had when she first set eyes on him at a white man's rendezvous long ago. He had talked about strange things, his God, his long imprisonment, his desperate escape, the sacredness of marriage, his quest for peace, his hatred of slavery, his loathing of war. He would fight if he had to, she had seen that often during the years with the fur brigades; fight with the bear medicine he had received if war came to him. But he found no joy in it, sought no honor, and fought only for survival—or his liberty. She had left him, found his world not enough, played dangerous games with Beckwourth, and had come to this.

Chapter 31

Victoria drifted into something like sleep that wasn't sleep, and when she returned to consciousness light leaked through the smoke hole and the women of the lodge were arguing about her. She didn't understand a word, but she knew. They were gesticulating, pointing, examining her. She lay inert, enduring pain, barely able to move. Her throat and neck were so swollen she had trouble swallowing.

She could imagine what was agitating these women: whether to feed her, kill her, torture her, nurse her, or throw her out. She was an enemy of the people, brought to these women by the master of this lodge—a trophy of war. She lay on the dirt, barely caring, feeling ants crawl over her body, find their way through the rents in her dress, and march across lacerated and abused flesh.

The warrior was not present. She was at the mercy of these Blood women, and knew them to be masterful in all the arts of torture and abuse. Better at it than the men. But then an old woman halted the chatter, dipped a trader's tin cup in a kettle of water, and brought it to her. She tried to sit up to drink it, but couldn't. The woman helped her and pressed the cup to Victoria's lips. She drank slowly, barely able to swallow. The raging thirst didn't leave her, and she drank more. The old woman brought her buffalo meat that had been boiled into a sopping softness and fed her a little. Victoria couldn't swallow it but managed to down some broth, which miraculously poured strength into her. So, for the moment, they were succoring her. But for what reason she didn't know.

There were five women in the lodge: the old one, no doubt someone's mother; what appeared to be three wives, perhaps sisters; and a girl of perhaps twelve winters. Victoria suspected there had been more men present once, but they had either died in battle or of diseases. Maybe they had died in fights against her own people.

The village did not move that day, and she lay in the shade of the lodge, grateful to be left alone. Her hurts dominated her consciousness. It wasn't really possible to think of anything else except all the ways she ached. The warmth built; she could see blue sky above, a golden summer day. But she scarcely moved, barely aware of the traffic in and out, brushing past her as they entered and left the lodge. Thinking took too much effort, so she drifted through the day without dreams of freedom, escape, revenge, reconciliation, or anything else except a profound hatred of these Blackfeet.

That evening, as twilight purpled the village, she heard the sounds of drumming, singing, and dancing. So the celebration of their great victory was continuing. She knew she would be a part of it. They had kept her alive for their celebration, and not out of mercy, though she thought she felt some small tenderness in the old one's touch. They had fed her again late in the day, giving her the strength to know her fate this night.

Outside the lodge, the drumming throbbed through the village, lifting to climactic moments when the war singers cried out their victory chants, their medicine, their prayers. This celebration had its own mesmerizing effect on all of them, and even on her.

Two warriors pushed through the doorflap into the darkness of the lodge. One was her captor; the other she did not know. They found her too weak to stand or walk, so they dragged her out and carried her to a meadow lit by a small fire, purely for illumination on a warm night. Here the entire village had gathered in a loose circle; the drummers around two large drums, the chiefs and elders in bright ceremonial dress, the dancers in breechclouts, women holding small children, and restless packs of older children.

They carried her to the center, near the fire, and she supposed they would throw her on the fire and she would die shrieking from pain beyond imagining. Instead, the dancers circled, approached, and counted coup, each warrior striking her hard, the blow stinging, with foot or fist or a coup stick. The blows rained down one after another, each convulsing her, shooting red pain through her. She had no refuge. If she covered her head, the next blow might crack her knee or land on her arm. She felt her body spasm, felt her flesh howl. And yet they had taken no blood and didn't even consider this torture. This was a matter of war honors.

The drumming ceased, and for a few moments the blows stopped, although the pain didn't. Then the drumming began anew, and this time the chiefs and elders counted coup, their blows as rough as those of the warriors. And when she could no longer endure these, the rest of the village began to count coup, the women first, yanking her hair, kicking her, pounding her arm. And after that the children, some of them more cruel than the rest, jabbing her with sharp sticks that did pierce her and bleed her. And then the very old, some of them gentle, ritually touching her and doing no harm.

She lay in a stupor, confused, her body a monstrous alien thing she didn't know and couldn't bear. Now they would toss her on the fire and listen to her death throes. But they didn't, for some reason. Perhaps they thought she was too far gone to know her own end. The drumming ceased; quietness came, and she sensed they were leaving her there to her fate. To die or not, the Absaroka dog among them. She could barely breathe; her lungs were almost paralyzed by the pain in her ribs and breasts. She could not swallow at all.

Then she was alone, and the coolness of the night took some of her fever out of her and lessened the pain a little. She felt the hard earth under her, unyielding, relentless, destroying exactly as much life as it nurtured, her few moments of life momentarily defying the rock and clay and water.

They had not tortured her, but the result was worse. They had feasted upon her, each coup an act of war, each blow rising from their primeval lust to destroy enemies.

It had been worse than torture. Now, after sustaining two or three hundred coups, more than she could count, she bore the venom of a whole village in her bosom. Each blow had taken something from her.

She drifted again, her mind awhirl as the night cooled and her body complained. She wished she could have a drink, but she could not manage to walk, or even crawl, to the stream. Was this war? Was this what Skye hated so much? She wished she had listened to him, instead of mocking him with a girl's foolish fancies. Tears formed in her eyes, but her face was too swollen to release them, and they clung to her lids, blurring her vision of the night, even as this night had blurred her vision of the world.

She sensed someone stirring near her, wondered whether she would now die of a knife wound. But someone—a woman—lifted her head, let her drink from a gourd dipper, and again. Cool water, yes, and more. Some distilled herb gave it a bitter flavor. Her benefactor pulled an ancient buffalo robe around her, rolling her onto it so that she was encased in it. The hands were young and soft. Now tears came, sliding down her cheeks, welling hotly in eyes that could not see. This one bade her to sip again, and she did greedily, slowly swallowing one sip after another. Who was this one, this Siksika woman? What sweetness—or pity, or mercy—inspired her to comfort her enemy? The woman cradled Victoria's head in her lap, crooning softly, wiping away Victoria's tears and washing her face gently, speaking in her unknown tongue, words miraculously understood.

"I am Magpie," said the woman. "Magpie, of the Kainah people, and I am here to comfort you. You are very brave and very beautiful, and you will grow strong again."

Victoria wept softly. Magpie, Magpie, her spirit-helper, the One she had defied, ignored, pushed away.

"You love your people as I love mine," the woman said, and Victoria couldn't fathom how she understood, but she did. "Your husband will find you," she said.

"He is gone," Victoria mumbled.

The woman didn't reply, but lifted the gourd dipper, and Victoria drank again. The herb was slowly and sweetly erasing her pain and making her sleepy.

The woman slid aside and arranged the robe. "When Sun comes, we will go from here. If you are well enough, you will go as a slave; if you cannot rise, you will die with one blow of the war ax, and your scalp will dangle from your captor's lance."

"Magpie," Victoria said.

The woman stood, and Victoria saw her staring down. Then the woman slipped into the blackness and Victoria lay alone, and yet not entirely alone. The herbal tea gave her rest and respite from pain, and she dozed in a cocoon of warmth. Somewhere in this village was a woman whose love reached even to the enemies of her people. Victoria wondered whether, among the Kicked-in-the-Bellies, there was any woman with such love. She wished there were. Maybe, if she ever returned, she would be such a woman. She was no longer the person she had been just a few hours earlier, accepting everything her people had taught her, laughing at Skye, never questioning whether other ways of life might be better. Now she questioned. A Siksika woman named Magpie had opened the door to a new life.

When she awakened in the gray before dawn, she found herself on the bare earth again, the robe gone. Perhaps she had imagined the succor she had received. She hurt.

And yet she knew that she had been restored to life and that some merciful woman among the Siksika had given her precious gifts. She made herself sit up, knowing she would soon be put to a test that could lead to her doom if she failed. She stood, blessed Father Sun, walked shakily to the burbling creek, washed, avoided looking at her reflection in the water for fear of what she would see, and stood again. She scrubbed her body, dipped her long jet hair in the chill creek and felt the water play with it, washed away the filth upon her even as she washed away the darkness in her heart. Skye had talked about something like this once. He had called it baptism, a washing and a dedication. Those were his ways, not hers, but now she remembered.

She could walk, but only in a sea of shocking pain. Her groin hurt. The muscles in her limbs howled. Her head throbbed, her throat barely permitted passage of air and water and food. And yet she walked. She walked a step, two, five, fifty. She paused, addressing Sun and Morning Star and the morning breeze, lifting her aching arms to them, her back arched, her fingertips reaching toward the heavens.

They were watching, but she didn't care. They were watching a new woman. She would give herself a new name, or maybe wait for one to come to her. If ever she saw the old seer, Red Turkey Comb, she would tell him her story, leaving out nothing, and ask him for a name. Many of them had gathered beside the meadow, along the stream, and now they all watched her. She stood in prayer, the sweetest and most urgent prayer of all her twenty winters.

She saw the black-and-white bird, its iridescent feathers glowing in the dawn sun, and apologized to her spirit-helper, and thanked the wise bird. Then she walked slowly, but like the woman of a great chief, slowly toward the lodge of her captor. She could barely remember the way, but she would find him and present herself to him, a woman of the enemy made new.

Chapter 32

Victoria found the lodge of her captor and entered. He was gone, probably collecting the horses that would transport his Blood family. The several women stared at her purpled and blackened flesh. One of them, a squinty, hard-faced woman, gestured for her to help. They were rolling up robes, stuffing things into the parfleches, dismantling her captor's backrest

No one offered her food. She saw some pemmican, shredded meat, fat and berries stuffed into buffalo gut, and she reached for it only to have the meal dashed from her hand. The woman shouted something at her, gesturing imperiously. Victoria expected to be beaten, but she hadn't the strength to work, especially without food. So she lay down in the place of least honor beside the oval door and waited for the blows to rain down.

She was not disappointed. The mistress of the lodge loomed over her with a whip and lashed it across Victoria's shoulder. But two younger women intervened, and a heated debate ensued. Victoria did not understand a word but hoped it would last long enough so that the new pain would fade a little. She curled on the bare earth, awaiting her fate.

One of the younger women gave her some pemmican. Victoria nibbled slowly, having trouble swallowing. She wasn't hungry after all. The other women ignored her, hauling parfleches out the door and then unpinning the lodgecover. It slid down the lodgepoles, filling interior shadow with sun. Victoria lay inertly, watching, grateful for the small mercy of lying there. Her captor returned, leading four horses, surveyed his women, studied her, and went off for more horses. It took many to move a lodge. The women talked with him about her but nothing came of it.

The women began bundling the lodgepoles and anchoring the bundles on either side of a swaybacked old horse. The household parfleches they hung on the packsaddles of the other horses. The heavy lodgecover they folded and laid on a travois. Around them, their neighbors were loading up in similar fashion, everyone working, even small children. The village was being swiftly dismantled, and very soon they would all be heading for the next place— wherever the seers, the village chief, the war chief, and the elders decided.

Her captor returned with four more ponies, better ones, all of them saddled. The women tied smaller burdens to these riding horses while her captor vanished one more time. The town crier drifted through the village, announcing something—probably the imminent departure of this Kainah village. Her captor returned, this time with his own mounts, five of them in all, some still painted with his war medicine.

Then the village began to form a column. The women of the lodge clambered into their saddles, hiking their skirts to ride. The youngest girl and the old man rode her captor's war and buffalo ponies. There were two horses left over, and Victoria wondered whether one would carry her. The man who had captured her barked words at her, and she understood them all right. Walk or die. She was the enemy.

This day she would die. She could not walk for long, not in her condition. She gazed at the instrument of her death dangling from her captor's waist. It was a war club, a shaped stone bound by rawhide into a forked haft. Sometime this day it would bash in her skull and they would leave her to the crows and coyotes.

Still, she would try. She would never surrender. She would walk until she dropped, and then get up and walk again. She would walk on her bare feet until they bled and every step tortured her, but she would walk. She would show these, her enemies, that she was worthy of their respect. She would show them what an Absaroka woman could be. So when the procession began, she forced one foot ahead of the other, step upon step, ignoring the pain that lanced through her with each movement. They watched her, curious, and that was good. She wanted them to watch.

They were heading east and south on a fine day in the month Skye called May, no doubt looking for buffalo and good prairie grasses to fatten their ponies, or maybe opportunities to torment their enemies. Victoria walked carefully, not wishing to wound her feet. Like all the People, she had walked barefoot much of her life and her soles had hardened. But now that her life hung by a thread, she took care where she stepped.

The pace was slow, accommodating the grandmothers and grandfathers, all the children, and the harried mothers who had to beat on slow horses, kick the dogs away, and see to it that nothing came undone or was lost.

The pace blessed Victoria. She could endure that but no more. Her captor rode a spirited white horse and disappeared for long stretches, mostly to ride in the vanguard with other leading men of the village. When he did return, Victoria took the opportunity to scrutinize this man whose whim governed her life—and death. He spoke little to the women, eyed her noncommittally, and showed every sign of being a powerful warrior, or a subchief. He lived for war, and maybe for the hunt, and wore the honors of battle, two notched eagle feathers, inserted in a bun of hair. at the nape of his neck. Who was this hard man, and what did he think of her?

The village settled into its travel routine, and now women visited with one another, children knotted together and raced up and down the procession making mischief and alarming horses until someone rebuked them. A few little ones rode in reed baskets attached to travois or in their mothers' arms. An old woman fell in beside Victoria and began talking in the Absaroka tongue, which astonished the captive.

"You are the one they talk about," she said. "I can speak the Absaroka tongue. When I was young, ten winters, your people took me away from my lodge and I grew up in one of your villages. I missed my people. One day I was married to one of your warriors and bore him two sons and a daughter. Then he died, fighting the Lakota. I went home; no one stopped me. Now I am a Kainah again."

Victoria knew that this simple story concealed much of a lifetime within it, but it was not the way of most people to dwell long upon such things. Maybe this was the one who came in the night with the herbal tea and the robe.

"Who are you?"

"I will not give my name to a dog. My name is for the People, not for you."

"They talk about me?"

"They say that for an Absaroka dog, you are brave."

"Who is my captor?"

"He is Grandfather of Wolves. That is his new name. Before, he was Cut Face. And before that, Little Fawn. Our chief, Crow Dog, gave him the name, which is sacred to us. Grandfather of Wolves is a name that makes people quiet when they hear it."

"Why was he given this name?"

"No Kainah is more like a wolf, and he is the grandfather of them all."

"Will he kill me?"

"You are an Absaroka dog."

"Did the Absaroka people treat you badly?"

"I was the enemy."

"Do you think your people should make war on my people?"

"The Absaroka are dogs."

"Did you feel that way when you lived with us?"

"Always."

"Were my people so different?"

The woman reflected a moment before replying. "They are not the People. We are the People."

"Then why do you talk to me?"

The woman laughed. "Just to find out."

"Will they put me to death?"

"They should. I myself would cut slices of flesh from you or burn you with embers. It would be good. But Grandfather of Wolves has not said it is to be done. Maybe he will soon. It is said you will bring misfortune on the

People, and maybe the chiefs will say it. Then you will die."

Victoria felt a new wave of weariness crawl through her. Only the slow pace of this procession kept her from stumbling to the earth. But they had not paused all morning, and she knew she wouldn't last no matter how strong her spirit was.

"I was married to a yellow eyes who hates war."

"That is the way of them. We will drive them away. He is a coward, then."

"No, he is the best warrior I have ever seen. He has the medicine of the bear."

The old woman grew agitated. "Then he is the fiercest warrior of all and will hurt my people. I will not talk to an Absaroka dog anymore," she said, and hurried away.

Victoria was glad to be left alone. She was desperate now, and needed to concentrate on walking, because to fall would be to die. She edged over to the side of a travois and leaned on it, letting her body rest against it and letting it drag her along. But the old woman of the lodge spotted her and shouted curses at her and threatened to club her until she withdrew her hand and stumbled ahead.

She reeled forward, stumbled, found her footing, and walked a while more, her flesh defying her spirit and her muscles like wax. They were traversing open plains, far from water or shelter, the long line of villagers protected by vedettes out to the sides, along with a rear guard and scouts ahead. There would be no escaping, no disappearing here upon an ocean of young green grass. She tried again to find support, this time behind a horse whose tail she caught and held. This time the fierce old woman caught her instantly and bounded toward her, a thick stick in hand, and arced it menacingly. Victoria let go.

She was all used up, scarcely half a day into this passage. She could walk no more. She glanced about, seeing the sunlit meadows rife with yellow wildflowers, bold blue sky, the brooding Sweet Grass Hills to the northeast, the circling hawks high above. Tears came unbidden, not because she was about to die but because of the aching beauty of this land, which stirred her heart. She had lost.

She reeled to the warm earth, which received her gently, the soil still soft from winter's snow. She pulled herself up so she might sit cross-legged and wait for the blow. And she began to sing her death song.

> I am Many Quill Woman.
> I am Victoria, named by yellow eyes Skye.
> I have seen the good world, and the flowers.
> I am one of the People.
> Now I will walk upon the long trail to the stars.

This she sang, once, twice, and again, scarcely aware of the Siksika gathering around. But then she found herself in shadow and looked to see what blocked the sun.

Chapter 33

I t was not her day to die. Her captor lifted her onto his buffalo-running pony, and that was that. She clung to the mane, barely able to stay on the lively horse, but this was the gift of life so she gripped the thick mane in small fists and hung on.

The Bloods stopped early that day beside a lively creek dotted with willows and brush. Grandfather of Wolves lifted her off the pony and took the pony away. His women ignored her, for which she was grateful. She wondered what he had in mind. Whatever her fate, she lay in warm grass now as the villagers set up camp for the night. Few raised lodges, because the sky was cloudless. They would cook and sleep in the open, even though the predawn chill might put frost on their robes. She hoped they would give her a robe against the night cold.

They seemed to be drifting out upon the plains, almost aimlessly but actually heading toward buffalo grounds. Or perhaps to make war on the Assiniboine, who lived in this easterly direction. Since she could not speak with these people, she really didn't know. She had not seen the old woman again, so she had no one to talk to.

Her body still hurt from the coup counting. She dragged herself to the creek, drank and washed, and then lay down. Her captor's women paid little heed. They would tax her with hard work later, when her body was ready. That they didn't demand anything of her now was clue enough: she would be a slave, a dumb animal put to their use.

Was that better than death? She faced loneliness until she could master their tongue, and she faced drudgery. But most of life was drudgery. Hard work absorbed the energies of any woman of the People. There was always too much to do: firewood, cooking, fleshing and tanning hides, making moccasins, preparing pemmican, berry gathering, root digging, beading, quilling, making lodges, making clothing, packing and unpacking lodges, dealing with horses, children, dogs, and guests. These things she would be doing for this Blood lodge. But it would be different because she would be under command and have not the slightest freedom of her own. Her life no longer belonged to her.

That is how the next suns spun out. As soon as her broken body mended they put her to work, always at the meanest and hardest tasks. They did give her a robe to sleep in; she would be of no value to them sickened by cold. Was this her life? She remembered the laughing girl in the village; the harder, lonelier life with Skye and all the trappers whose tongue she didn't know. But at least she had Skye then, and the trappers were friendly, not enemies forcing her into slavery. Those were idyllic times compared to what she was experiencing now.

The Moon of New Leaves passed, and the Moon of Buffalo Calves, and she toiled ceaselessly for the Bloods, who continued to drift south and east, enjoying the spring and anticipating the high, sweet days of summer. Each day, as the village drifted, riders rode out to find the buffalo, but they rarely found any except a few old bulls that had abandoned the herd or had been driven out. That meat wasn't good but it sustained them. No one ever went hungry, including their new Absaroka slave.

They reached the Big River, the river Skye called the Missouri, one afternoon. It ran high and swift, bank to bank, carrying the mountain snows far away. Skye said the water went to the seas, many suns away. The Blood seers and elders paused there, watching the swift cold waters, and elected not to cross. There was no need, and it would endanger the old ones, and the children, and maybe some horses, too. They would wait to make war on the Absaroka, and meanwhile look for buffalo and perform the spring ceremonies. Soon all the Siksika would gather for the opening of the beaver bundle. Then, in a while, would come the Sun Dance, the high, sacred time of the year. Skye had compared it to the Easter of the white men.

Maybe they would ritually torture and sacrifice her for that dance. But she doubted it. She was learning a little of their tongue—when the women of the lodge told her to cut wood or scrape hide, she understood. When they told her to leave or come or cook or not to think too highly of herself, she understood. Sometimes they were almost friendly—not that they spoke to her or attempted to befriend her. But a small smile or a little touch of a hand spoke worlds to her.

They camped on the Missouri a while, watching the Big River deliver its water to the lands far to the east. That was when Grandfather of Wolves came to her in the night. Two of his women were in the menstrual hut, so he came to her robes beside the doorflap and pulled the robes open and pierced her swiftly and forcefully. He had captured her; that was his right. She did not respond. Grandfather of Wolves would never be her beloved, and by lying quietly she let him know that. But he didn't seem to mind. In a moment he was gone, but those in the lodge, the grandfather and grandmother and the daughters, all knew, and so something had changed. Victoria did not hear the sounds of sleep for a while. She wondered if she would have the child that she and Skye never had. If so, it would be taken from her and raised a Blood. As a slave she could not even possess the child of her womb.

One day some Piegans visited the camp: fifty-six warriors, no women, and en route to the south, where they would kill Absarokas and capture many horses. Victoria watched them bitterly. These were powerful warriors, seasoned, mostly older men, ready to destroy her people if they could. They conferred with their Blood relatives, smoked in the lodge of the chief, a great circle of elders, war chiefs, leaders, and seers, and then the Piegans stripped, swam their ponies across the flooded river, having great trouble doing it, and collected on the other side, dripping cold water. Within a day or two they would make widows and capture slaves and kill many. She hoped the Kicked-in-the-Bellies—if that was the village to be assaulted—would be ready for a fight and that Beckwourth would defeat the invaders. But somehow she doubted it. Beckwourth loved to raid; he loved spoils, but would he defend a village?

The Bloods drifted along the river, finding deer and an occasional elk to feed them. The great river ran between steep bluffs, having cut a channel deep into the surrounding plains. Now the western mountains were no longer in sight. She wondered when the Bloods would settle down for a long encampment. Every day or two, they packed up and wandered once again, restlessly whiling away the sweet days. Soon after the summer solstice, when Father Sun reached highest in the heaven and had almost vanquished night, they and all the Siksika would gather at some prearranged place for the sacred dance of summer.

Then one day, out on a neck of land between the Big River and the one the Blackfeet called *Kaiyi Isisakta,* Bear River, they came to a small log cabin hastily thrown together from cottonwoods and chinked with mud. A pen for horses was attached. A narrow flat separated the post from the Big River. Some yellow eyes were building bullboats there and were nearly done. They had stretched hides over one willow frame and sewn them tight, and now were sealing them. So they would soon be leaving. She learned that this was a new trading post. The Piegans had told them about it. Not many goods left, but maybe some powder and lead and arrow points; maybe a war ax or lance point or two. Good things to have when killing the Absaroka. They would trade here.

So the lodges went up. They would stay a while. Victoria helped put up the lodge of Grandfather of Wolves and move the household items into it. But she was curious about the yellow eyes, as her people called them, and soon she would slip away to peek at them. There were only three, two lighter, one dark, almost like one of the People. But maybe there were more inside the cabin. The three stopped building and went into the cabin to trade. She hoped they had nothing to trade. The Bloods wanted guns and knives and hatchets and lance points to kill her people.

The women of her lodge did not let her leave it; indeed, they told her not to go to the white men or she would die. They were only three. If she tried to escape, they would kill her—and the white men. Victoria registered that and knew she must obey. So it was that the village traded and she stayed close to the lodge of Grandfather of Wolves. The Bloods grumbled because these traders didn't have much left and were about to go down the river, taking their pelts with them. Some of the younger Bloods wanted to kill the white men, take the pelts, and trade them at Hudson's Bay for lots of fusils and powder and balls.

All this she heard with her quickening understanding of the Siksika tongue. She learned there was an older one who was chief of traders, another who was dark and had warm brown eyes, and another who had blue eyes, a stocky build, and a big nose, the grandfather of noses. The description made her think of Skye, but he would not be here. This was not even the same white men's company. This was another company, not Fitzpatrick, or Bridger, or Sublette. Skye was far away, going to the place where he learned things. These traders were very cautious and did not much show themselves. They obviously feared the powerful Bloods, who could destroy them in a moment.

So the Bloods traded for the last of the goods, grumbled about the place, debated whether to destroy it so these traders could not trade with the Cree or Assiniboine or Lakota, and decided to let it alone. The traders had told them they had built the post to trade with the Siksika and would be back in a while with many more goods and would pay a good price for beaver.

The women of the lodge were disappointed. The traders had no ribbons or beads left, and only a little cloth, which the chief's wives took. Night fell, and word came from the crier that the Blood people would leave in the morning. She dreamed restlessly that night, her thoughts on Skye, her love for him building day by day as her captivity continued. She scarcely thought of Beckwourth. He had appealed to the girl; Skye had evoked the woman.

The next dawn the village dismantled itself, poorer in pelts and richer in the tools of war and implements of cooking. They had cleaned out the traders of every last pot and flint and fire steel and knife and arrow point. The traders rose early to watch the Bloods leave, and now they even wandered among them.

That was when she saw Skye. There was no doubt. That build, that rolling seaman's gait, that nose, those eyes. She stared unbelieving, speechless, as he and the dark one wandered past the busy Bloods.

"Skye!" she cried.

He whirled, saw her, mouth agape.

"Help me, Skye!"

The women of the lodge swarmed over her, shouting and pulling her hair and dragging her away from the white man.

"Victoria!" he yelled. He hastened toward the lodge, but Blood warriors casually blocked the way.

That was the last she saw of him.

Chapter 34

Skye stood, paralyzed. Victoria was a captive. He started toward the lodge where he had glimpsed her, but Blood warriors swiftly blocked the way. One, a large man with a scarred face, threatened to kill him—the gesture was unmistakable—if he proceeded.

That was the last he saw of her, but her cry to him seared his soul. Somehow she had been taken a prisoner. That was rare enough; the usual fate of an Absaroka prisoner was death. Skye watched the Bloods pack and saddle and depart, heading who knows where, with Victoria among them. There were a hundred adult women in the village, and he could not tell her from the others. And none of them looked back.

He knew he should forget it. She had abandoned him for another. She had been unfaithful. She had laughed at him and scorned his ways. He could not think of one good reason to try to rescue her. He had other plans now. He had debts to pay to two fur companies, a trip east in mind, and dreams of a life back in civilization. What's more, he couldn't just leave his two colleagues here; he was needed to take the peltries down to Fort Union.

That's what his mind told him. His heart spoke otherwise. Her cry for help tore him to bits. If she needed him, he would help her. Somehow, some way, he would free her. But how? Walk into a Blood village and—steal her? Buy her? Trade for her? No white man walked into a Blackfoot village alone, not even Berger, who had befriended a few of them. Skye knew what would happen if he pursued: the village guards would catch him, torture him to death as slowly as possible, making the torment extralong for a white man. He knew only a smattering of words and couldn't make himself understood. He knew the hand language, or some of it, but he doubted it would help him.

"What be ye staring at, Skye?"

"My wife, Victoria. She's a prisoner."

"A Crow. Forget it. Ye walk into that village askin' for her, and they'd slit her throat and hand her to ye. The Cree named'em Bloods for good reason. They got bloody hands. Some say it's because they paint up with red earth, but that's not it. You're talking about *bloody Bloods.*"

"I have to get her out."

"Skye, damn me, do ye like being hung by your feet from a limb and having your living brains roasted over a fire?"

"You could go after her—she's not a mile away. Here—trade my rifle for her."

"You're crazy, Skye. Forget her. Find another mountain wife if that's what devils ye."

"She cried out for help."

Berger contemplated Skye for a moment. "Come on

now, Skye. I've traded for a few bufflerhides, enough to build the second bullboat. Them Bloods don't have any too many horses, and they wouldn't trade. But they had hides aplenty. Now, I'm tellin' ye, get to work. We've got to get on down the river."

Berger was right. Skye knew he had to let go of the past. Victoria had been a happy interlude in his young life. It had come to a bad end, but he wouldn't remember that. When he was old and comfortable as a merchant, he might quietly invoke the memory of her glowing beauty, and the wild free days lived close to campfire smoke, and the sweetness of her kiss, and he would know he had been blessed.

He walked listlessly to the frame of the second bullboat. Arquette was already at work, shaping a green buffalohide to the frame.

"What be de trouble?" the Creole said, surveying Skye.

"My wife. I saw her in that village. She's a captive. She cried out to me but they hustled her off."

"Ah, one squaw's good as another. You wan' a good life, try variety, *oui*? We get you three, four nice Cree ladies and you forget this wan, I think."

"I love her."

"But she don't love you, eh? Not from what you tell us."

She loved him. He knew that. She loved him in spite of all that had happened with Beckwourth. He felt a weight on him so heavy he could barely lift his hands.

"Skye, we build dis boat now."

But the more Skye tried to work again, the more his mind wandered. He mostly just stared at the horizon where the Bloods had vanished, until Arquette roundly cursed him in two tongues.

"*Merde,* Skye! You not worth a sou this day."

Listlessly, Skye did work after that, his mind elsewhere. But one by one the hides were shaped, laced to each other, and the seams caulked. They could leave for Fort Union in the morning, Skye with his horses, Berger and Arquette each in a loaded bullboat.

The afternoon ebbed as the pair pulled the upside-down bullboat frame out of the earth and bound the hides to the gunnels.

"You no say ten word this afternoon," Arquette grumbled. "You deciding you go get yourself kill for a little Crow lady."

Skye had been deciding exactly that. He didn't respond. They finished the boat, tethered it with a line, and tested it on the swift current. They found half a dozen leaks, and set to work with tallow and pitch once again. Skye distrusted the miserable, light, leather-lined boats, and was glad he wasn't being required to steer one clear to Fort Union.

That evening he sank into a deep melancholy, saying not a word to either of his partners. Berger's sharp glances and headshaking told Skye what the others thought, but they left him alone and didn't try to dissuade him. If he was mad enough to get himself killed for a faithless little squaw, then there was nothing they could do about it. Skye didn't sleep that night. The image of Victoria, her cry for help, and the swift harsh response from the Bloods, returned to his mind over and over, keeping him up and deviling him. He rose in the morning in a black mood, weary and despairing.

They loaded packs of beaver into the bullboats and then added heavy packs of buffalo robes and assorted other peltries, including luxurious ermine, mink, weasel, otter, elk, and deer. The amazing little craft could haul enormous loads. Then Berger loaded Skye's packhorse with still more beaver plews, as well as Skye's kit.

"All right, Skye. We'll see you at the fort. Don't waste a minute. You'll beat us because of all the oxbows in the river." He squinted at Skye. "Don't let me down."

Skye nodded. So Berger had even discerned Skye's temptation and was warning him. Skye ached simply to ride away, forget the debts, forget his sixty-dollar income—which he would receive only if he completed his tour at this post—forget it all and go get her—somehow.

"I'll go straight to the post," he said.

"If you don't . . ." Berger didn't complete his thought.

He helped Berger and Arquette clamber into their wobbly craft and shove off. Each had a pole and crude paddle for steering and dodging rocks and rapids.

Then he was alone. Now Victoria was ten, fifteen, twenty miles gone. He climbed onto his black horse, untied the dun, and led it along a trail that soon took him far from the Missouri. He would rarely be close to the river all the way back. He rode listlessly, as if his whole life had bled away from him. If the world was a paradise in June, he didn't notice it. He had turned inward, seeing nothing but the images stamped upon his soul. He missed the last of the spring wildflowers, the red-winged blackbirds and meadowlarks, the emerald grasses swiftly growing their seedheads, the turtles and frogs in the sloughs, the antelope that watched him from the crown of a hill, and the constant signs of passage—the hoofprints of large Indian migrations. He had not eyes to see, and didn't know that a few ticks of the clock earlier—or later—he might have stumbled into the clutches of Lakota, Assiniboine, Cree, and any of several bands of Blackfeet.

Thus he progressed to Fort Union like a blind man, having lost all his wilderness caution. And yet Fate—or was it the magpies he kept seeing—spared him a fool's death. He had become the ultimate tenderfoot. He saw nothing in that sea of grass that could hurt him, though a thousand perils lurked in every league. Even the weather seemed to respect his madness: the looming thundershowers that built up each afternoon veered away, as if determined not to soak or chill a man out of his head. The winds, which normally howled through the empty grasslands, quieted themselves and politely eddied past him, having mercy upon an innocent.

His journey took him on a wide loop around the breaks of the Missouri, around the oxbows that doubled the water miles to the post, but he didn't notice. The hours slipped by in quiet march, and he knew that he would not go down the river to St. Louis, and he knew he would outfit again at Fort Union, using his sixty dollars, and go get her and take her home, wherever his home would be. He would find that band of Bloods and her, and nothing would come between him and Victoria ever again.

He rode into Fort Union unmolested. A long keelboat bobbed at anchor on the levee beside the post. It had brought forty tons of trade goods and resupply to Fort Union from the village of Independence, a thousand water miles distant, all of it hauled upriver by pole and sail and cordelle, employing wind and the muscle of the Creole voyageurs. He eyed the long low craft and knew he would not go down the river aboard it.

From McKenzie, who received him in his suite, he learned he had arrived ahead of Berger and Arquette. The iron-willed factor questioned Skye closely about how the trading had gone, and Skye answered. Yes, a good season. Sold out all trade items, garnered fifteen packs of beaver, plenty of other pelts, all very successful. And yes, AFC should build a permanent post at that site and trade with the Blackfeet. They had plenty of well-cured pelts. And yes, last Skye knew, Berger and Arquette were on the river in two large bullboats and due soon.

"Good. You've proved that our strategy works. The company owns the river. And now we'll own the Blackfoot trade clear to the shining mountains. Now, let's talk about you. What's the matter with you, Skye?" McKenzie asked. "Something sure as hell is wrong."

"The matter? Nothing, mate."

"I've talked with you for an hour. Where are you? You aren't here, that I know."

Skye shrugged.

"Did you see any Indians?"

"No, sir."

"Odd. We've had half a dozen bands stop here. And every day we pick up rumors of big fights, bloody wars, horse thievery, massacres . . . outrages. You must have seen a dozen war parties. We feared all three of you would perish."

"No, sir."

"It's a miracle you still have your hair."

"I've changed my plans, sir. I wish to draw my sixty dollars, pay you something, and reoutfit myself. I'll be staying in the mountains."

"Something happened. Tell me what."

"Nothing, sir."

McKenzie's piercing gaze missed nothing, but his keen mind missed everything. "You are mad," he said.

Chapter 35

It was madness. And it was love. In one piercing moment, as fleeting as a heartbeat, everything had changed. Victoria needed him.

In the post store, Skye replenished sparingly, but bought ample powder and precast lead balls for his rifle. The rest he agonized over: he needed something to trade for Victoria if it came to that. And peace offerings. He purchased ten plugs of tobacco for that. For trading he purchased a pair of blankets, which the Indians coveted, a kettle and knife, some awls, hanks of beads, and a bolt of red flannel. That was all he could afford, and it probably would not buy Victoria's freedom. He allowed himself some tea and sugar, paid fifty-nine dollars for the lot, and pocketed a dollar.

Kenneth McKenzie hovered about, wild with curiosity but shamming disinterest. "Where are you going, Mister Skye?" he demanded, abruptly.

"I'm going to the Blackfeet."

"The Blackfeet, are you? The Blackfeet! Then I've seen the last of you. I ought to prevent it, but I know better. Why are you going to the Blackfeet?"

Skye could not answer that one. There were things one had to do, however mad they seemed. "Just say I'm out of my head, sir."

"That you are. Well, I'll get the story from Berger. He ought to arrive today or tomorrow. Is there something about the Blackfeet I don't know?"

"No, sir."

"Which Blackfeet?"

"The Bloods."

"Ah, the Bloods, mostly living in British possessions. The Bloods, eh? Nice friendly people, the Bloods."

Skye laughed, loaded his new goods onto his pack-saddle, and tipped his hat. He lifted himself into the saddle and steered the horses through the massive double gate.

"Skye, dammit, I'll never see you again."

"That's right," Skye replied.

"Well, you're mad, but I wish you success, whatever you're up to. If anyone can succeed, you can." McKenzie offered Skye his hand, which Skye took. "Good-bye, Barnaby Skye," the factor said softly.

Skye rode west, feeling the stares on his back. He followed a trail that would take him past the little post on the Marias. It wound far away from the Missouri, across empty flats where there would be no place to hide.

Alone at last, he began to calculate the ways he might free Victoria, and the more he contemplated that task, the more daunting and hopeless it seemed. He knew a few words he had picked up trading, but these weren't enough to help him. How would he ask other Blackfeet where the Bloods had gone, and especially this band of Bloods? How would he say he wanted to trade for an Absaroka woman held captive by one of those bands? Who would translate, pave the way, help him? How could he make his peaceful intentions clear, keep himself from dying a lonely death on the prairies, find allies, enter a camp of people who relished the scalps of any white men they could find?

Did he have the courage?

He didn't. He was deathly afraid.

Why was he doing this?

For Victoria. It was utterly simple. It defied the sort of calculation of prudent men, weighing risk against reward. It came down to Victoria. He would do what he had to do. And probably die soon. Or worse, see her death as a result of his efforts.

Unlike his passage to Fort Union, he was alive to menace now. He scanned the rolling prairies for signs of trouble, studied the morning heavens for columns of smoke, kept below skylines wherever he could, examined each slough for fresh hoofprints. He saw more signs of travel than he wanted to see this far from the Blackfeet. He was still in lands dominated by Assiniboine and Cree.

He camped in hollows, built fires out of sight, studied the whole country before risking a shot at game. He watched his back trail, climbed hills where he could see for miles behind him. So far, at least, he had dodged war and hunting parties. But when would his luck run out?

One fine morning he reached the trading post on the Marias—or what was left of it. The Blackfeet had promptly burned it, and all that remained were some charred foundation logs. He shuddered. So little did they want traders in their land that they had destroyed the little cabin hours after it had been abandoned. The surrounding meadow glowed serenely in the blinding sun, as if nothing sinister had ever happened there. He was in Blackfoot country now, with no more plan than when he started. But one thing had been building in him: he needed a guide and translator, someone who could take him to the various bands of Bloods and help him negotiate. And keep him alive.

He knew of only one band of the Bloods, the Fish-Eaters, so named because they alone among the Blackfeet ate fish. Hardly any Plains Indians ate fish. Victoria loathed them, and stared appalled whenever the trappers filleted and cooked trout for dinner.

Where would he find a guide, and how would he pay for one? He did not know. But maybe if he rode a while, he would find one, or one would find him. He ransacked his skimpy knowledge of these people, seeking a way. Eventually he thought he might have one. He needed to find the Little Robes. They were nominally Piegans, but so independent of them that, in a way, they were almost a fourth nation in the Blackfoot Federation. Berger had said they were more hospitable to their neighbors—to some small degree. There were occasions when Absaroka and Little Robe hunting parties had feasted together, proclaiming a truce during a good buffalo hunt. Maybe a Little Robe would take Skye to the Bloods.

Then there were the Gros Ventres, mooching "cousins" of the Piegans, whose lengthy visits were not entirely welcome among the Blackfeet. Maybe Skye could engage one of those people to help him. But it wasn't an option he relished. He needed a bona fide Blackfoot Indian to take him into the heart of their country—and get him out alive, with Victoria.

For five more days he rode into Blackfoot country. The Stony Mountains formed a wall ahead, still tipped with white. The Piegans called it the Backbone of the World, a good description of a feature that sliced off the Great Plains from everything to the west. He startled with every flight of a crow, broke out in sweat every time an antelope ran, fought fear whenever he saw signs of horse passage. Yet he saw no one, and the imagined terrors loomed larger than any real ones.

He camped one evening on the Marias, which he had

followed northwest for days. He chose a well-concealed gulch with cottonwoods that would diffuse his woodsmoke and a seep for himself and his horses. The darkness seemed slow to come that time of year—probably July, though he had lost track—and light lingered across the northwestern heavens. He had been struggling to find food and had not used his rifle for fear of drawing Bug's Boys down upon him. But he thought he might fish the Marias for some trout. He slipped through dense cottonwoods to reach the river—and smelled woodsmoke. He ducked back into the twilight of the cottonwoods and studied the river flats. To the west was an encampment of some sort. His pulse leapt. He edged toward the camp, peering through a screen of alder and willow brush, and discovered twenty or thirty male Indians, either a war party or a hunting party, or both. They weren't painted. Most wore low summer moccasins, and he could not tell their color. He had learned anyway that most tribes made moccasins from the smoke-blackened upper hides of a lodge. The smoke and grease cured the hide, turned water, and added toughness to the leather.

His every instinct was to flee for his life. These men were tall, powerfully built, athletic, and looked entirely capable of murdering him on the spot. He crept away, his back itching with the anticipation of an arrow. Back in his own camp, he faced the dilemma: the Blackfeet terrified him, and yet he needed to make contact if he wanted to find Victoria.

There was only one thing to do: ride in. He would do it on horseback, because if he needed to escape, he would have his possessions with him and he could swiftly plunge into the safety of darkness just beyond the fire. He dreaded what he had to do. But the image of Victoria filled his mind, that searing moment when she cried out and was swiftly hustled away from his vision.

What was there but to go in? To live or die, he didn't know. Back in his own side gulch, he collected his horses, saddled up, loaded his kit, looked to the powder and priming on his flintlock, and then mounted, carrying his rifle loosely across his lap. But in his leathers he had a plug of tobacco, and in his kit some trade items—if he ever got that far.

It seemed like the longest ride he had ever undertaken, though the distance was less than a mile. The twilight had surrendered to blackness, though a band of blue still lingered above the Backbone to the west. Where were their guards? Would he stumble into the horse herders and be taken for a raider? He steered toward the trail along the river, scarcely knowing where he was going, the stars dancing pricks of light on the flowing stream.

Then, suddenly, the trees ahead reflected light, and he could make out moving forms.

"Hello the camp," he yelled, and kicked his black horse forward.

For a moment nothing happened, and he rued the folly of this quest.

"Hello the camp," he yelled again, giving notice, and this time he saw men stirring, racing for weapons, preparing for an intruder.

Then he rode in. In the light of the half-extinguished fire, he faced a phalanx of armed warriors, their faces terrible in the flickering light.

Skye's pulse raced so fast he wondered if his heart would burst. "Peace," he said, lifting a hand upward. "Peace." He remembered the plains hand sign for peace, but it was too late for that anyway. They could kill him in a trice. He saw nocked arrows pointing at him, a lance in the hand of a warrior. Several more stood with war clubs or tomahawks in hand. They were waiting for something, perhaps word from their headman. Skye looked for that one and thought he spotted the right one, a man with an imperious gaze, gaunt, hollow-chested, ugly and cruel, missing several teeth and an ear.

Skye lifted a plug of tobacco until it was plainly in sight of them all, and then walked his horse to the one he supposed led this party and handed it to the man.

But the unaccepted tobacco plunged to the ground.

Chapter 36

Skye stared at the plug of tobacco in the grass and swung the rifle in his lap around to point at the headman. That would give him a few seconds while the leader thought it over.

The headman's eyes focused on the bore of the rifle, and Skye saw some subtle change in his face.

"Who speaks English? Anyone?"

No one replied.

Skye didn't know how to proceed. He could not remove his hand from the trigger, yet he needed both hands to make some hand signs. During his four years in the mountains he had acquired a good hand sign vocabulary, but now it was useless. He ransacked his mind for a few Blackfoot words he had learned during the trading.

"Kainah," he said.

These warriors stared impassively.

Much to Skye's surprise, the headman resolved the dilemma. Slowly, his gaze on the bore of the rifle, he stooped over and picked up the tobacco plug and held it high, thrusting it first at Skye and then at the Blackfoot warriors.

Skye peered sharply into the faces surrounding him. No one lowered a bow or lance. It had come down to trust. Slowly he pointed the rifle downward and uncocked it. Then he slipped it into its fringed leather sheath on his saddle. He glanced around him. None of the Blackfeet had lowered their bows.

Slowly, using a combination of Blackfoot words and handsigns, he made his intentions known. He was a trader. He was looking for a band of the Bloods that had traded at the post on the Marias, *Kaiyi Isisakta,* recently. He wished to hire a guide to take him there safely. He wished to buy an Absaroka slave who was his wife. He would pay the guide well—a long knife and an awl and ten iron arrow points.

He wasn't at all sure he was understood, but at least they listened and watched his hands. Uneasily, he surveyed the bows and arrows in the hands of these warriors. No bow was drawn, but that offered him little comfort. In the space of two seconds he could be pierced by twenty arrows.

The Siksika are a great and powerful people, he signaled to them. One by one his hands formed words and ideas: He was glad they had accepted his tobacco. They would help a man who wished to buy his wife back. The Pikuni, Kainah, and Siksika were the most generous of all the Peoples.

They watched his hands, and listened to his occasional words, and stood in the flickering firelight without showing the slightest sign of acceptance or rejection, of friendship or murder.

His hands made new signs: If you will not help, I will go in peace.

The headman's hands made words: We do not know where Kainah are. Maybe we will see them at Sun Dance.

Skye responded: Where will the Sun Dance be?

"Mokwamski," the headman said.

The Belly River, Skye translated. Well up in British lands, a long, dangerous journey from here. The traditional home of the Bloods.

"Good. I am Skye," he said, making the sign for the sky and pointing at himself.

"Skye. Ah. I am *Istowun-eh 'pata,* Packs a Knife. We are *Nit-sitapi,* Real People, Siksika."

These were Blackfeet proper, then. A little more inclined to let a white man live than the Piegans, or Pikuni, as they called themselves.

The headman pointed at Skye's bear claw necklace and said something Skye could not translate. But he understood suddenly that the bear claws might have saved his life.

"Take me to the Kainah," Skye said, finding a few words.

But Packs a Knife shook his head, and with a flurry of words Skye couldn't follow made it clear that this party had other plans. He intuited that they were looking for some Cree scalps.

Very well, then. Time to escape into the darkness before things took an unexpected turn. He dug into his saddle kit, found an awl, and handed it to Packs a Knife, who nodded. Then Skye made the sign for going. He pointed to himself, then held his right hand before him, palm upward, and gestured outward three times. The headman nodded.

Skye turned his black away from camp, tugged on the line of his packhorse, and rode away, his back prickling. But no arrow stopped him. Swiftly the night cradled him in its safety. Not that the Siksika couldn't follow and kill him; they could go wherever he could go. But Skye sensed that he was safe. He had found the courage to walk straight into a Blackfoot war camp and ask questions. Suddenly, as the merciful blackness engulfed him, he felt the terror depart. His body sagged, his muscles released, and an incredible weariness stole through him. He wanted to dismount and lie in the grass until he recovered his strength. But he rode on, not really knowing where he was going except that his horse took him alongside the river. He wanted to put distance between himself and the warriors, so he rode onward in the deeps of the night. He didn't know where his passage took him, only that each step of the horses was a step toward safety.

He hadn't found out much. Sun Dance on the Belly. There was a lot of Belly River, and he could miss the whole affair. And what would the Bloods think of a white man showing up for their most sacred ceremony of the year? And in British Canada, where he was still a wanted man, as far as he knew? The Sun Dance would be held in the midst of that great fiefdom possessed by Hudson's Bay Company—which had a price on his head.

He had found out something this night. He could walk into the very camp of the Blackfeet and come out alive. If they had caught him running from them, he would be dead. But if he boldly walked into their company, he might live.

He rode into dawn, amazed to see another day. The

heavens grayed, forms began to emerge, and soon a hot sweet July day embraced him. He beheld a grand and open land, prairies laced with rushing rivers tumbling out of the great Backbone to the west. The Blackfeet claimed a mighty country, and it blessed them. He was too tired to continue, and the horses were dragging, so he turned up a side gulch, found a copse of box elder under a sharp low bluff, and made it home for the nonce. The shade would shelter him and the horses in the July midday heat; the innocuous grove of trees would conceal him from passing river traffic. He picketed the horses out of sight of the river, checked the warm slope for prairie rattlers, and curled up on a mattress of grass.

That whole day spent itself without the presence of Skye, who slept the sleep of the dead after his ordeal. When he finally did awaken, twilight was not an hour away. He studied the country, looking for signs of passage, and finally decided it was safe to water the horses. He led them to the river and watched them lap up water, pause, and lap up some more.

He felt lonely. For days he had traveled in solitude, enduring whatever fate was in store for him. He missed his old friends and knew they were gathering on the Powder River for the rendezvous of 1831. Maybe, if he raced south at breakneck speed, he might catch the tail end of it and enjoy one last hooraw with Jim Bridger, William Sublette, Davey Jackson, Joe Meek, and Jed Smith. The thought of that headlong plunge tempted him, but he knew he was already too late. He wouldn't show up, and they would wonder about him. Beckwourth would show up and brag about his triumph over Skye, and boast that he had even made off with Victoria. And the free trappers would figure Skye either went under or had fled the mountains, a whipped dog. Maybe it was just as well that he didn't go back this year. He scarcely knew where the Powder was, except that this rendezvous would be far to the east of the previous ones, out on buffalo plains, and closer to St. Louis.

Missing the rendezvous made him feel bad. Those were his only friends. He was still the lonely Englishman with no roots anywhere, adrift in an alien world. He had come to love the mountain life, and had endured four years of it, enough to make him a veteran of the fur trade. And yet, without Victoria, it had all turned to ashes.

He gathered his kit together, saddled his horses, and continued on alone, a solitary man who had never chosen to live out his life all alone. With the thought of rendezvous came the realization that real friends were more valuable than gold. Not all the wild beauty around him could assuage the hungers of his soul. No sweet wilderness or utterly free life in the midst of nature could equal the worth of a wife and friends.

He rode ever northwest along the river, through a sea of purple and lavender and blue, as the twilight tinted the Great Plains and painted the distant buttes and steppes with shadow and darkness. The scene was a good imitation of his soul, he thought. There wasn't much light within him.

He rode into the deeps of the night, guided by a thin moon and an inertia that carried him into the jaws of death almost against his will. But when the hour approached midnight, as best as he could judge, he called it quits and made camp. He was out of meat, and feared that he would have to subsist in the morning on his old emergency food, the ever-present and foul-tasting cattail root.

That night he sank into desolation. He couldn't help

it. The entire year since the previous rendezvous had been a disaster. From the time the Pawnees had stolen everything he possessed, to the time in the Crow village when he watched Victoria slip away from him and Beckwourth defeat him and frustrate his mission, to the bitter discovery of betrayal, to the long, hollow days and hours toiling eastward, to his miserable, lonely life as a trader in a remote cabin—all these things had crushed his hopes and dreams and had thwarted the life he had so bravely pursued ever since escaping the Royal Navy.

He had a good kit, was armed, had horses, had all the means of surviving in a wild land—and yet lacked the most important of all things. The will to continue. The thought of the rendezvous had sent him into a downward spiral that made him wonder whether Barnaby Skye had been God's mistake, an accident of Fate.

The thought of the presence of God in all the corners of the universe, even here, a thousand miles from the nearest settlement, didn't really comfort him. Where was God now, when he camped in the midst of the midst of the most dangerous tribesmen known to the trappers? And yet, in the soft silence and the midnight mists, he discovered the eternal stars, and with eternity came a vision of love. God loved him, and there was purpose in Skye's life, if only he could find it.

He could not remember the lucid and sweet supplications he once had read in the Book of Common Prayer long ago in London, so he recited the one he remembered, the one called the Lord's, and asked for the courage to pick up his cross and carry it when dawn came.

Chapter 37

Skye awakened to a benign world. The terrors and loneliness of the night had vanished, and now he gazed upon a glowing land. He felt refreshed and ready to travel to the ends of the earth to free Victoria.

Somehow, in the dawn of a sweet summer's day, the Blackfeet seemed different and approachable. Did they not have their own honor, love their children, defend themselves against enemies, just like all mortals? Surely all that he had heard around the brigade campfires had been exaggerated. How the trappers loved to tell a tale and embellish it until it barely resembled reality. Something within him this golden morning told him that with courage, love, and faith, he would find his straying wife and win her liberty—and her heart.

The trappers called them Bug's Boys, the Devil's boys, but there was a reason for that. Long ago, the Yank explorers Lewis and Clark had tangled with them, sowing the seeds of later trouble. But Skye wasn't a Yank. He considered himself a man without a country.

He packed his gear, paused at the riverbank to listen to whatever might be told on the breeze, and then he mounted and rode off, filled with a prescient belief that this very day he would make friendly contact with the Devil's boys. His path took him ever westward toward the Backbone of the World, which now loomed as a mighty rampart, layer upon layer of blue mountains that pierced the sky. He continued to follow the Marias, the stream that would lead him to the heart of the Blackfoot Federation.

At noon he topped a grassy knoll and beheld a village in the distance, forty or fifty brown lodges camped on a river flat near abundant woodlands. He paused, soberly assessing his chances and his fate, and then touched the ribs of his black and rode straight down the long grassy slope. A while later the village wolves, the guardians, spotted him and raced out to confront him. He knew that fear or flight would kill him, so he made a show of waving at them and proceeding straight toward the village.

They surrounded him, first two, then five, and eventually nine, the imperial warriors of the Blackfeet, all of them in leggings and little else. None threatened him; no one needed to. His rifle was sheathed, and they grossly outnumbered him. He held up a plug of tobacco, the universal peace sign. In spite of his renewed belief in the goodness of life and the comforts he had discovered in the past hours, fear crept through him. These warriors studied him, and none looked friendly. One of them, a leader no doubt, motioned him toward the village, so Skye spurred his horse and headed toward the lodges, surrounded by an imperial guard.

He in turn studied them, vaguely puzzled by something. They seemed familiar. He reached the outskirts of the village, and now the villagers crowded about, and once again he admired the people for their dignity and handsomeness. No Plains Indians he had encountered matched the Blackfeet in physical beauty, pride, grace, and carriage. They seemed familiar, and then he remembered: these people had traded at Berger's log cabin. Skye had met many of them across the trading counter. They knew him for a trader. A flood of relief ran through him. They would honor him within their village as a protected guest.

Piegans, then. And they would listen to his request.

He passed well-made lodges, remarkable for their decorations. Many had what appeared to be a row of stars around the base, and all of them displayed beautifully dyed totem figures and colored geometric designs that spoke of the owner's personal medicine. Their clothing showed the same care and elegance. They had fashioned it from a mixture of hides and furs and trade items, such as flannel, buttons, conchos, and jingle bells.

By the time he reached a sort of plaza, or open space in the center of the village, the elders and headmen had already gathered there. He handed his plug of tobacco to the chief, who stood ahead of the others, and it was swiftly accepted. He now had the safety and courtesy of the village. There followed the usual Indian smoking ritual, and Skye puffed the pipe as it passed by, deepening the peace. They took their time, and it struck Skye there was wisdom in it. They could assess each other, compose their thoughts, rest, and prepare for whatever would come.

Skye began with hand signs, plus the bit of their tongue he knew, and also a few English words. At Berger's post the Piegans employed a bit of English, probably picked up from the clerks at Rocky Mountain House, the Hudson's Bay post far to the north where many Blackfeet traded. These would suffice if Skye chose his signs and words carefully.

He told them he wished to be taken to the Kainah, the Bloods, in peace. A band of them, which had traded at Berger's cabin, had captured his wife, an Absaroka woman, and he wished to free her if he could by trading some things he had brought. He simply wanted his wife. He didn't even know the name of her captor.

"Grandfather of Wolves," the chief signaled. "He has the Absaroka woman."

Finally, a name. That was his first real progress.

"What band?" he asked.

"*I-sis-o-kas-im-iks.*" Hair Shirts.

"What are you?"

"We are *Sik-ut-si-pum-aiks,* Black Patched Moccasins, of the Pikuni. I am Bull Turns Around."

"I am Skye."

"Why would a man want an Absaroka wife? We have better."

"I love her."

"Let her go."

"I will give a good knife to one who takes me safely to the Hair Shirts and Grandfather of Wolves. And a hatchet if I succeed."

Bull Turns Around pondered that. The elders sat quietly, observing Skye with questioning faces. One of them leaned toward the chief and spoke at length in the Blackfoot tongue. The chief nodded.

"Every man should have a woman. But not an Absaroka woman. She must be a slave. We would like a trader in our band. We will give you a fine, works-hard Blackfoot woman, young and comely."

"I want only my Absaroka woman."

The chief pondered that. "We have among us Running Crane, *nisah,* elder brother, of Grandfather of Wolves. It is for brothers to decide." He turned to one of those sitting just outside the circle of elders and addressed the younger man at length. Running Crane stood, responded slowly, and sat.

"He will not go with the white man. It would cause trouble, asking for the slave. Grandfather of Wolves would be offended. Running Crane says for the pale man to turn around and go back now. This is not good."

Skye saw how this was going to end and lamented the defeat. But he would continue north, regardless.

"Tell Running Crane his counsel is wise. But I must try. I would like to learn the language of your people for a few suns. Will Bull Turns Around give me teachers?"

"That is a good request. We will teach you many words, but we cannot go with you to the Hair Shirts or help you. You will be a guest in my lodge."

So, miraculously, Skye found himself safe among the fearsome Piegans, in the very lodge of the chief of the Black Patched Moccasins. He intended to put every moment to use, mastering the tongue, absorbing the customs, picking up any bits of information that might help.

The visit turned out to be fruitful for both sides. The Piegans were starved for information about white men, especially the Yanks they hated so much. They knew many of the trappers by name or reputation, which surprised Skye. Somehow word filtered through the tribes. Ashley, Jed Smith, Jim Bridger were all familiar to them, and their young men dreamed of killing them all. They wanted to know where white women were hidden and why the men came alone. They wanted to know why the trappers armed the Crows and Shoshones and all the rest of the enemies of the Blackfeet.

Skye couldn't answer adequately, especially with his sketchy knowledge of their tongue and the hand signs. But the elders, who came to smoke with Skye each day, were patient, and whenever there was confusion or misunderstanding, they paused until Skye or they made themselves clear. Skye, in turn, learned much about the fierce Blackfeet; how they loved their children, how the husbands lorded over their wives, whose duty was to obey without question anything that their men demanded. Skye saw several terribly scarred women whose noses had been cut off. He learned that these women had been unfaithful, and cutting off their noses—making them forever ugly—was the penalty. Skye wondered how feisty Victoria could long endure under such a Blackfoot regimen. She would either be killed as a rebel or die of despair. He had to reach her, and soon.

But the delay helped. He began to understand the daily rhythms of life in a Blackfoot village; the habits of the horse herders, the war games played by young men, the equestrian skills of the warriors as well as the powerful religion and spirituality that guided these war-bent people. Each warrior had cried for a vision had a spirit-helper. But they worshiped Napi, Old Man, lord of the universe, but also something of a jokester who could foil their dreams and plans.

He learned words, but knew there would be too little time to become fluent enough to converse. He focused especially on family words, for these would be the ones he would need the most. The word he wanted the most was "wife": *nit-o-ke-man*. Just as helpful would be "husband": *no-ma*. "Father" was *ni-nah;* "mother," *ni-kis-ta,* while "son" was *no-ko-i,* and "daughter" was *ni-tun*. All that was good. He could now tell the Hair Shirts he was looking for his *nit-o-ke-man*.

Skye stayed until the village prepared to leave for a buffalo hunt. The Piegans were less committed to the Sun Dance than the Bloods, and often ignored the ritual. He learned that the dance was new to the Blackfeet, though well established among the Plains tribes to the south, including the Crows.

Skye didn't want to go on a hunt; he wanted to find Victoria, so he departed, giving gifts of awls to the chief's women, who had waited on him as if he were a duke. He rode north, while the Black Patched Moccasins rode south, toward the Judith Basin, where they knew the buffalo were thick.

It had been a good visit. He began to doubt all the terrible stories about the Blackfeet he had heard from the Yank trappers. These northern Indians were as amiable as any other, he thought. He would find the Blood bands gathered at Belly Buttes, near the Belly River, observing the sacred ceremony that involved purification, self-torture, an ordeal of endurance, and petitions to Sun for everything from healing to victory over enemies. Skye thought that would be a good time to deal with them, and so he rode north, refusing to worry about what fate might have in store.

Chapter 38

The Bloods found buffalo on Big Sandy Creek, west of the Bear Paw Mountains, and raised their lodges there for a hunt. These hides would not make good robes now, with the winter hair clinging in patches and the summer hair not yet grown, but the hides would make fine lodgecovers, clothing, saddles, and moccasins, while the meat would provide a feast. Some of it would be jerked into trail food for warriors on the warpath.

Victoria's young body healed, but her spirit languished. Day by day she drudged, doing whatever the women of the lodge demanded. Mostly they gave her the most miserable of tasks, scraping hair off a hide staked to the earth until it was naked leather, and then brain-tanning it. She was used to such toil. That was the lot of women among the Peoples. So she scraped with a metal-edged fleshing tool the Bloods had gotten from the traders, slowly peeling away hair and flesh, working on her knees in hot sun, enduring the smell and grease and clouds of green-bellied flies.

They gave her no respite. She was a slave, and if she sought a moment of rest they beat her with sticks or threatened her with knives. Only the old one, the grandmother, eyed her with any sympathy and offered the gift of an occasional fleet smile or a gentle touch of the hand. Once, when Victoria's ragged doeskin dress fell apart, the old one brought an awl and patiently repaired it, lacing a seam at the side with new thong.

But the other women, all wives of Grandfather of Wolves, vied with each other to make her miserable. His sits-beside-him wife, Sisoyaki, or Cutting Woman, was hardest of all to cope with, and was determined to set an example of meanness for the other wives to follow. The youngest wife, Going Out to Meet the Victors, Pi-ot-skini, looked as if she wished to befriend Victoria, learn Crow words, and help lift her burden, but the older woman ruthlessly crushed the slightest tendency toward warmth. And so Victoria toiled alone.

At least she didn't lack food. Even slaves needed food, and they didn't begrudge the tongue or hump meat or backfat she ate, though in hard times, which afflicted all the Peoples now and then, she would be fed last and least. But there was food for the body and food for the spirit, and of the latter she was starved. She was never so aware of her hungers as when twilight came and handsome youths played the love flute sweetly outside the lodges of their beloveds. She knew those melodies; they were the same for all the tribes of the young and tender. These Blood people were much more fastidious than the Absarokas, and watched their daughters strictly. The girls were virgins when they were given away by their parents. She found herself wishing she had been raised in such fashion, with none of the bawdiness and wanton conduct of her own people. She had been too knowing too young, and maybe that was one of the things that had led her life to this fate, this brokenness.

So she dressed and tanned the skins and saw some of them replace worn hides in lodges or turn into good moccasins. When darkness stopped her hide dressing, they gave her other tasks. One was to stuff buffalo beard hair into cushions and pad saddles. Another was to pound meat and mix in fat to make a trail food rather like pemmican, though it was too early in the year for the other ingredient, berries. Not until the master retired, often late at night, was she permitted to collapse on an old robe in the place of least honor. In a few scant hours she would begin the same routine over again.

Each day the younger women harnessed travois to ponies and went out to the killing fields, there to butcher the buffalo the hunters had killed. The Bloods wallowed in buffalo, eventually cutting only the tongues from them, and sometimes hump meat. They loved cow, which was tender, and sometimes brought back an unborn calf, whose soft hide was prized. Even the camp dogs had their fill and slept lazily instead of gorging on the carrion. Plentiful meat, the true food of these people, made them happy, and they began to slacken their efforts. All except the slave, who toiled on because she faced the lash or a stick if she paused. The village had more meat and hide than it could possibly use. The buffalo were so plentiful that a foray into the midst of them hardly disturbed the giant herd, which slowly grazed its way south.

Then the chief—she had found out that his name was Crow Dog—decreed that the Hair Shirts would go to the Sun Dance, and soon she found herself packing the lodge's wealth into parfleches, large rawhide containers, and loading them onto the ponies. The horses would be overburdened this trip, carrying all the jerky and pemmican that had been salvaged from the buffalo brothers and sisters, as well as fresh hides and tanned robes. It meant she would walk, but now that she was stronger she preferred to. Some of the bruises remained, yellow-and-purple reminders of her ordeal, which she wore like prisoner garb.

The walking gave her a chance to reflect on her life. As long as she didn't stray from the other women, they left her alone. She could not converse, even though she was mastering all the words she could. It was one thing to recognize words and commands, quite another to string words together and talk to these Siksika. So she walked through golden June days when the world ached with pleasure, her thoughts on the new reality she faced. She had lost dominion over her life; every minute of it belonged to her master and mistresses. She had lost the hope of many things, including husband, reputation, friends, esteem, and her freedom to organize her days as she chose.

The causes for all that lay in the past, in her folly, in her girlish worship of warriors and war, but those things could not be undone, so they were best forgotten. She still faced a future, however limited, and she would have to find some sort of bearable life among these enemies of the People, or else roll over and die. Skye was long gone. Why would he try to find her and save her from her own foolishness? Why would he come, after she had betrayed him? No, he was on his way to the east and the many-houses villages he had told her about.

She probably would have to make a life with the Kainah and then die. She had learned that *Kainah* meant "Many Chiefs" and that Bloods was a name bestowed upon these people by their enemies the Cree. On her war trip with Beckwourth she had departed a girl; now she was a woman. She had changed forever, a passage as real as her passage from freedom to slavery. As she walked, she came to understand herself as a woman who would not surrender. She would look for a chance to escape. Someday the Absaroka would show up in force and free her. Or someday when things were just right—an impending snowstorm, or chaos, or a desperate fight—she would walk away. Someday, sometime. And meanwhile, she could make life bearable by learning the tongue, avoiding abuse as much as she could, pleasing those who really didn't wish to be pleased, and perhaps even winning friends among those who wanted mainly to despise her.

She had never again heard from her benefactor, the woman who had saved her life the night of the coup counting, but she knew that somewhere among these people was a woman whose name was Magpie, and someday she would find and befriend that woman. Her other source of strength and courage was her spirit-helper. She found time for the traditional crying, and grew certain that her counselor was leading her through this ordeal for a purpose— maybe to make a beautiful woman of her. Magpie was wise; magpie did not flee south like other birds, but endured, even as she, Many Quill Woman, must endure this winter of the soul.

She learned to work without being asked or bullied.

By the time the village was settling down for the night, she had found firewood, unloaded parfleches, and spread the robes. The elder wife didn't really like this; she wanted to yell, and itched to beat the slave. So she found fault no matter what Victoria did, but the torrent of abuse slid by Victoria like leaves floating on a stream.

They traveled farther north than she had ever been, and now the Backbone of the World shown whitely to the west again. The Bloods possessed a good and bountiful land, though not half as sweet as the land of the Absarokas.

They came to a great grassy flat lying at the foot of mysterious and strange buttes, and there the Kainah were gathering. Several bands had preceded the Hair Shirts. Victoria beheld a great encampment, rather like the white men's rendezvous. The days had grown hot, even scorching, and the sun was driving the last of the green from the grasses. This had been a dry summer, for which she was grateful. She had almost no clothing; a tattered dress that was rotting away from her lithe body, and no more. With the coming of cold, they would either clothe her or let her freeze to death. She could not know her fate.

Her master, Grandfather of Wolves, had not come to her for many suns, preferring his own women, and that pleased her. Perhaps that was because she had been too still and submissive, giving him nothing. Whatever the reason, he left her alone, and she was able to sleep entire nights, rest her weary body, and awaken refreshed, even if desolation stole through her as she faced another hollow, brutal day.

They kept her far away from the sacred lodge they were erecting to worship Sun. This, the most arduous and sacred of ceremonies, was only for the People. She didn't wish to see any of it. They had stolen it from the Absarokas, who had honored Sun long before the Bloods. And before that, it had come from the Arapaho. She didn't know where it had come from before that. These Bloods were not a numerous people, the smallest nation in the Blackfoot Federation. And yet she admitted, reluctantly, that perhaps they were the handsomest and proudest, and perhaps raised its greatest chiefs, which their very name suggested.

The great blessing of the Sun Dance for her was simply that the Siksika ignored her. Sacred ritual absorbed these people. A woman of impeccable virtue was chosen to lead the Bloods in worship of Sun; there were prescribed dances, often lasting all night. They had built a sun lodge, a circular arbor with the traditional sacred pole in its center, to which the dancers would be tethered in the final act of ritual sacrifice.

Now the drumming never ceased, and along with it the eagle bone whistles and flutes. This mesmerizing throb filled the whole plateau with heartbeat, life's pulse. Had this been the ritual of her own people, her spirit would have overflowed with pride and joy. But these were not her Absarokas, and the ceremony had a reverse impact on her. With every beat of the drum, with each prayer and song lifted on eagle feathers to the Above Ones and Four-Foots, she was flooded with an ineffable sadness.

Chapter 39

Skye rode north, a solitary horseman passing through the land of the Blackfeet. The mountains, the Backbone of the World, rose ever present on his left, severing these featureless plains from whatever lay beyond. This was a brooding land, with perspectives so distant that it set the mind to thinking about eternity. Nothing but a few scattered buttes supplied features to a featureless land. From any slight hill he could see his fate in the day to come. This country made him feel small, as the sea had sometimes made him feel helpless.

He saw no Blackfeet, nor did he even discover signs of passage. Yet he was now in the heart of their country—and not far from British possessions. He had no way of knowing when he might cross that line, the 49th parallel, but it didn't matter. The Crown had no power here, and his escape from the Royal Navy frigate would be long forgotten. Trouble, such as it was in such country, would more likely be the crossing of a treacherous river or a sudden storm. He had crossed two northeast-flowing streams, and suspected they were the south and middle branches of the Milk, a river that rose in the western mountains, hurried north into the British possessions, and then curved south again to empty into the Missouri.

The long country evinced long thoughts, and the one that preyed on his serenity had to do with Victoria's heart. In that brief encounter at Berger's post, she had cried to him for help. And in his own fantasies, he had expanded that heart-cry into something it wasn't: a wish to return to him. She wanted help, escape, freedom. Not a word or gesture in that fiery moment had suggested love or caring. As he rode, he came to grips with that painful truth.

At first he believed it would have to be an act of faith; he would rescue her, drawing courage from his certitude that she loved him and would return to his arms, his hearth fires, forever. But then he knew even that was delusion. He simply did not know. She might be very grateful, quite distant, and once returned to her people, quietly shut the door to him again. So he wondered anew whether he was on a fool's mission. He could turn back, unscathed, probably find one of the Rocky Mountain Fur Company brigades and sign on—with his scalp on his skull.

The thought tempted him. Around his campfires, each skillfully hidden in a brushy coulee, he let the temptation run, wanting to see it whole. He owed her nothing. He loved her—nothing would ever change that—but faced rejection once again. Why had he set out on this fool's errand?

In the stillness of that sweeping land, when even the breeze seemed hushed and scarcely a bird sang, there came to him another reason: no mortal should live in captivity. Victoria's life was not her own. Why had *she* been set upon the earth? To be a slave? She was experiencing much the same ordeal as his own. He had not been in possession of himself. All he had, during his long burial in the crowded fo'c'sle of the H.M.S. *Jaguar,* was his dreams and his prayers. Nothing else. He owned not even the clothing on his body, and received a meal only when his masters felt like giving him one. What had sustained him then was hope. He had never stopped dreaming of the time when he would be a free man.

So it was with her. She probably was as much a slave as he had been. Perhaps her life would be better than his. At least she had land under her feet, and with it the chance of escape. And probably she did just about the same things she had done in her own village. She might even be given in marriage. And yet in some respects her lot would be worse than his. She didn't know their tongue; he and his shipmates and masters shared the English tongue, which had assuaged his loneliness.

Skye realized, then, that his purposes were larger and

more generous than simply the recovery of a woman he loved and had once possessed. He would free her if he could—and then offer her freedom from him. He would free her because of every bitter memory of being at the mercy of others, of the lash and whip that had befallen him whenever he resisted or failed to do what was required of him. He would free her because no mortal on earth should be forced into servitude. No one deserved that fate.

He studied the country as he passed through, uncertain whether he would know the Belly River even if he stood on its bank. The scant direction he had received from the Piegans scarcely prepared him to find his way in a land without landmarks. He forded another modest stream flowing northeast, and believed it to be the north fork of the Milk River. He topped a low divide and found himself in a different drainage, this one with scattered lakes lying ahead. Somewhere beyond the lakes would be the medicine line, the beginning of Grandfather's Land, as the Piegans had described it. From there it would not be far to the Belly River . . . and the Bloods.

They weren't pretty lakes, nor were they set in green forests. But they harbored thousands of ducks, geese, cranes, and white swans. One somber evening Skye made a meal of a Canada goose he shot as it lifted from the shimmering water. Skye didn't much like this silent country. It lacked the graces of beauty and surprise. Neither did he much like dining on goose. It took too long to gut it, pluck the pinfeathers, clean it, roast it, and saw it into edible portions.

He arrived at the northernmost of these lakes the next evening and beheld a campfire across the water. So, at last, he would make contact again, for better or worse. He waited for the darkness to settle, which was a long time coming in that latitude in summer. But at last he walked his horses around the grassy shore, edging closer. He wanted a good look before he made any decisions. He tied his horses to a juniper and negotiated the last quarter mile on foot. If trouble came, he would be shielded by darkness.

He saw that there were five or six standing around the fire, which burned brightly and too large for concealment. He spotted several horses picketed close by and what appeared to be packs on the ground. On closer examination, he discovered still more men sitting on logs near the fire.

"You out there, do you come in peaceably or do we hunt you down?" came the voice, startling and harsh in the velvet silence.

Skye sprang backward, fearing the firelight had revealed him.

"I know you're there. Every one of our beasts faces toward ye, ears pointed. You're not a catamount or a wolf. The beasts don't act like that except around mortals. Now, are you friend or foe?"

Skye watched the others casually lift weapons and settle behind the packs, which made fine barricades. He thought he detected some familiar ring to the voice, and what he heard did not remind him of Yanks.

"All right," he said. "I'm alone."

"Ah, I knew you jolly well weren't a red man," said the voice. "Ye speak the tongue known to us. Come then, and warm yourself at our fire, if that's your purpose. I will tell you straight off, we are Hudson's Bay men."

Skye paused. HBC once offered money for his capture. But that was four years ago, and the episode had long been forgotten, even by the HBC men he had encountered at the rendezvous since then.

"I'll come in," he said. "It'll be a few minutes."

He retreated to his horses, wondering all the while whether to leave them as a means of escape, and finally decided to bring them in. He wanted to talk to these men.

He collected the horses and led them toward the distant glow, and finally walked into camp. There he encountered others dressed rather like himself, in a mixture of flannels and buckskins, a wedding of native and European manufacture. Sitting on a log were several Creoles, dressed identically in red flannel shirts and blue trousers. They appeared to be voyageurs, and Skye spotted two large canoes nearby. They and the gents in buckskins all wore beards; some wore their hair shoulder length, like the Yank trappers. All but one. That fellow, amazingly, had outfitted himself in a heavy black swallowtail suit. That one looked for all the world like a duke. He had a ducal presence as well, examining the world about him as if he owned it. Now that penetrating gaze focused on Skye with obvious curiosity. Skye gaped at the apparition, this powerfully built gentleman in business attire in the middle of a wilderness.

"I'm George Simpson, governor of HBC. And who are you, sir?"

The name shot fear through Skye. Simpson was the most powerful Briton in the New World. Hudson's Bay had a charter that permitted it sovereign rule over a large portion of North America, and the governor of that fiefdom, who ruled not merely a business but operated a private government as well, stood before him. Here was the man appointed in London by the board of directors, a quasi-official of the Crown, the superior of Dr. John McLoughlin out in Fort Vancouver. Here was the man who oversaw an empire from his lair at York Factory on Hudson's Bay, as well as from Fort Vancouver itself.

And a man who might remember Skye's name, even after four years. But Skye doubted the man would remember the name of an ordinary sailor.

"Governor Simpson, I'm honored to meet you, sir," Skye replied. "I've heard much about you."

"And you, sir? Have I heard much about you?"

"No, you haven't. I am Barnaby Skye."

Simpson looked puzzled. "I know that name, yes. Somewhere, blast it. Well, come in and have tea. Yes, and the men'll put the horses up, and you'll tell us how a man like you rises like some wraith out of the wilderness and approaches a fire."

"I'm on my way north, sir, to the Belly River, where I wish to do business with the Bloods."

"What sort of business?"

"My wife is a captive. I wish to free her."

"Your wife? A white woman?"

"No, she is a woman of the Crows, the Absaroka. And I intend to get her back."

"You are an Englishman; quite plain in your speech. Yes, London. But not Billingsgate, not Cockney. What is it, then?"

"My father was a merchant, sir, import-export."

"Well, that's it, then. But you're not one of our men."

"No, sir. I'm not associated with any company at present, though I've trapped with a Yank brigade."

"Damned near treason, Skye."

"It's Mister Skye, sir."

"Mister Skye, is it? Now I remember. The Royal Navy. A damned deserter." He thrust a finger at Skye. "Seize him!"

Chapter 40

So it wasn't over.

Skye sprang toward Governor Simpson, wrestled the man around, and pressed his knife to the man's throat. The Hudson's Bay governor writhed until the keen edge of Skye's knife drew blood.

"They'll kill me, but you'll die first," Skye whispered.

"Don't move, don't move," Simpson bellowed.

Skye hated this. He had no quarrel with valid authority, only with injustice. He might die in the next moments. That couldn't be helped. He would not—ever—go back to England or spend his days in a dungeon. When he had finally escaped the Royal Navy, he vowed that no bars would ever come between his eyes and the heavens.

Around him, burly Hudson's Bay men stood frozen, ready to spring at him. Skye was one against twelve or fifteen. More than that. Simpson didn't beg, but stood composed, aware of the deadly blade pressing against his jugular.

"I will never be taken alive," Skye announced to the men, who even now were edging around behind him, preparing to spring. "And if you attempt to kill me now, Simpson dies."

They believed him. He could see their wariness in the flickering light. Yet he didn't know how to escape. With one arm around the governor, and the other holding the knife to the man's throat, he could not lead his horses away.

"For God's sake, be careful," Simpson said. It was a command to his men. The governor wasn't pleading and hadn't lost his composure. Skye admired him.

"I will make something clear," said Skye. "I prefer death to capture. Remember that. Mr. Simpson is a good and honorable Englishman. Don't cost him his life. He will have it if you heed me."

He wrestled Simpson toward the edge of camp, where the firelight dimmed. Simpson walked readily. The bores of several Hudson's Bay rifles followed. When he reached a place where some brush blocked the view, he steered the governor behind it.

"One man, bring me my horses," he yelled.

They debated a moment in the light of the fire.

"Tell them, sir," Skye said softly.

"Damned if I will."

Skye pressed his keen blade into the flesh of the man's neck. Simpson wilted.

"Bring his horses—you, McGill. Do it."

A man led Skye's black horse and the packhorse out of the firelight and brought them near.

"All right, go back," said Skye. "If you value the governor's life, don't follow. Sit down at the fire. Everyone."

Skye watched them reluctantly sit. He knew one or more lurked in the darkness, maybe even now circling around to pounce on him. He listened closely, hearing nothing.

Skye steered Simpson toward the horses. "Take the reins," he told the governor.

Slowly, Skye steered the governor into the deeps of the night, following the lakeshore northward. Water glinted on his right. A quarter moon spread pale white light over the darkened landscape. Skye paused frequently, listened for sounds of pursuit. He heard none.

"Are we in British territory?" Skye asked the governor.

"Where Hudson's Bay is, Britannia rules."

"Where were you coming from and where are you going?"

"I am returning from Vancouver and stopped to see Fort Spokane."

"And?"

"Up to the Saskatchewan River."

"And then to York Factory?"

"How far are you taking me?"

"You won't get lost. Not with that lakeshore guiding you back."

"You're an abomination before man and God."

"Think what you will."

"They should have thrown you into the sea."

"Quiet now. You're talking to give me away."

"I'll talk all I choose."

"You don't much care for your life, then."

Skye released him, took the reins, and prodded the governor forward at knifepoint. They traversed another mile or so of lakefront. Then, as the shore curved east, Skye turned north. A grassy slope took them out of the lake basin and onto prairie. The whole bowl of heaven lay over them.

"I'll let you go now," Skye said. "Go down the slope to the lake and follow the shore. And don't start yelling. As long as you are in my sight, you are not safe."

"I'll see you hanged, Skye."

"Be gone now. Do not yell. I am armed and watching. Remember that."

Sir George Simpson glared, whirled away, and marched off the ridge. Skye swiftly moved to his left and then swung north again. When he reached some brush he paused, mounted the black, and rode swiftly. He could scarcely imagine how he escaped. And he knew that at least some within Hudson's Bay had not given up their effort to ship him back to London.

He cut westward, putting the North Star on his right. The maneuver wouldn't long slow down an experienced mountain man, but Skye intended to do all he could to elude his followers. He rode swiftly through the night, intending to put distance and more distance between himself and Simpson.

He wondered what the Hudson's Bay governor was doing so far south of the usual voyageur's passage from Fort Vancouver to York Factory. But he didn't have to wonder long. Simpson was probably offering weapons and ammunition to any who would make relentless war on the Yanks. Hudson's Bay had been doing that ever since Ashley's free trappers penetrated the mountains. The British didn't want an American presence in the Oregon country, which ran from the Rockies to the Pacific and was under joint rule until a boundary could be established. Thus did Hudson's Bay further the imperial designs of the Crown.

Skye sensed he wasn't done with Simpson. The man might well show up at the Sun Dance. Where else could he stir up so many Blackfeet? If that was the case, Skye would be in even more jeopardy if he were to walk in to the great Blood tribal ceremony. If he intended to free Victoria, he would have to get in and get out before Simpson's large party showed up. Skye wished he had kept quiet about his plans back in those amiable moments when he first encountered Simpson. But it was too late to repair the damage.

He swung north again and continued until he felt the horses tire. Not long before dawn he made a dry camp in a coulee, picketed the horses well below the skyline, and rolled into his robe. He made no fire and went hungry. After four years in the mountains, he was inured to starving. He didn't sleep.

At first light, when the world was gray, he studied the surrounding country, which was open and grassy, and then collected his half-rested horses. He rode ever north, a solitary figure on a mission that seemed crazy. At every rise he paused to study his back trail, but saw nothing. The country began to change. Forest stretched along slopes, and the land seemed better watered. He supposed he was in British territory, but didn't know. A boundary had never been surveyed.

That afternoon he struck a goodly river that ran in a shallow canyon. Its clear cold water had the lingering taste of snowmelt. It ran northeast. Skye believed it was the Belly and he was close to the Bloods, but he couldn't be sure. From now on it would be guesswork. Very little the Piegans told him helped now, when one river seemed like another.

From a hilltop he studied the half-forested, half-grassed country. What he hoped to find was some distant buttes, the Belly Buttes—at whose feet the great Sun ceremony was even now proceeding. He saw nothing he could define as a butte or tableland, but maybe that was because he was too far west.

He sat his horse, examining a land so vast that a man could spend months mastering it. Somewhere, in some direction of the compass, was Victoria. He felt a helplessness once again. There were so many times, throughout his life, when he barely knew where to turn or what to do. He clambered off his horse and settled in the wind-rippled grass, letting himself absorb the country before him. He didn't much believe in intuition, but he did believe that if he opened all his senses to the world around him, he might get information, see or hear or smell the things he would otherwise miss.

One of these was buffalo. Below him, in the boxed valley of this river, he spotted a dozen of the great black animals peacefully grazing. They reminded him that he was hungry and out of food. These looked larger and darker than any he had seen before, and he wondered whether they were the woods buffalo the trappers had spoken of, a shaggy northern version of the plains buffalo to the south. From his vantage point he watched the shadows of puffball clouds plow the earth, roll over forests, climb slopes and disappear. He felt, as he sometimes did, that he was not alone, that the strangeness of his life had some hidden purpose he might yet fathom when he was an old man.

Below, a small barren cow grazed. He would eat her tongue and regret leaving so much more. It had been a long time since he had tasted the splendid, firm meat of the bison. He let his horses graze a while more, suddenly in no hurry, and then rode down a game trail into the narrow canyon. The herd saw him descend the canyon wall and trotted downstream, tails lifted, wide-eyed. Skye slid his mountain rifle out of its fringed sheath, checked the priming, which was dry, and rode easily downriver, driving the herd before him.

Then the cow he had his eyes on stumbled and fell, and he beheld an arrow in her side and a swarm of Indians boiling out of the bankside willow brush.

Chapter 41

They saw him just as he saw them. They barely paused at the fallen buffalo cow, and rode instead toward Skye, fifteen, twenty of them, all armed, some with rifles, most with deadly bows and arrows.

Suddenly Skye became the hunted, along with the buffalo. The howl of the hunters told him that. Swiftly, Skye kicked his horses straight up the slope. He intended to top the rim of the river valley, which was his sole hope of escape. But his burdened horse and packhorse lost ground to the buffalo ponies of these warriors. He saw an arrow hiss by and knew he was within range. He huddled low over the saddle to make a smaller target and urged his black up the steep slope, which it devoured with great leaps that almost unseated him.

The Indians had the advantage of the angle, and drew closer as he scaled the grassy slope. Another arrow reached him, this one smacking into the kit behind his cantle. An arrow struck the black, and it screeched. Sky saw a line of blood where the arrow had plowed a trench along the croup. Not a fatal wound, but the black horse kicked and screeched and bucked itself over the rim of the valley, and for a few seconds Skye enjoyed a respite.

His nearest succor was a patch of pines half a mile distant. But the lumbering packhorse was slowing him. He let go. His life was worth more than his kit. The horse thundered along behind Skye anyway, not wanting to separate itself from its companion.

The hunters spilled onto the grassy plain and fired volleys of arrows. Skye heard the packhorse wheeze. It grunted and stumbled to the ground, three arrows in it, one through the neck, one in the ribs, and the third into the rump. Another volley of arrows hit his black, and one arrow pierced his leather shirt. He felt the black buckle under him, shudder, and cave in. Skye pulled loose just before it collapsed, and found himself flat on the grass, the wind knocked out of him. He tried to unsheath his rifle, but it lay under the weight of the flailing, dying horse.

So this was it.

Moments later they swarmed over him, a dozen—more, twenty—powerful, tall, golden-fleshed Blackfeet, Bloods probably. They studied him, saw he was alive, and crowded around, each counting coup. Blows rained down on him. They kicked and pummeled, jabbed with coup sticks, knocked him about. The blows came so fast and hard he had no place to escape, no way even to fight.

Then the blows stopped. They had all counted coup. He supposed they would kill him now; a coup against a live enemy was worth much more than a coup against a dead one. He tried to sit up, but a foot smashed him to the ground again. He rolled over, beheld a circle of them over him, lances poised for the kill. But a sharp command of a headman forestalled that—for the moment. Skye wished they would finish the job. From the ground he saw them pillage his kit. They ripped open the panniers on the pack-horse and pulled out all the trading items he had planned to use to win Victoria: knives, awls, beads, pairs of blankets, powder, bars of lead, flints and steels, a bolt of trade-cloth. These they examined, sometimes glancing at him. He lay still, awaiting his fate. The leader of this band of hunters signaled two of them to roll the dead black over. He wanted to free the rifle. Moments later he possessed the prize, a fine, octagon-barreled percussion lock and a fringed and beaded sheath. He held it high, sighted down it, aimed it at Skye, and laughed.

"Shoot, Bug's Boy," Skye said.

But the warrior didn't. Instead he hefted the rifle, ripped Skye's powder horns from his chest, and took Skye's knife for good measure. The bear claw necklace caught his eye, and he examined it closely, plainly fascinated by the length of the dark claws. Now at last he examined Skye as a person, not just a white enemy. Then he said something Skye couldn't translate. The headman yanked at the necklace, trying to pull it loose. Skye resisted.

"That's mine; leave it alone, you devil," he roared.

The headman yanked harder, so Skye smacked him with his fist.

Surprised, the headman reeled back, sprang to his feet, and pulled out his war club, a mean weapon composed of a shaped piece of rock bound by rawhide in the fork of a haft. The warrior slashed down sharply; Skye rolled, and the club grazed his ear. Skye kept on rolling, got to his feet, and rammed toward the warrior, who brought the club back and down, smashing hard into Skye's shoulder. Skye went numb with shock. His shoulder felt as if it had been severed from his body. He pushed, and the warrior staggered back. Skye landed on him, but the tribesmen pulled him off, a dozen hands lifting him off the fallen chief by main force. They cast Skye into the dirt, where he lay panting, waiting . . .

When they turned to the chief to help him up Skye sprang again, his heart wild in him, his fists hammering at any flesh he could see—and he did not lack a target. Something berserk had loosed in him; his senses had become unmoored, and now he fought one and all, crazily, too powerful for any or several to grip him or topple him, though they tried. Then a sharp command stopped them, but not Skye. He was beyond stopping, and launched murderously after one, then another.

A blow to his head shot white through his brain, and then blackness. He knew nothing. . . .

He awakened now and then to the throb of a mighty headache, and knew from the pain that he lived. But he couldn't think and didn't understand what had happened. When he finally did come around, he felt only thirst and pain. He lay in a darkened place but couldn't focus his eyes enough to know where he was. His body gave him no comfort, but in spite of raw hurt he drifted into oblivion again. The next time he came to, he realized he was in a lodge. The poles at the smoke hole formed an apex. Blue sky lay beyond. The Bloods—if that was who they were—had taken him to this place. And spared him for reasons of their own. He knew their reasons, and wished they had killed him outright instead of the slow style they had in mind.

He heard a drumming and wasn't sure whether it was his angry pulse or the beat of a ceremony. He decided it was a ceremony and that the Sun Dance was under way, or about to begin, or in a preliminary phase. He closed his eyes again; to see was to hurt. He discovered that he still possessed his bear claw necklace, powerful medicine to these people and any other tribe. It lay across his chest, hurting him. The brush of a feather would have hurt him just then.

This night they would hurt him more.

He dozed. He was conscious of people entering the lodge, poking him, talking over him. One lifted his bear claw necklace and then dropped it. Some woman lifted his head and gave him water. He drank greedily and slumped back to oblivion. Let them examine him all they would; his life was no longer his own, and he had surrendered it. Maybe, when he could form words better, he would pray for a good death. No one much thought of the importance of a good death, but any mountaineer did, and a plea for a good death lay in the heart of every man he had met in these wilds. There were so many deaths of the other kind.

He lay awake in the quiet of the empty lodge, studying what had been stored within. He needed the means of self-immolation, a way to a swift sure death, without the pain of what was in store for him. He saw nothing. His captors had been careful. He was not bound in any way, but his moccasins had been taken from him. Nothing more was needed to keep him there.

No one bothered to feed him, but he hurt too much to care. All the long day he heard in the distance the dancing of the Bloods. For four days they would honor the Sun, perform ritual acts of repentance and sacrifice and cleansing. They would dance on a bed of fragrant sagebrush, around a Sun pole with buffalo skulls at its base. They would whistle with bone flutes, compose prayers to the powerful Sun, pleading for peace, for fruitfulness, for increase, for victory at war, for blessings. And some would beg Sun for darker things: vengeance, fulfillment of a bloody vow, death upon enemies. These were the most sacred hours in the liturgy of the Blackfeet, more sacred even than the opening of the beaver bundle in the spring. During all this, his captors would ignore him and fulfill their obligations to Sun and to the tribe.

Skye mended swiftly. His young body had been bruised and battered but not stricken by disease. Nor had any of his internal organs been damaged, or bones broken. He lay on his bed of grass, alert now, growing curious about his captors. He probably was in the lodge of that headman, the one who had led the buffalo hunt that supplied precious meat to this great tribal gathering. So many mouths to feed required relentless hunting for anything edible, and the buffalo Skye had hazed straight into the waiting Bloods must have seemed to them a gift from Sun himself.

On the third day of his captivity he wondered where Victoria might be and what her fate was. She probably was there, maybe within yards of him. No longer did he have the slightest chance of rescuing her. All his carefully hoarded stock of trade items intended to purchase her release had been taken from him. He lacked so much as a horse or a saddle—or covering for his feet. She would survive, tough and resilient and strong in her own way. Maybe she could fashion a life among these mortal enemies of the Crows. He knew it was commonplace for captive women to come to love their captors, marry them, become members of the once-hated tribe.

He was grateful she didn't know he was in the village, helpless. She didn't know he had tried, had plunged all this distance, taken all these risks, all because of a single plea to him before she was silenced. He didn't want her to bear that knowledge. But if she did find out—and she might during the torture—she would know that he had come. That was all. He had come for her. Let that tell her about his love.

They left him alone another night and slept outside the lodge because of the summer's heat. So he rarely saw the Blackfeet who held him. A woman fed him broth now, enough to sustain life—for the sport to come.

That day the sound of the drumming changed, the beat

darker and more tormented, interrupted by intense singing. It was the time of sacrifice, when those making the sacred vow fulfilled it. The flesh of their chests or backs had been pierced, a cord run through the incision and strung to the Sun pole in the sacred medicine lodge. And there the young men who were making their sacrifice to Sun danced and would keep on dancing until they ripped free of the Sun pole and lay half dead in a pool of their own blood. Maybe his captor had been one of those.

The drumming continued deep into the night, and then slowed, and finally stopped. A great and terrible silence fell upon the camp of the Bloods, and Skye knew the dance had passed and the next day might be his last.

Chapter 42

The yellow eyes had come to the great encampment of the Bloods, and Victoria caught glimpses of them as they presented themselves to the chiefs and headmen. The women of the lodge had told her not to go to the place of the gathering, so Victoria had to be careful. The white men had gathered before the lodge of the greatest of Blood chiefs, Sees Afar, over among the *Ah-kai-po-kaks,* the Many Children band. All the other chiefs and headmen had gathered there, including Crow Dog, chief of the Hair Shirts.

Still, Victoria found ways to glimpse all this. She drifted that way, lost among the crowds of Siksika women and children, and saw some of it. She risked a beating but what did it matter? She could live like a whipped dog or she could try to make some sort of life for her-self.

These were the other white men, from Grandfather's Land across the great waters. Hudson's Bay Company, the very ones who had chased Skye and tried to capture him years before. Most of them looked like the trappers she had seen in Skye's brigade, hairy men in buckskins. But she saw some darker ones, the Creoles who spoke an-other tongue, and these were dressed alike in blue pants and red flannel shirts, as if they were all eggs from one nest. They interested her, but not so much as the other one, the great chief of the Hudson's Bay men. This one wore black, except for a white shirt. Black from head to foot; a coat of black that dipped like the tail of a bird in back but was shorter in front. He had a meaty, cruel face, with bold eyes that missed nothing. He looked and acted like a great chief, too, a lord whose power and word won instant obedience.

She didn't like these men. These were the ones who had supplied guns, axes, arrow points, tomahawks, and all the rest to the Siksika so that they might war upon the Ab-saroka and kill off rival yellow eyes men in the fur bri-gades. She studied them closely; they were from Mister Skye's land and shared his blood.

She could see what all this was about: the black-clad man was seeking trade and giving gifts. He asked each chief to come forward, and gave each one a shining ri-fle. Those were mighty gifts, and they would assure that this company would have the Blackfoot trade for many winters to come. He was making a great speech all the while, and two translators were making his words into Siksika words so all could understand. All this was done with ceremony. One of the yellow eyes stood with a flag made of red with a certain sort of cross upon it. Skye had told her once that this company had a flag with the Cross of St. George upon it, but she didn't know what that was. Another man held up a pole with another flag, this one red and blue and white. Skye had called that one a Union Jack, and it was the medicine of these Beyond the Water men.

After that there were many speeches, as each of the Blood chiefs stood, had his say about friendship and peace and trade and the alliance of Hudson's Bay with the Siksika. She couldn't follow all of that. But she knew the gist of it: between them, the Hudson's Bay Company and the Siksika would drive out the other pale men from this land forever, and the Siksika would drive the Lakota and Cree and Assiniboine and Absaroka away, too, and be lords of the earth. She didn't like this gathering. The many-gifts white men were plotting and scheming, and the Bloods were dreaming of power.

The Blood chiefs rose. The gathering was dissolving and the pale men would soon be gone. But the grandfather in the black clothing was talking to Sees Afar about something. And the great chief talked to someone else, who talked to someone else. Then a Blood warrior came forth, a powerfully built man wearing war honors. He had counted many coups. The grandfather summoned his Hudson's Bay men to him, and soon they brought him another shining rifle and a pair of red blankets and other things. The warrior accepted these and vanished. Everyone stood there, waiting for something. Victoria wondered what it might be.

Then she saw what they were waiting for, and the sight sucked her breath from her lungs. They brought Skye to the grandfather man of Hudson's Bay. Skye! He looked weary and bruised. She wormed her way closer, desperate, wanting to cry out to him but knowing she couldn't. He had come for her. They had caught him. They had hurt him. He looked worn and wounded, but he stood alert and strong, something indomitable about him. His keen blue eyes surveyed the grandfather and the Hudson's Bay men. The warrior who had captured Skye pushed Skye the last few feet and sent him sprawling at the feet of the grandfather man. Hudson's Bay had bought Skye. They would take him back across the waters.

Victoria's heart ached and she felt a flood of anguish. She had to help him, somehow, some way. But how?

"Well, Barnaby Skye, we have you now," the grandfather man said.

Her man did not reply, but kept looking at the blue skies and the wild lands, as if not even seeing the grandfather man.

"It'll be the dungeon for a deserter, Skye."

"It's Mister Skye, sir."

The grandfather man laughed derisively. "Tie him up. We'll be off for York Factory," he said.

With that, some of the Hudson's Bay men bound Skye's arms behind his back.

Frantically, she maneuvered through the spellbound Bloods, who watched all this with intense interest. Only Skye's captor wasn't watching. He was cocking and uncocking his new rifle and sighting down its steel barrel.

She wormed forward, past the proper place for women and toward the warriors who crowded around Skye and the Hudson's Bay men. She had to let him know! A Blood warrior noticed her and barred the way. The council was not a proper place for a woman. He growled at her, and she stepped back, slipped away, and tried again at a different point, only to be rebuffed by more warriors who eyed her coldly for violating the custom.

She was on the brink of a whipping or death or torture, and yet she had to let Skye know she was there. Just one glance, one meeting of the eyes, that's all she could ask. She found a way, this time through a crowd of the Hudson's Bay men, trappers, and vogageurs, who stood amid their piles of gear and canoes. This time she darted through, stood not ten yards from her man, and waited, hoping that her spirit-helper, Magpie, would reveal her to Skye and conceal her from the eyes of the Siksika.

He did turn, did see her, and in one eternal moment they faced each other. In one moment that lasted forever and was written upon the stars, she and he saw each other, and it was like lightning from a cloud struck the earth so great was the force of their gaze. And then, after the briefest of smiles, he turned away—to protect her, to conceal the great event from these Siksika and Hudson's Bay. No one had noticed. She fled backward, her heart racing. She had to free him. She had to escape these people. She might never see him again. She knew his vow: they would not take him alive. If he had no way to escape before they put him in the big canoe and took him across the water, he would find a way to go to the land of the spirits.

Somehow in the confusion she retreated without rebuke or trouble, and soon stood among the women, once again looking through a wall of Blood warriors at the pale men as they prepared to leave. She choked back a flood of emotion. He had come for her. Alone, through the land of the dangerous Siksika, he had come. He had seen her at Berger's post, heard her cry, and had come. Tears welled. No man had ever given her as much. Skye's love had endured, survived even the cuts and wounds she had inflicted on it—and on him. Skye's love had triumphed over her own folly and unfaithfulness. Skye, not Beckwourth, had come to rescue her if he could. She could not stop weeping now, as she slipped quietly back from the gathering and watched from under the boughs of an aspen.

The grandfather's men were dividing into two parties. The trappers in buckskins formed one horseback party and headed west, while the burly voyageurs in the red and blue lowered their canoes into the Belly River and began loading them with mounds of peltries and supplies. Others lifted great packs they were going to carry. She marveled at how much one of these men could carry. They attached a pack to Skye's back and made him carry it barefooted. Soon his feet would bleed. And then a man with a strange device of metal and wood and cloth and leather, a sort of bag connected with a flute, made this device wail mournfully, its melancholic howl piercing the quiet. She knew about this thing that Skye called a bagpipe, and knew how that mournful noise spoke of war and blood and honor—and greatness. Only the white grandfathers had a piper who piped for them.

And so they departed after the piping of the man who squeezed the bag and made the beast howl. So terrible was the noise that all the camp dogs lifted their throats and howled, as if this was a great gathering of wolves. The black-clad grandfather got into a canoe with some of the voyageurs. Other voyageurs shouldered their packs and walked. She watched Skye walk away with them along the riverbank. He was stooped under the weight on his back and unbalanced because his hands were tied together. And yet he walked. He did not glance back to her.

Perhaps he was saying, Good-bye, my beloved; good-bye now forever, until we meet again on a distant shore.

She watched until the Hudson's Bay men and Skye vanished behind a wall of trees. Her heart walked beside him. The Bloods watched, too, and then the crowd dissolved. She hastened back to the lodge of Grandfather of Wolves, her mind awhirl with hopes. She had somehow escaped punishment—so far. But surely she had been seen. She hurried past the lodges where the Sun Dancers lay on their robes, recuperating. So great had been their ordeal that the various bands would not travel for a day or two. Grudgingly, Victoria admired the young men who had spilled their blood to honor Father Sun and thus win great blessings. The Siksika women were tenderly nursing all the dancers now, and honoring them for their courage.

No one was in the lodge of Grandfather of Wolves. She peered about, looking for any of her captors. How could it be? Were they all off visiting relatives in other bands, or collecting firewood, or doing one chore or another? A wild impulse struck her: go now, go swiftly, flee while she could. She forced herself to stop thinking such mad thoughts. They would find her and kill her. How could a small lone woman hide from warriors such as these? Surely they would know exactly where she went—along the Belly River behind the Hudson's Bay men.

But why would they think that? They didn't know that Skye was her man. They would think she'd fled south toward her Absaroka people, not north or east. But how might she survive? And how might she free her man? What would she eat?

Swiftly she surveyed the lodge. Everything she needed would be here—if she could only escape the village un-

seen. She knew she would try. Skye had given up his life
to save her; she would give up her life to save him. There,
hanging from a lodgepole, was the bow and quiver of her
captor. She had never touched it. If a woman touched a
warrior's weapons she rendered them powerless, polluted.
Skye had never felt that way, and enjoyed showing her
how to hold his rifle or his knife.

Heart racing, she examined what else she might take.
Skye would need moccasins, and there were several pairs
that would fit him. She needed a knife, flint and steel, anything she could carry that would help her and Skye escape. Swiftly she ransacked the parfleches, scooping up
jerky and a fat tube of pemmican. She found a sheathed
skinning knife and a flint and striker. She dug out two
pairs of moccasins, big ones for Skye, a spare pair for her,
plus some patching leather. She found an awl. Gingerly—
fear lacing her—she lowered the bow and quiver full of
arrows. She rolled all this into a light summer robe, one
she could carry, and tied it tight with thong. She peered
out of the lodge door, seeing only a sleepy encampment,
slowly recovering after the excitement and exhaustion of
the high summer gathering. The sun rolled lazily toward
the northwest. The day would fade in a while, and that
was good. Darkness might hide a small, lithe Absaroka
woman bent on fleeing the whole nation of Bloods.
Sharply she studied the People. Plenty of them were about,
tending their affairs, sunning, talking. She gathered her
breath and her courage and walked west, bearing the
rolled robe over her shoulder and carrying a woodcutting
hatchet. She did not look directly at any of the Bloods,
for fear they would register her passage, but instead penetrated the woods that grew back from the river, passing
two or three women who were industriously hacking at

branches. Then at last she was alone. She swung north, walking through pine forest laced with open parks, and emerged well north of the camp and almost around Belly Buttes. She knew she was on the river road the Hudson's Bay men had taken.

As she walked, she wept.

Chapter 43

Skye staggered under the pack they had loaded on his back. His bare feet bled and smarted, and each step shot pain up his legs. He bore the bruises of the beating the Bloods had given him while counting coup. His shoulders ached almost beyond endurance, and his legs threatened to collapse under him.

Sir George Simpson eyed him now and then when his canoe drew alongside or they portaged around rapids. There was smugness in his face but he said nothing. He had his man at last, and the Crown would be pleased—and so would the honorable directors of Hudson's Bay, back in London. The governor bore no burden, but had to walk like everyone else whenever walking was required.

Skye marveled at the voyageurs, burly Frenchmen who had carried two canoes on their backs across the Rockies for the forthcoming voyage down the Belly, Oldman, and South Saskatchewan Rivers, while others wrestled awesome loads. The party now consisted of Governor Simpson, two other Englishmen, and the French-speaking voyageurs. Skye supposed that the mountaineers and their horses were headed back to Fort Vancouver.

Skye contemplated his options. He would be swiftly tossed into a dungeon as a deserter from the Royal Navy, there to rot to an early death on the swill they would feed him. Or else they would simply return him to a man-of-war, there to slave away the rest of his days 'tween decks, the surly sea his prison. The navy was always shorthanded, and would make do with almost any sort of live body.

The overland contingent tramped along the rough banks of the Belly, which had incised itself deep into the undulating prairie above. They circled occasional sloughs that were choked with ducks, climbed steep bluffs where the river crowded passage, maneuvered through wooded hills to shortcut a bend in the river, but were never far from the Belly and the canoes of the rest of the party.

No one spoke to him until they halted for the night next to a glade of box elders back from the riverbank. Skye had somehow managed to endure, to make his battered body move, step by step, mile upon mile, to this place. He doubted he could do the same in the morning with his feet so badly lacerated.

"Well, Skye," said Simpson, "you had the good sense to come along and not fight your fate. You may live or die as you choose; it's of no consequence to me. Your feet are bleeding, and we'll fit you up with moccasins in the morning. You're a beast of burden, and that's your entire value to us."

"It's Mister Skye, sir."

Simpson chortled. "Caught by the Bloods. We knew we'd find you lurking about, just as you said you would. You haven't the brains of an ant. You could be safe in St. Louis or the States by now."

"Yes, I could have been safe long ago, sir. But I have

chosen to pay my debts, and I have chosen to help one I love."

Simpson looked faintly surprised, but only for a fleeting moment. "It's all nonsense, trying to butter me up so I'll feel some sympathy. Forget it, Skye. We'll feed you well—that's how one cares for a beast of burden—and then truss you up. Don't try to escape or it will go harder for you tomorrow. You see, Skye, the arm of the Crown reaches everywhere, even here."

Skye said nothing. Around him, the Hudson's Bay men made camp. They did a good job of it, settling down in a defensible place with shelter and firewood. He didn't doubt that these engagés were fully the match of the Yank mountain men when it came to survival. He settled into the grass, grateful to have the burden lifted from him. He hurt as much as he had ever hurt. No one spoke to him, but the whole company eyed him from time to time, their thoughts private. He suspected that very few spoke English.

In time he smelled roasting meat, and in a while they brought him some sizzling buffalo on a platter of bark. He would have to eat it with his fingers when it cooled enough. The scent of good meat made him dizzy. When at last he could handle the meat, he thought that it tasted better than anything he had ever eaten. He chewed mouthful after mouthful of the succulent steak, feeling the meat energize his wounded body and comfort him. They brought him more when he had downed the first helping, and he ate that, too, until he could not swallow another bite. The Indians had always said that buffalo meat gave them strength; they were right.

After he had his fill, they trussed his ankles with thong, and then his wrists behind his back. He would sleep miserably, but they were taking no chances. They did toss a robe over him, and the warmth comforted him. Full darkness settled over the camp, until he could see nothing but the twinkling stars in the vast heaven above. He had vowed once that there would never be iron bars between him and the stars, and now that vow lingered in his mind as the camp lay quiet.

He fought sleep because he needed to think. He might be a prisoner, but he had decisions to make, and his choice would be fateful.

Victoria.

She had seen him. She knew he had come. All that had passed between them had vanished in that terrible, beautiful moment. She knew what faithful love must be. He knew what it meant for her to renew her love. All of this lay beyond repentance and forgiveness, and in the realm where two souls meet and are inseparable to the end of time. Surely, surely, there must be a separate bower in heaven for true lovers. Maybe someday, beyond the beyond, he and Victoria would share that bower in the City of God.

He had no regrets. She had cried out to him, and he had come. If it meant tossing aside his life, then that was his destiny. It had all been worth it, this sweet interlude, an unasked-for wilderness idyll so far from everything he had known as a child.

He had a few options at that. He could refuse to take another step, refuse to participate in his imprisonment. If he chose not to walk, not to carry a burden, they could execute him, which he doubted they would do; flog him, which seemed quite possible, except that it would render him unfit to walk; bind and carry him on a packhorse, which was quite possible; or let him go, for want of means to take him to his destiny—which he deemed wildly improbable.

He had another option: cooperate, walk, gain strength on the plentiful food, heal his body, and look out for a chance to escape. He had jumped ship with almost nothing; he could do it again during this high summer warmth and the forthcoming time of berries, fruit, and roots. The engagés were skilled wilderness men, but so was he after four years in these wilds He might outsmart them.

He pondered both options as he lay there, trussed and uncomfortable. Walk or not walk. The decision was portentous. He was so young, yet he had always known he would give up that most precious of gifts, life itself, rather than submit to iron bars again.

The rest came in a flood of understanding. He had managed his escape from the Royal Navy only when he stopped resisting and seemed outwardly to cooperate. It had meant that he no longer was thrown into the ship's brig whenever they came within sight of land. They let him stay in his own bunk because they had seen the change in him. The implication was clear: for the moment, he would cooperate with them, give them no reason to think he might be plotting his escape. He would be cheerful, humble, accepting of whatever they imposed on him. And when at last their vigilance lessened, then he would escape—or die.

That was a somber thought, and he pushed it out of mind. He possessed the optimism of youth. He would find a way, and escape, just as he had done in the past. He felt sleep overwhelm him at last, but paused to ask his Maker for mercy and a way. Comforted, he drifted into a dreamless sleep.

The next morning they fitted him with moccasins, fed him gruel swiftly boiled over a campfire, and loaded him with an impossible burden again. The moment it sagged from his shoulders, he hurt anew.

"I can carry it, mates," he said.

No one replied. They had obviously been commanded not to traffic with the prisoner.

Simpson inspected him minutely. "Well, Mister Skye, you're going to walk another fifteen miles today. If you give us any cause, you may be certain blows will land on your head."

Skye nodded.

"I'll tell you something for your own profit. Behave yourself. Maybe you'll have a future, eh?"

Skye wondered what that meant. He remembered encountering the great Hudson's Bay man Peter Skene Ogden years before, and how Ogden had tried to recruit him. Hudson's Bay was as short of seasoned wilderness men as were the Yank fur companies. Skye suspected that Simpson's desire to make pence and pound for his lords in London exceeded even his loyalty to the Crown. And that Skye's cooperation might be the test.

It was going to be a bloody hot day, judging from the way the heat built within an hour after they had started out. Skye's back ached with the burden—he guessed sixty pounds—he bore. So heavy was his load that he stooped forward to balance it. He marveled that the voyageurs carried even more.

He fell in beside the two English-speaking mountaineers, each of whom shouldered a load. Was this how HBC got its furs out of the American Northwest? No wonder they didn't much bother with buffalo robes, preferring the more valuable beaver instead. They had to carry and portage and canoe everything from the Rocky Mountains clear to York Factory on Hudson's Bay.

He observed Simpson's heavily loaded canoe far ahead, and began talking quietly to the silent men around him. He supposed that the better they knew him, simply as a fellow mortal, the less likely they would be to hurt him. So he began simply to tell his story, keeping his voice low and quiet. He swiftly described his youth in London, the press gang that changed his life, his years in the Royal Navy, and his desperate escape. He didn't say much about his subsequent life with the Yank rivals of Hudson's Bay. They would know it anyway, and he didn't want to bring up a sore point. They listened silently, no one objecting, but no one giving any hint of sympathy either. And thus did a broiling day pass, and at the end Skye was never so glad to collapse into the grass and let his aching body find a moment of peace.

The voyageurs beached their canoes in a deep canyon of the Belly that hid the river from the surrounding plains, and were eventually joined by the men on foot. They fed him well and bound him again that night, and he dozed fitfully until he was awakened by something, he knew not what. And then he knew: he smelled the foul exudations of a bear, and then felt the snout of the animal nudge his robe and sniff his head. His spirit-brother had come.

Chapter 44

Victoria fled deep into pine forest. The day was still young, and this thin arm of woods that followed a gulch was all that concealed her. She padded far beyond the woodcutters and continued up a forested slope far from a trail. There she found a viewpoint and waited. She could not move far until darkness cloaked her.

For a while she saw no activity. Then four warriors rode casually north along the bank of the Belly River, on the trail taken by the Hudson's Bay men. They acted as if they didn't expect to find her going this way: why would an Absaroka woman go to the men from the grandfather's land who were allied with the Siksika? No, they would look for her to the south, supposing she fled toward her people. Still, they were taking no chances, and these young warriors had been sent to guard the trail in this direction.

They paused now and then, their senses keen, but they could not see her in her grassy bower, surrounded by pine, sitting so still that not even the birds gave alarm. But now these four stood between her and the Hudson's Bay men—and Skye. She settled into the thin grass, rubbing pine needles over her to subdue her own scent, and peering alertly in all directions, lest foot searchers came upon her.

She eyed the powerful bow she had taken. It was fashioned from yew, a wood that grew far to the west, which meant her captor had traded for it. There were few good bow woods in the land of the Siksika or Crow. The Sioux got Osage orange from someplace far east and south, but the People of the northern plains and mountains were hard-put for good bows. She did not feel she had done anything wrong by taking it. Her captor had taken everything she possessed when he caught her, including her horse. Still, it was wrong for a woman to touch an instrument of war. A weapon had to be purified by a warrior, bathed in the smoke of sweetgrass and offered to the Ones Above before it would recover its power. But now she had touched it—and the arrows, too. She wondered if the bow's power now belonged to her. She tried stringing it and found that her strength was barely enough. This was a bow for a strong warrior, not a woman. The long sinew, taken from the backbone of a buffalo, stretched taut and ready She nocked an arrow and waited, well armed against an enemy.

But no one came. She thirsted but was far from the river. It didn't matter. She could endure, and she wouldn't move until night enfolded her.

She had no plan, utterly no knowledge of how she might free Skye and how they might escape an intensive search by skilled men who could read sign as well as the People. But she would find a way and employ the night to conceal them. All doubt had vanished. She knew what she must do, and she would do it if she could. Her every thought was focused on freeing Skye and escaping. He might not want her, yet she would do it anyway. She would free him even if it meant that he would go east and never see her again.

When dusk finally came, she edged down to the river-bank trail that the Hudson's Bay men had taken, but stayed off it even though this caution slowed her passage. She was rewarded a while later by the dim sight of a warrior on horseback, sitting quietly, listening. He had heard her, and now moved slowly in her direction. She nocked an arrow, but settled silently into gloom beside some brush. He passed by without seeing her, never knowing that an arrow had pointed straight at his chest for a moment. She padded onward as the last light faded, and then stepped onto the trail, now lit only by starlight. She paced ahead, scarcely knowing where the trail took her, except that the North Star was on her left and as long as she followed the river, it would take her to Skye.

Then, suddenly, she found herself in the midst of horsemen, Siksika who had been waiting for her. They sensed her just as she sensed them, and rode her down. She whirled, loosed the arrow at one, heard a muffled cry, and dodged off the trail through grass and then brush, making too much noise. She pulled another arrow from her quiver, nocked it, and waited, feeling her heart race. She heard male voices, the clop of unshod hooves, groaning, and then nothing. She squinted into the murk, trying to discern what lay out there. They had probably left one behind to catch her. She edged closer, this time taking care not to make noise, and did finally make out what she thought might be a Siksika standing near something that was probably his horse. He was as alert as she, and no doubt as well armed, but she couldn't really tell. She chose to wait, and settled down right where she stood. Sometime he would leave, and then she would be free— perhaps.

He guarded that place a long time, and she knew he was waiting for Mother Moon to come and shed her milky light so he could see again. Indeed, she saw a glow on the horizon where the moon would soon appear from behind the edge of the earth. She had little time. If there was one, there probably was another she didn't know about. She dared not move, and simply sat quietly, not knowing what would come. When the three-quarter moon did appear, she saw the gray horse better than she saw the Siksika. The horse was staring at her, ears forward. That should tell a good warrior what he needed to know, but he was facing the other way.

Time passed, and the warrior mounted his pony and rode toward the east, toward the Hudson's Bay men. And another warrior joined him. She heard them talking, the two horses walking side by side. So the Siksika still lurked between her and Skye. They were following the trail, which lay clear now in the silver light. She watched them walk into the milkiness of the night, knowing what little chance a small lone woman had against them, even if she had a bow she could barely draw. They knew she was here and where she was going; they knew she had a bow and had hurt one of them. They would find her and kill her.

Slowly she stood, peering sharply into the duskiest places. She was in a hilly country with grassed valleys and wooded slopes, and gulches choked with brush. The trail ran through open meadows. In the white light, she could not approach the horsemen without being seen.

And yet . . . she would. She knew, suddenly, that she wanted those horses. One for her, one for Skye. And she would have to kill the Siksika to take them. And what chance had she? She flexed the bow, feeling its power, feeling it tug at her. She would try this thing, a frail woman against two powerful men. She pulled arrows from her quiver, wanting to touch them, invest her power in them also. She touched each arrow, making it hers, not her captor's. Somehow this was important. She slid her hand along the thin shafts, one by one, feeling the deadly iron points, the feathers that had been bound with sinew to the shaft, and the little slots that took the sinew of the bowstring.

She would do this thing! Her spirits soared. Some primeval power coursed through her, savage and wanton, hot and deadly. She had rarely felt this before; now she bathed herself in it. She might scalp these Siksika, a scalp from each, and let their spirits wander forever, without a spirit-home. She trotted after them, swiftly, deadly, silently, her moccasins somehow making no sound. She was a wolf trailing buffalo, a lioness gathering herself to outrun a deer and sink her teeth into its throat.

She saw them ahead, leisurely walking their ponies, a gray and a darker one whose color she couldn't make out. She would have to get close because she had little skill with this weapon. Close enough to drive an arrow into their backs. If she missed . . . what did it matter! It was a good night to die.

She walked boldly, no cover concealing her, onward toward these friends of Grandfather of Wolves who sought her blood and her scalp. She was close enough to put an arrow into them, but not close enough to be sure. So she walked swiftly, gliding like a magpie, spirit-driven. She gained ground, and now she could make out that one was thin, one stocky. They wore leggings, but their backs were bare.

Then one turned and saw her. He whirled, lifted his bow, loosed an arrow that seared her hair. He shouted as he turned his horse and pulled another arrow from his quiver. She pulled, feeling the terrible power of the bow, feeling her small hands wobble under such pressure, and loosed her arrow. It sailed home, burying itself in the warrior's side. He cried, coughed, drew his war club, and came on, kicking his horse. Now at last the other Siksika bore down on her, tomahawk in hand. She yanked an arrow, fumbled with it, finally found the bowstring, nocked and shot, all in one desperate moment. It missed. They both were riding her down. She ran sideways, leftward, but the tomahawk warrior easily steered his horse at her. She reversed herself, darting to the right as the horse came upon her. It hit her, bowled her over—and the Siksika rode by, without a target. She hit the ground hard, her breath knocked from her.

And then the other one rode her down, war club poised. But even as he approached, life fled him, and he tumbled to the ground almost at her side. He stared at her and then at nothing.

The other turned his pony with a violent yank of the hackamore, and the horse skittered and danced a moment. Victoria found her bow, stood, reached to her quiver, and met his furious charge with a well-aimed arrow that struck him in his thigh. He howled, spasmed, whirled past her, and clutched his gouting wound. She stood, shaken, trembling. It wasn't over. Blood boiled down his leg, dripped from his moccasin. His war club, its thong looped over his wrist, dangled. He turned his horse again. She saw a knife glint in his hand. She stood her ground, armed herself again, and stepped behind the body of the Siksika, knowing the horse would not step over it. The warrior yanked his horse toward her, but it dodged the fallen warrior, and he never came within knife range. She let him pass and released another arrow, which hit him in the shoulder and spun him off the horse. He landed hard, with a sob, and scrambled to his feet, soaked in his own blood. His arm was paralyzed and he couldn't hold his knife. He couldn't walk on his ruined leg. He writhed, settled into the grass, and stared at her.

She kept her distance, knowing how well he could lunge at her. Instead, she gathered the two frightened horses, quietly walking them down. She found the bloody knife glowing in the moonlight, and took it. She gathered the war club and bow and arrow of the dead Siksika, and found his sheathed knife as well.

She eyed the dead one. He was not her captor. She pricked the knife into his skull and took a ritual scalp, just a little piece. Her war honor. She did not dare approach the live one, and no longer felt like killing him, so she ignored him. He would probably bleed to death. Swiftly she tied her kit onto the back of the smaller pony, noting that she had acquired various things that had been tied to their saddles. She would find out what she possessed later, when she had put a night and more between these warriors and herself.

Chapter 45

Skye had rarely felt so helpless. He lay within a buffalo robe, hands and feet trussed, unable to flee the huge animal that was blocking his sight of the stars. A snout pushed and probed, exuding foul odors, sniffing at him, at his ear, his beard. He felt a tongue rasp his forehead, felt teeth clamp his shoulder. He lay too frightened and paralyzed to move or shout.

He did not know what sort of bear probed at him, black or grizzly. And then an odd thing happened: the bear licked his face, and Skye felt something had changed. For all his time in the mountains, he had sensed that he shared a brotherhood with bears, and this bear was being a brother to him. The bear whoofed softly and retreated, leaving Skye shaken and grateful to have survived such an encounter with Old Ephraim, as the men of the mountains called him. The stars returned and the night breezes calmed him. He could not say what mysterious thing had happened that moment but he knew that things would soon go better for him. It was as if that bear was a messenger of hope, sent only to him in that sleeping camp.

His fear and desperation left him, and he knew they would not return. All these things that had afflicted him in his short life had purpose, and had happened to him to strengthen him and prepare him for a life he could not yet discern. He fell into a sweet sleep, resting body and soul even on the hard ground, better than he had rested for a long time.

And he woke refreshed.

His captors came and rolled him over and untied his hands, which were lashed behind his back, and then his ankles. He rubbed his hands, restoring circulation.

"Well, mates, did a bear visit you in the night?" he asked them. But they didn't reply. Governor Simpson was sitting on a log nearby, watching closely.

"A bear poked his nose into my robes."

"No bear that I know of," said an HBC man. "But they's tracks, yes?"

Skye studied the grassy flat and found no sign of an animal's presence. The print of a bear looked oddly like the print of a stubby human foot, but the few barren places revealed nothing. And none of the packs lying about had been disturbed.

"Skye, you are not to talk with these men. You will not fill them full of stories or win their sympathies."

"A bear visited me."

"Dreams. Nightmares. Your past is catching up to you."

Maybe a dream. But Skye knew it wasn't. Maybe it was his spirit-bear. He thought back to what Red Turkey Comb had once told him: he and the bears had an affinity. All he knew was that something had changed, and he had some-how won a bit of leeway, or tolerance, from these men.

"If I can't talk to your men, I'll talk to you. I feel like

talking this fine morning," Skye said. "If you were at all interested in who I am, you might start with my upbringing. My father was a London merchant . . ."

Oddly, Simpson didn't stop him. He sat sipping tea, eyeing Skye with those penetrating eyes of his while his men boiled some gruel for breakfast and packed gear. Skye told his entire story—within earshot of the rest— and the governor let him do it. It was as if Simpson was seeing Skye for the first time.

"Very interesting, Skye, but not a word of truth in it. You're a clever one. You've read a few books in the ship's brig and learned to mimic your betters. I can't place your dialect, but Billingsgate comes to mind. London for certain. Born there, eh?"

"Yes, sir, Westminster, Kensington High Street."

"Rubbish, rubbish, Skye. You were born in the East End."

All that day Skye toiled under his heavy pack, saying little, his spirits actually buoyant. His body did not complain as much. His traveling companions seemed friendlier now, though none of them could converse with the prisoner. Something had changed.

They passed into country that was more level than not, and less forested than before. The Belly still took them northeast, toward its confluence with the Bow, and then the Oldman, and the South Saskatchewan River and ultimately Hudson's Bay. From one upland ridge, Skye discerned a valley choked with trees and suspected they were reaching the Bow, or perhaps the Oldman. He wasn't sure of anything now. Maybe they would load the canoes there, in much deeper water, and all crowd into the two vessels. But they would not reach the place until that night. Once the whole party was entirely waterborne, passage eastward would be swift and he would leave the mountains behind. The paddles would dip into the northern waters, and the canoes would race away from the country where he had spent several joyous years. Everything was coming to an end. Maybe his spirit-bear was telling him that.

That afternoon Simpson abandoned his canoe and fell in beside Skye, and Skye sensed that something was afoot.

"Skye, you tell an interesting yarn," the governor began.

"It's not a story, sir."

"I fathom that. Nonetheless, you're a deserter. In war you could be executed on the spot. The Crown wants you, and it's my patriotic duty to send you to your well-earned reward. However, Skye, there might be a different sort of future for you. I suspect a dungeon or another warship or maybe an Australian penal colony isn't quite what you had in mind for a life."

"No, sir."

"Maybe all that can be avoided."

"What is it you're proposing?"

"Perhaps nothing. It depends on you. HBC needs good men with wilderness experience. We never have enough."

"You're proposing that I join the company, is that it?"

"Maybe. Let's say that Barnaby Skye doesn't exist, but a man named Billy Blue does, and only I know the secret. Let's say that Billy Blue chooses to indenture to Hudson's Bay. Billy Blue gets all his needs provided for by the company; he agrees to ten years of service, after which he is free. He behaves himself, contributes labor and skill to the enterprise. He brings in the beaver. Billy's a young fellow. At thirty-five or so, he'd be a free man. Free to go live among the Yanks."

"And what's to keep me at my post, sir?"

"Your honor. I fathom you're a man of your word. Once given, it's kept. That's my gamble, not yours."

"And what would my wage be?"

"Your eventual freedom. We'd provide for your needs, outfit you. It would be quite costly, actually"

"And if I did well, would I advance?"

"Unfortunately, given the circumstances, we couldn't do much for a while. But maybe after six or eight years, we might offer some inducements. You could make a life career of it."

"And how do you feel about betraying the Crown?"

"Tut, tut. Life is expedience. If you wish, I will gladly return Skye to the Crown and consider it my patriotic duty."

"And what if there were—say—infractions? Billy Blue didn't measure up?"

"There would be no infractions. Billy Blue would measure up or face his fate, the fate that every step is now carrying him toward."

"And what sort of labor would this require?"

"Camp tender with a brigade. Or, since you're literate, clerk and supply depot work. Bookkeeping. Maybe other things. You're an Englishman. Your presence would help keep the Yanks out of the Oregon country. It's a matter of some concern."

"Ten years is a long time."

"Well, if you're especially valuable, we might parole you after seven. I could hold that out to you. Incentive, you know."

"I spent seven years in slavery to the Crown, sir. Isn't that enough?"

"Moot point. Accept or go to London and face the Admiralty."

"On the one hand, Governor, you seem to accept my story. On the other hand, you hold me for the Crown. Why don't you just let me go if you believe me?"

"Impossible. You're a common seaman and a blackguard."

"Whose word is his bond."

"You are toying with semantics."

"You don't see me as a person, but just as one of a class of commoners whose labor you wish to exploit."

"Of course I see you as a person, and I've given you a most generous opportunity, if I say so myself." He paused, pregnantly. "Maybe on good behavior I'd let you go after five. Give the company five good years and I'll review your case."

Simpson's offer sorely troubled Skye.

An HBC mountaineer named Belfast Berkeley halted the sweating voyageurs, and Skye gladly unloaded his burdens and stretched. The governor was clearly awaiting an answer, and Skye was ready to give it.

"The answer is no, sir."

"Then be damned, Skye."

"It's Mister Skye, sir."

George Simpson whirled away in a rage.

Skye watched him go. Simpson had tempted him. But he would not submit to seven years of slavery to Hudson's Bay, or even five, toiling for no wage and kept in line by fear of exposure to the Crown. It might even be a pleasant and robust slavery, out in trapping brigades. But it would be servitude, and he had had enough of that for several lifetimes. The decision should have saddened him, but it didn't. He felt elated. He would not give his word of honor or commit himself to a prospect he despised. Let them call him Skye; they would find out soon enough—somehow, some way—that he was *Mister* Skye.

Chapter 46

Victoria raced down the Belly River, driven by some urgency she couldn't entirely fathom. She abandoned caution, and no longer scouted the bankside path ahead or slipped into cover where she could. She had the feeling that time was running out, that she must find and free Skye at once—or lose him forever. She pushed her ponies hard, sitting light and lithe in the saddle, speeding them along as much as she dared. The ponies had not been well cared for, and they lacked the energy for sustained speed.

With every slight rise she peered ahead, hoping to glimpse the Hudson's Bay men—but she saw nothing. She had come across their campsites, saw where they had beached the canoes, and noticed that some men among them—Skye included—had carried heavy packs. She saw only moccasin prints, and knew they had given Skye some footwear.

Then she rode across a neck where the river oxbowed, and she did spot them, miles ahead, a tiny moving party, like so many ants, crawling along the Belly, while two canoes, black dots, rode the river well ahead of the ones on foot. There was Skye, if she could catch him. Now caution flooded her. She had to get close, but this was open country with few trees except in pockets along the river. Far ahead in the summer haze lay a green-clad valley of another river. She was approaching a confluence. Now she knew why she hastened: there would be deeper water after that, enough to float heavily laden canoes. She paused a moment, gauging the land and distances with an eye that understood space. The Hudson's Bay men would probably camp at the confluence. Even now Father Sun was setting. And in the morning, they would all crowd into the canoes and shoot downriver, propelled by currents and the mighty arms of the voyageurs.

She returned to the river bottoms, hoping she could stay close and yet avoid being seen by those sharp-eyed men. She hadn't the slightest plan, and didn't even know how to find Skye among them, free him if he was bound. She didn't know whether they posted guards through the night.

This was the land of the Crees, and she didn't much like it. The mountain vistas had given way to undulating prairies, with one or two buttes on the horizons. It seemed gloomy even in the hot summer sun. No wonder the Crees were such terrible people. They lived in a bad land. The Belly had cut deep chasms into the plains here, and the banks had eroded into fantastical shapes that chilled her and reminded her of spirit-places. Yet she would brave even these habitations of souls if it meant finding and releasing Skye.

She scared up pronghorns and coyotes and white-tailed deer that found their home in the bottoms. She saw countless meadowlarks, and the wild rose bloomed everywhere. Ducks filled every slough. The Belly flowed mysteriously eastward, carrying the waters from the Backbone of the World far away. Back in the land of the Bloods the water had been cold and clear; now it was murky and slow-moving, working through gravelly bars and shallow channels.

At dusk she knew she was close, and she walked her horses cautiously, lest she stumble upon the camp of the yellow eyes. She found a turnoff where she could ascend the bluff and took it, wishing to survey the terrain. She rode one horse upslope and tugged the other until she topped the bluff and beheld the vast, lonely plains. She let her eyes adjust to the gloom so she could see how the country lay. Just beyond was a wooded river valley, and she knew she was very close to the place where the Belly joined the Bow. She thought she smelled smoke on the night breeze. On foot, she led her horses along the bluff, and a while later was rewarded. Below, just beyond the confluence of the rivers, was the camp. A fire burned, and she could see the yellow eyes working around it. Two long canoes had been beached and turned over beside the large river.

Where was Skye? How would this camp be guarded—if at all? She saw no horses, and was grateful. Her own would not betray her with a sudden whinny, answered by whinnying from the camp. She stood now in the open, trusting in the dusk to conceal her small form from their eyes. She ached to spot Skye but couldn't at such a distance. She wanted to know where the black-suit grandfather was, too. He would give the commands. She eyed the canoes, thinking that if she couldn't find Skye, she could still delay these Hudson's Bay men by cutting great holes in the birchbark walls of the canoes.

Her horse nudged her, rubbing its forehead against her back, almost unbalancing her. She liked this horse, even if it was a Siksika horse and ill trained. What did they know about horses? Not half as much as any Absaroka!

She realized she had to adjust the packs so that Skye could mount immediately. There would be no time once she freed him to rearrange the load. So she quietly divided the packload between the two horses, tying half behind the cantle of each saddle. She needed to give Skye reins, too, and not just a lead line she had used to pull the packhorse along. So she made a loop of the braided line. Now he could sit the horse and steer it, and that was as much as she could do.

Full dark lowered, and the stars emerged one by one until all the spirit-people twinkled in the bowl of heaven. A night breeze lifted, already chill in these northern plains, and she felt a premonition of autumn although it was still the Moon of Ripening Berries.

If only she could find Skye, and if only they could reach these horses, they would have a good chance. The river men had no horses to give chase. She heard coyotes barking along the hill tops, and welcomed them. Coyotes were brothers, and tricksters, and they liked to laugh. At long last the men below settled down. She no longer saw movement, and the fire gave off less light. It was time. She brought the horses with her, knowing she would need them fast, especially if Skye were hurt or ill after being a prisoner so long. She saw no tents. These were good travelers, even the grandfather, and she knew they could get along with much less than many yellow eyes. She found a way down the bluff and penetrated into the bottoms again, which seemed darker and more foreboding. If they had posted a guard, she might be caught. So she walked gently, not even breaking a twig, as her people had always learned to do. And then, suddenly, as she rounded a bend, she spotted the fire dead ahead. She halted. Now she needed to conceal the horses and then wait for sleep to overtake the yellow eyes, because not much time had passed since the camp quieted. She strained to spot Skye, but couldn't.

She thought of all the things that could go wrong: wakening the wrong one, tripping over something, being caught by a guard, trapped by someone who had gone to the bushes. But it did no good to rehearse all these things, and she concentrated instead on what was right and what would go well. She decided on a clump of tall trees next to the river, no doubt cottonwoods, as a place of concealment where she would keep the horses. She walked that way slowly, her every sense alert, and wrapped the reins around a low limb. She knelt beside some brush and watched, aware that the constant gurgle of the river concealed her passage. The yellow eyes were careless. None of the People would camp so close to the water that they couldn't hear other things.

The camp slumbered peacefully. But as she crept out of the trees, she realized it had become much too dark. She could not tell one man from another, and they all looked alike to her anyway. In the blackness of the night she could not tell a bearded Frenchman from Skye. So she returned to the forest, waiting uneasily for the moon. She hadn't paid much attention to Mother Moon, and didn't know when she would visit. The horses behind her stirred uneasily, and she sensed that they were smelling something on the wind. Wolves maybe. They tugged back on their lines, making the leather groan and the branches creak. She didn't like that.

Whatever was troubling the animals didn't go away; her horses grew more and more restless until she feared they would awaken the whole camp or yank loose and stampede off. She stood, found the neck of one, and ran a hand under its thick mane, calming it as much as she could. Then she found the other, head back, line taut, ready to yank loose at the slightest provocation. She could not quiet that one. It stamped and jerked until she was sure the whole camp had heard.

Her vision was good; her eyes had accustomed themselves to the blackness, and she could make out the trees where they blotted the stars, and the meadow, a vaguely open area that hinted of space, and the orange eyes of the fire's last coals, which told her where these Hudson's Bay men were. But there was nothing she could do for the time being. So deep was the blackness that she could easily trip over one of the sleeping men.

There was Skye, so close, and yet so unreachable now, when she desperately needed to reach him. She sensed that someone stirred, but the night shrouded movement. Maybe that was good. What shrouded that one from her eyes would also shroud her from his.

A horse shrieked, pulled loose, and bolted. The other followed. She shrank into the ground with horror. The camp stirred. She could see nothing, but she heard voices, men grabbing their rifles. The glow of embers was blotted from time to time as men passed in front of it. She crouched, feeling helpless against such bad fortune. Had her wits deserted her, her spirit helper misled her? Mostly these men shouted in the tongue she didn't know, that of the Creoles, so she understood nothing. But the whole camp was awake now. No one threw wood on the coals for fear of making a target of them all, but men were up and about, walking.

"Where's Skye?" asked the voice of the grandfather.

"Here, mate."

Joy and anguish flooded through Victoria. He was

so close! She thought he was to the left of the embers, but she didn't know for sure.

"*C'est un ours!*" someone bellowed.

"It's a bear!"

"*Sacre bleu!*"

Now she smelled it. A bear. She thrilled to it. A bear, for Skye.

"Chase it away before it gets into the packs."

"I thought I heard horses."

"I thought I did too. But bears sound like anything."

"*Formidable!*"

Men scurried about. Someone threw some wood on the embers, but it didn't catch. One man loomed close, a shadow blotting out stars, and then she realized it wasn't a man, it was Grandfather Bear. She huddled still and quiet. The great hulk paused, sniffed, grunted, and went on.

She desperately wanted to run to Skye, but held herself in check. The wood on the embers smoked, the smell eddying her way, but didn't ignite. She waited until the camp quieted, aching to do something, anything. She needed to find the horses. They held everything she possessed except the quiver on her back and her bow, and the knife in her hand.

The night settled again, and she judged that the time had come. There was no sign of a moon, but for the moment she could walk among them and no one would imagine that the small figure looming above their robes was the woman of Mister Skye. She stood, padded resolutely into a camp that was fully awake, and hoped for the best.

Chapter 47

Victoria edged toward the camp of the Hudson's Bay men, wondering how she was going to do what she had to do. The night had cloaked Mother Earth, and she could not even see her own moccasins, much less the sleeping men who lay under stars, without a fire now. Should she simply yell for Skye? But what if he was tied up and could not get free?

She didn't know, and that made her faint at heart. Even the starlight had vanished, and she realized the sky was now overcast. How could she find him, find the horses, escape? Many of these men were awake. They had just dealt with a bear. How easy it would be for any of them to reach up and catch her as she passed.

She ached to find the fire, find an ember to orient herself, but not even that small comfort was afforded her. She compelled herself to walk forward, until she tripped over one of the men, who grumbled, muttered something, and fell silent. She could not go farther without stumbling over many more. There were twice ten men here, one of them Skye.

She backed away, knowing she had no recourse except to wait for moonlight or dawn—any sort of light that would permit her to drift through the camp without stumbling over the voyageurs. She would need light as well to find the horses.

The gloom persisted through the long night. She could see neither stars nor moon. She heard the gentle gurgle of water to her right and knew she was close to the river. When at last the day began to quicken, she realized she was too late. Some of the voyageurs were already stirring, standing, stretching, heading for the bushes. She retreated into brush and hid there, her heart heavy. On this day the canoes would take Skye away forever.

Then she realized this need not be. She stood, a figure as vague to the Hudson's Bay men as they were to her, and stumbled through the gauze of night to the river, with only her ears to guide her. There nearby were two long canoes made of the white men's fabric over the ribs and sealed with some sort of shiny paint. They rested side by side, upside down, not far from the riverbank.

She slipped her knife from its sheath and approached the vessels. The next task was easy, but noisy. She slashed the skin of the canoe, long stripes, the work of bear claws, one after another, on each side of the ribs, many slices. No one loomed out of the murk to stop her. She performed the same mutilation upon the other canoe, gouging great holes in both of them. Every stroke of the knife sounded like thunder to her, and yet she knew most of the noise was camouflaged by the omnipresent gurgle of the river. She could not yet see her handiwork and worried that it might not be enough. But she knew it would take the voyageurs a while to repair the damage and load the canoes.

But did it help? She could not say. Now she had to find her horses. Maybe, with horses, she could follow the river as fast as the voyageurs could paddle—though she doubted it. The voyageurs, going downriver, would speed Skye to his destiny. The day bloomed into a drab gray, and she retreated from the stirring camp and up a grassy slope to find her horses and hide. From the height she could see the general shape of the country—the thick band of woods along the river, the plains rising on either side, some rocky escarpments, insolated patches of pine.

And no horses. What would the Hudson's Bay grand-father do if they found the horses, each horse laden with Blackfoot gear? She hardly dared imagine. She felt hungry but put aside her needs, as she had long ago taught herself to do. Some things were more important than the howling of the body.

She settled into a small hollow in a slope, well concealed by tall grasses, and peered down upon the camp. She could not yet make out Skye, though most of the men were up and stirring about. And then she knew. The last one lying on the ground was Skye, because he had been trussed up and could not move. The light thickened a little, but it was still so dark she could barely make out forms. She examined the grassy ridges around her and spotted her horses a long way away, grazing together. They would be small dark dots to the Hudson's Bay men, but she feared the sharp-eyed white men would see them anyway. There was little she could do.

Then she heard the rasp of excited voices and saw the men head for the riverbank, plunging into a wooded area. She could not make out words but knew they had found the damaged canoes. The grandfather was visible now, a black spot in the vague light. Anger and suspicion floated on the quickening breezes. Several went to examine Skye—she could see him lying there now—and looked at the bound wrists and ankles. Maybe they thought he had done it. Maybe not. Maybe they thought Grandfather Bear had done it. She had cut the fabric in strips, as if bear claws had ripped it.

Two of the voyageurs lifted the canoes and carried them into the open meadows, to where the fire had been in the evening. So they were going to patch the holes, and she suspected it would not take them as long as she hoped.

She wanted the repairs to take all day, but white men had many tricks and did things that amazed the People. If they made guns of metal, they could repair canoes. As the day whitened—it would be gloomy at best, with thick gray clouds hiding Grandfather Sun—she saw the men at work on the canoes, cutting away the shredded fabric. Others stood about, examining the grassy hills, looking for signs of those who had done this thing. She froze, didn't move a muscle then, as she peered through the grasses. She prayed that they would not see the ponies. They didn't seem to look in that direction, back from the river, and she realized a swell of benchland hid the animals.

With the horses, she would follow them and keep up. Without them, she would fall farther and farther behind. They untied Skye's arms and legs, and she ached to signal him. He stood stiffly, barely able to use his freed body. He paid no attention to the canoes or the feverish work being done on them. Instead, he stood facing the hills away from the river, facing her almost. Then he slowly lifted both arms upward, toward her, toward one he did not see but whose presence he sensed. Ah, how much a torment that was, seeing him there, lifting his arms to her, letting her know. She dared not stand and could not reply. But then her friend the magpie flew close, alighted near her, and flew powerfully away. Then Skye was staring straight at her hiding place. She half stood one tiny moment and then folded back into the safety of the grassy hollow. Perhaps he had seen; perhaps not.

Thank thee, Magpie.

She could do nothing but hide. He could do nothing but perform his morning ablutions and eat the gruel the HBC men had boiled over a fire. A gray day ticked by while the voyageurs worked on the canoes. Some were shaping pieces of cloth and sewing them to the canoes. Others were collecting pitch from pines, heating it, and caulking the repairs. Soon they would have the canoes done and would be off. So her efforts hadn't amounted to more than a half-day delay. She squinted upslope, toward the horses, and found that they had vanished. She didn't know where they were.

Rain began, a mist at first, and then a cold pelting drizzle, and she huddled miserably in her unsheltered hollow. Below, the voyageurs ignored the wetness and continued their repairs. She watched the grandfather pace restlessly, a lion on a leash, wanting to be off. Her gaze was forever on Skye. He obviously possessed nothing but the clothing he wore, but he wrapped a robe around him to ward off the icy rain. The campfire began to smoke, and she knew the rain was extinguishing it little by little.

All that morning she debated what she might do. She had her bow and quiver of arrows, and contemplated ways she might use it: an arrow into each of the repaired canoes, for instance. But that would expose her to them. Now, with the rain wetting and weakening the sinew of the bowstring, she knew that she had no weapon at all save for her knife. Skye paused now and then and stared directly at her, or at least at the place where she crouched in wet, cold grass. She ached to know what he wanted her to do, ached to receive some sort of signal or instruction from him.

But maybe she had it wrong. Maybe he needed instruction from her. She needed a plan, and she needed to tell him. Escape would not be up to him: he could do nothing. It was entirely up to her. He knew one thing: who had damaged the canoes and why. She wondered if maybe he *was* signaling her. He walked about almost randomly, then lowered himself to the ground on the periphery of

the camp and lay down, imitating sleep. Yes, there was a
message in that. He would try to lie on the edge of the
next camp. She watched him repeat the whole thing and
lie down in the same place. In the next camp he would
sleep on the periphery, and on the upriver side. She swiftly
lifted her bow and quiver and lowered it, acknowledging
she had understood.

He lifted his bear claw necklace and pawed the air
with it. She didn't know what that meant. Could it be
that the voyageurs thought a bear had clawed the fabric
of the canoes? Did he merely mean that a bear had come
last night? Before she could grasp what that was about,
the grandfather came to Skye and ordered him to the
canoes. The voyageurs were testing one in the river and
loading the other. Soon they would be off, paddling easily down the Bow and then the Oldman River, many suns,
many nights.

All but Skye were now employed with packing and
loading the canoes, and none was remotely interested in
what might lie in the grassy bluffs above the river. That
was fine. She stood boldly. Skye saw her at once even
though the grandfather had made him carry things to the
canoes. She did not tarry, but trotted upslope and over
the crest, out of sight. The two horses grazed just a little
way away. She hiked through the cold drizzle, feeling
hunger and chill. Swiftly she caught her Blackfoot
warhorse, wiped the pad saddle dry, and climbed on, arranging her wide skirts. Then she collected the lead line
of the packhorse. Nothing had been lost. They had simply been panicked by the bear, broken their tethers, and
had drifted to this place after that. She repaired the reins
with a knot and rode downriver. If she hurried and kept
well back from the wooded bottoms, she might keep

pace—almost—with the swift canoes. That sustained her more than food or warmth ever could. Somehow, some way, she would rescue Skye.

All that day she drove her horses through rain and cold, barely noticing the protests of her body. She lost track of the canoes, and when she sometimes turned toward a bluff or promontory, she could not see the canoes on the whirling river. Now she feared she was very far ahead or far behind, and would lose Skye after all. She had to rest the horses, but the river never rested, and the canoes required little more than steering.

But it would not be like that. The Hudson's Bay men would stop now and then to stretch. They would cook a meal, maybe, or use the bushes, or just walk a little. No one was chasing them; they didn't know of her presence.

She saw that the river made an arc ahead, and cut across the neck of land late in the day, hoping to get ahead. But when she reached the river again, she found they were ahead of her after all. They were setting up camp straight down the bluff from where she sat her horse.

She heard a shout. In that one fleeting moment, they had seen her.

Chapter 48

Victoria knew she could escape if she chose; the voyageurs were on foot and she was horsed. She chose not to. Instead, she steered her two Blackfoot ponies straight down the slope toward the Hudson's Bay men. Skye watched alertly, his face a mask.

She didn't quite know what she would do. Nothing about her betrayed her Absaroka origins to the casual eye, and nothing about her horse furniture betrayed anything but Blackfoot manufacture. Nor would these men know that she was in any way connected to Skye.

They had unloaded the two big canoes and beached them. Piles of gear lay about, and a few bedrolls had been tossed into the bankside grass. There were many of them, and now they all stared at her, not overly concerned by the appearance of a lone Indian woman. She decided she would not speak but use the hand signs. Maybe she could stay the night. That was what she would ask.

The grandfather in black stared at her, his gaze relentless. He was a formidable man with the eyes of an eagle, his instincts keen. She would have to be wary of him. The others, the voyageurs, were big, muscular, dark men who spoke that other tongue, French. There were two additional ones from the grandfather's land who spoke Skye's tongue.

She peered at last toward her beloved, giving not the slightest sign of recognition. She saw Skye survey the spare horse, approving of the saddle and the goods tied behind its cantle. But none of what passed subtly between them was evident to the Hudson's Bay men. It was good to see Skye, even if he was so helpless. Soon he would be free!

One of the Englishmen made the hand signs, and she responded. She was cold and wet and hungry. The rain had made her bow useless. Could she share their food and stay the night?

Who was she?

She was a woman of the People, returning to her village after a visit.

Where were her people?

Far to the south.

What band of Siksika did she belong to?

She had lived with the Kainah, the Bloods. She would ride through the land of the Piegans soon.

The man translated his signs to the black-clad grandfather, who nodded. Skye had watched all this, reading the fingers and hands.

The signs continued. The man told her that this was a Hudson's Bay Company camp, very friendly with the Siksika, much trading, good to the People, and she was welcome. This was the camp of the greatest chief of the white men, and he was welcoming her for the night. She would be safe among his men. She was welcome to feast on a doe they had shot during the day. Soon they would have it hung and butchered. In the morning she could go her way and they would go downriver in their big canoes.

She nodded and dismounted. She untied her own bed robe, led her horses to grass a little distant, and picketed them. She hoped they would not notice that she did not unsaddle them. But Skye noticed. He also noticed the sheathed knife at her waist. That night he and she would escape—if all went well. Even now he was unrolling his robes as close to the horses as he dared. And laying his old robe in a way that would make his feet point straight at the ponies. Aiee!

The men had tied the doe to a box elder limb and some were gutting it, while others fed a hot fire. She and Skye exchanged glances, and she ached to know what stirred his soul just then. What did he feel for her? Was anything left? She would weep when she could, and tell him of her grief, her mistakes, her yearnings. Maybe he would reject her. But at least she would free him if she could. That would repay him a little for the sorrows she had given to him.

The grandfather in black told Skye to help with the butchering, so he did, paying her no heed at all. They were both going to great lengths to hide their relationship.

"Don't get any notions about escaping, Skye," the man said. "We'll be watching. I'm posting guards tonight. The squaw's horses may tempt you, but you're on your way to the Crown."

The grandfather stared thoughtfully at the prisoner. Perhaps he suspected something. She felt a chill run through her.

She feigned no knowledge of what she had heard in Skye's tongue, but was glad to learn about the guards. It was good to know of trouble.

The voyageurs eyed her now and then, not missing her lithe, young beauty. She grew aware of the darting gazes and ignored them. But they made her cautious. She decided she would ultimately bed close to her ponies that night, but would unroll her robe close to the camp at first.

The drizzle had dwindled to cold mist, and then, as the yellow eyes prepared a meal, quit altogether. It would be a wet, cold, miserable night warmed only by their cheerful fire. She doubted the heavens would clear, and this night would be as black as the last one. She did not know how she would deal with that. She ached to give Skye a knife, but doubted it would help if they tied his wrists behind his back. He had signaled that they did, holding his arms behind him, wrists pressed together. She would have to do it, in plain sight of the guards—somehow.

The voyageurs boiled the deer meat in a kettle, adding wild roots and herbs to season their stew, and soon they handed her a bowl. She ate with relish, utterly starved for want of food the entire day. She held out her tin bowl for more, and they laughed.

"Injuns got hollow legs," said one. "Feast or starve, that's the way of 'em."

She didn't let on that she understood, and knew it was a criticism. This was not a moment to reveal anything or show any displeasure. Instead, she smiled.

One filled her bowl again. They fed Skye well enough and then trussed him up. He never glanced at her, but stood with his back to her so she could see exactly how the thong wrapped his wrists. Then they let him sit down beside his robe, removed his moccasins, and trussed his ankles. One of them settled against a tree, rifle in hand, the guard she knew would watch that night.

It had grown dark. These men were weary, and so was she. In the last light she checked her ponies, making sure the saddles were tight and all was ready. Then she rolled up in her robe, oblivious of the stares and the almost palpable yearning for her that she felt around her. These were men without a woman. They weren't on the warpath, and they wanted her.

She waited for them to sleep, and almost succumbed to it herself. She could barely keep her eyes open and her mind clear after downing such a meal as that one. The embers died, and the night shrouded her, pressing down, the darkness suffocating her, a terrible weight

It *was* weight. One of the voyageurs had come to her robes. She cried out, rolled, stopped herself from cursing in his tongue, and fought as hands clapped her wrists and a massive weight pinioned her to the grass.

"Aiee!" she cried.

No one helped her. She heard no uproar in camp. She fought hard, bucking and writhing, biting and kicking, and won a momentary reprieve when she threw him off and he rolled. Swiftly she plucked her robe and vanished toward the horses—toward Skye. She could no longer tell exactly where she was because the blackness offered no clue.

"Victoria."

The quiet voice lifted from almost underfoot, so soft it barely reached her ears.

"Here."

She found him and dropped beside him, her heart hammering. She waited there for the sounds of pursuit but heard nothing. The utter blackness would foil her pursuer—if she kept quiet.

Slowly, softly, her hands found Skye's arms and followed them to the thong binding his wrists behind him. She choked back her terror, pulled out her keen knife, and gently sawed, working in blackness, afraid she might slice into him. But a thong gave, and she unwound the binding. She found his ankles and released them. He paused, found her hands, and pressed them between his. There would be more, much more, but the feel of his hands over hers, warm and tight, was overwhelming in its sweetness, and tears welled up in her.

Then came the hardest part, slipping away, making no noise, finding the ponies on an overcast and moonless night in which she could not even tell sky from ground. She gathered her robe and took the thong as well—it would have its uses—and tried hard to fathom what direction to go. Little by little she came to an understanding. The night remained as black as ever, but an interior vision formed within, some mysterious understanding of where she was and where the ponies would be. She knew Skye would not have this gift given to the People, and so she quietly helped him to his feet—better to walk than shuffle on hands and knees through grass, making noise. She led him confidently away from camp, her inward vision sure.

She smelled the horses before she came to them, their acrid odor familiar and joyous. They tugged back on their picket lines. She guided Skye to the one she had prepared for him and lifted one bare foot to the wooden stirrup. He climbed on, and the horse grunted and sidestepped. She feared the whole camp heard. She pulled the pony's picket while Skye found a rein.

Then the camp did erupt into shouts. They had heard. Someone put wood on the fire, but she ignored that. She freed her own pony, climbed on, and kicked it straight toward the bluffs. Skye followed, depending on the soft sound of hooves to guide him.

She heard talk, anger, and shouting behind her, but never paused to look back.

Chapter 49

Skye rode through darkness so thick he had no notion of where he was going. Victoria rode nearby but he could not see her. He thought they were going uphill, away from the Oldman River, but he couldn't be sure.

He rode through a tunnel without light, without direction, and it occurred to him that portions of life were like that, and that one penetrated various tunnels of life. He had spent much of his life in such darkness. He knew

Victoria was near, but only the soft rustle of her horse confirmed it. That, too, was familiar. For too much of their union she had been beside him but invisible to him.

And yet she was there. She had come, brought horses, found a way to free herself from the Bloods. He had come for her, and she had come for him. She had left him, only to return, and in the act of returning and finding and freeing she had said everything that needed saying. He felt himself rejoicing that she was near. Neither of them spoke, and he knew he was afraid to speak. Maybe she was, too. He almost dreaded the moment when they would speak, for fear he would use the wrong words—or hear the wrong ones.

Maybe she didn't really love him. Maybe she just wanted to help him. He realized he was simply tormenting himself, and stopped it. She was there beside him and what more needed to be said?

After a while he stopped. It would not do to ride too far, because they would probably trace a circle that would bring them perilously close to Governor Simpson and his men. Better to wait until the distant dawn, get their bearings, and ride away. Her horse stopped when his did. He strained to see something, anything, but the overcast hid even the heavens, and the night lay so thick that there seemed to be no other world. Only himself and Victoria. Maybe that was how it should be just now: no other world at all.

She touched his leg, startling him. He had not heard her dismount. He could not see her even that close. She said nothing, as afraid to talk as he was. He sensed she was standing right there, touching him, holding the rein of her horse, waiting for him to respond. Perhaps she was afraid. He found her hand with his and held it. He wished he could see her face, read it, understand what lay upon it.

The darkness held. His wife, his lover, his mate was there—yet not there to his eyes. Everything about this trip through the tunnel of darkness was an act of faith. Slowly he dismounted and stepped into cold grass, which poked between his toes and chilled his feet even more than they had been. The horse had been his salvation, his mobility when they had removed his moccasins from him to keep him within their wilderness cage.

He knew she was close, and hesitant to come closer, so he drew the small hand to him, and found all that it was attached to, and drew her to him in the blackness and held her. She held him, and in the sacred holding they renewed themselves. He kissed her, and discovered her face wet with tears, the tears he could not see. The wetness flooded down her cheeks and now filtered through his beard and wet his own cheeks, until the wetness from his eyes mingled with the wetness pouring from hers.

Thus they held each other for a long time, coming to the end of the darkness. She bid him to sit down, and a moment later he felt a robe enclose his cold feet and she joined him on the wet grasses, the warmth of the robe and love greater than all the coldness on earth. It was a good time to sit and hold her, an arm about her shoulder, and a time to say nothing in words because no words would do. She held the rein of one horse and he held the rein of another, and they heard the horses eat grass and wait to go somewhere else.

Life is like that, he thought. We walk through blackness, wanting to go where we will go. But in the blackness we cannot find our way, and we walk in another direction. Sometimes we find, when we come out of blackness, that it was a better direction after all, and it would have gone better for us to surrender to the unknowing, the uncertainty, than to insist upon the direction we had chosen. Maybe God permitted the blacknesses in all lives that we might let go, surrender, learn to trust in the guiding hand—or in no hand at all. Skye sat, content, knowing that the blackness had already passed. This Victoria, the chastened tear-stained woman in his arms, was not the Victoria who had followed her will into her blackness. He was not the same man, either.

Some time later the darkness began to soften, and with it their blindness. In time they found themselves on a lonely plain, without landmark, a vague place between heaven and hell, a place to choose a direction—any direction—and start on a long ride. They would have a long way to go through a dangerous country that was disputed by Blackfeet and Cree and Assiniboine. Chance, bad luck, a wrong turn could kill them. Daylight could kill them. But he wasn't really thinking about that. It was better to believe that they had already chosen a new direction. He would not go east and leave the mountains. She would not leave his side.

She pulled free, found some jerky in her kit, and handed him two pieces. They didn't assuage his hunger. Yet he didn't mind. She dug farther and extracted two pairs of Blackfoot moccasins. One set was too tight, the other too loose. He wore the tight ones, knowing they would stretch. She had thought of everything and found the means to bring it.

They had not yet spoken, and he was glad. All of this reunion was freighted with more than words would bear. But now she smiled, tentatively, half afraid. He drew her to him and held her again, and she held him very tight until their heartbeats were one. Then it was time to go.

The overcast denied him direction, but he wasn't really lost now They had ridden from the right bank of the Bow, or maybe the Oldman, which trended northeast. So they were not traveling in a northerly direction and could not without crossing the river. When the sun came, they would get their bearings. He wasn't sure where they would go. Maybe she would choose a path.

She was as afraid to speak as he, so they didn't. He helped her mount her horse, and he swung up on his, and they rode, two solitary figures over a sea of dewy grass, silvery in the softest gray light of dawn. The Hudson's Bay men might follow their hoofprints, so he did not tarry, but rode with Victoria into an unclear future. All that morning they rode without design, toward nothing they could discern. But then the overcast lifted piecemeal, a wan sun gave them shadow, and they turned pale shadow into compass and drifted southward under a patched sky.

Thus they continued through the quiet day, ever southward as best as they could tell. They watered themselves and their weary horses at an alkaline seep and continued until late in the afternoon, when they descended a grassy slope and discovered a slender stream of sweetwater at their feet, bordered with chokecherry and box elder and willow brush. They scared up a mule deer there, a doe, and regretfully Victoria pierced it with an arrow and paused solemnly beside it, saying some Crow prayer to the departed as it spasmed and died. A spotted fawn lingered there and then drifted away, frightened and alone.

They filled their starving bodies that evening, but the image of the fawn kept coming to him. It probably would fall victim to a coyote or wolf or lion, its small life truncated. He took the episode as an image of life, which was not fair, which upset one's hopes and dreams, which killed randomly. They spent much of the twilight butchering the doe, which was hard and slow work. They roasted the meat to preserve it, and stowed it in their kits. They kept the hide, which might be useful to two refugees with little between them but a few things swiftly gathered when she had fled the Bloods.

All that day, too, they barely spoke to one another. It didn't seem right to talk, and words seemed shallow. They were each participating in a sacred ceremony of reunion, and words would spoil it. For once, Skye didn't trust words. He trusted her smile, her tenderness, and the touch of her hands. She searched him constantly for signs of his acceptance and forgiveness, and he gave them to her in his touch, his hugs, and once by wiping away one of her tears. They needed understanding, and she gave him hers, and he was giving her his. But often they gazed upon each other, reading souls, peering into the wells of the eyes and drinking the cool water that lay there.

They did not make love that night beside the prairie creek because it wasn't what was needed. That would come sometime when they found their bearings. But they held each other through the darkness, under the sparkle of a heaven full of diamonds, listening to the coyotes, and he was glad when she fell asleep with her head burrowed into the hollow of his shoulder.

That night he spoke. "I love you," he said.

She cried and drew him tight.

The next day caution returned. They saw a distant movement, specks of humanity on a distant ridge, and hid in a slough, which upset the ducks. But nothing happened, and they rode onward toward a new life together. This day they talked now and then, and she told him everything that had happened, from the time she had been captured by the Bloods to that moment. And he told her all that had passed in his life. She faltered only when she mentioned Beckwourth. It did not matter. Someday he would see Beckwourth again, maybe at some rendezvous, and it would all pass by. She had chosen Skye, not the flamboyant Crow chieftain.

He estimated that some time that day they had crossed the 49th parallel and were back in United States territory, far east of the Rocky Mountains. He knew little of this land, except that it could be the home of Crees or Assiniboines, who probably were friendly. But they had to be alert for invading Blackfeet, who whirled out of the horizons and dealt death.

"Where do you want to go?" he asked.

"Wherever you go, that is where I want to go, Mister Skye," she said. "My home is where you are."

That reminded him of the biblical Ruth.

"Maybe Bridger and Fitzpatrick and Sublette will take me back."

"Then we will go there."

"If we can find any of them," he added.

"Our home is wherever we are," she said.

He liked that. Home was here, with Victoria.

"Then we are home," he said.